Back tae Auld Claes an' Porridge

Chronicle of an Edinburgh Family

BOOK ONE

A New Start

Jack Melrose

Jack Melrose Publishing

ISBN 978-0-473-62464-4

This is a work of fiction.
Names, characters, places,
and incidents either are the
product of the author's
imagination or are used
fictitiously. Any resemblance
to actual persons, living or
dead, events, or locales is
entirely coincidental.

Printing and publishing services provided by
PublishMe, New Plymouth, New Zealand
www.publishme.co.nz

Cover: *Front, the old Kirkgate in the 1950s*
Back, bairns at peevery beds in a Leith street in 1957

Contents

Foreword

We were born into working-class Leith and Edinburgh. It was a different time back then in the nineteen-forties. A different world as well. And not just because we had neither internet nor smart phones. The War and its aftermath touched almost everything: our thoughts and our actions; our songs and our games; what we ate and how much; what we wore; how we lived.

Our homes were poky two-room flats without bath, shower or running hot water in run-down Victorian tenements. Some of us might have shared a toilet with the family across the landing. Mod cons were few and far between: a plug-in valve radio, a gas cooker, maybe a clothes iron. Our dads worked long hours for small wages in blue-collar jobs. Our mums stayed home, cooked, cleaned, did laundry at the local steamie, and queued for hours to keep us fed.

We didn't live to consume; we consumed to live. Our staple diet was porridge for breakfast, mince an' tatties for dinner and white bread with margarine for tea. We'd heard stories about bananas; but they never appeared in the shops, so we began to wonder if they really existed. There was orange juice in small glass bottles from the chemist in Junction Street; but it was rationed to under-fives only. Cheese was cheddar, and that was it. Sweeties were still 'on the ration'. Ice-cream was a treat, banished to the occasional Sunday, if at all.

The upside was that there were upsides, at least for us bairns. Our lives were uncomplicated. We suffered few of the pressures and none of the angst of modern bairns; already at an early age we enjoyed freedoms they would envy, especially a licence to roam, for the City was a relatively safe place and it was our oyster. The fledgling welfare state looked after our health and wellbeing. Legislative reforms assured us of a solid Scottish education. Post-war society was in flux; opportunities abounded. So we were given the chance to make something of our lives. Now, in old age, we take our ease, marvelling at how far we've come.

This is just one story of one family during those times and beyond. Though a work of fiction, it's inspired by actual events.

Jack Melrose, New Zealand, 2022

For Janet and Ian
and the others
whose voices were never heard

Prologue
The shouts o' war

1941: The fire watcher

Janet Melrose stared westwards along the Firth at the faint red glow in the sky. Clydebank was getting another hammering. Though it was all of forty miles from Leith, she had a grandstand view from her lookout on the roof of MacFergus. Last night's raid on the town had been bad enough. The morning papers had been full of it. Total devastation, hundreds dead, thousands homeless. But March 13th had been only Episode One. With the familiar drone of approaching German aircraft, it had quickly become clear that tonight was going to be Episode Two, as if there was anything – or anyone – left for the Luftwaffe to destroy. She tried not to think about what those people were going through.

With a slight shock, she suddenly remembered that Dad had been called through to Clydebank the day before. Help had started to pour into the area from the Lowland fire brigades. An urgent call had been put out for search and rescue teams. Edinburgh responded. As a City employee, Dad had been the first to go on a special train the morning before. They needed people to deal with recovery, storage and identification of the dead. So, now he was there, bearing the brunt of the second raid along with the people of Clydebank. They hadn't always got along, but she found herself wondering if she'd ever see him again.

To be honest, her own situation wasn't much better. For she was standing on a powder keg, though whisky keg would be more accurate. Under her feet, stored in vats, were thousands of gallons of the choicest spirit, volatile, flammable whisky. And somewhere up there in the darkness were Heinkels, looking for targets for their incendiaries. Nor was it unknown for enemy pilots to strafe the odd building, just for the hell of it. She'd never felt so exposed. So far, the sirens hadn't gone off here in the City but it might only be a matter of time before the Luftwaffe switched its attention to the east. At just eighteen years old, fire watching alone in the dead of night wasn't something she'd ever imagined herself having to do. She wasn't exactly a shrinking violet.

From a large family, she'd lived through the hardships of the twenties and the thirties in working-class Scotland. She'd developed a thick skin. But this was different. It was war and she'd been thrust into the front line. Her nerves were starting to shred.

The glow in the western sky was getting brighter. From the roof she could see the dock area spread out below; factories, workshops and warehouses of every type on one side, the harbour and the sea on the other. The roofs of buildings were silhouetted against Clydebank burning. She bit her lip and wondered where Auld Beattie was. They'd been rostered on together for the night shift and it was getting on for midnight but he hadn't turned up. It wasn't like him and she hoped he was all right. March was a winter month in Scotland and it was freezing. As she stamped her feet to keep warm, the outsize tackety boots rang on the paving. She pulled at the blanket around her shoulders, glad of the old army greatcoat, the two jerseys, the extra semmit, long drawers, slacks and thick woollen socks. She longed for some of the tea from the thermos flask in the holdall at her feet but she'd better save that for later. The old steel helmet was uncomfortable. The chinstrap chafed under her chin and she had to keep tilting her head back to see properly. The soft brown waves she'd taken so much trouble to put into her hair were going to be ruined, she knew it. It had seemed pointless to be putting a helmet on for a bit of endless waiting around in the dark for something that would never happen but tonight she had to admit that Dad had been right to insist.

It had been only the year before, after the devastating blitz of London and then Manchester, that the British wartime government had finally woken up and made fire watching compulsory for all big businesses and factories. Incendiaries were a favourite weapon of the Luftwaffe. Dropped in their hundreds, they fell soundlessly onto their targets. On impact, a percussion charge ignited the thermite payload. The ensuing fire could burn for 15 minutes or more. 'Tile breakers' were designed to penetrate roofs and start fires within buildings. It stood to reason that a distillery with its attached bonded warehouse storing hundreds of thousands of gallons of spirit in vats and wooden barrels would be a prime candidate for a conflagration, should an incendiary make it onto or – God forbid – through the roof. It was common knowledge what had happened the previous September when a bonded warehouse at Tynecastle had been hit. Without a fire watch strategy in place it had gone up like a Roman candle. Such was the inferno that the firemen couldn't get near. Blazing whisky had run down the gutters and into the drains.

The management of MacFergus and Sons had asked for volunteers at a meeting of the workers in the bottling cellar. To set an example, the founder of the firm, old Mr Colin MacFergus himself, all of 76 years old, had been the first to step forward. To make a point, he'd accoutred himself with an ARP helmet, a stirrup pump, a shovel and a bucket full of sand and stood there with his gear, his gas mask haversack slung over his shoulder, smiling and clowning in all his self-deprecating glory. Crowded around him in a semi-circle, sitting on workbenches and leaning against silent machines, the distillery staff appreciated his attempt at humour.

"Well done, Mr Mac!"

"Dinnae forget tae take a wee dram up there wi' ye, Mr Mac!"

"The Jerries're shakin' in their jackboots, Mr Mac!"

In the wartime economy, most of the young men were gone, conscripted. The distillery relied on a workforce composed mainly of women and middle-aged or elderly men. Mr Mac's audience was overwhelmingly female. The seriousness of the situation wasn't lost on them despite the banter, so there was no shortage of takers. If the distillery went up in smoke, with it would go their livelihoods. It didn't hurt either that five shillings was paid for a full twelve-hour shift, six pm to six am. Janet was among the first women to put her name down. With Ian away in the army - God knows where - she felt she had to do her bit too, not to mention the fact that she wasn't going to turn her nose up at being paid overtime for a night spent hanging around on a roof doing, as she'd assumed, damn all. Then had come the mandatory day's training. They'd learnt what a German incendiary bomb looked like and how it worked. They'd learnt that it was easy to smother the life out of it if you acted fast, even with something as basic as a shovel and a bucket of sand or a stirrup pump. Upon 'graduation', they'd become proud recipients of an Air Raid Precautions Certificate. Janet had smiled to herself and wondered if she'd ever be called upon to put her newfound skills into practice.

She thought about Ian and wondered what he was doing. He'd sent a postcard or two but due to wartime censorship regulations wasn't allowed to reveal his location. She assumed he was still in Scotland. She glanced down at the cheap engagement ring on her finger, just visible, gleaming in the faint light. They'd met here at MacFergus and Sons, in this very building, two years before. Ian was a bonded cellarman and blender, she a junior on the production line. She was just going on seventeen, he was twenty-four. People frowned at the disparity in their ages but she didn't care. She was the one who'd pursued *him*. He wasn't used to being the quarry, especially when the hunter was a shapely young girl who was both outspoken and feisty. They quickly fell in love. With the outbreak of hostilities, Ian had been conscripted into the 52nd Lowland Division. Both their fathers had served in the same regiment during the First World War. All around them, with war closing in and the future uncertain, young couples were tying the knot, desperate to snatch a bit of happiness while there was still time. Separation accelerated matters and they'd decided to marry before it was too late. In four weeks' time, they hoped to be husband and wife.

Her mind went back to the last time she'd seen him. Somehow he'd managed to get five days' leave for Hogmanay. It had been his last day, Friday 3rd, the first Friday of the New Year, and freezing weather. They'd wanted to do something special. He had to leave by a late train from Waverley and had deposited his kit bag at the left luggage. Muffled up against the cold they'd met on the steps of Register House and walked down arm in arm to the Playhouse to see what was on. It was *Every Night at Eight* with George Raft, Alicia Faye, Patsy Kelly and someone they'd never heard of before, Frances Langford. They had no idea if it was any good, but at least it was somewhere warm and dark where they might be able to cuddle.

It was the second showing. An usherette with a torch led them into the gloom. There were still spare seats at the front. They sat down just as the picture started. It was a silly story from the previous decade. The fashions and the manners seemed terribly outdated now, a mere six years later. But the music was fabulous. There was an electrifying rendition of 'I Feel a Song Coming On' with the full orchestra, chorus, the trio of girls at the mike, and George Raft, for once out of his tough-guy persona, conducting the orchestra while performing a quirky step dance. Though the song might try to persuade them that their troubles were gone, of course, nothing could be further from the truth. Still, they allowed themselves to be beguiled as pint-sized Frances Langford sang the most memorable number, 'I'm in the Mood for Love'.

They'd walked back up to Princes Street struggling against icy winds funnelled by the tenements and picking over the actors, the plotline and the music. In the station tearoom over a cup of tea and an overpriced scone, they'd looked into each other's eyes, in love, hummed the melody and crooned the words. Then their time was up. They'd said goodbye on Platform 3, as what Janet now knew was the Aviemore train slowly groaned out of the station. At least she'd an inkling of Ian's destination but exactly where he'd end up was another story. That was the last time she'd seen him.

Her musings were cut short by a clomping of feet up the wooden stair behind her, then the sound of the door to the roof being forced open and slammed against the brick wall. She turned and quickly flashed her torch. The feeble beam picked out the grizzled but welcome features of Auld Beattie framed in a khaki balaclava. His upper body was swathed in an ancient tartan plaid that was fastened across his chest with a giant safety pin. Quickly killing the light, she gave a sigh of relief. Being alone up here in the dark was no laughing matter. The blackout was a golden opportunity for almost every type of crime. Burglary, looting, robbery, assault and even rape were not unknown as an unwelcome consequence of the wartime regulations. But Auld Beattie wasn't alone. A small, shadowy figure wrapped in a huge blanket was bobbing in his wake, panting and moaning after the steep four-storey climb to the roof.

"Hen, Ah'm awfy sorry," Auld Beattie managed to get out, stumbling into the open. He stood doubled up, out of breath. Between gasps, he managed to say, "Margaret here was havin' a bad time o' it wi' the raids. Ah couldnae leave 'er on 'er ain."

They didn't live far away. Auld Beattie had prevailed on her that he'd have to check on Janet. Either she stayed home on her own in the Anderson shelter or she came with him. She chose to come. Mrs Beattie, by now collapsed in a corner, gave out, "Ah fair raxed mahsel' oan they stairs!" In response to Janet's concern, she wheezed, "Ah'm awright hen. Ah just need a wee minute tae catch mahsel'."

When the newcomers had recovered, Janet reenged in her gas mask haversack and pulled out the Fire Watch Log Book and a pencil. She'd already signed in for the night and, pulling Auld Beattie back into the shelter of the stairwell, she got him to log himself in by torchlight. They returned to the roof and discussed the situation. Edinburgh didn't seem to be the target. Up until now, all the action had been in the west, in the Clyde valley. But who knew what the Luftwaffe had up their sleeve? Was it a diversion? Was there going to be a raid on the docks here, or another attempt on the naval base at Rosyth, or even a crack at the Forth Bridge? It was anyone's guess. Janet sneaked a look at her watch with the torch shaded. It was just after 1 am.

"Time for a wee break," she said. "Are ye hungry?"

She felt in the holdall for the thermos of tea and the meagre packet of corned beef sandwiches her mother had made. They sat together on the wooden bench in the lee of the half-roof. Auld Beattie and Margaret had brought some broth in a thermos, half a loaf of bread and some leftover stovies in a bowl. Groping around in the darkness faintly lit by the glow in the west, they shared out what they had.

"It's gey snell up here! Here, hen, warm yersel' up."

Auld Beattie was holding something out to her, but in the gloom she couldn't make out what it was. She reached out blindly and found herself grasping a small flat metal hip flask, which, going by its weight, was full.

"Git that doon ye! A wee dram," said Auld Beattie, "courtesy o' MacFergus an' Sons!"

Auld Beattie was a veteran distiller. He could have retired years ago, but he just kept on working. What he didn't know about distilling and blending whisky wasn't worth knowing. His job entailed constant handling of Scotland's finest *usquebaugh*. In a large distilling operation like MacFergus, it wasn't unusual for 'leakage' to occur. And naturally, some of that 'leakage' found its way into Auld Beattie's personal whisky flask. He should have been a raging dipsomaniac by now. But somehow he'd managed to maintain a sense of proportion, ensuring just enough of the precious liquid 'leaked' to keep him happy but not so much that it came to the attention of management or the Customs and Excise officer. No more, no less.

Surprisingly, Janet had never tasted whisky, despite the nature of her work. Still, here they were, exposed on a Scottish roof at night in the depths of winter with the Luftwaffe doing its best to terminate them. She unscrewed the flask, put the neck to her lips and took a cautious sip. She spluttered. Then a warmth, the like of which she'd never felt before, spread from her throat down into her chest and then through her entire upper body. She immediately felt better.

"Go on hen, hae anither one – dinnae stint yersel'!"

Auld Beattie's yellowing teeth appeared as he grinned in the darkness. She took a more generous mouthful, swallowed it down and the world suddenly seemed a much better place. That was the way to keep out the cold! She screwed on the cap and handed it back. Auld Beattie, then Margaret, took several swigs. Margaret started to cheer up.

"Tell ye one thing, hen. Thir's nothin' they Nazi buggers can dae against a wee dram. Nuthin' at aw'."

As if to spite her, the sudden wailing of the City air raid sirens split the air. It was the Alert. They might have deluded themselves into thinking the wee dram meant safety but it hadn't. It seemed it was now *their* turn.

"Oh mah Goad!" Margaret moaned. Auld Beattie put his arm around her and pulled her closer.

"Noo, noo," he murmured. "Dinnae fash yersel', hen."

With a half-eaten sandwich in her hand, Janet leapt to her feet, walked to the parapet and looked over the edge. The sound of engines revving carried from a couple of streets away. She looked up into the mirk. There was nothing to see, but she could hear a faint drone of aircraft engines. When the Alert sounded, fire watchers went up onto roofs while members of the public went down into air raid shelters. What to do about Margaret? The nearest public shelter was at Salvesen's in Bernard Street. But there was no way they could get her there, back down four flights of stairs and through dark, dangerous streets. Anyway, she, Janet, couldn't leave her post. Nor could Auld Beattie. Margaret would just have to tough it out with them on the roof. Searchlight beams split the air. The droning grew louder. The Fox Crag ack-ack opened up. From somewhere along the coast near Cramond, other batteries joined in. This was a raid good and proper.

At least they could take shelter in the entrance to the stairwell. Fighting to suppress bad thoughts, Janet hustled her two companions into the space. They sat on a blanket and huddled against each other in the darkness. Janet kept the door to the roof a crack open so that she could keep track of what was going on. For half an hour the cacophony of ack-ack and aircraft engines continued to the accompaniment of searchlight beams and flashes. They didn't talk. Janet didn't need to remind them that they were sitting on a potential bomb. If the distillery went up, they'd likely go with it. But she tried to be positive. Surely they wouldn't waste their bombs on Leith. Wouldn't they be more interested in Rosyth? Or The Bridge?

Eventually, it stopped. The droning engines faded away. The ack-ack wound down and the searchlights were extinguished. Minutes later, the All Clear sounded. The flat wailing tones brought a collective sigh of relief. They'd survived. Scrambling out of their refuge, they cautiously looked around.

Behind them, the half-roof above the bench seemed aglow. Janet froze for a few seconds, unsure of what she was seeing. At first, she thought someone was shining a light. But it wasn't a light. She could smell fumes. She shone her torch and immediately recognized what the shaky beam exposed. The metal casing with fins was familiar from her training. It was sparking and smoking. It must have bounced down onto the half-roof covered by the noise of the guns and was now resting snugly on pitch-encrusted tiles, covertly doing the job it was designed for. Her instinct was to panic. Then her training kicked in.

"Incendiary!"

She flashed her torch on the bomb as the Beatties turned in alarm. Auld Beattie, to give him credit, was quick off the mark.

“Ah’ll pump, you spray!” he shouted and made for the bucket and stirrup pump while Margaret, fearful, backed into the far corner. Dropping her torch into her greatcoat pocket, Janet grabbed the end of the hose, climbed on the bench and stretched up over the edge of the roof. Auld Beattie had begun to pump furiously. Luckily the bomb had lodged only a couple of yards away. With her left hand, she covered her mouth and nose with her scarf. With her right, she pointed the nozzle at the seat of the blaze just as Auld Beattie’s frenetic pumping produced the desired stream of water. Although she could breathe, her eyes were starting to sting from the fumes.

“Keep pumpin’!” Her voice was muffled by the scarf but Auld Beattie needed no telling on that score. Her wrist was starting to hurt but she kept the hose firmly pointed at the blaze. Surprisingly quickly there was a final flicker, a hiss and it was out. Janet lay there, half on the roof and half on the bench, staring at the steaming bomb casing and the charred roof tiles, now soaking wet. She half-turned and said over her shoulder, “Get the fire rake!” Auld Beattie was quick to oblige and between them they hooked the teeth of the rake around the bomb and pulled it down with a clatter off the tiles and onto the flat roof. They replenished the water in the bucket and soaked the whole area where the bomb had been, as well as the casing. As far as they could see, the fire had been confined to a small area of the roof.

Janet flicked her torch on. The three of them stood staring down at the sleekit, blackened, alien thing that had insinuated itself so noiselessly yet so violently into their lives. What had they done to deserve such evil? Janet’s thoughts were interrupted by a grunt from Auld Beattie. She flicked off her torch and looked up. He was pointing behind her. She turned round. Looking south, they could see a trail of small blazes reaching across the City. Their incendiary must have been among the first of a stack.

“Oh my God!”

With a sinking heart, it struck her that the bombs seemed to have fallen square across the western suburbs where her parents lived. She was mad with worry. Her Dad was in Clydebank. Her mother was alone. Auld Beattie immediately grasped the situation and was clear about what she had to do.

“Hen, ye have tae get hame. Go on wi’ ye, an’ look after yer mither!”

Janet was torn, but Auld Beattie insisted. The All Clear had sounded. She should be able to get home safely.

“Look, ye did the first half o’ the shift on yer ain,” he said. “Ah’ve got Margaret here.” He gave his wife a squeeze. “We can take care o’ the rest o’ the shift. Nae argie-bargie. Go on wi’ ye.”

She retrieved the Fire Watch Log Book, made some quick notes to record the events of the night, signed herself out and handed it over to Auld Beattie. Grabbing her holdall, gas mask and spare blanket, she made her way down the wooden staircase by torchlight and let herself out of the side entrance, making sure to lock it behind her. She stepped out into the blackout. Here, down in the sandstone and granite canyon of Commercial Street, the darkness was at its most intense. Leaving the hazards of the pavement and hugging the middle of the road, she started to walk, holding her torch in front of her. The sound of the cleats on her soles rang on the cobblestones and echoed back from the walls of bonded warehouses, rope works, cooperages and distilleries. She heard fire engines. But the streets were deserted. Somehow, being alone on the roof of the distillery now seemed a more attractive option. Foolish thoughts flicked in and out of her mind. She thought she heard footsteps behind her. *What* a *daft gowk*! She told herself to get a grip.

The road seemed endless. At last, she reached the bridge. Rats were scurrying along the breakwater. With a splash and flutter of wings, seabirds took off. Here, the river was tidal and from the smell, she could tell that the tide was flowing strong. That was when disaster struck. Her torch died. She cursed that she'd forgotten spare batteries. She'd planned to turn right along The Shore and up Coalhill to the Junction Street bridge but now, without a torch, that would have been foolhardy. The area had a shady reputation. Up ahead it narrowed to little more than a lane with a warren of slum tenements on the left and the river on the right. The chances of being jumped, losing her way or even stumbling into the tidal creek in the dark were too much. She'd have to play it safe, go the long way round, straight ahead then right into Constitution Street. The streets there weren't so narrow and were more likely to be patrolled by police and ARP. She went on in the gloom, tentatively feeling her way, hugging the centre of the street. Then, just as she was coming up to the turnoff into Constitution Street, without warning, the sirens started up. The Alert.

"Oh, God, no again!"

The ear-splitting wailing surged all around her. She had to get to safety. Now her eyes had adapted better, she'd a rough idea of where she was. She looked around her, straining in the darkness. She knew the Royal Bank of Scotland building was just ahead. She remembered that just before it was a block of Georgian apartments set back from the road with an archway and a passage leading through to a courtyard. She veered to the left and cautiously felt her way, tripping over the kerb and onto the pavement. Yes, there was the outline of the arch. She hurried beneath it. Further in there were massive oak double gates. They were firmly locked. But in the passage under the arch there was shelter. Here she'd be safe from anything except a direct hit. She spread the blanket in the corner between the wall and one of the gates. Pressing her back into the angle as far as possible, she waited in the darkness. All around was noise and confusion. The banging from ack-ack mingled with fire engine sirens and the growl of aero engines. She covered her ears with her hands and pushed her chin down into her chest, wishing it would all go away. It seemed to last forever. She lost track of time. After what seemed an age, it started to die down. The All Clear sounded. But still she didn't move. Head down, she hugged her knees, trance-like. Suddenly a powerful light flashed across her inert form and she was forced to look up, covering her eyes. The torch was quickly lowered.

"Sorry, lassie, Ah didnae mean tae blind ye. Are ye aw' right there?"

On receiving no response, the speaker turned the torch and shone it briefly on his upper torso and head.

"Look, there's no need tae be feared o' me!"

Janet gulped with relief. She could see from the letters on his helmet that he was an ARP warden doing the rounds. He was a middle-aged man wearing a black uniform. The straps from his haversack on one side and his gas mask bag on the other crossed on his chest. He was thin, with a hawk-like face, a prominent nose and piercing eyes.

"Ye shouldnae be here ye ken, lassie. Ye should be in a shelter. Can Ah help ye up?"

Nodding wearily, Janet allowed herself to be pulled off the ground, explaining she was a fire watcher trying to get home to her mother.

"Where does yer mother live?"

Janet told him. Warburton Crescent? He was going in that direction. He could light her part of the way if she liked.

"What time is it?"

"Gettin' on for five o'clock."

"Wis it bad?"

"What d'ye mean? The air raid?"

"Aye, that one just there – was there much damage?"

"There were some fires frae incendiaries in that previous one. Looks like Abbeyhill copped it. Damn Jerries. They probably dropped them in the wrong place. But this one, naw, none at aw'. It was just some o' they buggers on their way back tae Germany frae the Clyde, an' they triggered the Alert. The ack-ack took a crack at them. Dinnae ken if they got any, though."

They set off together at a brisk pace by torchlight, making quick work of the long artery stretching up to Junction street. Then, turning right at the statue of Queen Victoria, they walked on, passing the hospital and the picture house, then crossed back across The Water by the bridge. The further they went, the more Janet was able to relax. The warden, whose name was Jock Strachan, happened to know her father. (*Who doesn't in Leith?* she wondered.) Turning into Ferry Road, all was quiet. They plodded on, warmed up from the exercise, their breath steaming in the morning chill. The sky was beginning to lighten. Buildings and other features emerged from the gloom. Gradually other stragglers and early risers appeared as The City awoke to a new day. Jock had to turn off, but she could manage without him.

"Tell yer faither Ah'm askin' fir 'im, an' Ah hope he gets hame aw' right frae Glasgow."

Thanking him for his help, Janet pushed on for another half hour up the tree-lined avenue, past shops, schools, parks and still sleeping households, as the day broke around her. Buses were starting to run. At 6.30, she turned into Warburton Crescent, relieved to see no obvious damage. She mounted the steps into the entry, turned the key in the lock and walked into the flat.

"Mum? Mum?"

No answer. She dropped the holdall, blanket and gas mask on the linoleum, walked out of the flat, back into the entry and down the passage into the back green. It was deserted. She stood in front of the Anderson Shelter and banged on the corrugated iron.

"Mum, are ye there? Are ye aw' right?"

After a pause, the door opened and there was her mother with two neighbouring wivies. They stood shrouded in blankets, rubbing the sleep out of their eyes and blinking in the weak winter sunrise that was filtering through the bare-branched trees between the buildings.

"Oh, hello Janet, how are ye, hen?" her mother asked. Without waiting for an answer she turned to her neighbours. "Janet's been fire watchin' ye ken," she said proudly.

They all gazed admiringly at Janet. She realised she was still wearing her Dad's old helmet.

"Well, hen, thon was an awfy noisy night, wasn't it? Ye're lookin' a bit peely-wally. Did ye no manage tae catch any shuteye?"

Dazed and disoriented, Janet opened and closed her mouth but nothing came out. Suddenly it struck her how exhausted she was.

"Come on, hen, Ah'll make ye a nice cup o' tea, a bit o' toast an' a plate o' porridge," her mother said, taking her by the arm and leading her back into the flat.

It was then Janet realized that in two hours' time she was due back at MacFergus for the day shift. With a bit of luck she might manage an hour's sleep before she had to catch her bus.

1945: The sergeant

A hole suddenly appeared in the middle of Second Lieutenant Pearson's forehead the shape and colour of a small black flower. It was followed a split second later by the unmistakable crack of a Mauser Gewehr 98. Mr Pearson fell backwards with an expression of surprise on his face. The men dropped and snaked to the nearest cover, a shallow ditch below a bank. The shot had come from the low, mist-shrouded hillside above the road. Whoever had fired it knew how to use a rifle.

Sergeant Ian Swanston lay in the mud next to the dead officer and silently cursed to himself. Clicking his Sten to 'safe', he rolled over into the ditch. He sat with his back to the bank, cradling his weapon, and reviewed the situation. A light rain was now falling. Mr Pearson lay on his back in the middle of the road staring at the sky, his arms outstretched. His blond hair trailed in the mud. Blood was seeping from the back of his head, mixing with the rain and creating a widening red puddle. His helmet lay a few yards away. Ian had warned him about removing it in combat. Not that it would have been much help against this sniper's bullet. He looked along the row of mud-bespattered men of 'B' Platoon ranged in various attitudes against the hawthorn hedge lining the bank. Some were lying on their backs hugging their rifles. Others were sitting, their heads hanging between their knees, or crawling or looking around them. Of the faces that were visible, only a few appeared alert. Most were haggard after weeks and months of freezing, sleepless nights spent in barns, woods and water-filled slit trenches. A few were plainly afraid. Of the original thirty-odd men of this unit who'd started out seven months before, only three had made it this far unscathed. The rest had either been killed or invalided out.

Ian reflected on the events that had brought him here. This wasn't 'his' platoon. But when a German 88 shell had landed next to Lieutenant Purvis, the platoon commander, the day before, blowing him to unidentifiable bits, the platoon had suddenly been without a leader. The second-in-command was a green, nineteen-year-old 2Lt who'd been posted to the regiment only weeks before. There was no way they could leave him in command. The men would never have stood for it. Severely short of combat-experienced officers, Colonel Boswell had asked Ian to take over the platoon temporarily until a replacement could be found. Mr Pearson, with only three weeks' active service behind him, now lay in the mud. His war was over.

It was Friday 4th of May 1945. The strategic city of Bremen had finally surrendered to them the previous week. Yesterday, word had come through on Divisional radio that the German Fuehrer, Adolf Hitler, had committed suicide in his Berlin bunker three days before. The men of the 155 Brigade, 52nd Lowland Division, could be forgiven for believing that The War was finally over. But this was an illusion. No armistice had yet been signed. All around them, scattered German forces were still active - remnants of retreating Wehrmacht units, members of the Volkssturm and fanatical Hitlerjugend. They were armed and could still be dangerous. 'B' Platoon had been tasked with mopping up some of these units. Luckily, so far, operations had gone relatively smoothly. In most cases, the troops they'd had to confront had readily surrendered. Dirty, hungry and exhausted, they'd dropped their weapons, raised their hands and abandoned their positions, relieved that they'd been captured, as they thought, by *Engländer* and not the *Ivan*. Only later did they discover the 'Engländer' were actually Jocks.

This morning the Platoon had been sent out to investigate reports of units of the Hitlerjugend in some rough farming country to the northwest of Bremen near the town of Ottersberg. After one of the hardest winters Europe had known in many a year, spring had come late. But it had taken hold at last. Despite the grey, misty weather, the hedgerows were greening up, dog roses infested the verges and there were even some late daffodils around. Birdsong split the air as they marched away from the trucks that had brought them this far. Some members of the platoon might even have been thinking that summer was just around the next bend. It should have been a dawdle, rounding up a bunch of boys with obsolete weapons. They'd been advancing down a narrow defile with low hills of mixed pasture and heath stretching up on either side. Whether they'd grown careless, or whether it was just bad luck was anyone's guess. But when a halt was called to consult the map, any optimism they'd harboured was quickly shattered. This time, they wouldn't be going through the motions. There would be no easy surrender. The body of Mr Pearson lying in the mud with the life draining out of it was proof of that.

Ian weighed up his men. He knew what was going through their minds. It was written all over their faces. Nobody wanted to be another Mr Pearson. Nobody wanted to be an eleventh-hour casualty. Nobody wanted the dubious honour of being the last soldier in the Brigade - or the Division - to lose his life in this godforsaken war. Every one of them was a conscript. They hadn't asked to fight the German Wehrmacht. In Civvy Street most of them had had jobs, professions, careers. A couple of the officers were farmers, another was a lawyer, another a bank manager. Among the men there were civil servants, clerks, builders, warehousemen, shop workers and bus conductors. They weren't professional soldiers. Yet, they'd had to fight. In the long slog across the North German plain they'd encountered death and destruction everywhere they'd gone. Mates had died or had been maimed for life. For their part, they'd had to learn how to kill and how to live with death every day. They'd done their bit to defeat Fascism. But now they'd had enough. Any day now they expected to hear. Surely the Germans would surrender? Surely the armistice would come? Then and only then could they relax. Perhaps they could return to their families and take up their former lives where they'd left off. The main thing was to stay alive - for just a few more days.

Ian had stayed alive for all of eight months. He couldn't believe his luck. Up until 1944, one of the Division's main tasks had been rehearsing for the invasion of Norway. Stationed in the Scottish Highlands, they'd been trained in all aspects of a winter campaign in the mountains, from learning to ski and fight in the snow to winter survival.

Ian had every expectation that one day he'd be on a ship heading to Stavanger or Bergen. However, their military masters suddenly decided otherwise. Norway was no longer a priority. In September 1944, Ian unexpectedly found himself part of a full platoon of Jocks sitting in a Horsa glider at a Lincolnshire aerodrome with Dutch money in his pocket bound for Deelen airport, Arnhem. They were to join *Operation Market Garden*. Then, minutes before scheduled take-off, they were ordered out of the aircraft and told to stand down. In retrospect, Ian was relieved he hadn't been involved in that cock-up. Knowing the mortality rate among glider-borne troops, he had a fair idea of what his fate might have been had that glider taken off. The next change of plan was even more bizarre. The generals sent the mountain troops of the 52nd Mountain Division to fight below sea level in the Dutch polders on the island of Walcheren. *Operation Infatuate* was tasked with taking Walcheren as part of the clearance of the Scheldt estuary to free up the port of Ostend. This was the first time any of them had been in action. After an amphibious landing on the beach at Flushing, they found themselves up to their chests in seawater fighting their way across the flooded island, causeway by causeway, pillbox by pillbox, against a tenacious foe that employed snipers, fixed machine guns, 88mm cannon, and underwater mines. To say it was hell would be an understatement. Somehow, Ian survived. Once the island had been taken, the nasty winter war continued as 155 Brigade headed out across the Netherlands and into the snow of Northern Germany on a major slog against well-armed, dogged, battle-tested German troops in well-defended positions. They'd lost many good men in foolish gambits and ill-advised attacks. But finally, towards the end of April, they achieved their goal, capturing Bremen after two days' fighting. Again, miraculously, Ian had come through unscathed.

And now here they were. Somewhere up there was a sniper. Whoever he was, he wasn't going to give up easily. The standard MO in these situations would be a platoon attack, Bren gun on the flank, sections spread out. But Ian quickly dismissed this idea. Uphill, in unknown terrain, in the mist and rain? They had no idea how many other marksmen were up there. No support of any kind was available. They had no mortars. The tanks were miles away and the 25 pounders busy elsewhere. Air cover was out of the question in this weather. No rocket Typhoons today. It had become very still. He realized everyone was looking at him. He'd only recently had his thirtieth birthday. To most of the squaddies under him he was already an old man. He'd never commanded this particular lot before, but they knew him by repute. He was firm but fair, a strict disciplinarian but with a strong human streak and even a sense of humour. They knew he wouldn't ask them to do anything he couldn't do himself. The three or four youngest Jocks conscripted into the squad were only eighteen. With a couple of weeks' training under their belts and rifles shoved into their hands, they'd been shipped out to fill gaps in the Division. It was criminal. They tried to hide their fear but Ian could see it in their eyes. His next order could decide whether they lived or died. It was as simple as that. But a platoon attack was sure to result in casualties. He couldn't be responsible for any more deaths, not now, not when the end of this particular nightmare was so close. He made eye contact with two of the corporals and motioned them to him. They crawled over, keeping their heads down.

"What d'ye think?" he asked.

They easily read his mind and shook their heads in unison.

"The lads are knackered, Sarge," said Cpl. Murdoch.

"Nae fuckin' way, Sarge," echoed Cpl. Tait.

"Ah agree but we have tae try somethin'."

The corporals lay in the muck, staring at him expectantly. The contrast between them couldn't have been greater. Tait was 24, small, red-headed and pudgy but moved surprisingly fast. He'd been a butcher in Tranent before The War. Murdoch was older, 28, dark, lean and rangy. He'd crewed fishing trawlers out of Granton. Both had learnt the hard way how to lead men, how to kill and how to stay alive. Finally, Ian said, "First, let's find out where the bastard is." He unslung the binoculars case from around his neck. Normally only officers got their hands on binoculars, but he'd liberated these – a nice pair of Zeiss – from an Oberleutnant he'd had to kill in a particularly nasty firefight at a fortified farmhouse near the Dutch border. He handed the binoculars to Corporal Tait. He was to position himself in the ditch among bushes on the other side of the road. Cpl. Murdoch gave the signal. One of the men raised his helmet above the hedge on the butt of his rifle. Almost immediately the helmet was knocked off, followed by a crack.

"Did ye see 'im?" Ian asked Tait. They'd both spotted some movement they thought was a rifle barrel from a depression among some ferns. They went through the same procedure with the same result. Now they were confident they'd pinpointed his position. Ian left the corporals in charge and crawled a hundred yards back down the road until he was masked by the convex slope. He snaked up the bank, found a gap in the hedge, crept a further few yards up the hill and cautiously did a recce. There was a line of willow running from his position diagonally up the hillside to the left. The trees were heavy with new spring foliage and would provide adequate cover. There was a shallow ditch on this side of the treeline. The trees ended about twenty or thirty yards from the sniper's position. It was perfect. Ian crawled back. The two corporals were squatting beside Mr Pearson's body in the lee of a forsythia in full bloom covered by hyperactive bees. For a second or two, Ian reflected on the startling contrast between life and death.

"Right," he said to Tait and Murdoch. "It's on me."

"Ye mean...?" mouthed Murdoch.

"Aye, Ah'll deal wi' it."

"Are ye sure ye want tae dae this, Sarge?" offered Tait. "We could wait for support."

"Ye ken how long that would take. An' how many mair o' us is 'e gonnae clobber if we just sit here? We have tae finish this now."

Though Ian's words appeared self-assured, his stomach had dropped to somewhere below his boots.

"But Ah need one radio man in support wi' a Bren. A volunteer. No you guys. Ah need you tae be here. Whae d'ye think?"

Murdoch looked around. His eye fell on Murphy. He was one out of the box, an Englishman in a Scottish regiment. Ah yes, Private Murphy, who, despite his Irish surname, was from East Anglia. A maverick. And a first-class marksman. It was rumoured he was a gamekeeper in civilian life but he never admitted to this and some joked he was more likely to have been a poacher. Murphy, undersized, but sinewy and hard as nails. Murphy, who dressed like a gipsy in his non-regulation uniform. But nobody minded, least of all his officers. He was smart. He was resourceful. If there was a chicken to be found or a leg of ham or a bottle of schnapps, he'd find it. Most of all he was reliable, with a quiet courage. And he was one of the few that had survived all the way from Flushing. Murphy had been offered promotion many times but had always refused. "No, Sir," he'd say, "oi'm just one of the lads, and that's how oi'll stay, thank you."

Ian caught Murphy's eye. Murphy crawled over.

"What's up, Sarge?"

Ian briefly explained the situation. He needed to neutralise that sniper. Would Murphy volunteer to be his radio man and his cover? Murphy looked at him with a glint in his eye. There was something of the Irish in Murphy after all.

"You know, Sarge, it would be an honour," he said quietly.

"Right," said Ian, "three Mills Bombs each, Sten wi' spare mags for me, Bren wi' spare mags for you. Helmets off, cap comforters. Tell Finlay tae lend me 'is para smock. Set up the other Bren further up the road tae cover the hillside. Radio silence till ye hear from us, OK?"

He gave orders to the corporals about what to do should it all go wrong. They collected their gear and smeared cold mud from the roadside ditch across their faces. Murphy was helped on with the radio. They were ready to go. Ian took what might be his last look at the platoon. Despite the strain they were under, some managed to smile.

"Good luck, Sarge!"

"Thank you, Sarge!"

"Gie the bastard hell, Sarge!"

Mr Pearson's face had now been covered with a scarf.

"For Mr Pearson, Sarge!"

Closely followed by Murphy, Ian crawled back up the road, over the bank, through the gap in the hedge and entered the line of willows, keeping low. They were completely hidden from the sniper's position. But there was no way of knowing if he had support further up the hill and if so, how well that support could shoot. They'd just have to take their chances. They crawled along the ditch in the shelter of the trees, up and across the hillside, keeping a careful watch to their right. The pace was slow, Murphy struggling with his extra load. Finally, they reached a point where the willows petered out and lay down behind a shallow bank under low-hanging foliage. Before them was a slope of undulating, broken ground dotted with bracken and reeds. They could just see the left-hand edge of the dip in the ground where they thought the sniper was, straight ahead, twenty yards or more. Ian turned to Murphy.

"Ah'm gonnae take care o' this guy," he whispered. Murphy nodded. "Your job is tae take care o' *me*. Ah want ye wi' yer eyes peeled lookin' up that way." He pointed to the hillside above the sniper. "Get the radio off yer back, grenades ready, set up the Bren."

Murphy did as was bid, unlatching the legs of the Bren and setting it up facing up and across the slope. Positioning himself behind it, he flicked off the safety, snapped in a full magazine, quietly drew back the bolt and fed a round into the breech with a satisfying *click*. Ian settled his Sten round his neck on the long strap. He took a grenade in each hand, clamped his fingers over the safety levers and held his hands out.

"Pull the pins."

Murphy pulled the pins and dropped them in the mud. Ian nodded and turned to go. Murphy tapped him on the shoulder.

"Good luck, Sarge," he mouthed.

Slithering awkwardly out of cover, Ian half-crouched, half-crawled the distance to his target, making sure to keep a firm grip on the grenades. When he got close, he dropped onto his side, waited and listened. Nothing. He risked a quick look over the tops of the ferns. Sure enough, there was the end of a Mauser protruding from what seemed to be a serviceable sniper's nest dug into a natural depression. The walls and roof were of branches with ferns piled on top. A perfectly camouflaged position for a shooter. He looked round to see what Murphy was doing and got a nod in response.

"Well, here goes," he thought. For a fleeting second, his thoughts turned to his wife and child. Where was Janet? What was she doing? Then as soon as the image entered his head it was gone. Standing up, he calmly approached the shelter from the side. He released the spring lever in his left hand. As it flew over his shoulder, he threw the bomb through the front opening, quickly transferred the other bomb from his right to his left, lobbed it after the first, and dropped flat on his face.

Boom – boom!

The double explosion rang across the hillside but was muted by the mist and rain. Earth and broken branches cascaded down. He quickly stood up, took another two steps, pointed his Sten through the gaping hole in the shelter where the roof had been and emptied the entire thirty-two round magazine in a scything gesture, left and right. Dropping flat again, he put a fresh magazine in the Sten, cocked it and waited. The noise of the assault died away. He lay on his belly and looked round to where Murphy was. He was nodding. Ian raised himself, looked up and across the hillside, waiting for the expected bullet. But it never came. He walked round to the front of the shelter pointing the Sten, and carefully looked inside. The boy was about twelve years old. He had on an oversize grey overall with a Hitlerjugend swastika armband. His helmet, too big for his juvenile head, had been blown off by the force of the explosion and now lay dented and riddled with bullet holes in front of the bunker. He was on his side across his Mauser. Half of his head had been blown away by one of the grenades. A tangle of blood and blonde hair was all that was left. From this angle, he looked just like what was left of Mr Pearson down there on the muddy track. The other bomb had destroyed his lower legs. The Sten had finished the job.

Surveying the carnage he'd caused, Ian forced himself to suppress a pang of regret. He'd seen far worse in this rotten winter war. Women, children, incinerated in their homes by German Einsatzgruppen. Comrades reduced to a bloody mess by a single 88 shell. Friends with legs blown off by shoebox mines. Of course, he'd had close combat kills before. But never so young. He turned round, walked a few steps into cover and sat down, his head low. He retched but nothing came. A wave brought Murphy over, crouching under the weight of the Bren and the radio. He looked into the ruins of the shelter and simply said, "Well done, Sarge." They radioed down to the platoon to say that all was clear. Ian instructed the corporals to bring the men up by the same route and make a sweep of the rest of the hillside. His orders were carried out until they were satisfied the area was secure.

Later, as they made their way back down to the road, the men trooped past the shelter to see the corpse of the boy with the Mauser that had done for Mr Pearson. If they had any thoughts they kept them to themselves. But a few of them slapped Ian lightly on the shoulder as they went past. Ian recovered the Mauser, extracted the magazine, cleared the breech and broke the rifle over a nearby rock. The remains of the boy could be left to the recovery teams. It was a wet, weary platoon that straggled into the 155 Brigade HQ area in Bremen around 8.30 that night bearing the corpse of their young platoon commander on an improvised stretcher of branches and jackets. As they entered the regimental lines they could hear laughing, shouting, even singing in the distance. What was going on? A couple of orderlies ran towards them.

"It's over, it's over!" they cried, dancing around like madmen.

It took a few moments for it to sink in. The news had just come through over the radio. Unconditional surrender of all German forces in Holland, Denmark and Northwest Germany, signed just over an hour ago in Monty's tent on Luneburg Heath. It WAS over. They'd survived.

That evening, in the half-ruined hotel that passed for the sergeants' mess, someone had the BBC on and Vera Lynn was singing 'We'll Meet Again'. But Ian sat quietly. Word of what he'd done had got around. The Colonel had personally thanked him and talked of an award for gallantry, a DCM. Friends and fellow warrant officers drank his health. He had a few with them but stayed sober. The composure he'd always prided himself on had been sorely tested in this war, and particularly today. Despite that, he was determined not to let the day's events affect him adversely. The Germans had started it. Their actions had led to the deaths of men he'd known and liked and had forced him to kill them in return. So be it. The main thing was that he'd survived. He could return to his wife and daughter back home. He would never talk about this day. But a picture of the blond hair and the blood and the Mauser was now etched in his brain and was filed away, together with the hundreds of similar images amassed over the last eight months.

Ian never did get that medal. Before his CO could write his report, he was caught in a Werwolf ambush and his name became a *post hoc* addition to the long list of war dead. Without his endorsement, an award was out of the question. But Ian didn't care. Nor did he bother to collect the campaign medals that were his entitlement on discharge from the services. He resolved to put it all behind him and to get on with his life.

1946: A new start

Nineteen forty-five had come and gone. But Ian was still far from home. Though thousands of servicemen had been demobbed so far, his name hadn't yet reached the top of the list. Now promoted to Company Sergeant-Major and in a peacetime security role at Divisional HQ near Munster, Ian had yet more work to do. The Allies had won The War. Now they had to win the peace. There were prisoners to process; German cities to govern; civilians to feed; enemy weapons and armaments to locate and neutralise; war criminals to arrest. On and on it went. Finally, in May 1946, after a full year of this, he got to the head of the queue and his release from the British Army was approved. When he'd been conscripted in 1940 he'd had a full head of thick, wavy, chestnut hair. By the time the Army was finished with him at the age of 31, he was already balding. His final medical examination found him 'fit for further service in Medical Category A1'. His height was recorded at 5 ft. 8 ¼ ins., and his weight at 132 lbs. His military conduct was classified as 'Exemplary' and he received a personal, signed recommendation from none other than the General commanding the

52nd Lowland Division. Stamped at the bottom of his army service record was the entry: RELEASED TO CLASS 'Z' (T) ROYAL ARMY RESERVE. These words would come back to haunt him.

On his homecoming in 1946, Ian was immediately offered his old job back at MacFergus in Leith. He returned to a country that was bankrupt, a population weary of war, ground down and emaciated by deprivations that had not ended merely with the armistice in Europe. Rationing was still in force. Chocolate, bananas, coffee and oranges were fabled luxuries that had been plentiful in some distant pre-war world but which few had seen for years. Bread had never been rationed during The War. Suddenly, in 1946, bread rationing was imposed as the British took on the added burden of feeding starving Europeans. Housewives were incensed. They wondered when it was going to end. Bread continued to be rationed for another two years, sugar and sweets until 1953, and overall rationing, including meat, didn't end until 1954, a full 15 years after the start of The War and nine years after the end. Meals were basic, helpings were small and the food was often unappetising. Everything else was equally bland. Clothes were utilitarian. Petrol was scarce or unobtainable.

After six long years of war punctuated by brief, stolen periods of leave, all across Britain couples were having to acquaint themselves with each other all over again. Women were discovering that they no longer recognised the husbands that had gone off to fight. Men were struggling to readjust to a world without war. Some were wondering what had happened to the sweetheart they'd held fast in their memories. Children born when their fathers were away suddenly found a stranger living in their midst. Relationships foundered. Families fractured. The divorce rate shot up.

There had been a general election in 1945. Servicemen overseas had been able to vote. Labour had won a landslide victory and the wartime Prime Minister, Winston Churchill, to many a national hero, had been thrown out of office. A range of reasons was put forward for this somewhat unexpected result. Some said it was because people thought Labour would do a better job on the housing crisis. Others thought Labour would get servicemen demobbed faster. Yet others pointed to the wartime coalition cabinet, which had brought to prominence Labour politicians. But Ian had his own ideas and his own reason for voting as he did. He voted Labour – the one and only time he'd do so. It was a protest vote. Of course he'd supported going to war. When he'd been called up he'd been prepared to do his bit. But he was soon disillusioned by the levels of mismanagement and ineptitude he witnessed, from the waste and folly of sending mountain troops to fight in floodwaters, to

Market Garden, which he'd avoided only by the skin of his teeth. On reflection, he was sure he wouldn't have survived that particular fiasco.

As the 52nd Lowland Division had spread out over the plains of Northern Europe in the worst winter in eighty years, Ian and his fellow conscripts, most of whom had never been in combat before, had discovered how inferior their gear was. Occasionally, they'd bump into elements of the US Ninth Army operating on their eastern flank, exchange chocolate and cigarettes and swap stories. Ian always marvelled at the quality of the Yanks' clothing and equipment. Their overcoats, jackets and boots were heavier and thicker, better proof against the freezing weather. Their food was more plentiful, there was more variety, and it was brought up to the front more efficiently. Ian came to realise too how inferior their weapons were. His unit had gone into action without any kind of infantry artillery. By contrast, the Wehrmacht had the notorious 88, which could double as both an anti-tank gun and an anti-aircraft gun. This single German infantry gun alone, in the hands of German *Landser,* did dreadful slaughter among the Jocks of 155 Brigade. Then there was the only British-manufactured sub-machine gun, the Sten, which was vastly inferior to the German MP38 and MP40, the trademark weapons of German infantrymen. Against tanks, GIs had the bazooka. German troops had the infamous Panzerfaust, which was so simple to use that even the boys and old men of the Volkssturm were knocking out US, British and Russian tanks with it. By comparison, Ian and his men were given the PIAT, a cross between a mortar and a bazooka, which was heavy, clumsy and difficult to use. To his mind, he and his comrades had been hamstrung by the incompetence and lethargy of the British political and military establishments even before they'd fought their first engagement.

As well, lives had been squandered through First World War-style frontal attacks on fortified German positions without air or armour support. Not that he hadn't served with good men, effective soldiers, and capable leaders. But the latter, especially, had been few and far between. There had been far too many of the other kind; bad, weak, inexperienced and inept. The faces of comrades who'd lost their lives, as he saw it, unnecessarily, stayed with him. This was a burden he carried from his war, a level of bitterness he couldn't shake off for the rest of his life. But he kept it largely to himself. The extreme fanaticism of German troops had also been a shock, even though this was something they'd been warned to expect. An officer friend had once commented: "Whatever the Germans do, they do particularly well," and fanaticism, in Ian's book, was something they did particularly thoroughly. Their stubborn, often pointless, but almost always lethal resistance was, to Ian, incomprehensible. The Hitler Youth sniper was a case in point. On the day Ian had had to kill him, the Russians were already in Berlin. The German commanders knew it was over. Yet still, they ordered boys to resist – and to die. Why? Ian just didn't get it.

For her part, Janet had had her own struggle. Some might have said that her encounter with the incendiary bomb was nothing short of heroic. She and Auld Beattie had potentially saved MacFergus and the jobs of its workforce. But that very same night, all over Britain, thousands of ordinary people just like Janet were doing extraordinary things without reward or recognition. Instead, her reward was to have her wedding postponed. Ian simply couldn't get leave. Since the end of the Phony War, the 52nd Lowland Division had been tasked with the defence of the Scottish coastline. Ian was part of a team specialising in the defence of RAF stations in the South of Scotland. Pressure increased at the end of May with the loss of Crete. Landings by German paratroopers were expected at any time. All leave was cancelled. Then, suddenly, at the end of June 1941, Germany invaded the Soviet Union. With the Wehrmacht fully occupied on the Eastern Front, the threat of invasion started to ease. The 52nd Lowland Division could relax. Ian's request for leave to get married was finally granted.

The wedding took place on a Friday in August in South Leith Church two weeks after Janet's 19th birthday. It was a modest affair. Janet wore a powder blue two-piece suit with a knee-length skirt bought from Marks and Spencer with money saved from her meagre wages. Ian wore his dress uniform with tartan trews. Sister Effie, the single bridesmaid, wore an austerity outfit. Ian's brother-in-law and mentor, Jimmy, was the best man in his Sunday suit, especially dry-cleaned for the occasion. The only others present were Ian's mother, sister and stepsister and Janet's parents. There was no reception, just an afternoon tea at Warburton Crescent for a few family members. The newlyweds allowed themselves the luxury of a taxi to Waverley where they caught a train to North Berwick. Here they had the weekend for their honeymoon at a bed and breakfast before Ian had to report back for duty.

Janet soldiered on at MacFergus, the only memorable event in her daily grind occurring one morning on her way home from fire watch. For that was when she bumped into a uniformed, moustached, elderly gentleman who was just emerging from the Norwegian Sailors Chapel.

"Good morning, madam!" said the man in strangely accented English, raising his cap in apology.

"And guid mornin' tae you too, Sir!" Janet replied, bemused.

As his car sped off, she turned to the small group of onlookers, one of whom was carrying a large camera and seemed to be a reporter.

"Who was that then?" she asked, of no one in particular.

"D'ye no ken? That was King Haakon of Norway!"

She never tired of telling the story. As it happened, her time at MacFergus would soon end when she discovered she was pregnant. Two years after her wedding she gave birth to a daughter she named Effie after her wee sister. She brought the newborn home from the Elsie Inglis hospital to her parents' home in Warburton Crescent. But that didn't last long. Her father, Alexander Melrose, was by nature a difficult man. He and Janet had often clashed in the past. His mission to Clydebank had done little to help matters. Now, well into his fifties, he thought he'd left his personal horrors behind at Gallipoli and The Somme. But now he had a new horror: the memory of retrieving charred bodies of women and children from the rubble of Clydebank. He was sombre and withdrawn for some time after he returned. It was no surprise then that he couldn't cope with a new baby in the cramped, overcrowded flat. Wee Effie cried incessantly. Finally, Alexander unceremoniously told Janet to take the baby and leave.

Janet never forgave her father. She had nowhere to go. There was only one person she could turn to. Ian's older sister, Christine, and her husband had got one of the new council houses out at Sighthill. Childless, and amenable to having a baby in their house despite the practical drawbacks, they generously offered to take her and the newborn in. Caring for Wee Effie, Janet was able to work only infrequently when Christine – who had her own job as an office manager in the City – could step in. Even then, she had to be careful. Christine was kindhearted but she had little idea of how to care for an infant. Janet once walked in from work to find Wee Effie, at the age of three, standing on a stool in the kitchen in front of a chip pan bubbling on the stove, with Christine, a cigarette in her mouth, cheerily supervising. Diplomatically removing her bairn from the hazard, Janet reflected that it might, after all, be a blessing that Chrissie had been unable to have children.

Still, Janet continued to rely on her sister-in-law's charity while she scraped by on Ian's meagre soldier's salary. And so she battled on for another three years, lodging with her in-laws, seeing Ian only twice after the baby was born, getting censored letters with the return address *c/o Army Post Office*, then for a whole year, from 1944 to 1945, getting no letters at all. She had to make do with pre-printed postcards that merely told her that Ian was still alive. Only with peace in Europe did she start to receive real, uncensored letters that filled in the gaps of the previous two years. She was on tenterhooks as the day of Ian's arrival back in Scotland neared, but the military authorities had one last trick up their sleeves. For Ian's discharge to be formalised, he had to proceed directly to a military barracks in Troon and wait for the paperwork to be completed. Troon, Ayrshire, of all places, about the furthest away from Edinburgh that you could think of in the Lowlands, and about the most awkward to get to for someone without their own transport. After a gruelling bus and train journey via Glasgow, struggling with a suitcase and a three-year-old daughter, Janet arrived at the bed-and-breakfast Sergeant-Major Ian Swanston had booked in the town. After two years of separation, they had an emotional reunion. Seven days of passionate nights later, Janet had conceived a son and they'd successfully resumed their life as a married couple.

With Ian finally shot of the Army and back in Edinburgh at last, they tried to settle down. They were grateful for Christine's continued hospitality but knew this was only a stopgap. Four adults and a three-year-old bairn in a flat with only two rooms and a kitchen was a recipe for friction, especially as Chrissie's husband was beginning to tire of the arrangement. Besides, Sighthill was a long commute from Ian's work in Leith. The matter became even more pressing when their son was born in 1947. They'd definitely have to find something closer in. At a time of severe post-war housing shortages this wasn't easy. But after months of searching, they found a tiny flat on the third floor of a dingy tenement in Fife View, halfway between Leith and Newhaven. Before the Port Authority land reclamation, Fife View dropped steeply to a rocky, seaweed-infested shoreline. The Forth did its best to undermine the granite breakwater while the nor'easter that regularly roared in from the North Sea dashed salt spray against walls, windows, and into the open entry of the tenement. The flat comprised a bedroom barely larger than a good-sized cupboard and a cramped living room with a sink and gas stove. The toilet outside on the landing was shared with the neighbouring flat. The upside was that the rent was low, it was within easy walking distance of Ian's work and there was a stunning panorama across the Firth to Fife when the weather cleared. Counting themselves lucky, the Swanstons moved into their new home to start a life together with their two children. But they knew that what they had was only a temporary solution.

1 Brockit Brae

A room and kitchen

The heavy wooden tenement door of 11 Brecon Street leaned drunkenly against the entry, propped on a blackened sandstone flag that was worn concave by a century's passage of feet. No one could remember when that door had last closed. The tenement walls had been the colour of sandstone when new in the mid-Victorian era but a century of soot, dirt, salt-laden winds and landlord neglect had done its work. Now they were a begrimed mockery of what they once had been. The slates were loose, the lums were crumbling, the grannies didn't birl any more, the windows jammed and the panes were cracked. The entry smelt of urine, coal dust and boiled turnips.

Several steps in, the last rays of daylight quickly gave way to deep gloom that enveloped them as they mounted the stairs. Janet Swanston, a suitcase in one hand, clutched three-year-old James in the other as he clambered up steps designed for adult legs. Ian Swanston brought up the rear, a suitcase in each hand, shepherding Wee Effie, an independent-minded lassie of some seven years. Their eyes struggled to adjust to the dark. But as they climbed beyond the third floor the gloom lessened as a feeble light from a blackened skylight high above them filtered into the stairwell. By the time they got to the top floor, the fifth, it was just enough to fumble the key into the lock and push the door open. Now they could see normally again. They stepped inside onto the linoleum-covered floor and walked through the lobby and into the bare, unheated living room.

"Well, that's us," said Ian.

It wasn't much, but it was better than what they'd had in Fife View. What was supposed to have been a temporary solution to their housing needs had stretched out almost four years. The proof, if ever it was needed, that every cloud has a silver lining, came in the early hours of a March morning in 1951. Ian's mother died suddenly at the age of 61 of a cerebral haemorrhage in her flat at 11 Brecon Street. Putting their grief aside, the young couple realized that their bereavement had given them an opening. Granny Swanston's flat was free. It was much larger than the Fife View flat and, more importantly, it had its own toilet. As well, it was centrally located in the heart of Leith. Brecon Street was the only hope they had of improving their living conditions. The recent narrow Labour win in the general election wasn't going to change things any time soon. Labour under Atlee had already had five years to take action but hadn't produced any results that had helped the Swanstons. Like many, Ian had concluded that the vote he'd cast for Labour in 1945 had been wasted. This time round, he'd given his vote to the Conservatives under Churchill. Maybe next time they'd be able to take power and really get their teeth into the housing debacle.

The Swanstons' situation with two small children and their kinship to the previous tenant had stood them in good stead with the corporate landlord. Once the funeral formalities were out of the way, they took a tram up to the main office off St Andrew Square, signed the lease, paid a month's rent in advance and picked up the key. The flat was theirs. Apart from some tea chests containing bed linen, blankets, pots, pans and a teapot and kettle, crockery and cutlery, which still had to come from Fife View, the contents of the flat and of their three suitcases were all they had in the world.

Their new home was a so-called room and kitchen. The 'room' was one small bedroom. The 'kitchen' was a modest-sized living room off which was a tiny alcove scullery consisting of a scrubbed wooden bunker, a deep porcelain sink with a single brass tap that issued only cold water, and an ancient gas cooker with two burners, a grill and an oven, that was powered by the municipal gas supply piped directly into the tenement. At least they could tell themselves that they had a separate 'kitchen'. The living room window gave a view of tenement backs and so-called 'greens'. A single fireplace with a high wooden mantlepiece provided the only heating. The coal was stored off the lobby in a lumber-room, something the size of a large cupboard. Adjacent to this was a toilet, but no bath or wash-hand basin, so they had to wash themselves - and Ian had to shave - in the scullery. There was a single electric power socket in the skirting board of the living room, which powered the radio, but electric light had never been connected and the Swanstons had to be content to live by gaslight as the Victorians had done. The walls were covered with ancient flowery wallpaper that was peeling in places and brown with age.

Granny Swanston's meagre personal effects had been cleared out but her few sticks of furniture had been left for the new tenants. There was a bed, a wardrobe, an armchair, two dining chairs, a dining table and a decrepit, leather-bound bed settee. They found Granny Swanston's wooden ironing board in the press. As well as the brown linoleum, here in the living room they had the added luxury of a threadbare carpet that managed to cover about half of the area. The Swanstons stood there, unsure for a moment. They'd known this only as their mother's home – ultimately her last. But now it had become the step up they needed.

Brecon Street dipped abruptly from the spine of Junction Street and snaked down towards Bonnybrig Road. It was a long, narrow, cobbled thoroughfare, lined by dilapidated century-old tenements and workshops. So constricted were the five- and six-storey buildings that the street resembled a soot-encrusted ravine into which daylight rarely percolated, especially during the short days of the hard Scottish winters. So it was known locally as Brockit Brae. The lower half of the street, at the Bonnybrig Road end, was occupied by industry. The slate works were a vestige of the extensive eighteenth- and nineteenth-century manufactories of Welsh slate tiles that had given the street its name and had roofed half the tenements in Edinburgh. When the wind came from the south, aromas from the biscuit factory competed with yeasty odours from the breweries for the noses of the locals. A small foundry, a cooperage, a rope works, a metal works and sundry warehouses jostled for space. The upper half of the street was given over to tenements, shops, the Ebenezer Church and the Salvation Army Hall. Indeed, such was the concentration of commerce, rented accommodation and religion that Brecon Street was permanently busy with the comings and goings of church members, shoppers, tenants and workers, not to mention delivery vans, lorries, the odd ragman with horse and cart, as well as the scaffie with his push cart, shovel and hard-bristled brush.

The Sally was a major presence in Brecon Street. Its activities, which spanned the entire week, seemed to be unceasing. Bible classes, youth groups, family sessions, collections of clothing, food or household goods, there was always something afoot. Summer or winter, at least once a week, the Sally brass band would troop out into the street at the end of the working day, stand in a circle, half on, half off the cobbles, and play a repertoire of stirring Christian music. Within the narrow confines of Brecon Street, the sudden eruption of trumpets, trombones and tubas was compressed between the sandstone walls and amplified as if through a megaphone, startling the unaware into wakefulness and spooking carthorses far and wide. Support was provided by the vocal efforts of available Sallies accompanied by any passers-by that cared to join in the singing. Seductive but untouchable in her trim black uniform, her bonnet coquettishly tied in a bow at the side under her chin, a picture-perfect Sally maiden, smiling invitingly, went around with the collecting tin.

The tenants of Brecon Street were fortunate to have an abundance of shops literally on their doorstep. On either corner of Brecon and Junction Streets stood two of the commercial mainstays of the local community: Wilson's Newsagent & Tobacconist on one corner and Munro's Wine and Spirit Merchant on the other. Squeezed together opposite Number 11 were Guthrie's Pie Shop, Toni's Fish and Chips, De Marco's Ices and Murrell's Sweetie Shop.

But prominent within the cluster of retail excellence, the shining jewel was undoubtedly the Leith Provident Co-operative Society, otherwise known as The Provie. This cherished institution provided a wide range of goods for thrifty citizens of the working-class community. Each customer was a member and had a 'divvie' number. By providing this number every time they shopped at the Provie, they were ensured a modest dividend at year's end.

Diagonally across from Number 11 was The Provie's comestible branch, consisting of five departments; grocer, baker, butcher, fishmonger and greengrocer. The close proximity was invaluable to the tenants in the street. The men were paid their wages on Friday afternoon. Saturday morning at nine o'clock, queues of wivies were already starting to form at The Provie to shop for the week's groceries. The long, hard years of The War had beaten British housewives down and taught them the grim patience required to queue for hours on end. Leith wivies were no exception. Nor was Janet this first Saturday. She had shrugged on her coat and was now getting James ready.

"Where are we goin', Mum?" asked Wee Effie.

"Tae get the messages," replied Janet. *Aye,* she was thinking, *just another ordinary day o' queuin', queuin', queuin', tae keep the family fed.*

She shut the door quietly. In the gloom of the skylight, they could see well enough to grab onto the shoogly banisters and clamber down the steps. But the further down they went, the gloomier it got.

"Now be careful, and hud oan tae the railin'," she said, clutching her bags with one hand and James with the other, while Wee Effie made her own way. They warily entered the dark patch on the third and second floors, failing to see a coalman climbing up with a black face and a hundredweight sack on his back until the very last minute when he looked up and saw them coming down.

"Watch oot, hen, Ah'm comin' up!" he managed to grunt just in time as they darted to one side to let him brush past.

Soon, the light coming from below was enough to complete the journey safely. As usual, a bunch of local bairns hung around the entry, scouting for action. They looked curiously at the newcomers but the look on Janet's face put a stop to any suggestions of comment or banter. Mother and bairns made their way across the street and into The Provie. First, the groceries.

The large marble and wood vestibule already held a mob of about twenty wivies. They gradually formed themselves into a queue that shuffled forwards as those in front were served and left with their purchases. Most of the women were in overcoats and headscarves, some wore hats, and a few had curlers in their hair covered by a turban. In this neighbourhood, it was unusual to see a woman over the age of thirty go uncovered. After a lengthy wait, the Swanstons eventually reached the front. Three middle-aged male sales assistants wearing collars and ties under uniform cotton coats that had once been white were hard at work behind the polished wooden top of a massive counter that seemed to stretch from one side of the store to the other.

"Next, please," called the assistant nearest Janet, his pencil poised. She got out her list and stepped up to the counter.

"A quarter-pound o' cheddar cheese."

On the counter in front of the assistant was a block of blank invoices, each single blank triplicated with carbon paper.

"Yer divvie number?"

"Two-four-two-three-seven."

He wrote the number in the space at the top of the invoice.

"And yer ration book?"

"Oh, aye." Janet was already registered with The Provie for her rations. Flustered at her forgetfulness, she reenged in her handbag for her ration book and placed it on the counter. Although items such as soap were now freely available, some key staples such as sugar, tea, meat and cheese were still subject to rationing.

"And that was a quarter-pound of cheddar?"

"Aye."

He wrote: *1. ¼ lb cheddar.*

"Next."

"A packet o' Typhoo Tea."

He wrote: *2. 1 pkt Typhoo*

"Next."

"A pound o' sugar."

He wrote: *3. 1 lb sugar.*

And so on, down the shopping list. As she recited it, Janet could feel the eyes of the wivies behind boring into her back, taking in every detail of her weekly shop. When she'd run down the twenty or so items, the assistant busied himself fetching each one and ticking it off his list. The cheddar came from a large block sitting behind him on a marble slab. Using a wire with a wooden grip at one end, he expertly cut through the block so that a meagre slice fell on a sheet of greaseproof paper. He picked up the paper at both ends, ensuring he didn't touch the cheese, placed it on the scales and turned to Janet.

"A bit over. Is that all right?"

"Aye, that's fine."

He folded the paper and placed the packet of cheese on the counter. The sugar was kept in large open sugar sacks. He took a small aluminium scoop, dug it into the white sugar mass and poured the contents into a brown paper bag. He placed the bag on the scales, skimmed some of the sugar off until he was satisfied with the reading, closed the top of the bag by birling it round in his hands, and placed it next to the cheese.

This procedure continued until all the items on Janet's list were arrayed in front of her on the counter, including bags of lentils and split peas, a tin of Libby's corned beef, half a dozen eggs, two pints of milk, a packet of Stork margarine, Scott's Porage Oats, a block of Fairy laundry soap and two Izal toilet rolls. The assistant went down his list, filling in the price for each item. Then he added up the figures and wrote the total in a box at the bottom. Finally, he opened Janet's ration book and cancelled the coupons for the items she'd bought that were still 'on the ration'. He handed her book back.

"That'll be twelve shillings and eight pence, please."

Janet dug in her purse, pulled out a ten-shilling note and three one shilling coins, and handed them over. The assistant tore off the three copies of the invoice and placed the money on top. He turned to a contraption running up the wall behind him consisting of a vacuum tube and a number of empty brass jars with screw tops. He picked up a jar, unscrewed it, placed the money and the three copies of the invoice inside and screwed the top back on. He dropped the jar in a hole in the tube and pressed a button. There was a sucking sound and the jar shot upwards in the tube.

James stood on tiptoe with his fingertips clutching the edge of the counter, watching open-mouthed while all this was going on. When the jar disappeared, his eyes followed the tube and he saw that it ran up to a balcony where there was a glass-fronted office with several female clerks busy inside. He wondered where the jar had gone but guessed correctly that it was now in the hands of one of them. Meanwhile, Janet packed the groceries in her bags and tried to keep the bairns quiet. After a few minutes, there was a bump from the tube and the jar reappeared. The assistant went over, unscrewed the jar, handed Janet her receipt and counted out four pence change.

"Thank you. Next, please."

But they weren't finished yet. The same procedure was repeated at the greengrocer's where they queued for a fourpit of potatoes, carrots and onions, at the baker's where they purchased two well-fired loaves and four bridies, and the butcher's where the ration book allowed them a quarter pound of mince and some ham houghs for soup. Altogether, they'd queued and shopped for over three hours. The fact that they lived just across the road was a blessing.

Janet lugged the bags up the five floors while Wee Effie clutched James's hand in the darkness. They walked into the flat. There was Ian standing in the living room, staring at a letter in his hand, with a look on his face that was halfway between exasperated and angry, oblivious of the music that was issuing from his mother's ancient wireless. It was 'If I Knew You Were Comin' I'd Have Baked a Cake'. Janet produced a wry smile. Ian was a dab hand in the kitchen but she was yet to see him bake a cake and certainly not to welcome her back from doing the messages. She hastened to put her bags on the dining table, marched over to the set and demonstratively turned the brown Bakelite knob to kill the noise. But Ian remained oblivious.

"What's the matter, darlin'?" she said finally.

"Ye're no gonnae believe this!" he exclaimed, and handed her the letter. It had OHMS at the top and was from the War Office. Janet took in the heading: CLASS 'Z' (T) ROYAL ARMY RESERVE

For a split second, she was baffled. The form of words made no sense. What was this about? Then she read the second line:

RECALLED TO SERVE

And everything fell into place.

"Oh my God," she gasped. Suddenly, the day was no longer ordinary.

It had been in the newspapers. The Korean War had been raging for about nine months. The British Army, having discharged so many men since the end of The War, was now desperate for manpower. Conscription had been reintroduced in 1947. Since Ian hadn't been demobilised until 1946, he was still on the list of Army reservists and he was still under 40. That meant he could be called back to the army at any time. His status as a warrant officer with frontline experience made him particularly desirable.

Tens or even hundreds of thousands of other men in Britain had probably received the same letter. Ian was to report on a specific date to

Redford Barracks. He couldn't believe it. His frustration came rushing back. Six years, six bloody years they'd taken from his life. And five whole years after he'd been demobbed, just when he thought he had it all behind him, here they were dragging him in again. But there was nothing he could do. He was up against forces more powerful than himself. Plenty of other former servicemen were in the same boat. He'd have to grit his teeth and present himself on the date as ordered. The alternative would have been a visit from the local police. Janet tried to stay calm but she was seething internally. All the bitterness came back. How long could this, Korean, war last? Another six years? Her parents often referred to 'the big folk', the elite that ruled the lives of 'wee folk' like her family. The big folk were omnipotent and untouchable. They could do what they liked with you and there was nothing you could do, nothing. Well, it looked like the big folk, out of nowhere, had struck again. Her son and daughter were following the goings-on with interest.

"Will Daddy have tae go and fight in the war, Mum?" asked seven-year-old Wee Effie anxiously.

"Naw, Ah dinnae think so, hen," Janet replied evasively, even though she was asking herself exactly the same question. Despite her attempts to calm the situation, four-year-old James stuck his thumb in his mouth and began to suck furiously.

The appointed day came. Ian had to take a day off work, unpaid of course. After a tedious tram ride all the way out to Redford Barracks, then queuing for hours along with a mob of other affected former servicemen, his details were taken and he was given a medical examination. After that, he was handed a paper, which he had to countersign, that confirmed he was 'A1' and was liable for recall to the army at any time. They'd be in touch. Then he was sent home. The Korean War dragged on and the casualties mounted. It seemed that they couldn't escape this war, even though it was happening on the other side of the world. Daily reports in the newspapers. Daily bulletins on the wireless. Newsreels in the picture houses. And each time, Janet had a sick feeling in the pit of her stomach. When would the axe fall? Soon, she avoided newspapers and stopped listening to the news on the radio. It was too much. For his part, Ian seemed to be stoically accepting his fate. Things were going so badly, it was inevitable he'd be called up again. But he wasn't. The axe never fell. As the tide slowly turned in favour of the UN forces, and the Korean War advanced to its messy conclusion, the Swanstons dared to be increasingly optimistic. By the time hostilities ended in 1953, the cloud had at last dissipated. It had been hanging over them for two years. But Ian still wondered. Would the British military establishment finally leave him alone and allow him and his family to get on with their lives?

The Red Lady

Wee Effie had already clambered up onto the coping stones of the dyke. They were upright wedges intended to discourage climbing. But the edge was blunted and for a wee lassie just going on eight and already tall for her age it wasn't a problem. She sat looking down at the water while four-year-old James was jumping up, trying to catch the top of the stone with his elbows, but having no luck.

"Daddy!" he wailed. "Ah cannae see!"

Ian put down the jam jars and the canes. With one swoop, he lifted his son, set him down standing precariously next to his sister on the dyke and kept a protective arm around his waist.

"There, can ye see now?"

Satisfied, James nodded, looking down at the now visible stream with interest for the first time. His father glanced over to see how high the ground was on the other side then carefully lowered the boy onto a patch of grass on what passed for a riverbank. He grabbed his daughter and did the same with her.

"Now dinnae move till Ah get over!" he warned. He quickly negotiated the wall, handed the nets to Wee Effie, leant back over for the jam jars, took James's hand and together they made their way carefully down to the water's edge at the stretch of the Water of Leith that was known to the Brecon Street bairns as Puddicky. It was a Saturday afternoon in late summer. Janet had needed a break, so Ian had obligingly offered to take the bairns out for a couple of hours.

"We're goin' tae Puddicky!" he announced, much to Wee Effie's delight.

The last time they were at Porty, they'd got small fishing nets on long cane handles for the bairns at one of the shops on the esplanade. Ian found them again among the junk in the lumber room, located two empty glass jars under the sink in the scullery and wound string around their necks for handles. Getting the two younger Swanstons into jerseys – Janet had insisted – and wellingtons, he grabbed his jacket and wallet. Leaving a grateful wife to her rest, he shepherded his son and daughter out into

Junction Street and they caught the bus for Powderhall. It was a warm, muggy day, windless and overcast, what Ian called Saturday weather. Why was it that it was so often like this on a Saturday? Or was it just his imagination?

Getting off near Broughton School, they crossed the road, passed through the open metal gates and headed across St Mark's Park. The refuse station on the right, locally known as The Dump, was a wasteland of smouldering heaps emitting a haze of noxious blue smoke and a stench that pervaded the whole neighbourhood. The characteristic reek, the product of burning a collection of all manner of offensive household rubbish, including food scraps, was a constant, no matter how often he passed here. It was sickening. It wasn't so bad on windy days but on a calm day like today, the neighbours in Broughton Road and Redbraes would be keeping their windows tightly shut. Crossing the green iron Bailey bridge, Ian showed the bairns how to stamp on the planks of the walkway where you could look through the two-inch gaps at the girders below. The three of them jumped up and down to hear the bridge ring and echo. The bairns were thrilled to imagine that it moved as well below their feet.

As the path climbed, on their left, below and across the river, was Powderhall Stadium with its cinder track and odd scoreboard of what looked, from the distance, like six giant clocks in a row. Preparations were afoot for the meet that evening; trainers and staff paced around the tracks with greyhounds on leads and various teams of workers and cleaners were hard at work. Then it was down towards the housing scheme and across the bridge to the place called Puddicky. Here, just before it made its long loop north round the park, The Water of Leith ran straight for a few hundred yards on its journey from the foothills of The Pentlands, bounded on the south bank by the roadway, on the north by a massive cemetery wall of dressed stone that seemed to go on for ever. Here, generations of Edinburgh bairns had played, paddled and prospected for tadpoles and frogs. Ian's father had brought him here and probably his father before him. Here, the river was shallow and sluggish, especially now at its summer level. Here, bairns could be safe.

Rocks trailing gouts of green slime and clumps of freshet-flattened grass competed with chickweed and choice selections of Edinburgh's rubbish. Most of it seemed to consist of beer bottles and discarded cardboard but further upstream Ian could see what looked like an old bedstead with rusted springs poking out. Anyway, this spot was fairly clear up to the bridge and the bairns could go in. Even four-year-old James should be able to manage on his own, though he'd never ventured into a river before. Yes, he'd paddled at Porty, but that was with a parent holding onto him on a reliable bed of sand and the waves gently lapping his feet.

Here, as he discovered, it was different. With his feet in the element, even though the water reached only halfway up his calves, he felt the steady pressure, lethargic as it was, pushing against the backs of his legs, making them unsteady. The cold, even at this time of the year, penetrated the clammy rubber of his wellingtons. Not even his thick grey socks could keep it out. The river bed was uneven. Stones, rocks and clumps of underwater life abounded, just waiting to trip him up. As the brother and sister waded cautiously upstream, they dipped their nets in while Ian slowly walked with them, stepping from rock to rock or sitting watching, calling instructions. Meanwhile, the jam jars with the string handles sat on the bank in high hopes of some ballast soon enough.

"Look where the water's deep, on this side o' the rocks. That's where the taddies'll be."

As he tottered there, holding the cane with both hands, splashing his net through the mirk across the current, James checked each cast for a catch. At first, he just caught slime or chickweed each time his chilled, eager fingers turned the net inside out. But then, a sliver of life wriggled in the muddy mesh.

"Dad! Dad! Ah've got one!"

Ian hurried over with a jar, scooped some water into it and held it out. Plop! A tadpole dropped in. Together they admired the catch, the first of the day. Then it was Wee Effie's turn. Soon they had five tadpoles in two jars and they were starting on their second sweep up to the bridge, carefully placing their feet. That's when Wee Effie, in a mischievous mood and seeing their Dad was distracted, turned to her wee brother.

"The Red Lady's comin' tae get ye, ye ken!"

James looked at her in puzzlement.

"The Red Lady! She lives ower there!"

She pointed to ivy-encrusted cemetery walls louring silently above them and beyond, to where thickets of gnarled branches and tangled foliage presided over deep shadows. Even on a summer's day there was more than a hint of menace there.

"That's where she is! Ower that dyke! She'll come at night and take ye away if ye've been bad!"

James's eyes widened. Suddenly, a hint of fear had been injected into what had been, until now, a harmless outing. He looked warily up at the towering stone dyke. It seemed to be leaning out towards him. It wanted to grab him and take him to The Red Lady, whoever she was. He almost lost his balance. That got his dad's attention.

"Now watch yersel', son. Dinnae fa' in or yer mother'll kill me!"

James steadied himself with the cane and considered what Wee Effie had said. The Red Lady! Who was she? He turned to Wee Effie.

“But Ah’m *no* bad!”

“Aye, ye are, ye’re always bad. An’ The Red Lady kens that. She’ll come and get ye the night if ye’re no careful!”

With that, she wandered on towards the bridge with a studied air of innocence, busily trawling the waters, leaving James to ponder a potential nocturnal visit from The Red Lady. After seven tadpoles had been transferred to the jars, fatigue was beginning to set in. That was when Ian persuaded the bairns to release their catch. They’d turn into puddocks, he said, and what could they do with puddocks five flights up in Brecon Street? They’d hop around the floor and scare Mum. They laughed at that. Best let them go and be puddocks here where they were at home. The bairns agreed and as they squatted by the waterside, carefully emptying the jars’ contents back into the stream, they made their goodbyes.

“Ta-ta, taddies, we’ll see ye next time when ye’re puddocks!”

On the way home, on the big bench seat at the back of the bus, between his dad and Wee Effie, James was unusually quiet. He was thinking about The Red Lady and whether she’d come for him because he’d been bad. Had he been bad? He didn’t think so. He’d eaten his Brussels sprouts. He hadn’t wet the bed recently. He hadn’t got into an argument with his sister. Suddenly, he turned to Ian.

“Dad?”

“Aye, son?”

“Have Ah been bad?”

Ian considered while Wee Effie greeted the success of her seemingly casual remark.

“Well, Ah dinnae think so, son. Have ye?”

James didn’t answer but just stared out of the opposite window. As they lay in bed that night in the dark, James was finding it hard to get to sleep. Their parents made do with the bed settee in the living room while he and his sister slept together in a one-and-a-half-sized bed in the single unheated bedroom. In winter they were covered by Ian’s old army greatcoat but in summer a single blanket was usually enough. It hadn’t helped that Wee Effie, with a baleful whisper in his ear, had again uttered the dreaded name *The Red Lady!* before she’d dropped off to sleep. Unsurprisingly, some hours later the Swanston household was jolted into wakefulness by screams from James. Janet was used to him having bad dreams but this one seemed particularly distressing. Wee Effie, again the picture of innocence, pretended to look concerned as Janet sat on the bed cuddling James, asking him what was wrong.

“The Red Lady!” he sobbed. “She was comin’ tae get me!”

Janet was puzzled. Of course she knew The Red Lady but hadn’t known that her son knew her. It was only when the dream repeated itself the next night then the next, again turning their son into a sobbing wreck and ruining their sleep, that Janet began to get suspicious, especially as her daughter had kept an uncharacteristically low profile while all this was going on. It was after breakfast on the Tuesday morning that she took Wee Effie aside.

"Did you say anythin' tae yer brother about The Red Lady?"

Fearful of her mother's wrath, Wee Effie lied.

"No, Mum, Ah didnae say anythin'!"

"Then how did 'e ken about 'er? Ah said nothin', yer Dad said nothin'. Who else could've told 'im but you?"

Wee Effie said nothing but just hung her head.

"What did ye say? Come on ye wee besom! Ye're headin' for a skelp!"

But it was no use. Her daughter remained stubborn. When Janet talked to Ian about it, he twigged.

"It was probably when we were at Puddicky last weekend. Maybe she said somethin' tae 'im then, bein' pretty much on the spot. Ah mind 'e *was* a bit funny on the way hame, now ye mention it."

"What like?"

"Well, 'e asked me if Ah thought 'e'd been bad!"

"Ye're no serious!"

They chuckled over that but agreed there was nothing else for it. If they wanted a good night's sleep there was only one way to nip James's phobia in the bud. A visit to The Red Lady was on the cards. Janet took the opportunity the following Wednesday after an afternoon at Warburton Crescent. She and the bairns would take the long way home by way of The Dump. But this time they'd make one special call. As they walked down the hill towards the Puddicky bridge between the high stone walls she detoured, steering the bairns through the cemetery gates and into a stolen world. For this wasn't so much a final resting place as a vast secret garden on several levels that, while well maintained, concealed myriad mysteries among its ancient elm trees, snarled clumps of shrubbery and ivy-covered crypts. The fact that the place seemed deserted at this time of the week only served to magnify the sense of foreboding for the uninitiated. The bairns instinctively clutched their mother's hands tighter as they shrank from the tottering gravestones, creepy statues, weathered marble angels and deep, dark corners where who knew what - or who - might be lurking.

Janet, of course, had no fear, for she knew the cemetery well. She'd played here often as a member of the gang of Warburton Crescent bairns. It had been the perfect place for hide-and-seek and other games in that brief, distant time when she'd still been allowed to be a child. The gravestones and monuments held a morbid fascination, yes, but no dread. For her, a visit here was like coming home. As a young mother during The

War, she'd bring Wee Effie in her pram to this haven of peace and contemplation away from the rationing, dislocation, incessant bad news from the front and worrying about whether she'd ever see her husband again. It was then that she'd introduced her daughter to The Red Lady. Now it was time to introduce her son as well.

Soon, they came to a place where three paths met. In a grassy triangle stood what looked like a small chapel. It was striking because it seemed to be the only real structure in a cemetery of gravestones, statues and monuments. It was about ten feet long and five feet wide with a steep-pitched roof that topped at around fifteen or twenty feet. The walls were of faded white marble. On each side, four gothic arches, resting on slim pillars that had once been russet, framed blank, faux windows. Between the peaks of the arches, carved into the marble, were leaves of some sort, lilies or perhaps palm fronds. The narrow entrance, another gothic arch resting on pillars and barely two or three feet wide, rose up to intersect a lintel which ran all the way round above a carved frieze. A stout gate of iron bars that was secured with a padlock of recent vintage barred entry. But the strangest feature was the roof, for it was made of glass, sheets of dark-tinted glass that rose sharply to a ridge topped by a strip of delicate cast-iron filigree.

Janet had made it her business to find out the story. She'd once discovered the gate unlocked, gone inside and read the inscription cut into a weathered marble tablet on the wall. She was standing in the memorial to Mary Ann Robertson, the wife of a British Army officer stationed in India. She'd died in 1858 in Kussowlee in the Himalayas at the young age of thirty-two years, *excellently endowed with many gracious qualities and throughout life earnestly striving after all perfection...* Contemplating the tomb yet again, Janet couldn't suppress a twinge of sadness. Thirty-two! Almost ages with her. To think poor Mary had lived only that long then her life had been snuffed out. Janet had often wondered what had killed her. Consumption? Cholera? Smallpox? Or had she died in childbirth? She could only speculate. Nor could she understand how this young woman had merited such an elaborate, unusual, and probably very expensive memorial. Someone must have loved and missed her very much. While Wee Effie hung back, Janet ushered James forward into the doorway so that he could look

through the bars. He was at once thrilled and overawed by what he saw. For there, facing him, reclining on a marble plinth was the lifesize figure of a young woman. She wore some loosely fitting garment draped around her, the folds gathered up around her limbs and upper body. She appeared so realistic, her head tilted to her right, her eyes closed in peace, as if to inform the observer that she was merely asleep. Her hands were clasped over her stomach in an attitude of rest and repose. But the strangest thing of all was her colour. For though sculpted of white marble, she was enveloped in a deep red hue that suffused the entire chamber. It was only then that James realised the roof was of ruby-tinted glass. Janet bent down and spoke quietly in his ear.

"That's The Red Lady."

She gave her words a few seconds to sink in, then, letting her handbag and shopping bag slide to the ground, she picked him up.

"Isn't she nice?"

James couldn't help but nod, momentarily struck dumb, his mouth hanging open, his face catching the edge of the afterglow of the ruby interior, his small hands grasping the cold bars. This was definitely not The Red Lady of his nightmares.

"But what's she doin', Mum?"

"Well, she's asleep, isn't she?"

"But why is she red?"

Janet sighed, deposited him on the ground, picked up her bags and straightened up. James, at almost four-and-a-half years old, had reached the *Why?* stage in his development. Since his talking had progressed rapidly and he'd discovered the word, it was *why this?* and *why that?* all day long. Janet, never one to shun the opportunity to be creative, had evolved a particular strategy to deal with this torrent of *whys*. Her nimble mind simply made up an answer, the more outlandish, the more ridiculous the story, the better to silence the inveterate questioner once and for all. Once James had pointed to some writing inside a toilet bowl.

"What does that say, Mummy?"

"*Shanks*," said Janet after a quick look.

"But why?"

"Well," said Janet without hesitation, "when the man put in the toilet bowl, Ah gave 'im a cup o' tea an' a biscuit. He wanted tae say thanks, but 'e couldnae talk properly so 'e wrote *shanks* in the bowl instead."

James, apparently satisfied with the explanation, wandered off. Another time, they were on the train crossing the Forth Bridge.

"Mum, why do people throw pennies out the window?"

She could tell him the truth. She could tell him they did it for luck, but for a four-year-old that would be too abstract.

“Well, son, there’s a man down there in a rowin’ boat. ’E collects the pennies and gives them to the poor boys an’ girls.”

James nodded. Yes, it made perfect sense. Why otherwise would you be daft enough to throw money out of the window of a moving train?

“Why is she red, Mum?” asked James insistently, interrupting her thoughts. He’d pushed his right hand through the bars and turned it the same colour as the sleeping form by waving it from side to side as if trying to sever the beams of coloured light.

Actually, she didn’t know. She’d often wondered herself what had possessed whoever had commissioned the monument to have a ruby-red glass roof installed. It seemed to make no sense. But somehow she had to come up with an answer.

“Well, son, what colour are the Hearts’ jerseys?”

Even at the age of four, James was familiar with the sizeable community of Heart of Midlothian fans among the Brecon Street bairns, which had instantly won him to their cause. So the answer wasn’t exactly difficult.

“Red,” he said. Hearts’ jerseys were in fact maroon, but from a four-year-old, red was good enough.

“Aye, an’ that lady in there’s red because she’s a Hearts supporter!”

“Oh!” James gasped in delight.

The fact that the Heart of Midlothian FC wouldn’t be established for another sixteen years after Mary Ann Robertson’s demise was, to Janet, merely a minor detail.

“So,” Janet asked optimistically, “d’ye think she’s a nice lady?”

“Aye!”

“D’ye think she could ever dae anythin’ bad tae ye? What d’ye say?”

“No, Mummy, Ah dinnae think so. She’s a Hearts supporter!”

“So, would ye like tae come an’ visit ’er again?”

“Aye.”

“Right, we’ll do that next time we come tae see Granny, eh?”

“Aye,” was all he said, still spellbound, his face pressed against the bars as if he couldn’t get enough now of The Red Lady. In the background, Wee Effie merely glowered. That night, after the bairns were in bed, Janet shared with Ian their little jaunt to see The Red Lady.

“Was ’e feared when ’e saw ’er?” asked Ian.

“No!” scoffed Janet. “Mah son feared? Ah just told ’im she was a Hearts supporter!”

From then on, The Red Lady stayed out of James’s dreams. But she still figured prominently in his life. Rather like some great aunt living alone and advancing in years, she had to be checked on from time to time, just to make sure she was still there and still doing all right.

Miss Douglas

It was in the early autumn of 1951 when Janet decided to enrol James in Bonnybrig Primary School. He was barely four-and-a-half, but Janet had impressed on Ian that waiting another year would mean he'd be five-and-a-half and that could set him back. Besides, with James in school, she might be able to take a part-time job. Wee Effie had already been attending Bonnybrig Primary since they'd moved into Brecon Street the previous year. It was a typical nineteenth-century school of the type seen all over Edinburgh. A forbidding two-storied building of sandstone blocks, the Victorian authorities had seen fit to locate it among breweries, bakeries, and workshops, inserted neatly between the narrow confines of Bonnybrig Road and the main Leith-Newhaven railway line embankment. It was a tight fit. The school seemed to be saying, *Yes, I know I'm unseemly, but I'm here now, so you're just going to have to put up with me*. The pitched roofs were tiled over with grey slates. Three parallel, connected wings, each with its own mock spire, were topped off by a fake belfry. The triple sets of pseudo-gothic arched windows only served to reinforce the impression that it was in truth an oddly-shaped church. But this was contradicted by the sight of the wrought iron railings, a row of menacing, closely-spaced, six-foot spears that protected the school and its occupants against outsiders as effectively as a medieval schiltrom. Inside, the rooms were spacious to accommodate the oversized classes of the Victorian era. The ceilings were high. Much use was made of framed glass partitions to create separate teaching spaces. By the time James arrived, the original sandstone had degraded to the standard 1950's soot-encrusted façade, allowing the school to blend perfectly into the dingy industrial landscape.

The enrolment was brief. There was no objection to James's young age. After the formalities, Mr Bell, the Headmaster, sent for Miss Douglas, the infant teacher, to take James along to class. Mr Bell had barely time to explain that Miss Douglas was their newest young appointee who'd only recently taken over Primary One when the door opened. Glancing up in anticipation, Janet saw a tall, square-jawed young woman with a dusky complexion and a thick shock of black hair styled in a bob. She had on a loose cotton smock with a colourful pattern of large tropical flowers.

"Hello!" She smiled warmly. If her appearance wasn't enough, her friendly greeting, casual demeanour and unfamiliar accent instantly confirmed in Janet's mind that she wasn't from these parts. She bent down to where James was sitting shyly.

"Hello, James. I'm Miss Douglas, your new teacher."

He looked at her in wonderment.

"Would you like a lolly?"

A lolly? James wondered what that was, but his question was immediately answered when Miss Douglas reached into the pocket of her smock and produced a wrapped sweetie, which she pressed into his hand.

"Come on, let's go, shall we?"

And with that, she took James's other hand and expertly swept him off to class clutching his sweetie. He didn't even have time to say goodbye to his mother, about which she was quite relieved. No scenes, no tears, thank goodness. As she walked out of the school she reflected on James's teacher. Miss Douglas? She seemed a nice person but her accent was odd. A *lolly*? Janet wondered where she was from.

When Miss Douglas had arrived to take up her post at Bonnybrig Primary in August 1951, she'd found a dreary, grey Scotland, still struggling to overcome the economic impact of six years of war. Coming from a land of plentiful food stocks, well-fed people and a sunny, healthy climate, she was struck by the painful thinness of the Scottish people and their pale complexions. Looking around her classroom on her first day, she couldn't help comparing her sickly-looking pupils with the robust children she'd taught back home. But she had to remind herself that this wasn't New Zealand. Most of the infants in her class were from low-income families living in Leith tenements that not many years later would be declared slums and demolished. It was a situation she was just going to have to learn to live with and perhaps learn from.

Her full name was Marama ata Hapara Douglas but the pupils at Bonnybrig Primary knew her only as Miss Douglas. Her father had been a Scottish engineer who'd come to New Zealand to work on tunnels, dams and bridges in the South Island in the nineteen-twenties. Her mother was a Māori nurse from Te Aroha. They'd met when Andrew was hospitalized with a leg injury and Ngaire first nursed him, then bullied him back to health. They married, and their first child was born just before dawn at a full moon. So they called her Marama (moon) ata Hapara (dawn). Marama had something of a privileged education by New Zealand standards, graduating from a prestigious Christchurch girls' high school with distinction, and going on to qualify as a primary teacher at the Dunedin College of Education. Then she taught for a few years. By then, Andrew Douglas was serving as a captain of Engineers in the New Zealand Second

Division at the Italian front. He was killed by a sniper's bullet at Monte Cassino in January 1944. That was the start of Marama's hankering to visit the country of her father's birth. Several years later her opportunity came. Replying to an advertisement by British authorities in an educational gazette for trained teachers to work in Britain, she was accepted for a position at Bonnybrig Primary School to take charge of one of the infant classes. The sea voyage to Britain took five weeks.

Miss Douglas quickly realized that she was going to have her work cut out coping with the accent and the vernacular of the native Scottish people. With her soft New Zealand brogue, she was readily recognized as someone from somewhere else. But few locals made allowances. Needless to say, she had some problems at first understanding her flock. One day she was on playground duty when she spotted one of the infants standing in a corner of the playground sobbing bitterly.

"What's wrong with him?" she asked a nearby girl from her class.

"'E done a *toalie* in 'is *breeks*, Miss!"

"What... er, sorry... what did you say, darling?"

"'E done a *toalie* in 'is *breeks*, Miss!" the urchin shouted, much to the amusement of all around, as if upping the volume would somehow improve the clarity of the message.

Miss Douglas was nonplussed until one of the older pupils came up to her to interpret. Miss Douglas bent down and the girl cupped her hand and whispered in her ear.

"'E went to the toilet in 'is troosers, Miss!"

"Oh!" exclaimed Miss Douglas as the blood rushed into her cheeks and she hurried over to escort the distraught child to the toilet block.

Despite her newcomer status, Miss Douglas was made to feel welcome by almost everyone at Bonnybrig Primary. The exception was Miss Boyle. A spinster, Miss Boyle had been born when Queen Victoria was still on the throne. Through some strange osmosis, she'd absorbed much of the creed of that venerable monarch. Indeed, it would be fair to say that Miss Boyle was born not amused and she remained not amused for the rest of her life. The sight of a dark-skinned teacher in their midst certainly didn't amuse her and she said so in regular comments and asides to her colleague and bosom friend, Bunty Melville. But although Miss Douglas got wind of Miss Boyle's disapproval, as the most junior member of staff she successfully resisted the temptation to reciprocate.

That is, until, on a Friday in October 1952, an unfortunate concurrence of circumstances saw her enter the staffroom unseen and walk directly behind where her nemesis was sitting. Miss Boyle was holding court to a circle of acolytes, all seated in comfy armchairs around a low table upon which was an outsized teapot and an array of china cups and saucers. The ladies were celebrating a momentous event that had occurred the previous day. Tea rationing had officially ended after twelve long years. At last they could purchase and drink as much tea as they wished. Miss Boyle had immediately hurried off to secure a large supply of her favourite Darjeeling and had organised Bunty Melville to offer up her best china for a special tea-drinking session during the midday break. While delicately holding her sacred cup of unrationed tea, Miss Boyle happened to pass yet another remark about the new colleague from the colonies.

"Aih don't know what the world is coming to," she opined in her best Morningside. "Dark people in the staffroom at Bonnybrig Primary! What next!"

"Yais," agreed Bunty. "At least we don't have any in our classes!"

"Yet!" rejoined Miss Boyle.

Miss Douglas was stopped in her tracks. Initially unaware of her presence, Miss Boyle must have guessed from the expressions on the faces of her audience that something unpleasant was about to happen. And it did. Suddenly, there was Miss Douglas, gate-crashing the tea party, towering above her with a glint in her eye.

"Yes, Miss Boyle, you are right. I am a 'dark' person. But you might like to know that I am fortunate enough to descend from a line of fighters on both sides of my family."

Miss Boyle spluttered as if her tea had gone down the wrong way. She hastily put down her cup. But Miss Douglas was just getting into her stride. She folded her arms.

"On my mother's side, I come from a line of Māori warriors. My whakapapa is Ngāti Rāhiri Tumutumu. I'm descended from Rāhiri, a great Māori chief of the sixteenth century. On my father's side, Miss Boyle, I'm a Douglas, from a long and honourable line. If you remember your Scottish history, Miss Boyle, you'll be aware that my ancestor, the Black Douglas, fought alongside Robert Bruce at Bannockburn. When Bruce died, Black Douglas carried his heart to the Holy Land. He was killed defending it in battle, incidentally, together with Robert Logan, Lord of Restalrig..." She gestured around her. "...who once ruled over these very lands where we are now."

She paused for effect, staring calmly at her seated antagonist.

"So, don't you agree, Miss Boyle, that I have just as much right as you to be here? Well, Miss Boyle?"

But the mini-lecture on Scottish and New Zealand history had rendered Miss Boyle speechless. So black affrontit was she that she couldn't meet Miss Douglas's gaze nor that of her colleagues, for that matter. She gathered her things, stood up and flounced out of the room.

Miss Douglas stood her ground, glancing enquiringly at the seated schoolmistresses who, as if anaesthetised, were still clutching their cups of unrationed tea with glazed expressions, while coming to grips with the unexpected lesson on their own country's history delivered by a dark stranger from the colonies.

"Well," she said pleasantly, a smile curling up the corners of her mouth, "any questions, ladies?"

Their frozen attitudes were broken as if by a spell. They put down their cups.

"No, no, Miss Douglas!"

"Very interesting, Miss Douglas!"

"Thank you, Miss Douglas, for taking the trouble to explain that!"

And finally from the craven Bunty Melville: "Miss Douglas, do have a seat. Would you like a cup of tea? It's off the ration now, you know!"

Miss Douglas's main responsibility was the infant class, Primary One, which she'd be carrying on into Primary Two. The fact that she'd have the class for two years would allow her to acquaint herself with the children while helping them to boost their confidence in a teacher they knew well. The programme was elementary. Basic literacy, some simple arithmetic, bits of geography and history, singing, drawing, not to mention, for some, lessons in hygiene and simple skills such as tying their shoelaces. Miss Douglas interspersed this syllabus with her own special material. She narrated stories of New Zealand, of the explorers and how her Māori ancestors found Aotearoa, navigating by the stars across the Pacific. She showed them pictures of the country, its peoples and its breathless landscapes. Once, she recounted how, when she was a little girl in school, she was caught in a strong earthquake and had to shelter under her desk. Her charges were enthralled. Some took fright at the mere idea of an earthquake. She even had to take wee Aggie Simpson on her knee to comfort her. Miss Douglas, with her colourful smocks, beaming smile, gentle encouragement and casual colonial ways, was the perfect medicine for infants living in drab, post-war Leith. All the children loved her.

But especially James. She was kind. She never got angry or upset, even with the most obstreperous of her charges. Somehow, she managed, with her soft accent and her beautiful smile, to soar above everything. Adults sometimes asked James what he wanted to be when he grew up. But one day, an adult made the mistake of asking him what he wanted to *do*. James immediately sensed the subtle change in formulation, thought for a moment, then said, "Ah want tae marry Miss Douglas!" But he did have an admirer, albeit an unwelcome one. Her name was Margaret Mackie. Margaret was a wispy waif with bobbed yellow hair and a grubby, pale pink cardigan that was always undone. A happy bairn, when she wasn't smiling she was laughing. She wore new-fangled, national health spectacles. Because she had a squint, the left-hand lens was taped over with beige sticking plaster. She also drank from inkwells, so the other bairns taunted her, calling her glaikit. A song was making the rounds:

Margaret Mackie done a cackie
On her mother's knee.
Her mother said, "You naughty girl,
You'll have that for your tea!"

Margaret didn't care, because she was in love with James. So in love was she that she chased him untiringly during the jinking around in the school hall that passed for physical education while a beaming Miss Douglas saw to the gramophone and tried to keep order. James ran, literally, as fast as he could. It wasn't just Margaret's appearance but also her reputation that troubled him. She was glaikit. He wanted nothing to do with her. Now, if it had been Jeanette Scott, that would have been different. Jeanette was the bonniest wee lassie in the class. Her mother was friends with his mother but her father was dying in a tuberculosis clinic in Switzerland. Now if Jeanette were to chase him around the school hall he'd happily let himself be caught. Eventually, Margaret gave up. But when James saw her chasing Frankie Goldie, he couldn't deny a pang of jealousy. All thoughts of marrying Miss Douglas evaporated and for the first time in his life, at the tender age of five, he was obliged to wonder what might have been.

The back green

If ever there was a misnomer, 'back green' would certainly qualify. Although it was undeniably at the back of the tenement, green it certainly wasn't. It was simply a large trapezoid patch of hard-beaten brown earth. There was nothing green about it except rats' tails and docken leaves sprouting along the tenement margins where the water dripped from the gutters. If it had indeed ever been green, it would have been in days long past when the Victorian wivies from the tenement used the area as a drying green. But these days, it was far too risky to hang precious washing there to dry. For the back green was now the headquarters of the local tenement bairns. Any washing hung there could have reckoned its survival time in minutes. Besides, the posts for the washing lines had been wrecked or stolen long ago. So instead, the wivies now hung their washing on their ceiling pulleys in their flats, with buckets underneath to catch the drips, or in drying racks fixed outside the scullery window and projecting high above the melee of marauding bairns.

The back green of Number 11 Brecon Street was enclosed on two sides by the angle of the tenements between Brecon and Junction Streets, on another by the side wall of the Sally Ann and on the fourth by a high dyke separating it from an adjoining back green. The dyke was of dressed stone some eight feet high and was topped with capstones into which broken glass had been cemented. Why such extreme security measures were needed to protect one back green from another was anyone's guess. But the broken glass, the dyke, the tenements and the Sally wall quarantined the back green from the outside world. Narrow, congested Brecon Street was far from ideal as a playground, except in the long Scottish summer evenings when everything had closed down, commercial traffic had ceased and it stayed light until getting on for 10 pm. At all other times, the back green was the only space in the neighbourhood where the bairns could spread their wings.

From the time he was about five, James was allowed into the back green as long as his sister was there too. Janet could usually look out of the window and pick them out without too much effort. Off they both went, but it wasn't long before Wee Effie had disappeared among the squads of lassies, diligent at their songs and clapping games, and James was left to tag along with the local gang. In this way, the back green became his other classroom and here he served his apprenticeship.

His first lesson was to learn who the leader was. It was, of course, Jacky Johnston, chieftain of the entire Brecon Street clan. Jacky was definitely in charge but the strange thing was that he didn't fit the mould of a traditional top dog. He wasn't a bully. He didn't swagger or threaten. He didn't use his size against the smaller bairns. He didn't order them around. He wasn't cruel or sadistic. He wasn't repugnant to look at. No, Jacky was a most unlikely gang boss. At around fourteen years old, he was by far the oldest bairn around. Tall and lanky, he overtopped all of his followers. Indeed, his parents allowed him to wear longs when the other bairns had to be content with shorts. His longs had almost become a symbol of his authority. He had curly red hair, freckles, and handsome features. He was good-natured. But above all, he was smart. Intelligence and maturity beyond his years were the keys to his control of the Brecon Street bairns. He appeared to rule not by violence, intimidation or coercion but by the force of his personality, which, in the turbulent and potentially hostile milieu of the 1950's Leith underclass, was something of a miracle.

Jacky truly led a charmed life. When the Sallies spread the word that there was to be an event one Saturday afternoon just for boys and that there would be a special prize, James was tempted along to the Hall together with the rest of the gang. At the appointed time, around 40 laddies sat expectantly in packed rows, wondering what was going to happen. A young Sally officer appeared in his smart uniform and greeted them warmly. Then, as if showing a carrot to a donkey, with a flourish he revealed the prize. A large blank sheet of thick white poster paper was attached to a blackboard on an easel. The officer dipped a cloth into a bowl of water and carefully wiped it over the surface of the paper. Hey presto! As if by magic, the profile of a magnificent Red Indian chief in full headdress appeared in shimmering green. The audience was stunned. This portrait, the officer announced, would go to the best-behaved boy and the one who paid most attention. Well, at that, they all sat up straight, folded their arms and attempted to follow the talk with manufactured interest, encouraged by the sight of the carrot dangling in front of them on the easel at the side of the room the whole time. But it was a lot of boring religious stuff, which James was too young to understand. Of course he didn't win the prize despite his exemplary conduct throughout the ordeal. Appropriately, it went to another chieftain; who else but Jacky Johnston? Yes, it seemed that Jacky could do no wrong, even where the Almighty was concerned.

Under the tutelage of Jacky and his underlings, James learnt the rudiments of bulls; observed the knivies contests, though he was never allowed to have a pocket knife and anyway was alarmed at the idea of a blade sticking into his foot through his shoe; watched the conkers matches when chestnuts were in season and hoped that he'd someday have a bag of serviceable conkers. He was a keen spectator of the collie-buckie fights and even became a popular collie on a buckie because of his small stature and light weight. But when it came to halie-leavoi he stayed well away. It was far too rough for a wee laddie. Then, Davie Dow inducted him into the mysteries of making sugarellie water, from the visit to the sweetie shop for a pennyworth of liquorice, to chopping it up, adding it to bottled water and sugar, shaking the bottle, corking it and waiting for the delicious results a few weeks later.

When he was older and allowed out on his own, he tagged along when the gang made forays into the surrounding area, sliding down to the Water of Leith beside Junction Street Bridge to throw yockers and skiffers into the heavily polluted waters or, once, even as far as Vicky Park to fool around on the swings, vying to see who could make the best brankles then running off when the parkie came running to check them. Occasionally, one of them got wind of a wedding at a local church, usually on a Saturday, and they'd hang around outside, waiting for the poor oot. The doors were suddenly flung open, the bride and groom appeared but the laddies from Brecon Street still had to endure the rigmarole of the photo session until the pair finally got into the bridal limousine. Then the chant would go up.

"Poor oot! Poor oot!"

Five, ten, twenty, however many bairns had cottoned on, converged on the vehicle while the bridegroom wound down the window and scattered a handful of loose change onto the pavement. Usually it was pennies and halfpennies, occasionally a couple of threepenny bits thrown in, rarely a sixpence and very rarely a shilling. Nevertheless, the bairns were on all fours in a flash, scrambling across the granite pavers and into the gutters after every stray coin. James, being small, didn't usually do too well. A couple of pennies was usually par for the course but once he snatched a sixpence before it rolled down a syver and counted it his lucky day. Woe betide stingy or ignorant bridegrooms who snubbed the tradition. *What, nae poor oot?* At best, they'd be subject to insults or even the odd stone thrown in their direction. At worst, misfortune would dog them all their days and their marriage would be doomed.

The few gang members who could afford a ticket would attend the Saturday afternoon matinee at the State under Jacky's direction, returning immediately afterwards to the back green to act out on the hard beaten earth what they'd seen on the screen for the unfortunate remainder who hadn't been able to afford it. And so they became Audie Murphy in *Tumbleweed*; or Randolph Scott in *Man in the Saddle*; or Burt Lancaster in *The Crimson Pirate*; or Errol Flynn in *Objective, Burma!*; or John Derek in *Rogues of Sherwood Forest*; or Johnny Weissmuller as who else but *Tarzan*. They were in Wild West gunfights or in battle with a Tommy gun, fighting Jerries or Japs.

As the only nearby location with trees, Leith Links became Sherwood Forest where they shot bows and arrows made from cane and string at each other. The Links also doubled as the jungle where they attempted to swing from trees with branches low enough, beat themselves on the chest with their fists and competed to see who could make the best Tarzan yell. Probably the most popular picture was *The Red Beret*. Again, The Links came in handy. One Saturday afternoon, passers-by were bemused to see a group of laddies simulate parachute jumps off Giant's Brae and adjoining trees. But it was a contrite group that hirpled back to Brockit Brae, rubbing their elbows and massaging their wrists. Clearly, jumping out of Dakota aircraft was a pastime not without its dangers. In future, they'd leave it up to Alan Ladd.

James, a very junior gang prospect, observed from the fringes, trying hard to follow the progress of the various activities. When it came to bulls, he was puzzling over the significance of keppies when Davy McBean, the apparent winner of the game, broke off, poured his bulls back into their pooch and walked to the back wall of the tenement. He looked up.

"Ma, heh ma! Ma! Ma!"

No response.

"Ma, heh ma! Ma! Ma!"

At last a window on the third floor flew up. The impatient head of Mrs McBean, wrapped in a turban, appeared.

"What d'ye want? Ah'm busy!"

"Ma, can Ah hae a piece on jam?"

"Aye, just hud oan!"

Ten minutes passed. Then the turbaned head reappeared.

"Are ye ready?"

With that, a packet wrapped in newspaper and string sailed out of the window into the outstretched arms of the supplicant below.

"Thanks, Ma!"

Davy sat on the ground, undid the string and explored the contents of his air mail delivery. Lovely white bread pieces with strawberry filling. No margarine. No butter. Just the jam. He tucked in as his associates crowded round, hoping for a crumb or two. James took all this in. Why couldn't *he* have a piece on jam as well? All he had to do was shout up to his mother and he'd soon be eating one. He walked up to the wall of the tenement where he thought the windows of their flat were.

"Ma, Ma!" he shouted in his little five-year-old pipe. "Ma, Ma."

No answer. No window flying up. No head poking out. Of course there was a small difference between the third floor and the fifth, not to mention the difference between Davy's voice at eleven and James's at five. Plus the fact that he was shouting up in the wrong place. The Swanston's flat was the next one over. Anyway, even if Janet had heard him, it was doubtful that she'd have complied with his request. To throw bread into the back green was downright common. And that was one thing she was not.

Meanwhile, the lassies played their cryptic lassies' games, skipping their way through permutations of complex ropery, accompanied by calls and chants that none of the laddies had a hope of deciphering.

One, two, three aleerie
I saw Wallace Beery
Sittin' on his bumbaleerie
Kissin' Shirley Temple...

There was this perennial rope jumping favourite:

The wind, the wind, the wind blows high
Snow comes falling from the sky
Annie Davy says she'll die
For the want of the golden city!

She is handsome, she is pretty
She is the belle of the golden city
She is handsome, one two three
Come and tell me who shall be!

Between lassies and laddies existed a pre-pubescent, low-level guerrilla war, characterized by name-calling but rarely physical violence except for the odd push and shove. The lassies responded with mockery:

Skinny-malinky long-legs
Umberelly-feet
Went to the pictures
And couldnae get a seat.
When the picture started
Skinny-malinky farted!

And if anyone dared tattle to adults about some mischief their pals had been up to, the accused, when outed, was surrounded by chanting bairns:

Tell-tale tit
Yer mammie cannae knit
Yer grannie cannae walk
Withoot a walkin' stick!

Occasionally, things even got political. When Labour MP, James Hoy, defended his seat against the Unionist, Mekie, James found himself marching enthusiastically around the back green with the other tenement bairns, singing their rendering of the campaign song,

Vote, vote, vote for Mr Hoy
Who's that knockin' at the door?
If it's Mekie and his wife
Take a poker and a knife
And you won't see Mekie any more -
Shut the door!

But there was one game that couldn't be played in the back green. It was peevery beds, for that required a hard, flat surface, preferably of concrete. The beds were fields of numbered squares drawn in chalk, sometimes in a rectangle, sometimes in the rough form of an aeroplane seen from above. The peever was usually an empty Kiwi shoe polish tin.

The game was to hop along the squares, straddling some and shunting the peever with your foot from one square to another. But one thing was clear. In Brecon Street, this was a game for lassies and lassies only. The participation of laddies was

strictly taboo. Anyway, none of them could ever figure out how to play. Nor would any lassie divulge the rules. As a result, peevery beds took on the status of a secretive and obscure ritual which only the Sisterhood of Brecon Street were allowed to perform.

James stood among a rabble of young laddies, observing the peevery formalities with interest. The bed had been set up on a suitable stretch of pavement at the side of the Sally Ann building that wasn't encroached on by passers-by, local tenants or delivery men, not to mention dogs, the scaffie, or the folks from the Sally Ann themselves. One of the local lassies, Aggie Murdoch, was in charge. Aggie was taller and heavier than most of the other lassies. She had scraggly red hair, a sonsie face, and wore the standard peevery uniform for lassies: a thin floral skirt coming down below the knee, topped by a blouse and a dark jacket, and on her feet Mary Jane shoes over white ankle socks. Though she had a mild demeanour, Aggie was recognised as the repository of every arcane rule of peevery beds and took on the role of High Priestess at every peevery occasion. Whenever there was doubt about whether the peever was on a chalk line or not, the lassies looked to Aggie. If there was a question about whether a player was 'oot' or not, Aggie was the one to decide. And if the players started to quarrel among themselves, Aggie sorted them out. Without Aggie, it was impossible to play peevery beds in Brecon Street.

The hopping, skipping, straddling and shunting commenced. The players performed their energetic moves from square to square while James did his best to understand what was going on. But he couldn't work it out. Where was the peever supposed to go? There was nothing like goalposts or the hole on the putting green. Why were the squares numbered backwards? Why was that lassie 'oot'? He tried asking some of the other laddies but they just shrugged. They were as much in the dark as he was. There was only one thing for it. He walked over to where Aggie was standing, her concentration focused on the action. She towered over him and he had to tug the sleeve of her jacket to get her attention.

"Can Ah have a try?" he ventured in a small voice, looking a long way up at Aggie.

"Naw," she replied, staring down at him. "This game's only for lassies. Dinnae bother me again," and she turned away to continue her supervision of the game. A game only for lassies? Daft! James continued watching, but, ever more frustrated, his patience was exhausted. He was dying to join in. He should have known better but he was only five. Rushing onto the peevery bed from the side, he started mimicking the players, hopping from one square to the next and trying to kick the peever at the same time. The lassie currently 'in' was knocked off her stride.

"Oot mah road!" she yelled frantically, losing her balance.

Suddenly, mid-hop, there was Aggie standing in front of him. She gave him a gentle push in the middle of the chest. But a gentle push from Aggie was like a king hit from a normal-sized lassie. He went over backwards and landed, sitting on his bum in the middle of the peevery bed. He burst into tears. His bum was hurting but his pride was hurting even more. He bawled the first words he could think of.

"Aaaaah! Ah'll tell mah big sister oan you!"

The crowd gathered round him, lassies to the fore.

"An' whae's yer big sister then?" asked Aggie, now even taller, her arms folded across the front of her jacket.

"Wee Effie!" bawled James.

"*Wee* Effie?" repeated Aggie, with a snort. "Well, if she's wee, she doesnae hae much o' a chance against me, does she?"

The crowd howled. This was the funniest thing they'd seen in the street. Big Aggie talking down to this daft wee laddie. It was priceless. James's tears abated and he was beginning to grasp the gravity of the situation. Since Wee Effie had, at that point, not come to her attention, Aggie turned round and quizzed the members of the Sisterhood.

"Any o' you's ken this Wee Effie?"

There was a general shaking of heads. She turned back to James.

"Well, she's no one o' us so she'd better watch oot," warned Aggie.

Helpful laddie hands pulled James up. He stood in the middle of the crowd, humiliated, devastated.

"Now, go back tae yer mammie an' dinnae bother us again. This is a lassie's game, so keep oot o' it!"

James got up and, chastened, wandered home, rubbing his backside. He hoped that Wee Effie would never hear of this and tell his parents. But he'd learnt his lesson. Peevery beds was a lassies' game and that was final.

A wee flutter

"Fancy a wee flutter on the horses the day, hen?"

Ian sat across from Janet at the kitchen table scanning the racing section of the *Scottish Daily Express*, a warm buttered breakfast roll of the batch he'd just fetched from the corner shop in one hand and a cup of tea in the other. The bare scrubbed wooden surface of the table was set for only two. A lie-in and a lazy winter Saturday morning breakfast were the order of the day. It was already after eleven o'clock. The flat was slowly warming up from the coal fire burning in the grate. Wee Effie had already left to spend the weekend with her Auntie Christine. James, having devoured his bowl of porridge, milk and sugar, was on his knees on the carpet, playing with a little green metallic robot with red eyes and two antennae that Auntie Effie had given him for Christmas.

"Why no', darlin'?" Janet's eyes twinkled as she looked up from her *Woman's Own*. "Ye ken how good Ah am at pickin' winners!"

In their twelve years or so of marriage they hadn't had many common interests. But horse racing was one of them. It had started before The War when Janet and Ian had just become an item. What was a young couple to do when money was in short supply and they wanted to spend time together? In that era, the picture house or one of the many Edinburgh dance halls provided the standard solution. But Ian kept his options open when it came to showing a girl a good time. After long days in the gloomy cellars of MacFergus, an excursion into the countryside around the city was certainly an option, especially in view of the relatively inexpensive public transport system. For a few pence, the tram or bus took them to Cramond and, tide permitting, a walk over the sands to the Island; to Fairmilehead and a picnic at Hillend, weather permitting; or to Oxgangs and a pilgrimage into the lee of the Pentlands to Swanston Village, which Ian jokingly referred to as his ancestral home. Once they even scraped together enough for a day cruise on the *Thane of Fife* from Granton to

Burntisland in the summer of 1939, one of the last trips before war shut the service down.

One of their favourite outings was on a green SMT bus to Musselburgh. That town was famous for only one thing: the race track. The noise of the crowds, the tension in the air, the horses, the diminutive jockeys in their racing silks, plus the chance to place your bets and win a bob or two. Not that they could afford much, nor was it a trip that they could make often. But who knew how lucky they could be? Very occasionally, they backed a winner. Each time they did, a seed was planted that lay dormant all through the long war years. With all the turmoil, visits to Musselburgh, or any other racecourse for that matter, were out of the question. But they could still place a bet now and then.

From a legal standpoint, of course, the Swanstons were breaking the law, for in Britain, most off-course cash betting was illegal and had been since the Street Betting Act of 1906. Placing cash bets on horse races was possible only at racecourses on race days, which explains why race meets were so well frequented. However, these were mainly for the well-off. Few townspeople of limited means could afford the time or the money to travel all the way out to racecourses every time they wanted to place a bet. So, among the working classes in particular the law was widely flouted and a major underground industry based on race betting had flourished in almost every locale in the UK. Tipsters, bookies' runners and illegal betting operations abounded. Leith was no exception. Clandestine betting shops existed, and each had its dedicated clientele. If Ian or Janet wanted to place a bet, a visit to their bookie in The Kirkgate was on the cards.

However, first, they had to make their selections. For a couple who shared the same interest, their methods were strangely contradictory. Ian, on the one hand, studied form, basing his picks on what he considered to be a rational approach: the age of the horse, its record, the state of the ground, the trainer and, of course, the jockey, if known. Janet, by contrast, followed her intuition. As she scanned down a list of runners, the name of a horse would simply jump out at her. And strangely enough, going by results, her system appeared to work.

For the fact was that Ian had little or no luck. No matter what he gambled on, he never won anything. All his life he religiously did the weekly football pools but not once did he get eight draws, or anything near. All that money for nothing – except the thrill of the hope of being a winner. Janet, on the other hand, *was* a winner. It wasn't always a first prize or a valuable prize. But whether it was a raffle, a competition, or the horses, luck was invariably on her side. It swirled around her head. Under the circumstances, Ian, suppressing any chagrin he might have been tempted to feel, could only wax philosophical.

“Well, ye see, hen,” he’d say with a grin, “the fact is that Ah’m lucky in love and that’s good enough for me!”

They focused on two meets, Musselburgh and Ayr. Ian’s research led him to an Irish horse, Top o’ the Mornin’, that was running in the Novices Chase at Ayr. Janet, poring over the runners at Musselburgh, gave a whoop.

“Providential Payout!”

Ian looked at her, his expression the kind of question mark that only couples in love understand. Janet eagerly explained.

“Ah forgot tae tell ye. Ah just got mah divvie from the Provie this week.” It was her reward for a year of faithful shopping at Leith Provident, the sum of eleven shillings, seven pence halfpenny, not a lot, but also not to be sniffed at.

“Providential Payout – nae doot!” She laughed, quite convinced that the gods of luck were smiling on her. “Two bob each way?” she asked. Going to the sideboard, she opened the top drawer and pulled out her precious Basildon Bond writing pad, the one she used for her weekly letter to her wee sister Bella in Cheltenham. She sat at the table, flipped open the pad, folded the top sheet in two and tore it across. Picking up a pencil she wrote:

1. Ayr, Novices Chase, Top o’ the Mornin’, 2/- e. w.
2. Musselburgh, 2 o’clock, Providential Payout, 2/- e. w.

She looked up at Ian who was still busy with the newspaper.

“Anythin’ else?”

He thought for a moment then nodded at James, who by now was making his robot walk stiffly across the carpet and ‘talk’ in a booming, mechanical voice.

“How about givin’ Wee Jock a go?” he suggested playfully. Janet was immediately on board. Who knew, maybe her son had inherited some of her fey genes?

“James, come up here an’ pick a horse!”

Bewildered, James got to his feet and, still holding his robot, climbed on his mother’s knee. The racing page of the newspaper was spread out on the table in front of them. Although his reading was making great strides, it wasn’t yet up to deciphering a list of starters at the races. He’d need help.

“Try ’im at Haydock Park,” suggested Ian.

“Listen, son, d’ye want tae help us pick a horsey in a race?”

James nodded obediently, not quite understanding.

“Ah’m gonnae read oot the names of some horseys. Just tell me tae stop when ye hear one ye like. OK?”

James nodded absent-mindedly, distracted by the robot which was now marching across the surface of the table. Janet, settling for the two o'clock race, started to read, pausing briefly after each name.

"Turkish Delight, Frankie's Folly, Lancashire Lass, Valorum, Bonnie Prince Charlie, Pick My Brains, Pelorus Jack..."

"Pelorus Jack!" James interrupted.

Janet looked at her son in surprise.

"Pelorus Jack? Are ye sure?"

James nodded, his attention still focused on the robot, which was by now doing handstands.

"Pelorus Jack? What in the name o' the wee man is Pelorus Jack?"

She looked at Ian but he just shook his head.

"Sorry, hen, never heard o' it."

They both turned and looked at James. Janet prised the robot from his grasp. That, at last, got his full attention.

"Let the wee robot have a rest for a bit son. Now, who's Pelorus Jack?"

"A dolphin!" said James triumphantly. For the first time in his life he was telling his parents something *he* knew but *they* didn't.

"A dolphin?" repeated Janet, pretending ignorance with raised eyebrows, keen to test James's grasp of the subject. "What's a dolphin?"

"It's a kind of fish, a big fish."

"A big fish, really? Is it like a shark?"

"No, it's a nice fish. It likes people."

"Really? An' how d'ye ken Pelorus Jack's a dolphin?"

James looked at them seriously and spoke with authority.

"Because Miss Douglas told us!"

"Miss Douglas indeed! What did she tell ye?"

"Well, 'e was this dolphin in New Zealand. 'E was famous. Every day when the ferry sailed over tae the South Island, this dolphin swam in front tae show them the way."

Taken aback by the extent of their little son's knowledge, the two Swanstons silently made mock surprised faces at each other above James's head.

"And son," asked Ian, "why was 'e called Pelorus Jack?"

"Because Pelorus was the name o' the place where 'e lived."

The lecture complete, James returned to more serious business.

"Mum, can Ah have mah robot back now?"

"Well, that's us told!" laughed Janet, returning the toy and dropping her son back on the carpet. "Right, Pelorus Jack it is," and to the list of horses she added:

3. Haydock Park, 2 o'clock, Pelorus Jack, 2/- e. w.

Then, in the bottom right-hand corner of the paper, she wrote *Wee Jock*. This was now their betting slip and Wee Jock was their pseudonym. No one in their right mind put their real name or any other personal details on a betting slip. That was asking for trouble. The Swanstons' bookie had a method for recording every pseudonym without committing anything incriminating to paper. They could be assured that a winning bet by Wee Jock would be paid out to them. That was how the system worked.

"Right," said Janet. "Ah've got some messages tae get, so Ah'll be off up tae The Kirkgate first." As she was putting on her coat, she looked down at James.

"Want tae come, son?" When James hesitated, unsure, she added, "Ah'm goin' tae The Kirkgate tae put on yer bet. Pelorus Jack."

It was a typical grey winter morning in Leith. The wind off the North Sea surged down Junction Street into their faces as Janet briskly made her way past Dr Bell's, James grasping her hand at a fast toddle by her side. As they crossed the road to the Victoria Statue through busy traffic at the spot where four main roads met, the wind swirled and buffeted as if unsure where to go next. They turned left into The Kirkgate and suddenly all was calm in the narrow canyon of ancient, blackened tenements.

The Kirkgate, the historical centre, the beating heart of Leith, the main north-south artery long before Leith Walk, Constitution Street or Junction Street had even existed; the established route for travellers proceeding to Edinburgh from a landing at Leith Harbour. One thing Janet did know was her Leith history. She knew that Mary Queen of Scots likely rode this way from King's Wark to Holyrood on her fateful return home from France. It was said that a slew of historical figures had frequented The Kirkgate, including the tragic Mary of Guise, Regent of Scotland and Mary's mother, Charles II and Robert Burns. French troops had marched here during the Siege of Leith. Cromwell was said to have dined in a local hostelry. The grey stone hulk of Trinity House sulked on the left. Here in its vaults, the first pupils of what was to become The Academy had received their lessons from 'The Maister' 400 years before, until ejected by Roundheads. South Leith - St Mary's - Church sprawled among its lawns and gravestones on the right, as it had for half a century, Our Lady Kirk of pre-Reformation times and the spiritual hub of the Leith community.

Every time Janet walked here, she never failed to reflect on the street's significance to her family. Here was the church where she was married, the place where she and her eight brothers and sisters had been christened, not to mention both her children; not a few of her ancestors now slumbered in its graves. Her father had been born in Yardheads just over there and various uncles and aunties in Giles Street, around the corner. The Kirkgate had been their stamping ground, their territory, their home turf. For Janet, a visit to The Kirkgate was like coming home. There couldn't be a Leither alive that didn't have a connection to The Kirkgate in some shape or form. But now The Kirkgate had fallen on hard times. Neglected for centuries, a victim of economic recession, political dereliction, chronic poverty, and its own haphazard evolution, it now presented as a shambles of styles, from Victorian to Georgian to Jacobean and beyond, back into the mists of architectural time. Its mismatched, decaying buildings with their teetering chimney stacks and their soot-begrimed facades; its shabby shop fronts masking mouldering interiors; its dingy pends, giving into gloomy backyards, the legacy of a horse-drawn era; its corroded wrought-iron lamp standards. They all bore witness to what The Kirkgate had become: the detritus of history, its stature as Leith's principal thoroughfare now lost, its place as the traditional heart of the community threatened.

The Saturday lunchtime crowds were building as mother and son walked down the left-hand side of the street, passing almost every kind of shop imaginable: a tattoo parlour displaying photos of its artistic creations; a barber's doing brisk business beneath its red and white striped pole; junk shops with clutter spilling out onto the pavement; fish and chip shops and cafes emitting fatty, overpowering cooking smells; a children's outfitter with two child mannequins in the window; a men's outfitter selling cheap suits; a pawn shop brooding under three brass balls; salerooms with second-hand clothing on coat hangers out the door; butchers, bakers, fishmongers and fruiterers. Just about every branch of retail trade was on display.

Just as the road was starting to curve, they passed Kinnairds Tea Room and crossed over. There was no traffic to avoid for there was no traffic to speak of. Car ownership among the tenement dwellers of The Kirkgate was non-existent. Besides, the street was too narrow for twentieth-century through traffic. A hawker was selling paraffin from a horse-drawn cart. A solitary lorry was delivering to a grocer's. A couple of decrepit vans were parked against the kerb with open rear doors and nick-knacks for sale, little plaster statues of children, cats and dogs. Otherwise, the vacant roadway had been commandeered by groups of strolling shoppers and turned, by default, into an early species of pedestrian precinct. Two elderly ladies in ubiquitous blue-green raincoats wandered up the middle of the road, their black Labrador tugging on the lead, nose to the ground, busily cataloguing the tarmac's lingering spoors. A gaggle of bairns clustered round a toddler bawling in a pram. A grandmother in a headscarf struggled to control five-year-old identically dressed twin girls. At this time and on a cold day, Michael's Café was almost empty, the stocky, moustached figure of Mr Rocchio standing in the entrance, hands behind his back, looking enviously across at Kinnairds, which was beginning to fill up. At the Gaiety Theatre with its distinctive triangular stone escutcheon and sagging double gates, the box office was already open and selling tickets for the evening's performance.

Fifty yards beyond the Gaiety, they stopped in front of a nondescript shop front slightly elevated above the others in the street. The original name over the frontage had been painted out. The space above the doorway was blank. The window was empty of any display. Just then, the door opened and a middle-aged man in a trench coat wearing a flat cap and a knitted scarf barged past them without a word. James followed his mother up three stone steps. The door had once had a large sheet of glass in a wooden frame, but the glass had shattered long ago and the empty space had been blocked with bare wooden boards nailed onto flaking paint that had once been white. Janet pushed it open.

As they entered, an old-fashioned clapper bell on a metal spring was triggered. James looked around. This was a strange shop. The walls were unadorned and the shelves empty. The wide wooden counter on the left-hand side was bare. The room was cold, smelled of mould and was obviously unheated. But the anonymous exterior and the bland interior were belied by the hum and activity emanating from the partly curtained entry of a back room. Standing on tiptoe and looking over the edge of the counter, James could see four people seated at desks busily talking into telephones. There was a large chalkboard full of writing he couldn't make out from a distance. There was an insistent clack, clack, clack from some invisible equipment.

A woman emerged through the curtains in response to the bell. She was of full figure, looked to be in her late fifties and wore a flowery turban over her meagre head of grey hair. She had a lived-in face that had probably once been pretty and a chain-smoker's complexion. She wore a thick, grey turtleneck sweater over a long black skirt and had a Stewart tartan scarf swathed several times around her neck. Her expression was businesslike behind the fixed smile that gripped the Woodbine permanently wedged in the corner of her mouth. She squinted as the smoke irritated her eyes.

"Aye, hen, what can Ah dae fir ye?"

She was Rita Geddes, the sole proprietor, manager, director and general bottle washer of the nameless betting operation that ran from the nameless shop in The Kirkgate. None of her clients knew her surname. She went only by 'Rita'. Some wondered if it was her real name at all. Rita employed four staff who monitored the main race meets throughout the country, compiled the results, and processed the bets and winnings. Her back office had an array of cutting-edge equipment. There was a bank of telephones, a clutch of modern typewriters, a ticker tape machine and even an Olivetti teleprinter. Out of sight, half-hidden by a curtain, her boyfriend and partner, Tommy Campbell, an ex-boxer for Leith Victoria and bruiser of some competence, sat in an armchair with a cricket bat across his knees, providing security. Sophisticated as the Rita Geddes operation was, it was entirely invisible to the Inland Revenue Department. Rita had never been audited and paid no taxes. It was whispered that her continued survival owed not a little to the fact that officers of the local constabulary were among her best clients.

"Hiya, Rita," said Janet. Without formality, she retrieved the betting slip from her handbag and laid it on the counter. Opening her purse, she extracted three florins and placed them alongside. Rita grunted, picked up the slip and peered at it through her cigarette smoke.

"Three at two bob each way? Wee Jock?" she said, expecting confirmation. Janet nodded. Rita expertly scooped the money off the counter and into a leather purse that had miraculously appeared on a belt from under her sweater. Then, taking the slip, she disappeared into the back room, returning a few minutes later. With one hand, she reached under the counter, placed another slip of paper next to Janet's, with the other hand produced a pencil from the folds of her turban and wrote some numbers on both slips. Reaching under the counter again, she produced a rubber stamp to date stamp them. She handed Janet her receipt and filed Janet's slip away in some recess under the counter. At the top right-hand corner of the slip was the number 347. That was Janet's client number. Below was entered:

1 – 3
2 – 33
3 – 100

From this, Janet knew the odds she'd been offered were three to one for Top o' the Mornin', thirty-three to one for Providential Payout and a hundred to one for Pelorus Jack.

"Thanks, Rita!"

Janet went to leave. But Rita wasn't finished. Reaching under the counter again, she brought out a glass jar, removed the stopper, walked around the counter and held it out to James.

"Wud the bairn like a wee sweetie?"

"Go on," said Janet, "d'ye want one?"

Thrusting his small hand into the opening, James managed to extract a toffee doddle from the clump of sweeties inside.

"Say thank you tae the nice lady!"

"Thank you," said James shyly, then stuffed the toffee doddle into his mouth and started sucking.

"Aye, that's a bonnie wee laddie!" said Rita, and, "Guid luck, hen!"

"Thanks, Rita, cheerio!"

And with that, the bet was placed. Janet's receipt was enough to ensure she'd get her payout, should she have a winner. And should she be stopped by a passing bobby – she smiled at the notion, it was so ridiculous – all she had was a piece of paper with some numbers and a date. There was no evidence of betting whatsoever. As they left hand-in-hand, letting the door bang shut behind them, two young men with stylish haircuts came from the other direction and hurried up the steps into the shop. It was Saturday. Rita would be doing brisk business. Retracing her steps back up The Kirkgate, Janet reflected on what she'd just done. Six shillings! How extravagant! But she consoled herself with the thought that her part-time job in the DIY shop at Abbeyhill was bringing in another half wage, so maybe it was right to afford a wee luxury now and then.

Back home, Ian was interested in the odds they'd got. His horse was, of course, the favourite, and Janet's something of an outsider. Pelorus Jack looked to be a hopeless case – a rank outsider at a hundred to one. But, going by past experience he knew it was foolish to count his chickens. He'd wait and see. Janet, on the other hand, knew. She had in her heart a solid certainty that she couldn't dismiss. She went around with a smile on her face. James, of course, was oblivious to the chain of events he'd touched off with his unwitting knowledge of Pelorus Jack. Well, it was all predictable. At seven o'clock that night, Ian went out with James for fish suppers and a *Pink Edinburgh Evening News*. Janet had the tea and buttered bread ready when they got back. Dispensing with plates and cutlery, they unpacked the fish suppers and spread them in their newspaper wrappings across the bare table, salt and vinegar at the ready They tucked in, James sharing with Janet. After his first few mouthfuls and a gulp of near-scalding, sugary tea, Ian wiped his hands on a towel and picked up 'The Pink'.

"Now, let's see."

He thumbed past the mass of football results, then the rugby, and finally got to the racing section while Janet looked on patiently.

"Here we are. Racing from Ayr."

His finger ran down the page. Then it stopped and his face fell.

"Ye're not gonnae believe this! Mah horse came in fifth! Fifth! It was the favourite!" He scoffed. "Ah, well." He smiled at Janet.

"Still, lucky in love!" she said light-heartedly before *he* could. "Now what about Providential Payout?"

Ian turned the page and again ran his finger down.

"Ah dinnae believe it! Third!"

"See, Mister Smart Alec!" said Janet. "Mah so-called unscientific method seems tae work after aw'!"

They both looked at James.

"Let's see if Wee Jock has brought us any luck wi' Pelorus Jack."

Ian turned another couple of pages.

"Haydock, Haydock. Here it is, winner, two o'clock..."

He looked up at Janet, his face a symphony of emotions.

"Well, what dae ye think?" he demanded.

"Pelorus Jack won," pronounced Janet, as calmly as if she were stating they were going to have chips for tea. By now Ian's head was nodding in confirmation.

"Pelorus Jack won... Pelorus Jack won..." He shook his head in mock disbelief. "Ah dinnae believe it! Mah son can pick winners!"

"James, yer horsey won, it won the race!" Janet said, reaching over and giving James a sideways hug. "What a clever wee laddie ye are!" James just smiled and popped another vinegar-soaked chip into his mouth.

Because they'd chosen each way, the bet was split between a win and a place. At a hundred to one, James had won a hundred shillings, or five pounds for his win and a half of that for his place. He also got his original stake back. So in all, he won 152/- or £7-12s. Not bad for a two-shilling stake. Under the same system, at thirty-three to one Janet's third place had returned twelve shillings. Altogether, they'd won over eight pounds, more than her week's wages at the DIY shop. The following Monday, Janet didn't waste much time; by late morning she was already in The Kirkgate claiming their winnings. As she slapped their betting slip on the counter, her smile of satisfaction said it all. But as Rita counted out eight one-pound notes and change on the table she couldn't help but grumble. James's was the largest payout on a two-shilling bet that weekend.

"Ah'd like tae say Ah look forward tae seein' ye next time but now Ah'm no sae sure," she spluttered, but not unkindly, through rising cigarette smoke. Janet couldn't help herself.

"Would ye like tae ken whae picked the winner?" she asked.

"Aye, go on, hen, make it worse!" Rita chaffed.

"Mah wee laddie!"

"Thon wee laddie that was here wi' ye on Saturday?"

"Aye, that's the one! Mah wee James. 'E's just goin' on six."

If Rita hadn't been wearing a turban she'd have scratched her head in bewilderment.

"How come a wee laddie picks a horse ca'd Pelorus Jack – an' what does that mean, anyhow?"

Janet told her the story of Pelorus Jack and how James had learnt it from Miss Douglas at Bonnybrig Primary.

"Are you tellin' me Ah'm doon mair than eight quid because o' yer laddie's teacher frae New Zealand?"

"Aye, that's aboot the sum o' it!"

"That's a story Ah'll take tae mah grave wi' me!" Rita said, smiling sardonically.

That Monday afternoon, Janet was at the main gate of Bonnybrig Primary School at three minutes to three, waiting to pick up James. She was having a busy day. She'd taken the bus to the Royal Bank of Scotland Abbeyhill Branch to deposit £7 into their joint savings account. They were hoping to be able to have their first real holiday together as a family some time and this tidy sum would be a welcome addition to their nest egg. In her hand was a small, wrapped box. The electric bell suddenly made its shrill announcement that lessons were over for the day. The double glass doors flew open and groups of noisy pupils streamed out. She waved when she saw James.

"Hello, son, how was school the day?" she enquired.

Without waiting for an answer, she took his hand with her free hand and walked towards the blue side door of Miss Douglas's classroom. James looked at her in confusion. She was taking him back the way he'd just come.

"Dinnae worry," she said in response. "Ah just want a word wi' yer teacher."

Janet popped her head round the half-open door and knocked at the same time. Miss Douglas looked up from her desk, where she was making some entries in a ledger.

"Oh, Mrs Swanston, come in!" she said, standing up with a welcoming smile.

Janet approached hesitantly and, as she usually did in the presence of 'educated' people, lapsed into an attempt at Proper Speak.

"I've got a wee present for you." In response to Miss Douglas's puzzled expression, she added, "James here will tell you what it's aw' about." Then to James, "Son, tell Miss Douglas about the horsey."

By now, Miss Douglas was as bewildered as ever but, good-natured as she was, she turned to James with an indulgent smile playing around her lips, motioning Janet to take one of the two chairs at her desk and sitting down in the other.

"Well," said James, as if he were being tested on his catechism, "Mum asked me tae pick a horsey at the hay dog park..."

"Haydock Park, son," then to Miss Douglas by way of explanation, "It's a race track in England." Miss Douglas nodded. "Go on, son."

"...At Haydock Park an' Ah picked Pelorus Jack."

A light went on in Miss Douglas's head.

"Well, Ah went wi' mah Mum tae The Kirkgate an' we betted two shillins on it..."

"...Each way," interjected Janet.

"...an' it won the race!"

Miss Douglas's eyes had been getting bigger all the time and when James was finished she let out a cry.

"Well, I never! You remembered the story about Pelorus Jack!"

She was genuinely touched. If she'd needed proof that her lessons were getting through, here it was – straight from the horse's mouth.

"And your horsey – your horse – won, James, did it?"

"Yes, but it's aw' thanks to you, Miss Douglas. We, mah husband and me, had no idea what Pelorus Jack was..." She looked proudly at her son. "...but James did."

Then Miss Douglas asked a question that revealed some experience in these matters.

"And what were the odds?" she enquired.

"A hundred tae one!" replied Janet.

"Oh, well done! What a clever boy you are, James!"

Miss Douglas, ever the diplomat, declined to pose the indelicate question of exactly how much they'd won.

"And so," said Janet, "we just wanted to give ye a wee present as a thank you."

And she handed over the gift, which Miss Douglas carefully unwrapped. It was a box of Black Magic chocolates. Earlier that month, confectionary rationing had at last ended. People, and especially children, were revelling in being able to buy as many sweets as they wanted without a ration book. Those with a sweet tooth, which was about the entire population of Britain, had still not got used to the easy access to chocolate, so a gift like this was the height of luxury.

"Oh, how kind of you!"

Janet and James both beamed, relishing Miss Douglas's gratitude. What they didn't know, as had been evident from her question, was that Miss Douglas herself had been a keen follower of the horses back in her native New Zealand, influenced by her father who'd had a part-share in a racehorse, Rotorua Rose. But since her move to Scotland, there had been little opportunity to renew her interest, not to mention a lack of local knowledge about how to circumvent the draconian anti-betting laws. Well, here was her chance. She cleared her throat.

"Now, Mrs Swanston, can you help me here? How would one go about laying a bet on a horse in Leith?"

"Well, Miss Douglas, it's like this..." and she went on to explain how betting worked and gave her directions to Rita Geddes's.

"I've never been to The Kirkgate before. Would you mind drawing a little map for me?" And with that, Miss Douglas produced a sheet of ruled paper and a pencil. While Janet was busy sketching away at the teacher's desk, Miss Douglas turned to James.

"Now, James, it seems you have a knack. Could you pick a winner for me some time?"

And so began Miss Douglas's association with The Kirkgate and Rita Geddes. Her Saturday morning visit, combining a flutter at Rita's with a browse through the shops and tea and scones at Kinnairds, became a weekly fixture.

But as the 1960s approached, unknown to Miss Douglas, her Saturday outings were doomed, for Rita's days were numbered, as were those of The Kirkgate. On January 1st, 1961, off-course race betting became legal in Britain. Rita's thriving little empire was swept away almost overnight by the tsunami of national betting conglomerates that quickly seized control of the industry the length and breadth of the country. The nameless shop up the three steps with the bare shelves and the once buzzing back room now lay abandoned and empty.

Then the second tsunami arrived hot on the heels of the first. A new generation of city planners was now in charge up in Edinburgh, one that had little regard for all that had gone before. Swept up in the spirit of post-war regeneration and renewal gripping Britain, their mantra was *out with the old, in with the new*! Their methods were straightforward: flatten, concrete, high rise. With little or no forewarning, The Kirkgate was bulldozed almost in its entirety. Adjoining streets housing warehouses, distilleries, cooperages and workshops were razed to the ground. Only South Leith Church and Trinity House were spared. The rubble was dumped in the Forth for the land reclamation of the docklands.

Opinion in the population was divided. The Kirkgate had been an irredeemable, crumbling mess that had to go. And high time too!

But many were incensed. There was no consultation, no consideration, no regard for conservation or the long-term consequences. Centuries of history had been brutally swept aside, to be replaced by an ugly wasteland of soulless 1960s glass and concrete. As if to add insult to injury, the redevelopment was crassly named The New Kirkgate. Native Leithers got the message loud and clear. The old Kirkgate, *their* Kirkgate, was dead, and they'd just have to grin and bear it. But they couldn't bear it and they certainly didn't grin. Instead, they were grieving. It was as if their hearts had been ripped out. Of The Kirkgate they'd known, little or nothing was left. Leith would never be the same again.

The Cappy Club

"No matter what, keep a hud o' 'is hand!"

Janet bent down until her eyes were level with ten-year-old Wee Effie's.

"D'ye hear me?"

Effie returned the stare, nodding solemnly.

"Ye're a big girl now, ye have tae take some responsibility for yer wee brother!"

Janet straightened and stepped back, inspecting the two prospective cinema patrons. Wee Effie's ash-blond hair was in two tight pigtails. Her grey Fair Isle cardigan was patterned with a band of purple, green and white lozenges and had a pocket on each side. Only the top two buttons were done up. An off-white, thin, cotton poodle skirt with large blue polka dots reached below her knee and her white canvas shoes were slightly scuffed. Her face was scrubbed clean. Yes, she would do. Janet turned to James. He'd just turned six. His sandy hair was cut in a short-back-and-sides. He had on a long-sleeved grey cotton shirt under a sleeveless, beige jersey that had roughly the same pattern as Wee Effie's. Both garments had clearly been knitted by the same hands – Janet's. Wide grey shorts with deep pockets, grey socks and grubby black leather shoes completed James's outfit. Janet bent down and pulled the socks up from where they sagged around his ankles to just below his knees, hoping that the tattie she knew was in the left one wasn't visible. A couple of wide elastic bands did perfectly well as garters and kept a red sock flash in place on the outside of each leg. He stood patiently as she licked her fingers and rubbed away smudges of dirt around his nose. It was a pity about the shoes but she didn't have time to deal with them.

"Have ye got yer money?"

Wee Effie reached into her cardigan pocket and held out the two sixpences and two threepenny bits.

"Right, on yer way. Remember, keep thegither! An' be back by one o'clock!"

Opening the front door, she shooed her bairns out onto the landing and, arms folded, leaning on the banister, she watched them as they carefully made their way down into the gloom of the stairwell. Just as their figures were being swallowed up, Wee Effie turned round and waved, "Ta-ta, Mum!" Janet waved back with a twinge of anxiety mingled with the faint hope that she could trust them to go off on their own for a couple of hours on a Saturday morning, allowing her to catch up with some housework.

There was little in the way of organised entertainment for the Brecon Street bairns unless they had connections to organisations like the Sally Ann or one of the local churches or were members of sports clubs. But there were the pictures. Each of the two picture houses in Leith put on a children's programme at weekends, the Capitol on Saturday mornings and the State on Saturday afternoons. For some reason, the Capitol's offering was more popular, probably because the bairns' afternoons were tied up in other ways, especially if Hibs or Hearts had home games. So The Cappy Club, as it had become known, was a big attraction for the bairns of Leith, not to mention a blessing for parents who could get rid of their offspring for a couple of hours. Since not long after they moved into Number 11, Wee Effie had been going to The Cappy Club on a regular basis with a bunch of lassies from the tenement. Due to his age, James had never been allowed. But now, after putting up with weeks of his pestering, Janet had agreed to let him go, as long as he behaved himself and as long as he stuck close to Wee Effie the whole time. For her part, Wee Effie had mounted a stiff rearguard action. What lassie in her right mind would want to be seen out and about with their wee brother? But Janet had put her foot down. If James couldn't go, she couldn't go either. Wee Effie had caved.

Leaving the gloom of the stairwell, the two Swanston bairns joined up with the female Cappy Club contingent of around ten souls, already assembled and waiting outside in the street. Wee Effie had steeled herself for snide comments about the presence of James but was relieved to see that she wasn't the only member of the clique with a younger brother or sister in tow, and apart from a few funny looks, nobody said anything untoward.

"Hiya!"

"Hiya! Come oan, hurry, we'll be late!"

They set off in a chattering crowd, walking briskly along Junction Street, James's wee legs struggling to keep up with those of the big lassies. He wished they could have taken the tram but their allowance for today didn't stretch that far. Sixpence each for the pictures and threepence each for sweeties. Nobody was going to take a tram when there could be sweeties instead. The group turned into Leith Walk, crossed the tram lines and trooped into Christie's Confectioners to make their choices. Wee Effie had a Penny Dainty and a Sherbet Dab and still had a halfpenny change. For tuppence, Wee James got a poke of Soor Plooms. He loved Soor Plooms and knew that, once one was tucked in the corner of his gums, he could make it last forever. With the Soor Plooms in his left shorts pocket, he felt with satisfaction the penny change reposing in his right and considered what he could spend it on.

On they went, up Leith Walk and into Manderston Street. Already, a horde of bairns had collected in front of The Cappy, thronging on the steps, around the pillars and into the street. Without missing a beat, the Brecon Street lassies, led by the indomitable Mary Meikle, vectored into the mob with all the clout of a rolling rugby scrum, pushing and elbowing their way to the ticket counter. There was no need to speak. One after the other they slapped their sixpences on the counter, got their tickets from the grumpy wifie and formed another scrum to get into the auditorium.

"Tickets, please!"

The usher stood just outside the curtained entrance to the stalls.

"Hud yer horses, ye'll aw' get a seat!" he protested, tearing tickets in half at top speed and helping each bairn in with a push on the shoulder.

The stalls were already filling up fast and the Brecon Street bairns were lucky to get seats all together in two rows halfway down and in the middle. As the bairns crammed in, the noise level increased. By the time the programme was about to start at 10 o'clock, the theatre was packed and it was bedlam. Suddenly the lights went down and the first part of the programme started. It was, of course, cartoons. The bairns screamed, chortled and gasped at the antics of Mickey Mouse, Donald Duck and Pluto. Then came a couple of shorts each from Laurel and Hardy and Charlie Chaplin. Although the reels were monochrome, of inferior quality and plainly pre-War, the slapstick antics were timeless. How the bairns laughed. Tears streamed down James's face, he struggled to keep his Soor Ploom tucked into his cheek and worried that he might wee in his breeks.

After the programme's comic lead-in, it was time for something more serious in the form of the weekly serial which was always a thriller or mystery of some kind. This time it was Batman and Robin chasing around in their Batmobile after the villains of Gotham City. Again, the reel was monochrome, the acting hammy and the wobbly sets looked like they were made of papier-mâché, but it didn't matter. The bairns were enthralled. James was disappointed when the episode suddenly ended with a flourish of melodramatic chords and a voice-over preview. If he wanted to find out what happened next, he'd just have to come back the following Saturday.

The brief interval was followed by part three of the programme. It was always a full-length feature film. All through the first two parts, the noise level had remained stubbornly high with all the laughter, screaming and shouting. But when the big picture started, what passed for relative quiet descended on the auditorium, except for the rumbling of trains overhead on the Leith to Waverley line, for The Capitol was one of the few picture houses in Scotland located under the arch of a railway viaduct. This week's main feature was Roy Rogers, King of the Cowboys, and his clever horse, Trigger. Roy was trying to capture a golden stallion running wild with his herd in Texas, but then he got mixed up in diamond smuggling from Mexico, was wrongly accused and sent to jail. Of course, everything ended up happily ever after with the birth of Trigger Junior, but not until the bairns, on the edge of their seats, had been led through a series of thrilling adventures. James was mesmerized. He'd never seen a western before. The fact that it was in colour was a bonus.

When the session ended at 12.30 and the lights went up, there was something like a collective groan from the audience followed by a babble of exhilaration. It was all over – until next week. Then began the pushing and shoving to get out and get home. And that was when Mary Meikle, raising her voice to a shout above the hubbub, issued her fateful challenge:

"Last one oot's a hairy kipper!"

With that, all that mattered to the Brecon Street lassies was not to be last outside, and the race through the horde began. Nobody wanted to be a hairy kipper. As they regrouped outside in the street, Wee Effie heaved a sigh of relief. It wasn't her. It was Frances Goldie, the softy of the group. She was a real pushover and had been last to emerge from the melee. And now she was a hairy kipper. After reaching a consensus that Frances was indeed a hairy kipper, the lassies started to make their way home. Poor Frances.

But Wee Effie's relief at not being the hairy kipper was short-lived. Something was wrong. What had she missed? She suddenly stopped in her tracks and the others stopped with her.

"Where's James? Where's mah wee brother?"

Concerned expressions. As one, they turned round and looked back towards The Capitol. Bairns were still streaming out in clumps and knots, but there was no sign of James. Wee Effie hurried back with two other lassies tagging along, pushing up the steps against the current and into the foyer. No James. She turned to the usher, now leaning against the ticket counter picking his nose.

"Have ye seen a wee laddie?"

"Ah see lots o' wee laddies, especially on a Saturday mornin'," he opined laconically.

Wee Effie stamped her feet in frustration at the blatant sarcasm.

"It's mah wee brother!" she almost shouted. "Ah've lost 'im!"

She gave a description. The usher shook his head and suggested they go back and look in the empty auditorium. The three lassies ran in and patrolled the aisles, looking up and down the deserted rows of seats. No James. Wee Effie burst into tears.

"Mah mum's gonnae kill me!" she predicted.

Outside, the Brecon Street group had split up. One half that had to get home for their dinner hurried off. The remainder joined Wee Effie in scouring most of Manderston Street. No James. Someone suggested that he'd perhaps gone home on his own. Yes, that would be it, he must have gone back to Brecon Street. And having reached that obvious conclusion, the lassies smiled with relief and hurried off.

Meanwhile, James was wondering where he was. In the rush not to be a hairy kipper, his sister had done the one thing she was not supposed to do: let go of his hand. On reaching the foyer, Wee Effie had gone left towards Leith Walk while James, swept along by a crowd of bairns all much bigger than himself, had been carried to the right, down the steps and into the street facing the wrong way. The same throng had carried him all the way along Manderston Street away from Leith Walk. James tagged along thinking that he was bound to come out somewhere and that Wee Effie would be there to greet him. But when the crowd dispersed, there was no Effie and he was standing in a street he'd never seen before. Should he go left or right? He didn't know, did eetle ottle in his head and the result pointed him to the right. So he turned right and started walking. On and on. It didn't occur to him that he was going uphill until the road got noticeably steeper. That was strange. Wasn't Brecon Street *down* the hill?

He stopped at the next junction, not knowing what to do. He looked up. Above his head on the side of a tenement was a faded street sign. His reading had progressed sufficiently for him to be able to decipher it: Easter Road. Just around the corner was another sign: Albion Street. He thought for a moment. Easter Road? He'd never been in Easter Road before but knew that it was where the Hibs played. So this was Easter Road? Despite his predicament, he looked around with renewed interest. He took a few steps down Albion Street. Yes, there it was – the top of the stadium rose clearly above the surrounding tenements. Easter Road! The famous Hibs ground! Even though the Brecon Street laddies had already turned him into a Hearts supporter, he was awed at the sight. Buoyed by his discovery, he retraced his steps.

By now it was well past one o'clock and he knew his Mum would be worrying about him. He wondered what Wee Effie was doing. Did she even know he was gone? Realising he had to be going downhill, he walked back down Easter Road until he came to the next junction. He looked up. Albert Street. Ah, yes, Albert Street. He knew that. It was where Papa and Great Granny lived. He'd visited them there several times with his parents. As if following a homing beacon, he turned left and started to walk along Albert Street. He thought he might try and find his great grandparents but couldn't remember the number. All the tenement entries looked alike. Unknown to him, he'd already walked past the building where his mother had been born in the nineteen-twenties. Coming to the end of Albert Street, he could see there was a main thoroughfare up ahead. He walked on and round the corner, looking up at the street sign: Leith Walk. The penny dropped. Ah, Leith Walk. Now he knew where he was. He just had to walk down this way and he'd get to Junction Street. Looking both ways, he ran across the tramlines and started walking briskly down the other side of the street.

At the same time, Wee Effie was home and revealing her negligence to her horrified parents who'd just sat down to dinner, wondering where their bairns had got to.

"...An' Mary Meikle said last one oot's a hairy kipper an' naebody wanted to be a hairy kipper and when we got oot we couldnae find James!" she confessed tearfully.

"Ye wee besom!" scolded Janet. "Ah said tae keep a hud o' 'im!"

Without further discussion, the two Swanstons threw on coats, grabbed their keys and Wee Effie, locked the flat and hurried out of the building. They scoured Junction Street, Ian on one side and Janet on the other clutching her daughter by the hand. They turned into Leith Walk and searched all the way up and into Manderston Street until they reached the scene of the debacle at The Capitol.

Unknown to them, as they made the turn, a tired little figure was making his way down the other side of Leith Walk. They didn't see James and James didn't see them. While they were quizzing the staff at the picture house, James was already trekking along Junction Street. By now, Janet was up to ninety.

"We'll have tae get the polis!" she wailed, cursing herself for having trusted Wee Effie at her age to take good care of her son. Ian, never the one to panic, put his arm around her and calmed her down.

"Afore we dae that, let's gie Junction Street one more try."

They prowled back along the way they'd come, looking in all the shops and entries. Nothing. At their wits' end, they turned into Brecon Street. There was James, sitting stoically on the step of Number 11, exhausted from his Saturday morning adventure. Ian, ever the optimist, couldn't suppress a smile. Wee Effie felt the weight fall from her shoulders. Janet's profound relief was expressed in angry tones.

"And where do you think *you've* been, young man?" she demanded to know in her best Proper Speak, hands on hips.

But James, ignoring what looked like a scolding, was already standing up with a beaming smile on his face.

"Mum, Dad, guess where Ah've been! Easter Road! An' Ah saw the Hibs ground! An' Ah saw Charlie Chaplin an' Roy Rogers an' Trigger! Mum, can Ah have a cowboy outfit for Christmas?"

A fork in the road

June 1953 had been a memorable month for Britons. First, on June 2nd, there was a public holiday, for the new Queen, Elizabeth II, was to be crowned at Westminster to the general acclaim of her subjects. At Warburton Crescent, almost the entire Melrose family and half the neighbourhood had crammed into the flat and crowded around the tiny black-and-white TV, specially purchased for the occasion. That very same morning came the news that a British-led expedition had managed to place the New Zealander Hillary and the Sherpa Tenzing Norgay on the peak of Everest. At last, the highest mountain in the world had been conquered. It seemed, that month, as if Britannia really did rule the waves.

But Primary Two at Bonnybrig Primary School weren't celebrating, for they knew they'd have to say farewell to Miss Douglas. The tears were on both sides. Some of the children were emotional at the thought of leaving this lovely young woman in the flowery smock who had, at least for some, been almost a surrogate mother. She'd taught them the basics and now they were ready to go on to more complex learning. Miss Douglas, for her part, was equally emotional. This had been her very first class as a new teacher in Scotland. She'd been with these children every working day for the last two years. It had been frustrating and challenging at times, especially as she missed her extended family on the other side of the world. The upside was that her infants, for their part, had become a proxy.

When the formal goodbyes were over, Miss Douglas drew six-year-old James aside. She motioned him to follow her away from the clamour of the emptying classroom. They opened the sky-blue side door and stepped outside into the girls' playground. Miss Douglas had often used this special exit to give her class much-needed breaks in the fresh air and licence to unload excess energy. There was a wooden bench against the fence. Miss Douglas sat, and James was to join her. The blackened, weed-covered railway embankment rose steeply behind them but the June sun was warm on their backs. Miss Douglas had something in her hand.

"James, I wanted to say a special goodbye to you. I noticed how good you've become at reading." *Actually,* Miss Douglas was thinking, *this boy is the top reader in the class and is able to cope with material well above the reading level for his age.* "I hope you'll carry on. Here's something to help you. It might be a bit hard, but I think you'll manage."

She handed him a book. James held it in both hands. There was a colourful picture of five children, a dog, and a tent in the background.

"Can you read what it says here?" Miss Douglas pointed to the title. "If you can, I'll let you keep it."

James looked at the words and read them straight off.

"Five – go – off – to – camp."

"Well, that was easy, wasn't it?" said Miss Douglas. "Now you can keep the book. It's yours! What do you say?"

"Thank you, Miss Douglas!"

James would encounter many forks in the road on his journey through life. Unknown to him, he'd just negotiated one, as Miss Douglas shepherded him towards a passion for books and reading.

"Is your Mummy collecting you today?" enquired Miss Douglas.

"Yes, Miss!"

"Let's go and see if she's at the gate yet." They walked across the playground to the school gate. James ran ahead towards Janet.

"Mum, Mum, look what Miss Douglas gave me!"

"Oh, really!" Janet feigned amazement for James's sake and took the book from him. She read the title, relieved that it obviously wasn't new.

"What a lovely book. Did you thank Miss Douglas?"

"Yes, he did!" said Miss Douglas, catching up.

"That's very kind, Miss Douglas. Are ye sure?" Janet wasn't used to her children receiving gifts from non-family members out of the blue.

"Of course!" Miss Douglas came closer and lowered her voice. "I just wanted to let you know that James is the best reader in the class." She let that sink in, as Janet glowed with pride. "But he needs to be encouraged. Is there a public library near you?"

"Well, Ah'm afraid Leith Public Library isnae open at the moment."

Actually, it hadn't been open since April 7th 1941, when a German Heinkel, trying to evade RAF Spitfires, had dropped a bomb on it. "But there's the Macdonald Road Library."

"Well, they'll have a children's section and they're bound to have Enid Blyton. This book's one of the *The Famous Five* series. It might be a bit advanced for James, but you could borrow a few more and see how he gets on."

"Fine, thank you, Miss Douglas, that's very nice o' ye. Ah'll do that. And," she looked earnestly at Miss Douglas, "Ah want tae thank ye for what ye've done for James and aw' the bairns.' She paused. "Ah'm sure they must've been a handfu' at times."

Miss Douglas felt her eyes starting to smart and blinked. She'd told herself that she wouldn't cry when this day came. But in a job where she'd become used to being taken for granted, this was the first time a parent had ever thanked her.

"Not at all, Mrs Swanston," she said, regaining her composure, "I enjoyed every minute of it." At such a moment, little white lies were surely permissible. "Goodbye then." She bent down. "Goodbye, James."

And with her special smile, she walked out of James's life.

2 Auld claes an' porridge

A caravan in the Borders

"Where oan earth has Alistair got tae?" Janet fumed.

Alistair, her wee brother, was supposed to have been at 11 Brecon Street an hour ago but, so far, he hadn't put in an appearance. The Swanstons had no outlook onto the street, so Wee Effie had been stationed down in the entry to guard the family suitcases and shout up to her parents when he arrived. For the umpteenth time, Janet leant over the banister and shouted down the five fletts, "Is 'e here yet?"

"No, Mum, no' yet," echoed up the shrill response of her ten-year-old daughter in her best attempt at a yell.

It was a Saturday morning in late August 1953. The Swanstons were all set for a real holiday together, the first time away from 11 Brecon Street since they'd moved in, the first time since the end of The War, and the first time since before The War. The fact was that they'd never had a real holiday as a family before. Either they'd never been able to afford it, or they'd never had the time or the opportunity. Or The War had got in the way. But now they'd scraped together enough cash, the bairns were still on holiday from school, and Ian had been granted a rare two weeks' annual leave. They were supposed to be off. Supposed to be, but not quite. It looked like Alistair had let them down – yet again.

Alistair, Janet's younger brother, was the second youngest in a family of nine. He was eight years Janet's junior and, as a baby, had been her special responsibility for much of her puberty while her mother had toiled to keep the rest of the family together. Below military age during The War, he'd served out his eighteen months of post-war conscription in the RAF. What he did there was vague, but his curly red hair, handsome features, personable nature and smooth tongue had propelled him into some cushy RAF public relations position in London. Alistair took to the capital like the proverbial duck to water. To the son of an impoverished labourer's family from Scotland, the bright lights of London didn't just beckon, they swallowed him up entirely. With plenty of time off from his comfy employ and free at weekends, he lived the high life. The same personal traits that got him his RAF job, not to mention his exotic Caledonian brogue and his athletic physique, attracted the London lassies like bees to honey. He always had his pick of the prettiest, not least because, sporting a fashionable RAF moustache, he could even convince the more gullible that he was a pilot and had flown Spitfires when he was obviously far too young and had never been near an aircraft in his life. His period of conscription ended and, some homesickness setting in, he returned to Scotland and talked his way into another sinecure, this time with the Scottish Office based at St Andrew's House in some vague liaison role between Agriculture and Fisheries, without ever having been on a farm, or a boat, or having ever caught a fish. To say that Alistair was a bit of a con man might have been unkind. But in a parallel universe, he'd have been just that.

Back home, he continued collecting girlfriends like boys collected professional footballers' autographs. And now, as a young Scottish civil servant going on 24, his generous salary and single status allowed him to acquire something no one among his family or extended relations had ever possessed, namely a motor car. In the Leith community, private ownership of a car was rare and conferred considerable status. The fact that his cars were usually cheap bangers that broke down frequently was neither here nor there – he owned a car, and that was the icing on the cake as far as his female admirers were concerned. But there was one downside. Being the only car owner in a large extended family of folks without cars, meant that Alistair was often called on to ferry someone from here to there, to pick someone up at some ungodly hour or to make the car available for occasions such as a wedding or a family gathering. Alistair did his very best to avoid these commitments and his family soon got used to his excuses, the most common being that, yet again, his car had, unfortunately, broken down.

When the opportunity for a holiday for the Swanstons had arisen, there was just one problem: how to get there. Through some former workmates at MacFergus, they'd been offered a caravan for two weeks free of charge at the village of Adelstone, just 25 miles south of Leith in the Border Country. It was a godsend but how were they going to get there with two bairns and the luggage? There was a bus service, and a train that ran down to Peebles, but the times were inconvenient. They'd have to get a tram to Waverley Station or St Andrew Square before they could even start their journey, not to mention, at the other end, making their way on foot all the way to the caravan, which was on a farm some way out of the village. That was when Alistair came into the picture. Why not get him to drive them straight to their holiday destination, door to door, and pick them up again at the end, if they were prepared to pay for his petrol? It would be far more convenient and cheaper than return bus or train tickets for all of them. Given the attention she'd lavished on him as a baby, Janet, his surrogate mother for all these years, was adamant she was due some payback. It didn't take much for her to shame Alistair into acquiescence and the whole thing was arranged.

Or so the Swanstons had thought. Alistair's latest automobile was a black, pre-war, 1937 Austin Ten. It did indeed break down a lot. And, of course, Alistair was Alistair. Everyone knew how mercurial, how unreliable he was. He'd disappear for weeks. No one knew where he was. Then he'd turn up, as plausible as ever, cadge a meal or a cup of tea, tell an interesting anecdote or two about what he'd been up to, then disappear as quickly as he'd come before his hosts began to realise that, yet again, they'd been had. The suspicion that Alistair wasn't exactly on the level was aroused by the fact that he was in the habit of using his various relatives and friends as mailboxes. It seemed that he had multiple addresses. When mail arrived for 'A. A.' – Alistair Anderson – Melrose, they'd put it to one side, knowing that he'd be around to collect it one day. So when he didn't turn up at the arranged time, Janet wasn't in the least surprised. Only annoyed. Why had she been so daft as to trust such an important task as taking them on holiday to her capricious wee brother? She cursed herself. They should have just caught the bus.

"Mum, Uncle Alistair's here!"

Wee Effie's shout up the stairwell interrupted Janet's reflections.

"Ian, 'e's here!"

Acting fast, as if to snatch the opportunity before it disappeared in a puff of smoke, they grabbed their keys, coats, handbag, wallet and vacation gear including bats, balls and fishing rods, checked the windows were closed, the gas and electric turned off, locked the door of the flat, and tumbled down the stairs in the semi-darkness, Ian holding onto six-year-old James. As they emerged from the entry, there was Alistair. Typical! Anyone else would have been up the stairs in a flash apologizing for being an hour late. But no, not Alistair. There he was, leaning against his car, arms folded casually as if he'd always been there, holding court to a group of teenage locals, one of whom he seemed to know. The arrival of a motor car at the entrance to Number 11 had attracted a lot of attention, and Alistair was milking it for all he was worth, laughing, nodding and smiling in his princely, engaging way, as if he had all the time in the world. When the Swanstons appeared, he expertly ended his conversation with a "Sorry, lads, got to go" and greeted his sister and family with an extra special beaming smile.

Since Alistair had returned from London, then joined the Civil Service, his transformation had taken many forms. One of these was the noticeable change in his speech. When he'd been conscripted at eighteen, he'd spoken broad Scots with a Leith accent. Now, some years later, despite an enduring Scottish lilt, something had changed.

When locals said, "Ah'm gawn hame", Alistair would say, "I'm going home."

When locals said, "Ah'll see ye the morn", Alistair would say, "I'll see you tomorrow."

When locals said, "Ah'm fair puggled", Alistair would say, "I'm out of breath."

Alistair had morphed into a member of the anglicised Scottish intelligentsia.

"Hello, Sis, Ian and kids!" he said. "How are you all today?"

"Ye're no too auld for a skelp!" Janet shot back. "Where were ye?"

Meanwhile, James and Wee Effie rushed at Alistair, hugging him around the knees.

"Uncle Alistair! Uncle Alistair!"

He was their favourite uncle. Though he was rarely around, when he was, there was heaps of fun. Tickles, wrestling on the ground, being thrown in the air. Nothing was too much trouble for Alistair. The bairns loved him precisely because he was just like one of them. He was young, he was good-looking and he liked to laugh a lot, unlike their often-careworn older parents.

"Sorry about that," said Alistair. "I just got held up with something I had to do..."

Typical Alistair, and typically unacceptable. Save for a brief "Hello", Ian said nothing, retrieved the suitcases and stowed them in the boot along with the rest of the gear. They all piled into the car. The bairns were almost wetting themselves. They'd never been in a car before, let alone been on holiday in one. The excitement!

Ian sat in front with Alistair. The brothers-in-law had a good relationship. Ian was fully aware of Alistair's shortcomings but they didn't seem to bother him. In the Army, he'd had to put up with a wide assortment of human specimens, many far worse than Alistair. He was a minor irritation as far as Ian was concerned, so he was always civil in his dealings with him. For his part, Alistair, unknown to Ian, held his brother-in-law in considerable awe. The disparity in their ages undoubtedly had something to do with it. Alistair was in his early twenties. Ian was approaching 40. But there was more to it. Alistair had played at soldiers for 18 months in a cushy number in the RAF on the home front long after The War had ended. Ian had actually been a soldier – an infantry soldier – in wartime for six years. Alistair well knew that Ian had been an unarmed combat specialist and had trained ground staff of his, Alistair's, very RAF, at airfields around Scotland; that he'd been in the thick of the fighting during the winter war in Northern Europe; that he'd earned an NCO rank the hard way. Meanwhile, Alistair had remained the RAF equivalent of a private in a peacetime role. Alistair had done, well, next to nothing. Ian had done just about everything. So when Ian was around, much as he tried not to be, Alistair was a different person. Respectful, polite, he listened to Ian. Over time, their rapport almost came to resemble that between a father and a son at a time when Alistair's relationship with his real father was on the rocks.

Driving by the central city, through Morningside and Hillend, they took the road to Peebles. As they passed the Pentlands, a verdant, rolling, pastoral landscape opened out before them. Everything was different. There were cattle, horses, woods, little bridges over burns, farms, fields of wheat, barley and neeps galore. James actually did wet himself slightly when he saw a real, live sheep for the first time, but he didn't let on to his mother. The soot-encrusted tenements of Leith were left behind. This was new land. The trip was fast and unremarkable. They drove into Adelstone past the red-timbered Norwegian houses and turned into what passed for the main street. They'd been told to ask at the village shop for directions to the Reekies' farm at Meldon Knowe, where the caravan was located. It was just a short drive away, up the hill and round a couple of bends. They would see the farmyard. It was the only one in the vicinity. They did as they were told and soon the Austin Ten was parked in a dingy farmyard, surrounded by farm buildings, wooden gates, and an expanse of cow excrement. The biggest surprise of the day was that the Austin Ten had not broken down – this time. As Janet went to look for the farmer, stepping carefully, and wishing she'd brought wellington boots, a plump, middle-aged, grey-haired matron appeared in a doorway. She *was* wearing wellington boots under voluminous skirts that reached down to her calves.

"Mrs Reekie?" Janet asked.

"Aye, lassie, that's me. An' you'll be the folks frae oot the toon fir the caravan, is that right?"

Mrs Reekie spoke with the quaint inflection of the Border country. They exchanged pleasantries and Janet followed Mrs Reekie into a byre where the set of caravan keys was hanging on a wooden hook.

“Now, just drive back doon the brae and stop at the first gate oan yer left. The caravan is up there. But ye’ll have tae leave yer car at the bottom, it’ll never get up that track. Well, there’s bottled gas there for yer cookin’ an’ the watter’s piped doon frae the loch. Ye can get aw’ ye need at the village shop and ye can come here for eggs and fresh milk. Here, tak this,” and she handed Janet an aluminium can with a handle and a lid, shaped just like a milk churn but much smaller. “Ye can keep the milk in here. Just hand it back tae me when ye leave.”

They drove back down the hill, past an enormous raspberry bush heavy with fruit, and stopped at a rusty metal gate. They could see the caravan, about 50 yards up the steep, muddy track. It was situated in its own little fenced-in yard between two paddocks. The bairns couldn’t contain themselves. What an adventure! As soon as Ian got the gate open, they were up the track like a couple of rabbits. The adults lugged the cases and belongings up behind them and stood looking at their accommodation for the next fortnight. Its peeling paint and rusty hubcaps only served to emphasise its dilapidated state. Railway sleepers supported it at each end, and rickety wooden steps led up to the door. A mouldy, detachable awning was stuffed underneath. But the two Swanston bairns were still stuck at the fence.

“Dad, Dad!” shouted Wee Effie. “How dae ye get in there, Dad?”

“Ye use the stile,” was the reply.

“What’s a stile?”

Ian showed them the stile and how to climb over the barbed wire fence into the yard, holding on to the pole. Janet followed. She climbed the steps to the caravan and put the key in the lock, apprehensive at what she might find. Yes, the interior was dilapidated as well, and musty, but at least it was clean and it looked like it would keep the rain out. They opened the windows to clear the air, inspected the little cupboards, tested the bed and checked that the water supply was working. They’d brought their own sheets, but the blankets were supplied.

“What’s that, Mum?” Wee Effie pointed to a small, decrepit wooden outhouse at the other end of the enclosure, about four feet square and six feet high, with a rusty corrugated iron roof.

“That’s the bathroom,” said Janet.

The bairns were puzzled. It didn’t look like any bathroom they’d ever seen. The rickety door was hanging slack off handcrafted leather hinges and held in place by a rusting bolt that was supposed to slide into a hole in the door frame. The door handle was a cracked, wooden knob that had obviously been fashioned by hand and was held in place by a rusty screw. Ian grasped it and swung the door open. They were hit by the foetid stench of ancient faeces. There was no toilet bowl. Instead, a wooden crate against the back wall had a well-used wooden toilet seat nailed to the top of it. Squares of old newspaper hung on a piece of rusty wire hooked into a joist. The bairns held their noses and, in turn, peered warily down the hole under the toilet seat as if they expected to find a monster there. It dropped several yards into the earth and the bottom was caked with brown substances intermingled with decaying pieces of newspaper.

"Oh, Dad, is that where we have tae dae the toilet?" Wee Effie asked.

"Aye, it is that. But ye'll get used tae it," he added consolingly.

But the bairns never did. Even though they got proper shiny toilet paper, courtesy of Izal, they were afraid to go to the toilet, scared they'd fall down the hole. Every time they used it, a parent would have to stand outside with the door open a crack.

After the inspections were over, and the luggage stored in the caravan, Alistair said, "Well, I'll be on my way."

"Would ye no like a cup of tea afore ye go?" asked Janet.

But Alistair said not to bother. Secretly, he'd noticed a sign pointing to a licensed inn, The Black Douglas, and was looking forward to a more interesting beverage. Perhaps even a pretty Border lass? They arranged the day, date and time for him to pick them up.

"Now, Alistair." Janet looked at him with the severity of a schoolmistress. "Ye will be here in two weeks, Saturday, twelve noon. Now dinnae forget!"

Alistair promised he'd be there but they both knew what his promises were worth. Then Ian took him aside.

"What do we owe ye for petrol?" he asked.

"Oh," said Alistair, "well, ten bob should do it – that's for the two return trips."

Ian took out his wallet, opened it, selected a pound note and placed it in Alistair's, by now, outstretched hand.

"Sorry I haven't got change," Alistair muttered, embarrassed at accepting money from his brother-in-law.

"Ah dinnae want change, son. Just take it,"

There was to be no argument. Alistair gulped his thanks, whirled the bairns a couple of times and said his goodbyes, rapidly disappearing down the track and round the corner. They heard the Austin revving up, and he was gone. Their first real holiday as a family together. Janet couldn't believe it. Yes, the caravan wasn't much to look at. But there was a splendid view across the valley and everything was green. If you'd wanted to find the diametrical opposite of 11 Brecon Street, you'd have been hard pushed to find anything more opposite than this.

For two weeks they relaxed. The Lowlands produced their best late August weather in decades. No rain fell. The sun blazed and their sickly Brecon Street pallor was quickly replaced by a healthy tan. Ian clowned around in the cramped caravan kitchen playing the chef with a towel on his head. They went for walks over the paddocks, up the low hills, through darkling woods and crossed burns of peat-brown water that flowed out of muddy cleughs. Ian showed James how to set a snare to catch a rabbit, but they never had any luck. He taught him to guddle for trout in the Adelstone Water. They'd lie on their stomachs on the bank, half in the water, looking for trout to tickle, but they never managed to get one onto the bank. Better luck was to be had with the angling. Ian had learnt fly fishing from his other brother-in-law, Jimmy, his son James's namesake, the husband of his older half-sister, Rose. When the sun was low in the sky, Ian and James would wander along the banks of Adelstone Water, find a likely spot, and cast. Surprisingly, they were lucky, and, over the two weeks, caught five or six modest-sized trout, which ended up in Ian's frying pan.

Cows ambled up to the fence to greet them, to be rewarded with clumps of grass, which they expertly processed with their huge tongues. On the other side, flocks of ewes provided a wake-up call every morning. They marvelled at the teams of border collies racing up and down the hillsides, rounding up the sheep under the control of Mr Reekie, who leant on his crummock as he shouted gruff commands. Apart from the occasional call of a peewit, the baaing of sheep, the grunting of cattle or work sounds from the farm, they heard only silence. No traffic, no loud music, no bairns yelling in the back green, no Sally Ann band, no wivies shrieking up and down the stairwell. Just peace, perfect peace. They filled buckets of rasps at the big bush down the hill. The bairns guzzled until their chins and fronts were red and they felt sick. Then came a trip into Peebles on the local slow train and a day spent wandering around, shopping, going to the park and the museum, hanging over the parapet of the bridge over the Tweed, spotting the shadowy shapes of monster trout quivering in the peat-stained waters. Having afternoon tea and scones in a posh tearoom.

Every morning, someone would walk down the muddy track to the farm with the milk can to fetch the family's daily supply, straight from the cows' udders. Eventually, Wee Effie was brave enough to go by herself but James never was and it was all because of Mrs Reekie. That first morning, Janet had paid for their milk with a three-penny bit. Mrs Reekie took the coin, then, to James's horror, unceremoniously howked up her skirts, displaying a fine pair of close-fitting, navy blue, woollen knickers, which girded her monstrous thighs and stretched down to just above her knees. The knickers had a pocket at the front. Reaching into it, Mrs Reekie pulled out a brown leather purse, opened the coin compartment, dropped the three pence in and took out a halfpenny which she handed to Janet. Closing the purse and returning it to the pocket, she dropped her skirts and smoothed them down, as if it were the most natural thing in the world. The incident was enough to give a young laddie of James's age nightmares and to plant a phobia in his mind that could take years of psychiatric treatment to eradicate. Was it any wonder then that when Ian asked, "Whae's goin' for the milk?" James never volunteered?

The holiday was drawing to a close. It was the last Friday. As Janet was paying for the milk, Mrs Reekie said, "By the way, we'll be cuttin' barley in the top field this afternoon around four. There are always plenty o' rabbits. If ye're wantin' one for the pot, come on up. Ye can bring the bairns if ye want."

The Swanstons didn't know what to expect. How did you get rabbits out of a field of barley? At the appointed time they walked up, following the sound of a tractor engine. Mr Reekie had already started cutting the barley, working from the outside to the inside in concentric circles. Mrs Reekie was there, a couple of her sons and daughters, and some of the farm workers. Each one carried a stick or a club. The visitors leant on the fence and watched with interest. As the cutting progressed, the area of standing barley in the centre of the field got smaller and smaller. The farm folk had stationed themselves in a loose circle around the remainder of the crop. James then realized what was happening. There had been a host of rabbits in the barley. The mowing forced them further and further into the centre of the field until they were massed, trapped in their last refuge, around which the circle of farm workers got tighter and tighter. Occasionally a rabbit would make a break for it, only to be clubbed down. The final massacre was upsetting. As the clubs rose and fell, around twenty or thirty rabbits lay dead or dying on the stubble. Mrs Reekie came over, having noted their sombre looks.

"Ay, it may be an awfy thing tae watch fir folks fae the toon - especially the bairns," she added, addressing Wee Effie who was in tears. "But ye must ken that fir us in the country, the rabbits are a terrible pest. They dig into the parrochs and destroy everythin'. They're mair than a pest, they're the very plague!"

As the Swanstons nodded their heads in reluctant understanding, a burly farmworker wearing a cloth cap, leather jerkin and leggings came up. His face was beetroot from his exertions. From each hand dangled a surprisingly large rabbit by the leg. He held them out to the Swanstons.

"Fir you," he said, grinning broadly.

"Thanks, but Ah dinnae think we could manage two. Just the one'll dae," said Ian. The worker offered one of the rabbits to James.

"D'ye want tae cairy it, laddie?" he asked.

James gingerly took the corpse in both hands and gazed at it. He'd never seen a rabbit before except in pictures. Nor had he seen a dead one. As he held his first rabbit, his fingers dug into the soft grey fur and felt the plump body. The rabbit's eyes were glazed in death but it was still warm and floppy. Droplets of blood fell from a head wound.

"Say thank you tae the nice man," said Janet.

"Thank you," repeated James dubiously.

The next morning, after a last leisurely, but sad, breakfast, the Swanstons packed their things, cleaned out the caravan and got ready for Alistair to arrive to pick them up.

"'E'll no be here on time, if 'e comes at aw'," chaffed Ian.

"Ah wouldnae be a bit surprised," said Janet, as they sat outside, enjoying their last moments of freedom. As the minutes ticked towards noon, they began to kick themselves for believing that Alistair would ever be punctual, if he came at all. But at a quarter to twelve, to their surprise, they heard the sound of a car engine grinding slowly up the hill and a car stopping at the gate. A door opened and slammed shut. They couldn't believe it. Alistair here already! They hurried down the track to the gate. Yes, there was the Austin Ten, but who was this? As they came closer, they laughed and gasped in a mixture of astonishment and amusement. It wasn't Alistair but Janet's younger sister, Phoebe.

"What are ye doin' here?" they shouted, almost in chorus, crowding around Phoebe, kissing and hugging her. Phoebe laughed.

"Ah didnae think Ah'd find ye sae easily, so Ah left early this mornin'," she said. "Ah got directions in the village."

"But where's Alistair?"

"Ye winnae believe this, but Alistair's halfway tae Iceland by now!"

Phoebe might just as well have said that Alistair was on his way to the moon. As they stood, open-mouthed, she explained. Alistair had discovered that the Fisheries Protection Vessel, *Loch Fyne* was off to Arctic waters to show the flag in the simmering fisheries dispute between Britain and Iceland that would later become known as The Cod Wars. Alistair, being Alistair, had wangled a berth as a 'Ministry Observer'. The ship had already sailed last Tuesday and he'd be away for a month. He'd smooth talked his other big sister into being his stand-in for the Swanstons' pickup. Phoebe had been a WRAC driver during The War; there was nothing she didn't know about cars. She'd lent Alistair money to buy the Austin Ten but had never been paid back, so she was actually part-owner. She'd jumped at the chance to drive 'her' car down into the Borders for her sister and her family. And here she was. It was a perfect solution and no one was upset. But there was a shaking of heads, eye-rolls and laughter. That Alistair! Absolutely typical...

The journey home was uneventful but the mood was disconsolate. All the way, James held the rabbit on his lap. Rigor mortis had long set in but he didn't mind. Even in death, the rabbit was his last link to his fast-fading holiday. When they turned into Brecon Street, James could see the usual crowd of bairns hanging around the entrance to Number 11. As the car drew up, they became animated, backing off as the Swanstons emerged and following the unloading with interest. Finally, James got out, still cradling the rabbit in his arms, and stepped onto the pavement. The crowd parted as if he were Moses and they were the waters of the Red Sea. Familiar faces stood out. There was Kenny Ogilvie. And Mickey Meikle. And Fred Condey. Best of all, the chieftain of the Brecon Street Bairns, Jacky Johnston.

"Whoa!" "Jings!" "Crivvens!" "Whit's that?" "A deid rabbit!"

James swelled with importance. Although at the age of six he was only half the height of those around him, he felt twice as tall. He was going to burst. Ignoring the questions and comments, and showing no emotion, he held out the rabbit in front of him as if it were a religious icon, processed through the crowd like a high priest approaching an altar, and disappeared into the dark recesses of the tenement. His stock had risen. None of the bairns would look at him in the same way again. The erstwhile holidaymakers gained the top of the stairs, unlocked the flat and stepped inside. Dropping their suitcases, clothes and holiday gear on the floor, they gazed around at their dingy surroundings. The peeling wallpaper, the cracked ceiling, the scuffed linoleum, the threadbare carpet, the few scraps of shabby furniture, the flaking window frame that offered a dismal view of grimy tenement backs set against a grey sky.

"Well," sighed Janet, "it's back tae auld claes an' porridge!"

Ian, from his youthful rambles across the Pentlands, was already an expert where rabbit was concerned. James and Wee Effie squeezed into the scullery to watch with a mixture of fascination and distaste as their dad expertly skinned, gutted and prepared the beast on the bunker. They roasted it in the gas oven, salted and peppered and basted with butter. That evening, as if desperately trying to hold on to the final piece of their wonderful holiday, three Swanstons enjoyed their first taste of roast rabbit, while the fourth relished the familiar juices. But it was to be their last taste. Ever. Barely a month later, the first cases of myxomatosis were seen in southern England, and within a few years, 99% of the rabbit population of Britain had been wiped out.

Tonsils and adenoids

Has the bowel moved?" Sister Macdonald spoke with the lilt of the Western Isles. Half propped up in bed, the back of his head pressing up against a pristine pillowcase, James could only gape. It was a question he'd never heard in his life before and was never likely to hear again. A bowel? What was that? How did it move? And why?

Sister Macdonald was a severe woman of about thirty-five with a sour expression, as if someone had forced her to suck a lemon. She wore a white starched cap that by some cunning design remained firmly fixed to her austere, dark bob, no matter how much she moved her head. Peeping over the top of her blue, short-sleeved, starched tunic was a white starched collar buttoned at the neck. Enclosing the tunic was a white, starched, knee-length pinafore with a rectangular top that was attached to the front of the tunic above breast level with two enormous safety pins at each corner. A nurse's badge was attached to the left-hand pin and a small watch on a chain to the right-hand pin. The pinafore was held snugly around her waist by a wide, blue, stretch cinch belt with a chrome triple buckle. Thick black stockings encased her legs. A pair of black, shiny brogues with flat rubber soles completed the ensemble. So buttoned, belted, buckled, pinned and starched was Sister Macdonald that it was a miracle she could move at all, let alone carry out her nursing duties.

"I said, has the bowel moved? Well has it?" she repeated, hands on hips.

James's trance-like state continued. His mouth opened and closed but nothing came out. Sister Macdonald, her patience exhausted, approached the bed, bent down and spoke *sotto voce* in his ear.

"Have you been to the toilet?"

The penny dropped. James hastened to reply but all that came out was a throaty sound. Then he shook his head.

"Very well," said the Sister. "This is the third day. Time for some castor oil."

She was back in a trice with a large bottle of thick, ribbed, blue glass. To ensure that there was no doubt about its contents, the label read in bold capitals *CASTOR OIL*. The Sister produced a white ceramic measuring spoon, poured a full measure and said, “Open your mouth.” James did as he was told. The Sister quickly emptied the contents of the spoon into the open orifice. James spluttered and gagged as the sickly, greasy liquid went down his throat. When he opened his eyes again, the Sister was still there. She had re-filled the measuring spoon.

“And again!” was all she said. James opened wide, steeled himself, swallowed the liquid and gagged again, but this time less. And the spot where his tonsils used to be didn’t hurt so much.

He’d always been a sickly child, literally from the day of his birth. It hadn’t helped that a heavily pregnant Janet, already showing the first signs of labour, had had to struggle through deep snow to get to the Elsie Inglis Maternity Hospital, for Britain was experiencing one of the severest winters since records began. Freezing temperatures and blizzards were frequent from December 1946 to March 1947. The entire country was crippled. Power cuts, factory closures, widespread unemployment and even food shortages became the norm. And this, less than two years after war’s end, as if the British hadn’t suffered enough already.

And as if Janet herself hadn’t suffered enough, at the very moment she was pushing her new baby out into the world in the delivery room, an outbreak of gastroenteritis was sweeping through the maternity wing. James was among the first to be infected. He almost died. The fact that he didn’t was something of a miracle, for plenty of other newborns did. The doctors had told Janet he had only a 50-50 chance. But somehow Fortune smiled. The recovery took several weeks but even then, Janet wasn’t allowed to take her new son home; the risk of re-infection was too high. He’d have to be quarantined for several more weeks. By this time Janet had had enough. The thought of a month’s confinement to the hospital ward was unbearable. In a fit of post-partum pique, she discharged herself, returning daily for feeds.

The fact that the son she and Ian had so longed for had almost died at birth told on Janet. From then on, James’s health and wellbeing became priorities. To say that she was neurotic might have been unkind. But if she was, it wasn’t just because she’d almost lost James. As a child, she’d never seen a doctor, for doctors cost money, which the Melroses didn’t have. Yes, a couple of the other Melrose bairns had been lucky enough to see a charity doctor, but when they’d been struck down by the usual childhood ailments, their parents had simply had to battle through with the traditional home remedies. As for hospitals, they were only for absolute emergencies, which, inexplicably, never happened – or were never allowed to happen. Amid all the dirt, deprivation and hunger of the twenties and thirties, all nine Melrose children had simply had to endure, largely without medical intervention. And, inexplicably, all nine had survived. But Janet had never forgotten the misery of it.

Then, after The War, when the Tories were out, and Labour had got in, something happened that had changed her life, that of her children and of every person in the country. It was all due to the 1942 Beveridge Report that had been commissioned by the wartime coalition government. Britain, it said, should have a free National Health Service. It would be paid for by National Insurance contributions deducted from the wages of every working adult in Britain. Of course, at first, nothing happened. It was wartime. But when Labour had come to power in 1945, they'd put it at the top of their list of things to do. Suddenly, in 1948, the miracle occurred and the NHS was born. Now, you could visit the doctor any time you liked – for free. It was a new world and Janet had taken full advantage of it where her two bairns were concerned. For her, it was payback for all she'd endured during the hunger years. It was payback for what she and her family had gone through during The War. It was payback for the long separations from Ian and the fear that she'd never see him again. It was payback for the weekly deduction from Ian's pay packet. And she made damn sure the payback was sweet.

At the least sign of something wrong, she'd be along with James to the local general practice at the foot of Ferry Road where the family was registered. To be fair, Wee Effie wasn't left out. But she seemed healthier than James. So while she was at school, it was James who'd sit on his mother's lap in the waiting room of the GP surgery. It was James who'd be seen by gruff Doctor Wilkie. And it was for James that the prescriptions would be got from the chemist in Junction Street, including concentrated orange juice in little glass bottles and cod liver oil. Janet had no idea what was in it, but it was free, all of it. Then there was the sunray lamp treatment. It had been arranged by the GP's nurse who'd told Janet that children in northern climes needed more sunlight to stay healthy. So as soon as James was big enough, he found himself in a clinic on the other side of Leith Links, stripped down to his underpants, wearing a pair of large, clumsy goggles, sitting on the floor in a circle of bairns soaking up the white-hot rays of the sunray lamp. So convinced became Janet of the sunray lamp's benefits that she badgered Ian to find one of their own to use at home. It was a battered old thing, two carbon elements set in what looked like a large aluminium basin. When it was plugged in and the elements screwed to touching, the blinding white heat was frightening. But Janet was adamant. Once a week during winter, her bairns would be sat down, near-naked, in front of it, wearing only underpants, knickers and goggles. The plain fact was that Janet would go to any lengths to keep them healthy.

It wasn't surprising then that she'd willingly assented when Dr Wilkie had said that her son should go into hospital for an operation. James had had one infection after another. The solution, Dr Wilkie had opined, would be to have his tonsils and adenoids out. That would surely fix the problem. There was no waiting list. And it cost nothing. Only three days passed between the GP's notification to Leith Hospital and the hospital's letter to the Swanstons with the date for James's admission. It was only a week away.

James didn't quite know how to react to the news that he was going into hospital for an operation. Apart from his birth, he'd never been in a hospital before, not even as a visitor. He had no idea what an operation would be like and didn't know what questions to ask. The only indication that it would indeed hurt was when Auntie Effie, on being told of the impending surgery, turned to him with a big smile on her face and said, "Oh, ye lucky thing, ye'll get lots of ice cream." That's when James started to get suspicious, for ice cream was a rare treat, confined to occasional Sundays. When, at 8 am in the autumn chill of the appointed day, Janet walked him by way of Taylor Gardens and they passed through the massive front doors of Leith Hospital, his suspicions grew, for the air immediately took on an unaccustomed astringent character, concocted from myriad antiseptics mingled with the bouquets of chemicals, drugs, and gases. At once he was queasy. His angst increased as they negotiated endless echoing corridors of tiled walls, looked into sterile rooms full of stainless-steel apparatus, passed doctors in white with stern expressions and nurses in blue and white with even sterner expressions, and suffered sickly ambulant patients in dressing gowns puffing cigarettes in the stairwells.

Like worshippers entering a cathedral, they emerged into Ward Three, a vast gallery with a high, vaulted ceiling. The right-hand side was a blank, cream-painted wall. The left consisted of a series of large windows that stretched from floor to ceiling. Thick, opaque glass in the lower half of each frame ensured privacy but restricted the outlook to empty sky and nothing else. The beds, set a couple of yards apart, lined the walls. Most were occupied. A nurse on station directed them to one that wasn't. There, James suffered the indignity of getting undressed and into hospital garb in front of the entire ward.

"Less o' yer fussin'!" Janet chided at his groans and protests. "Naebody can see ye," when it was painfully obvious that his disrobing performance was being enjoyed by at least a score of pairs of eyes. By the time he was sitting up in bed, his unease was palpable. But Janet was unmoved. Yes, she was determined to see that her bairns got the best medical treatment available, but she never mollycoddled them. In comparison with what she and her brothers and sisters had gone through, this was harmless. James was seven. He was old enough to look after himself, just as she'd done at that age. He had to have the operation and that was that. Once he was installed, she wasn't allowed to stay but could return the following day during visiting hours. She smiled at her son, ruffled his hair, told him everything would be all right, said she'd return the next day, and left without looking back.

James watched his mother walk through the ward and disappear into the corridor. He was alone. He was in a strange bed, with strange, starched, bedclothes, in a strange place, among strangers. It wasn't even night time. The light was streaming through the high, uncurtained windows and he wasn't in the least sleepy. Everything was strange. He looked around him. For some reason he'd been placed in the adult men's ward, surrounded by patients in various states of wellbeing. Some appeared to be in a very bad way while others were sitting up in bed, unconcernedly reading newspapers or listening to the radio on headphones. In several places, nurses were busy at work behind screens. Two beds along from him, an ancient man who appeared to be demented kept jumping up from his bed, shouting incoherently, his gown riding up to reveal an enormous pair of testicles dangling between thin white legs. James had never seen mature testicles before. He'd barely seen his own, they were so undeveloped. The sight alarmed him even more. Two nurses rushed over, agile despite the starch, holding the disruptive patient down by the shoulders, while a third administered an injection. Soon all was quiet again. Nurses patrolled the aisles like jailers.

At 10 am, there was a small commotion at the glass-panelled room next to the ward entrance which served as the nurses' station. Matron had arrived. She was a large, middle-aged woman with a prize fighter's face and a formidable bosom. Her starched uniform resembled those of her nurses except for the outsized headdress, which made her look like a mother superior. The nurses were on their best behaviour. She marched around on inspection, her expression grim, snapping orders and making requests, the diligent staff nurse at her elbow making entries on a clipboard. When she stopped opposite James's bed, he pulled the covers up to his nose, hoping that he could escape notice.

"And who is this new patient, Sister Macdonald?" Matron demanded to know in a booming voice.

The Sister consulted her list.

"James Swanston, age seven, adenotonsillectomy!" she barked.

Matron approached. She stood beside James, pulled a hand from under the covers, gently grasped his thin wrist with stubby fingers and consulted the watch hanging from her safety pin. After a thirty-second wait, she gave a satisfied grunt. She looked at James. Despite her pugilist features, her expression was gentle.

"Don't worry, my child," she said. Then, "Surgery is timed for..." She turned to the staff nurse who hastily consulted her notes.

"Two pm, Matron."

"...Two pm," repeated Matron. "Then it will be over. Nothing to eat or drink until then."

She turned and swept off with queenly comportment, followed by her retinue of nurse courtiers. *Nothing to eat or drink*? thought James. He settled down to four hours of hunger, thirst and boredom, with only the four walls, the ceiling, and a bunch of sickly old men for company, eventually dozing off towards midday. Then someone was shaking him by the shoulder.

"Come on James, time to go."

He blinked and sat up. It was Sister Macdonald.

"First ye go to the bathroom, come on."

He got out of bed and walked barefoot through the ward feeling stupid in his hospital gown. Sister Macdonald motioned to a door with the sign *WC*.

"Go on, I'll wait for you."

James hated to wee under a time constraint. His inhibitions heightened by the Sister outside the door, he stood there and struggled, until at last a modest stream of urine came out. He dutifully washed his hands as his mother had taught him and opened the door. Sister Macdonald returned him to his bed. Five minutes later, two male orderlies appeared, pushing a stretcher on a trolley. He was to hop on. He did as he was told and was immediately tucked up in blankets. The trolley took off. He had a worm's eye view of various ceilings as they negotiated the corridor and a spacious lift and finally barged through a set of double swing doors into a brilliantly-lit room. They removed the blanket. One at his feet, one his shoulders, they swung him sideways as if he were a bag of fluff. He was lying on his back on the cold, hard leather surface of an operating table, wearing only his hospital gown. The light hurt his eyes. Anonymous masked faces in white surgical garb surrounded him. Only their eyes were visible. From behind his head, a black rubber mask was placed over his mouth and nose. The intense rubbery smell was overpowering. The anonymous face behind his head that was applying the mask, spoke. It was a man's voice.

"Breathe in deeply and count to ten in your head."

James did as he was told. The odourless gas had a keen edge, but the repulsive rubber mask was now compelling his breathing. He started to panic. He wanted to rip it off but his arms were being held. He wanted to retch but couldn't. His head was filled with a high-pitched whine the like of which he'd never heard before. The masked faces started to spin, ever faster. The whine became more intense. The faces were now a blur. He got to seven. The whine became a spinning white light that suddenly went silent and spiralled down into blackness.

He woke. He was in a small room by himself. His head was turned sideways and pressed up against iron railings at the end of the bed. There was no pillow. On the mattress, next to his mouth, was a stainless-steel kidney-shaped dish. There was blood in it. He wondered where it had come from. Then he realised it was his own. A further set of round, cream-painted rails fenced off the side of the bed. It was a prison cell. He had a splitting headache. His throat hurt. He realised he was partly covered by a blanket, but he felt cold. He couldn't move. His world consisted of the pain in his throat, the dish, the cream-painted railings, and through them, a view upwards through the grubby panes of a window to a murky autumnal sky. It was raining.

He lay there for goodness knows how long. He had no thoughts. Only the pain in his throat and the hope that the worst of his ordeal was over. Occasionally, he heard someone come in but no one spoke and he couldn't raise his head to see who it was. He could only guess it was a nurse checking on him. His mouth filled with blood. He tried to spit into the dish. He dozed off. When he awoke, the sheet next to his mouth was stained red. He still had the headache. He found if he pushed his head back, he could press his forehead against the cold metal bars and get some relief. He had no idea how long he'd been there, but he noticed through the window that it was starting to get dark. Someone came in and walked round the bed. It was Sister Macdonald. She bent down until her face was level with his. As she did so, the starch in her uniform crackled. Her voice was hushed.

"How are we, then, James? Feeling better?"

James grunted through a haze of pain. Sister Macdonald took his pulse and touched his forehead with the backs of her fingers. They felt cool. She stood up and pulled the blanket up to his neck. She picked up the dish and disappeared. He heard the sound of a tap running. She reappeared and replaced the dish next to his mouth.

"Just try and sleep," she said, and walked out.

It was about four o'clock when next James woke. The room was dark except for a faint glow behind him. He needed to wee. He wondered what to do. He still couldn't move. He was on the verge of just doing it on the mattress when suddenly a shadowy figure was there. He managed to turn his head. It was the night nurse. She had a small rectangular torch with a bare aluminium case fixed to her uniform. He couldn't see her face. He tried to speak but nothing came out. He managed to raise himself on his left elbow. Her face came into focus. She looked young. He pointed towards his genitals.

"Wee-wee," he managed to croak. She nodded understandingly and reached below the bed. A white ceramic receptacle, roughly the shape of a haggis, with a short, round open neck appeared on the mattress beside him.

"Here, ye can do it in that. Ah'll leave ye and come back when ye're finished."

James grasped what he had to do. He lay sideways on the bed, pulled back the blanket, held the container and put his wee robbie into the hole in the neck. As the urine flowed, he could feel the pot warming up. The relief was divine. He pushed the pot away and pulled the blanket over him again. After five minutes the nurse came back.

"All done?" she enquired brightly. James could only attempt a nod. She took the pot and James could hear running water. Then he dozed off again. Someone was shaking his right shoulder. He blinked in the glare. The ceiling light had been switched on. Outside, it was still dark. There was a hubbub in the corridors. Metal clashed, people gave instructions, voices replied, trolleys squeaked, doors opened and closed. They were serving breakfast.

"Six o'clock. Are ye hungry?"

James had never had breakfast so early before. Six o'clock? He didn't know if he was hungry or not. The pain in his throat was the centre of his existence. He wanted to stay as he was, on his side, looking over the dish and through the bars.

"Come on, try and sit up."

It was one of the nurses on the morning shift. She removed the blood-spattered dish, produced two pillows and helped him sit up. Despite his reluctance, it was a relief to be in a different position. Now, propped up, he could see where he was. It was a small, dingy recovery room with beige walls. His bed just fitted in. The only other thing in the room was a deep stainless-steel sink. He closed his eyes.

Suddenly the nurse was there again. Something was plonked in his lap. He opened his eyes. It was a wooden tray. Two tiny slices of white toast lay on a plate, together with a modest portion of scrambled eggs. There was also a stainless-steel dish with margarine, cutlery, and an empty china cup. The nurse disappeared and a second nurse came in carrying a jumbo-sized metal teapot. She poured tea into his cup. Then a third nurse appeared with milk and sugar. He drank. It hurt his throat at first but then started to soothe it. He picked at the food, discovered an appetite and ate the lot. That was when he realised his headache had gone. He was transferred back to the same ward later that afternoon, but to a different bed. The first person he saw was Sister Macdonald speaking sharply to some of the younger nurses, while they ran to do her bidding. She came and tucked him in.

"How are we?" she asked.

James just croaked. She smiled in her sardonic way and walked off. Most of the same patients were there but the bed next to James was empty. The skinny man on the other side pointed to it.

"Died durin' the night!" he said confidentially, as if it was a secret between James and himself.

From his prone position, James nodded his head dumbly. People died here! At 6 pm, people in street clothes started to fill the ward. It was visiting hours. His parents appeared with the latest *Hotspur,* a bar of Fry's Five Boys and a white paper bag. Mum handed it to him. Inside was a cardboard tub of Wall's vanilla ice cream with a small flat wooden spoon. So it was true! You did get ice cream. A pity he couldn't get his tonsils out again... He prised the thin card lid off the tub, plunged the wooden spoon into the white mass and thrust it into his mouth. Ah, what a cool, soothing sensation! After three mouthfuls, his throat was numb and his pain had been effectively banished. He was definitely starting to feel better but he still found it hard to speak. His parents didn't stay long. James wasn't exactly the ideal conversation partner. They said their goodbyes and promised to be back the next day.

They kept James in hospital for a week. Nurse Macdonald's castor oil had the desired effect. That very same evening, after an hour or two of warning stomach cramps, but to his enormous relief, James excreted three days' worth of hospital food down the toilet. After that, things got better. By the time his mother came to fetch him on the seventh day, his throat pain had almost disappeared. He could speak without too much effort. As they left to go home, Sister Macdonald was standing at the ward entrance in all her starched magnificence, her hands folded across her stomach.

"Well, you're off then, I see," she said, in her mildly mocking, but not uncaring, tone.

"Aye, we are that," said Janet brightly. "An' thank you, Sister, for aw' ye did for James,".

"Oh, that's all right, Mrs Swanston."

"Was 'e a good patient?" asked Janet mischievously.

"No, he wasn't," replied Sister Macdonald with a twinkle in her eye. "He talked too much." She paused. "But that's something you could cure with a good dose of castor oil!"

Back green concert

"Mum, can Ah go tae the back green concert next Saturday?"

Wee Effie's expression was pleading as she squeezed in beside Janet, who was washing dishes in the scullery.

"What back green concert? That's the first Ah've heard o' it."

"Well, some o' the lassies are puttin' it on." She paused. "It's at two o'clock just here in the back green. Can Ah, Mum?"

Janet considered as she swished a block of Sunlight soap into the tepid water to encourage suds. Actually, she had plans for next Saturday. She'd been determined, finally, to manage a trip to Campbell's the Butchers in Queen Street. The previous month, July, rationing had finally ended after fourteen long years as meat came 'off the ration'. They could now purchase as much as they wanted. Janet normally got her meat at the Provie in Leith, but her sister, Effie, now with Marks and Spencer, had sung the praises of Campbell's, the quality of the cuts, and the reasonable prices. So, as a belated celebration, Janet had put aside some of her housekeeping money and was minded to return home with a parcel of the best that Campbell's had to offer. Then they'd have steak and chips and all the rest, a slap-up meal, a rare treat that had been denied them, it seemed, forever. As well, she'd thought to pop round to C and A's or Marks and Spencer, for Ian needed a new winter overcoat. Normally, they'd be dragging the bairns along, but this might be an opportunity for them to spend some time together, just the two of them for a change.

"Where is this concert again, hen?"

Wee Effie took two backward steps out of the scullery and pointed to her right, through the window and into the back green.

"Just doon there, at the steps. Aw' the other bairns'll be there.

"Aye, awright, ye can go, but on one condition. Yer Dad and me'll be goin' up the toon for an hour or two. Ye dinnae move a muscle from the back green till we get back! And ye look after yer wee brother!" That made two conditions, really, but Janet wanted no repeat of the Cappy Club fiasco. "Dae ye hear? Ye look after yer wee brother! Period."

It was late summer of 1954. At the age of seven, James would get to see a back green concert in Brecon Street. It would be a modest affair and a far cry from the famous Spitfire back green concerts of the early years of The War. Naturally, it was the tenement lassies that planned, organised and staged it with help from their mothers. The Junction Street entry to the back green was used as a stage. It worked because here there was a difference in height of several feet between the back green and the base of the tenement back wall. Between the two was a wide concrete pan meant for drainage, then a retaining wall rising several feet to the back green proper. An area of the back green up to the retaining wall became the stage, marked out by four chairs at each corner, and the concrete pan made a serviceable auditorium, even though it was a bit tight. It also meant that the Junction Street flats overlooking the back green became balconies from which the privileged could view the performance in comfort through their open windows.

Janet had sent the two bairns downstairs at quarter to two and waited until, from the open living room window, she could see them taking their places against the wall of the Junction Street tenement. Wee Effie looked up and waved, the pre-arranged signal, and Janet waved back. Then, satisfied, she closed the window and she and Ian hurried out of the flat. Dame Fortune had smiled for, unusually, it hadn't rained for a week. The bare surface of the back green had hardened up and barring its normal quota of bumps, was now perfect for the intended purpose. The stage was set. James and Wee Effie were wedged between the tenement wall and the mob of 50 or 60 rowdy bairns fired up for the performance, plus a score of adults on the fringes and leaning out of open windows.

The Mistress of Ceremonies was one of the older lassies, Lesley Helliwell, who, at thirteen-going-on-thirty, had already formed a love of theatricals and was the brains behind this particular production. She was a tall, slim, bonny lass, whose standard summer attire was a pair of pale green slacks, a primrose blouse and a grey cardigan, and who wore her long, blonde hair in pigtails. But in honour of the occasion she now wore a long, black-and-gold patterned pseudo evening dress that her mother had run up on her Singer from some surplus curtain material. Not only that, horror of horrors, she'd been allowed to put on lipstick, her hair was down, and her flat, virginal bosom was adorned with a necklace of artificial pearls. Lesley made her entrance up the steps onto the stage. Although her sudden transformation to stylish elegance was undoubtedly at odds with her surroundings, her efforts garnered appreciative applause, hoots and calls of encouragement. She smiled and waved shyly to the crowd. In her hand she clutched the torn-out page of her school jotter on which she'd listed the acts in order of performance. As MC, she would call them out from deep in the back of the entry. Lesley's support crew consisted of her parents. Mrs Helliwell sat in one corner of the stage next to a rickety table that held a Decca 50 portable wind-up gramophone, a pile of 78 records and some of the new-fangled 45s. Mr Helliwell sat in the other corner with his accordion, providing accompaniment and filling in any gaps or delays with traditional Scottish melodies.

"Robert Helliwell – that's mah wee brother if ye dinnae ken – will kick off the festivities wi' 'is impression o' Johnnie Ray!"

Lesley gave a flourish to the entry and out came Robert, an eight-year-old male copy of his sister. He looked clownish in grey longs that had obviously been shortened and a jacket that was far too big for him. Under the jacket was a white shirt, with an unbuttoned collar and the tie hanging loose. His hair was slicked back with Brylcreem, but one lock had been allowed to dangle over his forehead. He ran up the steps and turned to the audience. Meanwhile, Mrs Helliwell had discreetly laid the first record on the turntable and wound up the gramophone. The unmistakable tones of Johnnie Ray singing 'Cry' issued forth. Holding a fake microphone made from the end of brush handle stuck into an old tennis ball, Robert did his best to mime, leaping about the stage, falling to his knees, pretending to tear out his hair and undoing some buttons of his shirt, with various contorted expressions on his face. The audience loved it. As the song reached its crescendo, so did the laughter. It then became even more strident as a bunch of lassies unexpectedly stormed the stage and pretended to rip Johnnie's clothes off, just as fans had done the year before in Glasgow. There was now pandemonium. Wee Effie was helpless with laughter and James couldn't contain his glee, although he didn't fully understand what the joke was. The fake fans had now managed to get off fake Johnnie's jacket, tie, and most of his shirt. Thankfully they stopped at the trousers, and Robert was allowed to leave the stage with his modesty intact, waving and acknowledging the cheers of the crowd at this clever conclusion to his act. Lesley leapt up the stairs.

"And now for somethin' completely different!"

With that, three lassies and three laddies appeared on the stage and took up positions. From the gramophone came the tinny sound of Jimmy Shand and his band, augmented by Mr Helliwell. It was the Gay Gordons. As they paraded, stepped and twirled, the three lassies looked competent while the three laddies tried hard not to look sheepish but failed miserably. The crowd didn't mind and clapped their hands lustily to the music. So much for the dancing lessons given by Miss Purvis to the senior students from Bonnybrig Primary. Next came several poetry recitations. 'I Have a Little Shadow' and 'Wee Willie Winkie' from two of the younger bairns with some prompting from parents on the side, and 'I Wandered Lonely as a Cloud' from another Bonnybrig senior pupil. Then, eleven-year-old Lilly Livingstone stepped up and said in a loud, confident voice, "Ah'm goin' tae recite 'Schule in June', a poem by Robert Bain." There was an immediate hush, which was quickly broken by Lilly's confident delivery.

There's no a clood in the sky,
The hill's clear as can be,
An' the broon road's windin' ower it,
But - no for me.

Not only was she word perfect; she also enunciated clearly and articulated the vernacular with a passion that breathed life into the poet's sentiments. The crowd was stunned. No one had heard these verses before, written in their own tongue, but they'd certainly hit home. As she completed the sixth and last verse, a relieved but ecstatic Lilly took a bow to prolonged applause. Mrs Livingstone stood proudly at the side, relieved that her insistent coaching had paid off. She had high hopes of getting Lilly into The Academy next year.

"And now, wi' apologies tae any Hibs supporters in the audience..." Lesley looked around with a mischievous smile, nodding knowingly at the cacophony of boos and a few cheers that greeted her words. "... here are three laddies frae Tynecastle!"

She stepped aside as the three named hurried up the steps and onto the stage. One of them was in a well-worn Hearts maroon football strip with white shorts and was clutching, to the envy of every laddie in the crowd, his own leather football. Though Easter Road wasn't far off, the fanatical core of Hearts supporters persisted in Brecon Street. Accompanied by Mr Helliwell and to the tune of 'After the Ball Was Over', first they sang:

After the ball was centred
After the whistle blew
Wardhaugh got up his temper
And off with the ball he flew,
Passed it straight to King Willie
Whae gave it to Alfie Conn
Between them, they fooled the goalie
And won the game aw' on their own!

Much applause. Then, to the tune of 'A Gordon for Me':

There are lads at Tyne-castle
Ye aw' ken their name,
Well known for their skill
At the auld fitba' game,
They play in the League
Twenty-two magic feet,
An' they hammer the Hibs
Every time that they meet!

After another chorus, which everyone except the few Hibs supporters in the crowd joined in, the three laddies retired with beaming smiles to rapturous applause.

"Now, for the Guy Mitchell fans..." announced Lesley.

She was drowned out by cheers and was unable to finish the sentence. But she didn't need to, for two weird characters had leapt onto the stage. They were barely recognisable as Kenny and Lizzie McBayne, respectively eleven and eight years old, from across Brecon Street. Kenny was dressed in an oversize suit that sharp eyes might have recognised as the same one Johnnie Ray had worn several acts before. But it was Lizzie that caused mayhem for her costume was outlandish: a skirt made entirely of long strips of brown crepe paper down below her knees, which barely concealed her modesty as her blue knickers were just visible; a fake bra made of two round pieces of black rubber that had been cut from an old inner tube and tied with string; around her neck a tatty red feather boa from her Auntie Senga; and a large fake flower of red papier-mâché stuck in her hair. And as if that weren't enough, she wore a thick layer of make-up and bright red lipstick.

You'd have to have been utterly ignorant of popular music not to know what was coming. Amid the cheers, laughter and catcalls, Mrs Helliwell already had the 45 on the turntable. There were a few jarring chords, then the powerful voice of Guy Mitchell and the backing group launching, unusually, into the chorus, bouncing off the tenement walls and filling the back green with 'She Wears Red Feathers and a Hooly, Hooly Skirt!' At the same instant, Kenny started miming, while Lizzie, standing at the front of the stage, did her best imitation of a hula girl, wiggling her scrawny little hips and waving her arms above her head. People were doubled up, howling and gasping, unable to contain themselves. Kenny continued, while this time Lizzie did a few twirls. Those in the crowd who could, sang and shouted along in unruly delight while Lizzie returned to her jerky hula movements. Three verses later and the crowd roared back the final chorus, scaring the pigeons and, some said, even making themselves heard in Junction Street. There was utter bedlam while the two performers took their bows, then ran down the steps and disappeared into the dark of the entry. Lesley thoughtfully gave the audience time to settle down, then stepped up brightly, lifting her skirts as she again mounted the steps to the stage.

"Well," she said, "now its mah turn. Ah'm goin' tae sing 'Blue Moon' by Jo Stafford."

At that, there was a sudden change of mood. The audience fell silent. Not a sound penetrated the tenement walls from outside. For a few seconds, the silence was pure. Lesley looked round at her father, who keyed an introduction. Lesley began to sing:

Blu-ue Moon!
You saw me standing alone,
Without a dream in my heart
Without a love of my own...
Blue Moon!
You knew just what I was there for
You heard me saying a prayer for
Someone I really could care for...
And then there suddenly appeared before me
The only one my arms will ever hold
I heard somebody whisper, "Please adore me"
And when I looked, the moon had turned to gold...

As she sang, adults who knew and loved the song looked at each other, eyebrows raised. This wasn't an easy song to sing, especially for an amateur. But Lesley handily mimicked Jo Stafford's modulation, her slight wailing, as the tones fluctuated between high and low, even the smoky quality of her voice. The entire audience was spellbound. Such a powerful voice coming from such a skinny wee lassie...

Blue moon!
Now I'm no longer alone
Without a dream in my heart
Without a love of my own...

The song ended. There was a moment's hesitation then the entire back green burst into ecstatic cheering. Not a few eyes were moist. Lesley stood there, blushing furiously, but managing to bow. From the middle of the crowd, someone shouted.

"Encore! Encore!"

The shout was taken up.

"Encore! Come on hen! Gie us another one!"

Then, from one of the balcony windows:

"How about 'You Belong to Me'?"

Flustered, Lesley turned to her father, mouthing a question in the hubbub. He nodded. Lesley turned back and raised her hands to calm her new fans. Smiling, she waited for quiet. The intro to 'You Belong to Me' sounded. Lesley began to sing. As the melody and the names of exotic locales washed over the crowd, eyes closed and people gently smiled. The Nile... The Pyramids... A tropic isle... The jungle... Algiers... For a few precious moments, the back green, a patch of bare earth within dingy tenement walls, became a magic space. Fathers who'd served overseas in The War looked thoughtful. A few of the wives of these fathers who'd endured the pain of separation became emotional. Yes, these were the kinds of songs that had kept them going at the worst of times during the awful 1940s. Lesley stopped singing and the back green erupted. She bowed shyly. When the applause had died down, she was able to announce the penultimate act.

"The McBaynes're back and this time it's wee Lizzie's turn!"

The McBayne bairns ran onto the stage. Eight-year-old Lizzie stepped forward. She was wearing her Sunday dress, green cotton down to her knees, with a wide white elastic belt around her waist. She was clutching a stuffed toy to her chest. She turned round and nodded first to Mr Helliwell, then to Kenny, who was in his normal summer street attire of shorts and a short-sleeved shirt and had positioned himself behind her and to one side. The accordion keyed an intro and she started to sing in her little girl, piping tones, 'How Much is That Doggie in the Window?' Then the audience, between laughing and cheering, realised why Kenny was there, for his sole function was to interject with *Woof! Woof!* The crowd were now joining in the choruses. Kenny had become redundant, for every time his part came, a loud *Woof! Woof!* came from fifty or sixty throats, effectively drowning him out. To loud cheers and applause, the two performers, smiling broadly, ran from the stage.

Lesley announced the final act. This time, more dancing from the seniors at Bonnybrig Primary and this time it was the last waltz. As the familiar notes of 'The Tennessee Waltz', sung by Patti Page, burst from Mrs Helliwell's gramophone and echoed around the tenement walls, the dancers waltzed around the stage, working hard to keep their step on the uneven surface. Then Lesley inserted herself among them, gesturing to the crowd, "Join in!" and partnering with her wee brother. Mothers grabbed their sons, the few fathers grabbed their daughters, and Wee

Effie grabbed James. “Come on!” she commanded, dragging him onto the stage to join the dancers, tottering around on the hard, uneven ground, and doing their best to copy the movements. The concert ended with an extended sing-song, led by Mr Helliwell with his accordion and beginning with an old favourite to get the audience tuned up:

Ye cannie shove yer granny off a bus!
Oh, ye cannie shove yer granny off a bus!
Ye cannie shove yer granny
For she's yer mammy's mammy
Ye cannie shove yer granny off a bus!

After several choruses of this, there was ‘The Quartermaster's Store’, ‘I Sent Her for Cheese’, ‘The Bonnie, Bonnie Banks o' Loch Lomond’ and finally ‘I Love a Lassie’. Of course, then they had to have the National Anthem. With the crowning of a new, young, queen the year before, patriotic sentiment was as yet undiminished, even in Leith. Everyone stood and gave their best rendering of ‘God Save the Queen’, though the Leith version was popular among some sections of the audience:

God save our Auntie Jean,
Long may she sell ice cream
In our back green!
May she have cones for you
Bashers and sliders too
But you might have to queue!
Go-od save our Jean.

With that, there was a round of applause, a few words of thanks from Mrs McBean, one of the leading tenement wivies, more applause, and the end of the festivities. Courtesy of Mrs Helliwell and her gramophone, the audience dispersed to ‘Walking my Baby Back Home’...

That night, the Swanstons tucked into a steak dinner: Prime Scotch cuts, chips, peas, and pickled beetroot. It was a rare treat. Ian had even splurged out on a bottle of Riesling at the off-licence. He'd acquired a taste for it during his enforced year trying to put Germany back on its feet. But for James, it was a doubly special day, for on this one day, there had been a first and a last. Not only had he got to taste steak for the first time in his life, but he'd also been privileged to witness the last back green concert in Brecon Street. By the middle of the nineteen-fifties, back green concerts were beginning to fade out of the lives of the tenement bairns of Leith. They'd simply become redundant, for there was no longer any need for the bairns to organise their own entertainment. Instead, television organised it for them. As well, affluence, longer vacations, the spread of picture houses, bingo halls and other entertainments made inroads into the very idea of playing outside in the back green or on the streets. And so, by the nineteen sixties, the tenement back greens were largely deserted and the streets inhabited only by a handful of bairns at peevery beds and bulls on the long summer evenings. If the wivies had wanted to, they could have reclaimed the greens for their laundry, but by now, in addition to washing machines, they had spin driers and the local laundrette. Anyway, a few years further on, the fatal frenzy that had gripped City planners would force the wholesale demolition of tenements that had housed generations of Leithers for a century or more, Brecon Street among them. And so, the back green, as James and the other tenement bairns had known it, would simply cease to exist.

Miss Boyle

When he was just on six-and-a-half, James said goodbye to Miss Douglas and moved up into Primary Three. His new teacher was none other than Miss Boyle. No longer Miss Douglas's homely classroom with its wall posters, miniature furniture, boxes of coloured chalks and sky blue side door. Now, he had to mount a staircase of 50 granite steps to the second floor, clutching a well-worn oak handrail, then walk along the corridor to Miss Boyle's room. Meeting the original requirement to accommodate enormous Victorian classes, it was far too big for the 1950s' equivalent of only 30 or 40 pupils, so only about 60% of the space was taken up by rows of wooden desks. Entirely bare of decoration of any sort, the room was segregated from the next classroom by a huge partition wall, the upper half of which consisted of framed panes of thick, rippled glass, allowing a distorted version of activities in the neighbouring classroom to be seen, and heard in muffled form. The windows to the outside, the converse of their external gothic counterparts, soared to the very top of the high ceilings, reinforcing the impression that one was sitting not in a school, but a church.

If Miss Douglas had been a balmy breeze from the South Pacific, Miss Boyle was a blast from the Arctic. The shock for James and his fellow pupils was considerable. If he'd been asked to create an exact opposite of Miss Douglas, the result would surely have been Miss Boyle. Small, dumpy, greying, grim-faced and hook-nosed, Miss Boyle dressed in severe tweeds and sensible brogues. But it wasn't just in her appearance that Miss Boyle differed from her colonial nemesis. Instead of warmth, there was cold. Instead of familiarity, there was formality. Instead of kindness, there was hostility. Nevertheless, it had to be admitted that with Miss Boyle, the education of the Primary Three students began in earnest, starting with the times tables. There were no books. Miss Boyle wrote the particular times table on the blackboard, which was perched on an easel in front of the class. The pupils would copy it into their jotters. Then they'd go through the table as a class, chanting the formulae: *Two ones are two, two twos are four, two threes are six* until they reached two twelves. The two times table was easy, but by the time they reached *twelve twelves are a hundred and forty-four*, it had become a marathon. On and on, they had it drummed into them until they could recite it in their sleep. Next came additions and subtractions, followed by multiplication, division and long division. They learned a lot. Discipline wasn't a problem for Miss Boyle. She could have used corporal punishment if she'd wanted, but she didn't need to. She simply put the fear of God into them with her tongue and her physical presence. All of her pupils were afraid of her.

Day after day, then on into Primary Four, James had to breathe in the toxic air of Miss Boyle's classroom. Working with an elbow on his desk, his head resting on his left hand, doing multiplications, he wished he could look out of the windows, just for a change of scene. But in their tiresomely meticulous way, the Victorian designers of the school had ensured that the lower panes of glass on the monster windows would be rendered opaque, in order to keep the pupils' attention focused on their lessons. So, instead, James risked a tilt of the head to gaze upwards through the top panes of glass which framed a blackened corner of the adjoining wing's roof, strutting pigeons, and a portion of grey sky. He felt as if he were at the bottom of a dark well, and would never escape.

Miss Boyle took out her frustrations on her pupils; James was a particular target of her ire. After two sunny years with Miss Douglas, he'd developed into a bright, chatty laddie with a modicum of self-confidence, despite his junior status in the class. Miss Boyle didn't like her pupils to be either bright or chatty or self-confident. She wanted them silent, in their place, and under her control. Things came to a head in the last week of October 1954. On this particular Monday, James was especially energised. Hearts had beaten Motherwell 4-2 the previous Saturday in the League Cup Final. Willie Bauld had scored a hat trick. For the laddies at least, it had been the main topic of conversation all day. Now, to finish off the afternoon's lessons, Primary Four were doing 'art'. Miss Boyle had distributed a blank sheet of drawing paper to each pupil. The 'art' class task was for the pupils to "draw someone you know". Meanwhile, Miss Boyle would sit at the front, marking jotters.

James, still on cloud nine from his football team's success, took to his task with enthusiasm. This was quite straightforward, for his subject was sitting right in front of him. It was Miss Boyle. James shared a double desk with Derek Montgomery. Although they were forbidden to talk, there were all sorts of ways of communicating non-verbally. As they worked, they looked at the progress each other was making, commenting and joking in their silent way. James had developed a surprisingly good talent for drawing with a pencil, considering his age. As his head-and-shoulders sketch developed, and it became obvious who the subject was, neither could contain his mirth, especially as James exaggerated some aspects of her features.

The climax came when James, having fashioned a good likeness, decided that Miss Boyle should live up to her name. He planted a huge boil on her nose. That was his first mistake. Then, carried away by the drawing's success, and adding insult to injury, he unwisely wrote under his drawing in capital letters MISS BOIL. Derek had to clamp both hands over his mouth to suppress his guffaws. Others craned from their desks, trying to see what the fuss was about. Then James made his third mistake. What on earth could he have been thinking? For he held up his drawing for others to see. The hilarity had suddenly become audible. Miss Boyle looked up sharply from her desk.

"What is going on here?" she snapped.

Immediately, there was silence. Miss Boyle saw, from the lingering smile on his face, that James was the centre of whatever mischief was afoot. She sprang from her seat and advanced on him before he had time to hide the evidence. Snatching the paper from his desk, she gazed at the drawing, her face contorting in black fury, barely able to speak.

"What is the meaning of this, you horrible boy?" she spat out through clenched teeth.

James thought she was going to faint. Derek hoped she would. But she didn't. She just ranted and raved. James cowered before her wrath. Derek had slipped so far down in his seat that he was almost under the desk lid. The rest of the class looked on in fear and awe. Miss Boyle – or Miss Boil – had fully taken leave of her senses. So loud was she that she disrupted Bunty Melville's sewing lesson at the other end of the corridor. Finally, she walked to the front of the class and turned round. With a smirk of satisfaction on her face, she stared down the class for a few silent moments, enjoying the shocked expressions and the bowed heads. Then suddenly, she dramatically ripped James's drawing in two, then four, then eight pieces, scattering the fragments on the wooden floorboards. She crooked her right index finger at James. He rose from his seat and came out to the front, terrified, afraid to look at her.

"Pick it up!" she commanded, pointing at the wreck of his artwork.

James dutifully got on his knees and picked up the pieces.

"Stand up!"

He got to his feet.

"Now put it in the bin!"

James did as he was told.

"Now sit down!"

James regained his desk with some relief. But worse was to come.

"The art class is suspended," announced Miss Boyle.

With a fixed, malevolent smile on her face, she went around the class collecting the pupils' efforts one by one, without bothering to glance at them. She then walked over to the rubbish bin and threw them in to join the tattered remnants of James's composition.

"Get your jotters out and open to a fresh page."

As they did as they were told, Miss Boyle was writing on the blackboard. When she was finished, she pointed to what she'd written.

Unruly behaviour of any kind will not be tolerated at Bonnybrig Primary School and perpetrators will be severely punished.

"You will each write this out a hundred times in your jotters in your best handwriting. I will be checking. Anyone who does not complete this work to my satisfaction will do it all over again."

She sat down. A stunned silence accompanied the expressions of disbelief. A glum mood settled over the room. Cowed and resigned, the pupils started on their group punishment. As he gripped his pencil and formed the letters of his first attempt at the sentence, James had only two thoughts in his head. One, was Miss Boyle going to belt him after the lesson? And two, what on earth did *perpetrators* mean?

When the bell rang for the end of the day, and it appeared a belting was not on the cards, James scuttled out, keeping as low a profile as possible. Then he waited for the Sword of Damocles to fall. But nothing happened. Was Miss Boyle too embarrassed to take the matter further or had she realised she'd over-reached? In any case, it was never mentioned again, though there was a bit of a backlash from classmates who blamed James for their aching wrists. Miss Boyle, for her part, ensured James was made a whipping boy from then on. Whenever there was a pretext to dish out lines or another tongue-lashing, she seized it with relish. James simply had to put up with it. As the autumn term dragged on, he wasn't looking forward to yet another term under Miss Boyle in the New Year. But a few weeks later, Fate would step in and emancipate him from Miss Boyle's bondage forever.

The usual

"Yer hair looks like a midden! Time ye had a haircut. A proper one!"

Janet surveyed James's head with a critical eye. It was a Friday afternoon. James's appearance had been allowed to deteriorate over the past month or so. If anything, Janet was determined her bairns look respectable when in public, but especially at school. James would need a haircut. And that meant a trip to Sanny Speight's. She got her purse, selected a sixpence, and handed it to him.

"Go on, ye're old enough to go yersel'."

He took the coin and stuffed it in the pocket of his grey shorts. Of course he could go to the barber by himself. After all, he *was* seven. And it was just along the road.

"Wash yer face before ye go. Dinnae forget behind yer ears." Even a barber deserved clean ears to work with. "And pit yer jersey on."

He did as he was told and, without a farewell, he walked out of the flat. Holding on to the banister, he made his way down the darkened, but by now familiar, stairs, past the usual pack of tenement bairns loitering in the entry, and out into the street. He walked slowly up the hill, turned the corner and draggled along Junction Street, distracted by the dingy shop fronts, and occasionally stopping for a closer look. There was a display of Diana air pistols in the window of the sports and bicycle shop. In another, a white terrier sat with cocked head, peering quizzically into the horn of a gramophone. James was able to read in large letters *His Master's Voice*. A shoe shop and a wine and spirit merchant's later, James checked his shorts pocket to make sure the sixpence was still there and turned into Bonnybrig Road.

Sanny Speight was the only barber in the neighbourhood, so his services were in high demand at a time when men's hair was fashionably short. Located at the top of Bonnybrig Road, his shop was sandwiched between a cobbler's and a cooper's yard. Outside was a traditional red and white striped pole. A large printed sign in the window announced:

HAIRCUTS - BOYS	Monday-Friday	6d.
	Saturday	9d.
HAIRCUTS - ADULTS		9d.
SHAVE		1s.3d.

James mounted the two steps through the entry into a long, narrow space. Three barber's chairs were located along the left-hand wall, with a large mirror in front of each. Only one was in use. On the right was a backless bench covered in cracked brown leather worn shiny by the passage of generations of bums. It ran the entire length of the wall except for a low, square table at the end piled high with old magazines and newspapers. Three men and a boy were already waiting. One of the men stared into space, smoking a Woodbine. Another pored over *Reveille*. The third was hunched over the previous Saturday's Pink edition of the *Edinburgh Evening News*. The boy was engrossed in an old copy of *The Rover*.

As James took his place on the bench, Sanny himself glanced over from the head he was working on and gave him a nod and a smile. He was a small, dapper man, clean-shaven with slicked-back hair and horn-rimmed spectacles. If he hadn't been wearing a white barber's coat and holding a comb in one hand and a pair of scissors in the other, he might easily have been mistaken for an accountant or a bank clerk. As each customer was done, the person sitting at the far end of the bench got up and took his place in the vacant chair, while the remaining customers awkwardly shuffled to their right without standing.

For once, James wasn't interested in reading. Instead, he sat back with his head resting against the bare wall, watching Sanny at work. The master barber danced around the object of his labour with quick, lithe movements, hardly appearing to touch the head in front of him, but clearly making a difference as the floor around his feet began to pile up with detached locks of hair. All that could be heard was the *click, click, click* of the scissors and the *clip, clip* of the hand clippers, overlaid with relaxed conversation as Sanny passed the time of day with his customer. The talk was about Hearts, Sanny being an ardent Hearts supporter. How would they do at the start of the season tomorrow? Of course, they'd wipe the floor with Dundee and then Falkirk next week. But what about Celtic in a couple of weeks? The Glasgow champs had pipped Hearts at the post for the Scottish Cup last season. What about this year? Would the signing of Crawford make any difference? James pricked up his ears and followed the discussion, memorising some of the juicier titbits he could use to impress the laddies in the back green.

When Sanny was satisfied, he put down his instruments, picked up the hand mirror in both hands, held it behind the head in question and enquired if it was satisfactory. The head affirmed with a nod that it was. Whipping off the protective cape and giving the neck a light going over with the brush, Sanny stood back to admire his handiwork. The fresh-faced thirty-something got to his feet, examined himself in the wall mirror, and went to put his hand in his trouser pocket. Then he paused and gave Sanny a meaningful look. Sanny responded in kind.

"The usual?" he asked softly, with a knowing, but discrete, smile.

The man nodded, grateful for not being obliged to spell it out. Sanny went over to the back of the shop, where a plain metal dispenser was screwed to the wall. He opened a sliding drawer in the bottom and extracted a small rectangular packet with writing on it. Keeping it hidden in his hand, he passed it over with his back to the rest of the room. The man furtively thrust the packet into the pocket of his overcoat, took a handful of change out of his trouser pocket and paid the barber. Another satisfied customer, apparently.

But James was curious. What was in the packet? He could have sworn one of the waiting customers had winked at him. He looked over at the dispenser in the far corner. No clue there. What could *the usual* be? Was it Brylcreem? Since almost every adult male he knew put Brylcreem on his hair, he guessed that must have been it. Did they sell Brylcreem in tubes? Maybe in a packet? Pleased with his deduction, he settled back on the bench.

When it was his turn, Sanny crooked his index finger. He reached down to a shelf below the chair, retrieved a polished wooden board and slotted it neatly into the upholstered arms of the chair. He bent down, picked James up and swung him onto the board. Seated at this height, James's head was almost level with Sanny's and was fully reflected in the large wall mirror. Tucking the cape around him, Sanny picked up his implements and smiled at James's reflection.

"What's it tae be, son?" he enquired brightly. "Just a short back an' sides? If Ah ken yer mither, that's what she'll want."

James just nodded and succumbed to Sanny's ministrations. As the barber fussed around him, snipping, clipping and combing, turning James's head this way and that with his free hand, from his commanding height James did his best to survey the area out of the corners of his eyes. On the wall to the side of the mirror there was a familiar black and white poster. It was about a foot square and depicted a row of three or four diminutive cartoon privates on parade quailing before the onslaught of an enormous, beefy, moustachioed sergeant major with a swagger stick tucked under his elbow, who was yelling at the top of his voice.

"HAIRCUT!" he screamed, making the very air around him vibrate in wavy lines. A private with particularly long locks showing from under his cap shrank back in terror.

"...AND A TRIXIE SHAMPOO!" added the sergeant major emphatically. And, as if to ensure the message was understood, a bottle of Trixie Shampoo was prominently displayed in the bottom left-hand corner of the poster.

This little spectacle confronted James every time he sat in the barber's chair. He couldn't explain why it fascinated him so. Maybe it was because he knew that his dad had been a sergeant major in the Army. But this cartoon sergeant major looked nothing like Dad. He wondered if Dad had yelled at the soldiers the same way this one did. He couldn't imagine it. Could Dad really make them have a haircut? And did the Army really insist that its privates use Trixie Shampoo on their hair? What was Trixie Shampoo, anyway? He risked a sideways glance along the wall. Between the mirrors were glass shelves with all manner of hair care products, toiletries and shaving soap for sale. But no sign of Trixie Shampoo. Well, it was something he wouldn't be using on his hair any time soon. Though his mother used shampoo from little sachets purchased individually at the chemist, it wasn't something men or boys would waste on their far shorter hair. A bar of soap had always done perfectly well and it would continue to do so.

His mind went back to his haircut. Sanny was completing the job and had just stepped back to admire his work. Without bothering to offer James the mirror, he whipped off the cape, brushed him down and swung him onto the ground. James waited for Sanny to ask if he wanted the usual. But Sanny kept his silence and merely held out his hand, palm upwards. James took the sixpence out of his pocket, relieved it was still there, handed it over and walked out. Sanny placed his earnings in the till and turned to the next customer. When James got home, Janet feigned admiration for his new haircut.

"My, that's fine. Aw' the lassies'll be efter ye on Monday," she chaffed.

But James had a question.

"Mum?" he asked. "Ye ken when ye go tae the barber's?"

"Aye."

"What's *the usual*?"

"Eh? What d'ye mean, *the usual?"*

"Well, the man before me... when 'e was finished... 'e asked Sanny for *the usual."*

But Janet was just as mystified. What could *the usual* be?

"Ask yer Dad when 'e gets hame," was all she could suggest.

"Dad, Dad, what's *the usual?"* was James's first question when his father walked through the door at six o'clock.

"Help mah Boab, let me in the door! What d'ye mean, son?"

James repeated the story he'd told his mother. Ian patiently listened to the explanation. Then the penny dropped.

"Oh, the usual," he said with a knowing grin. "THAT usual!"

Janet looked blank, then suddenly started to giggle. James stared at his mother, then his father, then back again.

"What's wrong?" he cried, exasperated. "Tell me!"

But they couldn't speak for laughing.

"Is it Brylcreem? Is it?"

"Brylcreem?" chortled Ian, "Brylcreem!"

"Well, it was the only thing Ah could think of, maybe in a tube?"

Ian, utterly failing to bring his mirth under control, was holding his stomach while Janet, helpless too, was wiping tears from her cheeks.

"Aye, son, that's right," Ian managed to get out once he'd recovered. "That's what *the usual* is. It's Brylcreem in a tube."

Satisfied at last, James wandered off, pleased that he'd cleared up another of life's little mysteries. And each time he returned for another of Sanny's masterpieces and Sanny held out his hand for payment, he was tempted to ask for the usual. But he never did, because he didn't actually like Brylcreem, that greasy, smelly stuff! Meanwhile, the sergeant major with the huge head was still screaming at the little shaggy-haired soldiers. And the soldiers still hadn't had a haircut, nor had they, it seemed, made acquaintance with a Trixie Shampoo.

The exchange

James happened to be sitting in the tin bath in front of a glowing coal fire when Mrs Waddell came to visit. The first he knew of it was when he heard a loud knock on the Swanstons' front door. It was already pitch dark at just after seven-thirty on a dreich Tuesday evening early in November. Unannounced visitors at this time of the day, at this time of the year, were rare. Discomfited, Janet got up quickly from where she'd been kneeling on the carpet bathing her son and dried her hands on a towel. Ian, who'd been relaxing in their only armchair, trying to listen to a new comedy programme on the radio called *Hancock's Half Hour*, quickly switched off the set and went to the door.

James heard the mumble of his father's voice, then the lighter, quieter response of a woman. With his fingers, he stirred the soapy water that barely covered his penis and wondered who the visitor was. He was going on eight and was blushingly self-conscious when it came to nudity - *his* nudity. He hoped that whoever it was would go away. But to his horror, he heard the front door bang shut, the sound of footsteps on the linoleum in the lobby, and suddenly there was a stranger standing in the doorway, in *his* living room. It was a small, middle-aged woman wearing a brown overcoat and a red woollen headscarf staring at him in some amusement.

"Oh, Ah'm awfy sorry. Ah didnae ken ye were bathin' the bairn!"

Ian, coming up beside her, explained, "Hen, this is Mrs... eh... Waddell... answerin' the advert in the *Evenin' News.*"

"Och, aye!" exclaimed Janet with some relief. "Pleased tae meet ye," she offered formally, but they didn't shake hands. Still clutching the towel, she gestured the visitor to a place on the settee. She seemed to have forgotten about James, who was having fits at the thought of a strange old woman and his nakedness together in the same room.

"Mum! Mum!" he wailed.

"Och, hud yer weesht. Mrs Waddell disnae mind ye, d'ye Mrs Waddell?" she chided.

Mrs Waddell disnae mind ME, but Ah mind HER!

"Mum! Mum!" He tugged the towel out of her hand, draped it around himself, and sat there stubbornly, as if in a tent.

"Well," explained Mrs Waddell, "Ah'm interested in the exchange. Have ye found anybody yet?"

"No," said Janet, hesitating, "Ye're the first tae... enquire."

Sitting in his watery tent, James reviewed what he remembered about the 'exchange'. After four years in Brecon Street, his parents wanted out. They'd had enough of the noisy street, the dingy tenement, the cramped flat and the lack of modern amenities. But they had few options. Private rentals were hard to come by. Anyway, a rental of better quality would mean higher rent. Buying their own home was unthinkable. They simply couldn't afford it. Nor did banks give mortgages to people of their class and their slender means. For many in their position, a council house at an affordable rent was the obvious solution, but there was a waiting list. A very long one. Janet had been up to the council offices in the High Street umpteen times, but movement up the list was glacial; with only two children, the Swanstons weren't a priority. In desperation, they'd put an ad in the *Evening News* for an exchange. It had become common practice, through the years of Edinburgh's post-war housing troubles, for tenants in rented accommodation to swap rentals in order to find something that suited both sides. In the current environment of housing shortages and numbing bureaucracy, movements between council and private rentals were tolerated by both local authorities and private landlords.

"Ye advertised for a council hoose, didn't ye?" Mrs Waddell went on. "Well, Ah'm in a council hoose oot at Fox Crag. Mah man passed away four months since and Ah'm oan mah ain oot there. The truth is, the place is too big for me and aw' mah family's here, in Leith. Mah daughter lives just roon' the corner in Junction Street." She paused and looked at them. "So wud ye be interested in Fox Crag? It's 68 Chesser Drive. It's a fine place, modernized wi' electric light, a livin' room, two bedrooms and its ain kitchen wi' a hot water boiler. There's a front an' back gairden as well. An' a dryin' green."

Ian and Janet quickly looked at each other. They said nothing but the sparkle in their eyes said, "Yes!"

"That certainly sounds like the sort o' thing we're after," said Janet at last. "What about this place here – is this what ye're lookin' for?"

"Aye," said Mrs Waddell, "but can Ah hae a wee look roon'?"

They nodded and Mrs Waddell got up.

"Mum! The water's gettin' cold!" moaned James, still clutching the towel around him. Janet went into the scullery and came back with a kettle of hot water which she proceeded to pour into the bath.

"Careful, now, dinnae want tae scauld yer wee robbie!"

James was wondering how things could get any worse. It was bad enough that they let a strange woman ogle him naked in his bath. But now they were making fun of his wee robbie. He almost wept with embarrassment and wished the bathwater would swallow him up. Wailing, he covered himself entirely with the towel. Janet turned to Mrs Waddell, who was struggling to hide her amusement.

"Go ben the hoose, have a look at the bedroom," she said.

When she'd left, James popped his head out of his towel.

"Mum, Ah want that auld woman tae go away!"

"Less o' yer peengin'!" she scolded. "Naebody's bothered about seein' ye wi' nae claes oan!" And she walked off to find Mrs Waddell. At the front door they briefly discussed practical details, the Swanstons made arrangements to go and look at the Fox Crag property, and Mrs Waddell left. Back in the living room, James was shivering in the rapidly cooling water, covered in the damp towel.

"She's gone, son!" announced Ian, tapping him on the head, and to Janet, "Yer son's easily embarrassed, isn't 'e?"

It turned out the rent of the flat at 68 Chesser Drive was only marginally higher than they were paying now; they could afford it. Mrs Waddell was keen to make the move before Christmas. With the formalities completed by the end of November, the Swanstons were able to flit on Friday the third of December 1954. A small removal van was hired to take their few sticks of furniture and tea chests of household goods. Alistair and his car were commandeered to drive them and their personal stuff to the new flat. The fact that it was almost midwinter didn't matter. They'd escaped Brecon Street at last. They were on their way, up and out.

3 Green grass, trees n' floors

A kind of utopia

There was a loud thump on the ceiling.

"Oh, God," said Janet. "It's Mon Sewer Renoir again! Effie, would ye go up an' have a look an' see if 'e's awright."

Wee Effie, now eleven, got up from the carpet where she was lying on her stomach reading a comic. Her look displayed reluctance but she said nothing. She went over to the sideboard, picked up a key, opened the door of the flat and disappeared. Monsieur Renoir lived above them at 68 Chesser Drive. A French socialist émigré, he'd landed in Scotland in 1940 on the run from the Gestapo. Unable to get him, the Gestapo had taken his wife and children instead. They'd disappeared into Ravensbrück concentration camp and were never heard of again. Inconsolable, Monsieur Renoir had spent the rest of his life in Scotland as a French teacher in a private girls' school. Now retired, alone and well past seventy, he spent his days daydreaming of his past life. In failing health, a corpulent man, he often fell over on the floor and, when he did, the Swanstons were immediately alerted, for his floor was also the Swanstons' ceiling. Wee Effie came back and replaced the key Monsieur Renoir had let them have so that they could check on him if necessary.

"It's OK, Mum," said Wee Effie. "'E's got up. 'E didnae hurt himself or anythin'." Then, adding, "'E's probably got too much fat on 'im," she dropped onto the carpet and continued with her comic. Janet grunted in acknowledgement, smiling inwardly at her daughter's cheek. The Swanstons had been relieved to find that the three other families sharing the building were relatively neighbourly. The Forresters next door were a childless couple who kept themselves to themselves. The Frasers had the other top flat next to Monsieur Renoir. He was a bus driver for the Corporation and she looked after their three teenage children. Monsieur Renoir was really the only concern, but between them, the Swanstons and the Frasers did their best to keep an eye on him.

Since they'd moved to Fox Crag, the Swanstons' lives had taken a decided turn for the better. Between the two world wars, Edinburgh City Council had demolished some of the more notorious slums in the heart of the City and had relocated the former slum dwellers to more salubrious habitats on the outskirts. Fox Crag, situated in the eastern suburbs not far from the Firth of Forth, was only one of several new council housing schemes developed in the 1930s for this purpose. The designers had been keen to implement some of the latest thinking on the improved housing of workers, their health, and quality of life. The streets were wide and tree-lined. Small shopping precincts had been strategically sited at appropriate intervals. Green spaces abounded. Buildings were low-rise and the distances between were generous. The number of flats in each housing block was kept to a minimum. Most flats had gardens, vegetable plots and their own toilets, almost unheard-of luxuries for slum dwellers. It would be no exaggeration to say that to families plucked from cramped, insanitary tenements, these new surroundings were a kind of utopia. And so it was for the Swanstons. After living so long in the dingy canyon that was Brockit Brae, they could now walk out into their own garden and enjoy a vast expanse of sky.

Number 68 Chesser Drive fitted one of the standard templates; a modest, four-apartment unit with pebble-dashed walls and clay roof tiles that had once been ochre, enclosed at the front and sides by a black, wrought iron fence. From the pavement, a gate gave access to a narrow path bounded by privet hedges. The single front entrance led up to two small ground floor flats and another two up the short flight of stairs. Each flat was an exemplar of efficient use of limited space. The Swanstons' front door gave straight onto a small living room. Off that was the kitchen - a real kitchen, and a far cry from the scullery of Brecon Street. Spacious enough to take a dining table, it would become the venue for family meals. Inexpensive electric washing machines were starting to appear in the shops but the Swanstons' budget still didn't stretch that far. So, for at least the first couple of years, they'd have to do laundry as they had in Brecon Street, namely by hand, in the kitchen sink, and on a washing board with a block of laundry soap and a hand-operated roller mangle to squeeze out excess water. But, luxury of luxuries, a back-to-back heater provided endless hot water, as long as the coal fire was on. Two bedrooms and a toilet/bathroom completed the interior. There was a front garden, vegetable plots at the side and back, as well as a back green, a real one this time, with real grass and five shared posts ready to take the tenants' washing lines.

Janet's first action, only three days after they'd moved into 68 Chesser Drive, was to enrol the bairns in the local school. James had been hoping she'd wait until the New Year, but Janet insisted; she'd be enrolling them both on Monday. That way, they'd have the two weeks to settle in and be ready to start their lessons properly when the school resumed in January. Fox Crag Primary School had been established between the wars to service the newly established council housing estate. The school was a reflection of its social environment and the new thinking in school architecture. No longer the dour, soot encrusted sandstone Victorian-era edifices of the central city with their vaulted ceilings, cavernous rooms, and cramped playgrounds squashed against local industry, schools like Fox Crag had been designed along modern principles of space and light but with economy in mind. A simple two-storey, red brick L-shaped building on a green field site, it was surrounded by a spacious playground that allowed the sexes to mingle during their breaks and enclosed on two sides by playing fields, as well as numerous green spaces. It was well ahead of its time.

Janet sat in the office of the Headmistress, Mrs Moncrieff, with the bairns standing beside her. Through the window, despite December grey, the playing fields managed to remain green and the tiled roofs of the housing estate stretched away to the distant horizon of Arthur's Seat. She always felt uncomfortable in the presence of educated people, especially those from a 'better' class and who talked differently. On the one hand, people of her class were expected to show deference to power, wealth and status, especially when it was seated behind a desk in an office. On the other hand, no matter how hard she tried, the gritty scrapper from the mean Leith streets of the 1930s, who'd made it into the 1950s, couldn't always be kept in check. Mrs Moncrieff leaned over her desk and studied the documents in front of her. Wee Effie had already been disposed of. At the age of eleven, she would, of course, go straight into Primary Seven. Now, what about James?

"He's seven years old is he not?" she asked in her best Morningside, staring at Janet over the frames of the gold-rimmed spectacles perched on the rim of her nose. Reading Janet's nod as affirmation, she went on, "Then he'll go into Primary Three."

"Well, actually," said Janet, summoning her best Proper Speak, "he's already done Primary Three. Should he no (*here a little slip-up*) go into Primary Four? That's where he (*recovery*) was, at Bonnybrig."

"Really?" questioned Mrs Moncrieff. "How is that possible?"

"Well, he started Primary One at four-and-a-half..."

"That may well be the case," interrupted Mrs Moncrieff, "but rules are rules. If he's seven, he should be in Primary Three and that's that."

The gritty scrapper, discarding Proper Speak, surfaced.

"Oh, no it isnae," Janet said, quietly but forcefully, leaning forward in her chair. "The laddie's always done well at school. What's the use o' 'im repeatin' the same lessons aw' over? Ah want 'im tae get on, and Ah want 'im where 'e belongs, in Primary Four."

Unused to being contradicted in so determined a manner in her own office, in her own school, Mrs Moncrieff sat back and, with a *frisson* of panic, took stock of this bothersome parent. She looked as if she could indeed cause trouble. She shifted her gaze to the boy. He was following the exchange with what Mrs Moncrieff judged to be an intelligent expression. She threw caution to the winds. Well, there was a place with Miss MacAndrew in Primary Four and, after all, it was Christmas.

"Very well, Mrs Swanston, if it means so much, Primary Four it is."

"That's very good of you," said Janet, successfully bridging the Proper Speak hiatus. "Can they start today?"

And with that, James was led off to join Miss MacAndrew in Primary Four, and Wee Effie placed with Mr Martin in Primary Seven. The decision to enrol James in Primary Four was to prove a fateful one. For the rest of his education, he'd be at least one year younger than every other pupil in his class. As Janet walked back to 68 Chesser Drive, she mulled over the meeting. She was pleased she'd got her way. She usually did. But there was something ticking away in the back of her mind that she couldn't put her finger on. What was it? She went over her exchange with Mrs Moncrieff again and finally it came to her. *MacAndrew*. Now, where had she heard that name before?

The proposition

On being demobbed in 1946, Ian had got his old job back as a bonded cellarman with MacFergus at his 1940 wage. But then, six years before, he'd been single, with no responsibilities or obligations. Now, he was married with a wife, a child and another on the way. The wage was barely enough for the family to live on. Since then, he'd been promoted to foreman in sole charge of the blending operation and had got a raise. But with two growing children to feed and clothe it was still inadequate. Not only that, Ian had changed. He was now a different person from the twenty-five-year-old who'd been conscripted in 1940. He'd risen from private to CSM, not merely because of his courage, but because his superiors had recognised his leadership qualities and organisational abilities. He knew what he was capable of, but saw there was no further scope for advancement at MacFergus. As well, old Mr Mac had passed away and with him had gone the original family atmosphere of the firm. It was time to start looking around.

A chance meeting changed everything. It appeared insignificant at the time, but was to have a lasting effect on the Swanston family fortunes. As a veteran of the First War, Janet's father, Alexander Melrose, was a long-time member of The Royal Scots Club in Edinburgh. On this particular day in late summer 1954, when they were still in Brecon Street, he'd invited Ian to have dinner and drinks there, together with a few old comrades. Ian had accepted, albeit reluctantly. The milieu of The Royal Scots Club wasn't exactly his cup of tea but the invitation had come from his father-in-law. Though Alexander was a difficult man, he thought highly of Ian. Between them was the unspoken rapport of a veteran of Gallipoli, 1915, and a veteran of Northern Europe, 1944-45. The Royal Scots Club had been crowded as usual on a Friday evening. As they sat waiting for their meal to be served, the talk was of the end of food rationing in July when meat had finally been freely available. Ian was savouring his Glenlivet when he saw a familiar face on the other side of the room at the bar. At the same time, the familiar face saw him. They both rose hurriedly and met in the middle of the lounge.

"CSM Ian Swanston!" said the other, putting out his hand.

"Captain Donald DeSantos!" proclaimed Ian, shaking it heartily.

Donald DeSantos was of small stature. His thick, jet-black hair was now shot through with grey. Square-jawed and brown-eyed with a military-type moustache, he couldn't have been mistaken for anything else but a former officer in The British Army. He and Ian had served together at the front. Don was one of the few with pips on their shoulders that Ian had respected, and the feeling was mutual. Attached to 155 Brigade as a forward observation officer, Don had spotted for the twenty-five pounder batteries in the rear. It was one of the most hazardous jobs, for he frequently operated in no-man's land. He'd been wounded several times and been awarded the Military Cross. Day in, day out, he and Ian had shared common dangers and now shared a common bond. Delighted at the unexpected reunion, they briefly updated each other on the last few years. When Ian mentioned that he was back in his old job at MacFergus, Don looked at him thoughtfully.

"Listen," he said, "I might have a proposition for you. He pulled a slip of paper and a pen out of his top pocket and wrote a few lines. "Could you come round to this address, say in a week's time?"

"What kind o' *proposition*?" a sceptical Janet had asked, using exaggerated pronunciation as if it referred to some kind of fraudulent activity. "Whae uses a word like that anyhow?" (*Especially somebody called DeSantos*, she was thinking.) It seemed she had visions of Ian becoming embroiled with the Mafia.

"Ah dinnae ken, hen," soothed Ian, "but it does no harm tae find out what it's about."

He'd managed to get off work at MacFergus half an hour early and took a tram up Leith Walk as far as Firth Street. Still in his work clothes and clutching his copy of the Daily Express, he searched the street until he found Number 17. It was a Georgian terraced house with a brass plate mounted on the black iron railings. It read *G. DeSantos & Sons*. A light went on in Ian's head. DeSantos? *The* DeSantos? Idiot. Why hadn't he twigged before? He mounted the steps, passed through the massive oak doors and checked in at the desk in a spacious high-ceilinged reception area. Two minutes later, he was led to an office where Don DeSantos was already coming out the door to greet him. As they sat down, Don's secretary entered with coffee, a bottle of one of DeSantos's premier sherries and two glasses. Although the sun hadn't yet dropped below the yardarm, it didn't seem to matter.

"Well, I suppose the cat's out of the bag?" commented Don wryly.

"Ah should have guessed!" Ian admitted ruefully, fingering his glass.

In their military superior-subordinate relationship, they hadn't delved deeply into what they'd done in civvy street. Don had an idea of what work Ian had done before The War and Ian understood Don had been a director of a firm in Edinburgh, but that was as far as it went. What Ian hadn't realised at the time was that Don was one of *the* DeSantoses, a prominent local family who'd originally been Portuguese. They'd provided vital support to the Duke of Wellington's army during the Peninsular War and had been granted British citizenship in return. They'd cleverly exploited their new status. The family had split into two branches, one to manage the estates in Portugal and the other to market their fine wines, sherries and ports in their principal market, Great Britain. Don and his three brothers represented the current generation of the British branch, which for some time had been located in Edinburgh.

"So," Ian went on, "what about this proposition, then?"

"Can I just ask you a few questions first? Would you mind just giving me a quick rundown of your time in the wine and spirit trade?"

Ian did as he was bid, breaking off to answer questions here and there as Don requested more details. When Don was satisfied, he briefed Ian on the firm's history. Then he got to the heart of the matter.

"The War really hit us hard, Ian. The company nearly went under. We're now in recovery mode, rebuilding and re-investing. Part of our strategy is to start a new blending and contract bottling operation here in Edinburgh, including marketing our own brand of Scotch whisky, something we've never tackled before. We need someone with experience to set it up and manage it. I'm offering you the position."

Ian was stunned at the unexpected development. He certainly knew his way around the Scotch whisky business and particularly the blending and bottling side but he'd never contemplated setting up and running an operation himself. His bemused silence was quickly filled by Don.

"You'll get every assistance. All the resources of the firm. And you'll be working mainly with me at first."

He then mentioned the starting salary he envisioned. It was more than three times what Ian was currently earning. Ian's eyebrows shot up and he finally broke his silence.

"And ye're confident Ah can do it?"

"Ian, you forget that I saw you in action in the worst possible circumstances. You impressed me immensely. I've consulted with my brothers and they are on board. They've left the final decision up to me. I've every confidence in you. But what about you? Are you ready to finally make the break with MacFergus?"

"Ah'll have tae talk it over with Janet, but Ah'm inclined tae say yes."

Don offered his hand and they shook.

"When can you start?"

By October, Ian had left his old job and had started with DeSantos. The new plant was to be set up in an existing building in Greenside that had been purpose-built for spirit production as far back as the eighteenth century. Although it was ancient, the bones were still sound. It needed only modernisation and refurbishment to bring it up to the standard required for the new function and to meet H.M. Customs and Excise regulations. Ian had thrown himself into his work with enthusiasm. For the first time in his life, he found himself wearing a suit and tie to work. A priority task was to recruit workers. Post-war unemployment levels were low. It was hard to get good staff, so Ian got in touch with four disenchanted former colleagues at MacFergus and offered them a better deal. There were Chrissie and Margaret Duncan, a mother and daughter, and Aggie Moracen, all three of whom had had long service on the production line at MacFergus, as well as John Leith, an experienced bonded cellarman who'd be offered the post of Ian's operations manager. None of them hesitated for a moment. The chance to work under Ian Swanston at significantly increased wages was too good to pass up. With that, they gave MacFergus the statutory two weeks' notice, and Ian had four experienced Scotch whisky specialists to form the nucleus of the new venture.

Christmas odyssey

"Now make sure ye look after yer wee brother. Ah dinnae want a repeat o' the Cappy Club nonsense!"

Janet was addressing Wee Effie over James's shoulder from the edge of the armchair where she was sitting buttoning up his overcoat. Wee Effie sighed wearily. At eleven years old, she'd been in a dwam about how grown-up she must look in her new beige winter coat, thick, knitted woollen scarf and Fair Isle tammy (both from Jaeger in Princes Street) and brand-new black winter shoes, all presents from magnanimous Auntie Christine. But now her mother had spoiled her reverie. She wondered when she was going to hear the last of that particular misadventure. Although she'd cried her eyes out at the time and had taken the blame, since then she'd convinced herself that it was actually James's fault. After all, he was the one who'd got himself lost...

It was Saturday, the 18th of December, the week before Christmas, 1954. The Swanstons were in a muddle, having been in their new flat at Chesser Drive for only two weeks. But Janet was determined that, as far as possible, things would go on as usual. The bairns were already enrolled in their new school. Ian's commute to work by bus was going smoothly. She'd been up town to the power company to switch over the electricity and gas bills. And, since they were in the depths of an Edinburgh winter, she'd organised for a coalman to bring three hundredweights to top up the nearly empty coal bunker. Now, she only had to finish unpacking the assembly of boxes and tea chests crammed into the empty front bedroom. But then there was the matter of the Parks Department Christmas Party to see to. Every year, Alexander Melrose's employer, the City Parks Department, held a Christmas party for employees' children and grandchildren. It was held in McDonald's Ballroom in Fettes Row. Since Wee Effie, and then James, had been old enough, Janet had taken them along. In the lean times of the late forties and early fifties, it was one of the bright spots in an otherwise monochrome year. There were games, songs, some dancing, lemonade and buns, and, of course, a visit from Santa Claus. The bairns had always looked forward to it. The problem was that it was Janet that had to take them, supervise them for a couple of hours, and bring them home again.

But now, with all the unpacking and rearranging to do, neither she nor Ian wanted to spare the time. So, Janet, reluctant to deprive the bairns of what had become a Christmastime tradition, made her decision. They'd have to go on their own. At eleven, Wee Effie should be old enough to travel on the bus by herself and despite the Cappy Club incident, she should by now be responsible enough to look after James as well.

At first, when Janet had told her, Wee Effie had hummed and hawed about going at all, for, almost a teenager, she was starting to balk at doing ring-a-ring-a-roses with tiny tots. She might not go, she'd said. But then, if she didn't go, James couldn't go, Janet had countered. And James wanted to go. They went back and forward and finally, Janet had put her foot down. Wee Effie didn't realise how lucky she was to be invited to a Christmas party at all. There were lots of bairns that would have given their right arm (one of Janet's favourite expressions) to go but couldn't. She ought to be ashamed that she wasn't prepared to take her little brother. Through her not-so-subtle blackmail, Janet achieved what she wanted short of issuing a firm edict. Wee Effie was shamed into submission.

"Now, have ye got yer bus fare?"

Wee Effie peeled back the red woollen glove on her left hand to reveal two one-shilling coins, enough for the return trip for both of them. Janet nodded approvingly. Wee Effie closed up the glove again.

"And what bus d'ye catch?"

Janet had to make a point of this question. They'd been at Chesser Drive only a brief couple of weeks. Much was still unfamiliar.

"The 35," replied Wee Effie, confidently.

"And where d'ye get off?"

"Henderson Row."

"Then where d'ye go?"

"Walk doon Dundas Street tae Fettes Row."

"When does the party finish?"

"Half past five."

"And what bus d'ye get hame?"

"The 34."

Janet nodded in satisfaction. Wee Effie was well-rehearsed. She turned to James, now rugged up against Edinburgh's worst in a second-hand child's overcoat, a grey woollen balaclava and grey woollen gloves. But he was still cold, for, like most boys of his age, he was made to wear short trousers, even with midwinter only a few days away. At least he had long woollen socks he could pull right up to below his knees. Janet looked him sternly straight in the eyes.

"Ye'll listen tae yer sister, d'ye hear!"

"Aye, Mum." James nodded vigorously.

"Ye do what she tells ye tae do!" Janet cut the air with her right index finger to emphasise the point. "Otherwise, ye'll have me tae deal wi' when ye get back!"

Suitably warned, James joined his sister. They walked out of the house with a quick "Ta-ta!" over their shoulders. Janet stood at the entry and waved them off up the street, struggling to quell a twinge of guilt, hoping she'd done the right thing. Surely there couldn't be a repeat of the Cappy Club incident? No, surely not. Lighting couldn't strike twice in the same place, could it? How little she knew.

The argument started when they got to the roundabout. Wee Effie made a beeline for the 34 bus stop which was diagonally across the large roundabout from that of the 35. But James hung back.

"It's the wrong bus stop," he said stubbornly.

"No, it isnae," replied Wee Effie.

"Mum said we had tae catch a 35," insisted James. "We have tae go over there," and pointed to the other bus stop.

"It wis a 34! And you've tae remember what Mum said!"

James hadn't forgotten. He was to do what his sister told him to do. Very well, he would. But he knew she was wrong. This would end badly.

They didn't have to wait long and took their seats on the bus. Wee Effie made a point of sitting on the long sideways benches intended for pensioners and disabled people near the exit so that they could get off quickly if need be. The downside was a continuous blast of arctic air. The bus lurched off. The route took them uphill, first up to London Road and then the Tron. As the bus ground slowly up the final gradient of Leith Street and around by the GPO, they looked along Princes Street where the bright lights of the grand shop fronts revealed pavements crowded with Christmas shoppers. Then there was the long loop south of The Castle, its ramparts dark and brooding against the December sky. The whole way, Wee Effie was keeping a keen lookout for Henderson Row. She'd know it when she saw it by the Georgian terraces. But where on earth was it? It should have been only about a fifteen-minute bus ride. Time was passing, they were somewhere in the wilds of Fountainbridge, and there was no sign of Henderson Row. As she peered anxiously through the windows, James sat grimly with his arms folded, saying nothing, slowly freezing, but savouring the worry written all over his big sister's face.

By the time the bus had reached Slateford, Wee Effie's anxiety was growing by the minute. They were clearly heading west out of the city and had been going now for almost half an hour. Her eyes were smarting from tears of frustration. Not just because they seemed to have come the wrong way, but because it was beginning to appear as if James had been right after all. When they were accelerating through Longstone amidst the thinning traffic, she was up to ninety. Looking out of the bus window, nothing was familiar. Just rows and rows of drab, soulless, council houses that complemented the darkening day. They were in a foreign country. They were lost. And she was in charge of her brother. What was her mother going to say? It would be the Cappy Club all over again...

"Are ye's aw' right, hen?"

The conductress had an inquisitive expression, her head cocked to one side, as she stood on the platform, nonchalantly hanging from a leather strap by her right hand, her body swaying in her black uniform to the rocking of the bus, her ticket machine dangling against her hip. She'd divined there was something not quite right about these two unaccompanied bairns. Her question pierced the silence between them. Wee Effie wiped her eyes with the end of her scarf. What should she do? She was swithering. She could ask for help. But being Janet's daughter, she was too proud to admit they were in trouble. They were in a hole, yes, but it was up to her to dig them out. So she just gulped.

"Aye, we're OK, thanks."

The conductress nodded, but the answer hadn't satisfied her. She'd keep an eye on them. To his credit, James was beginning to feel bad that he'd enjoyed his sister's distress. But the distress was catching and he was getting worried too. The party was supposed to start at three o'clock. It was now after three-thirty and the light was already starting to fade in the depths of the Scottish winter. The cold was gnawing at their bones and they weren't even there yet. Not only that, James had long realised that though she'd never admit it, his sister hadn't a clue where they were. He began to feel afraid.

Suddenly Wee Effie broke off from her constant peering and jumped up with a shout.

"Stop the bus please!"

Normally buses stopped only at regulation bus stops, but her cry sounded so genuine that the conductress, confirmed in her suspicions about the two and thinking it was a real emergency, pressed her special bell to alert the driver, who brought the bus to a screeching halt. Passengers not holding on were caught off guard and were thrown suddenly forward, some ejected out of their seats. There was bedlam for a moment. But Wee Effie, holding on to James for dear life, had eyes only for what she could see through the window. She pointed excitedly.

"Mrs Moran's hoose!" she exclaimed. "Come on, she'll help us."

Throwing a grateful glance at the conductress, who was thanking her lucky stars for the leather strap, she dragged James off the bus. They stood in the road in the gathering gloom as its tail lights disappeared in the distance. Unknown to James, who'd concluded that his sister had finally cracked, they'd reached Sighthill. Janet, with her newborn daughter, had lived with her sister-in-law, Christine, at Sighthill for some four years during and after The War. In fact, for Wee Effie, Christine's flat had been her first home and comprised her earliest memories. Sighthill was familiar territory. As she got older, she'd visited and slept over regularly before Christine and her husband had moved away to Trinity at around the time the Swanstons had moved to Brecon Street. She remembered the place well and particularly Mrs Moran, Christine's neighbour, who'd always been nice to her, and had made a point of feeding her home-baked jam scones through the time of rationing.

Incredibly, as she'd kept her eyes glued to the bus window, she'd seen what she thought was Mrs Moran's house suddenly come into view. Even more extraordinary, Wee Effie had recognised the building from behind, across several back greens and hedgerows, because it happened to back onto the road, which also happened to be the main bus route. James was dying to ask who Mrs Moran was. But, without bothering to explain, Wee Effie hustled him into a passageway between the pebble-dashed council houses. Walking a short way down Parkway Grove, they turned through a small gate and walked up a garden path.

As they approached the front door, a welter of thoughts ran through Wee Effie's head. Had she correctly identified the house in the creeping dusk among hundreds of others that looked exactly the same? After all, it was over five years since she'd last been here. Even if it was the right house, how were they to know that the Morans still lived there? Assuming they did, would anyone be at home? After all, it was Saturday afternoon near Christmas. A lot of people would be out doing Christmas shopping. What if no one answered the door? Or worse still, a complete stranger? Then they'd be high and dry. How were they going to get back into the City and, more importantly, how were they going to get to the party? By the time she raised her right hand to knock, she was so tightly wound up that tears were trickling down her slowly numbing cheeks.

The sainted Mrs Moran was dozing in her favourite armchair in front of the coal fire, music from the BBC Light Programme issuing quietly from the radio. She'd drifted off to the strains of Eddie Calvert playing 'Oh My Papa', blissfully unaware that what had become one of her favourite melodies was actually a German tune called 'Oh Mein Papa'. Had she realised its origins, she might not have been dozing so comfortably. Her spectacles had slipped down her nose and her knitting lay neglected in her lap. With Mr Moran and their son, Michael, away at Tynecastle where Hearts were playing Rangers ('Gers won 4-3), and her daughter gallivanting up the toon with her chums, she'd seized the opportunity for a quiet winter Saturday afternoon by herself with just the budgie for company.

Suddenly, her peace was shattered when a loud knocking jerked her out of her slumbers. Who could it be at this time, just on four, and on a Saturday, too? Pushing her knitting aside, she struggled to her feet, bleary-eyed. Imagine her surprise when she swung open the front door to find two tired, cold bairns on her doormat.

"Oh, Mrs Moran!" cried Wee Effie, gulping with emotion, and so relieved that the tears flowed even faster.

Mrs Moran was a kindly body, by now in her mid-fifties. Her dark, curly hair hadn't yet started to grey. Her face, like her spare figure, still gaunt from wartime rationing, had the look of someone permanently in charge. But now, she couldn't conceal a look of utter astonishment. She took a step back, blinked, adjusted her spectacles and glanced back and forth between the two little, anxious, teary faces.

"Wee Effie! Christine's niece! And whae's this?" Without waiting for an answer, she went on, "Is it wee James?" Wee Effie managed a nod. "What in the name o' the wee man are ye doin' away oot here?" Then, without waiting for a reply, "Come on in oot o' the cauld, the pair o' ye!"

Pulling them in, she sat them down in the warmth of the kitchen, and stood, arms folded across her peeny, glancing from one to the other.

"My, lassie," she said, addressing Effie, "Ye've a face as long as Leith Walk! Ye're goin' tae tell me what aw' this is aboot while Ah make ye some warm milk. Wud ye like that?"

The bairns nodded eagerly. While Mrs Moran busied herself in the small kitchen, putting a pan of milk to warm on the gas stove and opening a new packet of digestives from the press, a reassured Effie gabbled an account of their meanderings by bus across Edinburgh. When she explained how 'they' had caught the wrong bus, James's eyebrows shot up and he opened his mouth to protest. But then, sensing his big sister's embarrassment, he shut it again. It wasn't worth it. Mrs Moran, all the while listening sympathetically, served the milk in enamel mugs, together with the plate of digestives, then sat next to them at the kitchen table. As the milk and biscuits began to take effect, things started to look up for the two junior Swanstons. Whatever happened, here they were safe. But Mrs Moran was smiling inside. Poor bairns, it had been an easy mistake to make. When they'd demolished three digestives each and drained their mugs, she spoke.

"First things first. Ye'll be wantin' tae get tae Fettes Row in a hurry, otherwise ye'll miss yer party?" *And,* she was thinking, *Ah'll be wantin' tae get back tae mah armchair.*

The looks on the bairns' faces answered for them. Mrs Moran stood up, took her purse from the top of the sideboard. Sitting down again, she opened it and extracted a shilling, which she placed on the Formica table top. "Here's a shillin' for yer fare back." She pushed it over to Wee Effie who picked it up gratefully. "Now, aw' ye have tae dae is go across the road tae the bus stop and get a 34 back. It'll take ye right tae Henderson Row!" What they hadn't understood was that it was a circular route. In fact, if they'd stayed on the 34, although they'd have been late, it would have got them there in the end anyway, but from the opposite direction. Then James put his hand up as if he were in class.

"Please, Mrs Moran!" he said mournfully. "Ah need a wee-wee!"

"Of course, mah bonnie laddie! Come on wi' ye, through here."

After she'd got James sorted, Mrs Moran put on her big overcoat and tied a scarf over her head. Slipping her feet into her shoes, she ushered the two lost bairns back out again under dreich, darkening skies. They went back the way they'd come then crossed the road to the bus stop. After ten minutes' chittering in the cold, the bairns happily boarded the next 34 bus and the last they saw of Mrs Moran was her waving goodbye as she was swallowed up in the gloamin. Back they went into town and this time they seemed to be going in the right direction. By now it was after 4.30 and getting darker by the minute. Suddenly Wee Effie, who'd been anxiously monitoring the passing streets through the window the whole time, jumped up and grabbed the strap above her head. She ducked her head and peered out again to confirm it. Yes, there were the familiar elegant Georgian terraced houses. It was Henderson Row at last.

"Come on, we're there!"

They jumped off the bus and hurried down Dundas Street as a raw haar settled over the city, engulfing the street lights and blotting out the roofs of tenements and terraces on either side of them. They turned right into Fettes Row, walked a hundred yards, and there was McDonald's Ballroom, a beacon of light in the darkness. Judging by the noise and rowdiness coming from inside, the party was in full swing. Holding onto the rusty iron railing, down the steep steps they went, out of the cold and into a world of bright lights, warmth and good fun. The dance hall was packed with what looked to be a hundred or more children. Adults were supervising and a band was playing at the other end of the room. The hokey-cokey had just started, and the noise was deafening. They quickly peeled off their outer things at the wardrobe counter and entered the dance hall proper. Wee Effie, now to some extent recovered from the stresses and strains of the previous hour or so, walked purposefully across the floor looking left and right with James trotting along behind. When she found the person she was looking for, she reached up and tapped him on the shoulder. He turned round from his hokey-cokey supervision. It was their grandad. His eyebrows shot up.

"Och, ye're here at last!" he shouted, struggling to be heard above the racket of live music and loud singing. "Ah was beginnin' tae worry mahsel'!"

It was an excellent excuse not to give an answer. Wee Effie just smiled and waved at him. They never kissed or hugged their grandad, or anything like that. He just wasn't the type. The main thing was that he knew they were there. They quickly inserted themselves into one of the hokey-cokey circles and, holding hands, started to join in the fun at last. Then came 'In and Out the Dusty Bluebells', followed by 'The Farmer's in his Den'. The 'farmer' was the first volunteer in the circle. Then he chose a 'wife', who joined him. The 'wife' then chose the 'child', the 'child' chose the 'dog' and the 'dog' chose the 'bone'. The 'dog' happened to be Wee Effie, so, naturally, she chose James to be the 'bone'. His heart sank, for he knew from experience exactly what was coming. He was dragged into the centre of the, by now, crowded circle which closed tight around him and, towering over his diminutive form, everyone started to hit him on his back, his head and his ears, while singing the final verse:

Pity on the bone
Pity on the bone
Ay-o-mah-daddio
Pity on the bone!

Most of the hits were gentle, pretend hits, but it was intimidating all the same. When they were finished, everyone was laughing and patting James on the back to tell him what a good sport he was. He gasped with relief. He was glad that was over! Then there was the slightly less brutal musical chairs, although the two players left at the end did have a fierce little tussle for the final chair. The Swanston bairns had missed the lemonade and buns but had got there just in time for the ice cream. It was just Walls, in the wee cardboard tub with the usual wee wooden spoon, but it didn't matter; it was ice cream! There followed Scottish country dancing, with the adults showing the bairns how. Suddenly, in the middle of 'The Dashing White Sergeant', an official-looking Parks Department gent in a nice suit walked into the middle of the floor and waved his arms for the music to stop, which it did instantly. The band had been expecting the signal. All eyes were on him as he looked around in a practised way, enjoying the sudden hush.

"Well, children," he shouted, "who d'ye think has just arrived outside on his sleigh?"

"Santa Claus!" they roared back, as one.

And with that, amidst general jubilation, in walked the red-clad, portly figure of Santa Claus, swinging a bulging sack (actually a big brown GPO mailbag) on his back. He walked into the middle of the crowd, laughing and jolly through his long white beard, passing out wrapped presents to the bairns. There was pink wrapping for girls and blue wrapping for boys. The younger tots were open-mouthed with incredulity. Santa Claus! Right here! Helpers brought more sacks and when everyone had a present, the call went up, "Right, open yer presents!" There was a commotion as bairns ripped off the wrapping paper to see what was inside. These weren't expensive gifts by any means, a pen, a cheap book, a small doll, a Dinky Toy. But it didn't matter. When all that was over, and Santa had departed amid waves and cheers, the fun started up again.

There was 'Here We Go Round the Mulberry Bush', then some singing. They all joined in for 'She'll Be Comin' Round the Mountain'. The last dance was a slow waltz. Adults danced with adults, bairns danced with bairns, and adults danced with bairns, some of the dads balancing wee lassies on their feet. To James's chagrin, Wee Effie had found a boy of her own age to dance with. He felt abandoned as he stood with his back to the rough plastered wall of the dance hall and watched them waltz through the crowds as if they'd always danced together. But an auld auntie beanie, recognising his plight, took pity on him and swept him onto the floor. James didn't mind. She seemed a nice lady, even though his face was pressed hard against her considerable bosom the whole time and she reeked of lavender perfume.

Then, sadly, it was all over for another year. After getting their coats, they ran a gauntlet of helpers lined up on the stairs, one of whom was Grandad. Their job was to hand out the final batch of goodies. Each bairn got an orange, an apple, and a chocolate half-crown. It looked and felt just like a real half-crown but was tightly covered in gold foil. James was entranced. He'd seen chocolate coins before but not one as big and as heavy as this one. He carefully tucked it away in his pocket for future enjoyment. As he stood outside in Fettes Row under a street lamp, his breath condensing into clouds in the frosty air, juggling his Dinky Toy from Santa, his apple and his orange, Wee Effie buttoned up his coat and pulled his balaclava over his head. What a day! Suddenly Grandad was there to make sure they were all right. Wee Effie was canny enough not to offer any further explanation for their lateness but on the bus home, she suddenly turned to James.

"Are ye gonnae be a clypie-clappie?" she asked, trying to appear more threatening than anxious, which she really was.

James looked at her and considered. He had her on a hook. If he gave the game away to Mum, her life would be hell, for a time at least.

"What would ye gie me tae keep mah mooth shut?" he enquired, suddenly sleekit.

Wee Effie stared at him shrewdly, weighing up her options.

"How about mah chocolate half-crown?" she offered at last.

James said nothing, but with a satisfied expression, merely extended his open palm. Wee Effie handed over the coveted coin.

"OK? We're quits?"

"And," James teased, "ye have tae be nicer tae me!"

"Aw' right," Wee Effie replied, throwing in the towel. "Ah'll be nicer tae ye."

"Promise?"

"Aye, promise!"

Just to make sure, he made her crook and hook pinkies with him. And with that, the bargain was sealed. By ten to six, someone else was peering anxiously out of a window into the darkness and the yellow glare of Chesser Drive's sodium lamps. It was Janet, waiting on her bairns. They should be coming any time now. By six, she was starting to worry, but suddenly there they were, turning in through the gate of Number 68.

"Sorry, Mum, we had tae wait ages on a bus!"

"Well, did ye have a good time?"

"Aye, Mum, it was great!"

"Did ye have any problems?"

"No," Wee Effie lied smoothly, avoiding eye contact by pulling off her tammy and scarf, while Janet helped James with his buttons.

"Mum, Ah saw Santa Claus!" said James, hoping to distract his Mother from any other awkward questions like that.

"Did ye?" cried Janet making big eyes in mock surprise.

"Dad, look what Ah got!"

James emptied his pockets. A Dinky Toy from Santa, an apple, an orange and two chocolate half-crowns.

"Two chocolate half-crowns? How did ye get two half-crowns, son?"

James gulped. His face started to turn red.

"Ah gave 'im mine, Dad," said his sister quickly. "After aw', it's Christmas, is it no?"

"What a braw wee lassie ye are, hen," said Ian quietly, hugging her around the shoulders and ruffling her hair. "Ah always kennt ye'd take after yer auld man! Ah hope yer wee brother will turn out tae be as thoughtful as you," he added, looking at his son pointedly but with an impish grin. Striving to look innocent, James just dropped to the carpet to play with the tiny red fire engine, complete with a movable ladder.

Wee Effie tried to keep her promise. She didn't do a very good job but James didn't mind. He'd got her chocolate half-crown off her. That was more than enough. She never confessed to taking the wrong bus, to getting them lost in the outer suburbs, or about their surprise visit to Mrs Moran. And James, to his credit, kept her secret. Children that they were, they never stopped to consider the consequences of their lies, should Mrs Moran be in touch with their parents or Auntie Christine. But it never happened. Neither the Swanstons nor Mrs Moran had yet been able to afford the luxury of a telephone. They hadn't been in touch for years. Since Christine and her husband had moved to Trinity, all contact with Mrs Moran had been lost. So nothing was heard from her, away out there in the distant suburb of Sighthill.

Poor Mrs Moran. She never got her shilling back. It was only years later, when she happened to bump into Christine in George Street, that the story eventually came out about the two Swanston bairns appearing on her doorstep one afternoon in the depths of winter. By then it was far too late – both bairns were into their teens. When Janet and Ian got to hear of it, they had a quiet chuckle. Secretly, they were proud of the way Wee Effie had got herself and her brother out of the pickle they'd got themselves into, and how James had stood by his sister. Maybe the two of them would make something of themselves after all.

As it turned out, the 1954 Parks Department Christmas Party was the last of its kind for either James or his sister. By the following December, puberty had caught up with Wee Effie. A children's Christmas party was the last thing on her mind. As well, the trauma of that December day had stayed with her. There was no way she was going to reprise the humiliation of getting lost just to please her mother or her little brother. That left James. He was too young to go by himself. Janet couldn't take him, as her part-time job kept her busy Saturday afternoons. Nor would Ian; children's Christmas parties weren't exactly his thing.

Anyway, McDonald's Ballroom in Fettes Row had only a few years of useful life left. By the 1960s, it had closed down, and by the 1970s it had disappeared altogether, razed to the ground amid the general imperative to demolish that had gripped the Edinburgh City planners up in the High Street. So, for James, the Parks Department Children's Christmas Party at McDonald's simply languished and died, to survive in years to come merely as a fleeting memory.

The biggest back green ever

For James and the Brockit Brae bairns, the cramped area of bare, beaten earth squeezed between tenement walls had been the centre of their world. When his family unexpectedly relocated to Fox Crag, James's back green expanded exponentially in ways he could never have imagined. Not only did he now have his personal back green, as well as neighbouring bairns' back greens to play in, there was always uncongested Chesser Drive, which offered unlimited possibilities. But the jewel in the crown, just across from Number 68, was the biggest back green that James had ever seen: Fox Crag golf course.

The moorland waste of Fox Crag had been used for golf as far back as the seventeenth century, but it wasn't until the end of the nineteenth century that a golf course was formally laid out. By the time the Swanstons moved to Fox Crag in 1954, the golf course was in a parlous state. During The War, the War Department, seeing it as a perfect landing ground for German gliders and paratroopers, had taken it over and had rendered it useless to the enemy by digging pits and ditches, raising mounds and erecting other barriers. Then an anti-aircraft battery was added as part of the Forth defences that covered the two most likely Luftwaffe targets; the Forth Bridge and the naval base at Rosyth.

When the Swanstons moved into their flat in Chesser Drive almost ten years after the end of The War, half of the course had been reconstituted and nine holes were now playable. The other half was still covered in the abandoned reinforced concrete remnants of the AA defences: gun emplacements, pillboxes, command posts, gun pits, blast barriers and munitions storerooms in various states of dereliction. This wartime wasteland had become a playground paradise for the local bairns. They called it The Gun Park or The Gunnie for short.

As in Brockit Brae, James's first priority on moving to Chesser Drive had been to make contact with the local gang. In this particular section of Chesser Drive, there were two gangs, one at the top end, known as the Roundies, and one at the bottom end, known as the Foxies. When James had first arrived and was wandering around checking out the neighbourhood, he had, by chance, fallen in with some of the Roundies. They seemed a canny bunch of laddies but they warned him that full membership in their gang depended on the answer to one question. The day came when James's acceptance into the Roundies was to be decided. The members were gathered in a semicircle on the pavement. James stood facing them expectantly. The Leader had a serious expression on his young face as he posed The Question.

"What team d'ye support?"

James gulped. What should he say? He knew there were only two possible responses. *Hearts* or *Hibs*. He considered. Which one? Of course, he should have known better. Easter Road wasn't far away. Reason should have told him what the answer had to be. But his heart was still in Brecon Street where football was concerned, and in this particular instance heart won out over head.

"Hearts!" he blurted out, throwing caution to the winds.

The Leader frowned and there were scornful looks all round. The Leader spoke.

"Hard cheese. It's the wrong answer. We're aw' Hibs supporters. Ye cannae join."

And with that, the Leader turned on his heel and made for the gang headquarters, while his followers tagged on behind chanting "Hi-bees! Hi-bees!" and leaving James standing alone and open-mouthed on the pavement. However, as they say, *nil desperandum*, for that was when Billy Chalmers stepped into the picture. Billy lived at Number 66. He was two years older than James and a class above him at school but they'd quickly struck up a friendship. Billy was the leader of the Foxies. When he heard of James's rejection and the reason for it, the pathway was clear to Foxie membership, for the Foxies were all Hearts supporters. Since they were based in and around Fox Crag golf course, it quickly became James's new back green.

Out of their HQ, which was a concrete pill box capped by a former gun emplacement, the Foxies fanned out over the golf course for their regular forays. There were all kinds of warlike games. Cowboys and Indians was, of course, the mainstay. But when *King of the Wild Frontier* was running in the picture houses, Davy Crockett became the focus and coonskin caps were all the rage. Then there were battles between the Jocks on one side and the Japs or Jerries on the other. Naturally, no one wanted to play the Jap or Jerry. The golf course was perfect for best falls. It had bunkers, and bunkers had sand, so when you got 'shot' and fell, you didn't hurt yourself. Players used all sorts of contortions and theatrics to impress the judges to win the title 'Best'. You just had to make sure golfers didn't get in the way. In winter, there was sledging down the short, steep brae called The Back Breaker, and snowball fights. But the main focus was the golf course.

Even at a young age, most of the Foxies played golf. In Scotland, it wasn't unusual to see ten-year-old lads out on the fairways. Not much was needed – just a few clubs, a couple of balls and some tees. Like the other Foxies, James gradually acquired the minimum kit: an old cleek, crafted by the great-granddad he had never known, a number five, a number eight, and a putter, all wooden-shafted hand-me-downs from

Ian. Just four clubs carried in one hand or balanced on your shoulder. Naturally, the Foxies couldn't have afforded to pay for an actual round of golf but it was easy to play three, four or five holes on a quiet day without being caught, when the green keeper was busy elsewhere.

As well, some of the Foxies got involved in caddying. In those days, golf trolleys were a rare sight on Scottish golf courses. Most golfers still carried their golf bags slung over their shoulders. So, there was a modest demand among those who could afford it for laddies to do the carrying, at sixpence or even a shilling a round at weekends, especially as the young caddies could offer their adult clients advice about which clubs to play or the lie of a green.

When not playing or caddying, finding lost golf balls was on the agenda. The slicers and hookers didn't always have time to waste searching for lost balls in Fox Crag's notorious rough, but the Foxies had all the time in the world and often had a good idea where to find them. At a time when a standard golf ball cost up to five shillings, and a good one, seven-and-six, there was cash lying all over the golf course just for the taking. And some of the Foxies did the taking, making a nice little business out of selling lost balls back to golfers. Of course, it was frowned on by the golfing authorities, but what golfer would pass up the chance of new Warwick at half price?

And one of these golfers was Ian. His grandfather had been a master craftsman of golf clubs, with his own workshop on the edge of Leith Links in the late nineteenth century. For several of his uncles, cousins and in-laws, golf was the only game worth playing. Golf was in the Swanston DNA. Those influences had naturally driven Ian's early interest in golf. His step-brother-in-law, Jimmy, had taught him to play before The War. They'd spent many a happy hour duffing around the wild and woolly courses on the edges of the Pentland Hills, dodging the ewes and the stirks, where the green fees were affordable and the gradients so steep that you were constantly playing 'one leg up an' one leg doon'. Swanston Golf Club became their home from home.

Then Adolf Hitler came along and spoilt their game. During the fifteen-year hiatus of The War, its aftermath, marriage, family, homelessness, flitting and employment, golf had, for Ian, either been impossible, unaffordable, impractical or simply not a priority. But now, things were different. Life was, at last, settling down. Now he had the time. Now he could afford a decent set of Forgans. Now he had his own personal golf course practically on his doorstep. True, it was only nine holes. True, it was tame compared to some of the more challenging courses the City had to offer. But the green fees were negligible and it was only a stroll away. It was better than nothing.

Remembrance of things past

Janet and Ian Swanston's life together had so far consisted of a series of false starts: their courtship, abruptly terminated by Ian's conscription; their wedding in 1941; Ian's demob in 1946; the move into Fife View, despite its shortcomings, their first real home; the move to the larger flat at Brecon Street. It had been fourteen years of upheaval. Six years of war, six years of uncertainty, hardship, separation, death and destruction, stress and anxiety. Then the aftermath, eight years spent picking up their lives again, first, lodging with relatives, then putting up with dingy tenement living together with shortages of just about everything. The first sign of a change for the better had come with Ian's sudden and unexpected elevation into the ranks of management. Then, barely two months later, Brockit Brae was behind them, thanks to Mrs Waddell's unheralded arrival on their doorstep. Now, they had a comfortable flat with extensive gardens and all the space and fresh air that Fox Crag had to offer. The bairns were happier. James was flourishing in his new school, with his new teacher. Wee Effie would move up to secondary this year. The family appeared to be finding equilibrium at last. Three months after the Swanstons moved to Chesser Drive, Ian had celebrated his fortieth birthday. James and Wee Effie gleefully gave him his dumps while Janet looked on. As they thumped him on the back, he good-naturedly allowed himself to be manhandled and joined in the fun. Forty dumps! And when the forty were over, they finished with:

One for the day
One for the morn
One for the day that you were born
A kick, a tug and a nip!

James pulled Ian's hair, although there wasn't much left to pull, Janet gave him a very gentle kick on his bum, which Ian gallantly extended for kicking, while Wee Effie took the skin of his forearm between thumb and forefinger and gave him a pinch. The required formalities over, Ian was able to open his presents: a tie from Wee Effie, a presentation box of Warwick 7s from James, and a new dressing gown from Janet. Then, with the bairns' help, he blew out the candles on the modest birthday cake that Janet had found at a bakery in Abbeyhill.

When Ian was younger, he'd never had any particular ambitions. By 1940, his only ambition had been to marry Janet. Then, his life was taken away and he was put in the army. From the time of their marriage, his number one goal had been to survive The War, then to start a family with Janet, get a decent job and have somewhere nice to live, in that order. By the summer of 1955, he had, or so he thought, realised all these ambitions. The fact was, he now had no ambitions left. The War and its aftermath had sucked him dry of ambition. He was mentally and spiritually exhausted. He'd paid his debt to Life in full. More than that, he was well in credit. So, he switched off. Now he could relax, which was more or less what he did.

That's not to say he turned his back on life. Far from it. Some of his energies went into his new job. But he didn't drive himself. There was no need to. He easily mastered the requirements. He had a dependable workforce that liked and respected him. Despite the commercial realities, his bosses encouraged the kind of benign milieu typical of family businesses. There was little or no stress at work. Once the systems were in place, the operation more or less looked after itself.

He enjoyed turning 68 Chesser Drive into their ideal home. He improved the gardens, planted roses and vegetables, and a cherry tree. He gutted the kitchen and did a complete renovation, building all the cupboards and glass-fronted cabinets by hand. He ripped out the old stand-up wooden mantelpiece and installed a modern tiled version in its place. He and Janet tore down all the old wallpaper and completely redecorated the flat.

Not only did they have the time to do all this, they also had the money for, having starting married life destitute, they were finally managing to accrue some savings. Their social life was modest but lively. Not a week went by without them visiting friends and relatives. Very occasionally they took in a show at the Kings or the Gaiety. What energy Ian had left over was devoted to his one passion; golf. With Fox Crag on his doorstep, he had at least one regular foursome a week. When he started to teach John Leith to play, they'd venture further afield to some of the golf courses down the East Lothian coast, for John had a car. At last, Ian's life seemed to be settling into a gentle groove. There was just one catch.

Ten years before, The War had ended. But no matter in Britain where you looked, no matter what you did, The War was there, ever-present, inescapable. It wasn't just the ongoing global consequences: the Cold War and the threat of nuclear annihilation; The Korean War; the ongoing Allied occupation of Germany; colonial conflicts and decolonisation; the birth of new states, Israel, India. Or, closer to home, the austerity still snapping at Britons' heels; the damaged buildings and bombsites that hadn't yet been cleared; the struggling economy; the avalanche of books and films about The War; the bairns' war games in which the hated Jerries or Japs always had to lose; not to mention National Service from the age of eighteen, which would be in force for another five years.

Yes, it was all of these, but more, for like many who'd gone through the trauma of 1939-45, The War was ever-present in Ian's mind too. For six years he'd been in a different world and for almost one of those years, in a very different world. That was a place of death and destruction where, on getting up in the morning, you had to reckon with being dead by nightfall, where you regularly witnessed violent death or the aftermath of death or dealt out death to others. Then suddenly he'd returned to his old world. He'd been only one of the many ordinary people who'd been called upon to do extraordinary things, but on their return, there was little or no acknowledgement of their service. No assistance, no psychiatric help, no compensation, no thank you. Nothing. Switch off six years or more of your life and move on.

Compared to many others, Ian coped well. On the day of the armistice in North-Western Europe, he'd resolved to get on with his life and that's what he tried to do. He avoided talking about The War and his part in it because talking triggered remembering and that was the last thing he wanted to do. Unlike his father-in-law, he shunned any connection to The War such as Remembrance Day services or veteran's organisations. He'd had comrades during the conflict, some that he might even call friends, who'd shared the dangers, but he stayed in touch with not a single one after it. He'd turned his back on the whole thing. Overtly, it was as if it had never happened. Nevertheless, a thousand images were lodged in his brain, images he had no control over. The one of the twelve-year-old German sniper's shock of blond hair soaking up blood from the remaining half of his face recurred frequently. As for the rest, all it took was a spark and the past became the present.

On the 49 bus, on his way home from work, staring out through the window, as the tenements of Edinburgh sped by in the gloom of an early winter evening, the wrecked and abandoned German hamlet was menacing at dusk with snow on the ground. They'd been tasked to clear it, an insane order since it was almost dark and no proper recce had been done. Beside him, an eighteen-year-old boy from Dumbiedykes, Billy Henderson, just his second day with the platoon, nervously gripping his Lee-Enfield, bayonet fixed. On the other side, Corporal Slater, a veteran of Walcheren. A sudden crack and they all dropped. But Billy didn't get up again. A neat hole had been drilled through the side of his skull. Then the 88s started up. A stonk bracketed the platoon precisely. Slater was hit by shrapnel. Then came the order to fall back. Ian managed to drag him away. Billy remained where he'd fallen. His death had been mercifully quick. One killed, one wounded, yet Ian was unharmed. With a lurch, the bus came to a stop and he was back in Fox Crag again, quickly alighting, with another day behind him.

Standing next to a thousand-gallon vat of whisky, a measuring flask in one hand, a hydrometer in the other, he was pointing his Webley at the Bürgermeister of Fallburg, Westphalia. It was summer, 1945. Ian, now promoted to Company Sergeant Major, had been tasked with ensuring the feeding of displaced persons and former concentration camp inmates. The Bürgermeister, a plump, soft-skinned National Socialist who hadn't yet been de-Nazified, was refusing to release supplies from the town's warehouse. He needed them, he insisted, for the German population. Ian's interpreter, a seventeen-year-old Jew named Ben, who'd somehow survived the Holocaust, told Ian what the Bürgermeister had just said.

"Explain to him," said CSM Swanston quietly in precise English, "that if he does not obey my order, I will shoot him."

"Das ist ein Befehl. Wenn Sie nicht gehorchen, wird Der Feldwebel Sie erschiessen."

"Das glaube ich nicht," said the fat Nazi, shaking his head with a chuckle and settling back in his chair, mistaken in the belief that he was secure behind his enormous desk.

"He says he doesn't believe you," translated Ben.

"Stand up!" yelled Ian.

"Stehen Sie auf!" yelled Ben.

Startled, the Bürgermeister struggled to his feet like an automaton. Meanwhile, Ian was coolly unfastening his webbing holster and pulling out his Webley. He studiously broke it open and checked that there was a round in each of the six cylinders. Closing it again, he clicked off the safety, walked purposefully around the desk, raised his right arm, and, with his finger on the trigger, pointed the Webley to within a few inches of the side of the Bürgermeister's head.

"Ask him now if he still doesn't believe me," said Ian, his eyes filled with cold anger.

But there was no need for a translation. The Bürgermeister had collapsed back in his chair with his hands fluttering protectively over his head and was crying for mercy.

"Nein, nein, schiessen Sie nicht. Ich gehorche!"

Ian kept the Webley out anyway. It didn't hurt to show you meant business. The Bürgermeister signed the papers. Ian clicked the safety catch back on and carefully dipped the hydrometer into the flask of whisky. Yes, the specific gravity was right. He'd often wondered if he'd have shot the Bürgermeister. If he had, he'd have been court-martialled for sure. He didn't know. And the more time that elapsed, the more uncertain he became.

Wrapped up against the cold of the Scottish spring, he was walking briskly down the middle of the fairway having hit a useful 300-yard drive. As he reached the snow-covered bridge, he saw the chicken he'd been following. It had stopped to shelter in a deserted farmyard. He ran across the bridge and on up the road, his tackety books sinking silently into the snow, his breath smoking in the freezing air, unconcerned that he was running straight towards enemy lines. Reaching the yard, he realised he had the bird cornered. It only took a few grabs, a quick wring of the neck, and he was carrying it by its legs back to the bivvy. That night, some of his mates in the platoon had an unexpected feed of roast chicken to keep their spirits up.

The next morning, the advance was ordered towards Bremen. Ian had been allotted to the lead three-tonner. He climbed in beside the driver, a middle-aged volunteer from Dunoon called Rab. But when Rab turned the ignition key, nothing happened. Despite the pre-heating that had been done in the sub-zero temperatures, the diesel fuel hadn't yet thawed out in the pipes. Another truck took their place as lead vehicle while Rab got down to work on the problem. As the replacement crossed the bridge, it exploded with a roar. It had hit a Tellermine. The driver and his passenger in the cab were killed. As he pulled out his number eight iron and addressed his golf ball, Ian reflected on how fate had twice saved him from a minefield. His swing was true, the arc textbook. Dropping the ball neatly onto the green, he was confident that he could sink the putt with one stroke.

If it was The War that had impacted Ian's life, it was her childhood that had majorly impacted Janet's. For, unlike Ian, she'd never really had one. As soon as she'd been old enough, she'd been sent out with her older sisters to scour the streets of Leith for anything that would feed the family. They stood in the queue behind Crawford's biscuit factory first thing in the morning for handouts of broken biscuits. They crept into the alley behind the butcher's before the dogs got there, rummaging in the rubbish bins for old marrow bones for soup. They patrolled the streets looking for empty bottles they could collect the farthing or halfpenny deposit on. And when she was old enough, around the age of twelve, she was the one in charge, directing her younger brothers and sisters in the same activities. Like the rest of the bairns, she had only one change of clothes. Add to that a domineering father and a compliant mother who seemed to be permanently pregnant. The only bright spots in Janet's childhood had been school and the charitable activities such as the Sunday schools and occasional picnics arranged by Edinburgh philanthropists for poor children. As soon as she'd been able to think for herself, Janet had had a single ambition. To get out. To get away.

Upon leaving school at 14, she'd done whatever jobs there were, her meagre wages going straight to her mother. Then, after the move away from Albert Street, the family's fortunes started to improve. Alexander Melrose had been in permanent employment for several years and was bringing home a decent wage, though it wasn't enough to feed a family of nine children. But this was now supplemented by the wages of the older children who were beginning to reach young adulthood and had been put to work. This meant that, by the late 1930s, first one, then two, then three additional wage packets were coming into the home. They helped put food on the table and pay for occasional luxuries like ice cream on Sundays. The downside was that now eleven people, half of them adults, were living in a tiny flat that comprised only two bedrooms, a living room and a cramped kitchen.

Janet had landed in MacFergus at 16, working for a pittance, chained to the production line. When Ian walked past and smiled at her as she stood wrapping her three hundredth bottle of whisky of the day in tissue paper, her life changed. She was smitten. It wasn't just love. He was her saviour. He was her knight in shining armour. He was her ticket away from her home, away from her family, away from poverty and away from what had passed as a childhood.

It was no wonder she chased him. The only other mature male in her life had been her father. They'd never got on. As soon as she'd been old enough, she'd stood up to him and they'd had the most dreadful fights. At least Alexander, to his credit, was a teetotaller and only occasionally resorted to physical violence. But he could do a lot of harm with his tongue and his threatening presence. Ian was the exact opposite: gentle, calm, thoughtful, self-deprecating, but at the same time assertive and decisive, with a mischievous sense of humour. Janet's only wish then was that she could marry him and build an independent life for herself.

Yes, The War and its aftermath had affected Janet too. But not as much as her childhood had. Apart from a few scares, the suffocating austerity and chronic worry about the future, she'd weathered The War better than most, for it paled into insignificance beside the misery of her young years. It was almost as if the deprivation she'd suffered in the twenties and thirties had been training for that of the forties. Besides, she wasn't alone now. She had a husband, a baby, and support from her new in-laws. As well, the tough genes she'd inherited from her father came into their own. So, The War was nothing more than a deadly blip in her life, which she negotiated handily. At the end of it, she was still alive, she was married to the man she loved, she had a daughter and, most important of all, she'd liberated herself from her father.

But as the fifties matured, her past remained with her, too. While Ian had a thousand images of The War to contend with, she had a thousand images of her childhood. Her wealthy cousins visiting, eight-, nine- and ten-year-olds, dressed in the height of 1920s children's fashion, making Janet realise for the first time that her family was poor. Standing at the age of seven with her brothers and sisters in a row, being inspected like livestock for sale by a prim lady social worker sent by a philanthropic society and her mother, pregnant again, watching anxiously from the side. Again standing, this time in a queue, shivering with bare legs in the freezing cold outside the baker's at dusk on a Friday, waiting for cheap tea bread, chivvying her younger sisters Bella and Effie, who were whining and complaining and just wanted to go home.

Janet's images never left her. But as time went on, she found it harder to cope with them. Britain was recovering from The War. People were becoming better off. She saw children with fabulous Christmas and birthday presents. She saw teenagers, dressed fashionably, revelling in the attractions of an increasingly liberal society. She saw thin people grow fat as food went off the ration and became more affordable and they could eat as much as they wanted. She saw everything that she'd never had. And she was bitter. The fact that she and Ian too could have these things was clear to her. But it was too late, for she'd never had them as a child. She'd always been made to feel and look poor. She'd been routinely humiliated. And two or three decades later the humiliation still rankled. It never left her.

Like Ian, she rarely talked about The War. But she did talk about her childhood. She discussed it with her sisters every time they met. She took every opportunity to impress on James and Wee Effie how lucky they were, how easy their childhood was compared to hers and that of her brothers and sisters. At the slightest provocation, an anecdote would tumble out of her mouth. Modern psychiatry would suggest that talking about bad experiences is a useful therapy for patients who want to come to terms with them. In Ian's case, Freud's wisdom was never tested, for Ian declined to talk about his past. Where Janet was concerned, the theory foundered. For the more she talked, the more she remembered and the more she remembered, the more resentful she became on comparing her miserable childhood with that enjoyed by her modern counterparts. She begrudged everything they had and regretted everything she hadn't had. Instead of fading, her bitterness grew and would subsequently taint her entire outlook on life.

Miss MacAndrew

"Peter! Come on! You're supposed to be shelling those peas!"

Peter turned a bright crimson and started shelling. When Miss MacAndrew told you to do something, you did it. It was a rehearsal for the Primary Four class play. They'd perform it in front of the assembled school. It was a fairy tale about a woodcutter, a witch and a beautiful damsel. He had only a bit part. He had no lines to say but it was still a struggle for him. He was the youngest in the class and he'd never done anything like this before. His role was simply to sit on a chair in the corner of the 'kitchen' and shell peas at the appropriate time. Since members of Primary Four, many of whom were former tenement bairns, had only ever seen peas come out of a tin, Miss MacAndrew had had to induct them into the mysteries of how peas were cultivated and how they first had to be removed from their pods before they could be eaten. This turned out to be a neat little teaching unit and one of the spinoffs of the drama activities, the sort of thing Miss MacAndrew loved about her job. Peter started 'shelling' with gusto while the rest of the class looked on with critical interest. The fact that the 'peapods' were actually narrow strips of green crepe paper didn't matter. They were getting the message; this was acting. It didn't have to be real. What mattered was that you could make it look real. Miss MacAndrew, arms folded across her bosom and tapping her teeth thoughtfully with a pencil, turned to the room.

"What do you think, class? Is he doing it right?"

"No bad, Miss!"

"Miss, 'e needs somethin' tae put the peas in!"

"Of course!" replied Miss MacAndrew. "Irene, go to the class cupboard and get out one of those wicker baskets."

They'd been doing basketwork in the craft class and some of the finished articles were stored in the cupboard. Irene did as she was told, placed the basket in front of Peter, and went back to her desk.

"Thank you, Irene."

"Miss, Miss, 'e should turn more toward us! We cannae see 'is face!"

"Ah, yes, good point, Thomas. Peter, can you turn a bit more this way? And do look up! We want to see your handsome face!"

Peter blushed even more and did as he was told.

"Good, OK, let's try again."

Peter produced his best effort of shelling the peas into the basket.

"Very good, Peter, you can go back to your desk now."

Peter dropped the green crepe into the basket, scuttled back to his desk, and with a sigh of relief became James again. He hated having to do things in front of other people, especially when the people were his classmates. But he didn't mind doing it for his new Form Four teacher. In fact, he'd do just about anything for Miss MacAndrew. Since his emancipation from Miss Boyle's purgatory and his translation to a pupil in the blessed custody of Miss MacAndrew, the classroom had mutated into an unfamiliarly welcoming place. Undoubtedly, under Miss Boyle's domination at Bonnybrig Primary, his education had progressed. But he'd paid a high price. Now, here he was with Miss MacAndrew at Fox Crag. Not only had the pace of his learning picked up; the price he had to pay was also minimal, if anything at all. No longer was he down at the bottom of a dark well. Kind hands had hauled him up and now he was sitting blinking in the sunlight. James thought about his two previous teachers. They were so different. However, if it had been possible to merge ninety per cent of Miss Douglas with ten per cent of Miss Boyle, the result might have been Miss MacAndrew.

She was trim and attractive, of medium height, and in her mid-forties. Her naturally blonde hair was impeccably coiffured. Her skin had a translucent quality, her complexion the tone of fine ivory. In her day she'd undoubtedly been a beauty, and she retained a lingering charm that still turned men's heads. Her female colleagues tended to dress down for the rigours of the Scottish working-class teaching environment, where snotters, grubby fingers and even occasional head lice were the order of the day. Not Miss MacAndrew.

On this particular day in early summer, 1955, she wore a black silk blouse with pointed collar, subtle, high V-neck, three-quarter sleeves, and buttons down the front. She'd matched the blouse with a high-waisted, black and white check gingham swing skirt that came down below the knee and had pockets as a handy addition. The black ballerina, round-toed leather flats were practical for the classroom. Her necklace of natural Polynesian pearls matched her pearl earrings. On her left wrist she wore a slim, platinum Cartier watch, and on her right, an Art Deco bracelet of rubies and diamonds set in white gold that she'd inherited from her mother. Miss MacAndrew was a picture of ageing elegance.

Earlier that year, Miss MacAndrew had realised she'd served two decades at Fox Crag Primary School. However, she kept the fact to herself. Although she remained the most respected member of the school staff, there was no recognition of her service and no celebration. As a novice teacher in her mid-twenties, she'd been a founding member of the school when it had opened its doors to pupils in 1935. She'd gone into teaching with the support of her upper-class parents at a time when it was still fashionable for girls of her station to go into teaching as a career. Her father had been a bank manager and then a city councillor for the Unionist Party while retaining a directorship at the bank. At one time he was mooted as a future Lord Provost. Her mother had been a leading light in social circles in Edinburgh.

With her parents now both deceased, Miss MacAndrew lived by herself in the family townhouse in Heriot Row. A picture of Georgian elegance, her home was stocked with antiques, Meissen porcelain and collectible works of art. Her parents had left a sizeable fortune to her and her married sister. Her half of that fortune, shrewdly invested, provided a generous income over and above her meagre teacher's salary. She employed a part-time housekeeper, Mrs Cunningham, and Angus, an occasional chauffeur, who drove her to and from Fox Crag School every morning and afternoon during term-time. If anyone wanted to know towards the end of the day if Miss MacAndrew was still on the school grounds, they only had to glance into the school car park where, at a time when few in Fox Crag could afford even the most modest motor vehicle, her gleaming Bentley might be seen, discreetly waiting.

And yet, Miss MacAndrew continued to teach. She didn't have to. She could easily have survived on her private income. But she was of a special breed, for she regarded teaching as more than just a job. At a time when the perspective was beginning to be outdated, she was among the few who still regarded teaching as a vocation. Despite the frustrations, despite the upsets, despite the daily challenges of a class of unpredictable working-class bairns, she still genuinely enjoyed what she did. It wasn't merely a question of belief. She *knew* that she had the power to change the lives of some of her charges. And that was thoroughly satisfying. Perhaps the knowledge that she could walk away at any time was a factor in her equanimity.

Miss MacAndrew was also exceptional in her attitude towards corporal punishment. At a time when it was widely used to enforce discipline in schools, Miss MacAndrew had never used it. Not once. She didn't need to. Oddly, in that respect, she resembled Miss Boyle. But it was for an entirely different reason. It was Miss MacAndrew's combination of bright positivity, kindness and encouragement, together with quiet but steely firmness, that was somehow able to achieve a level of discipline and application in the classroom that no other teacher could. Her natural beauty and ladylike demeanour undoubtedly also played a role. Most of her pupils respected her. Some of them loved her. Even the toughest laddies from the back row would buckle under her implacable stare. Her colleagues envied her. Her reputation for keeping discipline without recourse to the rod was well known. How did she do it? How could they be like her? They didn't know.

It had to be admitted, though, that Miss MacAndrew's approach didn't work *all* the time. In almost every class there was one disruptor. Miss MacAndrew had to deal with these case by case. Usually, with effort, she could work out an acceptable outcome. In her present Primary Four, there was one such pupil. His name was Andrew Peterson. Andrew was nine, normally too old for this class. Miss MacAndrew had never enquired into the reason why Andrew's educational progress had been retarded in this way, but the fact was that he was one year older than most of his classmates and almost two years older than the youngest in the class. Perhaps as a consequence, he'd developed into the class bully and troublemaker. He was always getting into fights in the playground and more than once turned up proudly displaying a keeker. Miss MacAndrew had tried her usual gambits in such cases, but they hadn't worked. Stronger medicine was called for. One day at the end of class, she called Andrew over as the room was emptying. When they were alone she proffered a chair. Mystified, Andrew sat down warily, holding his army surplus haversack to his chest. Teachers never asked pupils to sit on chairs, well, hardly ever. Miss MacAndrew settled down and spoke in her gentle way.

"Andrew, what am I going to do with you?"

At once, Andrew caught on. *Here it comes. The usual 'talk'.*

"You're naughty. You disrupt the class. You don't learn your lessons. Isn't that true?"

Andrew just looked at her defiantly.

"Well, isn't it?"

"Yes, Miss," he managed to mumble, but he remained sullen.

"Well, Andrew, there's only one thing left."

His obstinate expression was immediately tinged with curiosity.

Miss MacAndrew began to play her hand.

"I must talk to your father."

Andrew started. She'd got his attention, but there was truculent disbelief on his face.

Miss MacAndrew placed her Queen on the table.

"Your father is Sergeant Malcolm Peterson of the City of Edinburgh Police, is he not?"

Andrew gulped, incredulous at her knowledge.

"Your father and I go a long way back."

It was true. Malcolm had been a twelve-year-old in Miss MacAndrew's very first class at Fox Crag Primary in 1935 when, for a few brief years, she'd taught Primary Seven. As with most of her pupils, she'd inspired a level of devotion in him that had stood the test of time. He was one of several former pupils who, to Miss MacAndrew's delight, dropped by Fox Crag every few years to update her on their progress. Now a brawny young police sergeant, he had a promising future with the City's police force.

Miss MacAndrew played her King.

"He is stationed at Queen Charlotte Street in Leith is he not?"

Andrew nodded again, consternation written all over his face.

Miss MacAndrew played her Ace.

"All I have to do is go down to the school office, pick up the phone and call him. The number is 2890, is it not?"

By now Andrew was in full panic mode. Miss MacAndrew revealed her entire hand.

"I will invite him to a meeting with myself and Mrs Moncrieff to discuss your behaviour. Here at the school. Is that what you want?"

It was a full house. Andrew was a busted flush. He caved. His eyes started to smart and a single tear trickled down his left cheek. He tried to wipe it away with the cuff of his jersey. Miss MacAndrew was touched. She could never recall ever having made one of her pupils cry before. Especially not a bully.

"Well, is it?" she insisted.

"No," Andrew muttered, his chin pressed down into his chest.

"No, what, Andrew?"

"No, Miss MacAndrew."

"Do we understand each other?"

"Yes, Miss MacAndrew."

"All right, you can go."

And with that, Andrew rose from the chair and scurried out of the room without looking back. Miss MacAndrew never had any trouble with him again, but she knew in her heart that it wouldn't last and that Andrew's next teacher would have his hands full.

Colleagues sometimes wondered, too, why Miss MacAndrew was still a 'miss' in her mid-forties. She was attractive, beautiful even, for her age. She must have been eminently eligible. Why had she never married? No one outside her close circle of friends knew the truth. In her late twenties, she'd become engaged to the love of her life, Major Hector Munro of the King's Own Scottish Borderers. They'd planned to marry in mid-June 1940. Then The War intervened. By May 1940 the British Expeditionary Force was in trouble in France. By June 4th it was all over, as the last of the BEF were evacuated from Dunkirk. However, a second British expeditionary force was landed in France four days *after* Dunkirk on June 8th. The ill-conceived plan was to stop the German invasion south of the Seine. Included in this new BEF was Hector's 157 Brigade. Of course, the whole affair was a fiasco. Advancing against streams of refugees and with little assistance from the French who were already broken, the brigade found itself virtually surrounded by a well-equipped, mechanised German army. Thankfully, the Jocks were evacuated in time. But Hector wasn't among them. He was listed as 'missing in action'. Devastated, Miss MacAndrew never married. A relationship with any other man was unthinkable. She resolved to stay single and to devote herself to her pupils. And that's what she did.

A re-acquaintance

The question continued to gnaw at Janet. Where did she know the name MacAndrew? She prided herself on her good memory. Leith was a small community and she was always bumping into people she knew from her past. She enjoyed going up to a stranger in the street and confronting them with a confident stare. "I know you!" she'd say, conferring gravity on the occasion with Proper Speak. Then she'd give chapter and verse. And enjoy it.

She startled one of her victims on a tram by addressing her by name, reminding her of her address twenty years before, what her father's job was, where she'd sat in class, and even – unbelievably – the date of her birthday. No surprise then, that this time her inability to place a name was frustrating her. Who was Miss MacAndrew?

The answer came out of the blue one day when Janet came to pick James up at school. She didn't usually do this, now that he'd just turned eight. But it was his first day back after an illness and she wanted to make sure he was all right. As she stood at the school gates, she saw a posh car in the staff car park with a driver in a chauffeur's uniform. Definitely not an everyday sight in a suburb like Fox Crag. When had she seen a car like that before? And a chauffeur? At last, her memory clicked into gear and transported her back over 20 years. She smiled broadly to herself. When James appeared among the outpouring of pupils at 3.30, she said, "Son, just wait here, eh? Ah'll be back in ten minutes." Janet wasn't one to let an opportunity slip. She walked into the school, stopped by the office, got directions and climbed the stairs.

Miss MacAndrew was tidying up in the Primary Four classroom at the end of another day. There was a knock at the classroom door. Thinking it was a pupil who'd forgotten something, she turned and called, "Come on in!" The door opened and an attractive woman with wavy brown hair stood there smiling. She looked to be in her early thirties. She had on a flowery summer flare skirt with pleats, a short blue jacket, a loose yellow scarf, and sandals. One of the mothers perhaps?

"Yes, can I help you?" Miss MacAndrew enquired politely, taking a step towards her. The person entered the room, still smiling.

"Miss MacAndrew!"

"Yes?" said Miss MacAndrew, wondering what this was about.

"Don't you recognise me?" Janet was in Proper Speak mode.

Miss MacAndrew took a few more steps towards her. She looked into the stranger's face, puzzled. Then her face lit up in recognition.

"Oh, my goodness me!" she exclaimed. "Janet Melrose! Is it you?"

"Yes, Miss MacAndrew, it's me!" said Janet with more than a hint of self-satisfaction. Her memory *was* still as good as ever. Yes, it *was* her Miss MacAndrew, twenty-odd years older, but just as beautiful. Miss MacAndrew put out her hand but they both needed more than a handshake. They hugged and patted each other gently on the shoulders.

"Oh, my goodness! Oh, my goodness!" Miss MacAndrew could hardly contain herself. "Janet Melrose! After all this time! Come and sit down my dear. Do! How are you?" Fighting back tears, she sat and gazed closely at Janet, trying to imbibe every feature of her face.

It had been in the early nineteen-thirties. Miss MacAndrew's father had been something of a philanthropist. While life in the New Town might have been more than comfortable, in the rest of Edinburgh there was widespread poverty due to the Great Depression. Her father had helped organise food distribution to the poor and he'd insisted that his two daughters also become involved; it was important that they understood how privileged they were.

And so, at around 20 years of age, Miss MacAndrew was confronted with extreme poverty for the first time. As a volunteer, she'd begun to notice an eleven-year-old girl who was a regular at the relief centre. The girl was gawky, had brutally bobbed straight brown hair and an expression that was too adult for a girl of her years. She always wore the same outfit: a worn, grey, polo-necked jersey a couple of sizes too big for her, a navy skirt that was too short, thick woollen socks, and a pair of tackety boots. Sometimes, a younger sister with red hair accompanied her. She was similarly dressed and was about eight. Miss MacAndrew learned that the girl's name was Janet Melrose and that she was collecting food on behalf of her numerous siblings. Her father was one of the many unemployed. She and her eight brothers and sisters lived with their parents in a room and kitchen in Albert Street.

Janet interested Miss MacAndrew. In material terms she possessed nothing. But she was street-smart, resilient and resourceful. She'd learnt to look after herself and her younger brothers and sisters. Miss MacAndrew was impressed by the way she organised, disciplined and protected them. She seemed more like a mother than a sister. Their acquaintance had a brief flowering. Miss MacAndrew racked her brains for other ways she could help Janet and her family. So she spoke to Councillor MacAndrew, who managed to arrange a job for Janet's father with the City Parks Department. However, when the Depression eventually wound down, the distribution centres and soup kitchens were closed and the volunteers returned to a more normal life. Miss MacAndrew had tried to stay in touch with Janet but when the Melroses moved away from Albert Street, the connection was lost. Miss MacAndrew had sometimes wondered what had happened to Janet Melrose. And now, here she was, sitting in her classroom. They reminisced about The War. Then Janet played her trump card.

"Miss MacAndrew, there's still somethin' that you don't know. My son's in your class!"

"What? Who?"

"James Swanston. Swanston's my married name."

"James? You know, I always thought he reminded me of someone. He's a lovely boy. A bit shy, but he works hard."

Then Janet looked at her watch. Proper Speak slipped.

"Oh, crivvens, Ah forgot aboot James! 'E's waitin' outside!"

They made their farewells, promised to stay in touch this time, and Janet hurried off. *Well, well,* thought Miss MacAndrew as she leaned back into the leather of the back seat of the Bentley. Janet Melrose! After all this time! She was delighted that Janet had managed to drag herself out of poverty. Of course, being Miss MacAndrew, she was far too unassuming to assign any importance to the part *she* had played in Janet's good fortune. Janet had found a good husband and had been able to start a family. *Start a family.* The merest pang of regret gripped her heart, as it always did when she thought of the family *she* would never have. Then it left her just as quickly, as it usually did. Never mind. She was helping to bring up Janet's son. And in that thought, she discovered her private gratification. She leant forward and tapped on the glass panel, which opened as if by magic. Keeping his eyes firmly on the road, her chauffeur gave her the attention of his left ear.

"Angus, would you stop by Jenners? I promised Mrs Cunningham I'd pick up her weekly order and some venison pâté for tea."

Louise

The rapid clicking of lawnmower blades ceased as James completed the last strip of back green grass. He stopped and took a breath.

He'd learnt that pushing a lawnmower around the lawns of Number 68 wasn't an easy task for a nine-year-old. It had been assigned to him as soon as his parents thought he was big enough to handle it. Not that he minded. It gave him a sense of proprietorship. Both the front lawn and the back green were his dominions. He decided how and when they'd be attended to. The most pressure he got to do the job was when Ian, looking casually out of the window, would opine, "Mmm, the grass is gettin' a bit long, isn't it, Jock?" He always called James *Jock*. No one else did, not even Janet. James never asked him why he called him that, but naturally wondered about it. One day he'd asked his mother.

"Well, son," she'd said, "we were goin' tae call ye John after yer grandfather on yer father's side, ye ken. But then yer dad discovered 'e had a cousin wi' a son called John. We didnae think it was a good idea tae have two John Swanstons in Leith, particularly in the same family. So we had ye baptised James, after yer Uncle Jimmy. Ah suppose yer Dad calls ye Jock – that's the same as John, ye ken – because maybe ye remind him o' *his* dad. By the way, if ye'd been a lassie, we were goin' tae call ye Anne!"

Red-faced, but suitably enlightened, James had wandered off to digest this new piece of information. Having two names made him feel special. *Jock* was his own connection with his father – and the grandfather he'd never known. Anyway, that was the signal, and within a day or two Jock would get the job done. James emptied the clippings out of the catcher onto the compost heap, opened the door of the little corrugated iron shed and pushed the lawnmower inside. He'd often wondered who'd put the shed there. It was only about four feet across, seven feet long and five feet high, with a rounded top where the curved metal sheets were bolted together. It had occurred to him that it might have been someone's wartime attempt at an Anderson Shelter because that's exactly what it looked like. He'd seen photos of them in picture books about The War. But it was entirely above ground, not sunk in as it should have been. Maybe they just couldn't be bothered. But it was certainly just big enough for a family to shelter in. You'd have thought Chesser Drive was the last place the Luftwaffe would have been interested in. Wrong. Several Luftwaffe bombs had, in fact, hit the housing scheme right next to Fox Crag School in 1942, not a mile from where James was standing, demolishing buildings and killing several residents. The sudden thought prompted James to look up at the sky. No

Luftwaffe today, thank goodness. Just lots of blue sky between brisk clouds scudding over solo from the Forth.

He was interrupted in his thoughts by footsteps on the path and someone clearing his throat. He turned round. There stood Monsieur Renoir. He was wearing his flat cap, a shirt stained down the front, a shapeless cardigan, baggy trousers, and had carpet slippers on his feet. As usual, he looked a bit doddery. He was carrying something with both hands.

"Ah, James, I thought it was you. It is nice that you mow the lawn for us, n'est ce pas?"

James smiled and said clumsily, "Bonjour, Monsieur." He blushed. He hoped he was saying it right. He'd learned it from Wee Effie who, at the age of 12 had already started French at secondary school and was becoming the family expert in all things French.

"Ah, tres bon, tu parles bien le français! Your French is very good!"

James blushed again and wished he could have said more.

"I teach you a few phrases, no?"

James nodded, embarrassed at an adult taking such interest in him.

"Maybe later but that is not why I am here."

He held out his hands. James saw four scaly legs, each with a set of claws, slowly and deliberately sawing at the air.

"Here, take it!"

James trustingly put out his hands, palms upward. Monsieur Renoir carefully made his delivery. The four sets of claws found James's skin but they didn't hurt.

"Do you know what it is?" asked Monsieur Renoir.

"A tortoise!" exclaimed James.

"She is for you if you want," he offered. "Yes, I think she is a girl."

"Ah'll have tae ask mah mum, but it should be OK!"

James was beside himself. He'd never held a live wild animal before.

"I have her from a friend who had to go into a home," Monsieur Renoir explained. "No pets allowed, so I offered to find a new owner."

"Thank you," said James lamely. "How d'ye say that in French?"

Monsieur Renoir smiled broadly. "Merci – merci beaucoup."

James tried to say it but it didn't come out right. Monsieur Renoir repeated it twice and after several tries, James managed to utter a fair imitation of the strange words.

"Formidable! Very good – I can see you are going to be a good French speaker!"

"Merci beaucoup!" repeated James, warming to the sound of the words.

"De rien! Alors, what are you going to call her?"

James thought for a moment.

"How about Louise? Isn't that a French girl's name?

A strange expression came over Monsieur Renoir's face.

"Louise... Aye, that sounds perfect!" James cupped the tortoise's under shell in his left hand, held her up and tickled her under her leathery chin with his right index finger. The grotesque head moved in response and the beady brown eyes seemed to be trying to meet his in some kind of weird reptilian greeting.

"Hello, Louise! Hello, Louise! Aren't ye a wee beauty!"

Lost in the unexpected gift, he fussed with the creature, pointlessly stroking her bumpy shell and trying to catch her eyes. Then something made him look up at Monsieur Renoir. He stood there, distraught. There were tears in his eyes and a pained expression on his face. James was well aware of their neighbour's history, health and state of mind. Janet had long ago briefed the family to avert any problems. They had a duty to look after him, she stressed. Since she didn't get on with her own father and since Ian's father had died when he was fifteen, she instinctively felt they had a responsibility for this elderly soul. So, James wasn't overly shocked. He'd seen Monsieur Renoir in an emotional state before, but he wondered what had caused it this time. He said nothing but looked at Monsieur Renoir anxiously. Monsieur Renoir took a large, grubby handkerchief that had once been white out of his trouser pocket, removed his glasses and dabbed his eyes. Then he lifted his cap, wiped his bald head and forehead, replaced his cap, blew his nose noisily and stuffed the handkerchief back into his pocket. He looked at James as if weighing up whether it was worth explaining his outburst to a nine-year-old boy. He decided that it was. As he spoke, his voice cracked.

"Louise was the name of my eldest daughter," he said. "She was a beauty, too." He choked and turned away, shaking his head.

James stood helplessly. *Was it his fault*? he wondered.

"Pardon, pardon, you should not see this."

Then, recovering himself, Monsieur Renoir turned back to James and spoke sternly, stressing his message by pointing his finger skywards in a Gallic manner.

"Look after her. There's plenty of grass here for her, but she would like a lettuce leaf every other day. Make sure she has water and get her a little box. She might wander, so you will have to watch her carefully. When winter comes, I will tell you what to do, OK?"

"OK," repeated James, staring at him, wide-eyed. As Monsieur Renoir shambled off round the corner of the building, James grasped the significance of his burden. Suddenly it wasn't just a tortoise he was cradling. It was Louise.

4 Fu' snug and bien

A gash an' faithfu' tyke

Louise had become a fixture in the Swanston household. She had her own little box in the cold frame behind the building. When the cover was off, James could look out of the kitchen window to check on her. He took her for walks and would lie flat, observing her determined, slow-motion forays through the grass forests of Number 68. Sometimes he caught Monsieur Renoir standing by his bedroom window curtain, observing them with a contented look on his face. Owning a pet had brought a new dimension into James's life. Now he was responsible for a living creature, as Janet never tired of reminding him. It was strange knowing that this being depended on him for everything. In Brecon Street, there had never been any pets that James was aware of, outside of the occasional caged budgerigar. No dogs, no cats, and certainly no tortoises. The War was partly to blame, for officialdom had frowned on wasting rationed food on pets. Offenders were prosecuted and there was mass euthanasia of pets as a result. In the decade or so since, pet ownership had struggled to reach pre-war levels. Nor did it enter the heads of those residents tasked with feeding their families to take on the extra burden of pets, particularly in the overcrowded tenements of a drab urban environment. But Chesser Drive was a different story. Here, there was a degree of affluence. Here there was space. Here there was grass. Here, as James quickly realised, there were dogs aplenty.

Number 68 had its own special dog. His name was Glen. He was definitely a Scottish dog, the archetypical towsy tyke. He had a thick, long, curly, salt and pepper coat, a round head, what appeared to be a permanent smile on his face, the waggiest tail you could imagine, and a gentle demeanour. He was of no particular breed but looked like an outsize Greyfriars Bobby on stilts. He belonged to the Frasers upstairs, or more accurately, they belonged to him, for Glen ruled the roost in every possible way. He demanded a daily meal of quality dog food. He demanded affection. He demanded a nice collar and lead. More importantly, he demanded a long walk every day, an obligation the busy Fraser family might have taken more seriously, for they never seemed to have time for this doggie essential. Unsurprisingly, given his new interest in pets, James soon made friends with Glen, hoping to have a dog like him one day. It was on an unusually warm morning in late July, with a whole blessed day of summer freedom stretching out in front of them, that Billy Chalmers made his fateful suggestion.

"Let's go tae Seafield."

From about the age of seven, the bairns of Fox Crag, just like their counterparts in Brecon Street, had discovered that they had a Licence to Roam, especially the laddies. Their parents were always busy somewhere with something or other: at work, doing the laundry, visiting family, doing the weekly shop at the Provie, up the town, at the doctor's, queuing in offices for this or that piece of paper, waiting on trams. Why should they worry? The city was a relatively safe place, especially when the bairns went off in a group. Often, the bairns didn't even bother to let their parents know where they were going. Often, *they* didn't know themselves where they were going. It didn't matter. As long as they were home by teatime and didn't get into any serious mischief, they could do what they liked. And they did. So when Billy suggested a jaunt to Seafield, James was immediately on board. His parents wouldn't be home till evening. He was locked out of Number 68. Wee Effie had the latchkey and she'd disappeared with the street lassies. But given his newfound interest in pets, he did suggest one addendum to the programme:

"Let's take Glen wi' us."

He was sure Mrs Fraser wouldn't mind. And he was right, for when they knocked on the Frasers' door and asked if they could take Glen for a walk, not only did Mrs Fraser not mind, she was delighted. If only more laddies would offer to walk their dog! But she had one proviso.

"Now listen," she cautioned, "Glen has a brand-new lead and collar. Ah dinnae want them gettin' clarty. An' forbye, 'e's just had a bath so dinnae let 'im roll in any muck."

With that, trusting Mrs Fraser handed over a freshly scrubbed Glen. His coat was fluffy and spotless, he sported a shiny, new, chrome studded leather collar with matching lead that must have cost a fair bit, and he smiled broadly, as if fully aware of how fabulous he looked. His doggy radar having already detected a walk in prospect, his tail was wagging enthusiastically. They were to make sure they were back by dinnertime, one o'clock at the latest. Mrs Fraser would have been wise to enquire into the experience of the two laddies in doggy matters and particularly in dog walking. For the fact was, they had none. She would also have been wise to enquire as to their destination. For, as she was to discover, handing over her dear pet into the care of two young novices of the canine arts was a serious mistake. But James and Billy were elated. They'd seen people walking their dogs on leads around the neighbourhood. Now they had one to walk too. And not just any dog. This wasn't a piddling dachshund, poodle or chihuahua. This was a real dog. A Scottish dog. A laddie's dog! And not just for a quick turn around the block. They were off on an expedition all the way to Seafield - and back, of course. But they hadn't told Mrs Fraser that.

They took turns with the lead. Glen was easy to walk. All he wanted to do at first was sniff then cock his leg, so it was a slow start through the Crescent where privet hedges enclosed fancy private bungalows. As they walked, they noticed an attractive lassie of about sixteen approaching. She was tall and slim. Her thick, wavy, auburn hair spilled loose over her shoulders. She wore a thin, high-necked, powder blue jersey over a white blouse. The tapering ends of her collar pointed down to a silver, heart-shaped locket that hung on a chain around her neck. Her baggy, faded pink jeans were rolled up to just below her knees, leaving her lower legs bare. She wore white ankle socks and red and white sneakers. The straw-coloured, long-handled, raffia bag that swung from her right hand was decorated with four large, stylised flower heads of purple, pink, turquoise and yellow, inside a leafy border.

"Hiya, Helen!" sang out Billy brightly, as they stepped off the pavement into the gutter to let her pass. But sixteen-year-old girls never spoke to nine-or-ten-year-old boys. Bonny Helen, without breaking step, merely produced a pained, artificial smile in response. They let her walk on a bit. Then as one, they turned round, and admired her retreating form, pert, aloof, a vision of beauty, defiantly swinging her raffia bag.

Meanwhile, Glen had discovered a fresh dog toallie and was submitting it to a sniffing extravaganza. Then, scenting freshly mown grass, he gave a jerk on the lead and they were off again and onto the golf course. The two adventurers cut diagonally across the second fairway. It was midweek, so there were few golfers around, but those who were playing shouted at them; dogs were banned from the course. But the pals stuck to their route, oblivious of the mayhem they were causing. Glen was on a lead, so what was the problem? At least they knew to skirt the greens and managed to exit the other side of the course without major strife. Crossing the main road, dodging the traffic, and struggling to keep hold of Glen, they walked directly onto the sea wall.

Instantly, their world opened out as strong draughts of cool air brought the familiar tang of salt water and seaweed to their nostrils. Choppy blue-green seas washed around Inchkeith and surged down the Firth of Forth. The Fife shore trended away hazily to the northeast. To the west, they could just make out the top girders of the Forth Bridge above the grey smudge of Leith Docks. Nearer, the Penny Bap emerged from the sands. To the east, across the bay, tiny but unmistakable, the pyramid of Berwick Law stood sentinel over the junction of the Firth and the open ocean. All three stood in silent contemplation, the humans open-mouthed, Glen, tongue lolling, enjoying a good pant after his exertions. Then Billy spoke for all.

"That's mair liker it!" he said. Then he pointed to the stone steps down to the foreshore. "Last one doon's a hairy kipper!" he announced, and disappeared at breakneck speed.

James followed, fighting to keep his footing on the slippery surface as Glen threatened to pull him over the steep incline. Then, reaching the bottom with a single leap, the dog frantically set to casting about, nose to the sand. He'd landed in a supermarket of smells and he was ecstatic.

"Let 'im off the lead, then!" shouted Billy as he trudged ahead through deep, dry sand.

"Naw, Ah'm feared 'e might run away," replied James and kept a tight hold of his charge. They wandered on, blissfully watching the tide go out and spotting ships in the sea lanes. It was when they came round an angle of the sea wall that the stench hit them. They squinted and tried to make out what it was. Ahead of them, covering the sand was a stinking brown glaur.

"What the fuck is it?" asked Billy, deeming that the situation warranted profanity. They stood, hesitating, scratching their heads, turning up their noses. But Glen, with a Canine Master of Science in Sniffology, was fast losing patience with the deficiencies of his human companions. Taking matters into his own hands – or paws – he suddenly ripped the lead from James's feeble grasp. With one joyous bound, he leapt into the deepest part of the glaur and plowtered around, spraying it up around him. Then, not content with that, and having quickly forgotten his recent bath, he turned over on his back and rolled royally in it, his four legs waggling in the air. In a heartbeat, Glen's fur went from pristine to putrid. Struggling to believe the evidence of their eyes and noses, the laddies suddenly twigged at the same time. As usual, it was Billy who was first with the words.

"Jesus!" he exclaimed. "It's toallies!"

And indeed, toallies it was. Acres and acres of them, raw, untreated human excrement that had been pumped out here at Seafield's Corporation outflow, probably overnight, and straight into the Firth of Forth. If the tide had been in, they wouldn't have known. But the tide was ebbing and the sewage had settled a half a foot deep in places all over the sands. The realisation left them speechless. Only one thing was worse than the smell: the fact that Glen was in the middle of it and didn't look as if he was coming back soon. As the sea slowly receded, more of the stuff was being revealed and Glen, his brand-new lead trailing beside him, was playfully trotting through it, heading for Fife, apparently.

They looked at each other, horror written all over their faces. What had Mrs Fraser said? They didn't have to struggle hard to recall her words. There was something with *clarty* in it and it ended with *muck*. How on earth were they going to get out of this? They tried calling Glen back, shouting themselves hoarse as his shaggy shape dwindled in the distance, but they might as well have been on another planet. He didn't hear over the sound of the waves, or pretended not to. They steeled themselves to step onto the field of toallies and follow him but neither could bring themselves to do it. Then, out on the verge of the ebb, they could see Glen make a right turn and wander along, prancing, frolicking and thoroughly enjoying himself where the toallies met the sea. Who needed humans to have a bit of fun? Frantically, they trotted on a parallel course along the foreshore, struggling through the deep sand, hoping desperately that somewhere up ahead the toallies would stop.

And inevitably they did. Puggled after their exertions, the pals were able to walk out onto clean, firm sand that was still wet from the receding tide. Now they could get much closer to the runaway. After a few calls and whistles, he came lolloping up. James managed to grab his lead, shuddering as his hand came into contact with the shite-encrusted leather. While Glen stood smiling, as if inviting compliments for his decisive action, James and Billy stood one on either side of him, surveying the damage. Unsurprisingly, Glen's once pristine grey and white coat was no longer pristine. It was now a melange of shades of cackie brown from his nose to the tip of his tail and he stank like fifty blocked toilets. However, the two inexperienced dog walkers, ignorant of canine behaviour as they were, were utterly unprepared for what happened next. For Glen did what all dogs do when their coat has become saturated; he shook himself, hard, endlessly, and with admirable efficiency. In doing so, he sprayed both laddies from head to toe with a film of brown excrement. Billy stepped back in disgust but James, still holding onto the manky lead, got the worst of it. They might just as well have jumped into the toallies with that damned dog! They coughed and spluttered, trying to wipe the stuff out of their eyes, their ears, their hair. Could things get any worse?

Cursing, they threw off their shoes and socks and waded a couple of feet into the sea where ebbing waves were languidly licking at the sand. They hopped around in the water, sluicing down their legs, James struggling to do it with one hand while the other clutched Glen's lead. They tried to wash their faces and necks but only succeeded in soaking their clothes and getting salt in their eyes and mouths. Then they tried to clean Glen up. Realising they'd have to let him go, they stood at the water's edge and threw everything they could find, chuckie stanes, skiffers, driftwood, buckies, into the sea to make him want to fetch and jump into the deeper water. But, smart dog that he was, he declined to immerse himself fully in the frigid waters of the Forth. Short of getting right in with him, there was nothing more they could do about his coat. They took off his collar and rinsed it together with the lead. By now, what had been a pristine collaboration of chrome and leather was a miserable reflection of its former self. Prolonged contact with human excrement and salt water was, apparently, not good for either. They refitted the collar around Glen's neck and clipped on the lead while he stood smiling gratefully and wagging his sodden, foul-smelling tail. Then they stood silent, looking at each other as seagulls tentatively landed around them then took off abruptly as soon as Glen showed interest.

"It was your idea tae bring the wee bugger!" said Billy truculently.

James didn't have an answer. It was true. The day was ruined and it was all his fault.

"What're we gonnae dae?" he asked.

Billy, older and therefore wiser, considered how to get them out of the predicament. Then, referring to the excrement that still clung to all three of them despite their collective ablutions in salt water, he explained his logic.

"It's wet. An' it stinks. So this is what we dae. We stay oot as long as possible. That'll gie it time tae dry and no stink as much."

James, with his nine-year-old brain, immediately grasped the argument. Yes, that's what they'd do. And by the time they got back to Number 68, they'd be in the clear. By now it was after midday and they were overdue. Well, that was too bad. They'd have to make the best use of the afternoon to waste as much time as possible. As Stage One of their Plan, they'd walk on to Portobello along the beach. So, off they went, Billy in charge of Glen, determined that this time he was not going to escape his grasp. But they soon realised Glen was having problems. Novice dog nannies that they were, they failed to realise how much a dog needs to drink, especially on a hot day. And today was turning unusually hot. After his long walk, his exertions and his encounters with excrement and salt water, it wasn't surprising that Glen was dehydrated and panting frantically. It was a man walking his dog near them on the beach that drew their attention to his plight.

"Heh, lads, yer dug looks like 'e needs a drink!"

The pals were embarrassed. They hadn't known and they hadn't noticed.

"Well," said the man, "away wi' ye up to the esplanade yonder, and ye'll find a public fresh water tap," and he pointed the way for them.

Thanking their Good Samaritan, they hurried up and through the deep sand, up the steps onto the esplanade and, sure enough, there was the tap. James cupped his hand to catch the trickle of water. Glen drank and drank. While this was going on, something had caught Billy's eye and he drew James's attention to it. On their right, between the esplanade and the main highway, they couldn't help noticing a wasteland of derelict buildings, half-demolished walls and twisted metal girders. They looked at each other. There was no doubt about it. Once Glen had drunk his fill they'd have to explore. The ancient, rusty, sharp-topped eight-feet-high metal fence had plenty of gaps where the palings had been ripped out. They crawled through, ably assisted by an enthusiastic Glen tugging on the lead. They couldn't believe what they found.

They were in a weed-infested wilderness of wreckage from a former era. There were what appeared to have been buildings, maybe warehouses, the remains of something like a hotel, going by the white paint; also the outline of what appeared to be a racetrack. But everything lay in ruins. What looked like a stadium was collapsing onto the raceway and of the other buildings only sections of walls were left standing. Girders, areas of roofing, corrugated iron, huge chunks of reinforced concrete, rotting wooden piles, creosoted railway girders lay higgledy-piggledy in piles. So densely packed and intertwined was this material that in some places it was impossible to get through. What a place! Climbing up onto a remnant of a bare concrete pad they were able to get a better view. Intrigued, James remembered photos he'd seen of the London Blitz. He half expected to see a double-decker bus sticking out of an immense hole.

"It looks like it's been bombed!" he announced.

But, no, the Luftwaffe hadn't paid a visit. What they were surveying were the remains of The Marine Gardens, an ill-fated project from Edwardian times based on the delusion that Scottish Portobello could rival English Brighton or French Cannes. The drive to turn Portobello into a posh holiday resort had been going on for about a century before that and had included a pier that lasted only forty years before it rusted away. The pleasure gardens, aimed at the middle and upper classes and including a ballroom, a zoo, cinema, theatre and ornamental gardens, were just another half-baked idea that had foundered in the face of the vile Scottish climate, a turbulent economy, and two major global conflicts. What James and Billy had discovered was the aftermath, left to rot and now used as a dumping ground. Yet again, The War was casting its long shadow. This was not to say that Porty was unloved, for it did have its devotees among the working classes. Here the less well-off families of Edinburgh and Leith could have a day at the beach for what amounted to the cost of a tram ride from the central city or the foot of Leith Walk. Porty could never be a Cannes or even a Brighton, but it could be a Scottish mini-Blackpool, and that was good enough for them. As James and Billy were about to find out, it wasn't just the folks of Edinburgh that flocked to enjoy Porty's beach during the summer.

The three adventurers squeezed back through the palings, relieved to be on level ground again, and walked on east towards the centre of Portobello. Up ahead, the beach was starting to fill up. The esplanade was getting busier, too. The foot of Bath Street was where all the action seemed to be. Crowds of noisy holidaymakers, mums, dads, grannies and granddads, aunties and uncles and, of course, heaps of excitable bairns clustered around a solitary café mere yards from the sea wall. Its frontage was festooned with beach holiday paraphernalia; buckets, spades, sunhats, sunglasses, beach balls and games. An irresistible aroma of bacon frying wafted out through the double glass doors and onto the esplanade.

A blackboard fixed to the fascia announced in chalk: *Hot Pies and Bridies, Hot Water, Bacon Rolls, Hot Pea Specials, Tea Trays.* The queue was out of the shop and round the corner into Bath Street. People walked out munching pies and bridies, licking ice cream cones, carrying jugs of hot water or carefully balancing tin trays, each with china cups and saucers, a sugar bowl, a milk jug and a metal teapot. This place looked to be a goldmine – at least in summer. Next to the shop, an elderly man was taking money and doling out deckchairs for hire from a large stack, as two girls of about twelve or thirteen helped carry them down to the beach. James and Billy now found themselves having to shoulder their way through the throng, James struggling with an exuberant Glen, who was in his element at doggy level sniffing through a forest of rolled-up trousers, bare legs and smelly, sandaled feet. But something struck James as very odd. As they negotiated the hubbub, he found he could hardly understand a word these people were saying.

“Lukarrwa-aturr - izzatnorerr?” said one mother, pointing at the sea for her little boy in arms, while he replied, “Ma, kinahgoinrawa-aterinraweeboa-at?” pointing at a little light blue pleasure boat that was taking on passengers from a rickety wooden gangway.

“Izzatrakew? – Och, amnostaunininra-at!” a dismayed father exclaimed to his wife outside the café.

Up until now the two pals had managed to keep their unhygienic condition to themselves but now, in a crowd like this, it seemed it was no longer possible.

“Ohmagoad, izzatnoawfy? Whitsratsmeww?” exclaimed one woman as they squeezed past her. Her son, a tough-looking fellow of about 18, covering his mouth with one hand, prodded Billy in the chest with the other and asked, “Heh, pal, whauryabeen? Doonracluggie?” while James stared at him, mouth open in utter incomprehension. Not only had he never seen so many people crowded together in his life before; he was now in among them, stinking to high heaven and not understanding a word they said. He was stranded in a foreign country. Panicking, he looked at Billy anxiously and held on tight to Glen. But Billy was smiling broadly. He dragged James out of the crush to the sea wall and spoke loudly into his ear.

“D’ye no ken what’s goin’ on?” he asked triumphantly, knowing exactly what was going on. “They’re Glaswegians!”

“Glaswegians? What’s that when it’s at hame?”

“Someb’dy frae Glasgow, ye daftie! Glaswegians. They talk different frae us.”

“But they’re frae Scotland?”

“Of course they are. They’re just different.”

Billy’s specialist knowledge of Glaswegians, he explained, derived from visits to his auntie in Drumchapel. People from Scotland who spoke a different language? Here? Was there such a thing? In fact, there was, for it was the Tuesday of the third fortnight in July, the height of the Glasgow Trades, the principal holiday of the year for the working folk of that city. While they streamed ‘doon the watter’ to Rothesay in their thousands, many headed in the opposite direction. A family could easily travel from Glasgow Central straight through to Portobello with only one change at Waverley Station. From there, it was just a short walk to the promenade. Porty had plenty of cheap B&B accommodation. Yes, the beach was susceptible to the fickle Scottish summer weather, but it was still a beach. The ambitious Lido was a big attraction. A massive swim complex that used cooling seawater from the power station, the artificial waves were switched on for five minutes every hour. Then there was a mini-funfair with dodgems and a wooden helter-skelter, the Tower

Amusements and, of course, the Skylark, the little motor launch running pleasure trips off the beach. Not to mention the pubs, cafés and restaurants that, during this fortnight alone, did a roaring trade. This was what the two pals had unwittingly stumbled into. They wandered up Bath Street, pushing against yet another influx of Glaswegians streaming resolutely down from the station, then spotted De Marco's. The queue wasn't so bad here.

"Wait wi' the dug and Ah'll get us ice cream," offered Billy.

He'd come prepared with sixpence in his pocket and, ten minutes later, he reappeared, a cone in each hand with raspberry topping. They walked back down onto the sands, picking a spot in the sun out of range of the shade cast by the tenements lining the shore, sat down, licking their cones and feeding dollops of ice cream to Glen on the ends of their fingers. The beach was a hive of activity. James had never seen so many white bodies in his life before. Families sat in little groups of deckchairs, the mother in charge, the father shirtless with his trousers rolled up and a knotted handkerchief covering his bald spot. Their bairns were paddling in the waves, building sandcastles or riding the donkeys for hire. Youngsters were throwing around beach balls. Impromptu games of football had started up. The pale blue Skylark was taking on more passengers.

They lingered until it was getting on for late afternoon. Aware that they couldn't stay away from home forever, they reluctantly decided they'd have to head back. Walking straight up to the highway, they crossed quickly and made for the main golf course entrance. By now, the course was busier and they aroused the ire of several foursomes as golf balls whizzed past their heads. Stage Two of their plan had been to spend as much time at the Gunnie as possible. After poking around the abandoned bunkers for some time, they sat on a concrete gun emplacement and applied the sniffing test to themselves and Glen. Nodding to each other smugly, they agreed that the result was negative. Satisfied that they'd got rid of most of the evidence, they decided they could risk a return to Chesser Drive. By now they were really hungry. James had to admit he was getting a bit tired of having to hold onto Glen. He just wanted to get home and have his tea.

Despite their confidence over the result of the sniffing test, their mood darkened as the inevitable reckoning with Mrs Fraser drew ever nearer. It was a bedraggled trio that turned into Chesser Drive. Glen, scenting home, was pulling hard on the lead. And who was the first person they should see coming towards them on the same side of the street but Bonny Helen? She was returning from whatever she'd gone to do, still swinging her raffia bag. This time Billy wasn't so keen on a meeting but neither was Helen, evidently, for she'd got only within a few yards of them when she suddenly stopped.

"Oh mah goad!" she exclaimed. "Where have you's yins been? Swimmin' in shite?"

She quickly stepped off the pavement and, covering her mouth and nose with her free hand, bypassed them and hurried off shaking her head. It was at that moment that James, his fantasy shattered, mentally wrote off ever having a future with Helen. Nor, going by her reaction, was it looking good where Mrs Fraser was concerned. It was then that Billy showed his true colours. His hand thrust into the pockets of his shorts, he simply turned into Number 66, announced over his shoulder, "See ye the morn!" and disappeared inside. James hadn't realised Billy was such a feardie gowk. Suddenly he saw him in a different light. So that was that. He was on his own. With a sinking heart, he opened the wrought iron gate of Number 68. Glen, home at last, yanked frantically on the lead as James struggled to tiptoe up the stairs so as not to alert his parents. He gulped and knocked at the Frasers' door while Glen wagged his tail furiously. It opened. Mrs Fraser stood there for a second or two, a fleeting smile on her face, just managing to utter the words, "Ah thought ye were lost..." before she recoiled with an expression of disgust.

"In the name o' the wee man, what on earth is that awfy smell?!" was all she could gasp. And in that instant, it was finally clear to James that the Plan had been an abject failure. Worse was to come. Glen, eager to greet his mistress after a whole day away, jumped up, planted both paws on her shoulders and gave her face a hearty licking.

"Oh, mah God, get doon Glen, get doon!" she commanded, lifting the end of her pinny and rubbing it over her face. "What *is* that smell?" she again demanded to know. She bent down, sniffed at Glen, wrinkled her nose and then gasped again. "Crivvens, what's happened tae 'is collar an' lead?"

Before James could answer, Glen ripped the lead out of his hand and hurtled past her into the house. Muffled shouts of distress could be heard inside as he greeted the rest of the family. Mrs Fraser stepped out onto the landing, closing the door on the sneck.

"Now," she said, with the most severe expression, folding her arms demonstratively across her matronly bosom, "tell me what ye've been up tae, an' for heaven's sake, tell me what that awfy smell is."

James hung his head and told her everything. As the story unfolded, Mrs Fraser couldn't conceal her displeasure. She was clearly put out, but her annoyance was directed more at herself than James. By now, James was almost in tears and the commotion had aroused the building. Even hard-of-hearing Monsieur Renoir had appeared, wanting to know what was happening, but remained in the shelter of his doorway as soon as the stench hit him. Of course, Janet was up the stairs in a flash when she heard James's voice, demanding to know what was going on. As soon as she got within range and saw the state of his clothes, her face clouded. The news that her son was covered in toallies from the Seafield corporation outflow didn't go down well.

"Get doon they stairs!" she shouted, "and think yersel' lucky ye dinnae get a skelpin'!"

James skulked away, wiping tears from his cheeks, but Mrs Fraser held his mother back. She was by nature a kindly soul and was wise enough to realise that she had to take some of the blame for entrusting her Glen to James at his age.

"Listen, hen," she said, "dinnae punish the bairn. D'ye no think 'e's been punished enough?" And with a smile, she demonstratively held her nose. Janet burst out laughing and had to admit, ruefully, that yes, Mrs Fraser had a point. But she insisted on paying for a new collar and lead. It would come out of James's pocket money. Mrs Fraser thought for a moment.

"Ah've got a better idea," she said. "First, we need tae get that glaur oot o' Glen's coat right away. D'ye no think that's a job for yer laddie?"

Without hesitation, Janet turned and shouted down the stairwell.

"James! Get up here! Now!"

A little face appeared, peering anxiously upwards. James had been dithering in the entry, scared to let his dad see him in this state. He mounted the steps slowly, hanging his head, expecting another row.

"Ye're tae wash Glen. Now!" his mother said, turning to Mrs Fraser.

"Just wait there, son," Mrs Fraser said and disappeared inside the flat. They heard some talk inside and running water, then Mrs Fraser's son Malcolm appeared lugging a large zinc mopping bucket full of steaming soapy water in one hand and a large rectangular block of yellow laundry soap in the other. Mr Fraser, keen to expel the stink from their home, followed up behind with Glen, still wagging cheerfully on the notorious lead. Everyone trooped downstairs and round the back of the building. Malcolm handed the soap to James while Mr Fraser tied Glen's lead to the fence then unwound a hose that was plugged into an outside tap. He showed James how to operate it.

"Right," said Mr Fraser to no one in particular, "we'd better stand back." Then, to James, "There's a mug in the bucket. First, ye need tae scoop warm water over Glen, then work the soap intae 'is coat."

James thrust his hand in the soapy water, felt around until he found the tin mug, then scooped and poured water over Glen's back. Malcolm showed him how to work the soap into an area of coat and then how to rinse it off with the hose. Then he retired to the others and let James get on with it. Glen stood, impassive, enjoying the pleasant feeling of hot soapy water on his skin and only getting frisky when it was time for the cold, snapping at the stream. Janet turned to the Frasers.

"Aye," she said confidentially, as James toiled away, getting filthy wet all over again, "this was the right thing tae dae."

Mr Fraser, who had a penchant for The Bard smiled.

"*Oh wad some Pow'r the giftie gie us, To see oursels as others see us*!" he intoned.

"Ah'm no sure aboot poetry," said his wife, "but isn't this what they ca' poetic justice?"

They all laughed, except James. *Yes, he had done something wrong*, he thought grimly, having reached Glen's stinking tail, *and now he was paying for it.* But somehow, it made him feel better. When they were satisfied with his work, Mr Fraser spoke up.

"Right, son, ye can finish now. Ye need tae gie 'im one last hose doon aw' over." He paused. "Then ye ken what ye have tae dae, or ye should ken by now!"

James looked, open-mouthed, uncomprehending.

"Stand back!" shouted all three in a co-ordinated chorus of laughter.

James did as he was told. When Glen had been well soaked, he quickly switched off the nozzle and took several steps back. Glen shook himself. But this time, James was out of range. He looked round, smiling at his mother for the first time. After the dog washing was over, Mrs Fraser made a suggestion.

"How aboot if James cuts the grass on oor half of the green as well? Ah've noticed 'e does quite a good job o' it on your side. Maybe 'e could do it for..." She did a quick calculation. "...three months? By then, 'e'll have earned enough for a new collar and lead."

Janet, pleased with the neat solution, nodded in agreement. Ian, who had, by now, been confronted by the filthy, stinking apparition that had once been his son and had heard about the escapade, couldn't stop laughing, much to James's discomfort. He wasn't used to his dad laughing at him.

"Help mah Boab," Ian said, "for goodness sake get intae a bath. At once! And tell yer mother tae throw yer claes oot. An' yer shoes. They'll aw' have tae be burnt!"

After he'd had a bath and had been thoroughly disinfected, James was allowed into the kitchen to have beans on toast and scrambled eggs. He wolfed it down. Then, in his dressing-gown and slippers he went round the back of the house. Another mild Scottish summer evening and it was still light. He fetched Louise from her box and played with her on top of the coal bunker. What a day! First seeing Bonny Helen - he paused a moment to savour the memory. Then the toallie disaster. Ugh! Then exploring the wasteland. Then seeing - and hearing - Glaswegians. Then, the worst part, having to return Glen in his polluted state. He was lucky Mrs Fraser had been so forgiving. Finally, the humiliation of having to wash Glen while the others watched and made fun of him. He'd considered asking his mum and dad for a puppy for Christmas, but, if truth be told, a single day with Glen had been enough. He couldn't go through that again, at least not for the foreseeable future. He'd stick to Louise for now. Tortoises were far less trouble. They didn't make a habit of jumping into toallies. They didn't have to be washed with hot soapy water. And, when wet, they didn't shake themselves, either.

A game won in yer heid

Ian removed the half-smoked cigarette from his lips and threw it on the turf. He took a stance addressing the already teed Penfold and swung smoothly. With a sharp click, the driver hit the sweet spot. The golf ball sped about three hundred yards straight down the middle of the fairway. He retrieved his cigarette, returned his Forgan driver to his golf bag, and stepped back to watch Alistair take his shot.

"Remember, heid doon, eye on the ball, swing the hips."

Alistair teed his ball then stood back, took the shaft of the club in his left hand, then carefully laid his right over it, ensuring the right thumb crossed over the left. He swung and hit the ball as hard as he could. It rose, traced a perfect curve to the right, and disappeared in the rough. Alistair's face clouded.

"Damn!"

With an exasperated groan, he thumped the ground moodily with his driver, then rammed it back into his golf bag. Sheepishly, he looked over at Ian for the anticipated expert analysis.

"Ye're tryin' too hard, son. Just puttin' aw' yer power intae it disnae mean the ball'll go further. Ye're fa'in' back from the ball just before ye hit it and that causes yer slice."

Alistair nodded, trying to understand. Ian looked behind him.

"There's naebody behind us. Take another shot, an' this time, dinnae try sae hard."

Gratefully, Alistair retrieved his driver, teed another ball, addressed it, swung, and hit with markedly less effort than before. The ball took off and did a pretty good job of flying down to the right-hand edge of the fairway about fifty yards short of Ian's.

"What did Ah tell ye?" Ian said. "Much better, son."

Alistair glowed in the praise. He re-bagged his club, then wasted five minutes searching for the lost ball. Alistair had wanted to learn how to play golf for a while. Many of his colleagues in the Civil Service were golf aficionados and Mondays were often reserved for post mortems of the weekend's game. Alistair felt left out. Although he was a keen swimmer, played football and did a bit of running at the Muirhouse Civil Service Sports Ground, it seemed that golf was the thing for both your social life and your career. He wondered how he was going to learn it, then remembered Ian. Jimmy had taught Ian and now Ian was teaching Alistair, playing a regular twosome two or three times a month across the newly reconstituted 18 holes of Fox Crag. However, the problem with Alistair was that he seemed to lack the temperament for golf, at least in his present condition. He reacted badly when his shots went wild and had once bent a five iron around the trunk of a small willow on the 13th fairway. Ian's calming influence was, however, having an effect and he was learning that golf, like tennis, has a psychological component. As they stowed their gear in the boot of Alistair's car, he turned to Ian.

"I wanted to ask you something, Ian," he said, obviously embarrassed about whatever it was he wanted.

"Aye, what is it, son?"

"I've entered for the Civil Service Novices Cup next month. Believe it or not, it's being played here at Fox Crag now that there're 18 holes. I wondered if you might be my caddy."

Alistair was aware that in golf tournaments, caddies didn't just carry golf bags for competitors. They were also an invaluable source of advice and information about the course being played on.

"If Ah'm free, of course Ah'll do it. But on one condition. Ah'm getting' a bit auld tae be luggin' golf bags around courses, even for you! Can ye no borrow one o' those new-fangled trolley things from one of yer Civil Service pals?" Ian knew Alistair perfectly well. If anyone could wangle a trolley, he could.

The Saturday of the competition arrived and Alistair's Austin Ten, fashionably fifteen minutes late, pulled up outside 68 Chesser Drive while an impatient Ian, togged up and ready to go, stood waiting at the gate with James beside him. Alistair got out, called a hello, omitted to apologise for his lateness, walked to the back of the car, leaned down, yanked the boot open and stood beaming. Inside was a golf trolley.

"Believe it or not, I cadged it off my boss, on condition that I give him a bottle of Drambuie if I win! Fat chance!"

"Aye, an' Jock here'll be taggin' along as yer second caddy in case Ah get tired! Ye can help Alistair look for 'is lost balls, can't ye, son?" Ian chaffed, grinning at his own joke.

As they parked and made for the clubhouse, they could see a crowd of competitors, spectators and officials already gathered. The Chief Umpire identified himself and briefly went over the rules. It was a handicap event. The competitors had had to hand in five verified scorecards from games they'd played in the past two months. The officials then worked out an approximate handicap for each player, relevant to this course, Fox Crag. The maximum was 24, and the minimum, since they were supposed to be novices, was 12. They'd play in twosomes, the first group to tee off in ten minutes.

"You will see that we have set up a player board with your names, your handicap, your twosome partner, and your tee-off time. Remember that the PGA UK/Ireland rules will apply unless superseded by a local bylaw. Finally, remember this is for the Scottish Civil Service Novices Cup, so Ben Hogan won't be making an appearance!"

The appreciative chuckles turned to laughter when someone in the crowd shouted, "What about Tommy Armour?"

"So, just get out there and enjoy yourselves!"

The crowd broke up and the competitors eagerly crowded the board. Alistair's handicap was listed as 18.

"What, only 18?" he muttered.

"Dinnae be daft," Ian said quietly, "that's gonnae give ye an advantage over anybody wi' a lower number!"

Alistair only added bitterly, "And look at my partner! Simon Jenkins."

Simon Jenkins was a colleague in the same department. Alistair secretly hated him. It wasn't that he was English; Edinburgh was full of Sassenachs and anyone living there had to get used to them. No, it was the fact that Simon was an awful snob, as well as being a pathetic suck-up to the bosses. Alistair suspected him of tittle-tattling on his fellows just to curry favour. He was the last person Alistair would have wanted to play with. On hearing the reason for Alistair's displeasure, Ian said nothing but pointed out that since they'd have an hour to wait to tee off it would be an idea to spend some of that time on the practice ground. Alistair did some shots with the driver and they worked on his swing. When he was satisfied, Ian looked at him.

"Listen, son, about that Jenkins fella. Dinnae let 'im put ye off yer game. Remember, many a game o' golf is won in yer heid, no in yer legs or yer arms." He paused. "Ye ken what Ah mean? Just take it easy."

Alistair nodded thoughtfully but James wondered if he'd really absorbed his dad's advice. The two players teed off. A nervous Alistair sliced his very first drive straight into the rough. He cursed under his breath and could almost picture Simon sneering at him behind his back, but he deliberately didn't look at him. The play went on. Jenkins, who was playing off the same handicap as Alistair, played a reasonable game. But, novice that he was he, too, had his share of hooks and slices, and neither player could avoid the dreaded rough. James helped out by spotting for any wayward balls and enjoyed the satisfaction of finding them. Ian had already taken James out a few times for a 'proper' game of golf. Nine holes had been enough for James at his age, but it was important that he learn not only golfing techniques but golfing etiquette, as well. One of the things Ian had schooled him in was identifying his golf ball if it landed in the rough. It was not unknown for a player to think he'd found his ball in the rough and to play it when it turned out to be someone else's lost ball from a previous game, or worse still, a 'live' ball from another player on the neighbouring fairway. Taking this to heart, James made sure that he peered closely at each ball to verify its identity.

Alistair seemed to have taken Ian's advice about golf being played 'in the heid' and was generally behaving, but he was becoming frustrated at his consistently poor driving and by the ninth hole had started berating himself loudly. Ian said nothing but plodded on behind him with the new-fangled trolley, pleased that he'd forced this condition on Alistair, and thinking that he'd like to get one for himself. As he took the eight iron from Alistair and handed him the putter he looked him straight in the eyes.

"Remember," he said, pointedly. "Ye drive for show but ye putt for dough!"

Alistair's face lit up at this golfing pearl of wisdom. Nodding earnestly, he addressed the ball, giving it his full concentration and, to his delight, sank the putt in one. Maybe he was going to be a decent golfer after all. They finished the round and compared scorecards. Alistair's face fell when he saw Simon's score. It was three strokes better than his. Alistair never expected to win the tournament. He'd have been content just to finish ahead of Jenkins. But since they both had the same handicap he wasn't going to have even that satisfaction. Thoroughly annoyed with himself, he nevertheless forced himself to shake hands, congratulating his colleague on a good game.

They assembled on the lawn in front of the clubhouse as the umpires made their calculations and ranked the players on the Leader Board. As the names went up or changed position, cheers went up from some supporters and groans from others. Eventually, the umpires were able to chalk up the two runners-up and the winner. They started with the Second Runner Up. It was Alistair with a final score of 90. He grinned at the unexpected result. But his pleasure was tinged with irritation at the thought that Simon Jenkins was either First Runner Up or, far worse, The Winner. Sadly, his worst fears were realised, first as Hugh Morgan was listed as First Runner Up with a round of 89 and Simon as, indeed, the Tournament Winner with a round of 87. Curiously, all three had the same 18 handicap. Alistair's achievement had been overshadowed. He turned away, choking back his disappointment. Meanwhile, James, who'd been taking all this in, turned to Ian who was waiting for the official announcement. Motioning Ian down to his level, James whispered long and earnestly in Ian's ear while Alistair looked on, not understanding a word. When James was finished, Ian stood up and patted him on the shoulder with a look of satisfaction.

"Well done, Jock," he said. "Just wait there," and walked off.

The uncle and the nephew looked on as Ian approached one of the umpires, got his attention, pulled him aside, and had a talk with him. The umpire looked grave, thanked Ian and went off to confer with his colleagues. That was when the Chief Umpire made an announcement.

"Er, just an administrative matter. Could Alistair Melrose and Simon Jenkins come to the front, please? We just need to check something."

James watched while a puzzled Alistair went to join the group of umpires, followed by an even more puzzled Simon. There was some talk and then the two hurried off to their cars and came back minutes later. What looked like two scorecards were flourished. There was more discussion with the umpires, this time heated. Suddenly, some kind of decision was reached. Simon stomped off, red-faced and angry. Alistair had an astonished look on his face. He came back just as the Chief Umpire stepped forward to make his announcement.

"With regret, and after an investigation, I have to announce that, due to an irregularity, Simon Jenkins has been disqualified. The new Winner of the Tournament is Hugh Morgan. Alistair Melrose is now First Runner up and Finlay Gillespie is Second Runner Up."

There was scattered applause and concerned looks as the audience reacted to the double-edged announcement, but Alistair was ecstatic. James had never seen him so happy. First Runner Up! That was good enough for him. Even better, though, was the news about Jenkins. He turned to Ian and emotionally shook his hand.

"I couldn't have done it without your help... Coach!"

"Och, away wi' ye. Go an' collect yer prize!" Ian pushed him in the small of the back and he went up to the dais to receive his trophy. It was only a small, nickel-plated cup but that didn't matter to him. He'd won a golf trophy – his very first. He stood proudly in front of the clubhouse while well-wishing colleagues came up with their congratulations. When they'd left, he turned to Ian with questions written all over his face.

"What on earth just happened?" he asked Ian.

"Nothin' to do wi' me, son," said Ian with a puckish smile. "Ask yer nephew."

"OK, I *am* asking my nephew!" said Alistair turning to James.

"Well, ye ken when Ah was helpin' ye find yer balls in the rough? The first two times Ah found Simon's ball, it was a Penfold 3. The third an' fourth time, 'e found the ball 'imsel'. But the fifth time Ah found 'is ball for 'im again. An' this time it wasnae a Penfold, it was a Warwick 7."

"The rat! He cheated!" gasped Alistair.

According to tournament rules, the details of the ball being played by a player at the beginning of the game had to be recorded on the scorecard. Unless something untoward happened, the ball a player started the round with should have been the ball he finished with. If for some reason he had to change balls midway he was supposed to notify his playing partner, who'd note the change on the scorecard. The umpires were supposed to check this at the end of each round, but it being supposedly the gentlemanly game of golf, and this being a Civil Service Tournament, they'd taken the players on trust. When they'd checked Alistair's and Simon's balls against their scorecards, Alistair's was given the all-clear, but Simon's wasn't. It wasn't the ball he'd started with. So he was disqualified. Ian explained.

"Yer pal Simon lost 'is ball in that rough on the fourteenth fairway. Did ye notice how long 'e took over it? James was busy lookin' for *your* ball. The bugger couldn't find 'is ball – the Penfold – an' craftily dropped the Warwick in its place..."

"...and avoided a one-stroke penalty for losing his ball!" exclaimed Alistair.

"Ye can thank James here for that!"

"Well done, James," said Alistair, "but... I'm mystified. How on earth did you work that out?"

"Well, mah dad taught me," James explained, looking up at Ian. "He showed me how to check the make and number o' the ball in the rough tae make sure it's yours."

"Every golfer should have a nephew like you!" exclaimed Alistair.

"But Ah'll tell ye somethin' else," said James quietly.

"What's that, son?" asked Ian, indulgently.

"Well, that Mr Jenkins. 'E didnae need tae cheat. If 'e'd been honest and told ye 'is ball was lost, 'e would just have had a one-stroke penalty and played a new ball." He paused for effect while the adults tried to follow his childish reasoning. "'E would've won anyway!"

Ian and Alistair quickly did the maths in their head. Eighty-seven plus one penalty stroke equals 88. The runner-up scored only 89. James was right. They looked at each other and burst out laughing again. Alistair actually fell onto his knees on the turf, he was so overcome.

"He didnae need tae cheat! He would've won anyway!"

Alistair tended to sound more Scottish when he was emotional. As they got to the car, he ruffled James's hair fondly.

"Well, Jock, you deserve an ice cream. Let's stop at De Marco's!"

James smiled. Ice cream! He'd get a double basher, especially if Uncle Alistair was paying. But one thing he definitely drew the line at. Being called 'Jock' by his uncle. That was a name reserved for his dad, and him alone.

The Official Secrets Act

What was it ye did during The War, Ulrik?" asked Ian casually.

"Sorry, old boy, can't tell you that," replied his brother-in-law blandly, puffing at his pipe.

Ian sat back in his chair, nonplussed. It was not a question he asked often, but usually he got an answer.

"Well," he said, deciding to try again, "what is it ye do now?"

"Sorry, old boy, can't tell you that, either."

Ian was beginning to get irritated. This was the first time he'd ever met Ulrik. He seemed a nice bloke and one would have thought that a simple exchange of harmless information would be part of the pleasantries and small talk in a new acquaintance. So, in his Scottish way, he persisted.

"Why not?" he asked.

"Because, old boy, I signed The Official Secrets Act," and then, jabbing the air with his pipe and throwing a manufactured smile in Ian's direction, Ulrik added, "twice."

It was true. Ulrik's first signed copy of The Official Secrets Act had been burned to a crisp in the London Blitz by Hitler's bombers. When, in 1946, the authorities had discovered this, they'd made him sign another copy. Ian settled back in his chair and gulped the sweetened tea from a fine bone china teacup the size of thimble while Ulrik, busy with his pipe, gazed thoughtfully out of the window. The Official Secrets Act? As far as Ian knew, every officer and non-commissioned officer in the British Army had to sign The Official Secrets Act at some point. He'd had to sign it himself on promotion to CSM. So what was the big deal?

He looked over Ulrik's shoulder at Janet, who was sitting on the other side of the room on the sofa with her sister, Bella. Both of them had been listening. Bella was smiling wearily, as if this was a conversation she'd heard many times before. Janet mouthed three syllables at Ian. He frowned and shook his head slightly to show that he hadn't understood. Janet tried again, this time exaggerating the movements of her mouth and jaws for the first two syllables. Was it "Em Aye"? Then she held up both hands, palms towards Ian, with all five fingers of her right hand outstretched but only the index finger of her left hand. It took a couple of seconds for him to catch on. MI6? Ulrik was with MI6? Stunned, he wondered why Janet hadn't told him before, but in her defence, she'd only just heard it from Bella and was sworn to secrecy. The fact that she'd then turned round and passed it on covertly to her husband didn't matter. Wives and husbands always shared secrets, didn't they?

Three of the Swanstons were in Cheltenham. By the summer of 1956, they'd scraped together enough money for another decent holiday. Janet's part-time job in the Abbeyhill DIY shop had continued to usefully supplement Ian's salary. Their bank account was starting to look healthy for the first time in their lives. The fact that they had a bank account at all was close to a miracle in itself. Janet had longed to see her wee sister, Bella, again, especially as she had a new-born daughter, Charlotte. They hadn't met for over a decade, though they'd each faithfully written a weekly letter. For James, it was his first time out of Scotland. Wee Effie had been left behind, at her own insistence. Now 14, she'd practically been adopted by her Auntie Christine and spent much of her free time over at her place.

Janet's wee sister had been fifteen when war broke out in 1939. By the end of 1941, the conscription of women in Britain had been mandated to help the war effort. Bella could simply have ridden out The War until she became 20, when she'd have been required to register. Not only that, she could also have avoided the perils of the military by opting for The Women's Land Army or some other non-uniformed service. But that wouldn't have been Bella. On her eighteenth birthday in 1942, much to her parents' dismay, and without telling them, she got a bus into Edinburgh, marched to the RAF recruiting office and volunteered for the WAAF. Bella was straining at the leash to do her bit. Also, like Janet, she was desperate to get away from the restrictions of Warburton Crescent. It wasn't only her father; the small flat was now crowded with teenagers who were becoming adults, in addition to the two parents. Squabbles and unpleasantness were becoming the norm. Bella, a bright, intelligent girl, had to get out.

After her initial training, during which her superiors had discovered how smart she was, Bella was posted, with her parents' reluctant consent, for she was still legally a minor, to the South of England. After a period of specialised training, she found herself in the Group Control Room at RAF Uxbridge as a plotter, in a workforce consisting mainly of women. They were responsible for the defence of London and the South-East of England. Bella helped process information coming in from the chain of radar stations around the UK and plot the movements of enemy aircraft on a huge map. The era of the London Blitz was past, but Britain still came under Luftwaffe attack. There were hostile aircraft to plot, bombers to guide home from raids over Germany, search and rescue missions to co-ordinate and, later, V1 and V2 attacks to deal with. Although the job was stressful and tiring, it was rewarding, and she made several lifelong friends.

Bella had always been the most beautiful among the six Melrose sisters, a fact the other five freely acknowledged. But when she wore her blue WAAF uniform, she looked even more stunning, her tunic pinched at the waist, brass buttons up the front and the blue skirt that came down to just below her knees. Add a pair of nylon stockings, if she could get them, black brogues, a dash of lipstick, her cap at a saucy angle over soft auburn waves, and she was ready for anything. Unsurprisingly, this eighteen-going-on-nineteen-year-old beauty with the glowing femininity and the lilting Scottish accent attracted men in droves. Captivated, they gathered like bees around a honey pot. She could have had her pick, but it was Ulrik she chose, ironically the one male who didn't make a point of chasing her.

Ulrik, despite his Scandinavian-sounding name, was an Englishman through and through. His Swedish forebears had landed in England in the middle of the nineteenth century, escaping poverty, political turmoil and religious oppression in their home country. They'd lost little time in becoming English though they never forgot their Swedish roots. Bella's future husband was as handsome as she was beautiful. Tall and dark with a lanky, spare figure, he sported a neat moustache that complemented his officer's uniform. His cultured RP-accented English matched the intelligence, reserve, and gentlemanly bearing that was expected of the archetypical Englishman. He even smoked a pipe. Ulrik was a major in the Secret Intelligence Service, more commonly known as MI6. With a background in engineering telecommunications and being widely travelled – apart from English, he was fluent in Swedish, German and French – he'd been active for a time in Section VIII, running clandestine operations with British agents in German-occupied Europe. When The War ended and he reverted to civilian status, his value to the British security apparatus ensured that he was retained on the payroll for the rest of his life at the Government Communications Headquarters in Cheltenham. What he did there remained a mystery to all who knew him, even to Bella. His family and friends assumed he was a spy but when they joked about it he'd merely smile enigmatically. His lips were sealed and remained that way for the rest of his life.

In choosing Ulrik as her partner, Bella had made a shrewd decision. Besieged as she was by handsome pilot officers, most very eligible, some obviously wealthy, a few even titled aristocracy, the temptation to incline towards one of them was strong. However, romantic as she was, reason whispered in her ear that pilots tended to have short life spans. In the radar plotting room of the Uxbridge base, word went round on a daily basis that so-and-so's plane hadn't returned or that his Lancaster had last been seen in flames over the Ruhr. The service was strewn with young widows bereft by the deaths of their new husbands. Bella resolved not to be one of them. She didn't just want an officer who returned; she wanted one who didn't leave in the first place, and Ulrik fitted the bill perfectly. An intelligence officer playing a vital role in the war effort who worked from the home base and would always work from the home base, that was all she needed to know.

So, unlike many young women around her, she felt no obligation to sleep with her sweetheart just because he might be dead tomorrow. Nor was she pressured into a hasty marriage. She'd take it slow, get to know him and marry when she was ready. After all, she was only nineteen and Ulrik was twenty-six. On becoming engaged, they'd agreed to postpone a wedding until The War was over. And so, it was in the summer of 1945 that they finally went to St. Paul's Anglican Church in Uxbridge and tied the knot with a few of Ulrik's fellow officers and some of Bella's WAAF chums in attendance.

Bella being at last honourably discharged from the WAAF, the newlyweds had moved to Cheltenham where the now ex-Major Rosendahl was to take up his new position at GCHQ. In a mere three years, Bella's life had changed almost beyond imagination. From a childhood of grinding poverty in a Leith tenement, then a crowded flat in a council house, she'd been transported, as if by a magic carpet, to a grand villa in an affluent garden suburb of Cheltenham. For, as she soon realised, her new husband was far from poor. It was true that both of Ulrik's parents had passed away at an early age, leaving him next to nothing. However, his godmother, Auntie Lottie, who, coincidentally, had lived in Cheltenham all her life, had more money than she knew what to do with. This was thanks to a husband who'd shrewdly invested in the armaments industry during the 1930s, had conveniently died of a heart attack on VE Day, and had left her his fortune. Lottie, now Ulrik's only living close relative, was getting on in years and was diplomatic enough to keep her distance from the newlyweds. However, in a generous gesture that was also designed to sidestep death duties, she'd signed over her spacious villa to Ulrik, together with a sizeable advance on his legacy and moved into a select retirement home for gentlefolk where she'd spend the rest of her life in comfort.

Not only had Bella gone from poverty to relative wealth. She'd also shot up the social scale faster than an express elevator in the Empire State Building. From being the daughter of an unemployed Scottish ex-soldier, she'd risen, thanks to her new husband, into the elite of English society. They attended concerts, functions and ceremonies. They hosted exclusive soirees in their villa. They rubbed shoulders with politicians and the Lord Lieutenant of Gloucestershire. As Bella's entry into Cheltenham society picked up pace, her native Scottish accent melted away as fast as the Caerketton snow on a hot May day. In no time at all, she talked like an English rose and acted like one as well. How Bella managed this miraculous transformation in just a few years is beyond the comprehension of mere mortals. Perhaps, underneath the unsophisticated Scottish exterior, a sophisticated Englishwoman had been struggling to get out. Perhaps it was a delayed reaction to her rough childhood. Perhaps it was the influence of Ulrik. Perhaps it was Kismet. But the fact is, so complete was the change that her sister Janet barely recognised her when they were reunited. Bella, the wee Scots lassie with the snottery nose, the one she'd chivvied on their foraging missions in the streets and back alleys of Depression-Era Leith, had metamorphosed into an English lady. Not that Janet minded; she was very fond of her sister. They shared a bond that no one would understand. So, together once more, they spent happy hours reminiscing on their childhood, laughing over this or that memory and marvelling at what they'd been and what they'd become.

Being wealthy, Ulrik naturally had a wealthy man's car. It was a very grunty Jaguar Mark 1, 3.4-litre saloon in fashionable British Racing

Green, a car intended only for export to the USA. But Ulrik, desiring this car above no other, had had a quiet word with a GCHQ colleague who happened to know a Jaguar director. And so, a Mark 1, 3.4-litre was reserved exclusively for Ulrik. It was a beast of a thing, with a spacious interior and plush brown leather seats. In his quiet, unassuming way, Ulrik showed it off to his new brother-in-law. He switched on the engine and lifted the bonnet. While they stood admiring the reassuring purr, Ulrik reeled off the statistical data. He opened the boot to show how roomy it was. He had Ian sit in the back and luxuriate against the plush leather. Then he had him sit in the driver's seat and test the steering wheel as he ran through the complex instrument panel.

"Want to take her for a spin?" he offered generously.

"Thanks, Ulrik, but Ah don't actually have a driving licence," Ian replied.

The irony was not lost on him. For six years, he'd driven around in almost every type of vehicle the British Army owned, from a motorbike with sidecar to a jeep, a three-tonner, to, even, a Bren Carrier. But he'd never held a civilian driving licence for, unlike Ulrik, he'd never known any ambition to own a car. Anyway, given their straitened circumstances up until the mid-1950s, there had never been any question of the Swanstons being able to afford a car. Ian, with his increasingly laid-back approach to life, had eventually formed the opinion that he didn't need one; Edinburgh had a good public transport service. He could catch a bus from virtually outside Number 68 to his work. As well, his war experience with military vehicles had taught him how unreliable the internal combustion engine could be. He just couldn't face all the hassles he knew were bound to occur, not to mention the expense. And anyway, he could always rely on Alistair or someone else to give him or the family a lift if necessary.

Ulrik had taken a week's leave especially for the Swanstons' visit and in his methodical way had planned a series of day tours. On the first day, they visited the ancient town of Tewksbury, strolled around in brilliant sunshine admiring the medieval buildings while Ulrik expounded on the city's past. They had lunch in a smart restaurant just off Church Street with Ulrik choosing a white Sauternes for them to try – Janet had never had wine before - and, of course, Ulrik insisting on footing the bill. Then they drove out to The Bloody Meadow. As the Jag slowly negotiated the traffic, Janet was feeling like royalty, never having been chauffeured in a luxury car before. Slightly the worse for wear now after her introduction to Sauternes, she decided that she *would* be royalty, wound down her window, adopted a fake royal smile, and started to greet pedestrians with the gracious back-handed wave of the monarch. Bella, equally well-oiled, joined in from her side of the car with impish delight. The giggles from the back and the scandalised stares of the pedestrians infected the others and it was a decidedly unserious group of visitors who alighted at the site of the Battle of Tewksbury. Janet had by now discovered that wine made her sleepy, especially on a hot day. She struggled to stay awake as she staggered arm in arm with Bella around the wooded battle site while Ulrik, standing in the lush grass, lectured them on the Wars of the Roses and the significance of King Edward IV of York's victory. James, however, was wide awake and was fascinated. History was beginning to sound interesting, especially the way Uncle Ulrik told it.

A tour of the beautiful Cotswolds had taken up another day, ending at the remains of a Roman villa in a beautiful valley at Chedworth. Ulrik explained that this part of England was saturated with Roman remains. He conducted James and his seven-year-old son, Paul, around the site while James peppered him with questions. Ulrik eagerly provided answers. He loved history and archaeology and there was nothing like a captive audience, even if it was only a nine-year-old nephew. Meanwhile, Bella, cradling Charlotte, sat on a bench seat together with Janet, half-dozing as the wine and the sumptuous food did their work.

Then the visitors were told that Ulrik had organised a picnic for them. They'd drive into the Malvern Hills to visit The White Lion. The Swanstons were intrigued, especially James. A white lion? Was there such a thing? What was it? Ulrik just smiled enigmatically while Bella went along with his little game. They'd find out when they got there. Bella had been busy in the kitchen and Ulrik had been down in his wine cellar. Ian had seen more than his share of wine cellars in Germany during The War. In fact, he and his men had sheltered in them while the 88s had searched them out, but it had been hard to keep the men's hands off the racks of bottles; alcohol and warfare didn't mix. But a wine cellar here in Britain! It must be one in a million, thought Ian.

"What would you suggest for our picnic?" asked Ulrik, aware of Ian's background in wine and spirits and giving him the respect due to an expert. After searching the racks, Ian emerged with a dusty bottle of Pinot Gris in one hand and an equally dusty Cabernet d'Anjou in the other.

"Ah don't know what we're havin' for our lunch," he paused, looking at Ulrik, quizzically, "but what d'ye think o' these?"

"Good choice, old boy," said Ulrik benevolently, patting him on the back.

Meanwhile, Bella and Janet had been filling a large wicker picnic basket with food, among which the wine took its place. Everything was packed in the Jag, the two families piled in and they were off. After yet another drive through beautiful countryside, the visitors found themselves getting out of the car in a car park at the foot of a small hill. Other cars were already parked and it was obviously a popular beauty spot. James noticed with interest that the field next to the car park was being ploughed. As the girls wandered up the footpath, baby and sons in tow, the two men retrieved the picnic basket from the boot and climbed up after them, each with a handle. As they neared the summit, James noticed what seemed to be their destination. It was a large white rock the size of a building and stood alone.

"The White Lion," Ulrik explained. "Here we are!"

The visitors were overawed. It was a massive outcrop of white quartz. Viewed from a particular angle, it was claimed, the silhouette looked like a crouching lion on a hilltop. As Bella and Janet spread a tartan blanket on the ground and unpacked the picnic basket, Ulrik couldn't help giving one of his mini-lectures on the geology and what had caused this unique landmark to be stranded here on a hilltop in the mists of time. Ian reflected on his brother-in-law. What a character! Here he was, an MI6 spy, who was cultured, well-connected, enjoyed fine dining, and appeared to possess a wealth of knowledge of just about everything. Was there anything Ulrik didn't know? They spent a few hours at the site, savouring their picnic lunch together with Ian's wine choices, chatting about everything under the sun but mainly family matters, and enjoying the sublime views of the Malvern Hills. On returning to the car park, James noticed that the tractor he'd seen before was now parked, and a plump, white-haired, elderly man, probably the farmer, was sitting on the low stone dyke enjoying a late ploughman's lunch. While the others were packing the car, James wandered over to look at the tractor.

"Hello there!" said the farmer. "Where be you from then, young fella-me-lad?"

"Scotland!" said James half-defiantly.

"Well, you've been an' come a long way, that's for sure! Havin' a good holiday, then?"

"Yes, thank you! That's mah mum and dad, and auntie and uncle. And this..." He pointed to Paul, proudly. "...is mah cousin!"

"Now, would a young lad like you be interested in history?"

James hadn't thought about it before but after being with Ulrik for nearly a week, he realised that, yes, he definitely was. He nodded. The farmer put down his half-eaten sandwich, wiped his palms together, put his right hand in his pocket then held it out to James. On his palm lay what looked at first glance like three small green buttons. James peered closer, unable to make out what he was looking at.

"But what are they?"

"Roman coins!"

The farmer placed them carefully on James's outstretched palm. James separated them with his index finger and peered closely at them. Yes, they were very small coins. They were thin and weathered around the edges but they were coins. He could see the outline of a head on one coin and some writing around the edge through the Verdigris. He turned it over. There was a tiny figure standing holding what looked like a staff. By this time, Ian and Ulrik had appeared. The farmer nodded towards them in acknowledgement as he munched his sandwich.

"They're Roman coins. Oi'm allus findin' 'em, every toime oi plough. Up they come! You can 'ave 'em!" he added.

James was speechless. Roman coins! And they were his!

"Well, son," said Ian at last. "Are ye no gonnae say thank you tae the man?"

"Thank you," said James recovering himself.

"Well, make sure you don't be losin' em!" said the man. "You look after 'em!"

And with that, he finished his sandwich, took a swig of cider, put his things back in his knapsack, got back on the tractor and rode off with a backward wave.

James held out his new treasures for his father and uncle to see.

"How old d'ye think they are?" he asked.

Ulrik carefully lifted one of the coins off James's palm, put it on his own and peered at it expertly, moving it around with his finger and turning it over.

"Probably fourth century," he said, quietly but confidently. "Emperor Constantine."

James was impressed. Was there anything Uncle Ulrik didn't know?

"So, come on, son, how old does that make them?" asked Ian.

James was flummoxed. Ulrik chimed in.

"What century are we in now?"

"The twentieth?"

"Good boy," said Ulrich. "So, what is the difference between four and twenty?"

"Sixteen," shot back James. Well, that was easy.

"So how old are the coins?"

"Sixteen..." started James, then stopped. He wasn't sure.

"...hundred years," finished Ian. "That's one thousand, six hundred!"

James couldn't conceive of anything that old. Back in the car, Auntie Bella gave him a paper napkin to wrap them in. He stowed them carefully in his shorts pocket and kept his hand there, clutching them, all the way home. Once they were back in Edinburgh, he took it upon himself to verify his uncle's opinion about the coins' provenance. Without telling anyone where he was going, he took a bus to Chambers Street and climbed what seemed like a hundred steps to the Museum entrance. Through the revolving door he found a uniformed attendant. Pulling out his precious cargo, he held out his hand.

"Can somebody tell me how old they are?" he asked, anxiously.

"Come wi' me, son!"

He followed the man up some stairs and along an endless corridor, past hundreds of exhibits in glass cases. The attendant knocked at a door and entered. An elderly man with a shock of white hair was sitting in a high chair examining something on a display table while a young woman with long, dark hair stood beside him. The attendant explained James's request. The old man smiled in welcome.

"Come on in and show us what you've got, young man!" he said in an English accent.

James stepped up, placed his small package, still wrapped in Auntie Bella's tissue, on the table, unwrapped it and stood waiting expectantly. The old man produced a magnifying glass, peered at the coins, turned them over and addressed James.

"Roman denarii. Fourth century. Emperor Constantine," he said with authority.

So, Uncle Ulrik had been right – as usual.

"Miss Rawlinson," said the man to the young girl. "Why don't you show this young man *our* collection?" and with that, he turned back to his work without another word. James followed Miss Rawlinson along some more corridors. They stopped at a tall glass case. Inside was a big bronze pot tilted towards them. Out of the mouth of the pot spilled hundreds and hundreds of bright, shining silver coins. Roman denarii! Dug up near Cramond, Miss Rawlinson explained, and these were almost identical to James's coins, only, they were in much better condition and had been cleaned up. James could only stare, speechless. And so, yet another strand of his life began to fall into place.

Meanwhile, back in Cheltenham, the Swanstons and Bergdahls were relaxing after a hard day's leisure. The sisters were doing something in the kitchen with the Light Programme on low volume. The dulcet tones of Jimmy Young could be heard singing 'The Man from Laramie'. Ian and Ulrik were in the library, a bookshelf-lined room that doubled as Ulrik's home office. Ian had something behind his back.

"After all yer kindness, and all the wine, Ah thought ye deserved a present from North o' the Border," he said playfully. He placed a bottle of DeSantos's best Scotch on the table. "Shall we have a wee dram thegither?"

Ulrik smiled in agreement, went to a glass-fronted cabinet, and extracted two chunky glasses of the best crystal. He picked up the bottle with the new-fangled aluminium cap.

"May I?" he asked with a grin.

"Go ahead!" said Ian. "There's nothin' like crackin' open a new bottle o' Scotch!"

The whisky made that unforgettable sound as it glugged into the glasses.

"To family – from North of the Border!" exclaimed Ulrik, raising his glass.

"Slainte mhath!" replied Ian. "No ice, undiluted, the only way to drink Scotch!"

They sat down, Ulrik nodding appreciatively, alternately puffing his pipe and tasting his whisky. They reviewed recent events. Did Ulrik think that Nasser's sudden nationalisation and occupation of the Suez Canal would lead to war? Ulrik didn't think so. What about Buster Crabb? Did Ulrik think he was still alive or would his body surface in Portsmouth harbour one day? Ulrik opined with a shrug of his shoulders that they'd never know. What did the sudden appearance of Burgess and Maclean in Moscow mean? Had their defection seriously damaged the work of British Intelligence? Ulrik didn't think so. Ian took his word for it. Ulrik, he could assume, had inside information. Also, like James, he was still marvelling at Ulrik's wide knowledge of just about everything under the sun. He was more like an Oxford professor than an MI6 spy. After the third dram, Ulrik was beginning to loosen up. After the fourth, glass in hand, he took his pipe out of his mouth and looked at Ian inquisitively. Suddenly, he spoke.

"Tell me, Ian, how do you make your Scotch whisky?"

Ian's first reaction was surprise. *Ye mean there's somethin' Ulrik doesn't know?* Then he thought for a moment, looking back at his brother-in-law with a puckish grin.

"Sorry, old boy, can't tell you that," he replied, in his best attempt at an English accent.

Ulrik's speech was beginning to slur slightly.

"But why not?" he asked emotionally.

"Because, old boy," replied Ian with a mock manufactured grin, "Ah signed The Official Secrets Act of the Scotch Whisky Association," and then, raising his glass, he added, "twice."

The black sheep and the prodigal daughter

"Did Auntie Flora really run away wi' a film star, Mum?"

James looked so earnest, Janet almost burst out laughing.

"No," she scoffed. "Where did ye hear that?"

"Ah'm no sure. Ah think Uncle Alistair told me."

"Well, Uncle Alistair's got an over-active imagination!"

"But she did run away?"

Janet paused as Ian smiled at her efforts to formulate an acceptable response.

"Let's just say she left hame."

"But Mum, *you* left hame and Auntie Bella left hame and Uncle Alistair left hame but ye didnae run away! Did ye?"

"Of course no, ye wee daftie!" She paused for reflection. "Let's just say she left hame, but didnae tell anybody she was leavin'. Now, is that enough for ye, Mr Nosy Parker?"

James sat back in his seat as the bus picked up speed between the traffic lights on Ferry Road. The four Swanstons were on their way to the annual New Year's Day family gathering of the Melrose clan at Warburton Crescent. As they usually did, they'd spent the previous evening, Hogmanay, with Ian's sister, Christine, his stepsister, Rose, their husbands, friends, and extended families. And, as usual, at midnight, they'd all stood to drink a toast to the year ahead and Absent Friends. Ian and Janet had also privately toasted the Old Year 1956, relieved that the November Suez Crisis hadn't led to another Z Reserve demand that Ian report for duty. In a couple of years, he'd be 45 and the whole issue would be behind him – a whole fifteen years after the end of The War.

There was another reason for visiting the Melroses on this particular day, for Auntie Flora would be there. James had never met Auntie Flora and had only heard her name spoken in hushed whispers. For the fact was that, while Flora hadn't actually 'run' as opposed to 'walked' away, there were elements of haste and subterfuge involved which could indeed be construed by some as 'running away' despite Janet's attempts to put a more acceptable gloss on it. Flora was the eldest of the Melrose girls. Born during World War One, she'd reached her majority in the late nineteen-thirties and like most of her sisters had had only one goal in life – to get out of Warburton Crescent as fast as possible. Her chance had come one evening at the Palais de Danse in Fountainbridge. Harry Roy's band from London had arrived in Edinburgh as a stop on their national tour. One of the saxophone players was a certain Des DeFranco. When pretty, twenty-one-year-old, Scottish Flora bumped into handsome, worldly-wise, English Des outside the cloakrooms during the first break, she was immediately as besotted with him as he was with her. They had a torrid three-day affair during which she lost her virginity and probably got pregnant. When the band moved on, Flora went with them. Without telling a soul, not even any of her sisters. One day she was there, the next she was gone, along with a small suitcase and a few of her things. Mirran, her next youngest sister, was the only one who guessed the truth, since she'd been there that fateful night in Fountainbridge and had gleaned some juicy details from Flora afterwards. While Mirran was able to placate her parents with what she knew of the affair, it was only when, two weeks later, she received a letter from her sister in London, that she was able to confirm it. Her parents were, of course, devastated. When a month later, Mirran received a second letter with the news that Flora and Des were married and Flora was expecting, Alexander Melrose's rage against his ungrateful daughter could be heard the length and breadth of Warburton Crescent. He swore to cut Flora out of his life. Her name would never again be mentioned in their home.

So, Flora became the Prodigal Daughter. Her brothers and sisters were forbidden to contact her, a directive they universally ignored. When Mirran followed her to London several years later, on marrying a smooth-talking Cockney sergeant major in the Engineers, the two sisters became more or less inseparable. Bella, too, on her transfer to Uxbridge was quick to re-establish relations with her big sister, whom she'd missed terribly. Alistair had done the same as soon as he was posted to London. But as far as the Melrose parents were concerned, Flora was persona non grata. For ten years, she'd had a good marriage but it had gone sour when Des had fallen for an eighteen-year-old soubrette who'd auditioned with the band. Still, Des turned out to be a good father. He was quite prepared to support his ex-wife and children and bought them a house in Wimbledon. As a top saxophonist, he earned good money, having virtually his choice of bands and doing regular session work at Abbey Road Studios. Janet, Ian and Effie had surreptitiously met him when he'd played again in Edinburgh in the late forties with another touring band. They'd taken an immediate liking to him and were upset when the news came through of the divorce. Des had a long and successful career, his face popping up on the TV screen from time to time, to Janet's delight, whenever some band or other was featured.

Then, somehow, after almost two decades of silence, a reconciliation was engineered. The Melroses, getting on in years, must have reached a point where they could forgive and forget. Flora, with three children and now long divorced, was eager to come home on a visit. It wasn't clear who'd arranged the reunion, but Effie was the most likely candidate, being the peacemaker of the family. And so here Flora was, on New Year's Day, 1957, back in the Melroses' living room, sitting in the second-best armchair, chatting with her parents. Although the atmosphere was, at best, only cordial, it was a start. James was bursting with curiosity. What was Auntie Flora like? He had to know.

As it turned out, he liked her immediately. With her ladylike charm and gentle ways, she seemed a far cry from the girl who'd run away with a big band musician in the nineteen-thirties. She was an older, more sedate version of his mother and through the London vowels, he could still detect a trace of a Scottish accent, unlike Auntie Bella. He quizzed her about her family. Her oldest son had just opened a clothes boutique in some place James had never heard of before called Carnaby Street. Her daughter was training to be a teacher. Des was hoping that his other son would follow in his musical footsteps when he left school. As they sipped their sherries and cordials and munched sandwiches, black bun and shortie, Alexander Melrose was still reserved. But after two decades, his rage had evaporated and he found himself looking forward to meeting the three grandchildren he'd never known.

Then Uncle George arrived, and the focus of the party quickly switched from Flora to her elder brother. For Uncle George was drunk as usual. The eldest of the nine, born just before World War One, he was actually a couple of years older than Ian. Now in his forties, he was unmarried and still lived at Warburton Crescent. He was of above-average height and in looks was a younger version of his father. In temperament, he was surly, unpleasant, and ill-mannered. He made little attempt to get on with people and went out of his way to offend. Ian had broached the mystery of George several times with Janet. What sort of man still lived with his parents at his age? Why was he so unpleasant? But Janet couldn't say. Her elder brother was as much an enigma to her as he was to Ian. In the 1920s and 1930s when they were growing up, he was almost ten years older. They'd had little in common. And now, twenty-odd years later, they rarely spoke.

George was a specialist technician with the GPO. When The War had broken out, his occupation had been listed as Reserved; he couldn't be called up for military service. So George rode out The War earning a good wage while fellow countrymen were being conscripted and sent to fight. Some of them were pals from his street. A few never came back. There was nothing to stop George from volunteering to serve in the armed forces in his civilian trade. There was also nothing to stop him from volunteering for the Home Guard, as many others in reserved occupations did. At a pinch, if he'd been persistent, he might even have wangled acceptance for active service, regardless of his privileged status. But he did none of these things. Legally, he was blameless. But morally he wasn't - in some folks' eyes, at least. One of these was his father. Alexander welcomed the contribution George's wages made to the household, but the fact that others were going to fight while his eldest son wasn't rankled with a veteran of Gallipoli and the Somme. His son had taken the easy way out. The honour of the Melrose family was impugned. And in Edinburgh, there were plenty of others who thought like him. *Their* sons, brothers and husbands had been taken to go and fight while others, like George, who seemed just as eligible, hadn't. Resentment was not uncommon towards those lucky enough to have, somehow, dodged the draft. But there was no way George was going to be so stupid as to put his life in danger when he didn't have to.

To make matters worse, it was Alexander's daughters who'd stepped up. Bella had volunteered for the WAAF though she didn't have to. Phoebe had joined the WRAC though she didn't have to. Even his married daughter, Janet, had volunteered as a firewatcher. Three of his girls were doing their bit, but his eldest son wasn't. The most obvious comparison Alexander made was between George and Ian, effectively his only son-in-law at the time. Ian had continued the family tradition, joining the local regiment. It didn't matter that he'd been conscripted; he hadn't tried to wriggle out of it. He was doing his bit, too. And here was his feckless son sitting at home, cruising through The War in safety.

The downside for George was that his guilt fed his innate paranoia, which only worsened as time went on. He imagined people were looking at him on the bus to work or talking behind his back. *Why isn't he in uniform?* He started drinking. Things only got worse after VE Day. Men started returning from overseas. The inevitable question was asked: *What did you do in The War?* George didn't have an answer. He'd done nothing except keep the telephones running. That may have been important work but it paled in comparison to what others had done. He turned in on himself, forming a dislike of Ian, which morphed into hostility, despite the fact that he didn't really know Ian. He just hated Ian for what he was and for what he, George, was not. By 1957, when Flora came home, he was an alcoholic. Ian recognised the signs. He'd seen enough of them in the Army, where alcohol was cheap in the

Sergeants' and Officers' messes: the pitted skin, the sunken cheeks, the pursed mouth and the glazed eyes. How George was able to do his job was anyone's guess.

On the day in question, George had been at the New Year's Day Hibs-Hearts derby. He was a fanatical Hibs supporter. When the game was over, he was ecstatic. Not only had Hibs won 2-0, but they'd done so at Tynecastle, the Hearts home ground. George and his cronies made a beeline for their local, Spence's, in Easter Road, to celebrate. There he did what he usually did every Saturday but today, in honour of the great victory, he did it in spades. He got plastered. And the drink did to him what it always did: made him aggressive and obnoxious. The convivial Ne'er Day gathering of the Melroses was suddenly disrupted when George burst in and single-handedly put a damper on the festivities. Ian just stood at the back of the room. He knew that George disliked him and didn't engage. That was until George started on James.

Over the period of Christmas, Hogmanay and New Year, James was used to getting gifts of money. A shilling here, a florin there, even a rare half-crown sometimes. This day had been no different. James, keen to share his good fortune, was showing everyone how much he'd got, happily displaying the coins in the palm of his hand to the feigned delight of his relations. But not George.

"Ye wee bugger, how come *you've* got money an' Ah havnae!"

Though some of those present might have been thinking that George would be better off money-wise if he didn't waste it all on booze, nobody said a word. James immediately thrust his coins back into his pocket and backed away. Uncle George always scared him. He took a step towards James and tried to grab him by the arm. Uncle George's drunken face leered over him. Then his Dad stepped in. Emerging from his low profile, Ian took George by the elbow and hustled him into the lobby away from the party. James had the presence of mind to follow, closing the door behind him. Ian was his usual calm self. He'd dealt with plenty of drunks in his time, mostly peacefully, but occasionally not.

"George, just take it easy. Why don't ye lie down?"

But George was having none of it.

"Ye fuckin' bastard, it's yer laddie that has aw' the fuckin' money."

He lurched menacingly in his nephew's direction but Ian grabbed him by the lapels and pushed him against the coats hanging from the rack fixed to the wall above his head.

"Don't you touch mah laddie or..."

"...Or what, ye bastard?"

"Ah'll knock yer block off," Ian said, matter-of-factly.

"You 'n' whae's army?" sneered George.

Ian had had enough. George was slightly taller, but taking a step back and bunching his right fist, he drove it sharply into George's solar plexus as he'd done several times before in last-resort situations. George's eyes opened wide, the colour drained from his face and he doubled up in pain. At that moment, the door to the living room opened and Alexander Melrose appeared in the doorway. Immediately sizing up the situation, he grabbed his son by the collar and thrust him through the open door of the bathroom, where he vomited all over the floor.

"Ye did the right thing, son," Alexander said, turning to Ian. "Somebody should've done it long ago."

While George slept it off, the party continued without him. There was a sense of relief. Somehow Ian had dealt with the situation. But James was the only one who'd witnessed exactly *how* Ian had dealt with the situation. His usually benign, restrained dad had revealed a side of himself that James had never seen before. Ian was the indulgent father. If anyone was the disciplinarian in the family, it was Janet. The occasional smack came from her, never Ian. But here he was, expertly taking out a drunk without any fuss. James knew his dad had boxed and wrestled in his younger days. He had a vague idea of what he'd done during The War. But he'd never seen *this* Dad. Suddenly, he realised he had two dads: the mild-mannered dad who snoozed on the settee after tea or who smiled with satisfaction after sinking a difficult putt or who laughed at his own jokes; and the other dad who, with quiet efficiency, dealt violence to another human being to neutralise an awkward situation. Though he'd suspected that this other dad existed, he'd never seen him in action before. Today, courtesy of drunk Uncle George, he had. It was to be the one and only time. James wondered what it meant. He now adored his dad even more. But he understood him less.

Alexander had had enough of his son's antisocial ways. The next morning he threw him out. Giving him two hours to pack his stuff, he told George he could stay with his drunken pals for all he cared. When George started to argue, Alexander played his ace.

"If ye're no oot o' this house by noon the day, ye'll be gettin' another dose o' Ian Swanston. Is that what ye want?"

George was gone by noon and he never returned. But Flora did. The reconciliation was the start of many return visits to the place where she was born. Then her children came, one after the other, over the years. Yes, they were English, born and bred in London, but, intrigued by their Scottish heritage, they made the trek north of the border to bond with their new Scottish family. When they did, James sometimes reflected back on that 1st of January 1957. In a single day, he'd lost an uncle and gained an auntie – and her family to boot. It was a good trade.

What's My Line?

Ian stepped up to the urinal and undid his ballop. As he stood enjoying the relief that can only come from a stream of warm urine splashing against white porcelain, someone stepped up and did the same at the neighbouring stall.

"Afternoon!"

Uncomfortable about talking while weeing, Ian merely grunted loudly, finished his wee, did his trousers up and walked over to the wash hand basin. The facilities were luxurious. The basins were spotlessly clean, endless hot water gushed out of gleaming chrome taps, there were liquid soap dispensers and individual hand towels on a side shelf, all reminiscent of a top hotel. As he took a moment to luxuriate, he glanced in the wall-to-wall mirror at the newcomer, who had come over to join him at the neighbouring basin. He was of medium height, in his early thirties, with dark, swept-back hair, a prominent nose, black, bushy eyebrows and quirky, smiling lips. He looked very familiar but that wasn't surprising considering Ian was in BBC Broadcasting House in Portland Lane, London. He rinsed off the soap, turned off the tap, walked over to the shelf, helped himself to a towel and dried his hands, taking the opportunity to examine his fellow toilet user more closely.

"Havin' a good day?" the newcomer asked jovially. His accent sounded vaguely from London.

"Aye," replied Ian, "havin' a wonderful time!"

"Would I be right in thinking you are one of our cousins from North of the Border?" the other suggested with a broad smile that produced wrinkles around his eyes

"Indeed Ah am that! From Edinburgh."

"Now, that's somewhere Ah've always wanted tae visit!" was the reply in a fake Scottish accent, that tended towards Glaswegian. Then it switched to Yorkshire. "Boot me Dad's from Yorkshire, ye know..."

Ian smiled appreciatively. There was an awkward pause, as both, still drying their hands, wondered what else to say. Then Ian spoke.

"Eh, Ah ken ye must be somebody famous, and ye look very familiar, but sorry, Ah just can't place ye. D'ye want tae help me out here?"

The other's smile broadened even further. His slightly prominent teeth appeared and his eyes twinkled as if he were preparing himself. Then he declaimed in a comical, high-pitched voice that could only come from one special person:

"You filthy rotten swine! You've deaded me!"

"Bluebottle!" exclaimed Ian without hesitation. "The Goon Show!"

"The very same, sir," confirmed the other.

"Then, which one are you?" By now Ian had dried his hands and was clicking his fingers in frustration. "Don't tell me... Not Spike Milligan..." Then it came to him.

"Peter Sellers!"

"Spot on, sir, spot on! And whom may I be addressing?"

"Ian Swanston!" They shook hands heartily, smiling with bonhomie.

"And what would you be doing all the way down here South of the Border within the august portals of Auntie BBC?" asked the comedian.

"Ah'm here for *What's My Line?* – a contestant."

"Well, you've already got one up on me," Peter said. "I've been trying for years to get on that show as the mystery guest and haven't managed yet!"

They both laughed and went their separate ways.

When Ian had come home from work one evening in early autumn and told Janet that he was going to be on *What's My Line?* her reaction had been predictable.

"D'ye think Ah came doon the Water o' Leith on a McVitie's Digestive?" she scoffed good-naturedly, blinking and holding the onion she was peeling at arm's length. Ian, still in his overcoat, gently took the knife and the onion from her and laid them on the bunker, handed her a towel to wipe the tears out of her eyes, took her by the arm and led her into the living room where he sat beside her on the settee.

"Hen, Ah mean it. Ah'm gonnae be on *What's My Line?* An' you're comin' wi' me tae London – unless ye'd rather stay here!"

A sceptical Janet did take some convincing. She remained incredulous, even when the full story was revealed. It turned out that an acquaintance of Vincent, the DeSantos brother who was based in London, was the BBC producer of *What's My Line?* or WML, probably the most popular television panel game in Britain at the time. Over drinks one night, he happened to be regaling Vincent with a particular difficulty of his: finding contestants from 'the provinces' for WML in line with the BBC policy of national inclusivity. After all, they were supposed to be the *British* Broadcasting Corporation. In short, they needed a contestant from Scotland. Vincent immediately offered the services of DeSantos, which his friend eagerly accepted. He phoned Don and asked if there was anyone in the Edinburgh HQ, possibly a manager, who could represent the Scotch Whisky side of the business in a future WML episode. None of the DeSantos brothers was willing or able to come to the party, so they asked Ian. When they told him it would be an all-expenses-paid, four-day trip to London, staying in a top hotel, and – the clincher – his wife could accompany him, he didn't hesitate.

To say Janet was ecstatic when the truth of Ian's story sank in would be an understatement. Ian, her husband, was going to be on national television. You might as well have said that they were going to stick him in a rocket with Laika and send him whizzing around in space. Janet had always been an up-and-down sort of person. When she was up, she was very, very up and when she was down, she could be, well, insufferable. But now she was on a very, very, very up trajectory that would last for weeks on end. The trip to London for the taping of the programme was only a month away. The whole time she walked on air. Everybody in the family had to know. She even walked up to the telephone box in Fergusson Avenue and made a very expensive trunk call to Bella in her fancy villa in Cheltenham, something she'd never dared to do before, to give her the news. Alistair, of course, he of all people, had to be impressed. Christine and her husband were told. Even Mrs Fraser upstairs. They all were made to share in her happiness. Of course, she'd have to have a new outfit for the adventure. It was worldly-wise Don who'd first mentioned it to Ian, well aware of what his own wife's requirements would have been in the same situation.

"Don't forget that you'll be meeting some important personalities down there. Get yourself a new suit, and a new outfit – no, two new outfits - for Janet. She'll need one for daytime and one for evenings. Send us the bill."

Janet could have splashed out at somewhere like Jaeger, but being Janet, extravagance was not in her DNA, even when she was spending someone else's money, so she went to Marks and Spencer in Princess Street. It didn't hurt, either, that her sister, Effie, was now well established there, and was able to give her a discount, which she honourably passed on to the DeSantos accountants. Her daytime choice was based on a sky-blue swing skirt with a royal blue bolero jacket and a white, long-sleeved, high-necked blouse. Her evening wear was a black cocktail dress, with a charcoal ermine-lined cape to match. Since it would be London in November, a warm winter coat in silver fox grey with a belt and a high collar completed the ensemble. The bill came to almost fifty pounds. Janet couldn't ever have imagined spending so much money on clothes at one go, especially for herself. She walked out of the shop into Princes Street with a bulging Marks and Spencer carrier bag in each hand. As she sat on the bus home it all felt unreal. Christmas had come early – just for her.

Meanwhile, Ian was taking it all with his usual equanimity. He'd been in London before, during The War, so that was nothing special to him. The thought of appearing on national television didn't faze him either, though he was a naturally shy person. He'd had to put up with much worse. He'd cope. They took The Flying Scotsman sleeper on a dreich November evening at 11 o'clock. Janet's sister, Effie, and James were at Waverley Station to see them off. Wee Effie had been parked with Christine in Trinity for the duration. James was to stay with his grandparents and Auntie Effie at Warburton Crescent. 68 Chesser Drive was locked up. Monsieur Renoir would keep an eye on Louise. Don DeSantos suddenly appeared as the train was about to leave and thrust a bottle of their premier whisky into Ian's hands through the open window. The prospective TV star already had an entire case with him as complimentary gifts, courtesy of his firm. This bottle was for Ian's and Janet's consumption.

Janet's elation over the past few weeks was now to attain, if it were possible, even greater heights. For the next four days she was swept along on a frenzy of new experiences, new people, and new places. First going to bed in a train – of all things – in a luxury compartment, with an attendant on hand to bring them anything they desired. As the train rocked and rattled through the south of Scotland and over the border, speeding towards the capital, she couldn't sleep a wink for excitement. She kept getting up to peer into the darkness, continually updating Ian on where she thought they were and robbing him of sleep. Breakfasting at six o'clock in the restaurant car, they steamed into the home counties and King's Cross Station, where a limousine was waiting to pick them up and convey them to The Strand Palace Hotel.

They had the morning to freshen up and would be picked up from the hotel at 2 pm for introductions at the BBC, but they weren't going to waste their short stay in London in a hotel room. Out they went and spent the morning doing a circuit down to the Victoria Embankment, up to Trafalgar Square, across to Leicester Square and Covent Garden and back to the Strand Palace. The weather was crisp and clear, perfect for a walk, but they missed the clean air of Fox Crag. After a sumptuous lunch, they were waiting on the hotel steps at 2 pm, when the same limousine drew up. This time, there was already another passenger in the back. He leapt out and introduced himself. It was young Vincent DeSantos, come to look after them.

They drove direct to Broadcasting House in the vicinity of Regent's Park, where they were warmly received. Vincent introduced them to his producer friend. Then, together with the other contestants (minus the mystery guest) they were given an overview of what would happen during recording and were given a tour of the Centre, including the WML studio. That was all for today, Tuesday. They'd return the following afternoon for rehearsals and the actual programme would be taped on Thursday afternoon in the presence of a live audience. Through all this, Ian displayed his natural reticence but Janet couldn't wipe the smile off her face, made humorous and sometimes inappropriate comments and flirted with the cameramen even though, being mostly southern English, they couldn't understand a word she uttered. That evening, the Swanstons had a quiet dinner together in the hotel and went to bed early, exhausted.

Wednesday morning there was a note from Vincent at the hotel reception. He'd organized a bus tour of central London for them, starting in an hour. Again, they'd be picked up. He also had tickets to the theatre that evening. He hoped they'd join him and his wife. That afternoon Ian went through the rehearsal at Broadcasting House. He'd prepared a piece of mime to illustrate his job, which had to be approved by the producer. Eamonn Andrews, despite his boxer's face, was precisely the charmer he appeared to be on TV. They used stand-ins for the panel members and everything went smoothly. After changing at the hotel they travelled by taxi with Vincent and his wife, Isidora, to the Theatre Royal, Drury Lane. It was a new musical that had premiered in April that year called *My Fair Lady*, featuring Rex Harrison, and a new young sensation called Julie Andrews. Janet was floating six feet above the ground. Not only was she in London, for the first time in her life she was among the cream of the entertainment world.

The taping of the show took place the next day, Thursday. This was the real thing. Ian was sitting calmly in the green room while Janet was on the edge of her seat in the front row of the studio audience. Ian was third up. The panellists were Lady Isobel Barnett, David Nixon, Gilbert Harding and Barbara Kelly. The first two contestants had beaten the panel. Now it was Ian's turn. He walked out in front of the cameras dressed in his new suit and signed his name with a black crayon on the large white paper wallboard. Then he mimed pouring whisky from a beaker into a measuring flask. When he sat down next to Eamonn, Janet was dizzy with excitement. Her Ian, being filmed for television!

To cut a long story short, Ian didn't have a chance. After hearing his accent and that he was from Edinburgh, it didn't take long for Gilbert Harding, holder of the title The Rudest Man in Britain, to ask if his job had anything to do with something specifically produced in Scotland. Of course, that was a 'yes', and when the questioning reached Lady Isobel, she of the razor-sharp intellect pursued it like a little aristocratic terrier, pouncing on the theme of Scotch Whisky and then shaking it until she had the answer. Of course, Ian was a Scotch Whisky blender, and they'd got him out in seven. But it didn't matter. Just being on the show was as important as winning. Ian had had his ten minutes of fame. After a firm handshake from Eamonn, it was all over, and he disappeared forever from the gaze of the British viewing public. Afterwards, there were cocktails. The contestants were introduced to just about everyone, including the panel. Janet had never been in the presence of British aristocracy before and in a humorously sarcastic aside to Ian wondered if she had to curtsy when she shook hands with Lady Isobel Barnet.

"Dinnae worry, hen, she's no really nobility," he confided. "'Er other name's Morag, she was born in Aberdeen, and she's a Lady only because 'er lawyer husband was knighted."

With that, Janet was relieved and was able to look Morag straight in the eye, woman to woman, Scot to Scot.

"I hear you're actually Scottish?" asked Janet politely in Proper Speak.

"Yes, my dear," said Lady Isobel, whose plummy put-on accent effectively disguised her origins. "I was ectually (she actually said *ectually*) born in Aberdeen and studied medicine at the University of Glasgow."

Janet just couldn't help herself.

"Well," she said, jettisoning Proper Speak, "Ah was born in Leith and Ah studied life at Leith Walk Primary an' the backstreets o' The Kirkgate."

"How interesting, my dear!" opined Lady Isobel and beckoned the waiter to bring her another pink gin.

That evening, Janet and Ian had a farewell dinner in a local restaurant with Vincent and his wife. As the train pulled out of King's Cross station the next morning and the drab suburbs of North London sped by, the euphoria started to dissipate. But much as their arrival back at the Chesser Drive flat on a freezing November evening was a *back tae auld claes an' porridge* moment, Janet remained on a high for weeks to come. She had so much to tell and so many people to tell it to, she'd enjoy herself all over again. But there was more to it than that. Janet had always envied Bella's elevation into the ranks of the wealthy. Not that she resented what her sister had achieved. She'd merely wondered if or when she and Ian would be able to attain anything like a similar status. As the fifties gradually drew to a close, all around, affluence was taking hold. People were now able to purchase consumer goods they could never have afforded ten years before. A fortunate few were now able to go abroad for their holidays. Even her sister, Effie, with her Marks and Spencer wages, had been able to vacation in Davos with a chum.

No, the Swanstons couldn't match the wealth of Bella. Nor were they yet able to take holidays abroad – it would be another twenty years before they could do that. But still, Janet thought, they'd achieved something. They'd been to London, stayed at one of the best hotels, attended the Theatre Royal and rubbed shoulders with establishment figures. Ian had been on television, and she had two fabulous outfits and a winter coat that would be good for many years to come. It had been the honeymoon she and Ian had never had. It had been unique. It wasn't Bella's. It wasn't Effie's. It didn't belong to anyone in her family or anyone she knew. It was hers and hers alone, to hold in her heart and to savour for years to come.

As someone who was invited to appear on one of Britain's most popular 1950s television quiz shows, Ian was a strange choice, for the fact was that the Swanstons didn't possess a television set. Of course, they'd heard of WML and had seen it a few times on other people's televisions. Oddly, the first to have a television in their extended family had been Janet's parents, with three solid wage packets coming into the house. Not surprising, then, that Warburton Crescent was the first to get a telephone, a television set, specially purchased for the 1953 Coronation, and an electric cooker. So if the Swanstons wanted to see Ian on television, that's where they'd have to be.

On Monday 26th January, the Melroses' tiny living room was packed with extended family as well as neighbours. The floor was a sea of bairns, heads tilted back and eyes glued to the screen of the new set the Melroses had bought specially for the occasion. Gone was the old nine-inch Pye that only received the BBC. Now, they had a seventeen-inch black-and-white Decca on slim rocket legs with a sliding door that also got the new ITV channel as well. WML started punctually at 7.30. Ian's sudden appearance brought a rousing cheer and the adults playfully raised their glasses, for, in honour of the occasion, Ian had supplied several bottles of DeSantos's best. Even Alexander Melrose, nominally teetotal, had been persuaded to have a dram. Janet and Ian had made a pact. They hadn't told anyone what the outcome of the panel game was, so everyone was on tenterhooks. Would they guess Ian's job? A groan went up when they did. Janet and Ian both had broad smiles. Folks patted Ian on the back and shook his hand. One of their own had been on television! Another first for the extended Melrose-Swanston clan. In the taxi home, James, perched on the jump seat, examined his mother's face, still ecstatic in the passing yellow glare of the sodium street lights. Even after all these weeks, she was still riding a high. He leant forward.

“Mum? Was there anythin’ ye *didnae* like about bein’ in London?”

“Aye, there was. Aw’ they BBC types fawnin’ ower ye, wi’ their fake posh accents. It could fair make ye boke!”

James sat back, considering her answer. *BBC types*. He wasn’t exactly sure what that meant but he expected he *would* understand some day. Meanwhile, Wee Effie cuddled sleepily up to Ian. She saw him in a new light. Her dad had been on television. He was famous. Wait till she told the other lassies in her class about this!

“Dad?” she asked.

“Aye, what is it, hen?” asked Ian, ever so slightly the worse for wear.

“What was the *best* thing about bein’ on television in London?”

Ian thought for a moment. Then his teeth flashed in the darkness.

“Meetin’ Peter Sellers in the BBC toilets. How many fellaes can say they’ve had a wee-wee wi’ with a Goon?”

The report card

It was just after 5 pm. The pupils were long gone and most of the teachers too. But Miss MacAndrew was still at her desk in her classroom. Brow slightly furrowed, she finished writing and put her fountain pen down. She was finalising the reports for Primary 5a and that was the last one. It was for James Swanston. Miss MacAndrew glanced down the rows and checked the entries on James’s report card. She mulled over his performance. Fourth in class. Not bad for a pupil so much younger and so much more immature than his classmates. And he was Janet Melrose’s son, here, in her very own class. It seemed like destiny. A circle had closed. James had done well and would go into Primary Six after the holidays, with Mr Martin. Ah yes, Mr Martin. That was another story. He was a nice person, with his tubby body, bullet head and continental ways. Odd how they were still kissing a lady’s hand in the middle of the twentieth century. Mr Martin and she sometimes sat over a cup of tea in the staffroom, conversing in French together. Strange, too, how so many Polish people seemed to speak fluent French. But that was as far as their acquaintance went. He seemed such a sad little man, in spite of an occasional volcanic outburst. Ah well, she’d done her best with James. Now it was time to pass him on. Aware that her Bentley would already be waiting in the car park, she quickly signed the report card at the bottom in her small, precise hand and added it to the pile. Just *A. MacAndrew*. She always signed report cards that way. There was no need for them to know that her first name was Arabella.

5 Shelter in thy honor'd shade

Mr Martin

As soon as the School Principal, Mrs Moncrieff, strode into the Primary 6A classroom on a dreich winter's day in 1951, the hubbub subsided and most of the forty-odd children started to rise. She planted herself squarely in front of the class, seeking out the malingerers, making small upward flaps of her right hand, palm up, until the whole class was on its feet. Then she stared around, daring the fidgeters into immobility until everyone was paying attention.

"Good morning, children," she said in a firm voice.

"Good morning, Mrs Moncrieff!" they chanted back in unison.

It was only then that the pupils realised Mrs Moncrieff wasn't alone. Beside and slightly behind her was a very short fat man dressed in a tweed jacket, tie and grey flannels, carrying a battered brown briefcase. He was bald, with a very large head, arched eyebrows and piercing blue eyes. Most of his neck had disappeared into his shirt collar. What was left over was strangely red and blotchy.

"Class, you may sit down!" said Mrs Moncrieff.

The stranger's fixed smile alternated with a look of quiet resolve. The children sat, some intrigued, some indifferent. Any potential chatterers were silenced by meaningful stares from Mrs Moncrieff. Then she began to speak.

"Class, this is your new teacher, Mr Martin."

She let it sink in. Some of the pupils were probably wondering where the previous Primary 6 teacher, Miss Cromarty, had gone, while others were weighing up the new person, wondering just how much they'd be able to get away with. Then she turned to Mr Martin. He took this as his cue. He stepped forward.

“Good morning, children.”

From these three brief words alone, the class could tell that this wasn’t one of their own. Mr Martin spoke funny.

“Mr Martin is not from Scotland,” went on Mrs Moncrieff. “Can anyone guess where he comes from? Hands up!”

A few hands went up.

“Yes, Morag?”

“Frae America, Miss?”

“No, not America. Duncan?”

Duncan Archibald, who had a fascination with crossbows, William Tell and the Alps ventured, “Switzerland, Miss.”

“Close, Duncan, but not quite. Mr Martin is from Poland.”

A muffled sigh went through the class. Poland... Yes, they knew Poland... There were even a few that knew Poland was the reason for The War, the reason their fathers and uncles had to go overseas to fight, and the reason some of them hadn’t come back.

Billy Tennant shot his hand up.

“Please, Sir, did you fight the Germans, Sir?”

Mr Martin said nothing but nodded his head grimly.

The class sat back on its heels. Mr Martin had fought the Jerries... Other hands started to go up but Mrs Moncrieff put her foot down.

“Enough! You’ll have plenty of time to ask questions, that is, if Mr Martin...” She inclined her head to Mr Martin. “...wishes to answer them. I know you will show Mr Martin how well Scottish schoolchildren can behave and how hard they can work.”

She turned back to the newcomer.

“Thank you, Mr Martin.” It was on the tip of her tongue to say, “Good luck”, but fortunately the words didn’t come out. He nodded gallantly and she strode out, to get on with what head teachers do.

Mr Martin had been born Antonin Martynowski in a small town in eastern Poland. A law student, at the age of 19 he’d fought in the Polish Russian war of 1920. He was a founder member of a political nationalist student organization. Once qualified, he’d married his fiancée, practised law and eventually became a district judge. When the Germans invaded in 1939, he’d found himself on assignment to the Polish minority in Danzig. Volunteering in the defence of Polish districts of the city, he received burns to his upper body and neck in an incendiary attack and was evacuated to a makeshift clinic. When defeat was imminent, there were only two choices: surrender or escape. Polish prisoners were being massacred by German death squads so the choice was clear. With the help of a friendly doctor, Antonin was smuggled aboard one of the last vessels that left Danzig bound for Sweden. Presenting himself to the

British embassy in Stockholm, he was spirited aboard a neutral freighter and landed at the Scottish port of Leith.

He wasn't alone. Wartime Britain had become a haven for tens of thousands of Polish sailors, soldiers and airmen who'd managed to escape from their homeland after it was attacked and occupied by Germany. The Polish First Corps, established in September 1940, had its headquarters in Perthshire. Antonin was one of the first volunteers. Due to his seniority and his previous military experience, he was immediately commissioned captain. The Poles were first tasked with defending the east coast of Scotland against the expected German invasion. After the Arnhem disaster, his unit, the 3rd Polish Infantry Brigade, saw active service in northern Europe.

Antonin somehow survived The War but his future was still uncertain. What had once been his home town had since been annexed by the USSR. Poland was now under Soviet occupation. At the February 1945 Yalta Conference, Britain had effectively recognized the Soviet-installed communist government of Poland. In July they followed up by withdrawing recognition of the Polish government in exile in the UK. This left more than 100,000 Poles in limbo. Britain, having welcomed their sacrifice during The War, now only wanted rid of them. Thousands did return home. But as an officer in the PFC, not to mention a Polish nationalist, as well as a judge, Antonin could expect to be put in front of a firing squad if he was among them. He was unable to locate his wife or any member of his family. His numerous enquiries through the Red Cross and other refugee organizations drew a blank. Gradually it sank in that they'd probably all perished in The War. Antonin was faced with a stark choice. In fact, there was no choice. Continental post-war Europe was in ruins. Over the past six years or so, Scotland had become his temporary home. Now it would become permanent.

Antonin returned to Scotland in 1946 at roughly the same time as Ian, and was eventually demobilised. He had nothing bar the clothes he stood up in and a few other bits and pieces in a small suitcase. He naturally gravitated towards Edinburgh, the Scottish city he knew best. Here, he thought, he could find shelter. Here, perhaps, would be his future. Through the offices of the Polish community and local authorities, he was settled in a hostel for displaced persons. Scotland was full of war refugees who for some reason couldn't or wouldn't return home. Poles and Italians made up a sizeable group. Because of his fluency in English and his background, he was offered the job of hostel warden and interpreter. This position paid a reasonable wage, but it wouldn't be permanent. What was he to do? The British government had allowed former Polish servicemen who couldn't return to Poland to settle in Britain, but only under strict conditions of employment. A possible option for Antonin might be to go into teaching.

Like the rest of Britain, Scotland was exhausted, war-weary and suffering serious skill shortages. A lack of teachers was one of them. The new Labour government had emphasised increased investment in education, but in post-war Britain there weren't enough teachers to go round, especially male teachers and particularly in primary education. The respected Edinburgh Provincial Teaching Centre, commonly known as Moray House, was right here in the High Street. Why not give it a try? The thought of becoming a teacher at once lifted Antonin out of his depression but filled him with apprehension too. This was like nothing he'd done before. He'd been first a lawyer, then a soldier. But to stand in front of a class of Scottish schoolchildren? Did he have the aptitude? Was his English good enough? Did he have the energy and commitment to endure perhaps several years of study yet again? Wasn't he too old?

He needn't have worried. Moray House, he learned, would look favourably on his application. His Polish academic qualifications could be credited towards a teaching degree. After much frustration he managed to obtain copies through the Polish Embassy in London. He'd also have to apply for UK citizenship. In his heart, he'd always be Polish. Giving up that special part of him was hard, but there was no alternative if he wanted to have a decent future here in post-war Scotland. So he went through the formalities. In light of his background and wartime contribution, he was granted naturalisation as a British subject. There was no fuss or fanfare, merely a mention in the official gazette in a list of fifty or so other newly minted citizens. But he had to have a new name. Antonin Martynowski didn't only have an alien look about it; to the British – not to mention the Scottish – tongue it was too outlandish, too hard to pronounce. So he became Anthony Martin. Once his documents had been translated and his qualifications accepted, Mr Martin, as he'd be known to his pupils, was ready for teacher training.

By now he was in his late forties. He'd always been small in stature and like most people during wartime had never had enough to eat. Free from these privations, he'd put on weight and lost much of his hair. As a result, his head increasingly resembled a cannonball. With a mercurial personality, which swung from agreeableness to fiery displays of temper, he became something of a phenomenon among the community of mostly younger Scottish students at Moray House. Behind his back they referred to him affectionately as *The Clootie Dumplin'*. Studying to be a teacher at his age could have been much worse. Fortunately for the newly created Mr Martin, there were others in the same boat – a mix of mature students, ex-servicemen and women, displaced persons, naturalised UK citizens, all striving to become teachers. They represented a clearly identifiable minority in the hallowed halls of academia. The institution catered for them through special classes and tutorials. Concessions were made to support their study. At the end of 1950, Mr Martin received the news that he'd passed the requisite papers and had been gazetted as a qualified primary teacher in Scotland. He was ready to be appointed to his first school.

In anticipation of a regular wage, he'd rented a modest two-room flat in Montpelier Park. There was a living room and scullery with a bedroom and bathroom attached. A small gas cooker and a gas heater were provided, along with a shilling meter in the lobby outside his door. He'd made some Scottish friends during teacher training, had found a circle of acquaintances in the local Polish community and was beginning to accept Edinburgh as his new home. Nevertheless, he approached his first teaching job with some trepidation. He'd never had much to do with children in his previous life; his brief spells of teaching practice had been in model classrooms in the primary school attached to Moray House. He'd never stood before a class of children in a real Scottish school. One day at the end of the academic year an envelope dropped through his letterbox. It was a notification from the Scottish Education Department informing him that he'd been assigned to his new school, Fox Crag.

Mr Martin presented himself at his new place of employment before the Christmas holidays. An interview with the headmistress, Mrs Moncrieff, and a meeting with some of his colleagues settled his mind about some of his more onerous concerns. Seriously short of male teachers, Mrs Moncrieff's priority had been to find a man of some maturity to take over what was traditionally regarded as a tough assignment because of its unruly nature, namely the senior class. That he was Polish, and with little teaching experience, was neither here nor there. With the start of the Spring term in January 1951, Mr Martin would take over Primary 6A immediately from the previous teacher, Miss Cromarty, continue with them as Primary 7A the following year, and would take them through to the final, qualifying examination.

Other people's children

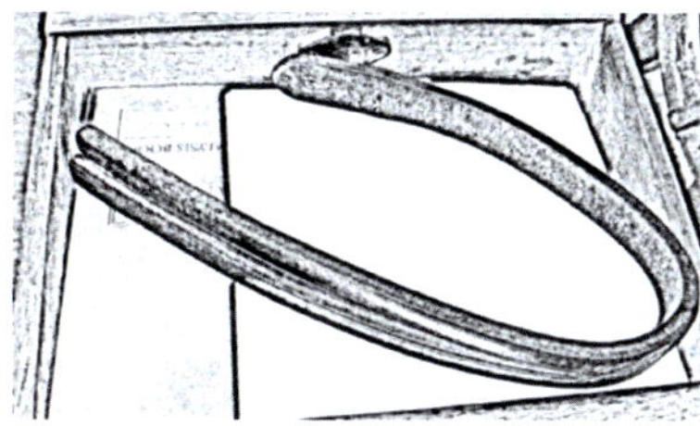

When Mr Martin joined Fox Crag, he was in his fiftieth year. He'd escaped Poland with the clothes he was wearing, his father's pocket watch, a battered brown briefcase and a wallet containing a small photograph of his wife. The previous ten years of his life had robbed him of almost everything he'd possessed: his family, his country, his culture, his native tongue, his career, his wealth, his property and his inheritance. Perhaps, even, his health. He was thankful that Scotland had taken him in. But his soul was empty. His heart nursed such a weight of grief and bitterness against the evil that had destroyed his family and his very existence that it sometimes overwhelmed him. Then, he'd quietly weep by himself in his flat in Bruntsfield, cradling the photo of his Magdalena. Of course, he had some friends. The Polish community was always supportive. The Catholic Church, too. But nothing they did or said could salve the hurt or fill the emptiness inside him.

He knew he wouldn't marry or be with a woman again, not at his age. He knew he was no longer attractive and that people would chuckle benevolently behind his back at his small stature, portly figure and large, round, hairless head. As he put on weight, he found it more and more difficult to get a shirt collar size to encompass his trunk-like neck and to hide his burn scars. Life was starting to be even more of a chore. Loneliness was starting to define him. The one bright light on the horizon was that he now had a new career, a different direction. Something he could focus on. Something, perhaps, that might take his mind off his cares. He'd long ago reconciled himself to the fact that he'd never have the children he and his wife were preparing to devote themselves to before their world collapsed around them. Was it possible, he wondered, that he could devote himself to other people's children?

As the first Monday of the Spring term dawned, Mr Martin rose early, lit the gas heater, shaved and washed, and donned sports jacket,

tie and grey flannels. He ate toast spread with imported tinned Polish strawberry jam and washed it down with a cup of Camp Coffee. Real coffee, Polish Mokka, was still impossible to get for ordinary folks in the British post-war economy. Putting on his overcoat, scarf and tweed cap, he thrust a packet of ham sandwiches into his briefcase. He locked his flat, walked out into the semi-darkness of the winter morning and strode up the hill to the tram stop. The Number 16 tram was crowded with early morning workers on their way into the city. Mr Martin sat clutching his briefcase to his chest, staring out as the bleak tenements and terraces of Edinburgh sped past. He liked to ride the tram. It reminded him of the single-decker trams of 1930s Warsaw, but he usually tried to get a seat upstairs for the view and the warmth. Around him, passengers scanned the morning papers, drew on cigarettes or just sat dozing quietly. As the tram clacked, rattled and swayed downhill through Bruntsfield, then Tollcross, he couldn't help thinking how lucky these people were to have survived The War with their city intact. Warsaw was a shattered, barely habitable wasteland by war's end. His thoughts were interrupted as the conductor fussed towards him and he held out his fare.

He quickly alighted near the Scott Monument. To his right, a freezing haar had settled over the low-lying Gardens, blotting out the monuments and the bandstand, but the Castle rose, sharply outlined in the clear morning sky, brooding above the city. To his left, the grand stores of Princes Street were still closed and shuttered at this hour. Lights burning inside told of cleaners at work or perhaps early-comer shop assistants setting up for the day. Pulling his scarf around him and tugging his cap against the cold morning air, he walked briskly eastwards. He didn't have long to wait for the Number 35 bus that would take him on the second leg of his commute. Since he was now heading out of town in the opposite direction, the bus was almost empty. As he got off at Kemp's Corner, the morning shift at Munrospun was underway as women in headscarves streamed through the gates. A smart-looking middle-aged man wearing a white coat stood in the doorway of the grocer's and gave him a friendly nod as he passed. He had a brief five-minute walk to the school through the council estate. Workers were emerging from the pebble-dashed houses with their shabby winter gardens. Then suddenly there was Fox Crag School. At this early hour, the playground and fields were deserted. The small staff car park was empty. The only other sign of life was the janitor sweeping the yard. Mr Martin gave him a good morning and made his way inside. After making his presence known at the school office and introducing himself to a colleague, another early bird like himself, he climbed the stairs and walked along the corridor to his empty classroom.

His first challenge had been to get a grip on his class. This was no easy task; the school had been built to service the council estate and his pupils were overwhelmingly from a working-class background. Mr Martin had become familiar with the peculiar class system in Britain, a phenomenon that didn't have an exact equivalent in his home country. He couldn't claim to understand all the nuances of an ideology that appeared to separate children, almost at birth, and allocate them to a particular social and economic future. But he was aware that a class of eleven- to twelve-year-old working-class children were likely to be boisterous, fractious, unwashed, malodorous and, sometimes, even, violent. At teacher training college, the problem had been raised and discussed with much reference to educational theory, the need to understand the children's origins, and the importance of making lessons interesting. After that particular session, however, Duncan Galloway, another mature student, had taken Mr Martin aside.

"Listen, Anthony," he said, "if I were you, I wouldn't bother with all that rubbish. It might work at The Royal High but not the sort of place they're sending us to. Take my advice; get yourself a belt, keep it in your desk drawer, and use it – often."

The Belt – or *tawse* – was the standard method of corporal punishment in Scottish schools. Consisting of a leather strap about a quarter of an inch thick, it was about a foot long, with an indented grip for the user at one end, and split into three or more thongs or tails at the other end. Sometimes described as 'Lochgelly's Finest' after its place of manufacture, it was the mainstay of any Scottish teacher likely to face discipline problems in the classroom. The victim was made to hold out his hand, palm uppermost, while the teacher brought The Belt down on the target. There was among pupils a time-honoured lore about what to do when faced with The Belt. Some said it helped to spit on one's hand beforehand. Some said after. Classmates were advised to make sure their shirt or jacket cuff was pulled well down, otherwise they risked the thongs snaking up their forearm and leaving painful weals. Others cautioned to choose carefully which hand to hold out. The effect of a single belting on a hand was plain to see and to feel. The hand was red, swollen and numb and could be useless for some time after.

At first, Mr Martin had been reluctant to take Duncan's advice. He was a kindly man by temperament and didn't naturally find pleasure in physically disciplining children. Besides, he'd experienced enough violence during The War to last a lifetime. Any proclivity in his nature towards aggression had been sucked out of him, or so he thought. So his first term at Fox Crag, he shied away from using The Belt, hoping instead to instil the necessary discipline through benevolence and rationality. However, sadly, he was to find that such was the potential for disruption in a classroom of eleven- and twelve-year-olds that teaching and learning would have been impossible without it. His vulnerability in this alien environment made him sensitive to perceived mockery on the part of class troublemakers. Then he'd fly into a rage. His cheeks flushed and the little pouches of skin to the right and left of his mouth began to quiver. As he got more enraged, the words tumbled out of his mouth and, predictably, his English would suffer, which in turn made his tormenters laugh all the more. Fearing that he was losing control of the class, belting the offenders was the only way, as far as he could see, to restore order. Eventually, towards the end of the term, he found himself filling out the form to order his Belt from an educational supplier. From then on, Mr Martin resorted to The Belt whenever a breakdown of class discipline threatened. Not that he belted pupils at will. But at least once a day, The Belt would appear from his drawer and some unlucky class member would be returning to his desk clutching his throbbing hand.

When Miss MacAndrew's Class 5A became 6A in the autumn term of 1956, Mr Martin's greatest challenge from a discipline perspective was undoubtedly Andrew Peterson. He quickly discovered that Andrew was the arch-troublemaker of the class. Unfortunately, Mr Martin possessed neither Miss MacAndrew's local knowledge nor her magic spell. The simple exchange of information between colleagues that might have neutralised Andrew in Mr Martin's classroom never happened. Furthermore, he was now a year older and more sure of himself. If there was any mischief going on between the rows of desks, Andrew was behind it; if there was any intimidation to be done in the playground, Andrew was the one doing it; if there were wild, violent games to be organised and staged, it was Andrew in charge; and if there were any nasty smells to be produced by farting in class, it was Andrew who was ready to oblige. Mr Martin lost count of the number of times he belted Andrew. Under Mrs Moncrieff's administration, the maximum number of permissible beltings at any one time for a specific offender was three. However, this became a regular occurrence with Andrew. And no matter how much, none of it seemed to have any effect. With his dark hair, intelligent eyes and mocking expression, Andrew sucked it up, laughed it off and returned to his seat, basking in the awe of the class. Andrew became, singlehandedly, the bane of Mr Martin's life at Fox Crag.

But it wasn't only rogues and bullies that were belted. Sometimes innocents too became victims of The Belt. Take for instance the incident of the gobstopper in Hairy Mary's knickers. Mary Robertson was a homely, buxom twelve-year-old, physically mature for her age. Her standard attire was a dirty pink woollen cardigan over a blouse and a dirndl skirt. She wore a ribbon in the dark, lank hair that fell around her ears in an untidy bob and her cheeks were permanently flushed. Aware of her unattractiveness, Mary enjoyed using her bulk and size to give her fellow pupils a hard time. As well as being a bully, she also had a reputation which had earned her the nickname Hairy Mary, for Mary was known to be good for a feel round the back of the toilet blocks in return for suitable remuneration. Since she had a sweet tooth, any laddie that had sweeties to spare might be a potential client. One day, Mary had been plying her trade as usual with the older boys during morning playtime. Her earnings for the session included a new, unsucked, gobstopper. James loved gobstoppers. However, had he known the provenance of this particular gobstopper he wouldn't have been so enthusiastic, for Mary was in the habit of keeping her earnings in her knickers. This was by far the safest place, considering she had no pockets. So when the bell rang, up went her skirt and in went the gobstopper.

Back she went to class and took her place at her desk. Whether her knickers had stretched, or whether she'd been careless about storage, no one could say. All they knew was that in the middle of Mr Martin's lesson on the geography of Canada the gobstopper suddenly escaped from its hiding place, dropped to the classroom floor and rolled back down the aisle between the desks. This successful jail break hadn't gone unnoticed by Mary's neighbours. Feet were thrust out in desperate attempts to block the runaway sweetie's path. It was Kenny Ferguson's foot that succeeded. Holding the gobstopper under the sole of his shoe, he waited until Mr Martin was distracted then bent down to pick it up. Wiping it off on the front of his grey cotton shirt, he was about to pop it into his mouth when Mary reminded him of its ownership.

"Hey, geez that back! It's mine," she said in a loud whisper.

"It wiz yours - it's mine noo!" he whispered back.

But then Neil Munro leant over and said in his ear, "D'ye no ken where that's been?"

"Aye," said Kenny, "oan the flair."

"Yeah, but before that, it was in Hairy Mary's knickers!"

Kenny gave an audible "Ugh!" and hastened to get rid of the offending object. Smartly turning round in his seat, he placed it on the desk behind him.

"What's this?" whispered the beneficiary of Kenny's largesse.

Before Kenny could speak, Neil chipped in.

"It's a gobstopper frae Hairy Mary's knickers!"

The recipient of the gobstopper screwed up his face in disgust and passed it quickly to his neighbour. And thus did the gobstopper do a tour of almost the entire classroom.

"Pass it on, it's frae Hairy Mary's knickers!"

By the time it landed on James's desk, the gobstopper had suffered badly from its odyssey. Its colour was now dirty pink, it was sticky with hairs and marked by numerous grubby fingers. He hastily passed it on, not forgetting to include the vital message. But Mr Martin was well aware that something was afoot from the giggles, whispers and suppressed turmoil that was going on behind his back as he attempted to work at the blackboard. He chose an opportune moment to whirl round. As luck would have it, wee Sandy Gibson, just in the process of passing the gobstopper on, was caught *in flagrante*.

"Alexander Gibson stand up!" roared Mr Martin.

Sandy sheepishly got to his feet.

"And what is that behind your back?"

"Nothin', Sir."

Sandy desperately tried to dispose of the evidence by dropping it on the floor. Sadly for him, the sharp click of a gobstopper impacting bare wood was clearly audible to the entire class and, more importantly, to Mr Martin. Nor did the camber co-operate, for the gobstopper rolled right to Mr Martin's feet. The teacher made short shrift. He crooked his finger at Sandy, beckoning him forward, then pointed down at the offending sweetie.

"Pick it up and put it on my desk!"

As he spoke, with his other hand he opened his desk drawer and withdrew the dreaded Belt from its lair.

"Hold out your hand!"

Sandy did as he was told.

Thwack! The Belt came down and Sandy whimpered.

"Now, go back to your seat and no more nonsense!"

Poor Sandy. Everyone else in the class – with perhaps the exception of Hairy Mary – was just as guilty as he was, but the belting had the required effect. A chastened class returned to copying the map of Canada, with the main cities, rivers and lakes inserted. But what, wondered James, had happened to the gobstopper? It was now nowhere to be seen and no one had the courage to look for it or ask. Mary was furious and blamed everyone but herself for her bad luck. Afterwards, the rumour went around that the gobstopper had ended up in Mr Martin's desk drawer next to his Belt; that even though it was foosty, he'd cleaned it up for his own use since he was partial to a boiled sweet for his breath; and that he'd sucked on it while marking jotters that afternoon after school. For how was he to know that its previous abode had been the moist, dark recesses of Hairy Mary's knickers?

Between two states of being

James took the move from Miss MacAndrew to Mr Martin in his stride, though it represented a major shift; for the first time, he'd be taught by a male teacher. From kind, doting Miss Douglas, to scary Miss Boyle, to competent Miss MacAndrew, James had got used to being under the authority of a woman. Now, not only was it a man in charge, it was a foreigner, too. Not that it made too much difference to him personally. Like most of his classmates in 6A, James would rarely if ever have come into contact with a foreigner during his primary education. The vast majority of pupils in government-run schools were likely to be taught by locals, or at least Scots. But now, following the massive dislocation of war and resultant teacher shortage, it was more common for a Mr Martin or a Miss Douglas to stand in front of a class of Scottish schoolchildren. Still, no one appeared to hold Mr Martin's foreignness against him. Yes, Scotland had its share of xenophobes of one stripe or another. Edinburgh wasn't insulated from the chronic, low-level anti-English sentiment that pervaded the ranks of Scottish society. Yet, there was no ill-will towards Mr Martin merely on account of his being Polish. His pupils accepted him just as he was.

It may be that Mr Martin himself contributed to this state of affairs. He dressed like most other Scottish male primary teachers – collar and tie, tweed jacket, flannels, even a flat tweed cap to protect his head in cold weather, which was just about always. The subject matter of his lessons was what could be expected from any local, for he followed the curriculum to the letter. He was a competent instructor. His spoken English was fluent, albeit accented, though outbursts of fury or passion caused his syntax to wobble. He belted troublemakers. He corrected his pupils' homework and tests. He dutifully filled out a report card for each pupil at the end of each term. No one in authority at Fox Crag Primary had told the pupils of the current 6A he was from Poland, nor had he. It was simply common knowledge. But he never projected his nationality. He never referred to his past or how he'd landed in Scotland. Unlike Miss Douglas, he never regaled them with tales of his native land. It was as if, at least in the classroom, Mr Martin had turned his back on Poland and all things Polish. His Poland no longer existed. It was as if with his flat cap and his tweed jacket he'd embraced Scottishness without actually being Scottish. It was as if he inhabited a no man's land between two states of being.

Yet, despite Mr Martin's success in downplaying his foreignness, his pupils couldn't avoid regarding him as anything but different. For a start, his appearance was odd. By the time James came under his care, he was 55 years old. The traumas of the past two decades had had their effect. He was prematurely ageing. He was shrinking in height while managing to remain just as corpulent. When James stood close to him he realised with a shock that at only ten or eleven years of age he was almost as tall. Mr Martin's head, entirely bald and round as a cannonball was, more than ever, out of proportion to his body. There were also the scars under his chin and on his neck. James was permanently fascinated by these scars. He fantasised that Mr Martin had been wounded while battling the Germans from behind a makeshift street barricade. Ironically, his fantasy was pretty accurate.

Then there was Mr Martin's overall demeanour in class. He was neither merely kind, nor merely grouchy, nor merely competent. He could be all of these things, depending on what time of day it was and what day of the week. James gradually discerned behind the stern, punctilious exterior a kind individual. There would be a friendly word here and a supportive gesture there. At times, Mr Martin even seemed to like being among his pupils, guiding and chiding them in a grandfatherly way. Yet, he appeared permanently on tenterhooks, as if waiting for something to upset the equilibrium of his world. When it happened, usually instigated by the likes of Andrew Peterson, he'd fly into a rage and become another person.

It would be unfair to say he was intimidating, as Miss Boyle was, for he was nothing like Miss Boyle; he didn't seem to have a vindictive bone in his body. But he had something to protect, something to conceal deep inside and, when pressured, his vulnerability was exposed. When they'd got used to his outbursts, most of the class, rather than being upset, merely reflected on them as something to be endured. Poor Mr Martin. That's how he was. Nothing would change him. Of course, none of them had an inkling of his past. None of them guessed at the traumas and tragedies he'd endured. None of them knew he'd lost everything. But despite their youth, they possessed sufficient humanity to be aware that he was defined by a lingering sense of sorrow that enveloped him and touched everything he did and said. It was as if he wanted to reach out to them but couldn't because of what he'd become.

For his part, over the past six years, Mr Martin had persevered in his original resolve to dedicate himself to other people's children. When he stood in class in the autumn of 1956, observing the newly constituted 6A, he saw 34 faces looking up at him, 18 girls and 16 boys on the verge of puberty, one of them James Swanston. Experience had taught him that a handful would be exemplary scholars; a handful would cause trouble; and the rest would swing whichever way the wind blew them, depending on the situation. He knew, now, how to run the classroom. He was more confident than he'd been at the start. However, he still felt ill at ease. What was he doing here? He wasn't a teacher by vocation. He'd become a teacher only through force of circumstance. There had been no other option. And there was still no other option.

The anti-NATO Warsaw Pact, signed in Warsaw the previous year, had, by its very name, yet again attested to the Polish subservience to Moscow. The ruthless suppression of the uprisings in Poznan the previous June had provided yet more evidence. Although they'd led to the rise of Gomulka, who'd promised more liberal policies, he was rapidly revealing himself to be just another Soviet stooge. It didn't take a genius to conclude that the situation in Poland would be, for him, just as dangerous as before. If there had ever been an iota of doubt in his mind, it was easily dismissed by depressing events like these. It was clear that there was no going back.

If things had been different, if 1939 hadn't happened, he'd probably by now be a senior judge in some small town in Eastern Poland. He and his wife would be prominent, respected members of the community. His wife would be active in local societies and charitable institutions. People would look up to him for advice and support. He might even be involved in local politics. They'd be well-off. They'd have a spacious villa, together, perhaps, with a cook and a serving girl, not to mention a chatka in the country for summer vacations. He'd drive a Mercedes. His children would go to a good Polish school and would be educated with traditional Polish values in mind.

Instead, here he was in a classroom in Scotland pretending to be a teacher, eking out a solitary existence on a teacher's salary. He knew he was a fraud. He knew was walking a tightrope. Any time now, the authorities would find out. They'd arrest him and deport him back to Poland to face the communist regime there. Before he began to panic, he mentally shook his head to clear his brain from such thoughts. The 34 faces were waiting. It was time to start the lesson.

Schule in June

When the class trooped in at 1.15 after the midday break, Mr Martin was standing with an open book in his hand and his back to the room, writing on the blackboard. As he took his place at his desk, James peered over the teacher's shoulder, curious to see what was there. He could make out the two words *Schule* and *June* in Mr Martin's large, looping script, but most of the rest was blocked by his body. *Schule*? What did that word mean? Mr Martin went on writing, giving the class a few minutes grace to settle down. Then he abruptly stopped, turned round, placed the book, still open, on his lectern and smacked the palms of his hands together several times in a cloud of chalk dust. All was revealed. Mr Martin had clearly been busy, for the entire blackboard was taken up with a poem. The title was in capitals: *SCHULE IN JUNE*. James scanned the first verse:

There's no a clood in the sky,
The hill's clear as can be,
An' the broon road's windin' ower it,
But - no for me!

James said the words under his breath, liking the sounds he heard. But where had he heard them before? He couldn't put his finger on it. Mr Martin spoke.

"This afternoon we are going to study a poem. This is a Scottish poem and you are going to have to help me because I don't speak Scottish."

It was an obvious attempt at a joke. Mr Martin didn't joke very often. As if to reward him for his unexpected levity, a polite titter rippled around the room.

"First, you are to write down this poem in your jotters."

A hand went up. It was, as usual, Henry Faulkner, the class swot.

"Pen or pencil, please, Sir?"

"Pen, and make sure you do it in your best handwriting. I'll be coming around to check your work."

The class bent obediently to the task. A *Scottish* poem! Of course, there were plenty of Scottish songs, but apart from Rabbie Burns, they'd never heard of a Scottish poet or Scottish poems before. James lifted the lid of his desk and got out his jotter. It had a pale grey cover of thick cartridge paper with the words Edinburgh Corporation Education Committee in large, black type. James found the notion of such an unwieldy, polysyllabic, four-word combination hard to grasp, let alone to say out loud. *Edinburgh Corporation Education Committee.* The name and its location on his jotter seemed to be sending out a warning: *You may think this jotter belongs to you, but it doesn't. It belongs to us, the Edinburgh Corporation Education Committee, and you may use it only with our consent.* It was as if he were renting the jotter. He had an image of a panel of dour old men (and a dour old woman or two) in black suits sitting on plush seats of red velvet around a heavy wooden table in a dusty committee room somewhere off the High Street, whose sole mission it was to oversee the distribution of jotters and to ensure Mr Martin adhered strictly to the rule that an old jotter had to be fully used up before a new one could be issued.

James opened his rented jotter with the lined pages. When new, the first task was always to take a ruler and a pencil and draw a margin on the left-hand side of every page. He turned to a fresh page with its newly-drawn margin. He picked up the pen from its cradle. It was about six inches long and consisted of a wooden wand with a rusty steel nib attached to one end. The small ceramic inkwell was sunk into a circular hole in the front right-hand corner of his desk. He dipped the nib into the ink, shook off the excess, and with the tip of his tongue poking out of the corner of his mouth he started writing laboriously, glancing back and forward from his page to the blackboard. First, the title, *Schule in June* at the top of the page. The first verse, and more dips into the inkwell. It felt strange, forming with his pen words he normally only heard spoken, like *clood* and *broon*. Then the second verse.

It's June, wi' a splurge o' colour
In glen an' on hill,
An' it's me wad be lyin' up yonner,
But then - there's the schule.

Meanwhile, Mr Martin, relaxed now his board work was done, patrolled the aisles, gripping each end of a wooden ruler behind his back with his still chalky fingers. Looking over shoulders, he critically examined his pupils' efforts, commenting here and there, and using his ruler to point out some writing misdemeanour. James had reached verse five.

A hop an' a step frae the windie,
Just fower mile awa',
An' I could be lyin' there thinkin'
O' naething ava'.

A hop an' a step frae the windae... He looked up to make sure Mr Martin was busy, turned in his seat and looked out of the window. The designers of Fox Crag School had broken with the Victorian convention of inserting rippled glass in the lower half of classroom windows to keep the pupils' attention focused on the lesson. Here at Fox Crag, the windows came down to desk height and were entirely transparent. It wasn't June. And there were plenty of cloods in the sky. Nevertheless, there it was – Arthur's Seat. It was as clear as can be, as if just *a hop and a step frae the windae.* And if he strained hard enough, he could make out *the broon road*, the Radical Road, just a dark smudge across the lion profile. He imagined himself on a hot June day, sprawling in the shade of the ruined chapel, engulfed by the fragrance of summer grass and buttercups, looking down at the wee lochan and the people clumsy at the oars of the rented rowing boats.

Suddenly sensing a presence at his elbow, he looked round cautiously. Out of the corner of his eye he could see Mr Martin studying his efforts. Flustered, he quickly moved on to the sixth and final verse.

"Do not press too hard with the nib." The ruler came down on the page. "Look, you are making tramlines!"

"Yes, Sir."

Mr Martin straightened up, turned to face the class and picked out individual pupils to read through the poem a verse at a time, while he stood, arms folded, head to one side, as if concentrating on the words.

"Now, who can read the last verse for us?"

Nobody offered. He turned back to James since he was nearest.

"Stand up boy and read verse six."

James got to his feet clutching his jotter. He gulped a couple of times then negotiated the verse, easily articulating the vernacular but feeling strange about having to do so in public. He turned red in the process as titters arose all around him.

Ay! -the schule is a winnerfu' place,
Gin ye tak it a' roon,
An' I've nae objection to lessons,
Whiles -but in June?

"Good, James, and now, can you tell us what the poem is about?"

James hesitated. “Well, Sir, it’s about a laddie who’s stuck in school on a nice summer’s day. An’ Sir, ’e’d much rather be up on the hill.” He pointed out the window. “Look, Sir, there’s the hill, right there.”

The whole class craned out of their seats to see what James was pointing at. Mr Martin, too, followed his gaze. Arthur’s Seat. It was as if he hadn’t made the connection before. There was a hush as a gentle smile crossed his face. He appeared to have switched off the present. Was he, too, wishing himself up there on the hill instead of here in the classroom with 34 fractious children to contend with? Or was he perhaps remembering another hill, in another place, at another time? A moment, then the spell was broken. Normal service had been resumed. Mr Martin cleared his throat and the craning pupils returned to their seats and their work.

“Yes, very good. Now, come on slow coaches, finish writing it out!”

“Please, Sir, Ah dinnae understand aw’ the words.”

“What don’t you understand?”

“Please, Sir, what’s *caller*?

“Let me see.” Mr Martin turned to his book, ran his index finger down the page and turned back to the class. “Caller means fresh.”

He let that sink in. Then he read the verse out loud in his best Polish-accented Scots:

There's a wude wi' a burn rinnin' through it,
Caller an' cool,
Whaur the sun splashes licht on the bracken
An' dapples the pool.

The whole class smiled. A stage whisper was heard from the back row: “Nae bad for a Polish!” Fortunately, Mr Martin was oblivious.

“You see,” he went on with enthusiasm, “it’s a burn (he pronounced it *bern*), a stream and it’s fresh and cool on a hot summer’s day.”

“Please, Sir, mah granny lives in Newhaven and sometimes she talks about caller herrin’. Is that the same thing?”

“Well, I suppose so,” said Mr Martin. But really, he wasn’t sure.

When the lesson was over, their homework was to learn one verse of the poem to be recited in class the next day. James put his heart and soul into it but Mr Martin never checked their homework. So he never learned how successful his Scottish poetry lesson had been. Still, James’s efforts weren’t entirely unrewarded. The poem remained fixed in his memory, to be taken out and dusted, mused over and enjoyed whenever there was cause to remember a June day in Scotland, a clear blue sky, and a distant hill calling him back.

The Martinis

Mr Martin had his favourites. They were the best-behaved pupils and usually the best performers in the class. In his second year with Mr Martin, it dawned on James that he'd become a member of this exclusive group. One of the benefits was being allowed to sit at the front of the class and right next to a radiator, which offered some small comfort to shivering children during Scottish winters in a poorly heated classroom. Another benefit was having permission to enter the school building early, before school officially started for the day. This privilege was extended to only four of Mr Martin's favourite pupils, Connie Purdy, Morag McKenzie, Malcolm McQuillan and James. Some of the other pupils, jealous of Mr Martin's special set, sneeringly dubbed them The Martinis. When he first heard the taunt, James, in his immature way, had no idea what a Martini was. But when it was explained to him, he thought for a moment. A Martini? Something that grown-ups like to drink? He was sure his mother had had one once. He decided he liked the name and he never let it bother him again.

For the rest of the school the day started at ten to nine. Before that, entry was strictly limited to authorised persons. On cold winter mornings, pupils would stand around shivering in the playground, longing to be allowed into the building. Suddenly, at the appointed time, a teacher appeared through the glass doors of the main entry carrying a heavy handbell. As soon as the cacophony of the bell was heard, class teachers walked briskly to pre-set locations while the noisy throng quickly ordered itself into twelve classes. Each class lined up in twos before its class teacher. Under the teacher's gaze, the noise and chatter quickly died down. When all classes were assembled, the teacher with the bell shouted, "Lead on" and the entire body of scholars would enter the school class by class, the most junior first and most senior last. When the playground was empty, the teacher in charge would have a last look around, re-enter through the glass doors and lock them. Thus was Fox Crag ready for the morning's lessons.

But by dint of their special status, James and his fellow favourites were exempted from these onerous requirements. Arriving some time before 8.15, they'd saunter up to the main entrance, through the glass doors into the relative warmth under the envious gaze of the mere mortals left out in the cold. They'd then make their way along silent, deserted corridors and past empty classrooms to Mr Martin's room. As they arrived, one by one, they'd usually find that Mr Martin was already there. However, there was a cost, albeit an insubstantial one, for the four favourites were tasked to be Mr Martin's helpers.

There was the milk to be brought up. By decree of the dour old men and women of the Edinburgh Corporation Education Committee, not only were jotters distributed to the pupils, milk was as well, a third of a pint per day for every pupil who requested it in small, handy glass bottles with tinfoil caps, a healthy option for growing children coming out of wartime austerity. While the girls were busy in the classroom, James and Malcolm made their way down the backstairs to the jannie's domain, where the freshly delivered crates had been stacked. They picked up the crate tagged 7A, one on each side, and made their way back upstairs. Each crate held 36 bottles but not everyone wanted milk so the crate was never full. It would be drunk during morning playtime. Sometimes in winter it froze and pushed up the foil caps. Some pupils liked it like that. The ones who didn't had their milk stacked along the radiators. That was Malkie's job. By the time playtime arrived at 10.30, it was nice and warm.

Then there were various tasks in the classroom. The blackboard had to be cleaned. The wooden-handled chalk dusters had to be taken down the back and beaten out against a wall. Jotters had to be distributed. Pencils were sharpened at the sharpener fixed to the teacher's desk. The inkwells had to be filled. The heavy glass ink jar was kept in the class cupboard. It had a red rubber stopper out of which protruded a glass tube. It was no mean feat to hold the jar in both hands and tour the desks, carefully filling each inkwell without spilling a drop.

By the time the jobs were done, it was getting on for quarter to nine and the four pupils were free to sit on their desks, swinging their legs and talking quietly amongst themselves, something that would never have been tolerated during normal class time. Meanwhile, Mr Martin, unconcerned, busied himself at the front of the classroom with his books and papers. Finally, he opened his desk, took out a paper bag and stood up. The children knew what was coming and stood up too, for what was about to happen was one of the very few concessions Mr Martin made to his homeland and his culture, one of the few indications to his pupils - but only to the favoured quartet - that he was indeed a native of Poland. As he did every morning, Mr Martin took a handful of sweets out of the bag, selected four, and placed them carefully side-by-side in a row along the outside rim of his desk. Then he looked up expectantly at the four Martinis.

"Well, help yourselves!" he said.

On first acquaintance, these were sweeties like James had never seen before. They were shaped like miniature rectangular boxes. Each one was individually wrapped. The waxed wrappers had strange foreign writing that James couldn't decipher. Each had a colourful picture of a different fruit; a raspberry, strawberry, apple, and so on. The sweetie inside had a hard, glazed shell, but when you bit into it there was a soft fruity centre that melted on the tongue. Each flavour matched the colour of the sweetie and the wrapper. They were Polish sweeties, juicy drops of delight. For James and his friends, sugar rationing was still a memory and any sweeties at all were still something of a luxury. But these sweeties were extra special. Not only were they deliciously tart, but they were also a reward for effort. They'd come all the way from Poland and they were from Mr Martin. Malcolm guzzled his without hesitation but James couldn't bring himself to rip off the stylish wrapper. So he stored his rewards in his school bag and ate them at his leisure, secure in the knowledge that he was probably one of only two boys in Scotland that day sucking a sweetie from Poland.

Then disaster struck. Every Friday afternoon, as a way of closing off the week, Mr Martin held a spelling test.

"Get out your jotters. Number from one to twenty in the margin. Let's see if your spelling has improved..." He paused while the class did his bidding. "... Number one..." Then they got to number seventeen.

"Number seventeen – *recognise*"

James wrote it down: r-e-c-o-d-n-i-s-e.

"Now exchange jotters with your neighbour and mark their work."

"Ah bet ye dinnae get them aw' right," mocked James's neighbour, Ricky Jameson.

"Bet ye Ah do," whispered James. Since he usually scored full marks, he felt himself on solid ground. They marked the test. So far James had not a single mistake, while Ricky had four. Then they came to question seventeen. Mr Martin wrote the correct answer on the blackboard: r-e-c-o-g-n-i-s-e.

"Ha, ha," mocked Ricky again, "got one wrong! Cannae spell *recognise*!"

"Ye didnae mark it right," James shot back and tried to grab his jotter while Ricky held it from him at arm's length, laughing quietly. But they were incautiously getting louder, which was enough to get the attention of a Mr Martin already at breaking point after a normally stressful week.

"What are you boys doing?" he barked angrily. "Stand up, the pair of you!"

They stood sheepishly.

"Well, what on earth is going on?"

James looked at the blackboard behind Mr Martin's head and saw: r-e-c-o-g-n-i-s-e. He looked at his jotter, which he'd grabbed back from Ricky and saw: r-e-c-o-d-n-i-s-e.

“But Sir, you said *recodnise*, r-e-c-o-d-n-i-s-e.”

“No, I did not,” said Mr Martin.

James threw caution to the winds. Had he become too presumptuous about the exact nature of his relationship with Mr Martin? Injudiciously, he began to argue.

“But Sir, you *did*...”

Forced to work in a language that wasn’t his native tongue and uneasy that he had in fact pronounced the word incorrectly, Mr Martin’s already flushed face became redder than ever. Some pupils started to giggle, others were turning in their seats and exchanging comments. Mr Martin hated being made to look foolish. Especially in front of a mob of unruly children. He exploded with rage. Shaking with emotion, he put down his chalk, pulled open the desk drawer, took out The Belt and motioned to James:

“Come out here, you insolent boy!”

James couldn’t disguise his shock. His face went as pale as Mr Martin’s was crimson. He was going to be belted. *He* was... By Mr Martin. As if in a dream, he walked to the front of the class.

“Hold out your hand.”

Of course, he forgot all the advice he’d been given. He was right-handed and he automatically held that hand out. He forgot to spit. He forgot to pull down his cuff. As the belt came down, for a split second he glimpsed the full fury of Mr Martin’s expression before he closed his eyes in anticipation of the blow. Whack! The noise seemed to echo around the room. Involuntarily, tears sprang into his eyes. His hand felt as if it had been caught in a vice inside a furnace. He could feel the stinging all the way up to his elbow. His arm dropped to his side and he winced, shaking it out to try and reduce the agony.

“Now go back to your seat.”

The rest of the class, shocked into silence for once, stared in awe, not so much because of the punishment itself but because of the identity of the victim. It was James Swanston, one of the Martinis. It sank in. Mr Martin had belted a teacher’s pet... And with that, Mr Martin had gained new respect in the eyes of the members of Class 7A.

Somehow, James got through what was left of the afternoon, nursing his shattered hand and barely able to hold a pencil. He was in a fog of pain, resentment and shame. Mr Martin had belted *him*. Worse still, he hadn’t got full marks in the test... But that wasn’t the end of it. When the bell rang at 3.30 and the class was dismissed, James was hoping to slink out unnoticed. In vain. Mr Martin, standing by his desk, crooked a finger to call him over. From the look on his face and his jumbled grammar, it was obvious how angry he still was.

"You do not to come any more help in the morning. No! Finished!" he said. "Not any more, from Monday!"

James was in disgrace and had never felt more embarrassed. Come Monday, he got to school at the usual early hour but had to stand in the playground chittering in the cold as the three remaining Martinis, one by one, swept past him into the warm. When the bell was rung, unaccustomed to lining up, he was confused about where to go and some teachers shouted at him. Eventually, he tagged along after the others as his class entered, lowering his eyes to avoid the gaze of Mr Martin.

James never did get his privilege back as Mr Martin's helper; Henry Faulkner was appointed in his place. In time, James sensed that Mr Martin regretted what he'd done. Of course, he never said so. Gradually their relationship seemed to heal, though it was never the same as before. The bond had been broken. But for James, the worst thing was the loss of Mr Martin's daily sweetie. Once the supply of juicy drops of delight from Poland had dried up, his life was never the same again.

The Qualy

Summer was on its way and the Qualy loomed on the horizon. It was the practice in Scottish schools to triage pupils at the age of 12 by dint of an examination – the Qualifying Examination or Qualy, as it was known. For the pupils in government schools, primary education ended with the Qualy. Success in the Qualy meant the opportunity of a further six years of academic education at a grammar school with a view to university study and a possible future in one of the professions – teaching, law or perhaps even medicine. Failure meant three years of vocational education at a secondary modern school for a possible career in one of the trades (boys), or for positions in areas such as retail, office work or, in special cases, junior positions in the civil service (girls and boys).

Courtesy of the wise heads of the Edinburgh Corporation Education Committee, the majority of pupils in Fox Crag would be sent to one of two secondary schools: those who passed the Qualy – usually a small elite - were sent to The Academy and those who didn't found themselves at Lothian Park. One or two top students would do particularly well in the Qualy. Their parents would be advised that not only did their brainy offspring qualify for a grammar school, but it might also be possible to arrange a scholarship at one of Edinburgh's top private, fee-paying schools such as The Royal High School for boys or George Watson's Ladies' College for girls.

Class 7A would be the next cohort to take the Qualy. There was no specific preparation, no study of previous papers, no advice on how to pass, in fact, no information at all about the content for either the parents or the pupils themselves. All that happened was that one day in spring, Mr Martin announced that the following Thursday they'd all take the Qualifying Examination. And that was that.

James's parents had no particular expectations with regard to their children's education, but there was one thing Janet was clear in her mind about; she wanted her children to have a better start in life than she'd had. Ian shared her outlook. Like most working-class youngsters of their generation, Janet's and Ian's education had ended at the age of 14. From then on, they'd been expected to find work to help feed their families. For people like them, neither the financial support nor the educational framework existed for further education of any kind, let alone university entrance. Now, in light of the educational reforms of the last two decades, both James and Wee Effie had far better opportunities than their parents had had. Like many working-class parents, the Swanstons didn't pressure their bairns to excel educationally. Wee Effie had taken the Qualy three years previously and was now at Lothian Park. The fact that she'd failed to make it to a grammar school didn't come as any great shock to her parents. They bore the unwelcome news much as one would have to put up with the announcement that the Russians had launched Sputnik. There was nothing they could do about it. Not that they even made the effort. The gods had spoken. They had no choice but to acquiesce. Now it was James's turn. They'd just have to see how he got on.

When James announced to his mother that they'd sit the Qualy the following week, she merely nodded and said: "Well, Ah ken ye'll dae yer best, son." Secretly, though, she was hoping for more than that. She'd observed over the years that James and his sister were made of very different stuff where schoolwork was concerned. James was already an avid reader of books from the age of six. Wee Effie, by contrast, confined herself to comics and later to girls' magazines like *Valentine*. Their thrice-yearly primary report cards had also told a different story. While James hovered near the top of the class, Wee Effie hovered between the middle and the bottom. So, Janet was keeping her fingers crossed that there wouldn't be a second fail in the family.

James knew from playground chatter that if he failed the Qualy he'd end up at Lothian Park; if he passed he'd go on to The Academy. For years he'd watched the elite of The Academy, first in the streets of Leith and then in the avenues of Fox Crag, making their way to school in their smart royal blue blazers with the embroidered badge on the top pocket and the blue-and-white striped school tie. But the notion that one day he might be permitted to wear that blazer seemed as preposterous as running a four-minute mile or conquering Everest. The Academy was the shining city on the hill, distant, unattainable and enigmatic. What went on there? The only way to find out was by passing the Qualy. It was a simple as that.

The appointed day dawned unusually mild, a perfect spring day in Scotland. After the midday recess, Class 7A sat wordlessly as the sunlight filtered into the classroom. They knew they were about to sit the Qualy. But none of them had any idea what it entailed. They'd never sat an examination before. Only a few of them understood its full significance; only a few grasped the wider implications it could have for their futures. Blissfully ignorant, the majority lolled in their seats and awaited their respective fates. Mr Martin entered with a stranger in tow. He was an elderly man with glasses, in a suit and tie, holding several thick manila envelopes to his chest. Without any greetings or preliminaries, Mr Martin turned to the class.

"This is Mr Henderson. He has come to administer the Qualifying Examination." He glared at the rows of upturned candidate faces. "No talking. All books and papers off your desks. Pencils only. Do not touch the paper until we tell you. The examination will last one hour. Do not forget to write your names on the cover page."

With that, the papers were distributed. Mr Martin was staring at Mr Henderson who was staring at his wristwatch. Then he nodded to Mr Martin.

"You may start," announced Mr Martin, and took his place, arms folded, against the wall at the back of the class while Mr Henderson, in the teacher's chair at the front, adopted an even more serious expression and directed watchful looks around the room.

James had never seen an examination paper before. This one consisted of an A4 question-and-answer booklet, stapled down the spine, with the ubiquitous heading *Edinburgh Corporation Education Committee* across the top of the cover page. James found it strangely comforting that the dour ladies and gentlemen around the table in the dusty room in the High Street who provided his jotter and his daily milk had also had a hand in his Qualy. Fascinated, he gently fingered the fine quality paper and delicately turned over the pages filled with printed questions and blank spaces for the answers. The sections seemed to be about his knowledge of arithmetic, written English and problem-solving.

He wrote his name, turned to the first page, and methodically worked his way through. He finished with a few minutes to spare. He thought he'd done everything. Putting his pencil down, he cautiously looked around the room. Some of his classmates were finishing up, some were still frantically writing, and others appeared to have given up, leaning back in their chairs with baffled expressions. Henry Faulkner was sitting straight up, staring into space and biting his nails as usual. He'd finished long ago and had that bored, confident look of someone who already knew he'd done well. James looked out of the window. A small flock of seagulls had taken over the playing fields. Arthur's Seat was still there, clearly etched in its leonine pose. He looked through the booklet. He didn't think there was anything he could change.

"Time up!" said Mr Martin. "Pencils down!" He paused to ensure all had complied. "Stay in your seats until we have collected the scripts!"

Along with Mr Henderson, he toured the aisles, piling the completed scripts on the teacher's desk. With Mr Martin looking on, Mr Henderson counted the scripts, checked each one had a name, then counted heads. He nodded to Mr Martin, placed the papers back in their envelopes and left the room without another word. Mr Martin turned to the class.

"All right, we'll now have a special break of ten minutes and carry on after that. Don't make a noise in the corridor!"

Nothing happened for a couple of months. Most had forgotten that they'd sat the Qualy and there was a distinct lack of curiosity about the results. Then, one Friday afternoon after the midday break, Mr Martin walked into the classroom with Mrs Moncrieff. They all got to their feet. Only in exceptional circumstances would the Headmistress and a class teacher enter together. James wondered what was going on. Little did he realise that this would be one of the most important days of his life, for what happened in the next few minutes, one way or another, would determine his future, not to mention that of everyone else in the class.

"Sit down!" said Mr Martin. He paused. "We have the results of the Qualifying Examination." A quiver of excitement went around the room. "When I call your name, you will stand."

He started calling names from a list in his hand. The first name was that of Henry Faulkner. James's was the third or fourth. When eight pupils were standing and twenty-six still sitting, Mr Martin stopped, took a step back, and nodded to Mrs Moncrieff. You'd have had to be of limited intelligence not to know what was coming, for everyone standing belonged in the top tier of the class. Nevertheless, James remained apprehensive. He leant forward, his knuckles pressing on the cold, polished, wooden lid of his desk for support. His ears were buzzing and his stomach felt as if it were doing a highland fling. Mrs Moncrieff stepped forward. She looked around closely into the faces of the eight. In the split second before she spoke, James tried to read what was in her expression. But he saw nothing.

"All of you will be going to The Academy," she said as matter-of-factly as if she were confirming that the sun would rise tomorrow. James felt his heart give a leap. He'd done it. He joined in the smiles of relief among the Chosen Ones. There were gasps and sniggers from those sitting. Someone muttered, "Sooks!"

"The rest of you will be going to Lothian Park."

This time more gasps and one or two crestfallen expressions. Mrs Moncrieff lowered her spectacles to consult a paper in her hand then, as if she'd already forgotten, asked, "Where is Henry Faulkner?"

Henry, standing only a yard or two away from her, raised his hand.

"Here, Miss," he said impassively.

"The rest of you may sit." She waited for this to happen. "Henry, Mr Martin tells me you are the dux of 7A and now you have come out top in the Qualifying Examination."

But Henry already knew. His face remained expressionless and he merely nodded in his condescending way.

"It also means," went on Mrs Moncrieff, "that you will be offered a scholarship to a better school."

Henry again nodded, as if she wasn't telling him anything he didn't already know. Of course, that had been the plan all along, as drummed into him by parents who were inordinately ambitious for him, despite their working-class roots. *A better school*? thought James. No sooner had it been announced, than his own achievement had been cheapened.

"I will be in touch with your parents in due course. Sit down."

Henry sat, silent and self-assured in his private world.

"As for the rest of you," announced Mrs Moncrieff, scanning the upturned faces, "your parents will also get an official letter in the post."

And with that, she swept out of the room. Like Mrs Moncrieff, Mr Martin had betrayed no emotion. True, he'd had what appeared to be a fixed smile on his face the whole time but that could have meant anything. There had been no suggestion from either of them of congratulating those successful pupils or consoling the rest. That had not been the purpose of the exercise. It had been merely to impart information. James, meanwhile, took a moment to reflect on *his* success. Regardless of Henry Faulkner, *he* was going to The Academy. Now, he was going to be one of *them*. It was an odd feeling. Was it really the same James Swanston in this body who had graciously been granted a passport to a different future? Or was it some other James Swanston? It took him some time to grasp the reality. Then, as it sank in, he started to feel elated.

But there was a cost. In the invertedly snobbish world of Edinburgh working-class society, attending a grammar school the likes of The Academy was considered by some to be tantamount to betrayal of your class. In Class 7A, there were not a few adherents to this mindset. It was rumoured that certain pupils deliberately 'threw' the Qualy in order to ensure that they were sent to the 'right' school, that is, Lothian Park. There were even said to be pupils who'd passed the Qualy but had declined to take up the place earmarked for them at The Academy, preferring instead to accompany their less able chums to Lothian Park. No wonder there had been some hostile reaction to the naming of the eight new Academicals. They might as well have been eight Covenanters from Rullion Green, lined up on the scaffold at the Mercat Cross for the pleasure of the Edinburgh Mob. Once outside, and on the way home, the sniggers became comments and snide remarks that continued for some time. But James didn't care. He was euphoric. He'd be going to The Academy in the autumn.

When he got home, he found his mother in the kitchen preparing Scotch broth for the next day's dinner. Mrs Kirk's *Tried Favourites Cookery Book* was propped up against the milk jug open at page three. On the bunker, there was a cup of barley, together with a packet of split peas, carrots, and leeks but no onions, as Mrs Kirk directed. The large soup pot heating on the stove already contained the marrowbone and the salt and was just coming to the boil. Janet was busy skimming off the scum with a large metal cooking spoon.

"Mum, we got our Qualy result the day."

Janet paused, spoon in her hand, steam rising around her face, and looked round at him wearing a guarded expression, not sure if she wanted to hear this.

"Well?" she asked, trying not to sound impatient.

"Ah passed."

He paused for effect, but she merely nodded once, as if what he'd just said was expected confirmation of what she'd already guessed. So he went on, just in case she hadn't understood.

"Ah'll be goin' tae The Academy next term."

She smiled brightly.

"That's very nice, son," was all she said, and turned back to skimming off the scum.

But secretly she was over the moon. The Academy! The stigma of her ‘lack’ of education still ran deep. No one in her extended family, none of her eight brothers and sisters, none of their children, none of her cousins, none of her in-laws’ children, not a single one had ever got into a grammar school, let alone one the likes of The Academy. Now, her James would be the very first. As she added the barley and the split peas to the bubbling brew, she savoured her triumph. But there was one small problem – how Wee Effie would take the news. She hoped the Qualy wasn’t going to be the cause of a rift in the family. As soon as Ian got home from work, she took him aside and told him.

“Help mah Boab!” he exclaimed. “The wee devil. ’E’s done well!” Then he grinned mischievously. “’E obviously takes after ’is auld man!”

“Aye,” Janet said, ignoring his feeble attempt at humour, “but watch what ye say. Dinnae make too much o’ a fuss, otherwise Wee Effie’ll be in the huff. And,” she added, “ye dinnae want yer son gettin’ too big for ’is boots.”

The class photo

A few weeks before the end of term, Mr Martin announced that a photographer would be in school to take class photos the following Friday. He’d been summoned specially from a studio in Leith. There was a schedule of 15-minute slots for each class to have the photo taken. 7A’s slot would be just before the midday break.

“It might be a good idea to make sure you wear something nice. You will want to look your best, won’t you?” he added.

“Whae wud want tae dress up for a school photie?” scoffed an anonymous voice. Thankfully, Mr Martin didn’t hear, or pretended not to. On Thursday, James remembered to tell his mother.

“Mum, we’re havin’ a class photo taken the morn. Mr Martin says we should wear somethin’ nice!”

“Well, does ’e now?” replied Janet, taking from James’s rendering of what Mr Martin had said an implied insult that they normally didn’t wear ‘something nice’. Which, she thought, on reflection, was probably not far from the truth, for plenty of mothers on the Fox Crag estate sent their bairns to school on a daily basis looking like a midden. Well, *she* didn’t, and she’d make sure her son was smart for the occasion.

The morning lessons seemed to drag. Mr Martin appeared especially jumpy. He’d never supervised 7A outside the classroom before and wasn’t relishing the prospect. Even for a brief span of twenty minutes or so, out there in the unknown there was no Belt and therefore no discipline. When everyone was wearying of long division, at 11.40 he laid the chalk on his desk and, as usual, smacked his palms together to remove the chalk dust.

"Now it is time for the class photograph. You will stand up, quietly get into twos in the corridor behind Malcolm McQuillan and Henry Faulkner..." He glanced meaningfully at the two boys. "...and make your way downstairs and out the back entrance to the playground. No talking. No chatter. No nonsense." He scratched the back of his bald pate as if he'd forgotten something. "Oh, and take with you anything you need over the midday break. You won't be coming back until afterwards."

He gestured to Malcolm and Henry to get out first, while the class rose, collected their things and, entirely ignoring Mr Martin's instruction not to chatter, proceeded to chatter excitedly. Once, a couple of years back, a photographer had come to take individual school portraits, but they'd never had a class photo taken before. On the one hand, what was better than being let off lessons twenty minutes early on a Friday and being allowed to go outside into what was turning into a spectacular Scottish June day? But a few, those approaching or already in the midst of puberty, were beginning to rebel against symbols of adult-imposed conformity and being made to pose for a group photograph was one such symbol. So reactions were mixed.

"Mah goad, mah hair's a mess!"

"Is mah face aw' right? Ah thought Ah saw a plook comin' up this mornin'!"

"Look at Raymond, never seen ye wearin' a tie before! Sook!"

"D'ye ken how much this photie's gonnae cost us? What a waste o' time!"

"No noise!" thundered Mr Martin, to no avail. He stood in the corridor, chivvying them into line, then, when it was good enough, he told the two boys at the front to lead on. The binary crocodile made its noisy way along the deserted corridor and down the back stairs. As they walked, some of the girls pulled combs out of their bags and awkwardly tugged at their mops, trying to impose some sort of order. For practical reasons, Edinburgh council estate mothers usually kept the hair of their daughters short. In a time and a place devoid of showers, shampoos, or hair dryers, hair washing for working-class women and girls was a time-consuming, messy business at best, relegated to once a week, usually on a Monday evening. As a result, only three or four girls in 7A had hair that came below the level of their shoulders, and with one exception, that was either tied back in pigtails or a ponytail.

The exception, was, of course, Daisy Myers. Daisy was a tall, spindly, gawky lassie but she had one saving grace: long, flaxen tresses that reached well down her back. If her mother had taught her to look after this endowment it might have been an asset, but since she hadn't, Daisy's hair was merely a mass of clumps, tugs, knots and wayward curls that swirled around her head in the slightest breeze and got into her eyes. Yet, Daisy, like most of the girls, had taken to heart Mr Martin's suggestion about wearing 'something nice', or her mother had, for she was wearing a neat black jacket with tiny metal buttons up the front over her salmon blouse with the long, tapering collar tips. Even Hairy Mary had made an effort. Instead of her usual grubby cardigan, today she had on a unique dress that combined a pale green waistcoat incorporating faux pearl buttons, and a gingham check green and cream flared skirt over a white blouse with a black fake bow tie. Not only that, her black hair was tied back neatly and held in place by a hair comb and her face was freshly scrubbed. It was a surprising transformation.

But where the boys were concerned, the opposite was almost universally the case. Only four of them, Henry Faulkner, Malcolm McQuillan, Raymond Porteous and, of course, James, appeared to have made the effort. Henry, Malcolm and James were wearing their Sunday jackets. Raymond was wearing a rare Fox Crag school tie of red and gold stripes with his neat white shirt. James also had on a clean, white, open-necked shirt, his best grey shorts, long socks and his Sunday shoes, buffed to a shine. His short-back-and-sides was neatly combed and his cow's lick flopped over his right eyebrow. But despite Mr Martin's suggestion, the rest were universally clad in the same shabby shorts, shirts and jerseys that were commonplace wear for normal school days.

The class burst out through the glass double swing doors and into the unaccustomed sunlight. There in the distance was a middle-aged man, standing at the edge of the grass. The playing fields rose half a foot or so above the playground and were separated by a narrow concrete rim. At this point, a set of three stone steps about three yards wide gave access from the lower area of tarmac to the upper area of grass. The steps were the obvious location for a group photograph. The large Leica stood on a tripod with a remote shutter release dangling from its front. There was a small collapsible wooden table with the photographer's other bits and pieces. Next to the table was a chair from one of the classrooms. The photographer, Mr Fleming, was ready and waiting. By now, 7A had dissolved into a disordered mob, Mr Martin anxiously darting and snapping at its flanks like a neurotic border collie. This was going to be worse than he'd feared. But he needn't have worried. Mr Fleming was a small man but he had the weathered countenance and the presence of a sergeant major, which is exactly what he'd been during The War, as a member of The British Army Film and Photographic Unit. In peacetime, a veteran of countless photoshoots with unruly groups of every shape, size and composition, on every occasion, from weddings to company staff functions, graduation ceremonies and military gatherings, he immediately took charge and proceeded to bully the mob into shape just as he'd have done on the parade ground at Redford Barracks.

"Right, you lot," he commanded in a stentorian voice that could be heard by many a wifie hanging out the washing in the neighbouring back greens, "listen up!"

There was immediate silence. Even Andrew Peterson was deprived for a few seconds of his stock defiant expression. Mr Martin allowed himself a mental sigh of relief. *Dzięki Bogu!* He stepped back and folded his arms to watch, revelling in his enforced redundancy as the photographer waved his arms rather like Malcolm Sargent at a Henry Wood Promenade Concert.

"Boys here," he pointed to the area at the side of the table, "girls there!" he pointed to the top two steps.

He paused while his commands were obeyed. Then, turning back to the boys, now huddled in a group, he barked, "Don't move!" and proceeded to organise the girls. They were to arrange themselves standing in two rows on the steps and the grass. As they mingled, muddled and disordered, he expertly separated them into tall and not-so-tall. The tall girls would constitute the back row, the not-so-tall ones and the really short ones, the front row. Unceremoniously, he grabbed elbows and pushed and shoved them around, standing back, gauging their height, and rubbing his chin in concentration. While this was going on, the laddies looked on, some with interest and amusement, but others, mainly in the Andrew Peterson camp, full of devilment, started making comments just loud enough for the girls to hear and intended to do maximum damage.

"Look at thon Daisy! She's an awfy-lookin' ticket."

"She cannae even staun straight!"

"Did ye no ken? She's humphybackit!"

Daisy, in reality no wilting flower and near enough to have picked up the hurtful comments, turned, stared daggers at her critics and mouthed, loud enough to be heard, even though no sounds appeared to issue from her mouth: *Away an' raffle yersel'!*

Mr Fleming stepped back and examined his placements. He had a row of the tallest girls at the back, anchored by Jean Tulloch at one end (she was a long skinnymalinky) and Anne Gunn at the other, with the largest, Hairy Mary, holding the centre. The second row were all diminutive girls, with the smallest, Wee Minnie Mackay, strategically placed in the middle. Satisfied with his work, Mr Fleming walked over and picked up the chair. He placed it in front of Wee Minnie, then gestured the boys over. Since they'd all be sitting down, less work was required. He got them into two rows on either side of the chair, the back row consisting of the taller ones sitting half on the concrete rim and half on the grass among the rats' tails and dockens, and the front row with the shortest sitting cross-legged on the hot tarmac. Since it was a dry summer's day, no one seemed to mind, though a tiny voice was heard muttering about getting a *sair bum*.

All this time, Mr Martin had been standing observing the arrangements with his arms casually folded, enjoying his few minutes of not being in charge for a change. A mellow smile on his face, he didn't mind that he'd forgotten his flat cap, for he luxuriated in the rare warmth of the sun on his baldness. The sudden fine weather was reminding him of summers near Stara Kamienna, deep in the eastern Polish countryside. There, at his parents' summer chatka, where the sunflowers grew tall along the rustic fence and the strawberries were plump and juicy, he and his fiancée, Magdalena Laschweska, would cool off in the meandering stream on the hot days. In the late afternoons they sat at the rickety bench in the shade of the linden, chewing nalesniki washed down with pivo and nalewka, good-naturedly arguing with student friends about the future of Poland well into the evening. Little did they guess that Poland, *their* Poland, *had* no future... Suddenly, his reverie was interrupted. Mr Fleming was waving to him. He walked over.

"Almost ready!" Mr Fleming said. "Now, if you would just take a seat, Sir?" He gestured to the chair he'd placed directly in the middle of the group. Apparently, Mr Martin was to take pride of place in the photo. But Mr Martin baulked. Expressionless, he took the photographer by the arm and walked him out of earshot of the class. A brief conversation ensued. Then they both returned. Mr Fleming removed the chair and got the boys to move sideways to fill the gap. Meanwhile, Mr Martin smartly walked round the back of the tall girls and reappeared at the left-hand end of the line next to Anne Gunn and behind Joyce McCluskie. It appeared that Mr Martin had absolutely no wish to make an exhibition of himself for all the world to see. Now, only the top half of his head was visible.

"Ready? Now, how about a nice big smile for your mums and dads!"

And with that, the photographer captured the moment for posterity. Most of Class 7A, including James, had complied with the request, smiling and looking nicely into the camera lens. But there were exceptions. Georgie Patterson, who was a bit of a serious character anyway, had seemingly concluded that this was a serious matter and decided to put on his most serious expression. Three of the tall girls who'd had to stand around the longest made their frustrations clear with disapproving expressions. Wee Rab Forrester and Sandy Kilgour, seated in the back row of boys, were caught laughing into each other's faces, apparently sharing a joke.

But for sheer insubordination, who else would it be that took the biscuit? None other than Andrew Peterson. Sitting at the opposite end of the back row of boys from James, Andrew managed a cleverly-timed piece of sabotage. Just as the camera shutter was about to click, he raised his left leg and deposited his shoe-clad left foot on the left shoulder of Raymond, he of the pristine white shirt and the school tie who was sitting in the front row, cross-legged, with his right arm around the shoulders of Serious Georgie in a comradely fashion. At the same time, Andrew contrived to raise his left hand containing his playpiece above the crowd of boys, thus displaying to the whole world, with a scornful expression, a corned beef sandwich. And so, yet again, Andrew Peterson had neatly and effectively shown his contempt for 7A, Mr Martin, Fox Crag School, and the world in general. For him, it was par for the course, but a blemish on an otherwise near-perfect outcome. Just then, the school bell rang for the midday recess.

"Thank you!" shouted Mr Fleming amid the clamour.

The group dissolved and all went their separate ways. Briefly thanking Mr Fleming, Mr Martin slowly made his way back inside to the staff room for his sandwich lunch.

A couple of weeks later, after paying his sixpence at the school office, James received a large envelope with his copy of the class photo. Eagerly, he opened the flap and pulled it out. There he was with his 33 classmates, young, bright, and hopeful. Most were cheerful, smiling or grinning obligingly, innocently oblivious of what the future had in store for them. Some would lead long and happy lives. Some would lead dull, ordinary lives of dead-end jobs and broken marriages. Some, like Serious Georgie, would be hugely successful and become wealthy. Some, like Wee Rab Forrester, thanks to success in the Qualy, would discover hidden talents and become an eminent architect or engineer or sculptor. Daisy Myers, she of the flaxen locks, would metamorphose from gawky schoolgirl to famous beauty, her looks gracing many a magazine cover, and modelling contracts would be strewn in her path. Hairy Mary would fall pregnant at an early age, be forced into marriage, have further children whom she would raise with care and devotion, get divorced, and discover late in life a new career as a useful member of Edinburgh society. Andrew Peterson, whom all had roundly predicted would end up either dead or in prison, would discover fertile ground for his devious talents and end up as a prominent politician in the Scottish National Party. As for James, well, his future was still unwritten.

When he brought the photo home to show Janet, she was pleasantly surprised as she took it in both hands. There was the group of 34 pupils standing and sitting at the edge of the Fox Crag playing field with plenty of smiles evident. And there was James, sitting right at the front, to Janet, the neatest, smartest, best-looking among all the boys there.

"But where's yer teacher? Where's Mr Martin?" she asked.

"There!" James pointed.

All she could see above Joyce McCluskie's head were two squinting eyes surmounted by a large, round, earless, hairless dome.

"That's Mr Martin?" she gasped. "Why did 'e hide 'imself like that?"

"Ye've never met Mr Martin, have ye, Mum?"

"No, Ah havnae. Ah've only seen 'is name on yer report cards."

"Ye ken 'e's Polish?"

"Aye."

"Well, 'e's just different. The last thing 'e'd want tae do would be tae make a fuss." He paused but she was still nonplussed. "Never mind. That's where *he* wanted tae be in the photo. At least *Ah* ken where 'e is."

Anyway, as far as Janet was concerned, it was a good result and well worth the sixpence outlay. She'd have the class photo framed and placed on her best china cabinet for her and Ian to enjoy in years to come.

The last lesson

Word had gone around that Mr Martin was leaving Fox Crag. James wondered why. Was he going back to Poland? But the truth was that Mr Martin, now in his late fifties and not in the best of health, was finding his five-times-weekly commute across to the other side of Edinburgh more and more of an effort. For quite a time he'd been keeping an eye out for vacancies in primary schools in his immediate area. When a position was advertised at a Catholic primary in Bruntsfield, he applied, was interviewed, and to his surprise, he was offered the job. Not only had it stood in his favour that he was a baptised Catholic, but the Mother Superior was also eager to appoint a male teacher to relieve her nuns of the onerous task of teaching the senior class with its quota of rough boys. They needed someone like Mr Martin who was well acquainted with The Belt.

A week before the end of term, in the playground beside the toilets, five or six future Academy pupils were discussing what to do about Mr

Martin. He was leaving and they wanted to give him a present. They didn't want to let anyone else in on their plan. They were the ones that had had a closer relationship with him than anyone else. They assumed they were the only ones that would want to thank him. But how? They'd never done anything like this before and wondered how to go about it. As they scratched their heads, there was an unceremonious irruption into their circle. It was Andrew Peterson in his overbearing, swaggering way. They reeled back while he claimed the middle ground as if he were the centre of a playground game.

"Well?" he stared around at them. "What're ye talkin' aboot?"

Andrew had an uncanny nose for secrets. How had he guessed they were up to something? None of them wanted to talk. It was their idea, theirs alone. Why was he sticking his neb in? He was a keelie and he was destined for Lothian Park, then prison most likely. No one spoke. Andrew started to look threatening. He stood, his fists clenched, glaring around the circle of faces, searching out the weakest link. He stopped at James. He took a step towards him, thrusting his face into his.

"Well, are ye gonnae tell me or no?" he growled.

James thought he was going to wet himself. He'd never found himself in such close proximity to Andrew's face before and it wasn't pleasant. He was afraid. He had no choice but to spill the beans. They were planning a leaving present for Mr Martin.

Andrew thought for a moment then asked, "Whae's in charge?"

They looked at one another. No one was.

"OK," said Andrew, "just leave it tae me." And with that he swaggered off.

The group turned on James.

"Why did ye tell 'im?"

"It was oor idea, no his!"

They broke up in disarray and went their separate ways. James hurried to the boys' toilet block. Some days later, the news went around that Andrew was collecting for a present for Mr Martin. They couldn't believe it. Andrew! The worst troublemaker in the class had hijacked their idea. Why? They quickly came to the conclusion that the whole thing was just one of Andrew's little schemes.

"It's a swindle," said Morag. "'E's gonnae keep the money for hissel'."

They all agreed. They wouldn't contribute to Andrew's racket. They wouldn't allow themselves to be coerced either. In the end, whether they all did or not wasn't clear. James couldn't avoid Andrew and had tuppence extorted from him, knowing full well that he'd never see it again. Probably some of the others did too but they never admitted as much. Among the rest of the class, Andrew seemed to have received a surprisingly positive response to 'his' idea of buying a gift for Mr Martin. Of course, most, like James couldn't afford more than a penny or two.

Friday, 4th July: The last day of term came. Mr Martin had intended to leave with a minimum of fuss. Mrs Moncrieff had merely said a few kind words in the staff room during morning break, praising his near decade-long service to the school. For his own part, he'd make a brief address to his class at the end of the day, then he'd put on his coat and cap, pick up his briefcase and leave. With that depressing thought, Mr Martin addressed himself to his last session with the 34 pupils he'd spent most of his waking hours trying to teach over the past two years. To get them focused on their careers, he'd decided to devote the last session to the question: "What do you want to be when you leave school?" One by one, the members of the class had to stand up and make their confessions. Most of the responses were predictable – fireman, policeman, nurse, typist, and so on. One or two were unusual.

"Ah want tae a be a newsreader on Scottish Television," announced Joyce Jamieson.

That gave food for thought. For those whose families had televisions, the first Scottish commercial TV channel had come on air the previous summer, opening up possibilities that had never existed before.

"Ah want tae be an engineer an' work on the Forth Road Bridge," added Rab Forrester, alluding to the new Forth crossing that had been in all the newspapers. Final plans had been approved and work was just about to start.

Some of the more ambitious among them ventured doctor or lawyer but were met with sniggers or sarcastic comments from the back of the class. After that, those with such ambitions simply lied, toed the party line and repeated the expected mantra. Then it was James's turn. He stood up. The party line wasn't for him.

"Ah want tae be a farmer," he said defiantly.

The class collapsed in fits of laughter. They hooted, they cried, they wept tears of derision. A farmer! What a joke!

"How're *you* ever gonnae be a farmer?" rang through the carnival of hilarity.

James didn't know. Ever since their holiday at the caravan in Adelstone, he'd dreamt of being a farmer like Mr Reekie. He'd pictured himself driving the tractor, then herding sheep, cromach in hand, out on the hills with his faithful sheepdog – Glen from the Frasers upstairs, of course. Calmly, he sat down, folded his arms and, with a grim smile, stared down his detractors, all of whom were Lothian Park bound anyway. He didn't care. *He* was going to The Academy. *They* most definitely were not.

Mr Martin did his best to restore order. When the class had finally laughed themselves out, he held up his hand for silence.

"Now, I have something to tell you," he said, looking around the room. "I too am leaving Fox Crag."

One wag at the front piped up, "But Sir, we ken already!"

That was the cue for Andrew Peterson to stand up. Mr Martin stared at his nemesis and his heart sank. What final stunt did the class troublemaker have up his sleeve for his last day? Couldn't he have left him alone, just this once? But what followed was quite unexpected. Andrew raised the lid of his desk and pulled out a packet inexpertly wrapped in brown paper and loosely tied with string.

"Sir, we've got a present for ye!" he announced, holding it up for all to see. Boldly, he walked to the front of the class and handed it to Mr Martin who took it gingerly, wondering if this was some kind of trick.

"Sir," went on Andrew, half turning to the class, now the self-appointed spokesman, "we want tae thank ye for aw' ye done for us."

Mr Martin, resisting the impulse to correct Andrew's grammar, remained dumbfounded at what he'd just heard. This, from the class troublemaker-in-chief? The boy he'd belted more than any other? Prime fodder for Lothian Park, not to mention Saughton Prison?

"Go on, Sir, open it!" came a voice from the back.

"Yes, Sir, open it!"

Mr Martin cautiously unwrapped the parcel. Dropping the brown paper, he held up a round tin of Crawford's shortbread. A highlander stared out from a green and red tartan background.

"It's no much, Sir, but we hope ye like it, as a wee mum... a wee mom... a wee somethin' fae us aw'."

Having made his speech, Andrew went back to his desk, sat in his seat and grinned triumphantly round at the class. It was his very last performance at Fox Crag Primary, and, true to form, he never failed to surprise. James wasn't the only one stunned by what had transpired. There were so many questions. Was there some good in Andrew after all? Or had it indeed been a scam to skim his 'commission' from the contributions he'd solicited? If it was all above board, why would Andrew, of all people, be so eager to organise something for the benefit of Mr Martin, of all people? It just didn't make sense.

James's thoughts were interrupted by the sound of sporadic clapping. Others quickly joined in. Soon the whole class was applauding and cheering Mr Martin, who stood there wordlessly, clutching his tin of Crawford's shortbread, tears by now streaming down his cheeks. The applause seemed strangely out of place in a classroom. Some of the pupils were beginning to look embarrassed for they'd never seen a teacher cry before. This was truly a day of firsts and lasts. Mr Martin put the tin on his desk and, pulling an enormous white handkerchief out of his trouser pocket, he dabbed at his eyes and blew his nose loudly.

"Dziękuję bardzo, dzieci. Nigdy cię nie zapomnę," was all he said.

The shrill ringing of the school bell interrupted the festivities. It was the bell for the end of the last lesson at the end of the last day of their last term of primary school. Mr Martin made no attempt to impose order. The cheers intended for him morphed into cheers for the end of school. There was bedlam, as, caught up in the sheer joy of it, pupils gathered their things and stormed the classroom door, cavorting along the corridor, down the stairs and out into the playground, yelling at the tops of their voices. A few of the more considerate ones lingered behind to say a personal farewell, a final thank you, to their teacher from Poland – probably the only one they would ever have.

James remained at his desk, overcome by the moment. Despite all that had happened, getting The Belt and losing his Polish sweetie privileges, he felt no animosity towards Mr Martin. And now, seeing him in tears, he couldn't help feeling sorry for him. They had something in common; for each, a chapter of his life had ended. For Mr Martin, a new school and a new chapter, perhaps the last of his career. For James, a new school too, but a very important new chapter at The Academy and one that would be life-changing.

He dug in his schoolbag and pulled out a small notebook, bound in an elegant wine-red cover. The word *Autographs* was etched in large gold leaf letters, as were his initials, JS, in one corner. This was a birthday present from Uncle Eddie who was a bookbinder in a printing works at Stockbridge. The autograph book was still full of blank pages because James had been too shy to ask anyone for their autograph yet. But he'd brought it to school, determined to overcome his fear and with one purpose in mind. When all the well-wishers had finally left, he gathered his things, plucked up his courage and walked up to Mr Martin, who was still standing at his desk as if in a trance with a strange expression on his face and tears lingering in his eyes.

"Excuse me, Mr Martin? Sir?"

James held out the autograph book.

"Could Ah have yer autograph please, Sir?"

Mr Martin started, as if woken from a reverie. He said nothing but smiled brightly, sat down at his desk and took the autograph book. He opened it at the first page and smoothed the paper clumsily with his fleshy fingers. Then he ceremoniously removed his fountain pen from his top pocket and unscrewed the cap, replacing it on the other end. He gripped the pen near the nib and looked up at James expectantly. Then, slowly and carefully, he made his entry at a 45-degree angle across the page. He checked what he'd written and seemed satisfied. He re-screwed the cap on the pen and returned it to his top pocket. Then he turned the book round, holding open the pages by the edges to let the ink dry. He looked at James. At the same time his eyebrows arched and he smiled a puckish smile that James had never seen before. It was then that James knew he'd been forgiven.

"Is this all right?" asked Mr Martin.

The message was signed simply *A Martin*. The words were written in Mr Martin's large, looping, continental script, first in Polish:

Powodzenia w nowej szkole
Mam nadzieję, że mnie nie zapomnisz.

The English translation was below:

Good Luck in Your New School.
I Hope You Will Not Forget Me.

James never would.

6 Nicely bred wi' education

The school uniform

"Can Ah help ye, hen?"

The motherly sales assistant called over as she vectored in at an angle of forty-five degrees. Janet was striding purposefully through the men's and boys' section of the Provie haberdashery department trailed by a bashful-looking James. She turned her head and stopped abruptly. The assistant, in her grey and black tunic over a white blouse, caught up, smiled, and tilted her head in an enquiring pose.

"Aye," replied Janet. "Ah'm wantin' an Academy uniform for mah son here."

To anyone else, it might have seemed like an unremarkable sort of utterance. But to Janet, it was a form of words she'd never used before and till now could never have imagined herself using. Yet, here she was, making a statement that was pregnant with significance. Her son – *her* son – was going to The Academy. And he had to have a uniform. She was bursting with pride at the thought but no one would have known.

"Yes, the school uniforms are down here, hen," offered the assistant, making an ushering motion, but Janet already knew exactly where she was going. Since it was just across the road from Brockit Brae, she knew this haberdashery department inside out. And now she and James had had to make the pilgrimage from Fox Crag back to their old haunt because clever Provie managers had engineered a monopoly on selling a range of school uniforms, including that of The Academy. She walked on through a wide, curtained entry and five steps down into the School

Uniforms Department, followed by the assistant and an even more apprehensive James. He hated being the centre of attention. He'd never had a school uniform before. Neither Bonnybrig nor Fox Crag primaries had made uniforms compulsory. Most bairns attended in their everyday street clothes. But The Academy was different. It was a grammar school. Full school uniform was essential. It was simple: no uniform, no admission.

He found himself in a small annexe. The middle of the room was empty but the walls were swathed in a colourful array of secondary school uniforms arranged in sections by school. The blue and white of The Academy contrasted with the green and gold of Holy Trinity, the black and white of Lothian Park, the black and yellow of Donald Kirkwallace (known locally as *Daft Kids*), and the grey and maroon of Dunedin High. Janet pulled a sheet of paper from her handbag and consulted it as the assistant stood expectantly, her hands folded over her stomach.

"Ah'll be needin' the full Academy outfit. Blazer, shirt, tie, shorts and socks."

Blazer. It was a word entirely disconnected from her class and her world. Blazers were worn by wealthy yacht club members; by England cricketers; by schoolboys at Eton and Harrow; by the Oxford and Cambridge rowing teams. But blazers didn't figure in the lives of working-class people. They didn't own blazers. They didn't wear blazers. They didn't need blazers. She'd never spoken the word in her life before. But there it was, on the typed list they'd got in the post from The Academy and here she was saying it. *A blazer*. Her son needed *a blazer*. The assistant sized James up with a professional eye.

"Let's start wi' a small."

She bustled off to the rack of blue and white uniforms, selected two royal blue blazers and brought them back. Displaying them to Janet on her forearm, she looked at James and said, "Best to take yer jersey off, son. Yer blazer should be worn over yer shirt." Even more embarrassed, James pulled his jersey over his head, gave it to his mother and surrendered to the lady's ministrations.

"Hold out yer arms, son."

James did as he was told and the assistant deftly threaded his left arm into the left sleeve, walked the jacket around his back and threaded his right arm into the right sleeve. She adjusted the collar at the nape of his neck, stepped around to his front and tugged at the lapels. James felt the weight of the blazer settle down on his shoulders and fit snugly under his armpits. He'd never worn a blazer before. It felt different. Janet and the assistant stood back and surveyed him critically.

"That was the small, was it?" asked Janet.

"Aye, d'ye no think it's a good fit?"

"It is, but 'e's a bit tae grow yet. Have ye got a medium?"

They went through the same procedure with a medium. It was clearly too big, but Janet was insistent.

"At his age 'e's growin' fast. 'E'll grow into that in nae time. Go an' look at yersel' in the mirror, son." She nodded to a tall standing mirror in the corner. James walked over and stood staring at his reflection. He barely recognised himself. The brilliant royal blue of the blazer had transformed his puny body. The shoulders were wide. The cuffs came down to the tips of his thumbs. He half-turned. His bum had disappeared under the tail of the garment. In this magnificent blazer he was a different person. He returned to Janet, smiling for the first time. She smiled back at him.

"D'ye like it, son?" she asked fondly. James nodded, took off the blazer and handed it to the assistant who carefully laid it out on a heavy, wooden worktable. Janet then asked the most important question.

"How much is it?"

"Six pounds."

Six pounds? Janet hadn't been so naïve as to think an Academy uniform would be cheap but *six pounds*? That was half a week's wages for some folk. Even though Ian was now in a good job and she was working part-time, it still seemed a lot of money. Thank the Good Lord for Auntie Effie.

In addition to being his Auntie, Effie was also James's godmother. It was natural that Janet had offered her the honour. Younger than Janet by a couple of years, she'd been, apart from Alistair and Bella, Janet's other charge in the mean streets of twenties and thirties Leith as they foraged for food together. They'd stayed very close. Since Christine, Janet's sister-in-law, had bagged the coveted prize of godmother to their firstborn, it was only fair that Effie should be godmother to their secondborn. Effie revelled in her new status. She never married and never had children of her own, so there was always a special place in her heart for James. As he grew bigger and stronger, and she grew older and weaker, she never tired of chaffing him: "Aye, son, Ah remember the day Ah carried ye in church!" and would gesture to the framed black-and-white photo on her sideboard. Here was a much younger, much skinnier Effie dressed in a 1940s austerity ensemble with short skirt and padded shoulders, beaming and proudly cradling months-old James in his christening robe while Ian, Janet, and the Minister of South Leith looked on. And it was Effie who, several days after hearing the news that James had passed the Qualy and was going to The Academy, had said to

Janet, "Listen hen, Ah'd like tae pay for James's school uniform." Janet was scandalised.

"Ye will *not*!" she stated emphatically. If there was one thing she wouldn't take, it was charity. She'd taken enough of it in the twenties and thirties and had never got over the humiliation. The thought of having to be beholden to anyone else for money still rankled.

"Ah'm 'is godmother. Ah'm earnin' good money. Let me do this."

Effie was a very gentle person. But she gazed defiantly at Janet in the way only wee sisters look at big sisters when they're putting their foot down for the very first time. Effie wasn't offering. She was demanding. And it was Janet's wee sister being charitable this time, not some faceless philanthropic organisation that made you jump through hoops for their largesse. Janet loved her sister and was touched by her generosity. Though reluctant, she conceded graciously. What would a complete uniform for James cost? But Effie had already worked it out. She'd been down to the Clydesdale Bank with her bank book first thing that morning to withdraw what she calculated were the necessary funds. She opened her purse and laid three crisp five-pound notes on the table. Janet gasped at the sight. She rarely saw a single five-pound note, let alone three at once.

"Are ye sure it's gonnae be that much?" she'd asked.

But Effie, already well into her retail career with Marks and Spencer, was far more worldly-wise than Janet where the prices of such things were concerned.

"Take the money, and if it's less than that ye can give me the change," she said.

Janet thanked her, gave her a hug and stuffed the notes into her purse. Secretly, despite her views on accepting charity, she was relieved. She'd heard stories about the cost of school uniforms. The Academy's was supposed to be one of the most expensive. And, of course, it wasn't going to be a one-off outlay, for over the course of four years - or six if she dared be optimistic - James would grow. He'd need regular replacements.

"Will ye be wanting the badge?" the assistant broke into her thoughts. It seemed the badge was an extra. James was looking at her, pleading with his eyes. The badge, the coveted badge, was sewn onto the top left-hand pocket. Without the badge, the blazer was just a fancy jacket. *With* the badge, it was a uniform. No self-respecting Academy pupil would wear the blazer without the badge.

"How much it is?" Janet couldn't help herself even though she knew she wouldn't have to foot the bill.

"Fifteen shillings."

Fifteen shillin' for a badge? She could do a week's shopping at the grocer's for that. But she'd seen the look in her son's eyes and had understood.

"We'll take it," was all she said.

The assistant went to a large oak storage cabinet and opened a wide industrial drawer. Apparently, it was The Badge Drawer. She methodically flicked through the contents and fished out a small tissue paper packet. She walked over to the worktable. Opening the tissue paper, she revealed an Academy badge, which she reverently laid in its proper place on the top pocket of the blazer. Then she stood back admiringly, as if inviting Janet and James to share the moment.

Janet had never seen an Academy badge close up before. She stepped up to the table. Gold, dark blue and white, a medieval sailing ship on the left balanced a turreted castle on the right. In between stood a bearded warrior leaning on an enormous broadsword with the cross of St Andrew behind him. He seemed to be guarding three wine tuns grouped in a triangle. On a scroll below was the motto: 'Nemo Me Impune Lacessit'. Now, seeing it for the first time, in all its splendour, she fully understood James's look. It was beautiful. It was the icing on the cake.

The Academy tie had wide blue and white diagonal stripes. The long socks had a similar motif, two blue stripes enclosing one white which were revealed when the top of the sock was folded over at the required height, just below the knee. They bought two white cotton shirts in James's standard size. Then he had to try on shorts. The assistant produced two pairs of Academy regulation grey shorts of different sizes.

"Go an' try them on, son."

She escorted him to a cubicle, pulled back the heavy green curtain and ushered him inside. James's distress showed on his face. Janet knew exactly what was bothering him.

"Dinnae be daft! Naebody's gonnae see ye. Look, ye can close the curtain," and she closed it for him. Hoping no one would open it while he was disrobing, he quickly took off his old shorts and put on the first pair he'd been given. He heard the assistant's muffled voice.

"How're ye gettin' on, son?"

He didn't answer but opened the curtain and warily stepped outside. Again, the two females critically appraised him, as if they were art experts verifying the authenticity of a suspect Breughel. They turned him around, checked how the shorts fitted his backside, peered at his crotch (more mental agony on his part) and quizzed him about how comfortable they were. Again it was decided to go for the larger medium size. Janet took two pairs while a relieved James was able to get back into his old shorts and resume his normal life. Now the items were assembled on the worktable.

"Will that be all?" asked the assistant.

All? Isn't that enough? thought Janet. But she merely nodded politely and smiled. The assistant retrieved her receipt pad and a biro from the pocket of her tunic, laid it next to the purchases, and totted up the amounts.

"That'll be thirteen pounds, fifteen and six, please."

Janet gulped. Another week's wages gone. She delved into her purse and handed over the three five-pound notes Effie had given her while James looked on, marvelling at his mother's sudden wealth. The cash and copies of the receipt were speedily transported to central accounting by way of the Provie's compressed air system. The assistant carefully stowed the purchases in two large paper carrier bags with string handles proudly displaying the name Leith Provident. Just as she finished, the receipt and change landed back in the metal basket with a bump. Janet gave a sigh of relief, handed the carrier bags to James to manage and thanked the lady for her help. But they weren't finished yet. The new Academy pupil also needed shoes. They made their way downstairs to the shoe department.

"We need some shoes for mah son," said Janet to the assistant, this time an eager-to-please young man in a neat grey suit. "He's starting at The Academy next week. Ah suppose ye have the right ones," she added, waving the typed list at him.

"Oh, how nice!" the young man said. "What a clever laddie!"

Even though he *was* still a laddie, an indignant James turned beetroot at being referred to as one and wished the shopping would end. It seemed that black was the order of the day. James was told to sit on a low, leather-topped stool with convex brass studs, while the salesman sat on another stool and helped him to try on the shoes with a long, yellow-beige shoehorn and to tie the fresh, new laces.

"Are they too tight? Can ye wiggle yer toes?" asked Janet.

James wasn't sure.

"We'll soon be able to tell," said the salesman. "Just come over here, young man."

James smiled grimly. In a matter of minutes he'd been promoted from a mere laddie to a young man. He was ushered over to a strange-looking piece of furniture. It was a small wooden platform covered in linoleum with two steps up, and something like a lectern attached.

"Just get up here," said the salesman, guiding him by the shoulders.

In the stiff new shoes, James hobbled up the steps.

"Now hold on with both your hands and put your feet in here."

He showed James how to shuffle his feet, clad in the new shoes, forward into a little dark hole. When he looked down, he realized that the top of the lectern thing he was holding onto had a screen in it. The salesman flipped a switch and, abracadabra! James saw a magical emerald green image appear on the screen.

"There! D'ye know what that is?" asked the man.

James stared, mystified.

"It's your feet in your new shoes!" He turned to Janet. "It's our new gadget, an x-ray machine for shoes," he announced proudly, as if he'd invented it himself. Janet stood on the floor beside the platform and took in the strange green image of James's feet inside the shoes while his face was lit green from below by the glow.

"Just wiggle yer toes, young lad," said the salesman.

Ignoring the fact that he'd now been demoted back to a lad, James obeyed and marvelled as he saw a green rendering of his toes moving inside the outline of the shoes.

"Aye," said the salesman, "there seems to be plenty of room there. Is that all right?

Janet agreed but she still got James to walk around.

"Are ye sure they feel OK?" James nodded.

"How much did ye say they were?"

"That would be seventeen and six, madam."

They were slowly creeping up to Effie's fifteen pounds, but it couldn't be helped. As the salesman was re-packing the shoebox, Janet got a pound out of her purse and laid it on the counter. He wrote out the receipt and when the tube returned their two-and-six change they walked out of the shop. As they sat on the 34 bus back to Fox Crag, Janet suddenly said, "Listen, son, d'ye ken who paid for yer new school uniform?" Hadn't his mother paid for it? No, Janet explained, this was a present from his godmother, his Auntie Effie. James didn't know what to say. He'd seen the three five-pound notes lying on the table at the Provie. He was old enough to know what a large amount of money it was. Janet let that sink in then turned to him again.

"How are ye gonnae say thank you to yer auntie?"

James thought hard, then it came to him. Auntie Bella in Cheltenham was always generous where presents for James and Wee Effie were concerned. Whether it was because of her special bond with Janet or whether all her nieces and nephews were so fortunate, James didn't know. But every Christmas, every birthday without fail, a parcel or an envelope with a Cheltenham postmark would drop through the letterbox at Number 68. Sometimes it was a postal order for five or ten shillings, but there were gifts, too, often educational gifts that had consequences. Once, she sent James a tiny travel chess set. Books were a favourite. But last birthday, she'd sent him the most incredible gift of all.

It was a camera, a brand-new Kodak Brownie 127. It resided in a yellow box together with a soft bag and an instruction manual. Made of black Bakelite, it took a roll of film that produced 12 black and white snaps. He knew nothing about cameras but this one was perfect for a novice. In the back was a small, round, red Perspex window. You wound the film on until you saw the number 1, then you were ready to take a picture by pressing a little white button. You just had to remember to wind it on after each picture, otherwise you'd get a double or triple exposure. James had learned this the hard way. Yes, it was basic and next-to-useless indoors, but outdoors was fine. He'd got some super snaps of Louise, and of his dad digging in the garden. Although he didn't know it at the time, thoughtful, kind-hearted Auntie Bella had set him on a path that would last his whole lifetime.

"Mum?" he said.

"Well?" a distant Janet enquired, staring out of the window as Hawkhill passed them by. "What have ye come up wi'?"

"How about if Ah put mah school uniform on? Then we go out in the garden an' Dad takes a photo of me wi' mah Brownie frae Auntie Bella? Then we could have it framed and give it tae Auntie Effie as a present."

Janet carried on looking out of the window to mask her reaction. She never failed to be intrigued by the ideas and notions James came up with on his own. She tried not to look delighted but she was.

"Aye, son," she just said, "that would dae fine."

The Sunday before James was to start at the Academy was a crisp, sunny, early autumn day. He felt odd in his stiff new clothes, the blazer with the newly sewn-on badge, the tight shirt collar and the tie choking his neck. But he looked in the mirror and was pleased with what he saw. Out in the back green, Ian took three pictures of him against the pebble-dashed wall. When the film was used up they had it developed. They chose the best of the three, took it back to the photo shop with the negatives, and asked them to make an enlargement. After two weeks, they were back in the shop again choosing a frame. There was James, his blazer, the badge, the tie, and a nice big grin for his Auntie. James made a special trip to Warburton Crescent by himself to hand over the gift. Auntie Effie was overcome.

"Oh, son," she said, with tears in her eyes, "it's the best present Ah've ever had!"

She placed it on the sideboard next to the photo of her holding James in Church, and never tired of telling visitors with undisguised pride that this was her godson and that he was a pupil at The Academy.

A new world

James gulped and swallowed hard. He stood alone on the pavement before the eight-foot-high black and gilt gates of The Academy's main entrance. Slung over one shoulder was his 'new', near-empty schoolbag, actually a used khaki army surplus gas mask bag that he'd bought for 3s6d from Millets with his saved-up pocket money and, had he only known it, one not unlike the one his mother had used during fire watch on the roof of MacFergus. It was 8.30 am on the first day of the autumn term, 1958. The streets around the school were a hectic of blue, white and grey uniforms and the clamour of hundreds of returning academicals streaming down approaches in the early morning sunshine, alighting from buses, cycling down to the bike sheds and gathering in the playgrounds. They strolled along the pavement behind James, chatting and greeting each other, casting amused, pitying or condescending glances in his direction. But strangely, not one of them entered the school through this apparently exclusive entrance.

Between the gates and the intimidating crowds of pupils, some of whom appeared almost as old as his Uncle Alistair, James was, to put it mildly, terrified. Yes, he was decked out in his new school uniform. But he knew he was an imposter. He didn't belong here. His pass in the Qualy had been a mistake. They were sure to find out. Everyone would see through him and he'd be sent home in disgrace. He almost turned on his heel and walked away, but something stopped him. What would Auntie Effie say after paying for his uniform? What would his dad say? After all, he'd offered his son his best advice: *If anybody tries tae bully ye, knock 'is block off!* What would his mother say after seeing him off for his first day at The Academy?

She'd stood with him in the entry of Number 68, knowing not to embarrass him in front of the whole street. She'd looked him up and down, mentally ticking off the first-day-at-the-new-school checklist. As she noted the discrepancy between his appearance in his smart uniform and the trepidation written all over his face, her heart was bursting with emotion for him. But she didn't show it. She'd done so many things for him. She'd borne him, breast-fed him, cherished him and loved him. She'd taught him right from wrong. She'd ensured he had three good meals a day. She'd worried constantly about his health and pestered the doctors. She'd got him sunray treatment. She'd rubbed Vicks on his chest. She'd made sure he got his daily dose of National Health Service cod liver oil. She'd managed his primary schooling as best she could. But this new chapter of his life she couldn't do for him. It was beyond her abilities. He'd have to do it by himself.

"Well, son, off ye go," was all she'd managed to say, smoothing down the arms of his blazer and stifling any hint of tears. Then, as an afterthought, "Ah ken ye'll be a credit tae me and yer dad."

She hadn't waved as he'd walked up the street, even when he'd looked round. She'd just stood in the entry with her arms folded, smiling and nodding encouragement. Then he was on his own.

Movement at the edge of his vision interrupted his thoughts. Someone was standing next to him. He looked sideways. Another new boy by the looks of him. Everything about him was new. The flawless school uniform. The shiny shoes. The near-empty school bag. The short haircut. The scrubbed, over-young face. He stuck out a mile. *Just like me,* thought James and even *more* terrified, going by the expression on his face. But the other boy's palpable show of fear combined with his own vacillation before the gates had an unexpected effect on him. Suddenly, he felt brave. Determination welled up inside him. It seemed he'd inherited some of his mother's genes after all.

"Come on," he said with a touch of impatience directed more at himself than the stranger. "What're we waitin' for?"

And with that, he pushed open one of the gates, resolutely mounted the steps, and passed between huge oak framed glass doors which were latched back against the wall, unaware if the other was keeping up with him but certain that he was. They stopped in a vast, marble-floored vestibule with a high ceiling and oak panelling surrounds. They were enveloped by the fragrance of wood. They'd been told to enter by the main gate and report to the school office just inside the entrance. Buoyed by his newfound confidence, James stepped inside the open door and walked up to the polished oak counter, the other new boy still in tow. An efficient looking lady in her forties wearing a grey Jaeger cardigan over a blouse and skirt came up to her side of the counter with a businesslike smile.

"Good morning, boys!" she said loudly and cheerily, and, without bothering to enquire, for it was obvious from their pristine school uniforms and their demeanour exactly who they were and why they were there, she went on, "Admission forms, please!"

They scrabbled in their bags, retrieved the required documents and handed them over to Mrs Tulloch, for that's who she was. Taking them to her desk, she consulted a list, did some ticking, made some notes then came back to the counter.

"James Swanston?" she enquired. James raised his hand as if he were in class then quickly lowered it when he realised how ridiculous he must look.

"And Bernard Lamont?" The other boy nodded eagerly.

"Now, boys, just one thing. Today, you came through the main entrance for that's what you were told to do, but from now on you must never use that entrance. It's only for teachers, visitors, prefects, and sixth years. Otherwise, you'll always enter the school by the side entrance from the playground. All right?" They nodded. She consulted her paper. "You'll both be in class 1a1 with Mr Flockhart. Turn right into the corridor, go past the stairs and it's classroom G7." As they stood hesitating, taking in the complex directions, she added, "Go on then, your teacher will be waiting!" And off they went briskly, almost bumping into two new girls, going by their similar, pristine, uniforms.

As they walked side by side along the corridor James felt his confidence grow. Finding G7, he knocked on the wooden frame of the rippled glass window then, without waiting, he turned the door handle and strode in. The room was almost full of around thirty fledgling twelve-year-old-or-so academicals, all in smart new uniforms and most looking apprehensive. Some were just sitting at their desks staring into space while others were conversing in hushed tones as if they were in church. James took one of the last remaining seats in the front row and Bernard sat across from him. They looked at each other properly for the first time. Bernard was even smaller than James, though he must have been older. He had tight red curls and a freckled, pinched face like a pixie. James took the plunge.

"Where are ye from?" he ventured quietly.

"Willowbrae," he answered back. "And you?"

"Fox Crag," said James.

"Any idea what happens now?"

"Search me. Ah suppose we'll find out soon enough..."

No sooner had the words left James's lips than they were realised, for suddenly the classroom door opened and an adult swept in, the tails of his black academic gown swirling up behind him in his wake. Closing the door, he walked up to the front row of desks. He was about 45 years old, of average height and weight, with thinning dark brown hair cut unfashionably long but leaving his ears free, a matching moustache, bushy eyebrows, and a smile on his face which was a cross between apologetic and conspiratorial. When some started to rise from their seats in anticipation he flapped his hands for them to sit down again.

“Good morning, boys and girls. Welcome to The Academy. I am Mr Flockhart, your Register Teacher. In addition, as Head of Foreign Languages at The Academy, I will be teaching you French.”

The novice Academicals sat forward as one in their seats to offer their new teacher their undivided attention.

“There’s no need to stand up when I come into the room – or any other teacher for that matter.” His smile got even broader, then a bit more serious. “But you must always stand if the Rector, the Deputy Rector or the Lady Advisor enter the room. Is that clear?”

Thirty-odd young heads nodded dutifully. Yes, it was clear – even though most had no idea who the Rector was, or his Deputy, or the Lady Advisor.

“Every morning at 8.45 you will be here in your seats for registration. At five to nine, the bell will ring and you will make your way as quickly as you can to your first class of the day. Is that clear?”

Again the thirty-odd young heads nodded dutifully.

“Now, is there anyone here that’s already familiar with the Academy buildings?”

He looked around the room. Blank expressions. Then, after some moments, a single hand hesitantly went up.

“Yes, stand up, boy,” said Mr Flockhart.

The boy unfolded himself from his desk. He was well over average height for his age, with a face correspondingly old beyond his years, a worried expression, and a shock of thick black hair that flopped over his forehead in a cow’s lick.

“What’s your name?”

“Eric Livingstone, Sir,” said the boy, shuffling his feet, obviously ill at ease. “I did the orientation course, Sir,” added Eric helpfully.

The Academy ran a summer two-week programme called *Orientation to Study at The Academy* for keen students whose parents could afford to pay for it. Apparently, in 1a1, Eric’s parents were the only ones that could – or Eric was the only pupil prepared to admit that they could. As a result, it seemed he already knew his way around the labyrinthine corridors of the school.

“Fine. You will now be the temporary Class Monitor.”

Eric flinched at the edict. It was plainly not his kettle of fish.

“It will be your task to take charge of 1a1 and guide your fellow pupils to the correct classrooms when you move from period to period throughout the day. Is that clear?”

The class were beginning to grasp that this was one of Mr Flockhart’s favourite expressions. Eric nodded reluctantly.

“Good. You may sit.”

Apparently, Eric had no choice in the matter. He sat, squirming down in his seat as if trying to conceal his lofty form.

"The bell will ring for the start and end of each period. For the first couple of weeks, at the end of the period, you will line up in twos behind Eric and he will take you to your next class. This will ensure that none of you gets lost and that you get to your classes on time. Normally, registration period is from 8.45 to 8.55. I will take attendance and deal with any other administrative matters. As I said, you will then proceed to the first period at 9 am. However, since today is your first day we will need a bit more time, so you will not be starting lessons until the second period, that is at 9.45."

Mr Flockhart's next task, as Register Teacher, was to record attendance, which he did briskly, holding a large, green, leather-bound register in one hand, a pencil in the other, going down the alphabetical list and making an attempt to memorise some of the names. Then he had to give the pupils their timetable. Crooking his finger to a couple of nearby boys to help, he went to a cupboard, unlocked it and handed each of the pupils a stack of brand new, grey-covered jotters to distribute to the class. James was pleased to see the familiar heading Edinburgh Corporation Education Committee above the name The Academy. The dusty old men and women in the committee room off the High Street had kept him company onto the next stage of his life. The thought was strangely comforting, for James was now realising that the black and gold gates of The Academy were in fact a portal to another world and that he'd emerged on an alien planet. Here, everything was different.

For a start, the mere idea of a timetable was new. At primary school, there had been no such thing. Though their teachers might have had a timetable in their heads, it was never written down. All learning had taken place in one room with one teacher. But here, they'd move from classroom to classroom, with up to seven different subject teachers a day. Mr Flockhart had already prepared a timetable blank outlined on the blackboard. He instructed them to copy the blank with ruler and pencil on the last page of their jotters while he filled in the empty spaces on the board in chalk. They were then to complete the timetable.

The school day comprised seven periods of 40 minutes each, with a five-minute break between each one to allow movement between classrooms. There were four periods in the morning, with a twenty-minute break at 10.25, and three in the afternoon, with a one hour and ten-minute dinner break at 12.10. School ended at 3.30. James started on his timetable blank, then enjoyed filling in the spaces with the names of exotic new subjects - chemistry, physics, French, Latin, P.E. - and for each subject the name of the teacher and room number.

The school building would also take some getting used to. The current Academy building and that of Fox Crag both dated from the 1930s and both used red brick in their construction, but there the similarity ended. Simply put, Fox Crag was budget while The Academy was luxury. The plain, two-storied, elongated construction at Fox Crag paled into insignificance beside the three-storeyed elegance of The Academy with its carefully groomed façade, its pseudo-baroque four-faced clock tower and its neoclassical entrance. Essentially, it was a large building of brick, dressed stone and slate for the roof, roughly pentagonal in shape, encompassing a large gymnasium. In addition to standard classrooms on all floors, the school offices were on the ground floor, together with rooms for technical subjects, while the second was given over to science and the third to art and music.

It took some weeks for the newcomers in 1a1 to become accustomed to all this. Unless Eric was supervising, they were constantly getting lost. The fact that a one-way system operated on all floors and staircases only made things worse. For some reason, at some time in the past, it had been decreed that pupils (an exception was graciously granted to prefects) would move in an anti-clockwise direction along the corridors. In addition, there were 'up' stairs and 'down' stairs. For James and the other newcomers, this led to endless walking. For example, G7, their registration room and French classroom, was just past an 'up' stair on the anti-clockwise side. This meant that on leaving to go to another class on an upper level, the pupils couldn't just turn left, walk ten yards, and go up the stairs. No, no, no, that would be contravening the anti-clockwise rule! Instead, they had to turn right, make a circuit of the entire school along the ground floor corridor, arrive almost at the point where they'd started, then mount the correct staircase. After a year of this, James concluded that the one-way system was a cunning ploy by some previous rector to ensure his pupils got enough exercise.

The sheer extent of The Academy's facilities was overwhelming. The gymnasium was of gargantuan proportions. It was actually a double gymnasium, each half separated by a huge, electrically operated wooden partition. A game of netball could be going on in one half, while there was gymnastics or even cricket practice in the other. The whole could be then opened out for theatrical performances or special events such as prize-giving and was designed to cater for the entire school community at once, getting on for a thousand souls. To James, the number of dedicated classrooms for subject areas such as science, domestic science, technical subjects and the arts seemed endless and he was constantly getting mixed up. There was even a language laboratory, one of the many achievements of Mr Flockhart. The first time they were timetabled in there, 1a1 had no idea where they were. Mr Flockhart, who was already waiting, gestured for them to sit, each in a glass-walled booth. They marvelled that the strange contraption integrated into the desk turned out to be a tape recorder and gingerly fingered a gadget plugged into it, which only a few had ever seen before in obscure photos of people in BBC studios, namely headphones. Giving them a brief overview of the lab and its functions, Mr Flockhart proudly told them that in that year of 1958 they were the only pupils north of the border to be privileged to be sitting in a language laboratory and one of only a handful of classes with access to one in the entire country. At that, they brightened up and felt very special indeed.

As an Academy pupil, James was expected to master a new language. Like his primary school teachers, their Academy counterparts were almost exclusively native Scots who spoke in an educated tongue, a form of Proper Speak. Some were devotees of *Morningside*. Like Uncle Alistair, they said 'I' and 'you' and 'he' and 'not'. They ended their participles with 'ing'. They used correct forms of the past tense and present perfect. They rarely used Scots words and expressions, not to mention Leith or Edinburgh patois. Instead of *Can Ah hae a sybae wi' mah tatties?* it was *Can I have a spring onion with my potatoes?* James's primary school teachers had made little or no effort to correct their pupils' speech, but here at The Academy some teachers did, for educated speech was expected of the pupils as well. It was early on that he got the message when he was publicly shamed by Miss Tranter, the RE teacher, for daring to utter the sentence *They've went tae the toilet, Miss,* when explaining some pupils' lateness. He soon learnt that on the rare occasions he spoke up in lessons, or when he plucked up the courage to address a teacher privately, Proper Speak – or a close approximation – was the only acceptable medium. It was a steep learning curve. He found himself inhabiting two separate worlds. Under the roof of The Academy, while in class, he was obliged to produce grammatical, properly pronounced English, while at home, colloquial Scots was still the norm.

Not only was James expected to speak English, but he was also expected to follow a curriculum that was strongly English-oriented. In six years of English literature, it was Chaucer, Shakespeare, Keats and John Masefield all the way. No Robert Burns. No Robert Louis Stevenson. Not even Walter Scott. It wasn't literature in English. It was truly *English* literature. Apart from a smattering of Scottish themes, history lessons focused on English history. Given the wealth of history right on their doorstep in Leith and Edinburgh, it was disappointing that James graduated from The Academy ignorant of most of it, except for what he'd bothered to find out for himself. Yes, the school choir sang 'Step We Gaily' to entertain visitors. And yes, they were taught Scottish Country dances in preparation for the fourth-, fifth- and sixth-year dances. But these activities didn't reflect what they were taught in class, nor what they were examined on. They were a veneer. He valued his Academy education but did wonder if his time there was the first step, not only in making him *speak* English but in making him *be* English.

Life at Fox Crag had been plain and unvarnished. The only teacher you knew was your class teacher and extra-curricular activities were unknown. Suddenly, everything was different for, as James soon discovered, he was now a member of a large and complex academic community. The Academy was ruled over by a triumvirate consisting of the Rector, the Deputy Rector and the Lady Advisor. Dr Drysdale, the Rector - a decorated war hero - was a completely bald bulldog of a man who reigned, godlike and distant over The Academy. But his Deputy, Dr Small, had more than enough hair for both of them with plenty to spare. Despite his advancing years, his large head was covered in luxurious grey waves of it, matched by a grey Kitchener moustache, tinged orange by his chain-smoking. As if to defy his surname, Dr Small was large and corpulent. If James had bothered to give the matter a moment's thought, he might have wondered what the Rector and his Deputy actually did. They didn't appear to have any teaching duties. They didn't interact with students. They were rarely seen in the school corridors or classrooms. They were, to all intents and purposes, invisible, except when called upon to appear on stage at an assembly or ceremony, or for annual photographs.

In stark contrast, Miss Fyffe the Lady Advisor was very visible indeed. In fact, visibility was almost her middle name for her role required a good deal of lurking around the school, busily attending to the 'welfare' of the female pupils who made up a good 50% of the school population. Miss Fyffe, half-affectionately known to the pupils as 'Miss Fluff', almost matched Dr Small, not only in terms of height, for she was easily over six feet tall, but also for her own rich coiffure. In her fifties when James arrived, she had a fine head of sandy curls which looked incongruously youthful around her middle-aged face with the orange-framed spectacles anchored by the slender gold chain hanging around her neck. So incongruous were Miss Fluff's tresses that it was rumoured she wore a wig, but no one could prove it either way. She'd patrol the corridors wielding a giant wooden ruler for measuring skirt lengths. Since she was never seen without her black academic gown, she'd swoop down, bat-like, on any girl who was deemed to have offended against uniform regulations. Without number were the girls summoned to her office to answer to Miss Fluff for too short skirts, for the wearing of lipstick and mascara or for even worse. Miss Fluff had a fearsome reputation that she probably didn't deserve. Invariably with a smile on her lips, she seemed a kind person at heart. It was even whispered that she'd helped fifteen-year-old Margaret Finlay, who, finding herself with a bun in the oven, was being pressurised by her dysfunctional family to have a back street abortion. Margaret, God bless her, had had the presence of mind to seek out The Lady Advisor. Miss Fluff had taken the girl under her wing, organised legal safeguards, and had her admitted to a special clinic in The Borders that handled such cases, where she was able to give birth in safety. She then returned to complete her studies at The Academy, having given the child up for adoption.

These three godlike Academy executives ruled over a community of some 60 teaching professionals, almost all with solid academic qualifications from reputable universities or teacher training colleges. The nature of these teachers was probably the single most important factor impacting the pupils' learning, their daily lives, and even their future prospects. James was soon to realise that there were two basic types of classroom teacher at The Academy, namely the ones he feared and the ones he didn't. He used two simple litmus tests to tell them apart. One, did they call pupils by their first names or surnames? Two, did they use The Belt? The ones he didn't fear usually addressed pupils by their first names and belted sparingly or not at all. They ranged from those who couldn't control their classes to those who blended competence, understanding, kindness and humour to earn their pupils' respect. The teachers he did fear always used surnames, sometimes even for female pupils (but this was rare), and belted with regularity. They ranged from the merely uncaring to the positively terrifying, heartless, tyrannical, and sometimes even cruel, who belted untiringly, all day and every day. There were, of course, exceptions, such as teachers who put the fear of God into James but never belted, probably because they didn't need to. He'd meet a couple of these in the course of the next six years. But, in general, his classification scheme held water.

With relief, James gradually came to realise that most of the teachers in whose care he'd landed were in the first category. And fortunately for Class 1a1, among them was Mr Flockhart. Although James soon developed some doubts as to his effectiveness as an instructor, he was humane and affable, and his very affability was the key to maintaining the discipline required for learning. But pre-eminent among competent, caring instructors was undoubtedly Henry M. Neil, James's Latin teacher. No one knew what the M stood for and no one cared, for his pupils universally referred to him behind his back as

Henry. Henry was about 45 years of age. He was unusually tall, thin and rangy. His high cheekbones and gimlet eyes gave him a Slavonic appearance but his good-natured smile marked him out as friendly and approachable. His head of thick, wavy hair was prematurely white because, it was said, his ship had been torpedoed by a German U-Boat and he'd spent several days floating in the Atlantic before he was rescued by a Sunderland of Coastal Command. Unlike his male colleagues who wore the standard grammar school suit, he unfailingly sported a Harris Tweed sports jacket, flannels, and tie. Nor, unlike most of his peers, was he ever seen in an academic gown in class despite the MA after his name that entitled him to don one. These quirks earned him the reputation of being a bit of a maverick. Even among the teachers James liked, Henry was unique, for he had the knack of treating his pupils as equals without sacrificing his authority, cleverly blending humanity, humour and competence to such a degree that not only was he an effective teacher, he was widely respected and even loved by some.

On the first day of Latin, the pupils were in their places waiting for the teacher. After the first few periods of French, the class had concluded that while it seemed easy, the pronunciation tied their tongues in knots and overtaxed their nostrils. Now, they were keen to find out what Latin would be like. The door opened. Henry strode in, introduced himself, turned to the blackboard and wrote in chalk 'Nemo Me Impune Lacessit'.

"Now," he said, turning back to the class, "who can tell me where you'd see this Latin phrase?"

Eric Livingstone's hand shot up first.

"Yes," said Henry, pointing to Eric, "and what's your name?"

"Eric Livingstone, Sir."

"Well, Eric, what's the answer?"

"It's the school motto, Sir. It's on our badge – here!" and he pointed to the pocket of his blazer.

"Well done, Eric, and can you tell us what it means?"

It was one of the few times James was to see Eric stumped. With a frustrated expression, the future Dux had to shake his head.

"Well?" Henry enquired with a smile, looking around 1a1, his eyebrows arching even more than usual. "Who can tell us the answer?"

There was a hush. No one, apparently, knew the meaning of 'Nemo Me Impune Lacessit'. No one, that is, except James. He was bursting to answer. But in his shy way, he was afraid to speak out. He waited. Henry waited. The class waited. Finally, from goodness knew where, James plucked up the courage. He put up his hand. Henry turned to where he sat in the front row next to the door.

"Yes," he said with a grin, "here's someone who knows. Or does he? What's your name, young sir?"

"James Swanston, Sir," said James, having had the presence of mind to stand up.

"Well, James, are you going to share your knowledge with us?"

"Sir, it means *No one shall touch me with impunity.*"

There was a collective gasp around the room. How was it possible that this little nonentity, James Swanston, could confidently provide the answer, let alone know a word like *impunity*? Against their better instincts, they had to admit they were impressed.

"Well done, James, quite correct. Have you studied Latin before?"

"No, Sir."

"Would you like to tell us how you know this, then?"

"Well Sir, mah Dad taught it tae me. It was the motto on 'is cap badge in the army durin' The War."

"Ah!" exclaimed Henry, "Of course." Then, turning to the others, he said, "Really, I'm surprised none of you knew that. Well done, James. You may sit and, by the way, go to the top of the class!" In that instant, Henry endeared himself to James for years to come.

"So," said Henry, "we have established that the school motto, 'No one shall touch me with impunity' or..." Henry's eyes twinkled. "...in our Scots tongue, *Wha daur meddle wi' me*?..." Smiles and some laughter from the class. "...is written in Latin. Would anyone like to explain why?"

Hands went up. Henry chose one.

"Because it's an important language, Sir?"

"Why? Isn't it a dead language? Who speaks Latin these days?"

"Sir, doctors have to know Latin!"

"True, but do they speak it? When they want a fish supper, do they ask for it in Latin?"

There was universal laughter. James immediately pictured himself going into Luigi's in Junction Street and asking for a hot pea special in Latin. But the class were stumped. There seemed to be a use for Latin, but it was true, nobody actually spoke it these days. Eric decided to help them out. He put his hand up.

"Sir, some modern languages like French and Spanish come from Latin, don't they?"

"Ah!" exclaimed Henry, "Lux ex tenebris! Well done, Eric." He turned round with his chalk and wrote it on the blackboard. Turning back to the class, he translated. "Light from darkness. Yes, you are right. So, if you know Latin, you'll find it easier to learn French, Spanish, Italian, and, if you think about it, you'll realise a lot of English words come from Latin. I wonder if anyone can give an example?"

Joyce Carnie shot up her hand.

"Sir, mah uncle has an antique shop. Does antique not mean old in Latin?"

"Very good!" exclaimed Henry. "Now we're making progress!"

And so as the dialogue progressed, the new scholars began to understand why there might be some point in learning Latin and Henry had done an effective job of selling the rationale for his existence.

"Now," he went on, "already, we've learnt quite a few Latin words. Let's make a list on the board. Now, remind me..."

Hands shot up, pupils opened their jotters, busily started writing, and James's first Latin class was well underway.

Henry was a stickler for homework. Every day there was a vocabulary list in their textbook to be learned. Every morning, Henry would go around the class, orally testing them on yesterday's list. If a pupil couldn't answer, he was given another chance at another word. Then another chance. But that was all. James never forgot the one and only time he failed to answer the three questions.

"Sorry, James," said Henry with a regretful smile. James wondered how many teachers would apologise in advance for having to punish him. "You know what to do!"

James knew perfectly well. Plenty of Latin vocab delinquents had made the Walk of Shame before him. He stood up, unable to hide his embarrassment. Slinking to Henry's desk with his face averted from the class, he took the blank sheet of ruled foolscap paper Henry was holding out to him.

"Three times, please," Henry said with a smile, his eyes piercing through James at the same time. James returned to his place, hanging his head. He'd have to write out the entire list three times and hand in his work the next day. But didn't bear a grudge. Far from it. He should have done his homework. He'd learnt his lesson.

At the other end of the spectrum, surely the two nastiest teachers in the school were the boys' Physical Education (PE) teacher, Mr Hamilton, known to the students as Hammy, and the Technical Drawing teacher, Mr Dunbar, simply known as Duggie, from Douglas, his first name. For sheer depravity, there was no one to equal them in The Academy. They were both sadists, each in his own way. In his first week at The Academy, James was introduced to a novelty in his education: a dedicated PE class run by a specialist PE teacher. In primary school, there had been no physical education to speak of. In the dour post-war years, state-run primary schools focused on getting the products of the baby boom through the system. Organised sports at the primaries James attended were rare. Boys who showed promise at an early age might be encouraged into a sports club like Leith Athletic, Leith Victoria or The 1930 Club, but these would be a tiny minority. Where girls were concerned, the situation was even more dire. Real sports were only for the very talented or the oddballs. The promotion of sports within the education system was left mainly up to secondary schools, especially the private, fee-paying ones who could afford the facilities and the equipment. As a result, the weekly dose of sports at The Academy came as a shock to many novice Academicals who'd never participated in sports in their lives. Suddenly, they were confronted with a level of physical exertion that many found at the least, challenging, at the most, brutal.

Boys and girls were separated for PE. For first- and second-year classes, there were four periods of PE a week, one in the school gymnasium, plus an entire three-period afternoon at Hawkhill sports ground. In the gymnasium, they did what amounted to circuit training. At Hawkhill, they were introduced to the only winter game permitted boys at The Academy, namely rugby. Come summer, it would be cricket. In the first week of the new term, in their very first PE session, Hammy made no mistake about putting his stamp on the fledgling male scholars from 1a1.

On the Tuesday, Eric had dutifully led his charges to the boy's changing room for the last period of the morning. They were allowed only seconds to sit on the wooden lockers before the door burst open and Hammy came charging in at full tilt. The boys leapt to their feet, not out of respect, but out of fright. This was an emotion they'd get used to when Hammy was around. James saw a hard-bitten, flinty individual in his fifties dressed in an open-necked white shirt, light grey flannels, and gym shoes. His significant physical attribute was that he was short. Every boy in 1a1 overtopped him except James and Bernard Lamont. Maybe his diminutive stature in a tall world explained why Hammy was the way he was. He didn't bother to introduce himself.

"Get your PE kit out. Come on! On the locker in front of you!"

The pupils scrabbled to obey while Hammy looked on.

"Please, Sir?" It was Raymond Maconachie, already marked out as the class pansy. "Ah'm excused PE, Sir."

If a pin had dropped they'd all have heard it for they were focused on Hammy's face which was a wonder to behold, since it was in the process of turning several furious shades of red. Then he erupted.

"No one is excused PE without a note from a parent or doctor!" he bellowed. "That was stated clearly in your enrolment briefing!" He held out his hand and his voice dropped a few decibels. "Your note?" Despite the question mark in his voice, it wasn't a request. It was a threat.

By now, Raymond was beginning to realise he'd made a serious misstep. He gulped several times before he could get the words out.

"Ah don't have one, Sir," he managed to utter. There was a suppressed sigh around the room. Raymond was in for it.

"Stand over there." Hammy pointed to the other end of the room. He turned to the kit laid out on the lockers. Boys were required to have a pair of white shorts, a white singlet and a pair of gym shoes. Hammy passed along the lockers like a sergeant major doing barracks inspection. Several boys had incomplete kits.

"Where're your gym shoes?"

"Ah forgot them, Sir."

"Go and line up with that boy over there."

Hammy's long experience in the game had taught him that there were always boys who'd do anything to avoid PE. The most common excuse was that they'd forgotten their gym shoes. Hammy always used his first session as a lesson in forgetfulness. Inspection over, four boys had joined Raymond. Fortunately for him, James wasn't one of them. Hammy went to a cupboard, opened it with a key on a chain dangling from the pocket of his flannels, and brought out the largest, meanest Belt James had ever seen.

"Hold out your right hands, palms uppermost!"

Crestfallen, the boys did as they were told. Hammy went down the line and whacked each of them once across the palm of the hand. As whimpers resounded behind him, he addressed the rest of the class.

"Let that be a lesson to those that think they can get out of PE! This time, I was generous!" He turned and looked at the offenders who were variously shaking out their wrists or blowing into their cupped hands. "This time, it was only one. Next time, it'll be two, and the time after that, three! Now, the rest of you, get changed!"

Shocked and intimidated, James and the others quickly threw off their uniforms, got into their kit and silently trooped across to the gymnasium. The hall was immense and cold. The massive partition was closed. On the other side, the girls were already busy with Miss Merrylegs at netball, by the sound of the shouts and calls. Hammy supervised the boys as they set out mats and ropes and positioned vaulting horses, split them into groups and inducted them into circuit training. As he toured the gym barking orders, he amused himself by mocking those too weak to complete, or too scared to attempt, the assigned exercises. A master of biting sarcasm, his special technique, once he'd learnt all their names, was to allot a nickname to each member of the class and berate him in exaggerated Scots.

To James: "Come on, Swanny, ye wee jeely piece, get up that rope!"

To Eric: "Ah havnae seen yer muscles the day, Krankie, did ye leave them at hame?"

To Bernard: "Get yersel' next door Lame-ington, ye wee jessie, an' play netball wi' the lassies!"

By the end of forty minutes the boys had had enough and Hammy released them. Sweating and sore, they trooped back to the changing rooms, hurriedly pulling their uniforms back over their sweating bodies, desperate to get away and into the fresh air of the midday break. They'd certainly learned a few things. One was never again to forget a piece of gym kit. But for sheer malice, Hammy's special version of gate duty took the prize. The boys' playground gate had to be locked at 8.45 am; latecomers got detention. Most teachers on gate duty made allowances, keeping the gate open for stragglers, but Hammy had his own special torture. He'd stand holding the gate half open, glancing at his watch and up the road. Then, just as his victims arrived, panting and red-faced, he'd slam the gate in their faces, lock it, and grin at them through the bars. To Hammy, it was all a game; the boys existed for his amusement. Some claimed he was insane. Maybe he was. Or maybe he was just a sociopath who took out his shortcomings on his pupils.

Of Hammy, it could at least be said that he delivered his sadism with a dash of humour. No such thing could be said of Duggie Dunbar. Where Hammy was just plain nasty, Duggie was frightening. Fortunately, he taught only the non-academic B stream but such was his notoriety that his exploits were broadcast far and wide. Duggie was malicious and dangerous. He was so violent that he might just as well have had a Belt grafted onto his right arm instead of a hand. In fact, it could be said that his lesson menu consisted of a main course of belting with a side serving of technical drawing instruction. He didn't need a reason to belt. He just belted because he could. Almost every boy in his classes had tasted the stinging caress of his custom-made Lochgelly's Finest. His favourite trick was to pick out a boy not paying attention and to throw the chalk duster at him. The duster, a misnomer if ever there was one, was a block of wood with a piece of felt glued to one side. If you were lucky, it was the felt that made contact with your head. But not a few lads walked out of Duggie's classroom nursing a bruise to the forehead.

Unlike Hammy, Duggie was large and stout and in his mid-forties. His cropped hair and wire-rimmed spectacles anchored by protruding ears underlined his resemblance to a Gestapo torturer. His flushed cheeks and florid nose only reinforced the impression that he was permanently angry. Older boys claimed he was an alcoholic and kept a bottle of Bell's in his class cupboard. Maybe he was, but if so, he managed to keep it well hidden from the school authorities. James often thanked his lucky stars that Duggie's name didn't appear on his timetable. Just one single time, James and Duggie happened to be in the same room together when Duggie had to stand in for an absent teacher in the academic stream. There was no lesson, just a period of supervised 'work' but it was the most frightening 40 minutes of James's time at The Academy. He kept his head down and never moved a muscle while Duggie, in his choler, busied himself picking on boys for his special treatment on account of minor infractions.

Duggie's victims knew there was nothing they could do about his excesses, not to mention those of Hammy and his ilk, for teachers were all-powerful. The thought of complaining never entered their heads. Anyway, there was no mechanism to do so. If pupils were intimidated, threatened, belted, or otherwise assaulted by the teacher, the last thing they'd do was tell their parents, for the stock parental response would be, "Well, if ye got belted, ye must have done somethin' wrong!" In the end, they simply had to put up with it, knowing that these were the actions of a minority, and hoping that as they grew bigger and stronger, they were less likely to be easy targets.

The elite

In James's primary schools, prefects hadn't existed, but here at The Academy, they were an integral part of the disciplinary system. The Academy prefects were the elite at the pinnacle of the school. Among the common plebs, they enjoyed the status of minor deities, together with members of the boys' First XV rugby team, members of the girls' First XI hockey team, and the top scholars. Anyone able to combine all three states in their person - prefect, sports and scholastic excellence - enjoyed even more elevated status. The ultimate was to be Head Prefect, Captain of the rugby or hockey team and Dux of the School, a trifecta that would confer a godlike status approaching only that of the Rector. This clique of prefects, athletes and duxes, la crème de la crème de la crème, was the real powerhouse of The Academy. It was they who kept order among the pupils outside the classroom; it was they who were the impetus behind the sports teams, clubs and societies; it was they who, as much as the Rector and the teachers (some might say even more), shaped and nurtured the culture of the school. When James joined The Academy, there were around thirty prefects, split roughly fifty-fifty between males and females. All James knew about them was that they wore a special badge on their blazer lapel, posed annually for a group photo with the Rector, and could tell him what to do when not in class.

They could censure him for a breach of uniform regulations or for running in the corridor. They policed unruly behaviour and stopped or prevented fights. Punishment usually consisted of lines or, if more serious, being reported to the school authorities.

From his lowly perch in the hierarchy, James struggled to understand how someone got chosen to be a prefect. What were the criteria? What was the process? If there was one, it was never divulged to the pupils. As far as James knew, it wasn't a position you applied for or were elected to. Instead, soon after the start of a new school year, individual chosen ones would mysteriously appear with badges in their lapels. There was no announcement. It was only when he flipped through the group photos of the prefects and sports teams, and the lists of prize-winners in the school magazine that he made the connection: either you excelled at sports or you excelled scholastically, or both. A curious, time-honoured feature of the system was that male prefects didn't police female pupils and vice-versa. This practice hadn't arisen through regulation. It was simply an unwritten law. Or so James thought. That was, until the day Cassiopeia Clover came into his life.

Cassiopeia's father's fondness for astronomy had led him to persuade his wife to name their firstborn after the mythical Greek queen known for her beauty. No name could have been more appropriate, for, taking after her mother, a Swedish scientist, at the age of seventeen Cassiopeia was already famed throughout The Academy for her incredibly good looks. A thick cluster of natural golden locks framed her lovely features. Her pleasing form displayed curves in all the right places. She was gorgeous, with an engaging personality and intelligence to boot. Nothing and no one could be more perfect than Cassiopeia. However, there was one thing she did insist on. Any attempt by her peers or even her teachers to take a shortcut with her name was firmly put down.

"My name is Cassiopeia," she'd politely remind the offending person, "not Cassie. Five syllables, not two. Would you remember that please?"

Every year, her name, all five syllables, appeared high on the list of Academy prize winners. She was captain of the girls' Hockey First XI and, to cap a successful scholastic career, she'd been selected as a fifth-year prefect. It was in this capacity that, one day in just his second week at The Academy, she bumped into James – literally. Somehow, he and Bernard had become separated from that essential school guide to the newly formed 1a1, Eric Livingstone, along with the rest of the class while on their way to art with Mr Helliwell. Completely lost and forgetful besides, for they were charging the wrong way up the one-way corridor on the third floor, who should they crash into coming round a corner but the incomparable Cassiopeia in company with her best friend and fellow-prefect, Haida Henrichsen?

Haida just happened to be another product of the Scandinavian School of Beauty, but this time the Norwegian department. There had been close ties between Scotland and Norway going back to Viking times and beyond, as attested to by the presence in Leith of the shipping and whaling conglomerate and major employer, Christian Salvesen. Haida's family was a consequence of those ties. Like Cassiopeia, she was a stunner. But where Cassiopeia was blond, Haida was dark. Where Cassiopeia displayed generous curves, Haida was elegantly slender. And where Cassiopeia had a sweet personality, Haida tended to be sagacious. They complemented each other perfectly.

Nonetheless, it was Cassiopeia that James physically made contact with. The moment of impact with that cloud of blonde hair, soft curves, Academy blazer and feminine fragrance stayed with him forever; he'd collided with an angel. Cassiopeia had just come from the library. It didn't matter that James was a head smaller. In his eagerness to get to class, he'd cannoned straight into her, scattering her selection of Shakespearian commentaries all over the floor. Apologetic in the extreme, he recovered his schoolbag which he'd dropped in the mêlée.

"Oh, Ah'm sorry, Ah didnae mean tae..." he managed to get out.

Cassiopeia looked down at him with a mixture of surprise and pity. She could see right away that he was a wee first year who probably didn't have a clue where he was or what day of the week it was. But it was Haida who stepped in to manage the mishap.

"What's your name?" she demanded in an officious tone.

"James Swanston, Miss..."

His confusion was understandable. Haida was seventeen and had matured early. She could easily have been a junior member of the teaching staff, had she not been in school uniform. She whipped out a biro and a slip of paper from the top pocket of her blazer while Cassiopeia was scrabbling around picking up her library books. Apparently, as a freshly minted prefect, Haida was quite prepared to carry out the practical duties of her office regardless of some arcane Academy convention, unwritten or not.

"Is that Swanston with or without a 't'?" she asked.

"With..." replied James with trepidation, having suddenly been made to grasp the seriousness of the situation, not to mention the fact that not only were they were already late for class, they couldn't remember where the classroom was. Bernard, meanwhile, looked on in awe, relieved that it hadn't been him doing the colliding.

"Right," said Haida, "I've now taken your name." It sounded terribly formal, like something a policeman – or woman – would say. She turned her attention to the hapless Bernard.

"And what's yours?"

"But, but Miss... Ah didnae do anything!"

"You both broke the one-way rule. You should have been going *that* way..." With her biro, she pointed over his shoulder back down the corridor. "...not *this* way. *And* you were running. Your name?"

Bernard reluctantly offered up his name. Haida carefully wrote it down, taking her time over it and making sure that he was sufficiently intimidated. By this time, Cassiopeia had collected her books and was looking on, thoroughly amused. Poor wee laddies, you had to feel sorry for them. And they were probably late for class as well. Ah, the joys of being a first year! She stepped forward. Giving Haida a slight nudge and a knowing look, she took charge.

"You realise you could get into trouble for this?"

She tried to make her voice sound harsh but didn't quite succeed. The two boys gazed at her and nodded, wide-eyed. But a strange thing was happening. They knew they were in trouble, but somehow it didn't matter. Not one little bit, for those they were in trouble with happened to be two goddesses descended from Heaven for their pleasure alone. Neither of the boys had ever seen them before, but it was clear they were two of the greatest beauties in The Academy and they were actually taking the time to talk to *them. Them!* They'd been led to understand that only male prefects would exercise discipline over them, but even if their antics resulted in some punishment from these two stoaters, who cared? Not them. They were actually starting to enjoy the experience. Taking a big breath, James spoke up for both of them.

"We're *really* sorry... er... Miss..."

He looked up at Cassiopeia with his best appealing expression.

"We got lost and we're late for the art class with Mr Helliwell..."

Cassiopeia's heart almost melted. She had a wee brother about the same age as these two who, for his sins, went by the name of Sirius. She loved him dearly though he was always messing up too. She looked at Haida with raised eyebrows and a wry smile. Her friend got the message. Anyway, they both knew that it wasn't the done thing for girl prefects to punish boys. Not only that, but they also couldn't stand around wasting time in the corridor like this. They both had to be somewhere as well.

"Right," Haida said, "this time, we'll let you off. But if we catch you at it again, we'll report you to your Register Teacher."

"Thank you, Miss!"

"And stop calling us 'Miss'. We're not teachers, we're prefects!"

"Sorry, Miss..."

The girls struggled not to laugh. What a pair of clowns!

"Er, could ye direct us tae Mr Helliwell's class, please?"

Cassiopeia pointed back where they'd come from.

"Back down the corridor and go past the stairs. It's the first classroom you'll see. Better hurry!"

But James had been bitten. He just couldn't help himself. Anything to prolong this propitious encounter, even by just a few seconds.

"Sorry, but..."

He was about to say 'Miss' again but stopped himself just in time. He gulped and tried again.

"Could ye tell us yer names?" he blurted out.

"If you don't get out of here in one second it's a hundred lines for both of you!" warned Haida, as Cassiopeia struggled to suppress her mirth at James's cheek. The two boys turned and scurried off into the distance, fortunate that Mr Helliwell the art teacher, a kindly man who was by no means either a Duggie or a Hammy, was prepared to make allowances so early in the term for lateness caused by unfamiliarity with the Academy's labyrinthine corridors. Afterwards, marvelling that the heavens had smiled on them in the forms of the two anonymous angels, James and Bernard couldn't wait to let Eric in on their escapade. From their descriptions, Eric knew at once who the two angels were.

"Cassiopeia Clover and Haida Henrichsen. You lucky dogs! And *they* took the time to talk to *you*?"

"Aye," replied Bernard, "can ye credit it? An' the best part is, we didnae even get any lines!"

From that day on, James did his best to catch a glimpse of Cassiopeia wherever he was in The Academy building. Besotted, he just couldn't get her out of his mind: her sweet face; her softness; her curves; her hair; her fragrance! He hatched a plan. At the right place and time, he'd deliberately go the wrong way along a corridor again and contrive to bump into her 'by accident'. Even if he got lines he didn't care. Just to be with her for a few brief moments would be sufficient compensation. But, no matter how he tried, despite forays down various corridors and much work with his watch and notebook, the hoped-for encounter never took place. Apparently, Fate had somehow determined that eleven-year-old boys and seventeen-year-old girls had no business being in each other's company. Before James knew it, Cassiopeia was in the Sixth Year, then, sadly, she disappeared altogether. She'd graduated and moved on with her life. Nevertheless, the moment of their collision was permanently etched in James's memory and her star would shine bright in his firmament long after she'd forgotten that he'd ever existed.

A junior playing in a senior league

One aspect of James's new life at The Academy was to affect him more profoundly than any other. It was what the Academy expected of him as a scholar. At Bonnybrig and Fox Crag Primaries, his progress and test scores had seen him regularly ranked among the top pupils in his classes without much effort on his part. He'd sailed through. He'd been the proverbial large frog in a small pond. Here at The Academy, he was, as he was to discover, a very small frog in a veritable Loch Lomond.

Class 1a1 was at the top of the academic stream; every one of its members had passed the Qualy and more. Some had already won bursaries or special prizes for their scholastic prowess at primary school. A few had been Dux. They were already the *crème de la crème*. The realisation hit hard. He was a junior playing in a senior league. He was Leith Athletic playing Rangers at Ibrox. For the first time in his life, he struggled to keep his head above water. For the very first time, he didn't put his hand up but kept his mouth firmly shut. For the first time in his life, he felt stupid in class.

But it wasn't just the fact that he was suddenly in competition with his academic peers and betters. It was the fact that he didn't know what to do about it. Thanks to his mother's historical machinations he was at least a year younger than his fellows. Not only was he naïve, but he was also uninformed. No one had taken him aside and explained what was expected of him. No one had given him tips on how to study, how to pass exams, or even explained the significance of exams. No one had offered a plan, a strategy, a programme. He had nothing, nothing but himself.

Some would have suggested this was his parents' job, but what were Ian and Janet to do? With their working-class roots and ignorant as they were of the learning techniques and methods of study required for a grammar school, they had little to offer him, especially in a world that had changed so markedly in the twenty or thirty years since they'd left school. Who else could help him? Not the school, which had offered an orientation only to those pupils who could pay. Not his teachers, who blithely assumed that their charges already knew everything there was to know about navigating the stormy waters of academia unaided. Not his peers, some of whom would surely, just like him, be struggling, too. There was no one. It seemed he'd have to work it out for himself.

The reckoning came at the end of the first term. Examinations had been held in all subjects the week before. When the pupils of 1a1 received their results from their subject teachers throughout the final week, it slowly dawned on James that he'd failed in every subject. Then, during registration on the penultimate day of term before the Christmas recess, Mr Flockhart came in with a stack of envelopes.

"This morning I have your report cards," he announced to the room without preamble. There was an instant hush. "You will hand this to your parent or guardian and obtain a signature to confirm that he or she is aware of your results and your progress. You will ensure that you return it to me in January on the first day of the second term."

Amid worried whispers and confabs, Mr Flockhart toured the room, distributing the envelopes.

"No opening the envelopes here!" he warned. "What you do afterwards is your own affair, but for now they will go in your schoolbags and stay there for the rest of the day." Downcast looks. "Is that understood?" Nodding heads.

On his way home, James made a diversion to Lochend Park. The report card had sat in his bag all day like a lump of kryptonite. His parents wouldn't be home for at least another hour and a half. A freezing December day meant that the park was all but deserted, especially with night not far off. He made for a small lookout that was roofed over; at least he could sit on the bench without getting his bum wet. The loch, actually a large pond, hadn't yet frozen over. Ducks waddled up, hoping to be lucky. Ignoring their scolding, he furtively retrieved the envelope. The flap was loose. He pulled out the pale green card folded in two. There they were again: *Edinburgh Corporation Education Committee* in underlined capitals at the top. The dusty old men and women were still with him. Then, the heading, *Pupil's Report Card* and *The Academy*, in bold letters. He opened it. He already knew the subject marks listed on the left-hand side. On the right-hand side was Mr Flockhart's entry:

Number in class: *34*
Place in class: *34th*

He was stunned. For the first time ever, he was bottom of the class. Bewildered, he stared across the water and into the gathering gloom. Arthur's Seat was rapidly fading as a haar settled over the city. The ducks were still optimistic. Then an old woman wearing a moth-eaten fur coat and a tammy, with a walking stick in one hand and a brown paper bag in the other, appeared from the direction of the gate. Apparently, the ducks knew her. Lifting their siege of the shed they waddled frantically in her direction, giving voice to their hunger. As she opened the bag and started throwing bits of old bread on the grass, James watched, willing himself to be distracted by the feeding frenzy. He wondered what he was going to do. Such was the depth of his shame that his juvenile brain could construe only one course of action; he decided he wasn't going to tell his parents. Not yet, anyway. After sitting there as long as he could bear it, he stuffed the envelope back in his bag, got up wearily and wandered slowly home. Behind him, surfeited ducks surfed into the water and the old woman was nowhere to be seen.

However, James's agony was only just beginning. A number of Academy teachers liked to arrange the seating in their classrooms according to pupil achievement. Mr Flockhart was one of them. So, the next day, the last day of term, a grand re-shuffling took place based on the results of the examinations. Mr Flockhart stood at the front of the class doing the directing, the results on a paper in his hand. The new top pupil was to sit at the front right-hand desk next to the window and the radiator. The bottom pupil was sent to the back left-hand desk next to the bare wall. That way, everyone knew his or her place. Having failed miserably in every subject – he'd scored only 43% for French - James's place was, naturally, at the back against the wall in place number 34. He'd never felt more humiliated in his life as he picked up his school bag and slunk off to claim his new desk in the scholastic wilderness. Mr Flockhart was not unsympathetic.

"What happened, James?" he asked with a concerned expression.

But the question was metaphorical. James just bowed his head and sank into a morass of defiance and despondence; and there was still the report card to deal with. He had three weeks' grace, hoping at the same time that his parents wouldn't ask to see it. After all, how would they even be aware of its existence? He wondered if he could get away with forging his mother's signature. However, Fate was to take a hand and deliver a strange and somewhat disturbing twist to the affair. And it was Wee Effie who'd play a central role.

Since James had started at The Academy his relationship with Wee Effie had languished. The reason wasn't hard to find; she was plainly miffed that James had become the centre of attention in the family. It wasn't exactly barefaced jealousy, just a grinding resentment that *he* had secured entry to a grammar school - and not just any grammar school, The Academy - and *she* had not. She was now just past her fifteenth birthday. She'd stay on at Lothian Park into the New Year and leave at the beginning of the first or second term, depending on what opportunities life threw in her path. She'd have had just three years of secondary schooling and would depart with a leaving certificate issued by the school but without any formally recognised academic qualifications. That wasn't to say she wasn't smart; she had a natural intelligence and had done well in her Pitman shorthand and typing assessments. She might be able to pick up a job as a junior somewhere in an office, but the direction of her life was already mapped out. Not for her university; not for her any of the professions; not for her the high salaries, unlike her brother, whose path, quite a different path, was already predetermined, depending, of course, on his ability to persevere and succeed.

It started when Wee Effie came into possession of information that she quickly realised was explosive. It happened like this: Despite the academic gulf between a secondary modern like Lothian Park and a grammar school like The Academy, she and James did have something in common; they both learnt French at school. And it just so happened that Wee Effie's French teacher at Lothian Park was none other than Mrs Esmée Flockhart. Yes, that Mrs Flockhart, the wife of the very Mr Flockhart who was Head of Modern Languages at The Academy, and was both the 1a1 Register Teacher and teacher of French. The very Mr Flockhart who'd marked James's French exam, the same Mr Flockhart who'd placed him at the bottom of the class, and the same Mr Flockhart who'd sent him to sit in the wilderness. *That* Mr Flockhart.

And if anyone doubted that at the end of each day husbands and wives gossip about their respective workplaces over supper, the Flockharts were living proof that such doubts were unfounded. Somehow, the Flockharts had discovered that they were teaching a brother and a sister from the same family, not an unusual occurrence in a close community like Leith. As if they had nothing better to do, they fell to tittle-tattling about the respective merits of the brother and sister. Esmée Flockhart happened to be Wee Effie's favourite teacher. Strongly suspecting this, Mrs Flockhart flattered herself by playing something of a mentor to Wee Effie. Perhaps, too, she saw something in Wee Effie that others didn't. Anyway, it was the last day of term at Lothian Park. Mrs Flockhart, who was on playground duty, happened to get into conversation with her youthful protégé, and Mrs Flockhart proceeded to let the cat out of the bag.

"Wasn't it a pity about your brother?" she just happened to say.

"Ye mean mah wee brother, James, Miss?"

"Yes, of course, you have only the *one* brother, don't you?"

"Yes, Miss. What about James, Miss?"

"Well, his disappointing exam results at The Academy, of course."

Wee Effie, sensing a juicy piece of gossip, dug deep.

"How were they disappointin', Miss?"

"He failed everything. Didn't he tell your parents?"

The unexpected disclosure went off in Wee Effie's head like a hand grenade. But with great presence of mind, she kept her composure. Guessing accurately that Mrs Flockhart had this startling information from her husband at The Academy, but with the family honour in peril, she countered with a lie.

"Ah'm sure 'e told mah mum an' dad, Miss, but 'e didnae tell me."

Realising she might have over-reached, Mrs Flockhart grasped the proffered lifeline.

"Oh, well, that will account for it, of course!" she said, with a slight feeling of relief. And with that, the subject was closed.

For her, it might well have been, but not for Wee Effie. For, inwardly, she was struggling to contain her sense of triumph. James, the pampered family pet, the crown prince of scholars, the one that had got into grammar school when she hadn't, had fallen flat on his face. Yes, she'd lied. James hadn't told his parents the truth about his results. If he had, she'd have known for sure. But he'd kept it to himself. The wee devil! It just didn't get better than this. She was dying to tell on him. She didn't care if she was being a clypie-clap. Her schadenfreude at his misfortune overcame any shred of loyalty she might have felt towards him. But she was going to choose her time, enjoying every moment of anticipation, calculating correctly that the longer James held on to his secret, the worse it was going to look for him when it eventually came out into the open.

She waited till the week before Christmas. The four Swanstons were at table in the kitchen, having their tea. Wee Effie finished her scrambled eggs, put down her fork and knife and turned to her brother.

"Oh, by the way, James, when were ye gonnae tell Mum and Dad about yer exam results?" she asked archly.

James, taken utterly by surprise, choked on his toast and felt as if the roof had fallen in. All he could see were three faces staring at him; his sister enjoying his discomfort with a malevolent smile, his parents shocked and uncomprehending. He blushed scarlet and bowed his head. His fork slipped from his fingers and fell with a clatter onto his plate. His chair scraped across the linoleum as he stood up and fled from the room. Picking up his parka, he opened the front door and hurried into the gloamin, zipping up his jacket, his eyes smarting from the cold and the tears. Behind him was chaos. Ian, quickly grasping the situation, turned to Janet.

"Dinnae worry, hen, Ah'll go after 'im." He grabbed his overcoat and a scarf, jammed his bonnet on his head, slipped on his wellingtons and banged the door as he left. Janet turned on her daughter.

"Ye wee besom!" she spat out. "What *have* ye done?"

Wee Effie was only just beginning to grasp the gravity of the situation. The smile was quickly wiped off her face as Janet let her have it with both barrels.

"Ye just cannae let the laddie be, can ye? Just because *he* got intae The Academy and *you* didnae! Ye should be proud o' yer brother, no vexin' 'im aw' the time!

Unable to withstand the onslaught, Wee Effie threw a full teenager tantrum, kicked back her chair and stormed off to her bedroom.

"Aye, go on, run off tae yer room! That's aw' ye're fit fir!"

Fuming, Janet went into the living room, drew back the curtains and peered into the December darkness of Chesser Drive, eerie in the glare of the yellow sodium lighting. It didn't take long. Two figures emerged slowly from the mirk and made their way up the path of Number 68. Tragedy had turned to comedy when James realised he'd walked out in his carpet slippers. There was black ice about under the thin covering of snow. He hadn't got far. Ian had found him in The Grove, clutching an iron fence for support. Janet let them in and helped them off with their outer things, Ian, grim but calm, and James, embarrassed. Wee Effie stayed in her room, sulking. Janet sat him down and took off his soaking wet slippers, wrapping his chilled feet in a towel. Ian produced the tonic that helped in almost every situation. A hot toddy. Whisky, hot water and demerara sugar. As James sat on the couch, stirring the sugar in the bottom of the glass and sipping carefully at the strong spirit, Janet sat in the armchair staring at him with a worried expression while Ian stood warming himself to the fire, his hands clasped behind his back. His face didn't betray any particular emotion. Finally, Janet spoke.

"Is there anythin' ye want tae tell us, son?"

Saying nothing, James stood, put down the glass and went over to his school bag in the corner. He opened it and took out the concealed envelope, walked over to his mother, handed it to her, his face a blank, then sat down on the couch again and continued to sip at the toddy. The warmth was beginning to spread through his chest and stomach and, strangely, as he watched his mother open the flap and remove the pale green card, he was starting to feel some relief. At least his secret would soon be out in the open. Janet finished reading the report card. She said nothing and handed it to Ian. He glanced through the numbers. His only reaction was to clear his throat with a thoughtful "Hmm." James sat and waited for the roof to fall in for a second time, but it never happened. Instead, Ian walked over to Wee Effie's bedroom door and turned the handle. The door was locked. He knocked on it firmly.

"Effie. Get oot here. Now!"

Without waiting for an answer, he returned to his place by the fire. The door opened and, her tantrum burnt out, a subdued Effie appeared.

"Sit doon," said Ian, pointing to the couch. She took a place on the couch but as far from her brother as she could get.

"Hen," he said, "yer mum an' me have only one question." His tone was unusually conciliatory. Typical Ian. But Janet, still fuming at Effie, was thinking, *Actually, darlin', Ah've got a lot mair than one!* But she held her peace while Ian went on. "How did ye ken all this? About yer brother's results?"

"Mrs Flockhart told me."

There was an intake of breath from her parents. James, who'd already worked out who the source must have been, just nodded wryly. To Ian and Janet, it seemed implausible at first, but immediately they knew they had to believe her. It was the only possible explanation. They knew full well that the Flockharts taught their bairns at different schools, but this had always been just one of those strange coincidences that they had smiled over, especially when Effie came home with this or that story about her favourite teacher.

"What?" exclaimed Janet, her fury finding new heights. "Are you tellin' me a teacher in one school is passin' oot confidential information aboot a laddie in another school?"

They were appalled. Was this the sort of thing that went on at secondary schools these days? But they could do nothing. They had no power. The Academy was untouchable. Lothian Park not much less so. It never entered their heads to consider a complaint or anything resembling one, but their faith in the education system was shaken. An institution previously considered an ally had suddenly become an enemy. And their son, James, was the victim. As for the report card, Janet didn't react. Neither did Ian. Surely they were disappointed, but they had the decency not to call James to account. He'd been through enough. Presumably, they grasped why this had happened, the fact that James was now playing in a different league. Maybe they blamed themselves. So, without a word, Janet signed the report card in her firm, slanting script, tucked it into the envelope and handed it back to James to return to the school. They kept their counsel. James's secret was safe with them even if teachers were not to be trusted, but 'the talk' was still definitely on the cards. Janet waited into the New Year. Then, one evening in the first week back at school after James had dried the tea dishes, Janet sat him down at the Formica dining table in the kitchen. Wee Effie was out and Ian was having his snooze on the couch.

"Listen, son," she said. "Ah had nae education tae speak o'. Ah *was* good at school." She paused at the apparent contradiction. "But we never had the opportunities *you* have. There would be this or that teacher that would take an interest in ye." She paused as if remembering names and faces. "But it never led tae anything. Can ye believe yer mother was good at English? And Ah was athletic. Ah could dae a summersault – and a handstand. What Ah'm tryin' tae say is that we never had your chances. We could have been somethin', yer dad an' me, if we'd had the qualifications."

She paused and looked at James with a pained expression. She seemed embarrassed at her unaccustomed frankness about herself. James knew that his parents' education had ended at the age of 14. He'd reach that age himself in a couple of years. He was locked into a system that assured him solid educational qualifications unless something drastic happened. He had at least another three-and-a-half years ahead of him at The Academy, and then another two on top if he made the grade and was able to take his Highers. After that, who knew? He tried to imagine what it would be like if his schooling suddenly stopped at the age of 14. He couldn't.

"It's OK, Mum," he said. "Ah get the message. Ah'll do mah best."

"That's aw' we're askin' son. Now go an' dae yer homework."

Then, as the year got underway, James discovered that he wasn't alone after all. Curiously, it was Eric Livingstone who came to his rescue, for it was Eric who was now top of the class. It was he who had the honour of sitting at the front next to the window and the radiator. To put it mildly, Eric had turned out to be something of a genius, sailing through the end-of-term exams in all subjects. And even more curiously it was Eric who had struck up a friendship with James. The Dux of the class and the dunce. Who'd have thought it? But, oddly, they had something in common. Eric's obvious academic ability hadn't made him many friends so far. If he'd come top in one or two subjects it might not have been so bad, but he'd swept the board in everything. Literally. Not a few noses were put out of joint among the class elite. Nor were the lower orders impressed. Who wanted to be friends with the class swot? By the same token, who'd want to be pals with the dunce? So, somehow, they found themselves drifting together.

The fact that Eric was an only child might also have had something to do with it. He'd been a longed-for son that had unexpectedly come into the world when his parents had almost given up hope. Unsurprisingly, they spoilt him silly. Not that being spoilt had spoilt *him*. He had, against the odds, turned into a sensible, thoughtful lad who'd managed to keep a level head, but never having had a brother or sister seemed to have affected him. Due to the quirks of birth dates, school admission deadlines and Janet Swanston's plotting, Eric was almost two years older than James, even though they were in the same class. Maybe, in James, he saw a little brother who needed a big brother.

Like everyone else in the class, Eric was fully aware of James's very public car crash start to his Academy career. When the optimistically named Spring Term started in January, Eric took it upon himself to tutor James in the basics of his own scholastic success. It was simple. James had to prepare himself. He wasn't to rely on hectic, last-minute swotting and expect to pass. He had to make a point of regular study, every week throughout the term. Three criteria were important. First, taking or finding the time to study regularly. Second, having a fixed location to study, a place where you could be private and which put you in the correct frame of mind. Finally, application – the will to stick at it to achieve results. As he filled in the details, Eric found in James a receptive ear and a questioning mind. His eyes suddenly opened by an obliging friend, Eric's new disciple started to plan his comeback.

As far as James's parents were concerned, they had little to offer in the way of praise or encouragement. Platitudes like *good*, *excellent*, *well done*, *we're proud of you*, were never offered up, even though the thoughts might have entered their heads. This type of encouragement was simply not in their DNA, nor the Leith they'd grown up in. Perhaps they themselves had received so little praise as youngsters that they didn't grasp the value of giving it. Perhaps they felt that if they praised their son too much he'd become big-headed. An old adage says *You don't miss what you've never had*. And the fact was that James didn't miss it. Indeed, he'd probably have been embarrassed had he been showered with bogus praise. Maybe it wasn't in *his* DNA, either. This wasn't to say his parents didn't care, only that the support they offered was of the practical sort rather than empty words.

In their wisdom, the school authorities decreed examinations at the end of the first term and the third, but not the second. It was examination-free. This seemed a well-thought-out policy. The first term examinations gave pupils - and their parents - an early indication of how they were performing. Then they had a whole two terms to make any necessary adjustments, around five months. James was determined to take advantage of the breathing space he'd been given, but he had nowhere at home to study. Both bedrooms in the small Chesser Drive flat were taken; his normal sleeping arrangement was on the bed settee in the living room. His parents immediately offered their bedroom. But he had to be undisturbed. No problem. They'd leave him alone for two hours every night and keep the volume down in the living room. What about a desk? Sorry, not possible. But then Ian brought home a clean, rectangular piece of thick marine ply from work. It was the size and shape of a small desktop. James could sit in the cane chair with the board on his lap. He could have the gas fire on for heat. Would that work? Grateful, James said yes it would.

And so, that winter and spring, from January to late May, five nights a week and at weekends when there was time, James sat in his parents' bedroom in front of the gas fire, his board on his knees, his books and notebooks on the carpet. In addition to the prescribed homework, which was set for four nights a week and the weekend, he followed his own course of study. There was nothing to base it on. No scheme of work for the exam. No list of topics. Nothing. He made it up himself. He conjugated French strong and weak verbs. He declined Latin demonstrative adjectives. He memorised lines of English poetry. He tackled algebra and geometry problems - not that it did much good - learnt portions of the periodic table and equations for chemical reactions, and worked on sample mechanics problems. He had no one to help him; Eric's advice stopped there. The rest was up to him. He struggled, particularly in maths. And in between, he celebrated his twelfth birthday. Another year and he'd be a teenager.

At the end of the summer term, examinations in all subjects came and went. James had felt more confident than last time. As before, Mr Flockhart distributed the report cards. And as before, James strayed from his route home to digest the contents in Lochend Park. This time, in early July, the park was a picture. Groups of mothers with prams and toddlers were feeding the ducks. The old lady in the fur coat was nowhere to be seen. Choosing a dry spot against the trunk of a plane tree, he opened the envelope and removed the same folded green card. His results for Term 1 were still there in the first column with his mother's signature below. The results for Term 3, in a different colour of Mr Flockhart's fountain pen – he'd gone for red – were in the third column. James's confidence hadn't been misplaced. He'd got an A in English, Latin, French and, surprisingly, art. His French mark had gone from 43% to 82%. He even managed a C in maths even though he hadn't a clue. But best was his new place in class. No longer was he 34th. He'd moved eleven places to 23rd. With an overwhelming sense of achievement mixed with relief, he sat in the spring sunshine, enjoying the quiet, the loch, the ducks, the mothers and the toddlers. Something had changed. Winter was past. Summer had arrived at last. He stood up, dusted himself down and prepared to go home. Suddenly, the old woman appeared, walking in front of him along the path around the loch. She still had on her fur coat and tammy despite the warm weather. Now that she was closer to him, it struck James that she looked like Wendy Wood. Was she taking time off from firebombing Royal Mail post boxes? The ducks swarmed towards her, quacking loudly. Wendy, if that's who she was, started calling shrilly and throwing her crusts onto the grass.

Mr Flockhart did a quick re-arrangement of the class seating before the summer recess. James now found himself a third of the way closer to the front. As those behind him abjectly took their new places, Mr Flockhart couldn't help but offer them words of wisdom from The Book of Samuel. “How are the mighty fallen!” he intoned with a wry grin. They were not amused. James wanted to share the joke, but it was a struggle. His sentiments towards Mr Flockhart had undergone a sea change. Once he'd been on his way to being James's favourite teacher, but James now regarded him with suspicion. What other tit-bits of school gossip was he tattling to Esmée over a bottle of Beaujolais after school? It was a salutary lesson for James as he grew up. He'd learned the hard way that he had to be careful about whom to trust.

His relations with his sister suffered a similar fate, not that they'd ever been particularly cordial. Wee Effie had played the Big Sister role for a while, but only under pressure from Janet. Really, she hadn't much time for James. They'd little in common. Her frequent sojourns with Auntie Christine just widened the gulf between them. Her betrayal had been the final straw. The loss of face would eat at him for years to come. As far as he was concerned, from now on he'd lead his own life. Nothing his sister said or did would matter any more.

When Ian and Janet got to examine James's report card, they were quietly pleased. They'd known instinctively that he'd pull himself together. After all, he was their flesh and blood. He'd done exactly what they'd have done. He'd got stuck in, just as they'd expected he would. James now understood what he had to do. He had the formula right. His programme of self-study stretched out another year and paid further dividends. But, even with all the effort, his ranking in class never rose beyond the midpoint. He just had to admit that about half of his fellow scholars were better than he was. At least he had one consolation; his art grades had stayed strong. He'd never considered himself a talented artist, but Mr Helliwell seemed to have a different opinion. Without doing a scrap of study or preparation, James had gained the top mark in art for the entire Second Year. There was no prize, just an informal announcement from Mr Helliwell to the class in the last session. There were murmurs of “Well done!” He was astonished. He'd actually beaten Eric at something. He could end the school year with a warm glow inside. There was at least something he was good at.

7 Tae mak a tour an' tak a whirl

The shivery bite

Mum, it's Uncle Alistair!" Wee Effie called as she peered through the lace curtains into the winter darkness of a Monday evening, alerted by the sound of a motor car pulling up at Number 68. But the car door had already slammed, footsteps hurried up the path, the front door opened and there was Alistair, his bright, cheery self, framed in the kitchen doorway where James and his mother were clearing away the tea things. Both looked up in surprise. Alistair dispensed with greetings.

"I've come to take my nephew swimming!" he announced with a broad smile, without preamble. Before his open-mouthed sister or nephew could say anything, Alistair spoke again. "D'ye want to learn to swim, Jock?" he wanted to know.

Typical Alistair. No warning. Just barging in, taking over, without a by-your-leave. But you had to laugh, really. James's smile flashed over his face.

"Can Ah, Mum?" he asked, clutching a dish towel and a wet plate.

"Aye, of course, if yer Uncle Alistair is prepared tae take ye!"

Janet was secretly delighted. She knew her wee brother up and down, back to front. After all, she'd virtually brought him up. He had many failings, but one thing could be said for him; he was a good uncle to the bairns. To his expanding tribe of nieces and nephews, he was still Uncle Alistair, heaps of fun, and ready for anything. Neither Janet nor Ian could swim. It was yet another of the many experiences that had passed them by in childhood. Learning to swim required time, money and opportunity, not to mention a teacher. For the two Swanstons, none of these things had been forthcoming in their Leith of the '20s and '30s. Yes, there were the Victoria Public Baths or the Vicky Baths as they were commonly known. But even though it cost only a few pence, entrance on a sufficiently frequent basis to learn to swim had been quite beyond their means and that of their parents. By the time Alistair was old enough, second youngest of the Melrose brood, the forties were near, the entrance money could be found, as well as someone, apparently, prepared to teach him. As a result, he was the only one of the nine siblings who could swim. If he could pass on what he knew to James, that was all to the good.

James was just coming up to his thirteenth birthday and would complete his second year at The Academy in a few months. Despite the strong emphasis on sport, swimming wasn't a skill The Academy chose to teach. Yes, there was an annual swimming gala for those who could already swim but no lessons for those who couldn't; the task was left up to families, friends and clubs. A glance at the list of the gala champions revealed the same names over and over again. It seemed that excellence in swimming was something that was limited to a select group of Academy pupils, so the chance to learn to swim and to be taught by his uncle, was something James jumped at.

"Go on then, yer uncle's waitin'!" said Janet, "Ye can leave the rest o' the dishes. Yer big sister can finish them off."

James could see Wee Effie making a face over her mother's shoulder. Janet had already asked Alistair if he wanted anything to eat, but no, they had to get away to make the most of the session otherwise they'd be too late. Over Alistair's protests, she'd also given him a shilling to cover James's entry. It would easily be enough.

"Mum, where are mah trunks?"

They scurried around, James throwing on another jersey and his duffle coat and woollen scarf for the winter night and Janet stuffing his trunks and a towel in a small duffle bag while Alistair stood chatting to Ian. As she handed the bag to James, she said, "Ah've put a shivery bite in for ye." He'd be cold and hungry after being in the water. Uncle and nephew hurried out to the car.

"Be back around nine!" called Alistair. He climbed in and turned the key in the ignition. That's when James realised his uncle had a new car. Not, of course, a brand-new car, but a different car.

"Have ye got a new car, Uncle Alistair?" he asked.

"Yes, well spotted. Do you know what model it is?" Then without waiting for a reply, for he knew James would have no idea, "It's a Triumph Mayflower."

James was thinking how odd it looked, just a pale grey upright box.

There seemed to be square corners everywhere. If a competition existed for ugly cars, this model would definitely win. With only two doors, it was sure to be a struggle to get into the rear passenger seat. But the interior had a touch of luxury. The driver and front passenger shared one unbroken red leather bench seat, for the gear lever was in the steering column.

“Is it a good car?” James asked innocently, knowing absolutely nothing about cars.

“Good enough,” replied Alistair as he accelerated up Chesser Drive and took the roundabout with élan, heading for Lochend Road and Leith. What he didn’t say was that the car was yet another of the long line of cheap used cars he drove. This one had been a bargain considering it was only eight years old, for it had been a disastrous mistake on Triumph’s part. The British and US public had rejected it. After miserable sales figures, manufacture had ceased in 1953 after only four years. Any remaining models could now be had for a song. Right up Alistair’s street.

As soon as they got out of the car in Junction Place, they could tell from the commotion inside the Vicky Baths that the session was in full swing. Alistair paid at the kiosk and James followed him into a spacious changing room tiled from floor to ceiling. After they’d quickly got into their swimming trunks, Alistair handed James what looked like a loop of thick red rubber. James held it in his hand and examined it, then looked at his uncle, uncomprehending.

“Come on, I’ll show you what it is,” said Alistair with a chuckle.

He took James to the lockers, selected one, and stowed his things while James looked on. He then locked the door and removed the little brass key. Taking his loop of red rubber, he slipped it over his wrist and pushed the key into a slot in the rubber. Alistair had got a junior size for James at the kiosk. He slipped it awkwardly over his left wrist and after he'd stowed his things, Alistair helped him tuck the key away safely. They were ready to swim.

James’s first impression was of a vast open space, an overpowering stench of chlorine and bedlam, as the noise from the swimmers bounced and echoed off the white-tiled walls. Pale bodies were everywhere, in and out of the water, some female, but mostly male. Water churned, surged and splashed. The pool itself looked enormous and there was a gallery for spectators. Hesitantly, he followed his uncle to the shallow end. Alistair motioned him to sit beside him on the edge of the pool. He started the lesson by giving him some pointers. The main one was how to breathe, keeping his mouth closed under water, then taking a breath on surfacing. They did a dry run together, Alistair doing a demonstration of holding his breath under water, then breathing out and in, exaggerating the motions just to make the point. James did his best to mimic Alistair's performance. Then they got into the water. It was freezing and a shock to the system.

Alistair went through the basics of the breaststroke, first the arm and then the leg movement. Supporting James under his belly, he walked across the shallows with him, dodging other learners, as his nephew flailed at the water, coughing and spluttering, and had the pleasure of swallowing large amounts of chlorinated water as all beginning swimmers do. After numerous repeats, James was beginning to get a feel for it, the most difficult part being co-ordinating his leg and arm movements with his head and shoulders and his breathing. But by now he was dead beat. As he was pushing his face into the water for the umpteenth time, he suddenly realised Alistair wasn't there any more. He was on his own. Such was his surprise that he immediately lost his concentration, plummeted to the bottom of the pool, and swallowed a few more pints of Vicky's water. Then there was Alistair dragging him up by the back of his trunks and standing him upright. He shook the water out of his mouth, nose and ears, coughing and fighting for breath. They stood looking at each other. Alistair was smiling.

"Well, Jock, you were swimming!"

He walked his nephew to the side of the pool. James leant against the rim, gasping and spluttering.

"Now, have a wee rest, then I want you to see if you can do it yourself. One width." Alistair cocked his head to the side. It was one of his mannerisms when he was concentrating. "Think you can do it?"

James nodded wordlessly, his chest still heaving from the effort. Alistair climbed out of the pool and walked around to the other side, making sure to have a leisurely chat to the odd acquaintance on the way. Meanwhile, James was psyching himself up for the next ordeal.

"All right, Jock!" Alistair shouted at last, and gestured through the hubbub. "Swim to me!"

Taking a deep breath, James plunged into the water again, struggling to avoid the tangle of bathers infesting the shallow end and at the same time trying to remember everything Alistair had taught him. Head down, mouth closed, kick back with his legs, push out with the arms, head up, breathe, down again. After what seemed like an age of thrusting, pushing and kicking in a maelstrom of wet chlorine and underwater limbs of both genders, suddenly his head bumped against something solid. It was the other side of the pool. His feet found bottom and he surfaced, gulping for air. He looked up, wiping the water out of his eyes and clearing his nose. There was Alistair, looking down.

"Well done, Jock! Right, have another wee rest, then I want you to swim back again."

Alistair retraced his steps to the other side of the pool and waited a minute or two for his nephew to catch his breath, then he gestured again. James set off. Another splashing, spluttering effort and this time it was his hands that found the other side of the pool first. He gripped the rim and pulled himself upright, looking up at Alistair.

"Well, son, it looks like you can swim!"

James was exhausted but ecstatic. It was hard to believe, but it seemed he'd learnt to swim... He'd never thought it would be so easy. He waded through the shallows and wearily mounted the steps.

"Right," said Alistair. "Enough for now. I'm going to do some lengths. You can watch for a bit, but don't get cold or your mum'll kill me. Go and have a shower."

Alistair walked around to the deep end, took a stance and executed a perfect racing dive into the water, disappearing entirely for a second or two. When he resurfaced, he was doing the crawl. It seemed lazy, effortless, and yet there he was, already touching and turning at the other end of the pool for his second length. James watched in admiration. He was starting to shiver now but couldn't pull himself away; he'd never seen Alistair swim before. As the head with the red curls cleaved the waters, the body turning sideways and the arm bent languidly at the elbow, James realised what a consummate athlete his uncle was.

Then, overcome with cold, he rushed into the showers. They were crowded. There were only two showerheads and one wasn't working. Eight white, wet, adult male bodies crowded around the single meagre stream of lukewarm water, jostling for room. None of them had soap or a sponge. No one was actually washing himself. They were all simply desperate to drive the chill out of their bodies before they dried off. James pushed himself as close as he dared. Inevitably, his cold, wet skin came into contact with other cold, wet skin. It was as if someone were prodding him with a dead fish. Ugh! He gave up and rushed to the changing room. Thankfully, his wristband was still around his wrist and the key was still inside. He opened his locker, dried himself briskly and got dressed just as Alistair appeared, dripping wet, his eyes bloodshot from the chlorine.

"How many lengths did ye do Uncle Alistair?"

"Just ten, this time."

James wondered if he'd ever be able to do one length, let alone ten. A length must be about three widths and he'd done two of these already. But

– and it was a big but – he'd rested in between. What would it be like to do three widths without a rest? He decided there and then that would have to be his next goal.

"Can we come back next week, Uncle Alistair?"

"Sure, I think so. Same time?"

They returned their wristbands to the box near the kiosk and stood putting on their coats. Alistair suddenly gave James a nudge, bent down, and spoke quietly in his ear.

"See that old guy over there?"

A small group of men was standing chatting on the other side of the vestibule. The oldest was a small, stocky, white-haired man in an overcoat and flat cap who looked to be in his mid-sixties. James nodded.

"It's Ned Barnie!"

James had no idea who Ned Barnie was but nodded again nevertheless. Alistair finished buttoning up his coat, wound his scarf around his neck, picked up his bag and, with a sidewards glance to James which he interpreted to mean 'follow me', walked purposefully over to the group. The men stepped back as he approached, immediately taken with his professional smile and his public relations demeanour. As usual, Alistair knew exactly how to be charming in a crowd. He stuck out his hand to the white-haired man.

"Ned Barnie!" he said simply, his smile becoming even broader, then, by way of introduction, "Alistair Melrose!" Then, "I'm Alexander Melrose's son."

Though at first taken aback by the stranger's intrusion into the circle, Ned Barnie quickly recovered his composure on Alistair's announcement of his origins.

"Alexander Melrose!" he exclaimed, shaking Alistair's proffered hand warmly, "Ah havnae seen 'im in years! And you're 'is son! Michty me, ye dinnae half look like 'im at the same age!"

As it turned out, Ned and Alexander had been in the same regiment during the First World War and had seen each other since at reunions.

"And this," Alistair turned to James, put his arm around his shoulder and pulled him forward, "is my nephew and Alexander's grandson."

Ned smiled broadly, putting out his hand. At his age, James seldom shook hands, but when he responded, he felt his fragile, thirteen-year-old hand engulfed in a massive, leathery paw that gripped firmly.

"And what's *your* name, young man?" asked Ned.

"It's James, Sir," replied James.

Ned, still holding James's hand, beamed around at his friends.

"Sir! 'E called me Sir!" Then to James, "It's Ned, James, ye can call me Ned, just like everybody else!" And he released James's hand.

“He’s just had his first swimming lesson,” Alistair volunteered, and then, “One day he’ll swim the Channel, just like you, Ned!”

Everybody roared at that one. In response, Ned put his hand in his trouser pocket, pulled out some change and selected a shilling which he held out to James between massive thumb and forefinger.

“Well, James, if ye’re gonnae swim the Channel, ye’ll need a decent shivery bite. Here’s a shillin’!”

At this, there were smiles while James, thanking Ned, pocketed his shilling, awed at getting money from a complete stranger. But Alistair, ever the diplomat, knew not to overstay his welcome.

“Thank you, Ned. I’ll tell Dad I saw you next time I see him!”

“Aye, and tell ’im Ah’m askin’ for ’im!”

They walked out into the night, their breath smoking in the haar, and got into the Mayflower.

“Uncle Alistair, who’s Ned Barnie?” asked James, right on cue, before his uncle could even start the engine. Alistair told him how Ned was a famous swimmer, a local hero, though he wasn’t strictly a Leither, being from Portobello. As the Mayflower negotiated the darkened streets, he explained how Ned had been one of the first people to swim the treacherous currents of the Firth of Forth, from Granton to Burntisland, how he was the first person to swim the English Channel in both directions and held the record for being the oldest person to do it. James tried to imagine what it must have been like to swim through the Forth’s freezing waters – the Vicky Baths were bad enough.

But he was also musing on his uncle. This was typical Uncle Alistair. If there happened to be a prominent person somewhere in a public place, Alistair would spot them, go up to them and brazenly introduce himself. He was inexorably drawn to major events and famous people, like a wasp to an open jar of raspberry jam on a summer’s day; he just couldn’t help himself. When the Scottish Open had been held at Muirfield the year before, Alistair had had to be there. Having driven out to Gullane for the day, there he was in the *Edinburgh Evening News* photo of Gary Player holding up the cup, smiling broadly in the second row of the fans crowding around their hero. Notorious events with notorious characters would do just as well. When Peter Manuel, the serial killer, was on trial in the High Court in Glasgow, Alistair took the day off work, caught a train from Waverley Station and stood in the queue for ages to get a seat in the public gallery. He sat patiently in court all day, following the legal arguments and watching Manuel conduct his own defence, then he caught the train home again. When asked about the experience, he commented, “Manuel? He’s just a Glesca keelie!” When Manuel was found guilty and hanged, he was philosophical: “He deserved what he got.”

As well, Uncle Alistair was a fund of local knowledge that he was happy to pass on to his nephew. There was always a story to tell, something interesting to point out, or someone famous to spot in a crowd. But there was something about the way he did it that James found unique. In 1950's Scotland, Victorian norms persisted. The thinking that children should be seen and not heard was still widespread, but not as far as Alistair was concerned, for he was never patronising. *He treats me just like another grown-up,* James suddenly realised. On making that discovery, he settled back in the plush red leather of the Mayflower and decided on a scientific experiment. Opening his bag, he took out his mother's shivery bite. Unwrapping the packet, he pulled the bread apart into two pieces, roughly equal in size.

"Alistair?" he ventured.

"Yes, what is it?" replied Alistair, concentrating on the road.

"D'ye want half o' mah shivery bite?"

"I wouldn't mind!"

Alistair was always hungry. James waited for an opportune moment, then handed over half of the cheese sandwich.

"Thanks, Jock!" smiled Alistair, accepting it with his left hand and munching away while steering with the right. Meanwhile, James sat back and analysed the results of his experiment. Had Uncle Alistair not realised what he'd just done? He'd deliberately called him *Alistair,* not *Uncle Alistair*, but his uncle hadn't reacted. He'd accepted it. It was proof. To Uncle Alistair, he was just another adult. And anyway, he, James, allowed Alistair to call him *Jock* so why shouldn't he get to call Alistair, *Alistair*? From then on, James never called him *Uncle* again to his face. It was always *Alistair*, but he often wondered if Alistair had registered the change; he never showed it.

From then on through winter and spring, Monday evening swimming became a fixture for uncle and nephew. Mostly they'd head for the Vicky Baths but if they'd missed too much of the session, Glenogle would do just as well. James made rapid progress, and soon he was able to swim a whole length doing the breaststroke. Then two, then three. Next, Alistair started him on the crawl. This was far harder; not only were his shoulders still too puny, the movements were more complex and the breathing sequence trickier. Eventually, he could manage a couple of lengths but only with supreme effort. As for the backstroke, that was a lost cause. Alistair did his best; it was a style he himself had mastered, and performed elegantly. James tried to mimic his uncle's demonstrations, but it was no use. After sinking countless times and swallowing half the pool, he concluded that he simply lacked the physical wherewithal for the backstroke, so he stopped trying. But it was on the back burner. He'd get to it one day.

A time soon came when their Monday night sessions had to end. Alistair had taught James all he needed to know for the time being and, anyway, he was now, it seemed, going steady. His love life was obviously more important. But James didn't mind. He persevered by himself, even joining The 1930 ASC Club so that he could get to swim lengths in fixed lanes without bumping into other bathers all the time, eventually easily managing ten lengths and more. He was gradually turning into a confident swimmer. Then he had an idea. The Academy swimming gala would take place later in the year. He thought he might enter – just for a laugh. He didn't tell his parents or Alistair. Instead, he went to see Mr Hamilton after school on a Friday in June. It had been a hard week for the PE teacher with plenty of belting to do. James found him tidying up in the gym. By now, James was almost two years older but he was still leery of the pocket tyrant. He swallowed as he walked across the noisy wooden gymnasium floor.

"Excuse me, Sir, have ye got a minute?"

"Aye, what can Ah do for *you*, Swanny?" said Hammy in his semi-sarcastic tone.

"Sir, can Ah take part in the school swimmin' gala this year?"

Hammy asked the obvious question.

"Can ye swim?"

"Ah can do the breaststroke fairly well, Sir. Mah uncle taught me."

"Yer uncle taught ye." He stared at James, nodding sardonically as if weighing up the veracity of his claim. "But that doesn't mean ye're good enough for the gala. It's a high standard ye know."

"Ah'm a member of The 1930 Club, Sir."

Hammy's eyes narrowed.

"That's different. Show me yer membership card."

Luckily, James had it on him. He pulled it out of his bag and handed it over. Hammy perused it, scratching his chin thoughtfully.

"Mmm, well, Ah might allow ye to enter the heats. They'll be in early September. If ye're good enough, we'll see if ye can get into the finals in October."

And so it was arranged. James was entered in the heats. He'd only be 13, so he'd be entered for the under-14 breaststroke. Still, he told no one about it. The heats were scheduled for an afternoon in September in the Vicky Baths. He'd never raced before and was as nervous as a kitten when he stood ready at the starting pistol. He was glad Alistair hadn't just taught him to swim but to dive as well, including the flat racing dive. Well, he needn't have worried. He came in second in the first of the three heats. That meant, much to his surprise, that he got a place in the final. He was over the moon. But the final would be a different matter. He now knew what he was up against. The gala took place on a Friday evening late in October. He told Ian and Janet about it a week before.

"Well, son," said Ian, "we wish ye'd told us earlier. Yer mum and me have arranged tae go to a meeting that night." Then he said, "But we'll be interested to see how ye get on!"

James was disappointed and relieved at the same time. If he made a fool of himself coming in last, he didn't want his parents watching. Fine, it didn't matter. He could manage on his own. The day of the gala arrived. The Vicky Baths were packed to the roof. The noise was incredible as friends and family cheered on the swimmers from the gallery. James sat in the changing rooms with the other competitors, a towel around his shoulders, nervously waiting for his race to be called. He was wearing his new red swimming trunks with the 1930 badge that he'd sewn on, strategically located over his genitals, but he felt sick. Maybe he should just withdraw.

"Under-fourteen Boys' Breaststroke!" came the sonorous call from Mr Laidlaw, Race Steward for the night.

Too late. He got to his feet along with the other five. They all looked confident as they stretched and bent their limbs. James did his best to mimic their moves and their confidence but he failed miserably. They walked out into the hall in a single file in lane order. The cheering started. James discarded his towel and took his place in lane three. As he stood shaking out his arms, waiting, he heard his name being called through all the clamour.

"James! James Swanston!"

He looked up at the gallery towards where he thought it was coming from. There were his mum and dad in the crowd, waving at him. What were *they* doing here? What about their meeting? Really, sometimes his dad went too far with his pranks. He could only grimace. Not only that, there next to his parents, unmistakable with his ginger curls, was Alistair with his arms around a gorgeous girl. Now he definitely would have to perform. But at least somebody would be cheering him on. Then Mr Laidlaw called out their names from his clipboard and they were under starter's orders. The starting pistol sounded and they were off.

It's said that a swimming race can be won at the initial dive. And so it was. Ian Bremner was the first to surface and was well out in front. In this, a mere two-length race, he was already the winner. The others tried to keep up. James surfed through the water, his head bobbing up and down, his arms thrusting, legs kicking frantically, Alistair's voice constantly there over his shoulder. *Breathe, down, thrust, kick*. All he was thinking was, *Please don't let me be last!* Touch and turn at the other end, one more length to go. Now it was all out. His arms worked like they'd never worked before. His legs took most of the strain. He swallowed a few more pints of the pool. He had no idea where the others were. He just kept going. The cheering reached a crescendo and suddenly he touched. He fell back in the water, his face hot from the exertion, for once enjoying the freezing water of the Vicky pool, gasping, staring up at the ceiling high above and the faces of the crowd. There was no doubt that Ian Bremner had won. But where was *he* placed? There was a confab among the umpires, then the announcement. It was a dead heat for third place between James Swanston and Alan Rankin. Stopwatches were consulted, the confab continued, then there was a decision. Rankin had touched a split second ahead. James had come in fourth.

The inevitable award ceremonies followed. Some worthy from the Academy's board of governors, all fake smiles, presented the prizes to sustained applause from the crowd. Through it all, James hung around the edges with the other losers. It would have been 'bad form' to slink off before the formalities were completed. But, still in his trunks, his damp towel around his shoulders, he chittered with cold and silently cursed to himself. Vicky's feeble, overburdened showers would never get him warm and the worst was that he'd forgotten to pack a shivery bite.

When he emerged from the changing rooms, a huge crowd of family and friends were packing the vestibule, standing on the steps and overflowing into the October night, chattering excitedly, congratulating their sons and daughters, admiring the modest trophies. James squeezed past and found his family standing under a street lamp, Ian wearing his trilby hat and with a copy of the programme in his hand, Janet excitable as she always was on such occasions, Alistair, holding back, his girlfriend, whom James had never met, smiling demurely.

"Great racing dive, Jock," said Alistair.

"Well, there's one thing, son. Ye can swim a lot better than yer faither," said Ian.

"Thon Lady Advisor's a gey queer-lookin' fish!" said Janet.

"Sorry, folks, there isnae a prize for fourth place," confessed James with a rueful expression.

"D'ye ken what, son?" Ian said. "Ye're wrong. There *is* a prize for fourth place!"

James looked at him and, for about half a second, almost fell for it. Then, knowing his Dad and his penchant for corny jokes, he grinned.

"OK, what is it, Dad?"

"It's a fish supper at Luigi's, just round the corner!"

Everyone burst out laughing. Ian paid. James didn't have the fish. Instead, he had a white puddin' supper with extra brown sauce and two jumbo pickled onions. But it was still the best shivery bite he'd ever had.

A walk with Doctor Frost

As James strode briskly down Swanston Road, staring up at the ragged rim of Caerketton, stark against the southern morning sky, he couldn't help repeating the verse to himself under his breath:

There's no a clood in the sky,
The hill's clear as can be,
An' the broon road's windin' ower it,
But – no for me!

He allowed himself a smile that put a skip in his step. There were just two things wrong. There was no *broon road* on Caerketton - in fact, there was no road of any description; and it was, most definitely *for* him. It had looked like it might be a warm day, so he'd forced himself out of bed to make an early start while the rest of the family were having the statutory lie-in. Bolting down a bowl of cornflakes, he'd hurriedly made himself a flask of Maxwell House, opened a tin of Fray Bentos and buttered and filled a pile of corned beef sandwiches, blanched the two eggs he'd been hard-boiling, retrieved the KitKat and block of Kendal Mint Cake he'd been saving up, and stuffed them all into the Bergen. It was large, grey, tattered and battered but had a stout aluminium frame, another of the relics of Ian's mountain warfare days that he'd liberated and brought home with him in 1946. It *had been* Ian's. But it was now his. Together with the supplies had gone his rain gear, spare socks, spare jersey, a balaclava, map, compass, Ian's old Zeiss binoculars and the heavy, grey, angler's clasp knife he'd got from his Uncle Jimmy because Uncle Jimmy didn't need it any more.

He'd caught the 49 bus at just after eight o'clock in Chesser Drive. It had taken him up to Princes Street where he jumped off near the Scott Monument, walked along to the next bus stop and stood waiting for the Number 4, impervious to the stares of passers-by bemused at the sight of a boy with a huge rucksack waiting for a bus at this time and at this spot on a Saturday morning. He was in luck. One arrived within minutes and he swung himself aboard. Hurrying up the spiral staircase, he found the coveted big rear bench seat empty, shucked off the rucksack and settled down next to it. This was his favourite spot. Not only could he watch the city go by, but he could also observe the other passengers as well without being observed himself. The journey had taken the better part of half an hour. All along the route, the Number 4 had shed its meagre load of passengers until, by the time it was racing along Oxgangs Road, it was almost empty and James had the upper deck to himself. Suddenly, his stop came into view. He jumped up, slung the rucksack over one shoulder, hurried down the narrow stairs and stood on the platform clutching the vertical handrail, enjoying the rush of cold morning air on his face and hoping the conductress had seen him. She had. Giving him a conspiratorial smile as if to say she fancied coming with him but knew perfectly well she couldn't, she pushed the bell and the bus screeched to a halt. He was the solitary alighting passenger, for who in their right mind would get off here in the middle of nowhere at this time in the morning and on a Saturday, too?

He leapt off, settled the rucksack on his back, and stood adjusting the straps as his transport disappeared up the hill towards Fairmilehead in a cloud of black diesel smoke. Then, looking both ways, he hurried across the highway and into Swanston Road. The two or three elegant bungalows on either side quickly petered out and he found himself on what was little more than a narrow track of rough asphalt between low hedges and bare ploughed fields empty of human or animal life except for the odd seagull. It was a half-mile straight with a long incline. Invigorated, he stepped out, his boots ringing on the road surface. As he walked, his eyes were fixed on Caerketton and the massive amphitheatre of the Pentlands that reared up before him and filled his horizon from left to right. He was being pulled inexorably towards it like a wayward iron filing towards a powerful magnet. The road dipped and started to rise again past some decrepit farm buildings and the mixed stench of pig and cattle manure. The long summer's day stretched out before him.

Caerketton was the most prominent summit of the northern ridge of the Pentland Hills, with its black rock face above silvered scree slopes, towering above the T Wood. It was visible from virtually every corner of Edinburgh, a dark smudge in summer, snow-capped in winter and sharply outlined against the southern sky. To most inhabitants of Edinburgh, Caerketton *was* the Pentlands though few could claim to know its name. The sound of the word alone was magical. But what did it mean? James hadn't a clue. He only knew it was Celtic and was very old. For James, Caerketton was his closest point of entry when the Pentlands became his personal playground. It had been Ian who'd originally introduced him to Caerketton and the Pentlands. As a teenager himself in the 1920s and 1930s, he'd been influenced by the spreading belief in British society that the public should be allowed more general access to the countryside. Like many other young folk forced to spend most of their time in the grim tenements and factories of industrial cities, the urge was strong to get out into clean air and areas of natural beauty. It had all come to a head in the mass trespass at Kinder Scout, Derbyshire, in 1932. The movement hadn't been quite as strong in the country districts around Edinburgh. But Hillend and the Pentlands were only a tram ride away and access didn't seem to be a problem. So, Ian and his pals would make the trip whenever they had time and the spare cash for the fare. That's how he'd discovered Swanston golf course where he'd learned to play. Though no longer a club member after The War, when James was little he'd occasionally take his son all the way out to Swanston Village, nestled in the lee of the hills, walk him onto the course and reminisce about his younger days. These excursions had planted the seed.

When James was twelve, he'd bought a Bartholomew's map of the Pentlands at Thin's for 4s6d. The sky-blue linen cover had a line drawing of a shepherd with a flock of ewes. Then, poring over it night after night, he'd started to plan expeditions. At first, Ian and Janet were a bit leery of allowing him all the way out there on his own. But since he'd turned thirteen and had officially become a teenager, they'd gone along with it. He'd disappear for an entire day. Somehow, they trusted him to be sensible. Somehow, they assumed nothing would happen to him. He had no idea where their trust came from. For the Pentlands, although only a stone's throw from the city, presented a largely trackless wilderness of steep slopes, desolate moorland, deep reservoirs and muddy cleuchs, with the odd crag and rocky waterfall thrown in for good measure. There were no public telephones, no buses, no public roads and few dwellings, apart from scattered farm cottages; nor was there vehicle access, apart from a gated, dead-end private road from Flotterstone, built to service the reservoirs. In those days, the Pentlands were unknown, unexplored and undeveloped. Even at weekends they were almost entirely devoid of people, except for the odd farm labourer, Water Board worker, or, on the military training grounds at Castlelaw, soldiers. In this empty country it would be easy to disappear and never be found.

Unless you had a car, the only way to get to the edge of the Pentlands was by bus or tram, which could take up to an hour, depending on the time of day and the state of the traffic. Anyway, what sane person would take pleasure in slogging across miles of bleak hill and moorland, especially in the unpredictable east coast climate? Weren't there far more important things to do in your spare time in the comfort of the City? Go to the pictures, drink in the pub, window shop in Princess Street, watch a Hearts or Hibs game, or, increasingly by the end of the fifties, sit glued to the television? Though James did occasionally come across other lunatics in the Pentlands, they were few and far between. He could easily walk an entire day with only ewes, rams, stirks, and curlews for company. As a result, a twisted ankle, a bad fall, and what had seemed like a carefree day out could easily have ended in disaster, or at the very least, inconvenience.

For his part, James, in his naïve way and barely into adolescence, had profound faith in himself. He'd borrowed books about hill climbing from Leith Public Library, had read them avidly and had taken their advice. He made sure he was prepared. He had good ex-army boots and rain gear. He took plenty to eat and drink and always had a backup of a couple of chocolate bars. He had a map, a compass and a wristwatch. If a winter walk was planned, he even packed a sleeping bag in the Bergen just in case, and wore his thick, waterproof parka. As soon as he'd seen it hanging on the rack in Millets with the fleece lining and hood with the fake fur border, he'd had to have it. It had cost a fortune, nearly £5, but he'd gladly raided his hoard of pocket money. He timed his walks, made sure that he didn't overextend himself and that he was off the hill well before nightfall. Whether his preparations paid off, or whether he was just lucky, in all the years he traversed back and forth across the Pentlands, not once was he to suffer any mishap. The worst that ever happened was missing the green SMT bus home to the City and having to wait ages for another one.

Swanston Road had almost run its course. He strode on, glanced up to his right at the golf clubhouse on the knoll, walked through the tiny car park, empty at this hour, and climbed the steps through the trees to Swanston Village. Every time he stood here on the gravel path surrounded by the low thatched cottages with their dingy, supposedly whitewashed walls, he couldn't suppress a feeling of belonging. He'd once imagined this was where his family name had originated. Even though he'd since discovered it hadn't, he still felt a connection. He'd read that Edinburgh Town Council owned these cottages. Maybe that was why they looked so run down and deserted. Not once had he seen anyone else here. The village was closed off from the open hillside by a rusty iron fence that had once been black. The kissing gate always prompted a wry smile. Each time he sidled through, scraping the Bergen in the narrow gap, he wondered if the day would ever come when he'd put it to its proper use. Almost at once, the ground rose steeply towards the T Wood. James had already discovered when he'd got above it that it was actually in the shape of a cross, but from the City, because of the lie of the land, it looked like a T. There was a story that it had been planted as a war memorial. But it seemed to him the explanation might be rather more prosaic – here on the exposed north-facing slope, its cross shape had more likely been intended as a windbreak, a shelter for stock, especially in the hard winters. He walked up over the upper reaches of the golf course parallel with Swanston Burn, secure in the knowledge that Ian had played these very fairways in the days before The War had interrupted his game. Leaving the burn and the fourteenth green behind, he headed straight up towards the highest point of Caerketton through long grass still dew-soaked, scattering ewes and arousing the curiosity of grazing cattle. There was no track here. He could have taken the easy way up by detouring to the right, then walking up the gentler ridge of Allermuir. But there was no challenge in that.

Now the slope was getting even steeper. He was beginning to get puggled and had to stop several times, hands on hips, sucking in the sweet upland air. Despite the time of year, the ground was soft and slippery. He dug in the edges of his boots to give himself a better grip and zigzagged. Though he was still climbing on grass, he was only yards from the right-hand edge of the scree slope. The crags towered over him on the left. He'd sometimes thought he discerned a cave up there, in among the vertical rock walls, but had decided it was just too dangerous to explore without a rope and all the gear, especially on his own. Towards the top, the slope was still grass covered but it was so close to the vertical that the only way he could make headway was by half-crawling and grabbing tufts of grass. His calves were aching, his breathing was reduced to spasmodic gasps, his chest was on fire and his rucksack seemed to be pulling him backwards. One false step, one slip, and he'd slide, roll or – if he was unlucky – fall a hundred feet. Here in the lee of the hill it was dead calm and though he'd started out cold, he'd long broken a sweat in the June morning sun.

One more step up, and suddenly a waft of cool air hit him full in the face. He was starting to breast the ridge between Caerketton and Allermuir. A few more steps and he was able to veer left up towards the true summit. Struggling to keep his footing now, he battled on against the buffeting south easterly that regularly scoured the crest. A few more steps and suddenly to the south a breathtaking panorama appeared of Pentland tops emerging out of a cloying morning mist like a string of enchanted islands. On his left rose a mighty ridge of green and grey, reaching its highest point at the giant, Scald Law, and ending at the distinctive pyramid of West Kip. In front, and below, was the bulk of Castlelaw and behind that, to the right, the brooding high moorland of Black Hill.

First things first. He bent down, picked up a rock, and, walking up to the sizeable cairn that marked the highest point of Caerketton, he placed it on top. He had this little ritual from Ian. He didn't know why you did it. You just did. He walked back from the cairn to where, over time, previous hillwalkers had built up small walls of rock for shelter around natural depressions. Shucking off his rucksack, he turned round and smiled in anticipation, knowing what was about to unfold. He'd deliberately averted his eyes as long as he could. If the panorama of the Pentlands to the south was memorable, the outlook north was even better.

For, spread out so far below him that he might have been viewing it from a helicopter was the entire City of Edinburgh, still waking from its Saturday slumbers. There was Arthur's Seat, looking like a molehill from this height, as well as the geometric angles of the Castle on its Rock. Almost every suburb of the City was visible, from Corstorphine in the west to Portobello and Musselburgh in the east. He always had fun spotting Fox Crag, which wasn't hard to do, especially through Ian's binoculars. He just looked for the brick-red Munrospun tower. Behind the City, the Firth of Forth, deep blue in this light, stretched from the clearly visible Forth Bridge in the west to the tiny but distinctive equilateral triangle that was Berwick Law in the east. Beyond, to the northwest, he could just make out Perthshire and a hazy ridge that marked the start of the Highlands. Straight ahead and on his right, to the north and northeast, the plains of Fife rolled away from the Lomond Hills towards the Firth of Tay and the North Sea. He'd been up here several times already and was yet to encounter another living soul. It was as if this view had been created for his pleasure alone.

As he was putting on his spare jersey and preparing to enjoy his first snack of the day, he suddenly spotted movement below him, just above the top edge of the T Wood. He squinted and tried to make out who or what it was. Reaching down for the binoculars, he walked to the edge and focused them on the hillside below. It was another person coming this way. He - or she - was climbing steadily straight towards him taking the very route he'd taken. Dumbfounded, he lowered the binoculars. This was one for the books. Another walker, here! It was a first, especially so early on a Saturday morning and especially on this rather demanding route. He wasn't going to have his view to himself after all. His curiosity aroused, he settled down on his rain jacket out of the wind, facing north. First, a boiled egg, cracking the shell against a rock then sprinkling salt from the little paper twist he kept in a pocket of the Bergen. He washed it down with a few sips of hot coffee. He could afford to take his time. It might be interesting to meet a kindred spirit. So he sat in the morning sun, enjoying the moment, expecting that he'd have to wait at least half an hour.

Imagine his surprise when, after barely twenty minutes, a head appeared, bobbing above the crest of the hill. Then moments later the attached body came into sight, moving effortlessly. James stood up and showed himself, the wind battering into his back. The person came closer, noticed him at once and waved a greeting from twenty yards away. James found himself confronted by a small, tanned, elderly man who looked to be in his late sixties, at least. He was wearing a thick, dark blue windcheater, brown corduroy climbing breeches that were strapped below his knees over long, red, diced woollen stockings, stout, expensive-looking hiking boots with what looked like rubber soles, a faded khaki kepi on his head of the type James had seen in photos of soldiers in the Afrika Korps, and carried a small frameless day rucksack on his back. He smiled and waved again.

"Good morning!" called James over the rushing of the wind.

"Guten Morgen – good morning!" called back the little old man, and came up to him looking as fresh as a daisy and barely out of breath. He was about as tall as thirteen-year-old James, who didn't need two guesses to work out where he was from.

"Pleased to meet you!" exclaimed the stranger, his accent immediately giving him away. He stuck out his hand, apparently expecting James to shake it. James was amused and nonplussed at the same time. Not only was he rarely called on to shake the hand of an adult, but he'd also never done so on a hilltop before. It all seemed so comically formal. But he reciprocated automatically.

"Pleased to meet you," he said, shaking the other's hand, surprised at the firm grip.

"My name is Frost!" shouted the man, "Doctor Frost!"

"And mah name's James! James Swanston!"

James gestured to join him in the lee of the rocks, where they could talk without having to shout at each other. Doctor Frost took off his rucksack, spread a waterproof and settled down next to him. James took the initiative, and only one thing was on his mind.

"Are ye maybe from Germany?" The words tumbled out of his mouth.

"That is right!" replied Doctor Frost. "From Kassel."

"Mah father was in Kassel just after The War."

"Ach so, how interesting! He was in the English Army?"

"No, the *British* Army!"

"Of course. Verzeihung, sorry, the *British* Army!"

They both sat silent, an unspoken thought hanging between them in the pause, but neither of them gave voice to it – yet. James stared out at Fife in the far distance as the wind blasted over their heads. How many innocents had been killed by the German Luftwaffe? How many times had he shot at Germans in their war games in the back green at Brecon Street? How many German soldiers had been wiped out in the myriad black-and-white war films at the Cappy Club? How many evil Germans had been expunged by the likes of Rockfist Rogan in his boys' magazines? And now, here, right beside him, was one of them. A German.

The German was busying himself with his rucksack, pulling out a packet of waxed paper. Opening it, he extracted what seemed to be a sausage. But it wasn't like any Scottish sausage James had ever seen. It was longer, was a rich dark brown colour, and was square in cross-section. The Doctor hesitated and looked at him.

"You would like some Jägerwurst?" he suggested politely.

Fascinated by the odd-looking delicacy, James nodded.

"Have you a knife perhaps? I have forgotten the mine."

James put his hand in the side pocket of the Bergen and, pulling out the big grey clasp knife, he opened it and handed it to the Doctor, handle towards him.

"Danke," said the Doctor, and, slicing off a generous piece of the Wurst, which he let fall into the waxed paper, he offered it to James. Intrigued, James put it to his mouth and bit into it. It was tough. He tore off a piece with his teeth and started to chew. It was definitely nothing like any sausage he'd tasted, for it was sharp, with an infusion of herbs and spices. Suddenly he had a vision of a picture he'd once seen. It was somewhere in the Alps. Folks in national costume were sitting at tables, drinking beer from enormous beer jugs and chomping on something like Jägerwurst. Mmm, so this was what German sausage tasted like?

"Gut?" asked the Doctor, who was chewing away on the remainder of the sausage, holding it as if it were a carrot.

"Very good!" agreed James, nodding to show his approval. "What did ye call it again?"

"Jägerwurst," replied the Doctor. "It means, er... hunter's sausage?"

James liked the sound of foreign words. He enjoyed getting his tongue around French and Latin words and phrases. Festina lente! Or the tongue-twisting Qu'est que ce, que cela? Uppermost in his mind was that since a recent interview with Doc Flock, he'd very likely be starting German at The Academy after the summer break. Now here was Jägerwurst, his first German word. He tried to say it out loud. The Doctor laughed.

"Sehr gut, very good, you can speak German!" he said encouragingly. Then he paused, and while James continued to say *Jägerwurst* under his breath, he looked at him with a quizzical expression.

"But you are very young to be up here alone, nicht wahr?" he asked. "Know your parents that you are here?"

James smiled. Before leaving home, he'd opened the door of Janet and Ian's bedroom just enough to put his head round it, and had spoken quietly into the darkness.

"Mum, Ah'm just off up the Pentlands. Ah'll be back around six."

He'd been answered by a groan he knew came from his mother that he took to mean, *That's fine, son, have a good time.*

"Of course, they do. Ah'm thirteen ye know," he countered. "Is that too young in Germany to go into the hills on yer own?"

Doctor Frost, caught off-guard, thought for a moment.

"I am not sure," he said, "for you see, in Germany the most people like better to do things in groups!"

"But what about you? Ye're not in a group now!" James exclaimed.

The Doctor smiled at his clever response. Then he started to explain. That was because he wasn't in Germany. He was on holiday on his own. His wife had only recently passed away and, wishing to put some distance between himself and his grief, he'd decided to visit Scotland, a country he'd long wanted to see. It seemed that in his younger days he'd spent many a happy hour climbing in the Wilder Kaiser, and now, in his old age, he still enjoyed getting into the hills whenever he could. In his Edinburgh hotel, he'd read about the Pentlands in his guidebook and decided to come and see for himself what they were like. James was impressed at his resourcefulness. He must have caught the very next Number 4 bus and had known exactly where to get off, apparently. Not bad for a stranger and one who was no longer young. Doctor Frost had probably spotted him climbing from Swanston Village and had followed him up. He decided to risk a question.

"Can Ah ask how old *you* are?"

He did feel a bit uncomfortable asking but after all, he'd told the Doctor *his* age, so why not? The Doctor replied that he was seventy. James had barely had time to process this information, when, happening to glance at his watch, he stood up in haste. It was a quarter to ten. He'd been up here far too long. He'd have to make tracks if he wanted to keep to his schedule. He hurriedly threw stuff back into his rucksack and retrieved his knife. He looked down at the Doctor.

"Sorry, but Ah have tae go."

He swung the rucksack on his back.

"Hope ye have a good day!"

The Doctor stood up, taken aback by James's sudden activity.

"But where do you go?"

James pointed and the Doctor followed his outstretched right arm.

"There!" said James, gesturing southeast in the direction of Scald Law, clear as ever above the haze. The Doctor looked at him searchingly.

“May I to come with you?” he asked.

James swithered. He wasn’t used to having companions in the hills and, to be honest, didn’t like to. He preferred to be on his own. Others, he’d discovered through bitter experience, could be a positive nuisance. They thought flimsy clothing and gym shoes were suitable attire for hiking, so they froze, got soaked through or blistered their heels and held you up. They moaned and complained that you walked too fast. They wanted to rest all the time, especially girls. They talked too much. They wanted to go a different way, not the way he wanted to go. They cramped his style and restricted his freedom. They intruded into his mood and distracted him from the solitude around him. They were just a pest and a hindrance. And besides, this was a German.

“Well...” he began, but he stopped when he sensed a hint of pleading in the Doctor’s eyes. His wife had just died. He was alone, but it seemed he didn’t want to be. Was it just his German way, of wanting to be part of the group, even if it consisted only of James? Or was he genuinely lonely?

“Ah’m goin’ a long way,” said James, deliberately speaking slowly to emphasise the point. “Ah’ll be walkin’ all day an’ won’t be back in Edinburgh till tonight.” As the Doctor looked at him, silent, he added, “Ah’ll be goin’ up some steep hills,” but immediately realised how foolish that sounded. The doctor had just ascended the steep face of Caerketton like a rabbit in the hundred yards. He was properly equipped. He seemed more than competent. And there was that look on his face. James began to relent.

“If ye think ye can manage and don’t mind bein’ away all day...”

“Young James,’ the Doctor said with a long-suffering expression, “almost every year I am walking a tour in the Alpen! And I have nothing other to do today. No one waits me at the hotel. I have all the day time!”

Despite the minor imperfections in Dr Frost’s English, James got the message loud and clear.

“All right,” he said, “as long as ye think ye can manage...” *And,* he was thinking, *as long as ye dinnae talk too much an’ spoil mah day!*

At that, Doctor Frost cheered up, hurriedly repacked his rucksack, threw it on, and turned to James with a broad smile on his face.

“Lead, my young friend and I follow!”

James made for the wire fence that ran along the ridge, selected a suitable spot and clambered over it. Doctor Frost followed nimbly, looking, to James’s amusement, like a mountain goat. Out in the open, the south easterly blasted into them, making conversation impossible. James merely pointed west across the slope. They’d work their way across the back of Allermuir and drop down the shoulder of Capelaw to Glencorse Reservoir. He mouthed *follow me* and plunged down.

There was no track. It was a bleak hillside sparsely populated by blackface ewes. James picked his way, bounding from clump to clump of heather, choosing the easiest route, trying hard not to turn his ankle, assuming that the Doctor was close behind but stopping to check from time to time that he was. Continuing his imitation of a mountain goat, the Doctor seemed to be having no problems and James reflected that the professional-looking pair of climbing boots on his feet probably had something to do with that. Half an hour later, they struck Phantom's Cleuch and bore left, heading straight down a narrow, muddy track bounded by steep slopes, towards a large sheet of water. All the way down, the Doctor had uttered hardly a word and James was beginning to think that their temporary partnership might work after all.

Soon they were over the stile and standing on the narrow tarmac WB road that ran along the shores of the reservoir. They paused for a moment's breather, admiring the view and enjoying the stillness. Down here was sheltered. Only a small breeze coming north up the valley ruffled the surface of the waters. Looking to their left, they could see an islet in the distance. James was remembering his first visit here with Ian when he was about six. They'd walked up from Flotterstone and Ian had told him the story.

"What is this place?" asked the Doctor. "Is it one of the famous Scottish locks?"

"*Lochs*," James corrected unconsciously but immediately realised it had gone over the Doctor's head. "No, it isnae a loch," he added, "this is Glencorse Reservoir."

"I am sorry, I did not understand."

"Glencorse is the name, and it's a reservoir."

"*Reservoir*," Doctor Frost repeated. "I do not know this word."

"It's drinkin' water, for Edinburgh!" James explained, miming drinking from a glass.

"Ah, Trinkwasser! Ein Staudamm."

James pointed at the middle of the reservoir.

"Under the water over there, is a chapel, a small church," he said, pausing to make sure the Doctor understood. "Its name is St Catherine and it was built by Robert the Bruce. Have ye heard of 'im?"

But this was too much for the Doctor. He shook his head.

"'E was the Scottish king that beat the English at the Battle of Bannockburn in 1314."

"Ach so, ach so!" said the Doctor, nodding vigorously. He stroked his chin and stared hard at the spot in the water as if expecting St Catherine to appear from below the surface or perhaps even The Bruce himself. Having settled that, and having had enough of standing still, James turned and set off up the valley, his new companion doing a good job of keeping pace with him.

"Where does it go to now?" he asked.

"We have tae go along this road for a bit, then we go up there."

He pointed up to their left where Carnethy and Scald Law rose almost perpendicularly from the valley floor. The Doctor looked up, following his outstretched arm and gave a grunt of what sounded like satisfaction. They continued wordlessly at what amounted to a comfortable quick march on up the tarmac road, all the while taking in the reservoir to their left. The water was a deep metallic blue, hinting at depth and contrasting with the paler blue of the sky. As James had expected, it was turning into fine summer's day. Their jackets had disappeared into their rucksacks back at the cleuch and they were now walking in rolled-up shirt sleeves.

After about twenty minutes, the reservoir had petered out and the valley was now occupied by the Logan Burn. A few hundred yards further on, James started searching for a good crossing point. He suddenly swerved left down the bank. Without pausing, he leapt the burn, took a few steps, then turned round to ensure the Doctor was following. They paused for a moment. James pointed up to the right. They'd do a traverse across and up the flank of Carnethy Hill and onto the summit of Scald Law. It would be a long, hard slog, especially as there was no track. The Doctor merely nodded and smiled. This was his bread and butter. They set off again. James knew what to expect. It was hot in the lee of the ridge. As they gradually gained height above the valley floor, the panorama started to open up around them. They could look back to the summit of Caerketton. The dreary wilderness of Black Hill was slowly sinking below them. Eventually they reached the saddle between the two tops and were crossing a narrow track that led due east down into the lowlands around Penicuik. More hard work and at last they were on the top of Scald Law. It had taken them about three-quarters of an hour. Red-faced and out of breath, they stood leaning against the white-painted concrete of the trig point, smiling, enjoying their achievement, their faces pointing directly into the wind. Now they could appreciate the entirety of the Lothians spread out below them all the way to the North Sea. The Doctor was enchanted.

"Wunderbar, wunderbar!" he kept repeating under his breath.

James pointed down into the valley they'd just left.

"There's a lovely wee waterfall further along. We can stop there for our break. It's too windy up here!"

The Doctor nodded in agreement and, putting their jackets back on, they headed downhill again in a south westerly direction, first on to the rounded East Kip which was a midget compared to Scald Law, then on to the West Kip which was equally small but oddly pyramidal in shape. This was more or less the southern terminus of the north-east-south-west Pentlands ridge for from here the land fell away to low hills and rolling farmland. For that reason, James deliberately paused. This was the last vista they'd be able to enjoy. Southeast Scotland stretched out before them and disappeared in the haze of the Border country. Far below were roads, fields, woods, small towns and villages that appeared so civilised when contrasted with the brutal wasteland of the almost entirely treeless Pentlands. They plunged down the shoulder of West Kip, passing the source of the Logan Burn, then followed it for fifteen minutes until they reached a small upland glen, a col, where the burn speeded up between high banks and then plunged over a waterfall. It was beautiful, and one of James's favourite spots in the Pentlands. Here they stopped for their midday break. It was nearly one-thirty. Reclining against the grass and heather slope above the burn, facing southwest with the sun on their faces, they made a start on their provisions. As James munched one of his corned beef sandwiches and gulped hot coffee from a plastic thermos cup, a doubt still hung in the air between them. His curiosity finally overcoming his shyness, James decided it was time.

"Doctor Frost..."

He was immediately interrupted.

"*Also*, James, in Germany we have a... Sitte..." He searched for the English word. "... a custom. When we make a new friend, we shake our hands and call us *Du* – that means *you* or *thou* in English."

"Is that just like French, where ye say *tu* to someone who's yer friend?" suggested James, after a moment's hesitation.

"Exactly!" beamed the Doctor, a piece of black Pumpernickel in one hand and another Jägerwurst in the other. "So, now we are friends, yes?"

"Yes," smiled James. Yes, he thought he could say that.

"So now, I say you my name is Hermann and we shake hands!" He put down his Jägerwurst and extended his right hand. James shook it. "Now you must call me Hermann! And I call you James!"

The Doctor appeared delighted with his little ceremony while James puzzled over the whole thing. Here in Scotland, if you had a friend, you had a friend. You didn't have to say it and you didn't have to shake hands. He was beginning to grasp that Germans were different.

"Well, Doc... Ah mean Hermann... Ah just wanted to ask..." *Here it comes*, he thought. "Did ye fight in The War?"

But Doctor Frost appeared unfazed by the question.

"Which war do you mean, James?"

He enjoyed James's confusion, then carried on.

"You see, I was at all the both wars, The First and The Second!"

James paused, took a bite of bread and corned beef, and considered this fascinating piece of information. Both his granddads had been in The First, and his dad had been in The Second, but here was Hermann, who'd been in both. How was that possible? Hermann explained. It was simple. He was born in 1890. To James, that sounded like a million years ago. He'd been 24 when the First World War had broken out. He'd been a young teacher of Latin and Greek in Kassel, just out of teacher training. He'd been conscripted, sent to the Russian front to join an artillery company and got caught up in the Battle of Tannenberg. Then Russia had collapsed and signed an armistice. For the rest of the war, Hermann had been kept at his post in the east with little or nothing to do. He'd been lucky. James digested this new information. He'd have to find out about this battle, Tannenberg. But what about The Second? Hermann had been 49 in 1939. Because of his artillery experience he'd been pressured into joining up again. By then he'd been a school principal but it hadn't saved him, for he'd made the mistake, though he hadn't regretted it, of never having joined the National Socialist Party. Again, he'd been lucky. This time, he hadn't been sent to the Russian front, which would have been akin to a death sentence. Instead, he'd spent most of his time in France, in a staff role, on the construction of The Atlantic Wall. When the Allies had invaded in 1944, he had, much to his relief, quickly been captured and made a prisoner-of-war.

"The British were to me good!" he exclaimed. "And, I forget to say, James, the soldiers who made me as a prisoner - they were Scottish!"

James almost laughed. What a thought! If things had been different, it might have been *his* Dad who'd captured Hermann. He sat back and considered his story. All his short life, through films, radio and TV programmes, books and comics, he'd been conditioned to fear and to hate Germans. Though The War had ended fifteen years before, its abundant after-effects were still being felt, so James had a fairly good idea that the Germans had been responsible for pretty much all of the ills that had befallen Britain. Before Hermann, he'd never met a person from Germany. Now here he was and if James was being honest, he didn't seem to be all that much of a threat. James found it hard to imagine him doing any of the terrible things he knew the Germans had done during The War. But he was now reading widely. He was beginning to learn about The War for himself, and the events leading up to it. Even at thirteen, he understood that a single meeting with a single German wasn't necessarily of any significance. So there was still a sizeable, lingering doubt in his mind about Germans and Germany. At least Hermann had, with his account, answered James's unspoken question. But now, in between bites of Jägerwurst and Pumpernickel, he had one of his own.

"What about your father? What did he in The War?"

James had to confess he only knew three things; his father had been an infantry sergeant major; he'd fought on a Dutch island called Walcheren; and he'd been an unarmed combat specialist.

"My dad... 'E was a sergeant major in the infantry and fought on an island called Walcheren." James didn't know if he'd pronounced the name correctly.

"Ah, Walcheren!" exclaimed Hermann, turning the "w" into a "v" and hardening the "ch" to make it sound Germanic. "Walcheren! That was, as the English say, no picnic! Not for the Tommies, not for our boys!"

James was dying to ask why but decided he'd rather hear about it from Ian or a book than from Hermann. Having polished off his lunch, he lay back in the heather, soaking up the June sun, mulling over what Hermann had told him and feeling decidedly dopey. Hermann was talking again, but his voice faded away as James nodded off. Then he woke with a start when a fly landed on his nose. Stretching out and yawning, he looked over to see Hermann with his back to him, sitting on the bank of the burn with his shoes and socks off, soaking his feet in the chilly, peat-brown water. Looking at his watch, James saw with a shock that it was past two-thirty. Time to make tracks.

"Hermann, time to go!"

"Ah, my young friend, at last awake! Want you not to join me?"

"No thanks. Ah'm not sure if Ah'd get mah boots back on again! Anyway, we'll need another couple o' hours tae Balerno, so we should make a start."

They repacked their gear, threw on their packs, and with James leading the way, walked along the side of the burn until it disappeared over a flat rocky outcrop. Hermann walked to the very edge and gingerly looked down.

"Ach, wie schön!"

It was the waterfall. James showed him how to skirt the rock and climb twenty feet or so down the near-vertical slope, gripping onto plants and tufts of grass. Once again on the flat, they turned round and admired where they'd been. This was one of the secret beauty spots of the Pentlands. Although few people knew about it, the ones that did came again and again. This was the one place where James occasionally encountered other hill walkers. But not today.

They set off again. It turned into a hard slog. As usual, even in dry weather, the Green Cleuch was a morass. It seemed to be a watershed where the water refused to shed; it just sat there, collecting in bogs and stagnant pools, some surprisingly deep, waiting for the unsuspecting walker to put a foot wrong. James had been right to hurry Hermann along.

He'd known they'd be held up here, and they were. After a good half an hour of hopping from one peat mound to another, falling in and floundering, they eventually made it out the other side. Both had mud up to their knees. Then James began to see the point of Hermann's continental choice of clothing for, as soon as he was able, he sat down, dragged off the filthy, mud-encrusted stockings, pulled a fresh pair out of his rucksack, and put them on, carefully tightening the little leather straps at the base of his breeches. Meanwhile, James was left to enjoy his muddy trousers all the way home.

Not long after, they began to emerge from the Pentlands and enter farmland. Barren hills of heather, gorse and whin gave way to pasture. Soon they were on the sealed road that led past Bavelaw Castle and across Threipmuir Reservoir. They stood on the causeway, relishing the silence on the waters of the late afternoon. Swallows were flitting across the surface catching dragonflies. Unlike Glencorse, the banks of Threipmuir were thick with dense foliage. A dark and secret place, James always thought, where dastardly deeds could be done. He turned round for a last look at the Pentlands before the road plunged into the wood that would block their view. From this angle, the hills didn't look much, lacking the drama of the far side, low and insignificant, sinking into the haze of the early summer evening.

The last section of the asphalt road was long, straight, and tree-lined between high banks. James was thinking about the walk. Doctor Frost had turned out to be almost the perfect companion. He'd been reticent much of the way, though James now knew he enjoyed talking and, it seemed, knew when to talk and when to remain silent. He hadn't complained. He'd kept up. He knew what to do in the hills. He was clearly physically very fit. Funny, thought James, he'd never imagined that a man, and a German to boot, older than his grandfather, would turn out to be the one person he could bear to have with him in the Pentlands. He decided that the Doctor had earned the opportunity to talk.

"Tell me about your family in Germany," he said.

There wasn't much to tell. He had two married daughters. One was a teacher at a *Gymnasium* (that was a grammar school, explained Hermann) and the other was a civil servant. Both had children of their own. The Doctor lived by himself in his small flat not far from one of his daughters.

By now they could look straight down the road and into Balerno. Every time he came this way, at this particular point James would be on the alert, for the bus terminus was on this side of the village. From about a mile away, you could tell whether there was a green SMT bus waiting or not. If it was, James would start running. If he missed it, there could be a half-hour's or even an hour's wait, depending on the day of the week. Today they were in luck. The bus was there, sitting like a large green cat, purring away, waiting, preparing to tease them into hurrying and then to take off as soon as they approached. He turned to the Doctor. Could he run at the age of seventy, James wondered? If he made him run, might he kill him?

"There's our bus!" he pointed ahead. "We have tae hurry!"

He doubled his pace. Doctor Frost doubled his. Then he broke into a gentle trot, his rucksack bouncing on his back. Doctor Frost trotted beside him. James kept expecting him to stop or stumble or clutch his chest. But he never did. He just kept trotting. At least it was downhill. They reached the bus and stood by the open door, gasping for breath, smiling at one another. The driver had just been about to leave when he'd spotted them.

"Aye, ye did well, lads! Which one o' ye's Roger Bannister?"

No sooner had they climbed in, got their tickets and thrown themselves into a bench seat, than the engine roared, the green bus completed its turning circle and they were off down Balerno high street. As they headed into the City, Doctor Frost, still red-faced from the exertion but having regained his breath, turned to James.

"I want to ask you something, young James!" He paused with a strange look in his eyes. "You told me of your father in The War. I would like to meet him. What is your opinion?"

James was silent, for he didn't know what to think. His father's almost permanent taciturnity about The War must mean something but he didn't know what. Although Ian was welcoming with strangers when necessary, his innate diffidence kept him apart from them if he could help it. James couldn't say a definite yes.

"Ah'll ask 'im," was all he said.

The bus dropped them off in St Andrew Square at five-thirty. It was a perfect, mild, golden summer's evening in the capital city, a rarity that enticed people out into the streets. They stood incongruously on the pavement, a Scottish boy and a German pensioner, mud bespattered and carrying rucksacks, among theatre-goers and concert-goers, visitors looking for restaurants, pub crawlers, tourists exploring the New Town, and people out simply to enjoy themselves. James ignored the funny looks. When the Doctor told him he was staying at the North British, he whistled to himself; it was the poshest hotel in Edinburgh.

"What is your telephone number?"

James had to confess shamefacedly that they didn't have a telephone at Chesser Drive. The Doctor suggested that he come by the hotel the following day to give him an answer to his request but James again had to demur. He had exams in two weeks' time. He'd in good conscience been able to take Saturday off, but Sunday was different. Janet and Wee Effie would be off to chapel, then visiting family. Ian would be on the golf course. It was perfect for swotting at home.

"What about Monday, after school? Ah could come at, say, four o'clock."

And so it was arranged. James was to ask for the Doctor at reception. They did a good afternoon tea at the hotel. Would James join him?

It was after six when James walked into the flat at Chesser Drive. Janet was in the kitchen making tea. Ian, just in from the garden, was washing his hands at the sink. James dropped his rucksack onto the settee, walked into the kitchen and sank into a chair.

"Well, son," said Janet, attending to the bubbling chip pan, "did ye have a good day?"

"Aye, Mum, Ah did. Ah walked from Swanston right across tae Balerno." He paused. "And Ah met a German."

He might just as well have said there was an unexploded bomb in the back green.

"What?" Janet exclaimed, taking her attention entirely away from the browning chips. "A German? What kind o' German goes intae the Pentlands?"

Ian said nothing but turned his head to look at James with a strange expression, his hands still under the running tap water.

"A seventy-year-old German," James replied, smiling because this was more or less what he'd anticipated. He gave them a précis of his day, of his walk across the Pentlands with Doctor Frost, including mention of the Doctor's wartime experiences. Not entirely relieved, Janet turned back to the chip pan while Ian dried his hands and sat down wordlessly, apparently digesting James's story.

"Away ye go an' have yer bath," said Janet suddenly, pushing the fish slice under the eggs, "and hurry, before yer tea gets cauld!"

James said nothing about Doctor Frost's request that evening. Not only was he tired, but he also sensed that his narrative of the day's events had not gone down too well, particularly as both Ian and Janet stayed tight-lipped, neither displaying a hint of curiosity about the stranger from Germany who'd accompanied their son across the Pentlands. He waited until the following day. He judged Ian would be more relaxed after a day on the golf links, and so he was. Because everyone except James had been away, dinner had been postponed until six o'clock. Wee Effie was still at Christine's. The three remaining Swanstons sat together in the living room digesting the roast beef, Yorkshire pudding and Brussels sprouts, Ian scanning through the latest scandals in *The People* and James chuckling over the escapades of Oor Wullie and The Broons from *The*

Sunday Post, while Janet was knitting and listening to music from the Light Programme with the volume turned low. James waited until he thought the time was right.

"Dad?"

"Aye, what is it, son?" said Ian absentmindedly.

"D'ye ken Doctor Frost, mah German... friend?"

James hesitated over the word. But after all, there at the waterfall, they'd shaken hands on it. Apparently, at least in German eyes, they were officially friends.

"Aye, what about 'im?"

"Well..." James struggled with the right formulation. "'E wondered if ye'd like tae meet 'im."

Janet looked up from her knitting but the clack-clack of her needles continued as if by remote control. Ian stopped his reading and glanced at James expressionlessly.

"Naw, Ah dinnae think so, son," he said, and returned to *The People*.

And that was that. James, despite his young years, was smart enough to know not to push the matter. He went back to *The Sunday Post* but his mind was somewhere else. Funny, Doctor Frost wanted to meet Dad but Dad had no interest in meeting Doctor Frost. What did it mean? Soon, Ian got up and went out into the garden to take advantage of the long summer evening and hoe the rows of potatoes. Janet had used up her ball of wool and needed a new one. She got up and came back from the bedroom with a fresh hank. When he saw her holding it up enquiringly in his direction, James knew what he had to do. Getting the stool, he placed it next to her and sat down facing her. She looped the coil over his wrists, found the end of the yarn and began to roll it into a ball, while he held his arms apart to keep the coil taut. Half-hypnotised by the ball of wool growing between his mother's hands, he was aroused by the sound of her voice.

"Ye should ken yer father by now," she said quietly, without preamble, "'E disnae talk a lot about it, but it still affects 'im. Even after fifteen years."

James didn't have too much trouble surmising what the 'it' was.

"When 'e came back in forty-six, 'e did talk a bit. Told me some stories." She paused, continuing to wind the wool around the four clenched fingers of her right hand. "Awfy stories. Things ye couldnae imagine. Friends o' his, mates, gettin' killed, right beside 'im." She risked a glance at James. "Can ye no imagine what that does tae a person?"

James couldn't really. He just sat staring at the growing ball of wool.

"D'ye ken, once, they were held up in thick snow. Somewhere in Germany. They couldnae move, somethin' up ahead was blockin' the advance. Then yer dad saw a chicken. A chicken!" She had James's attention. A chicken? What had that to do with *awfy stories*? "A chicken. They were hungry, ye see. Hadn't had anythin' decent tae eat for a while. So 'e ran after it up the road, ower the snow. Tried tae catch it."

"And did 'e?" asked James, suddenly snapped out of his trance.

"Oh aye, *he* caught it awright, ye ken yer dad. 'E wrung its neck, brought it back, and cooked it for him an' 'is pals. Well, next day, they got the order tae advance. *His* lorry was to be in front but for some reason it wouldnae start, so another lorry took its place."

The ball was now enormous and the winding was almost done.

"It blew up. On a mine. A mine that had been buried in the road yer father had run along tae catch the chicken. Killed both men in the cab. Blew them tae bits."

Now she was done, James could lower his arms. With the ball in her lap, she picked up her knitting, knotted the end of the yarn, looped it onto the knitting needle and skilfully grafted it onto the existing woollen garment that was slowly taking shape. No one would know what it was or whom it was meant for until she was finished. As she clacked away again, she looked straight at James.

"It was supposed tae be yer dad in that cab. If 'e *had* been, just think son, Ah'd be a widow, an' *you* wouldnae be sittin' here now."

She bent her head to the task and knitted on, expressionless. Yes, she'd stated the obvious but she'd made her point. In his mind, James struggled to process the facts as she'd laid them out. Only by a fluke, a coincidence, the merest minuscule molecule in the enormous complexity of human affairs, was he alive and where he was today. It was too overwhelming to process. So he said nothing. Nor did he comment on the wider implications of the story, for he already had an inkling. Why else would his father keep The War locked up inside him, fearful that if it did escape, it would infect his thoughts, infect his actions, infect his life? He understood better now. But he regretted it, too. There was so much he wanted to know. And as he grew older, he'd want to know more and more. But he couldn't and he wouldn't. It would all stay locked up and only Ian would know, and he'd take it with him to his grave.

The next day at 4 pm, an apprehensive James was standing outside the North British Hotel dressed in his school uniform, clutching his canvas schoolbag. He'd been in few hotels before, let alone a five-star hotel, not to mention the fact that he was wearing shorts. At least it was summer. But next term, thank goodness, he'd start the Third Year and would be allowed to wear longs. The doorman seemed to be going to bar his way, then, appearing to recognise his Academy uniform, he stepped aside and let him pass. He got the same reaction at reception. Within moments of the receptionist's call, Doctor Frost was bounding down the wide staircase and into the foyer. Beaming from ear to ear, he advanced on James, his right hand held out.

"Guten Tag mein lieber Freund!" he exclaimed cheerily.

James took the proffered hand, but a split second before he could return the greeting, the Doctor spoke again.

"Did you not say you will learn German at school?" James nodded. "Then you must say, *Guten Tag*! Try it!"

"Guten Tag!" He tried to copy the Doctor's pronunciation.

"Sehr gut! Soon you will good German speak! Let us have tea."

And with that, followed by James, he strode into a grandiose lounge full of pillars, aspidistras and frescoes. Cafeteria tables clothed in the whitest table cloths were set with the porcelain cups, saucers and plates, accompanied by silver cutlery and fashionably-shaped linen napkins. Elderly ladies with hats on sat at the tables, drinking delicately, conversing loudly in refined accents. The friends were ushered to their seats by a matron in black with a dainty, white, frilled pinafore.

"If you'd just laike to accompany me... Full afternoon tea, Sir?"

"Jawohl... yes please... and, just a question. Have you some of these delicious... mmm... those with *Marmalade*, no, I mean... jam?"

"Scones?" She pronounced it *scoanes*.

"Ah, yes, scones, yes please!"

As she hurried off, James felt decidedly uncomfortable but took heart from his elderly companion who was smiling broadly like a child who'd been let loose in the largest sweetie shop in Scotland.

"First, I must thank you for Saturday. You had... pity... for an old man. You took me with you in the Hills of Pentland. It was a very good day for me! For you too, no? *Also*, did you ask your father?"

"'E said no," said James, trying to look apologetic.

Doctor Frost didn't seem too surprised but was nevertheless downcast. There was a long silence between them, during which James examined the sugar bowl and the Doctor stared straight ahead as if assessing the artistic worth of the murals.

"This is pity. I hoped he said yes." There was another long silence. "But do not worry. I understand why. The War. It is too early. Many people are still in their hearts bitter."

The tea and scones arrived. A waitress did the honours with the silver teapot. There were plain scones, date scones and cheese scones. There was clotted cream, butter, strawberry jam and Scotch marmalade. When Dr Frost instructed James to help himself, he needed no second telling. It was a relief to be busy with something and not to feel obliged to talk.

"Well, The War is still in *my* heart too," said the Doctor suddenly, in between sips of Darjeeling. "Do you know that, my young friend?"

James shook his head, wondering what he was supposed to say.

“You know why? You want to know why, James?”

James didn’t know if he wanted to know why but said yes anyway just to please the Doctor.

“My only son has fallen at Stalingrad.”

James’s immediate thought was, *Did he hurt himself?* But he didn’t say anything. He only wondered why the Doctor was telling him this. He hadn’t mentioned a son before, only two daughters. His son’s fall must have been a serious one. But what was the Doctor’s son doing at Stalingrad? He’d vaguely heard of it. He thought it was a city somewhere in Russia but he wasn’t sure. In geography lessons at The Academy, they hadn’t yet covered Russia – if they ever would.

“He was shot in the head from a Russian sniper.”

James almost choked on his date scone. He had to cover his mouth with one of the fancy napkins while he recovered his composure.

“He was only nineteen years.”

With understanding came embarrassment and dismay; embarrassment at his ignorance and dismay at the circumstance. What was he supposed to say?

“Sorry,” he said quietly, looking down at the table cloth, trying not to feel it was his fault that Dr Frost’s son had fallen, and *he* had not.

The Doctor sat silently, busying himself pouring them a second cup of tea and buttering a cheese scone. Then he looked at James pensively.

“You are wondering, no? You ask yourself, how could Hermann fight for the Nazi? How could Hermann’s son fight – and die – for the Nazi?”

James didn’t know whether to nod or shake his head. No, he hadn’t been wondering that exactly at that very moment but the general principle had crossed his mind, starting back at the waterfall. How could Hermann and his father have been enemies, trying to kill each other? And that led, logically, to Hermann’s question. So, yes, he *would* be interested to hear the answer.

“You understand why, James, when you live in a strange country. Here in this country is only one leader. Here is only one radio station. Here is only one newspaper, one... how to say, *verdammt*!... source... for information. Here is only one truth, what the leader tells you. So, even good people believe the lies, because the truth is a lie. Here, everyone is afraid. Neighbours betray neighbours. You are killed for your believe. Or you disappear for your thinking. This was my country, James. Before The War. During The War. Not anyone was free. All you had to do was what they told you. There was no freedom. You just had to obey. If you did not...” He picked up the silver knife from the tablecloth and brandished it melodramatically across his throat, “... *kaputt*!”

James didn't know the meaning of the word but it wasn't hard to guess. He spoke it silently to himself. It sounded like a useful word. Hermann placed the knife on his plate.

"I will not see this again. I am too old. But you, perhaps you... Perhaps you will live in a time when your thinking be not be free. It can happen not only in Germany. Here in Britain can it happen also. Like Germany, 1933. One day you have democracy. On the next, you do not. When they tell you what you must think, punish you for bad thinking. When they tell you what you must believe. When the truth is a lie that is given to you like the truth. But still, you begin to believe it yourself. Then, you must agree. If you do not..."

"...*Kaputt*!" James finished the sentence for him.

"Exactly!" Doctor Frost exclaimed, thumping the table cloth and causing some dames at a nearby table to look up sharply. "Now you understand. Now you know why!"

Yes, James did understand. At last. It all fitted perfectly. In such a world, even decent people like Doctor Frost would have no choice but to do what they were told. He was relieved, for he'd wanted to like the Doctor, but it had been difficult because he was a German. He couldn't deny that he still had doubts. But after what the Doctor had said, it was easier to like him. He tried to think what it would be like to live in such a country, at such a time, not only that, to lose your only son into the bargain. He hoped he'd never have to live like that. They said their farewells in the hotel foyer. The Doctor would return to Germany the day after tomorrow, by sleeper to London and the boat train with connections to Cologne and Kassel. He gave James a little square of paper. On it was stamped in purple-blue ink:

Hermann Frost, Oberstudienrat, a.D.,
Ludwigstr 47
3500 Kassel
BR Deutschland

"You will write to me, no?" he insisted. "We will be, how do you say it, letter friends..?

"Pen-pals!" corrected James.

"Ah, *pen-pals*, that is for me new!" And he repeated the phrase several times as if to stamp it into his elderly brain.

They shook hands formally.

"I will ever remember you - and the Pentlands!" the Doctor assured him, blinking back tears, while James tried to hide his embarrassment.

"Auf Wiedershehen, James! That means until we meet again!"

"Auf Wiedersehen!"

As he went out onto the pavement, he turned and looked back. Doctor Frost was waving with his right arm, a curious left-right wave with fingers spread, as if to a child.

"Do not forget me!" he called.

Funny, thought James, *that's exactly what Mr Martin said...*

A summer place

The velvet tones of Cliff Richard issued from the jukebox, proclaiming that he now had a livin' doll that not only cried and walked but slept and talked as well.

"Oh, no again! Haven't we heard enough o' Cliff an' 'is livin' doll?" complained Janet, spooning more ice cream topped with raspberry syrup into her mouth.

Wee Effie disagreed. But she said nothing. Why would a devoted Cliff fan interrupt her pop idol right in the middle of his Number One hit that had been in the charts for six weeks and had been the best-selling UK single of 1959? She simply sat there, her cheek resting on her hand and her elbow resting on the Formica of the café table with a dreamy look on her face, her banana split neglected for now.

"Well, 'e's got a doll 'cos 'e cannae get a *real* lassie!" opined James, who'd almost demolished his knickerbocker glory. "That's Cliff for ye!"

If Wee Effie had been younger she'd have stuck her tongue out. But she'd be seventeen soon and such behaviour was now beneath her. So she just ignored her wee brother as she'd long ago learned to do. But her wee brother persisted.

"'E's got tae lock 'er up in a trunk so she disnae escape. Poor wee doll, Cliff's the last fellae she wants tae be seen wi'!"

Ian, meanwhile, drank his coffee in silence, calmly impervious to his bairns' banter, and scanned a story in this morning's *Daily Express*, Francis Chichester's record solo transatlantic crossing in *Gypsy Moth* in 40 days. There was a closing guitar riff and Cliff was done at last. Janet gave a sigh of relief, put down her spoon and got out her purse.

"Here, son!" She slid a sixpence over the surface of the Formica to James. "Put on mah favourite!"

Taking the coin, James pushed his chair back, stood up and obediently went over to feed the insatiable music machine. The coin went in, he pressed button F and button 7, there was a click, clack, the 45 dropped onto the turntable and the café was filled with the unmistakable sounds of the violins of the Percy Faith orchestra. James returned to his seat. Wee Effie rolled her eyes and returned to her banana split. But Janet was already in ecstasies.

"Daah, da-da, da-da, a summer place..."

There were no words. It was an instrumental. But Janet sang it anyway. Not only was *Theme from A Summer Place* the runaway hit in Britain that year with its laid-back melody and aura of serenity, but it also seemed to epitomize the glorious holiday that the Swanstons were enjoying together in the summer of 1960. It had all started during the Congregational Chapel annual picnic at Colinton Dell only a few weeks previously when Janet had happened to fall into conversation with a fellow chapelgoer, Mrs Heriot.

"An' d'ye have anythin' planned for yer summer holiday?" Mrs Heriot was asking, as they stood behind the trestle table overseeing the distribution of tea from the giant teapot and iced buns, buttered tea bread and sausage rolls from plates.

"Actually, we dinnae," said Janet. Secretly she was annoyed that they didn't. Why did they always have to put things off until it was too late? If they'd wanted a holiday, they should have organised it long ago. "We just havenae found anythin' yet!"

Mrs Heriot nodded understandingly.

"Well," she said, "if ye ever want a good holiday up north, just let me know. Mah sister has a wee bed'n breakfast in Burghead."

"Oh, aye?" said Janet, immediately interested. *Burghead*? She normally prided herself on her knowledge of her native land but had never heard of Burghead before.

"An' where's that?"

"Oh, ye ken Inverness? Well, Burghead's just along the coast towards Lossiemouth, near Elgin. Aye, it's a lovely spot. Me an' Mr Heriot've had a few good holidays there!"

It turned out that Mrs Heriot's sister, Mrs Moray, had married the captain of a fishing trawler out of Burghead. The two sisters had grown up in Forres. Mrs Moray had stayed in the district but Mrs Heriot had moved to the bright lights of the Capital when she herself had married. Her sister had lived in Burghead for almost twenty years now, and had three children. As a side business, she'd started a B & B.

"Ah don't want tae blow mah sister's trumpet," Mrs Heriot said, "but it's a lovely wee bed'n breakfast, very clean and tidy, and she puts good, plain food on the table." Then as an afterthought, "An', her charges are very reasonable, Ah can tell ye."

Janet was now more than interested. The Swanstons hadn't had a proper holiday together since the caravan in Adelstone. To Janet, a *proper* holiday was one that didn't involve throwing yourself on the mercy of your relations. Yes, they'd had a good time in Cheltenham with Bella and had stayed with Ian's other sister in Lancashire a couple of times, but it wasn't the same. She longed for a real family holiday where they could just be themselves, laze around, and didn't have to worry about other people.

"That sounds just what we're lookin' for!" she exclaimed. She took the plunge. "D'ye think yer sister would have a vacancy for two weeks, say at the end o' July or the beginnin' o' August?"

And with that, the holiday was as good as arranged. Mrs Heriot obligingly made a trunk call to her sister that very evening. The Swanstons were in luck. Due to a late cancellation, accommodation was indeed available for the last week in July and the first week in August. A £10 deposit would secure their booking but they'd have to be quick. Janet hurried to the post office first thing on Monday morning, placed a £10 postal order in an envelope, together with a note for Mrs Moray, and sent it off by registered post to Burghead at 37 Baird Street. Ian received Janet's executive decision and subsequent actions without a murmur. As long as he didn't have to be involved in organising it, that was fine. James immediately pulled out his school atlas to find out where Burghead was.

"Mum, it's a wee village on the Moray Firth! On a peninsula! Right next tae the sea!" he reported, keen to be going on holiday anyway, but especially when it was an exotic-sounding fishing village in the 'remote' northeast of Scotland. Wee Effie, however, wasn't so enthusiastic.

"Ah cannae go," she flatly announced. "Ah've been told Ah have tae work up tae the end o' July."

To Janet's and Ian's relief, Wee Effie had taken to her job as office junior like a duck to water, and it had now become the central focus of her life. On leaving school at fifteen the previous year, she'd been fortunate to get a position in the Department of Health for Scotland. Considering she had only a school leaving certificate, to land even an entry-level job in the Civil Service was certainly no mean feat. However, she'd done well in the Pitman shorthand and typing exams at Lothian Park and her prospective employers had been impressed by her feisty, no-nonsense demeanour during the interview.

"But ye could take leave in August, couldn't ye?" insisted Janet.

And so it was decided. Wee Effie would stay with Auntie Christine for the first week of the Swanstons' holiday and join them in the second week. It seemed a sensible arrangement all round. But Wee Effie still wasn't chuffed. She'd be seventeen in September. She was getting too old to be traipsing along with her family on holiday. She longed to get away from them with her friends. Somewhere nice. Somewhere fashionable. But she just wasn't yet quite old enough to be challenging her parents on the matter. And anyway, she couldn't afford a holiday away on her own. Her new savings account at the Clydesdale Bank would have to be a bit more flush for that to happen. So, she just swallowed her frustration and prepared for a week of boredom with her parents and her tiresome wee brother in some dead-end village in the middle of nowhere.

Saturday 23rd July, ten-thirty in the morning, and it was time to go.

"Right, James, up the Avenue and call a taxi," said Janet.

As he walked up the hill, James wondered when they'd be getting a phone at Number 68. He was getting tired of having to go up to the phone box in the Avenue whenever they had to contact someone urgently. Anyway, public phone boxes always had that funny smell about them. He couldn't accurately describe it, something like a metallic mixture of dust, urine and dried sweat. The taxi arrived promptly. All that remained was to shut up the flat. Louise was in the care of the Frasers upstairs. Sadly, M. Renoir had had his last fall the previous year. Mrs Fraser had found him comatose on the floor of his flat. He'd been rushed to hospital but it was too late. The funeral had been a simple affair at Seafield Crematorium with only Janet, Mrs Fraser and a few members of the émigré French community in attendance. At Waverley, they caught the train for Aberdeen. As they clacked slowly over the Forth Bridge, Janet looked at James.

"D'ye want tae throw a penny out for luck?" she asked.

He looked at her disapprovingly.

"Don't ye think Ah'm gettin' a bit too old for that, Mum?"

At Aberdeen they changed trains and within the hour they were in Elgin. Walking straight out of the station with suitcases in hand, they took the first taxi on the rank. In a situation like this, Ian never mucked around. Somehow, he always seemed to have money for a taxi when necessary. As they sped north through flat farming country, then thick Forestry Commission plantations of fir and pine, the Swanstons looked around them with interest. This was new land for all three. Not even Ian had been in this part of Scotland before, known as Morayshire. It was only a fifteen-minute ride, and soon they were entering the outskirts of Burghead. Ian wound down the window on his side.

"Can ye smell it, Jock?" he enquired with a grin. "The sea!"

Low cottages built of sandstone blocks lined the narrow main street that climbed steadily, straight as an arrow.

"What was the address again, hen?" the driver enquired. Janet already had her piece of paper out.

"It's 37 Baird Street," she said.

They took a right at the top of the hill, drove fifty yards or so and stopped outside a neat little whitewashed cottage with dormer windows built into the slate roof. It must have been a hundred years old at least. There was a low wall at the side, behind which was a small garden with clematis creeping up a trellis. As they emerged from the taxi, the front door of the cottage was thrown open and there stood an attractive, buxom woman of about fifty, with greying hair that had once been blonde, wearing a flowery pinafore over which her hands were folded. It was obviously Mrs Moray.

"Welcome, welcome," she called in her Morayshire lilt. "Now did ye have a guid journey here?"

As Janet and Mrs Moray instantly became friends, the taxi driver unloaded the cases and Ian reached for his wallet. Meanwhile, James had got out of the other side of the taxi and turned away from the cottage. He crossed the narrow roadway in a few short steps and stopped in awe of what lay before him. Here the road ended. He was standing near the summit of the promontory on which Burghead was built, looking northeast. It was hard to tell where the blue of the sky met the blue of the ocean. Battalions of waves marched in, each rank equidistant from the one behind. If his eyesight had been freakishly good, he might have made out the Norwegian coast across the North Sea, for there was nothing in between. He looked to his left. The land fell steeply away from its rocky height. Far below was Burghead harbour, a narrow finger enclosed by two massive breakwaters, where trawlers bobbed in safety. Beyond, across the Moray Firth, was a line of low lying coast, the Black Isle. And here, curving west away from Burghead, was a bay of golden sand about eight miles long that would have put a Saracen's scimitar to shame. This was spectacular. With some reluctance, he had to admit that this view might even trump the one from Caerketton. Might.

"C'mon James!"

Janet was calling. He turned back. Mrs Moray was ushering them into the cottage.

"Now, Ah expect ye'll be wantin' a cup o' tea efter aw' yer travels but Ah'll just show ye upstairs tae yer rooms first."

They followed Mrs Moray up the small, cramped staircase into what was a low-ceilinged second storey wrung out of the slate roof. There were three rooms, two tiny singles and a more substantial double. James claimed the single with the dormer window facing the harbour. There was the same view. He could stand taking it in day after day if he wanted to. Mrs Moray pointed to a door at the end of the narrow corridor.

"There's a wee hoose here for visitors and another doonstairs if ye need it."

A wee hoose? Wordlessly, James looked at his dad for the answer. Ian pushed open the door.

"It's the bathroom, Jock!" he said with a grin.

A house with *two* toilets? That was something new.

They stowed their cases, freshened up and joined Mrs Moray in her front parlour. Her 'cup o' tea' turned out to be a splendid Scottish spread set out on a white tablecloth of Irish linen, replete with the mandatory home-baked scones and sultana cake, butter and clotted cream, two kinds of marmalade, and home-made damson jam. The parlour was in the northwest corner of the house. There was a large double window set into the angle, obviously intended to make the very most of the panorama. As she poured the tea and offered round the scones, Mrs Moray told the visitors of her life.

"Mah man's a trawler captain. If ye look, ye can see 'is boat in the harbour, the one wi' the sky-blue stripe. *Norseman.*" As the three Swanstons craned forward to look, she added, "In fac', they're just aboot tae put oot tae sea!"

And, as if Mrs Moray herself, from her lofty height, had mysteriously transmitted a message to Mr Moray at the helm, *Norseman* started to move. As they watched, the large vessel slowly manoeuvred through the gap in the two breakwaters, breasted the waves, picked up speed and headed out into the blue. The visitors were entranced. But during the two weeks they stayed with Mrs Moray they never saw Mr Moray. He was like a ghost who came and went at all hours but never when they were awake or were there.

"Aye, they'll be away frae Burgheid fir days, weeks sometimes," she explained, "efter the herrin'. Oot intae the North Sea or up towards Norway an' Iceland. Then they land thir catch in Fraserburgh or Aiberdeen, wherever's closest. As ye can imagine, it's no regular hours!

Particularly at this time o' the year, fir wi' the lang summer nichts they'll be fishin' as much as they can!"

Apparently, there was good money in it. Very good money. Not only were both the trawler and their cottage mortgage-free, but the Morays also owned two other cottages in the village that were rented out. Then she told them of her family.

"Ah have a loon an' twa queynes," she said.

It was here that she lost James. Having kept up thus far, he was now bamboozled. Ian interpreted.

"Here it's a *loon* an' a *queyne*, Jock! At home in Edinburgh we'd say a *laddie* an' a *lassie*. Is that no right, Mrs Moray?"

Mrs Moray laughed heartily.

"Aye, that's right, Mr Swanston." Then to James, "Efter twa weeks here, loon, ye'll be talkin' the lede!" She went on, "Noo, mah loon's Geordie, then there's mah aulder queyne, Sheila, she's nearly twelve, an' the wee one, Iona, she's seven."

It seemed that Geordie helped on the trawler from time to time but by law he was too young to get his ticket as a bona fide deckhand. Next year, he'd leave school and join his father at the helm of *Norseman*. Sheila would be catching the school bus to the secondary in Forres after the holidays and Wee Iona was at the primary here in the village. The women chatted, exchanging information about themselves, while Ian and James sat gorging themselves on the spread and staring out of the window as *Norseman* dwindled to a speck on the horizon. Then there was a loud noise as the front door was forcefully opened and banged shut again.

"That'll be Geordie," said Mrs Moray. "'E was doon at the harbour helpin' tae cast off the boat."

Fifteen-year-old Geordie suddenly filled the doorway. He turned out to be a gentle giant with red hair, a freckled face and an outlook on life beyond his years. For the moment, introductions were in order. Then, not one to stand on ceremony it seemed, Geordie honed in on James.

"D'ye fish?" he asked bluntly.

Taken aback, James managed to stutter some sort of reply. But he was soon to discover, as if the intelligence had previously escaped him, that fish were the mainstay of life here in Burghead. If you weren't out in a trawler catching fish, you were either pottering around the harbour mending nets or collecting fish boxes, or you were on the end of the breakwater with a fishing rod, or you were selling your catch, or you were scaling and gutting it, or, finally, you were eating it. Everything, but everything here revolved around fish.

And with that came for James the first stumbling block to his love affair with Burghead. For he couldn't stand fish. Yes, as a boy at Adelstone he'd fished for trout. But the truth was that there was a difference between catching them and eating them. It had all started - and ended - with kippers. For some reason, since the early days at Brecon Street, Janet had served up fish on Fridays for their dinner. Why it was Fridays in particular James had never understood. They weren't Catholics. There was nothing in the Swanstons' belief systems that said Fridays should be meat-free. Once, though, he'd heard Janet defending her Friday choice of fish to Ian. The reason was, she said, that on Fridays the fish in the fishmonger's was of better quality. Whether that was true or not, some form of fish dish had become the standard Friday fare and often it was kippers cooked in milk.

James soon discovered that though kippers were tasty, he always had a bone to pick with the fish on his plate. Literally. For he quickly discovered that kippers have numerous small bones. As if picking through these spiny obstacles to separate out the flesh wasn't bad enough, it was when he'd got a kipper bone stuck in his throat that, as far as he was concerned, fish were off the menu - forever. The sensation of choking, his mother thumping him on the back and the expulsion of the bone onto his plate were traumatic enough for him at the age of seven to decide that never again would he touch fish – of any kind. Nothing would move him, not his mother's cajoling, not even her threatening. The fact was, he'd rather go hungry than eat fish. And that's exactly what he'd done once or twice when Janet had refused point-blank to serve up an alternative for him. So, there it was. If he wanted to enjoy his stay in Burghead, he'd just have to accept the place fish played in everyone's lives. Little did he know that for just a single day of that stay, fish would play a significant role in *his* life.

But for now, the Swanstons' priority was to get out and explore their new surroundings. Before they did, Mrs Moray gave them her basic information for tourists. At the top of the headland were the ruins of a Pictish fort dating back over a thousand years. Before about 1800, Burghead had been a small fishing village, then a new village had been laid out and built on the peninsula. There were a couple of interesting old wells and an annual ceremony called The Burning of the Clavie which might be linked to ancient Pictish or heathen Viking rituals - no one really knew - but since it took place in winter, the Swanstons would have to take her word for it. With that, she stood up. Over her protests, Janet and James helped clear away. Then, shooing Janet out of her kitchen at the very thought of her helping with the washing up, she gave them directions for a walk, first up to the headland then down through the village to the harbour.

After marvelling at the Pictish remains and the spectacular view from the headland, they walked down through Burghead to find that it consisted almost entirely of one- or two-storey stone-built cottages with slate roofs. Whoever had designed the layout had had a very geometrical mind. Every street, it seemed, was straight. Every angle was a right angle. Every block of cottages was a perfect rectangle or a square. There was a village shop that doubled as post office and newsagent. There was a primary school, a church and a public house. And that was Burghead. The next morning, after a Sunday lie-in and a lazy breakfast, they had planned to explore further afield. But they soon discovered that the Sabbath in Burghead was kept even more strictly than in Edinburgh. Nothing was open. No buses ran. Nothing happened. Anticipating this state of affairs, and that her guests would be at a loose end, Mrs Moray had put packed lunches and two flasks of tea into a raffia bag.

"If ye want mah advice, ye'll heid doon tae the beach an' spend the day there. It's just the day for it and the weather's done ye proud."

Mrs Moray was right. Since they'd arrived yesterday, the sun had shone and would continue to do so for the rest of the week. It was perfect beach weather. She let Janet have a latch key, "in case we're no here when ye've had enough o' the beach," stood looking critically in the hall mirror fastening her best Sunday hat to her hair with a hatpin, then marched off down the road to church with her handbag over her arm, Bible in one hand and the other grasping the hand of Wee Iona, while Sheila draggled along at her side. No sign of Geordie. But there was one other member of the family to consider. He was the Moray's dog, a cross between a Russell terrier and something else, who'd originally been called Rusty but who'd acquired the nickname Terror due to his rapidly developing mouse- and rat-catching skills. Terror found a ready welcome in his excursions in and around Burghead for he was widely acknowledged to be the reason the village was free of vermin. Now, since he wasn't a particularly pious dog and had long foresworn churchgoing, he'd decided the best thing was to latch himself onto the tourists from Edinburgh for the day.

With Terror in tow, the three Swanstons made their way down the hill, following Mrs Moray's directions for the beach. Ten minutes later, they stood ankle-deep in fine, golden sand, gazing west in wonder at the perfect crescent that constituted the shore of Burghead Bay and a sea that was several shades of azure and green depending on the light. But there was something else that immediately caught James's attention.

"Dad, what's that?"

He pointed, but he didn't need to, for the subject of his question was in plain sight. Along the top of the beach, just where the sand dunes commenced, as far as the eye could see, was a succession of huge, square concrete blocks, roughly equally spaced, facing the sea. James estimated they measured around 10ft by 10ft. At intervals between the blocks were what James recognised as pillboxes similar to the wartime gun emplacements on Fox Crag golf course. Most were sitting level but some were leaning at drunken angles, undermined by the action of the waves.

"Well, what d'ye *think* it is?"

James didn't answer but was mentally scratching his head. While Janet spread the old blanket Mrs Moray had lent them on the sand and unpacked their things, father and son stood surveying the phenomenon with Terror between them, already wagging his tail at the prospect of some fun. At last, Ian explained.

"The square concrete blocks are tank traps. They're barriers tae stop any tanks that might land on the beach. An' ye ken what thon pillboxes are. There would be machine guns in there, nae doot aboot it."

They walked up the nearest dune, examining the tank traps more closely, then stuck their heads into one of the pillboxes. It was half-buried in sand and the entrance, which must have been at the back, had disappeared. Joined by Terror, James slogged up the dune, walked onto the flat roof, shaded his eyes with his hand and stood looking up the beach. The tank traps and pillboxes seemed to go on forever.

"But Dad, why are they here?" James asked as they wandered back to their chosen spot against a convenient bank of sand and dune grass.

"Of course, it was durin' The War. In 1940, it looked like the Germans would invade any minute. This bay..." He nodded towards where the sea met the shore. "...would have been a perfect spot for them tae land. The invasion force could have come from Norway – ye ken the Germans had occupied that? Well, these tank traps and pillboxes were supposed to be gonnae stop them." He smiled wryly. "At least that was the plan. If ye ask me, they wouldnae have stopped a longboat full o' Vikings!"

"So they were put here tae stop the Germans but they never came?"

"No, thank God, but they did come in useful as Ah seem tae remember. It was 1943. Ah was stationed in Aviemore wi' the Mountain Division. Everybody knew D-Day was comin'. An' it was here in Burghead Bay that the Third Division practised for it. They had tae test their tactics, ye see, an' their equipment. We know what was goin' on. But ye werenae allowed tae speak of it on penalty of bein' jailed. They even evacuated the whole population o' the coast for the duration."

"What equipment, Dad?"

"Well, amphibious tanks for a start. At that time they had the Valentine and they'd converted some tae an amphibious role." He nodded again towards the sea. "This is where they tried them out. As usual, it was a cock-up. They turned out to be useless an' had tae be replaced wi' Churchills an' Shermans. Ah seem tae mind there might be a few still out there, ones that never made it from the landing craft tae the beach, wi' bodies still inside!"

Suddenly, the incoming waves seemed less innocuous. James stared at them with renewed interest, morbidly fascinated by the thought of the rusty turret of a tank poking up from below and picturing skeletons of dead soldiers inside, still seated at the controls. Who knew, maybe at Halloween, the ghostly tanks and their crews drove, with eldritch groanings and clankings, up on the beach to celebrate with Auld Nick? He smiled at himself for his weird imaginings, shook his head to clear his brain of the image, and set to, digging a hole in the sand with Terror, who was already busy, eagerly excavating as if he knew there was a nest of rats down there that just had to be got out.

It turned out to be a fabulous week. They lazed on the beach. They lazed in Mrs Moray's front parlour. They spent a day in Forres and lazed in the nice café they'd discovered that happened to have, of all things, a jukebox. They walked the eight miles or so along the beach to Findhorn, lazed at the river estuary eating their picnic lunch, then telephoned at the village shop for a taxi back to Burghead. They wandered around Elgin, had lunch at a fancy restaurant and lazed in Cooper Park on the banks of the River Lossie, licking ice cream cones. It was the perfect lazy holiday Janet had envisaged. Until Wee Effie arrived, that is.

The following Saturday they got the morning bus to Elgin, met her off the afternoon train and went home in the ubiquitous taxi. Suddenly, at least for James, the light-heartedness went out of the holiday that the three Swanstons had enjoyed together so far. For Wee Effie was in a peevish mood. It was one thing to know you had to go on holiday with your parents and wee brother in the middle of nowhere, but it was another to have to actually do it. She'd already made up her mind not to enjoy herself and did her best to ensure that the others didn't either. James's reaction, after a few choice comments, was to give up on his sister. Ian's and Janet's reaction was to seek ways to make their holiday Wee Effie's holiday too.

But in unpretentious Burghead, with little other than a fantastic beach, terrific views, fishing trawlers and friendly locals, this was a big ask, especially when it was a teenager who was being pandered to. That was why, after an awkward Sunday, with much moaning from their daughter about there being nothing to do, they hit on the idea of a day trip to Forres by bus on the Monday. A café, and with a jukebox too. That should be right up Wee Effie's street. But despite the café and despite the jukebox and despite Cliff Richard's dulcet tones issuing from it, Wee Effie was still not entirely mollified and she showed it. It was only when Ian asked her to fetch him another coffee and a bacon roll that everything changed. For that was when Fergus Stewart briefly entered her life.

As she stood at the counter waiting for the order, she had the feeling someone was looking at her. She turned her head and saw that she was right. He was only slightly taller than she was with a Latin look about him. He had thick, black, wavy hair, a complexion burnt brown by sun, wind and waves, and an infectious grin that was hard to resist. But any self-respecting Leith lassie who felt she was being stared at unduly had only one recourse. It was to ask a question. A certain question. And Wee Effie asked it. She just couldn't help herself. It was in her DNA. Anyway, she was still in a peevish mood.

"What's wrong wi' *you*? D'ye want a photo?"

Normally the offending starer would be so perplexed that they'd stop their staring and wander off. But the more persistent ones might attempt to answer the question. There were two possible answers: *Yes* or *no*.

If the starer said *yes*, the stock response was *Well ye cannae have one*!

If the starer said no, the stock response was *What for no? What's wrong wi' me?*

Either way, the person being stared at usually won the war of words.

But this time, it was Wee Effie who was nonplussed, for the answer that came back didn't fit the standard template.

"Aye, Ah'd love one, but make sure it's coloured!"

She was immediately disarmed and, summarily jolted out of her bad mood, couldn't help smiling.

"Well, ye're out o' luck," she countered, "Ah've only got a black-and-white one!"

With the ice well and truly broken, they got chatting. From his oiled woollen polo-neck sweater it was obvious he was a trawlerman. He looked to be in his mid-twenties and was a deckhand on the *Crimond* out of Fraserburgh. She was a civil servant out of Edinburgh, here with her family. Did he want to join them? Certainly. Wee Effie made the introductions. Fergus was charming. Janet was charmed. Ian was polite. James was suspicious. What did this guy see in Wee Effie? Yes, James had to admit, he supposed she had her attractions, but he was battling a brand-new phenomenon. A male who seemed to be interested in his big sister. How was he supposed to deal with that?

Fergus told them about his life at sea, posed intelligent questions about Edinburgh, for he'd never been there, and when the time came to leave, he asked them if they wanted a lift back to Burghead. For Fergus, being a trawlerman and earning good money as all trawlermen did, had his own car. He was on his way back home to Lossiemouth. Burghead was on the way. It was no problem to drop them off. They gratefully accepted. With Wee Effie in the front seat of his blue three-litre Rover 80, which, Fergus proudly told them, was only two years old and had a top speed of 83mph, and the rest of the Swanstons in the back, off they raced, for Fergus was, if anything, no Sunday driver. Dropping them off at the Burghead post office, since Janet had postcards she'd clean forgot to post in Forres, Fergus left the engine running and stepped out onto the pavement to address Wee Effie.

"There's usually a dance on in Elgin on Wednesdays. Would ye like tae come?" he enquired brazenly, entirely unconcerned that her mother, father and wee brother were party to his approach. "There's a live band and they play the latest hits. Even Cliff's!"

Wee Effie blushed and suddenly discovered that her peevishness had evaporated. She'd never been asked to a dance before. Especially not by a mature, handsome man who drove a Rover and appeared to have all the sophistication of a well-to-do city dweller despite his somewhat swashbuckling occupation. She didn't have to ask permission. She'd be seventeen soon. Asking permission was a thing of the past, as far as she was concerned.

"Aye, that would be nice," she replied, trying not to sound too eager.

"Pick ye up at seven?"

"Great!"

He gave them all a cheery wave - "See ye!" - climbed back into his Rover, revved the engine, and raced off. That night, Wee Effie went to bed dreaming of Fergus and wondering if he might be the start of something new in her life. The next morning, as three Swanstons were having breakfast at 8.30 and Wee Effie was having a long-lie, there was a sudden commotion at the cottage door. It was, as usual, Geordie.

"Mackerel's up!" he shouted through the house loud enough for everyone to hear and stamped around busily, talking to his mother excitedly at the same time. Then he was filling the door to the front parlour with his large frame. In each hand he had a long fishing rod. Around his neck and across his chest were the straps of a couple of large canvas bags. On his head was a red woollen toorie. On his feet were wellington boots.

"Mackerel's up!" he announced again, his eyes lit up, his expression eager, but this time to the Swanstons. Then to James, "Want tae come?"

James knew that mackerel was a species of fish. He had no idea what Geordie meant by the fact that they were 'up'. Nevertheless, it certainly appeared to be something exciting that he shouldn't miss.

"Aye!" he shot back, wondering what he'd let himself in for.

"Just be careful," said Janet, "and put a jersey on!"

Entirely in the dark about what exactly he had to be careful of, James gobbled down the last piece of toast, drained his teacup, threw on a jersey and hurried after Geordie who was already out through the front door and hurrying down to the harbour, Terror, who'd cleverly cottoned on that something was up, trotting by his side, tail wagging expectantly. Had Janet been fully aware of what mackerel being 'up' entailed, she might not have been so relaxed about letting her son go. For, as Geordie hurriedly explained on the downhill rush, a shoal of mackerel had been spotted in and around the harbour mouth and anyone in the village with the time and a fishing rod was rushing to take advantage of this unexpected piece of good fortune.

"They migrate along the coast, ye see," he explained. "Sometimes they come really close in tae feed. But ye have tae be quick!"

They hurried down onto the flat along the seemingly endless western breakwater. Then Geordie suddenly stopped and turned.

"Terror, go home!"

Terror stopped dead and looked up at Geordie with a hurt expression. What, he couldn't go with them?

"Ah said go home!" and Geordie stamped his wellington-booted foot on the concrete. Now, displaying classic hang-dog body language, Terror turned and slowly, reluctantly ambled back in the direction they'd come, stopping a couple of times and looking over his shoulder to see Geordie still staring threateningly at him.

"We cannae have 'im wi' us," explained Geordie. "Ye'll see why."

When Terror had at last disappeared, the two boys carried on at a high rate of knots to the end of the breakwater, then out to the end of the narrow stone pier that jutted yet further into the sea. James, who was almost running now beside Geordie, suddenly fetched up puggled beside his new friend, next to a small lighthouse. It was the very end of the land. He looked around him. They'd come so far from the village that they were almost entirely surrounded by surging blue-green water, as if stranded on a rocky islet in the depths of the Moray Firth. A cool easterly was whipping up the waves and the sky was louring. The word had obviously got round. A small crowd of about seven or eight had already gathered despite the early hour. They were Burghead men of all ages, from boys younger than James to pensioners, all clad in hastily donned warm clothing. They hurriedly fiddled with their gear, throwing banter around as they glanced keenly out to sea, willing the mackerel to stay just a bit longer. Red-faced and sweating after the unexpected exertion so soon after his breakfast and in his thick woollen jersey, too, James caught his breath and stood aside to watch.

The first thing he noticed was that the fishing rods were completely different from the simple fly-fishing rod he'd used at Adelstone. For a start, they were far longer, over nine feet, and clearly more robust. Nor was there a simple reel. Instead, there was a complicated contraption the likes of which James had never seen before. Geordie explained in between assembling his kit. It was a spinning rod and the reel was a spinning reel. The reel caused the line to spin. On the end of it was a lure. Geordie had a whole box of these. They were small, shiny metal shapes of different sizes and colour combinations, each with a wicked-looking hook attached, meant to fool the mackerel into thinking they were real fish darting through the water, but controlled by the spinning reel. Geordie would use a different lure, depending on the fish to be caught, the state of the sea, the time of day and the weather. As he spoke, he carefully selected what he judged was the right lure and proceeded to attach it to the line. Even though its surface was near-flat with only a slight curve, it was so lifelike, James could easily imagine the mackerel taking it for a real fish with its artful blue, red and silver colouring.

Then, telling James to keep well clear, Geordie stood at the rail, glanced behind him to make sure there was no one there, then made a powerful cast, skilfully avoiding the lines of others who'd already started. It helped that the wind was coming from over his right shoulder. The lure, much heavier than the fly used for trout, took the line with it, soared what seemed to James like a hundred yards, flickered feebly for a fraction of a second in the ambient light off the waves, and plunged into the sea. Geordie stood calmly, turning the spindle to turn the spool to pay out the reel and make the lure spin in the water.

For a few moments nothing happened. Then there was a shout from the far end of the rail. The first mackerel had been hooked. From then, it was a frenzied spectacle. The shoal of mackerel was circling right in front of the pier, chasing sprat or some other prey. Flocks of seagulls were screeching, circling and diving. Silver streaks could be glimpsed just beneath the waves as the shoal hunted perilously close to the surface, oblivious of the danger posed by a posse of human anglers with all the latest fishing gear. Once the first mackerel had been caught and landed, the rest followed in quick order. No sooner had an angler unhooked one fish, dropped it behind him and re-cast, than he caught another. The fish, still with plenty of life in them, were bouncing and thrashing on the stone surface of the pier in their fives, then tens, then twenties.

Women and girls had by now turned up to help, and were dispatching the hapless creatures in short order by bashing their heads on the railing or the links of the massive cast iron chain, then throwing them into fish boxes and baskets. Others were gutting them on the spot and throwing the entrails to the screaming clouds of seagulls. James stood as if mesmerised, overwhelmed by the numbers of mackerel that were so rapidly being dumped onto the pier and the utter bedlam that surrounded him. This was nothing like fly fishing on a placid Scottish river, where the fruit of several hours' careful casting might be a single trout. He couldn't help feeling sorry for the fish. They hadn't a chance. This was quite simply a slaughter of enormous proportions. He was suddenly jolted out of his inertia by Geordie.

"Quick, gie me a hand!" he yelled over the wind as he detached yet another huge mackerel from the hook and dropped it on the ground. He had no girl or woman to help him. Only James. He'd have to step up. As he did, the thought crossed his mind. That was exactly why Geordie had asked him to come along. His friend had already got three. They were thrashing around helplessly on the cold, wet stone as the life ebbed out of them.

"Bash thir heids on the rail and throw them in the bag!" Geordie instructed, then, yet again, he cast his lure far into the waves.

Doing his best to overcome his revulsion, James bent down and tried to pick up one of the mackerel with one hand. Despite himself, he had to admit it had a certain beauty. It was far larger than any trout he'd seen, iridescent blue-green above, with a silver underbelly, wavy black stripes running across its long body and a forked tail. But it was slippery and slid out of his fingers to continue its thrashing on the ground. He tried again. It slid again. Then, with two hands he scooped it up and, clutching its cold body to his chest, walked over to the rail and prepared to dispatch it. He could have sworn a black eye looked straight at him in the split second before he brought its head down hard on the rail. Immediately, its twitching stopped. James couldn't help feeling a pang of regret, but he did as he was told, threw the dead fish into the canvas bag and turned to the next.

Now there were five, all in different stages of flailing their lives away. By the time he'd dealt with them, there were already another three waiting. In no time, the first bag was full, a bulging jumble of silver-blue scales, blood, dead eyes and the occasional final twitch. He started on the second bag. As he filled it, the sweat started to trickle from his forehead and drip off the end of his nose. He tried to wipe it off with the sleeve of his jersey. Around him, the mad scramble of catching and killing continued in an atmosphere that was at once businesslike and carnival-like. There was joking, ribbing and repartee as boxes and baskets filled up and the body count mounted. Gutting knives flashed, blood flowed, seagulls wheeled and called, fish jumped and flopped, anglers cast, pulled, and cast again. The Burgheaders were smiling. They already knew they'd feed well tonight.

Then, it was all over. Just as abruptly as it had started, it stopped. Fishing lines, previously taut, were suddenly hanging slack in the waves. Anglers, previously straining with effort at their rods, were now still, leaning on the rail, staring dubiously out to sea, looking at each other for answers, raising eyebrows and shaking heads. No one spoke. There was a long pause. But it was no good. The sea had spoken instead. The shoal had moved on. There would be no more mackerel today. Lines were reluctantly reeled in. Catches were packed away. Gear was returned to bags and cases. James looked around him in a daze. Both bags were full. In the frenzy of killing, he'd lost count but Geordie, who'd by now resigned himself to the sudden halt to the carnage, was squatting down, counting on his behalf. His catch totalled 35. James was stunned. 35 fish in what couldn't have been more than half an hour! Suddenly he became aware of his hands. He raised them to his eyes. They were sticky with a slime of silver-blue fish scales and blood. And they stank. As he wiped them on his jersey, he wrinkled his nose in disgust. But Geordie was in seventh heaven. What a start to the day!

The clouds were breaking up and the sun was struggling to come out but the easterly was still fresh. The early morning anglers and their helpers were now packing up their gear and leaving the pier, lugging boxes, baskets and bags heavy with mackerel. The two friends joined them, walking slowly now back along the pier and the breakwater carrying a bag each, sharing the load. That, explained Geordie, had been the easy part. Now came the hard part. James was mystified. What could be harder than catching a fish? All you had to do now was gut it and fry it. Wasn't that right?

"Tae a point," replied Geordie, "but ye have tae be careful wi' mackerel. Ye see, they spoil easy. If ye dinnae eat them right awa' on the same day, ye'll have tae throw them oot. For once they spoil, they can gie ye food poisonin' if ye eat them."

"Then," asked James with a hint of sarcasm in his voice, "how are you, yer mother an' yer wee sisters gonnae eat 35 mackerel the day?"

"We're no," replied Geordie bluntly. "What we dae now is look for fridges wi' freezin' compartments tae store them in!"

He explained. Freezing the mackerel would make them safe to eat in future. They'd stuff his mother's freezer with as many as they could. Mackerel were big fish. He guessed maybe six or seven at most, including what could be eaten today. Then they'd tour the relatives and friends in Burghead with fridges that had freezers. Not everyone had them, and of those who did, only a few would be big enough. In exchange for their available storage space, they'd get a share of the mackerel. It was a well-established practice in the village.

And so, all that morning, as the sun rose in the sky and the summer heat bounced off the stone walls, Geordie and James trudged uphill and downhill with their catch of fish, begging storage space in freezers. And, as Geordie had predicted, it wasn't as easy as it might have seemed, for everyone else who'd been pulling mackerel out of the sea that morning was doing exactly the same thing. Sometimes they were told "Sorry, too late son!" when someone else had got there before them, which wasn't seldom. But eventually, towards noon, by offloading a couple here and a couple there, they had got the job done. The full complement of mackerel was safely stored away. Geordie, in his efficient way, had made a note of where they all were and how many were there. He – or his mother – would go round in the coming weeks and months on a tour of Burghead's freezers to collect their bounty from the sea whenever they fancied a meal of mackerel.

As for James, he was exhausted. Barely able to finish his breakfast, and without warning, he'd been thrust into a world of fish and ferment that he'd never known before. Then had come the unexpected tour of Burghead's back streets toting a load of smelly catch, the straps of the canvas bag biting into his shoulders the whole time, sweat running off him and his face getting burnt redder by the sun. Now he knew what the hard part was. Now he could begin to understand what the Newhaven fishwives must have had to endure. When the lads turned up back home, and Janet saw the state James was in, she almost chucked a Charlie. But when Ian, with one of his looks, reminded her they were on holiday, she just laughed instead. Holding her nose, she insisted he remove every shred of clothing, to be thrown in the washing, and mandated an immediate bath. Not even bothering to eat, a much less smelly James sank gratefully onto his bed and slept the afternoon away.

For their tea, everyone in Mrs Moray's household enjoyed a plate of fresh, fried mackerel. Everyone, that is, except James. He, who'd been a prime mover in securing the catch in the first place, wasn't included and that suited him fine. Even the smell of the fish being cooked on Mrs Moray's stove made him queasy. Instead, he tucked into a plate of her stovies, Brussels sprouts and sausages at a picnic table specially set up for him in her back yard. As he lay in bed that night trying to sleep, he imagined he heard the village of Burghead groaning as it burst at the seams with all the mackerel stuffed in its freezers.

The next day, Wednesday, was particularly hot. The Swanstons spent the morning on the beach. Wee Effie was noticeably milder-tempered than before. They didn't have to ask the reason. All she could think about was tonight and her date with Fergus. But it being an unusually windless day, and with no shade, by about one o'clock it was unbearable and they trekked back to Mrs Moray's in search of cooler climes and cold drinks. That was when Geordie appeared again at the front parlour door.

"Can ye swim?" he enquired of James in his usual forthright manner. Could he swim? James had to laugh. Of course he could swim.

"Want tae come for a swim off the pier?"

A swim *off the pier*? That was an odd expression. How did you swim *off a pier*? But James didn't argue. On such a stifling day, even though he wasn't exactly sure what it was, if it involved immersing himself in the Moray Firth, it seemed the perfect thing to do. Without bothering to ask permission from a very drowsy Janet, who was, for the first time in her life, contemplating a siesta, he grabbed a towel and his swimming trunks and hurried out after his friend. The sun bounced off the stone and concrete as they made their way back out to the very spot where just yesterday, they'd pulled 35 mackerel out of the sea. Whatever they were about to do, there was a small crowd of local bairns and teenagers already assembled with the same thing in mind. And it was then that James discovered the meaning of *swimming off the pier*, for it had already started. One by one, the loons and queynes of Burghead were throwing themselves gleefully off the end of the pier into the sea, swimming round into the harbour mouth through the incoming waves up to a rusty, barnacled ladder, climbing back up to the pier, and doing it all over again. Mmm. James was in two minds. Jumping a couple of feet into the water of the Vicky Baths from the side of the pool was one thing. Jumping off a pier into the Moray Firth some 50 feet below was quite another. Despite his love of hills and mountains, when it came to a sheer drop, he'd always felt a bit uneasy.

But there was another, more pressing problem. Unlike the Vicky Baths, the stone pier in Burghead harbour had no changing rooms. How was he to get from his clothes into his swimming trunks, not only in public but in the middle of a dripping horde that included plenty of queynes? His mind shot back to that November evening in 1954 and his humiliation when Mrs Waddell had walked in on him in the tin bath in front of the fire. He'd been seven. But still, nothing had changed. He was just as squeamish, just as terrified of being seen unclothed in front of others, even when they were all the same sex as himself. What made it worse was seeing how lustily Geordie was throwing off *his* clothes, apparently entirely unfazed by being seen naked in public.

"What's wrang wi ye?" he asked as he thrust down his underpants and stood in all the glory of his birthday suit. "Get changed!"

James stuttered and stammered. At last he managed to get it out. How was he to get changed with so many queynes around, some within touching distance? How could he expose his wee robbie to the prying eyes of women? It was then that Geordie, who indeed had a shrewd take on life that defied his young years, gave James a piece of homespun Burghead wisdom that would stay with him for the rest of his life.

"Listen," said Geordie as he stood with his swimming trunks in his hand, oblivious to all around him, "if it's the queynes ye're scared o', there's one thing ye have tae remember. If they've seen a wee robbie before, yours is just another yin."

He paused, looking thoughtful, while James hung on his words.

"An' if they havenae seen a wee robbie before, well, there's always got tae be a first time!"

Geordie's words hit home like a bolt of lightning. Of course! Suddenly all was clear. Like an ice cream cone on a hot day at Burghead beach, his chronic bashfulness melted away. Yes, that was it! He tried to remember the words: *If they've seen one before, yours is just another one. If they haven't seen one before, there's always got to be a first time.* Nothing could make more sense. Without giving it a moment's more thought, he dropped his pants, stood in his naked glory and quickly stepped into his swimming trunks. There. It was done. And having done it, he was mystified. Why had it bothered him so much all those years? He quickly followed Geordie who, without any hesitation stepped up to the edge of the pier where there was a convenient gap in the railing, and jumped in. Flying through the air with what sounded like a Highland yell of the sort given out by clansmen at Culloden, he disappeared entirely below the waves, bobbed up again and yelled at James who was standing apprehensively in the gap.

"What're ye waitin' for?"

James gulped. He was looking down. The surface of the water was a mile below. For a split second he was as if paralysed. But he knew that if he baulked, he'd be shamed in his heart forever, not to mention in Geordie's eyes. With that fleeting thought in mind, James took his life in his hands and jumped, at the same time letting out an ear-splitting yell, the likes of which Burghead pier had never heard before. If he *had* to go, he wasn't going to go quietly. The sensation of falling was amazing. A rush of air, then he was plunging into freezing salt water, down, down, then clawing back up again.

A veteran of the effects of the Vicky Baths' chlorine, he'd had the presence of mind to pinch his nose between thumb and forefinger before take-off. Shaking his head to clear his ears, he trod water, ecstatic. Not only had he conquered his fear of being naked, but he'd also overcome his fear of heights as well, all in a few short minutes. He broke into a fair imitation of a professional-looking crawl that was the envy of Geordie, who was clumsily doggie-paddling his way round. Slicing through the waves, he reached the ladder first, clambered up, ran through the throng to the gap, and jumped in all over again.

That evening, promptly at seven, Fergus's Rover drew up outside the Morays' house. It was Wee Effie's big evening. Not expecting to experience anything remotely glamorous in somewhere as mundane as Burghead, she hadn't exactly packed a cocktail dress, so it was a scramble to find something suitable. But by combining her own wardrobe with her mother's and Mrs Moray's, between them they managed to come up with a presentable enough blouse and skirt combination, with a cardigan and earrings to match. Mrs Moray, who had numerous hidden talents, had styled her hair into a beehive, one of the latest fashions. Fergus, as charming as ever, chatted animatedly to Ian and Janet on the pavement as he waited for her. James, in the background, held back. There was something about Fergus he couldn't put his finger on. He was just too smarmy for his liking. But he hadn't been the only one with doubts. After witnessing Fergus's public invitation to her daughter on the Monday, Janet had voiced hers that very night as they'd got ready for bed.

"Are we doin' the right thing lettin' 'er go oot wi' that Fergus?" Janet had asked.

"Well, what's wrong wi' 'im?" countered Ian.

"'E's a good bit older than her for one thing. 'E must be 24 or 25 if 'e's a day."

Ian looked at her fondly.

"And tell me, pray, mah darlin', how old were *you* when ye started makin' eyes at *me*?"

"That was different!"

"How was it different?"

"Ah was far more mature than Wee Effie is now."

Ian scoffed.

"Ye were sixteen goin' on seventeen, almost exactly the age Wee Effie is now. Ah was twenty-four. An' a doubt if you were any more mature than yer wee lassie. Sounds familiar, does it no?"

Janet conceded without another word. Maybe he was right. She shouldn't judge. But it was the prerogative of a mother to be worried about her firstborn. This conversation would come back to haunt both of them, for not long after Fergus's Rover sped off down the High Street with Wee Effie on the front passenger seat, headed supposedly to the dance in Elgin,

Mrs Moray appeared with a worried but apologetic look on her face. She asked if they'd step into the front parlour for a moment. James wasn't included in the invitation, but he listened at the door anyway. Bidding her guests, who were wondering what this was about, to take a seat, Mrs Moray started to speak.

"This may be none o' mah business, but Ah feel Ah have tae get somethin' off mah chest."

By now the Swanstons were getting alarmed. What was going on? Had James done something wrong? However, it wasn't about James, not by a long chalk.

"It's aboot that lad that just picked up yer lassie. 'E's Fergus Stewart, is 'e no?"

The Swanstons nodded in unison. Janet realised that it had never occurred to them to share the name of Wee Effie's new beau with their landlady.

"Aye, Ah thought Ah recognised 'im. 'E crewed for mah man for a while. An' now 'e works a trawler oot o' Fraserburgh, does 'e no?"

"Aye, so 'e told us. Is that no right?"

"Oh, aye *that's* right. But did 'e tell ye as weel that 'e's mairrit?"

The Swanstons blanched visibly.

"What?" exclaimed Janet.

"Aye, it's the God's honest truth. Not only that, 'is wife lives in Lossiemouth an' she's got twins, wee queynes!"

The Swanstons were now speechless.

"The fact is, Ah ken the wife's mither through the kirk, like. That Fergus is a known..." She searched for the right word. "...philanderer. Aye, that's right, a philanderer. He leaves 'is wife at hame an' gallivants wi' fancy women."

The Swanstons' speechlessness had now escalated to looks of horror.

"Ah dinnae want tae worry ye needlessly..." Here she paused, gauging whether she'd be going too far or not. But the looks on their faces encouraged her to continue. "...but they say there's mair than yin lassie 'e's put in the family way."

Right then, if he'd had a car, Ian, who was now in a quiet rage, not least at his own stupidity as he saw it, would have been ready to drive after them. But he didn't have a car. No one did. Even if he managed to get a taxi, no one had had the presence of mind to enquire exactly where they'd gone, or to check that there really was a dance on in Elgin that night. There was no way of locating them or of getting in touch with them. So all they could do was sit and wait and worry. James, who'd retreated to the back garden after he'd heard enough, pretended to be ignorant and passed his time teaching Terror to shake hands and fetch a hidden ball.

The wait was long. It was near midnight before they heard the sound of Fergus's Rover screeching to a halt outside the Morays' residence. James, sent to his bedroom, had forced himself to stay awake specially, with the window facing the street open, hoping to enjoy the fun. Now, sitting in the dark, he had the best seat in the house. Both Ian and Janet were out on the pavement in a flash. If Fergus had been looking for some snogging time, he was to be sadly disappointed. Wee Effie's parents had decided to split the workload. Janet, to Wee Effie's astonishment, wrenched open the passenger door.

"Get oot, hen. Just get oot." She said it calmly, unhurriedly. Bewildered, Wee Effie slowly climbed out of the car. Janet put her arm around her and steered her with some force through the garden gate into the house, past Mrs Moray, who'd turned the front outside light on and was standing, her arms firmly folded over her bosom, with a glint of satisfaction in her eye. Meanwhile, Ian had wrenched open the driver's door with roughly the same directive.

"Out!" was all he said, however. Fergus, beginning to realise he'd been lumbered, stepped warily onto the pavement, leaving the engine of the Rover running, just in case. Ian gave him short shrift.

"When were ye gonnae tell mah lassie ye were married?" he asked pointedly. It was then that Fergus noticed Mrs Moray in the background, like a solo Greek chorus. All became clear. He nodded to himself and smiled with wry comprehension, his perfect teeth glinting in the street light, but said nothing. Ian went on.

"Dinnae come near mah lassie again," he said simply.

"An' how are ye gonnae stop me?" Fergus shot back.

Ian took one step forward. *Oh-oh,* thought James, grinning to himself as he leant comfortably at the open window with his elbows on the sill, soaking up every moment of the show, conveniently illuminated by Mrs Moray's outside light and the Burghead street lamps for his particular delectation. *Looks like Uncle George all over again!* He knew exactly what his dad was going to say.

"Ah'll knock yer block off," answered Ian calmly, staring coolly into Fergus's eyes, his fists already bunched.

Fergus's smile changed to a craven smirk. Although he appeared younger and fitter than Ian, James doubted if he was stronger. He was just dying for Fergus to get what he deserved, delivered courtesy of his dad. It would be the highlight of his holiday. He could just imagine telling Eric and the others at school about it. His dad! But he was to be disappointed. Fergus had calculated that Ian was just one angry father too far. He took two steps back.

"Dinnae worry, pal. She's no exactly Diana Dors, is she?"

And with that, he scuttled back into the driver's seat of his Rover like a startled mouse, slammed the door, put the engine into gear with an expensive-sounding grating, and took off at high speed. However, in his haste, he'd forgotten that the passenger door was still open. As he braked to take the corner too fast, the door suddenly swung out with such force that it ripped itself entirely off its hinges and clattered noisily across the road surface, waking not a few neighbours and causing multiple bedroom lights to come on. But Fergus didn't stop. The broken car door lay illuminated by the street lights, a glittering, incongruous trophy of Ian's triumph over evil while James, now hanging out of the bedroom window, betrayed his presence by roaring with delight and adding to the commotion. Ian stepped back, put his hands on his hips and looked up at his son, smiling for the first time that evening.

They had an earnest talk with Wee Effie in Mrs Moray's lounge over hot cocoa, with Mrs Moray in attendance. James had tiptoed down the stairs and was again doing his favourite trick of eavesdropping. By now, with Mrs Moray providing the evidence, his sister knew everything there was to know about Fergus. No, she assured them, it was just a dance. Nothing had happened.

"If he *had* tried anything, Ah'd have knocked 'is block off!"

That's mah wee lassie! thought Ian, but he said nothing.

Consoling themselves with the fact that Fergus had undoubtedly had an uncomfortable drive home, plus a sizeable bill for a replacement passenger door, not to mention a new gearbox by the sound of it, the Swanstons put the affair to rest and, thanking Mrs Moray once more for her timely intervention, retired to bed.

On the Friday morning, the taxi was waiting to take them to Elgin to catch their train back to Edinburgh. Mrs Moray got emotional, saying they were the nicest guests she'd ever had and dabbing her eyes with the border of her pinny. Then Janet got emotional, gave her a hug and told her they'd definitely be back for another holiday. But of course, they never were. Geordie thanked James for helping him catch the mackerel and said he'd definitely look him up if he was ever in Edinburgh, but of course, he never did. And, on being asked, Terror assured James with several wags of his tail that he'd keep on catching rats as long as he lived in Burghead. He was the only one to keep his promise.

Janet and Ian agreed that despite the unpleasantness with Fergus, it was the best family holiday they'd ever had, especially as the notoriously fickle Scottish climate had, for once, played along. Wee Effie, however, was non-committal. Her adventure with Fergus had been a bright spark, a hint of danger in an otherwise humdrum week. But of one thing she was sure. It was definitely her last holiday together with her family. As for

James, well, as the train sped south, he sat back in his seat, staring out over the rich farmland of the northeast, and silently went over the past two weeks. Without a doubt, the unexpected holiday in Burghead had been unforgettable. The almost permanent sunshine had, of course, had a lot to do with it. But other things would stick in his mind as well. The fantastic ocean views. The Second World War beach frozen in time, with its tank traps, pillboxes and ghosts. The slaughter of the mackerel. Swimming off the pier. Conquering fear of nudity and fear of heights at the same time. Not to forget Mrs Moray, her lede and her cooking, Geordie with his homespun philosophy, and the loons and the queynes. So much in such a brief moment of time. He knew he'd have other holidays, perhaps more adventurous, perhaps more exotic, perhaps, even, more glamorous. But, he wondered, would any of them measure up to that magic fortnight in a Summer Place?

8 A' yer jargon o' yer schools

Among scholars

For two years, day in, day out, James had been one of thirty or so fledgling academicals, each with different credentials, expectations and abilities, in a classroom that was nothing like that of primary school. Before, he'd sat together with pupils. Now, he was among scholars. He'd quickly resigned himself to the fact that he'd never be top of his class or anywhere near it. He was up against boys and girls who were simply better than him, most of whom actually took their studies seriously. In a masochistic moment, James savoured the irony. At Fox Crag he'd been the one belonging to the elite. He'd been the one shunning the losers in the back row who were all bound for Lothian Park. Now, in this new, topsy-turvy Academy world, *he* was the one sitting in the back row. *He* was the one being shunned. *He* was the loser. It was hard to accept and took some getting used to. In fact, for all of his six years at The Academy, he never quite did.

The minds of the members of 1a1 and 2a1 were focused on one thing and one thing only: excelling in their studies. After all, they were still too young to make any of the sports teams, too untutored to shine in the Literary and Debating Society, too immature to be considered for a leadership role. At this point in their journey through The Academy, passes in exams, class rankings and subject prizes were to be the centre of their existence. In the foundation programme they had two years to prove themselves. In the Third Year it would be different. Then, they'd be permitted to take electives, depending on their prior performance. But in order to secure their places, they were expected to put their noses to the grindstone and most of them did.

Several top pupils typified this mindset in 1a1/2a1. One of them was, of course, Eric Livingstone. But chasing him down was a clique of elite scholars who held themselves aloof from the mediocre rest. Prominent among this select few, and Eric's closest rivals for class honours, was a trio of girls, Aileen Herkes, Drinda Chalmers, and Shelagh Macfarlane. These weren't lassies from Leith tenements or the council estate, but from the posh villas at Marionville. Graduates of independent, fee-paying primaries, they naturally considered themselves a cut above anyone else who wasn't. Aileen and Drinda were best friends who shared an identical, unwavering pursuit of scholastic achievement. But in physical respects they differed. In the poker game of life, Nature had been kind to Drinda, dealing her rich, wavy, raven locks, a sweet face and a curvaceous form she knew boys found pleasing. By contrast, Aileen had been dealt a far weaker hand based on plain features, a flat chest and that standard teenage affliction, acne.

Strange to say, of the two friends, it was flirty, shapely Drinda who was more successful in giving Eric a run for his money in those first two years. For, come the third term of the First Year, she'd snatched the prize of Class Dux from his grasp and left him floundering with the Rector's Prize for Progress as his consolation. His mother and father, quite aware of how gifted their son was, closely supervised his scholastic endeavours and were his greatest fans. Naturally, they were disgruntled and urged him to greater efforts. But, much to their chagrin, Drinda had repeated the feat in the Second Year, taking the Vanda Ferguson Memorial Prize as Class Dux and again pushing Eric into second place.

However, by the Third Year, Drinda's scholarly star would start to show signs of waning. And, sadly, it would be her popularity with the opposite sex that would lead to her downfall for, passing the age of fifteen, her physical allure only intensified. Who could forget the time she caused uproar among the pubescent and post-pubescent males in the school (not excluding teachers) on a hot day in June when she discarded her blazer for the afternoon to reveal a black bra encasing her ample breasts under her white, regulation Academy blouse, which, even myopic members of The Academy community perfectly well knew, was see-through when the light was right? Miss Fyffe was not amused. Seduced away from her studies by boys, much to her ambitious parents' displeasure, Drinda would eventually leave the field clear for Eric.

It was for entirely the opposite reason that her friend Aileen's scholastic star would, instead, blaze more brightly. So far, Aileen had always been a second runner-up. Third place got you no accolades at The Academy. For the first couple of years, Aileen gritted her teeth from the sidelines as Drinda and Eric carved up the major prizes and awards between them. Her frustration mounting, and under pressure from her lawyer father and schoolteacher mother, Aileen then made a shrewd move. For the Third Year science elective, she'd choose whatever the other two were either not good at, or not interested in. After some research, she ascertained that Eric and Drinda had something in common; they both disliked biology. Further discreet enquiry revealed that none of her close rivals was likely to be in the biology class either. Aileen realised that the annual Biology Prize was there for the taking. So she decided to take it.

It wasn't that hard. Having passed fourteen, she'd found no amount of medicated soap was able to budge the spots erupting on her face. Her junior bra had done little to augment her spare figure. It was clear that, this year at least, there would be no distractions where boys were concerned. There were some advantages to being plain after all. She couldn't admit to any genuine interest in biology, but she enrolled in the class anyway. To her satisfaction, not to mention that of her ambitious parents, her scheme to take the Biology Prize would bear fruit, and her name would appear on the Academy prize list unfailingly, year after year from then on.

Shelagh Macfarlane, in contrast to the other two girls, was something of a paradox. If a girl had been sought to represent a stereotypical swot, she'd have got the job. With curly, sandy hair and a pinched, plain face, her eyes were abnormally magnified behind the thick lenses of her spectacles. She was shy and retiring. So insignificant was she in class that she was more of a mouse than a girl. The key to understanding Shelagh was the fact that she'd been born into a family of swots. Her father, a chemistry teacher at The Royal High, had been Dux of Duns Academy. Her mother, likewise, had been Dux of James Gillespie's. Shelagh herself had been Dux of her independent primary school. Her two little brothers, carbon copies of herself - mousy personality and thick-lensed spectacles - had followed in her footsteps as Duxes. Being a Dux was simply in the Macfarlanes' DNA.

Like Aileen, Shelagh had been a third runner-up in the foundation years. Always near the top of the rankings, she was never close enough to claim one of the sought-after prizes awarded to Eric, Drinda and others. And like Aileen, it wasn't until the Third Year that Shelagh began to show her mettle. But unlike Aileen, there was no guile or strategising in her method. The plain fact was that, as the years passed and the subject matter became more complex, Shelagh began to excel in subjects Eric and the others were beginning to struggle with, such as mathematics and physics. So, while Eric continued to sweep the board in English, history, geography, chemistry, modern languages plus a host of special prizes such as religious knowledge, Shelagh quietly did what she did best: addressed herself to problems of trigonometry, algebra, mass, temperature and dynamics. By focusing on her strengths, Shelagh ensured her name appeared regularly on the prize list.

But oddly, it wasn't just swotting that Shelagh was good at, for, despite her mousy persona, she happened to be a top swimmer as well. Not only that; thin and spindly in the First Year, by the end of foundation she'd filled out to such an extent that she caused consternation among the third-year boys at the Vicky Baths one day during a special PE mixed swim session in preparation for the Annual Gala. As usual, some pupils, including James, had been excused participation for various reasons. From their vantage point on the running balcony, they were allowed to watch the goings-on below in the pool. When Shelagh the Swot stepped out of the ladies' changing rooms in her maroon one-piece bathing suit there were gasps of admiration from the idlers above, for the ugly duckling had become a swan. Not one among them could have guessed that under her bland exterior, studious demeanour and Academy uniform, Shelagh had been concealing the body of a juvenile Jane Russell.

To say that James and his fellows were stunned would be an understatement. Instantly, they were turned from spectators into voyeurs as they followed every movement of Shelagh's pale form in her maroon swimsuit in and out of the pool, eagerly jockeying for position to get the best glimpse down her cleavage. Indeed, so hectic was the jostling that Alfie Strachan almost did a henner over the railing and into the deep end. In an instant, unlikely as it seemed, Shelagh the Swot hadn't only acquired a new persona, she'd also accumulated a cadre of male admirers who'd compete to be her escort at the next school dance. Unsurprisingly, her name featured prominently in the list of winners from that year's Swimming Gala. James was entranced. Not that he was attracted to Shelagh, but the episode gave him much food for thought. It seemed you couldn't always judge a book by its cover.

Among the 1a1/2a1 boys, Eric's one and only serious rival was undoubtedly Tony Magnus. Tony's record was impressive, for he was yet another of the elite who'd been Dux of his private, fee-paying primary school. His strength was literature. His regular poetry contributions to the school magazine would invariably be published without question, even though the editor - Mr Fluke, the English teacher - must have been scratching his head over the weird language as well as arcane themes that revolved around post-apocalyptic nuclear wastelands and nightmarish creatures from dystopian dreams. But maybe that's why his poems were published. Throughout his time at The Academy, Tony twice took the English Prize off Eric and, once, the French Prize, too.

The strange thing about Tony, though, was that he looked nothing like a typical swot. He didn't wear spectacles, for a start. Then there was his hair. As the nineteen-fifties were winding down to the new decade, men's hair was only just starting to be fashionably longer. Tony was at the forefront of this trend. His rich, sandy hair curled over his forehead and licked down the back of his neck, over his shirt collar and even onto his blazer at times. More than once he was pulled up by prefects and got lines for overlong hair. But, despite his hirsute offending, he was particularly careful of his appearance. His hair was always neatly brushed with a parting at the side. He wore his uniform with elegant panache. His Windsor knot was always symmetrical. His shirts were clean and nicely ironed. His blazer was regularly dry cleaned, then replaced when he grew out of it. From the Third Year, his longs were always pressed with a knife-edge crease. To complete the ensemble, his black winkle pickers were buffed to a high shine. The fact was that, some years before the term gained general currency, Tony was something of a Mod.

The only evidence that he was, in reality, a swot, were his pasty complexion and bleary eyes from hours alone with his textbooks. As well, regarding himself as potential Dux material, he naturally associated exclusively with the clique of top scholars who were all swots like him. From the rest of the class, he kept his distance, his single concession to communication being his standard Cheshire Cat smile that seemed to say he knew something they didn't know but he wasn't going to tell them what it was.

Another peculiarity of Tony's was that his name wasn't actually Tony. On their very first day at The Academy, Mr Flockhart had been checking attendance. Going down a list of unfamiliar names in the class register, he'd reached Tony's name.

"Bruce C. Magnus?"

Tony put his hand up.

"It's Tony, Sir, not Bruce."

"Oh, you mean your first name is Anthony?"

"No, Sir, it's Tony."

"But here it says Bruce! Is that a mistake?"

"No, Sir. But my name's Tony."

By now Mr Flockhart was frustrated, but being a kindly man at heart, he made an exception since it was the first day of the new term.

"You mean your name is Bruce, but you prefer to be called *Tony*?"

"That's about it, Sir."

Mr Flockhart ran the sharp end of his pencil through his thinning scalp, then made a note in the register.

"Prefers the name *Tony,*" he muttered to himself.

Why Bruce C. Magnus affected the name Tony to his classmates and teachers was a mystery. Most people would understand William wanting to be Billy, or Andrew, Drew, or Frederick, Fred, but why would Bruce want to be Tony? No one knew and no one ever found out. Tony's urge not to conform had been evident in his very first months at The Academy when he'd discovered a photo of Cliff Richard with sideburns in his weekly copy of *Melody Maker*. For - yet another of his idiosyncrasies - unlike his fellows among the scholastic elite, Tony actually made time in his life for something other than perfecting his ink homework and swotting for exams. He'd been a firm fan of Cliff since 'Move It' had reached Number Two in the UK Singles Chart in the autumn of 1958. Secretly, he thought he looked like Cliff. He habitually made minor alterations to his appearance in an effort to resemble his idol. That way, he surmised, despite his small stature, he'd be more attractive to girls.

With 'Move It' being played endlessly on Radio Luxembourg, Tony, in addition to being one of the first in the queue at the HMV store in Junction Street willing to spend 6s6d for a precious copy, had decided that more was needed to cement his loyalty to Cliff. He decided to grow sideburns too. For, much to his delight, at twelve-going-on-thirteen, he'd discovered that hair, albeit sparse, was beginning to sprout on his cheeks and around his chin, thanks to the genes inherited from his father, and that he was having to 'shave' about once a fortnight. By dint of careful sculpting with his dad's razor, he could look more like Cliff than ever. And attract girls more than ever.

After much primping and mirror gazing, by October, Tony had managed to produce a meagre but just barely visible result: a pair of downy, russet sideburns gracing his pale, youthful cheeks and stretching down to level with the tip of his nose. However, the lifespan of his new facial accessories was brief. One Monday morning, he'd been quick-marched into the Deputy Rector's office by the Head Prefect. The instruction was plain and unadorned. He had to get a haircut. But not only that.

"You will also shave off these things on your cheek. Now. Until they are gone, you are suspended from school."

Tony had left school and, as per instructions, had gone around to Sanny Speight's for a trim, at the same time requesting, with regret, removal of the offending items. He'd returned to The Academy bare-cheeked but defiant and resentful. This was not, to his mind, how potential Dux material deserved to be treated. But it was when Duncan Dunmore stepped into the picture that Tony's sideburn troubles only got worse. Duncan lived not far from James in The Grove and they walked to school together occasionally. He was a handsome, dark-haired boy with an air of sophistication and an odd accent because he'd been born and raised in England to Scottish parents. Duncan, being a devotee of who else but The King, Elvis Presley, despised Cliff Richard. James had lost count of the number of times he'd had to put up with Duncan's rants against Cliff, denouncing him as a cheap Elvis copycat who couldn't sing a note. To add insult to injury, Cliff had chosen to kick off his career at the very time when Elvis had patriotically allowed himself to be conscripted into the US Army for two years.

"He could've got exemption!" Duncan griped. "But he did his duty!"

Cliff, the dirty dog, had sneaked in by the back door and was making himself popular off Elvis's enforced absence from the music scene. Duncan was incensed. And he wasn't the only one. A hard core of Elvis fans in The Academy shared his sentiments. Now James, like most of his fellow pupils, hadn't had even a glimpse of Tony's embryonic sideburns before they'd been consigned to Sanny Speight's rubbish bin forever. But Duncan happened to be among the few who had, and it was Duncan, seizing on an unwise remark by Tony about the reason for them, who'd fanned the flames. The story had spread around the school like wildfire. Tony Magnus had been suspended because he'd grown Cliff Richard sideburns! The reaction was a cross between outrage and ridicule. He was mocked in the corridors, especially by those female Elvis fans.

"Is that a wee moose on yer cheek, Tony? Oh, no, it's a sideburn!"

"Tony, haven't ye dropped somethin'? Oh, no, it's just one o' yer sideburns!"

Poor Tony. They'd given him a hard time, but he was determined to re-grow the sideburns eventually. That was until the latest *Melody Maker* arrived. There on the front page was a photo of Cliff taken just days before, surrounded by a bevy of female admirers but *minus* the sideburns. Tony scanned the story. Apparently, Cliff had been told to remove the sideburns by a record producer *so that he'd look LESS like Elvis*! Tony was over the moon. The Academy had unwittingly done him a favour and had saved him from a serious faux pas. He'd cheered up and, smiling his Cheshire Cat smile, he kept writing his weird poetry for the school magazine and plotting his next class prize.

Nine words

James cursed to himself as he hurried along the corridor on level three, the bell ringing ear-splittingly for the first period. *Damned one-way system*! He was late. It was Monday morning at the end of August 1960, on the first day of the new autumn term in his third year at The Academy. The Third Year! This was when everything changed. New classmates, new teachers, new subjects. The class, now renamed 3a2, had shrunk from 34 to 23 scholars. Some had come and some had gone; some had swapped streams; some had left The Academy and switched to the likes of Lothian Park on the realisation (or strong advice of the school managers) that The Academy wasn't for them. The elite from 1a1 and 2a1 remained in place, plus some mediocre, hopeful middle-rankers such as James, and a smattering of new faces.

Their new Register Teacher was Mr Laidlaw, their physics teacher. Morning registration took place in his lab. This was a much more relaxed arrangement, for they all got to loll on lab stools like bar patrons and there was none of the kind of enforced ranked seating of Mr Flockhart's classes. New subjects meant that the third-year scholars would drop some subjects and pick up new ones while continuing with core subjects such as English and maths. Ironically, one of the subjects James had dropped was the one he'd done best in, art. Even at this young age, he was sufficiently aware to realise there was no future with art. As a hobby, yes, but how would he ever make a living from it? He had absolutely no regrets, for he'd realised it was modern languages that he wanted to focus on. He'd done better in the Second Year in French and Latin and had applied to do an exciting new subject, Russian, as his elective.

And who should the Russian teacher be but Henry M. Neil, his erstwhile Latin teacher? Henry had been at the forefront of the drive to introduce the teaching of Russian in Scottish secondary schools. Originally a Classics teacher, it was said that he'd taught himself Russian before The War. It was even rumoured that he'd been Churchill's interpreter at Yalta, but the more he thought about it, the more James wondered if this were true. He'd seen a grainy newsreel of Yalta on TV and there was no one hovering between Churchill and Stalin that looked remotely like Henry. Regardless, he was looking forward to another few years with the person who was now, without doubt, his favourite teacher. However, his hopes were to be dashed. One day at the end of the previous term, he'd got a message to say that Mr Flockhart wanted to see him after school.

"Listen, James," said the French teacher, brandishing a piece of paper. "I understand that you've applied to do Russian next year as your other modern language elective?"

"Yes, Sir," replied James, wondering what was coming.

"Well, I'm sorry to have to tell you that there's a problem."

He paused, looking at James as if he expected some reaction but none came.

"The thing is this," he continued. "Though your marks improved in Latin and French last year, across the board they've been less than satisfactory. Russian's a very difficult language. It's only for the top scholars."

Yes, James had already guessed that, since Eric, Drinda and Aileen had already been accepted without question. And he was fully aware that he was far from being a top scholar. You'd have to be thick not to know where this was leading.

"So, I'm sorry but The Academy's Modern Languages Committee has rejected your application. You can't do Russian but you can continue with French. And, for your other foreign language you can take German. It's much easier than Russian."

This last statement, as James would come to conclude later on in life, wasn't entirely true and probably a matter of opinion. But for the present, it looked like his dreams of studying Russian were scuppered. There was to be no argument. There was no right of appeal. The decision had been made and it was final. German it would have to be. So, come the first Monday of the new autumn term and the first of the new school year, as registration ended with the urgent ringing of the bell for the first period and the scholars headed out to their first classes, James felt a pang of envy for the elite, strolling off in a tight-knit group for their first Russian class with Henry, while he headed off all on his own in a different direction to find his consolation prize, the German class with Mr Grossart. At least, maybe he'd soon be able to write letters to Doctor Frost in German. As he mounted the stairs to the third floor in his new grey longs, his bag over his shoulder, he suddenly felt grown-up, especially when he saw the little scared-looking first years in their shorts being convoyed around in groups to their first lessons. It seemed only yesterday he'd been one of them. It was when he got to the top of the stairs and checked the number of the classroom he was looking for that he realised he'd have to go almost all the way around the entire building to get to where he had to be. *Damned one-way system!*

But then occurred another of those encounters that appear trivial at the time but that can have far-reaching consequences. And so it was for James on this first day of the new school year. As he hastened along the corridor obeying the rules and taking the long way round, his frustration mounted, for the period bell had stopped ringing and he knew now for sure that he'd be late for his very first German lesson. At that moment, who should appear hurrying in the opposite direction against the flow (he was a teacher, so that was all right) but Henry M. Neil, a canvas bag in one hand and a briefcase in the other, on his way to his first Russian class of the term with those elite students James had seen off in the other direction. On catching sight of James coming towards him, Henry stopped dead in his tracks, his bag and his briefcase swinging with the loss of momentum.

When he thought about it afterwards, James realised that believers in predestination would claim that Fate had arranged the meeting; believers in God would say that He had had a hand in it; those that believe in just reward for good behaviour would say that it was all down to James obeying the school's one-way rules, while those that believed in none of the above would say that the encounter was pure chance. Whatever the case, it was one that would profoundly change James's life. Not having seen James for some two months, Henry threw him a hearty greeting:

"Hello, James! What are you up to?"

He'd easily divined from James's anxious expression and hurried gait that he was hot and bothered. James's face lit up. He paused in his step.

"Hello, Sir... Ah think Ah'm lost." He turned his head and glanced back down the corridor. "Ah'm looking for mah German class!"

Then came nine words that would entirely alter James's future.

"Why don't you come and learn Russian with us?" Henry said from his lofty height.

James, I am inviting you to become a member of the community of the elite. You may join the Russian class. James couldn't believe his ears. Was it that simple? His application for Russian had been rejected. Mr Flockhart had told him so. But here was Henry throwing all of that out of the window. Henry looked at him searchingly, the question mark in his voice hanging pregnant in the air.

"Sir, Ah *wanted* to..." James stammered, at a loss for words. "Ah did apply for Russian... But Mr Flockhart told me Ah couldn't do it." He paused, daring himself to go on. "He said Ah'm not good enough, Sir."

He looked at Henry with a mixture of hope and dread, dread that Henry would say, *Yes, he was right, you aren't good enough.* But he didn't say that.

"Don't worry about it!" he said instead. "Just leave it to me."

Then he smiled what James liked to call *the golden smile*, for when Henry smiled broadly, he revealed the gold crown he'd had fitted to his first left bicuspid by a Soviet dentist during his last visit to Moscow.

"Well, are you coming?"

And without waiting for an answer, he loped on up the corridor with his long legs and giant steps. As if in a dream, James found himself turning, then trotting after him, this time going the wrong way round the one-way system. He supposed it would be all right as long as he was with a teacher? Then Henry was briskly going right and entering through the open door of a classroom. The new Russian class of third years was sitting waiting. Only nine pupils, among them Eric Livingstone of course, plus Aileen Herkes, Drinda Chalmers, a few other members of the crème de la crème and a couple James didn't know. He'd be number ten.

As Henry entered, the faces of his prospective pupils brightened in recognition, but a few expressions quickly changed when James appeared from behind Henry's back. Frowns and puzzlement. James knew exactly what they were thinking. What on earth is *he* doing here? Suddenly, their achievement of getting into the Russian class seemed not so special after all. But Eric was the exception. Sitting by himself at a double desk next to the window at the back of the class, he was lost in thought as he often was. On catching sight of James, he perked up, curled up the corners of his pursed mouth in what might have been a smile, extended the fingers of his right hand in greeting and pointed downwards to the empty seat beside him. James went around the back of the class and sat down warily as if expecting the seat to bite him. Henry put down his bags on the table.

"Good morning, class," he said. "Ready to learn some Russian?"

Without more ado, and without any reference to James, he opened the bag and started to distribute textbooks, jotters and handouts. It appeared that as far as Henry was concerned, it was no one else's business. Eric simply raised his eyebrows in surprise for he knew full well about James's rejection, but they didn't speak about it until afterwards. While Henry was setting up and the pupils were examining their new materials, one girl did turn round and give James a look. It was a furtive look, tinged with malevolence. James just happened to catch it. The girl's name was Gertrude Cordiner and she was from the south of England. James knew she'd already taken a dislike to him during the First Year. He didn't know why, exactly, but suspected it had something to do with his less than perfect speech. Maybe she felt pupils at grammar schools should speak flawless Queen's English, regardless of the fact that they were in Scotland. His pronounced local, working-class accent singled him out as vulgar. Snobbery was indeed alive and well in The Academy. Gertrude regarded herself as one of the elite but had never won any prizes and was on shaky ground with her marks. Nevertheless, when the look came, James didn't flinch. He simply returned it until, flustered, Gertrude turned away and pretended to be busy with the new English-Russian pocket dictionary her parents had ordered from Thin's as a reward for her getting into the class.

In the next few days, James kept wondering when he'd get the summons from Mr Flockhart to tell him that Henry M. Neil had overstepped the mark and James would have to leave the Russian class immediately. Surely Mr Grossart had been, at the very least, peeved, perhaps even outraged to discover that one of his prospective German pupils had been poached by the Russian colleague, and flagrantly too, in the school corridor not ten yards from the very classroom where Mr Grossart was already calling the register? But no summons came. Somehow, Henry had done it. He'd gone against the fiat of the Modern Languages Committee and admitted James Swanston, patently unfit, to his Russian class. How he'd wangled it, James never found out. Nobody said a word. James marvelled. Eric was similarly bemused. The whole affair simply reinforced their impression of Henry as a maverick. He did what he liked and the rest be damned.

But there was more. With those nine words, Henry had changed the course of James's life. Though James didn't realise it at the time, he'd do things he'd never have done, know people he'd never have known and go places he'd never have gone, had those nine words never been uttered. Mesmerised by the incident itself, James was at first ignorant of the fact that a major shift had occurred. Everything would be different now, and it was all down to Henry. That night, he told Janet what had happened.

"Mum, Ah'm studyin' Russian. Mr Neil got me into the class!"

"Well," she countered with a satisfied expression, "me and yer dad would much rather ye study Russian than German anyway."

Naturally, The War still took centre stage, nor was the Doctor Frost episode forgotten, and Janet was delighted that she had yet another anecdote for her cronies about her son at The Academy.

"Aye, did ye hear aboot mah laddie, James? (Of course they had, for the umpteenth time.) Well, 'e's in the Third Year at The Academy and 'e's learnin' Russian! It's only for a select few, ye ken."

There were murmurs of admiration, but other reactions too.

"Is 'e learnin' tae be a spy or somethin'?"

"Is the teacher Mr Krushchev, then?"

"Better watch out – 'e'll disappear one day an' turn up in Moscow!"

Fanciful though such comments might have been, they did raise a serious issue. It was the middle of The Cold War. Despite a residual thread of anti-German sentiment running through British society, the public was well aware that Russia was now the real enemy. The Soviets and NATO had huge stockpiles of nuclear weapons. War could break out at any moment. Three years before, the Soviet Union had launched Sputnik, the first artificial satellite, into space. The same year, *From Russia with Love*, Ian Fleming's James Bond novel about the evil Soviet SMERSH organisation had been published and would soon appear as a film. The following year, the Russian cosmonaut, Yuri Gagarin, would be the first man to orbit the earth in space. The Cuban Missile Crisis wasn't far off. Russia could trigger a nuclear holocaust. Russia was uppermost in everyone's minds. It didn't matter that learning the language of your enemy might build bridges. People were downright suspicious of the motives of anyone who had anything to do with Russia.

But as far as the class was concerned, the parlous state of East-West relations was the last thing on their minds. They were among the chosen few who'd had been given the opportunity to study a challenging new language. It was an opportunity they grasped with both hands and with one simple goal in mind. At the end of two years, if all went well, they'd get the chance to sit the new Scottish Certificate of Education O-Level Russian exam. That was the gateway to the Highers, which in turn were the gateway to university. Henry prepared them well. Owing to the small class size, the teaching was intimate and informal. James discovered that their two years of Latin had been excellent preparation for the complexities of Russian grammar. Once he'd mastered the orthography, it wasn't all that difficult. He was captivated by the strange Cyrillic characters such as Ж and Ч and Я and Ю. The fact that *с* was *s*, *р* was *r* and *н* was *n* took some getting used to. But it was fascinating. It was like a secret language.

Because the teaching of Russian in Britain was in its infancy, there was a dearth of Russian teaching materials. Henry made up for this by preparing his own handouts. Since the school possessed only one small Banda spirit duplicator, the results were not of particularly high quality. The paper was cheap and thin and the letters were always fuzzy and stained purple, but the pupils loved Henry's handouts for one special reason; the alcohol in the spirit was particularly fragrant, especially when the printing was fresh off the Banda. The first thing to be done was to run their nostrils across the sometimes still slightly damp paper, self-indulgently breathing in the fumes. Thus did many a Russian class get off to a jolly start. In addition to conventional grammar and vocabulary, Henry introduced them to songs and poetry with the help of a small Italian Geloso tape recorder. He played them recordings of a Russian choir singing 'Kalinka'. They studied the lyrics and learnt them. Then came 'Stenka Razin', the song about the Cossack robber baron, and other Russian standards. But one day Henry came into class and played them the best, the absolute best, and the only, Russian pop song they'd ever heard. It was called 'Moscow Nights, Podmoskovnie Vechera'.

First, Henry said nothing. He simply switched on the tape recorder and played the song straight through. To put it mildly, they were blown away. The melody! The violins! The Slavonic accordion! The balalaikas! The choir! The ambience! Without much difficulty, they could easily imagine themselves at a lover's tryst, lingering just off Red Square on a balmy Russian summer's evening. Then, haltingly, they deciphered the purple-tinted lyrics on Henry's handout and translated them. Finally, they sang them together, accompanying Vladimir Troshin, the deep-voiced vocalist on the tape. 'Moscow Nights' had been number one in the Russian hit parade it seemed like forever, yet the British public was entirely ignorant of it. After all, this was Soviet Russia. Those romantic Moscow Nights were taking place behind the Iron Curtain. But then, a year later, an instrumental version called 'Midnight in Moscow' appeared in Britain and the US. It was a huge hit. But it wasn't the same. It was a cheap, jazzed-up knock-off. It had none of the magic of the original and meant nothing to novice Russian scholars, for they already had the words and the music of the real, the original 'Moscow Nights' locked up inside them, to be enjoyed again and again.

At the end of the autumn term, they had their very first Russian exam. There was a translation from Russian into English, a short prose passage to write, and some questions on grammar. Then there was an oral test including a famous passage by Turgenev about the beautiful Russian language to be learnt by heart and recited. James had prepared as best he could, but he was competing against a small group of top scholars. His expectations weren't high. The class average was 73%. He scored 70%, which equated to a B+. He didn't know where he stood in the class rankings because Henry, unlike Mr Flockhart, didn't go through that particular exercise. But one thing he did know. By chance, overhearing the girls gossiping in class, he discovered that Gertrude Cordiner had scored only 58%. She got a C. James was overjoyed. At least he knew he couldn't be bottom of the class. Not only that, he'd bettered an arch-enemy. There couldn't have been a more satisfying conclusion to his first term of the Third Year at The Academy.

Tommy Steele and Mussolini

Why do you have to listen to this terrible rock and roll?" demanded Mr Longmuir for the umpteenth time, breaking off from his chalk rendering of the Carse of Gowrie, which was, apparently, important to the Scottish jam-making industry, and glaring around the classroom. Mr Longmuir's bitterest enemies were Tommy Steele, Cliff Richard and, of course, Elvis, in that order. "Why can't you enjoy folk music and folk dancing like the Danes?" he went on. Whether his question was rhetorical or not was unclear. Anyway, no one hazarded an answer. Instead, the class bent to the task of copying the map into their geography jotters.

Mr Longmuir was an odd fish. A colourless, humourless disciplinarian in his mid-fifties, he eschewed The Belt because he was a practising Christian. He explained the mysteries of the Tropics of Cancer and Capricorn, introduced them to meanders, loess and igneous rock, and even inducted them into his personal interest, astronomy. All well and good. But he also took it upon himself to make no secret of the fact that he was a great Danophile, spending every summer in Denmark pursuing his other hobby, Danish folklore. It seemed that, hooked on a diet of Vikings, folk-dancing and Hans Christian Andersen, Mr Longmuir had concluded that Denmark was paradise on earth. And he constantly preached that very message to his pupils in between drawing colourful maps on the board of the Rhône-Saône Corridor and the South Island of New Zealand.

James pondered Mr Longmuir's words. There were sure to be Danes who liked Cliff as well. Who could deny the possibility of Hank Marvin and The Shadows backing him while he crooned to a gaggle of blonde Danish maidens? Why couldn't you like rock *and* folk music? Or the eightsome reel and jive, for that matter? But more importantly, why did Mr Longmuir bother unleashing his tirades on his pupils? He must have known they were of a different generation. He must have guessed that their tastes in just about everything were likely to be very different from his. He must have realised he was on a losing wicket. But still, he persisted.

The Academy offered a palette of after-school activities for pupils. Each full-time staff member was expected to be involved in at least one club or society. Mr Longmuir, unmarried, his life revolving around school, astronomy and Denmark, had put his hand up for three. First, there was the Politics Club. James had no idea what went on there. It seemed to be a bunch of serious-minded swots who spent their time endlessly debating the boring ins and outs of British politics in Mr

Longmuir's geography lab after school. Politics didn't particularly interest him, despite his struggles to understand the regular political shenanigans reported in his dad's daily *Daily Express*.

Second, Mr Longmuir ran the Astronomical Society. There was a lively programme of guest speakers, practical sessions and excursions around the city. The Astronomical Society, under the guiding hand of Mr Longmuir, was probably one of the most active and successful non-sport societies in The Academy. Ever since his collision with Cassiopeia Clover, the stars and planets had definitely been on James's radar so he hadn't hesitated to join. One of the highlights of the programme was the annual night visit to Calton Observatory. The City Astronomer would be revealing to them the mysteries of the night sky. They'd meet Mr Longmuir at Register House and then make their way as a group up to the Observatory. Janet was hesitant about letting 13-year-old James out on his own on a winter's evening, particularly up to Calton Hill. The area had an unsavoury reputation after dark. But after being assured that he'd get the 49 bus just outside the door, there would be others there too, and he'd be supervised by his teacher, she'd relented. As twenty or so boys and girls from the Society stood on the Register House steps waiting for Mr Longmuir, cheerily chatting, swathed in duffel coats, gloves and scarves, their breath condensing in the freezing November air and the steely glare of Princes Street's impressive illumination, James found himself being drawn into the spirit of fellowship. Here they were, pupils from every school year, in amity, mingling, talking, laughing, doing something enjoyable, something interesting. They weren't in a classroom. They were out in the world. But they were still The Academy. Suddenly, James had an overwhelming sense of belonging.

Another regular event was the annual Society ascent of Arthur's Seat on the first of May. The point was to be on the summit by sunrise to witness a common astronomical event few of them ever got to see. This would require James to get out of bed before 4 am. He'd then have to get to Arthur's Seat to meet the others before starting the climb. But here, Janet put her foot down. There were no buses at that time. He couldn't walk there in the dark. Short of getting a taxi or asking Alistair to drive him (not only very unlikely but unreliable into the bargain) there was no way he could make it on time. Sorry, this time she'd have to say no. But James wasn't too bothered. He'd already been up Arthur's Seat plenty of times and already considered it small fry.

Mr Longmuir's third after-school commitment was the Christian Union. For a while, James and Eric Livingstone attended the weekly Tuesday meetings after school in Mr Longmuir's geography lab, but it was really only on account of Miss Lindsay, the new, young, twenty-something English teacher and an absolute stoater, who also happened to be a committed Christian. There was a rumour going around that her fiancé had been killed in a plane crash and that she was available. The beautiful Miss Lindsay had quickly become a pillar of the CU at The Academy, resulting, much to Mr Longmuir's delight, in a massive uptick in applications to join, bolstered mainly by pubescent male pupils who came to salivate at her at close quarters over their hymn books during 'Lead, Kindly Light'. However, James's interest soon palled when he saw how much competition there was for her affections and he broke off attending, contenting himself with admiring her from afar in the school corridors.

That left the Astronomical Society. It was interesting, but... Yes, there was a but. James couldn't put his finger on it. Activities were well organised; Mr Longmuir obviously put his heart and soul into it. It seemed he was more successful outside the classroom than inside. But there was something about him that James's young mind couldn't get to grips with. He was so earnest as to be uninspiring. He was entirely lacking in the charisma of a Henry M. Neil. Of course, there was surely much they could learn from him, but James couldn't reconcile Mr Longmuir's tirades in class with how he was out of class. If he was so dismissive of his pupils' teenage belief systems, why did he go to all the trouble to organise three clubs for them, not to mention give up so much of his time, when he didn't need to?

The question lay unanswered in James's mind. It was when he suddenly caught the flu that things came to a head. It was in the summer term of his second year at The Academy and just past his thirteenth birthday. He'd been off school for several days but was now slowly on the mend. He was home alone at four-fifteen on a Thursday afternoon, lying on his parents' bed in his dressing gown nursing a sore throat and didn't expect any of the family back until five-thirty at the earliest. Suddenly there was a knock at the door. Getting up, he tied the cord of his dressing-gown and stumbled blearily across the living room, wondering who it could be. He opened the door. There stood Mr Longmuir. He was hatless, wearing a gabardine raincoat and clutching a leather briefcase under his arm. He was wearing his usual earnest expression but appeared ill at ease.

To say James was surprised would be something of an understatement. Through the fog of his flu his head filled with questions. The first three were: Why was he here? How did he get here? What did he want? In answer to the first, for a second or two, the thought crossed his mind that Mr Longmuir had come to give him homework. But just as it popped up, he dismissed it. How ridiculous.

Teachers didn't bring homework to sick pupils, at least not unless it was a long-term condition. He'd never heard of a teacher visiting a pupil at home before, let alone one who was off sick and especially without prior notice. His association with Mr Longmuir was nothing out of the ordinary. He didn't do particularly well in his class. He was a mediocre student. He was definitely not one of Mr Longmuir's favourites or among the geography elite. That was a privilege reserved for the likes of Aileen, Eric and Shelagh. He wasn't a leading light of the Astronomical Society. He just tagged along behind the rest, following, not leading. So what had he done to deserve the honour of an unannounced visit by Mr Longmuir? Was Mr Longmuir checking up on him to make sure he was really sick? That sounded equally far-fetched. Did Mr Longmuir make a habit of visiting sick pupils in obedience to his Christian beliefs? Really? Bemused, James stepped back, opened the door wide and, pulling the woollen scarf tighter about his throat, he managed to croak something.

"Oh, Sir... Come in..."

Other than that, he was lost for words. What do you say in such a situation? Teachers were for school. Teachers were for classrooms. Teachers stood behind desks, or, in the case of Mr Longmuir, behind a large, raised bench in the geography lab. Teachers walked along corridors in their academic gowns or stood on the stage at assembly. They most definitely didn't stand in the tiny living room of James's parents' cramped flat. But here he was. James closed the door behind him. Mr Longmuir stood in the middle of the room wearing an expression now exuding concern. But the sense of uneasiness remained.

"I didn't want to intrude," he said at last. "I heard you were sick and I just wanted to see how you were."

"Thank you, Sir," James managed to croak. "Gettin' better."

How on earth had Mr Longmuir got his address? He wasn't his Register Teacher, so either he must have gone to the School Office or Mr Flockhart for it. For some reason, James didn't want to ask him to sit. So they just stood, looking at each other. In the last few months, James had put on a spurt of growth. He suddenly realised that he was a touch taller than Mr Longmuir. This made the situation even more bizarre. His small teacher was standing in his home looking at him.

"Mah mum'll be home soon," James managed to get out at last in a poor attempt at Proper Speak. "Did ye want to speak to her, Sir?"

He didn't know why he'd said that. It was a lie. His mother wouldn't be home for at least an hour. But he had to say something.

"No, it's all right. It was you I was worried about."

There was another awkward pause. Then breaking the spell, Mr Longmuir turned towards the door.

"Well, I'd better be going. Get well soon, and maybe till next week?"

He managed a smile. James hastened to open the door. His teacher stepped outside into the entry. He turned again.

"Goodbye, James."

"Thank you, Sir. Goodbye."

And Mr Longmuir walked off briskly up the path between the hedges and out into the street. By the time James had closed the door again and peered through the net curtains, his teacher had disappeared. Perhaps he'd parked his car somewhere nearby. James sat down on the edge of the bed and went over what had just happened. He was left with a strange taste in his mouth and it had nothing to do with his sore throat. It was weird, inexplicable. He was surprised to realise he felt guilty, as if he'd done something wrong, but he didn't know what. So he never told his parents or anyone else about the strange visit from Mr Longmuir to his sickbed. He kept it to himself. It was his secret.

He was back at school the following week. Mr Longmuir didn't particularly acknowledge him in class. He just went ahead with the lesson on the benefits of the St Lawrence Seaway in his usual diligent manner. There were only a few weeks of the term left. Up to now, James had just scraped by in geography. But this time, for some reason, he didn't bother to study for the exam. He got an E. It wasn't until he landed with a new teacher, Miss Keith, in the Third Year, that his marks improved. As for the Astronomical Society, he'd enjoyed the sessions, especially the excursions, but come the new school year he didn't return. He and Mr Longmuir never saw each other again.

James struggled to understand why he managed to keep his head above water in physics but had failed so miserably in geography, a subject that actually interested him. If he'd felt like shifting the blame, he might have said it had something to do with the teachers. For his physics teacher and new Registration Teacher, Mr Laidlaw, was nothing like Mr Longmuir. A pleasant, popular teacher in his late forties, Mr Laidlaw was tall and handsome, with a shock of greying hair that had once been black and a thin moustache. Married with a family, he had none of Mr Longmuir's strangeness about him. His no-nonsense approach worked fine for James, putting him at ease and making him feel his physics teacher was treating him just like another adult whenever they had to converse. A competent and inspiring instructor, Mr Laidlaw was one of those teachers who had no need to impose discipline in class to keep order. So respected were they, so riveting were their lessons, that their pupils disciplined themselves.

Strangely, Mr Longmuir and Mr Laidlaw did have one thing in common; they were both committed Christians. The difference was that

Mr Laidlaw strictly separated his job from his faith. No CU after school, no proselytising. He confined his Christian activities to assisting his wife, an ordained Baptist minister, at a chapel somewhere in Comely Bank. She was small and slim, with unfashionable short, black hair. She'd lost her left arm in the London Blitz as a Red Cross nurse when a building had collapsed on her. That experience had led to a life in the ministry. Mr Laidlaw always brought her to school dances. James would watch, awestruck, as they waltzed elegantly among their ungainly pupils, tall, handsome Mr Laidlaw and his petite wife, he holding the stump of her left arm, she smiling radiantly and confidently.

But there was another obvious difference between the two teachers. Unlike Mr Longmuir, Mr Laidlaw never brought his personal opinions into the classroom and in this respect, he resembled most of his colleagues. It was as if the hallowed halls of The Academy were hermetically sealed from the outside. James found this curious, for it was apparent to his young mind, fed by the articles in his father's *Daily Express*, as well as BBC news broadcasts, that events were taking place at home and abroad that could have an impact on him, his family, and the country. It was a time of change and upheaval. At least some of the teachers must have had strong opinions about what was going on. If they did, they kept them to themselves.

Henry M. Neil was a case in point. He clearly had links to the Soviet Union. That led James to assume, rightly or wrongly, that he must have had left-leaning opinions. The issue of whether he was a communist was mooted more than once in James's presence. Nor could the uninformed avoid drawing the erroneous conclusion that studying a language equalled imbibing the ideology of the people whose language it was. But in all the six years that James knew him both as a Latin and Russian teacher, Henry never expressed any personal opinions in class or attempted to influence his charges in any way. The focus was on learning the language and, to some extent, the culture. The same applied to Mr Flockhart. If anyone was likely to foist his opinions on his pupils, it would surely have been him. Amid the conjugation of French irregular verbs, the gender of French nouns, false friends and the delights of the *passé historique*, Mr Flockhart's lessons were peppered with off-the-cuff remarks and anecdotes. The risk of an opinion slipping out here and there was very real. But it never happened.

So Mr Longmuir with his tedious sermons on Denmark and his pupils' taste in music appeared to be an exception. Well, he would have been if it hadn't been for Miss Keith, James's other geography teacher. Whether it was exclusively geography teachers who had awarded themselves the monopoly for indoctrination, James had no idea. Be that as it may, Miss Keith was just as keen as Mr Longmuir to ensure her classes heard her point of view on various subjects. One of them was Mussolini. In the years before The War, Miss Keith had spent several magic summers in Italy, perfecting her Italian, touring the cultural delights of Florence, Pisa, Siena and Venice and enjoying clandestine liaisons with virile young locals. Her love of Italy and all things Italian had never left her, despite the events of 1939-45. Perhaps, as a result, Miss Keith was unable to make a secret of her admiration for Il Duce. But by the late fifties, The War had been over for over fifteen years, Mussolini's crimes unmasked and he was long dead. Yet, Miss Keith, that everlasting Italophile, persisted in her reverence.

"Did you know that Mussolini suppressed the Mafia?"

Of course they didn't, but no one had the presence of mind to say so.

"Under Il Duce, crime rates dropped and all the Mafia bosses ran off to America," she went on. "That's something you'll never read in your history books!"

Then, as if remembering that she was supposed to be teaching geography, not history, she added a more relevant titbit.

"What they never tell you is that Mussolini drained the Pontine Marshes!"

None of the class had any idea what the Pontine Marshes were or even where they were. They were marshes, right? Boggy areas full of water. So what? Nor could anyone be bothered to put up their hand and ask. They merely nodded wearily. But James had an instant mental snapshot of the bald little tyrant in wellington boots, up to his knees in water and mud down in a ditch, busy shovelling away, cursing in Italian, while Adolf Hitler, hands on hips, barking commands and hurling Germanic slurs, supervised him from dry land. As if reading his thoughts, Miss Keith's voice broke into his reverie.

"If he hadn't got mixed up with Hitler, just imagine the good he'd have done for Italy!"

Since she didn't elaborate on what that 'good' might have been, the class were left mystified. What impact Miss Keith's opinions had on her pupils it was hard to say. Anyone of James's age who showed an interest in The War knew that the Germans and the Italians had been the enemy. Why would Miss Keith be praising an arch-enemy of Britain? He had no idea. But he did wonder about Miss Keith. Unlike her colleagues, she seemed to see part of her duty as a teacher to breach that invisible cordon sanitaire between The Academy and the outside world, even if it did mean exposing her biases to her pupils. And her homilies did seem to have some basis in fact, unlike Mr Longmuir's tirades, which were merely expressions of his disapproval of his pupils' lifestyles. Was Miss

Keith trying to provoke a reaction out of them? Was she trying to make them think? Maybe, just maybe, there were two sides to every story. Maybe, just maybe, there had been a tiny bit of good in Mussolini after all. And maybe, just maybe, Miss Keith was pointing it out to force them to think beyond the obvious. Maybe.

French and Faust

Miss Ross marched into the class punctually at one minute to ten and placed her bulky brown leather briefcase on the teacher's table. She waited to ensure she had the class's attention then smiled and addressed the packed room of expectant students.

"I am Miss Ross, your new French teacher."

Most of the pupils sat up. A new French teacher after two years! James immediately catalogued her as a nice teacher. She was small of stature, in her late thirties, was wearing a Fair Isle cardigan under her academic gown and, where looks were concerned, could be placed somewhere between plain and pretty in a mousy way. She seemed a pleasant person. But, as the French B stream were to discover, she was also made of steel.

"First, we'll distribute the jotters."

She went to the class cupboard, unlocked it and, pointing to the pristine stacks inside, called on a couple of pupils in the front row to assist. Almost every subject had a dedicated jotter with the unforgettable designation *Edinburgh Corporation Education Committee* ingrained in the grey cover in the usual large, unmissable, bold black letters. The French jotters were of the standard type with lined pages and no margin. The geography jotters had a mix of lined pages, blank pages, and pages of graph paper. The science jotters were similar to the geography jotters inside, but had hardcovers, were thicker and were referred to as 'lab books', which James found extraordinarily exciting. He always felt important when he had to say something like, "Ah just need to get mah lab book" or "Where's mah lab book?" Then there were the music jotters, which had lined pages, blank pages, and, of course, pages of manuscript for musical notation. For French, each pupil got two jotters. Miss Ross's helpers had each taken half the room and were busy distributing them.

While that was happening, Miss Ross picked up a piece of chalk and turned to the blackboard. She drew a vertical line on the left-hand side, neatly separating a third of the surface area from the rest. In this upright rectangle, she proceeded to write a heading in block capitals: *HOMEWORK FOR THE WEEK*, reaching up from her small stature to the very top of the blackboard to do so. She turned back to the class, who, most with their new jotters open and pens and pencils poised, were looking at her expectantly like eager secretaries about to take shorthand for their bosses.

"Every Monday," she explained in an equally businesslike manner, "I will write up your homework on the board. You will copy it down. That will be your programme for the week." She paused and looked around the upturned faces of her new scholars, who were just beginning to grasp the mettle of Miss Ross. "I will be personally correcting some of your homework and recording the marks."

Furtive looks and murmuring from the class. Well, this was something new! Miss Ross turned back to the board and, referring to the notebook in her left hand, she proceeded to write up the homework for the five days of that week, the book title, pages so-and-so, exercise so-and-so, numbers so-and-so. As he copied down Miss Ross's homework programme, James couldn't hide his admiration. No other teacher did this, not even Henry. No other teacher gave them the entire homework programme a week in advance, and written down too. He immediately grasped what this told him about Miss Ross. She knew exactly what she was going to teach in each period – all six of them. She knew exactly how far she'd get in the allotted time. And she knew how much homework she could expect from the class. No other teacher was so well organised. Usually, at the end of the lesson when the bell had started to ring, the teacher would throw the evening's homework at them through the clanging and the babble:

"For tomorrow, do page 35, Exercise 6!"

"What did he say? Page 55?"

Not Miss Ross. Those first few minutes with her amounted to a microcosm of her method. A careful, meticulous instructor who demanded application and industry from her charges, she clearly visualised her task as being the elevation of these second-raters to the first-rate. They were all suffering from the same malady. Strong medicine was needed. She was the remedy, or her methods were, for weak scholars needed structure.

The Third Year, with its new subjects, new teachers and differentiated classes was certainly a brave new world for James. It was as if another door had opened. It was still The Academy, yes, but everything else was different. A major change was the reorganisation of the French class into an A and a B stream. The A stream, taught by Mr Flockhart, were the high flyers from several classes, including Eric and the rest of the 1a1/2a1 class elite. The B stream consisted of the mediocre rest. Naturally, James found himself in the B stream with Miss Ross. As James was to discover, she was the antithesis of Mr Flockhart. He was disorganised; she definitely was not. He was distracted; she was focused. He tended not to prepare his lessons; she did. This wasn't to say that Mr Flockhart was a bad teacher. Far from it. But it was obvious to James that he winged it, making an impact more by his personality, humour and inventiveness than by a methodical approach to his work, unlike Miss Ross. The difference couldn't have been more marked.

There were two types of homework; pencil homework and ink homework. That's why they'd each received two jotters. The pencil homework would be done from Monday to Thursday in their pencil jotters. This homework would be checked mostly in class, either casually by Miss Ross, by the pupils themselves, or by swapping jotters with a neighbour. Occasionally, she might collect some of it for marking. Ink homework was to be done over the weekend in their ink jotters. This was usually more substantial. Since Miss Ross would be collecting it every Monday morning for marking, and since it would count towards their final grade, it had to be done in ink.

The Academy had already abandoned the wooden-handled, nibbed pens and inkwells that had still been in regular use at Fox Crag Primary. The vacant round holes at the right-hand corner of every desk were mute reminders of the impact of obsolescence. Here, pupils now had fountain pens filled from their private bottles of ink purchased at the local stationers. Some had the more practical cartridge pens. A few even possessed the newer ballpoint pens, but these were frowned on by the more traditional sort of teacher who stipulated fountain pens for ink homework, and no argument. Miss Ross, being a bit more progressive, allowed either.

For that first year and the one following, she drove the class in her quiet, single-minded way. She checked their homework as she'd warned. She called on them in class and made them repeat the words over and over until they got the pronunciation right. She patiently explained the grammar and drilled them in it, as well as springing regular vocabulary tests. And she never once had to resort to The Belt. James doubted if she even possessed one. Most of them thrived under her tutelage, James included. He was learning more, faster, and everything was clearer than with Mr Flockhart. The sharp increase in the class average mark by the end of the year was evidence of her efficacy.

But Miss Ross had one weakness. It was obvious to James and he wondered if it was obvious to anyone else. The fact was that Miss Ross had a crush on Mr Flockhart. When they were together, discussing admin matters in the classroom or bumping into each other in the corridor or at an assembly, she openly made cow eyes at him. When, as Head of Department, he walked into the classroom during one of her lessons, she got all flustered, not because she was worried about being observed. Of course not. It was just because *he* was there. She couldn't help it, nor could she disguise it.

For his part, Mr Flockhart, with an unusual accumulation of denseness in one so intellectually gifted, appeared oblivious of the fact that he had an admirer so close by. After all, he was happily married to Esmée, with three almost-grown-up children. So, her love unrequited, despite the fact that that was the respectable thing, Miss Ross was left to suffer in silence. Except that she took every opportunity to praise Mr Flockhart to the skies in the public space that was the classroom and to her captive audience of pupils.

"Mr Flockhart is a very intelligent man, you know."

"Mr Flockhart studied at the Sorbonne. Now, who can tell me what that is and where it is?"

"During The War, Mr Flockhart was engaged in something very hush-hush in France."

James was left to wonder what she meant. Had Mr Flockhart been in the French Underground? Come to think of it, he did look very French with his straggly black hair, bushy eyebrows, bushy moustache, conspiratorial smile and whimsical ways. Even his shoulder shrugs had a Gallic quality. All that was missing was the stereotypical French beret.

One Monday at 10 am, Miss Ross came into class with an indescribable expression on her face. It was a mixture of rapture and excitement. James thought she'd had some sort of religious experience. Or won the football pools. Though he could never imagine Miss Ross doing the football pools. She put her bag down on the teacher's desk, turned to the class and gulped hard. She was obviously about to make an announcement. This was unprecedented. Pupils looked at each other in wonderment. Where was the week's homework programme to be chalked up on the blackboard, the priority every single Monday morning? What Miss Ross was about to say must be very important indeed. She immediately had their attention.

"From today," she announced, breathlessly, "you must not call Mr Flockhart *Mr Flockhart* any more."

She paused. For a moment, James was baffled. *Not call him Mr Flockhart? Has he changed his name*? But that wasn't it.

"From today," Miss Ross continued, struggling to contain her emotions, "if you address him, you must call him *Doctor*! Yes, he is now *Doctor* Flockhart!"

A doctor? thought James. *Does that mean I can go to him if I'm ill?* But his question was immediately answered, for Moira Buchanan had shot up her hand.

"Please, Miss," she asked, "he's not a medical doctor, is he? Doesn't it mean that Mr – Ah mean *Doctor* – Flockhart now has his *Pee Aitch Dee*?"

"Yes, that's right, Moira," replied Miss Ross, nodding eagerly. "His dissertation on *Marcel Pagnol's conceptualisation of social rituals in a cinematographic dramatisation of Lettres de Mon Moulin by Alphonse Daudet* was examined last week in a viva voce at Edinburgh University. He passed with flying colours and is now a Doctor of Philosophy!"

After all that, she had to pause to catch her breath. James thought she was going to have some sort of seizure. He didn't have a clue what she'd just said or what it meant, but it certainly sounded important, especially when she mixed English, French and Latin words together like that in a single sentence. Nor did he fully understand what a *Pee Aitch Dee* was, but he wondered if one day he'd have one. Whatever the case, now that Mr Flockhart was *Doctor* Flockhart – or *Doc Flock*, as he was instantly dubbed by his pupils – it was clear that Miss Ross was more than ever head over heels in love with him. Poor Miss Ross. James fervently hoped that one day she'd be helped to get over her infatuation by some nice young man, perhaps another *Pee Aitch Dee,* otherwise she was inevitably destined, as his mother would put it, to become an auld maid in a garret.

Despite her unique vulnerability, James felt a strange attachment to Miss Ross. He couldn't explain why. She never paid special attention to him. She wasn't particularly attractive or engaging. Unlike Doc Flock, she never contrived silly in-jokes like *Why are a French sailor's trousers like French towns? Answer: Too Loose and Too Long*. She never taught them French songs like 'Alouette'. She never told anecdotes about French food or wine, French life or her visits to France. No, she did none of these. Nevertheless, what she did do worked, at least for the heap of no-hopers in the French B stream and especially for James.

After that first year of Miss Ross, they discovered that they'd continue with her into the Fourth Year. She'd prepare them for the dreaded Scottish Certificate of Education O-Level French examination, the first they, or any pupil in Scotland for that matter, would ever sit. Whether James passed or not would be largely up to Miss Ross. But later in life he was to discover a strange thing. He could speak and understand French. Several times in France, in Alsace or Haute Savoie, he'd find himself in spontaneous conversations in shops, in cafés, in the street, using the right words, remembering the grammar, speaking confidently. It was inexplicable. Where did it come from? He had no idea. But one thing he did know. It was Miss Ross who'd put it there.

If Miss Ross was the epitome of organisation, Miss Goudie was the epitome of disorganisation. If Miss Ross was an example of a competent teacher, Miss Goudie was, unfortunately, not. That wasn't to say that she wasn't a nice person. She was. Very nice, in fact. The problem was that she was too nice. Miss Goudie was, for most of his time at The Academy, James's music teacher. But her lessons, if they could be called that, were so disordered that even someone who enjoyed music as much as James learned little from her. Miss Goudie attempted to teach them musical theory in her grand studio on the third floor of The Academy building, she on the stage with her Bechstein, the rest of the class seated in the mini-auditorium. However, she was stymied by pupils who appeared to regard the weekly period of music instruction as a waste of time and an excuse merely for a skive-off from serious study. Disrespectful and distracted, they'd disrupt the lesson with titters and giggles while poor Miss Goudie attempted to keep order. Typically, the session would descend into chaos.

James felt sorry for her. How could this happen here at The Academy? How could normally self-disciplined scholars behave like this? James decided there was a simple reason. For music, there was no examination, not even the odd test to keep the class in line. So, to preserve her sanity, Miss Goudie would abandon the Bechstein and put on a classical record instead, and the scholars would calm down under the spell of one of the masters. Thus did Miss Goudie manage to tame the beast and thus did James learn to appreciate Ravel's *Bolero*. But Miss Goudie did have one saving grace. Like Mr Longmuir, she was more successful outside the classroom than inside. Outside, she came into her own. She organised concerts. She ran the school choir. She even directed small operas. One day in the autumn term of James's second year, fifteen minutes from the end of the lesson, she dismissed the girls. Then, turning to the remaining boys, whose curiosity was well aroused, she proceeded to tell them that they were going to be in an opera.

"Edinburgh Operatic Society is putting on Gounod's *Faust* in Leith Town Hall. They need a Soldier's Chorus. You will be it."

She didn't ask them. She told them. Grandly designated The Academy Junior Boys' Choir, together with boys from other second-year classes they'd take the stage and strut their stuff in front of a large audience of Edinburgh's finest. It didn't seem to matter whether they could sing or not. That wasn't an issue. Just being there and opening their mouths was the issue. James was terrified. He hated having to do things in public. The thought of hundreds of people staring at him scared the pants off him, but it seemed he had no choice. Reluctantly, he dragged himself along to rehearsals after school in the studio, where a very different Miss Goudie first had them each 'sing' a few bars solo as she played chords on her piano. James enjoyed singing in Chapel. Belting out 'Onward Christian Soldiers' was exhilarating. But in Chapel, he could hide among the congregation. Having to stand up and sing solo in front of thirty or so sniggering boys was the most nerve-wracking thing he'd ever done. At least there was an outcome; he discovered for the first time that he was a tenor, whatever that was.

Then they had the elements of 'Glory and Love to the Men of Old' drummed into them. At least, thundering out the song again and again did have a beneficial effect; it helped to get rid of your inhibitions. The choreography was next, if it could be called that. They were summoned to the school gym after school. There, under the joint command of Hammy and Miss Merrylegs, they were drilled in the required movements - the entrance, the gestures, the exit. After several weeks, Miss Goudie joined them at the piano in the corner of the gym and they put words and music to the movements, marching and singing ad nauseam until finally she pronounced that she was satisfied. They were ready for a rehearsal on a real stage. Though James had been squeamish at first, he was surprised to find that he was gradually beginning to enjoy the whole thing. Together, the boys and the teachers had created something out of nothing. It was a miracle.

But there was better to come: the first dress rehearsal in the newly constituted Leith Town Hall. It was a Saturday afternoon in early December. James had never been in anything approaching a real theatre before. He was bombarded by an abundance of new experiences. As the boys trooped sheepishly into the auditorium shepherded by a solicitous Miss Goudie, they were welcomed warmly by their fellow amateur performers of the Operatic Society. After all, what would *Faust* be without 'The Soldiers' Chorus'? Probably relieved that the key missing element of their oeuvre had at last turned up, the cast plied them with kindness and care. James was entranced. He was suddenly part of a troupe of glamorous artistes. He'd never been among such people before. Then to be backstage, to be schooled in all the little rules, the practices, the etiquette of the theatre. To sit and wait your turn in a corner of the stalls, mesmerised by the rehearsals going on, the stage directions, the singing, the lights, the curtain, finally understanding how the contribution of The Academy Junior Boys' Choir fitted into the overall performance under the guidance of the energetic, long-haired young director.

There were two full dress rehearsals. During these, The Academy boys became acquainted with their costumes, puffy red and blue uniforms with matching floppy hats. For the first time in his life, James was made up for the stage. His make-up person was a black-haired actress in her thirties with devilish eyes. Only his mother had ever held her face so close to his before and he was flustered at first by her careful attentions, the scent of her skin, the shape of her eyebrows, the curve of her nose. He blushed under the greasepaint. But then, suddenly, at the tender age of thirteen, he found that he was beginning to enjoy it. He felt a stirring inside him. It became hard to sit still. He was glad when it was over but then discovered a feeling of regret. He was looking forward to the next time.

When he'd told his parents he was going to be in an opera their reactions had been understandable. Since James had started at The Academy, they'd vicariously shared all the new and strange adventures that had come his way. Just as it was for him, it was for them a different world. In their rushed and stolen lives, up to now, their only link to the theatre might have been the odd occasion when they were able to afford a seat in the stalls at The Gaiety or The King's. But now, here was their son, actually in an opera. Janet, of course, couldn't help herself.

"Well, ye ken mah James. It's amazin' what 'e gets up tae at The Academy. Now 'e's in an opera!"

By the day of the first performance, James's imminent fame must have been known to half of Leith and a goodly chunk of Edinburgh. Of course, Ian and Janet had to be there. The parents of the boys got special concession tickets and there was even one for Auntie Effie. The big night came. That first performance, James was crushed with nerves, but it helped to be one of thirty. They simply did what they'd been trained to do. He stood on the stage, singing his heart out, staring through the stage lights at what seemed to be a thousand faces in the packed auditorium, marched off the stage with the others to rapturous applause, then wondered what he'd been so worried about. Meanwhile, Janet, well back in the stalls, struggled to pick out her son from among the thirty identical youthful medieval warriors returning from battle in war paint and floppy uniforms. She kept bothering Effie.

"That's him, third frae the left!" she claimed in a loud whisper, nudging her sister with her elbow. Then, "Naw, it isnae, that's him fourth frae the right!"

Anyway, it didn't matter. Their son was somewhere there, in the chorus. He'd performed in an opera. They couldn't have been more proud as they stood around on the pavement outside, their breath condensing in the frosty air, discussing and critiquing the performance, most of which had gone right over their heads. *Faust* wasn't exactly *The White Heather Club*.

Looking back, James was grateful to Miss Goudie. She'd given him something new, something unique, yet another exploit to tuck under his Academy belt. He almost forgave her her pointless, anarchic lessons, for he did like music. But he wished that somewhere along the way she could have managed to teach him something to help him understand music better. It might have come in handy some time.

In the remedial class

Late again Mister Briggs?" barked Mr McCluskie as he whirled round from the blackboard, the ends of his black academic gown swirling round the trousered legs of his bespoke Burton's suit. His familiar sardonic tones hovered over the heads of the Third Year Remedial Mathematics class, who were already bent over their jotters, copying their teacher's workings from the blackboard. James risked a glance over his shoulder. There was Gordon Briggs, swinging his canvas schoolbag, Academy uniform dishevelled, top button of his shirt undone, tie loose, his face betraying the fact that he'd been caught in flagrante as he attempted to slide unnoticed into a desk in the back row.

As usual, Mr McCluskie's aim was spot on. The piece of chalk, only just out of its box, all of three inches, spinning end over end, struck Gordon squarely at the point where his unruly red hair flopped over his forehead. Mr McCluskie's feat was all the more remarkable, for he'd launched his projectile precisely while Gordon's torso was still in sideways motion, much as a surface-to-air guided missile is programmed to hit an incoming rocket. Gordon flopped onto the seat as if nothing untoward had happened. The chalk rebounded, executed a perfect curve, dropped onto the wooden desk then rolled onto the wooden floor, breaking neatly into two unequal pieces in the process.

“Well,” said Mr McCluskie impatiently, “bring it back!”

Gordon got up again, retrieved the two pieces of chalk, and, walking to the front of the class, obediently placed them on the teacher’s desk. Turning, he winked humourlessly at the class and returned to his place.

“Right,” said Mr McCluskie, apparently satisfied with his penalty for lateness, “now, where were we? Ah yes, isosceles triangles!” and he turned back to the board.

James had never been any good at maths. Arithmetic was no problem. Ian had always excelled at mental arithmetic, dazzling James with his speedy calculations. Somehow, James had inherited a modicum of that faculty. But when it came to maths, he was a hopeless case. He didn’t know why. He just didn’t get it. From the very first week in the First Year, there had been separate arithmetic and mathematics classes. The former was merely an extension of what he’d done in primary school and never fazed him. But algebra and geometry? And it would only get worse. Later would come trigonometry, then the dreaded calculus. They were like foreign languages he’d never been taught but was supposed, instinctively, to understand. In class, maths seemed to be merely an endless series of ‘problems’ which, somehow, you were expected to solve. It wasn’t so bad if he could see the point of the problem:

Refer to the diagram, which depicts Mr Smith’s yard. He wishes to concrete the yard to a depth of 1½ feet. Referring to the dimensions and angles of a trapezium, calculate, 1) how many cubic feet of concrete Mr Smith needs for the job and 2) the cost of the job excluding labour if concrete costs £2 7s 11½d per cubic foot.

Well, this sort of thing almost made sense. But when he was confronted with a jumble of letters, *a, b, c, d,* minus, plus, multiplication and division signs, all enclosed in a maze of brackets and equals signs, then given the dreaded task, *Solve for x,* he just didn’t have a clue. The marks on his report card told the story: 47%; 39%; even 24%.

Janet had wondered if it had something to do with her son’s one-year-plus age deficit. Without asking him, she’d arranged some private tuition with an Edinburgh University student she happened to know. Josephine, a pretty blonde in her early twenties, lived with her parents in a council flat in Boswall Parkway. James had gone along with his mother’s suggestion, surprised at her unexpected zeal on his behalf. But as he knocked at the door of Josephine’s parents’ flat with the blue chintz curtains and was let in by complete strangers, he found it hard to conceal his feelings of embarrassment. The hour-long lessons had been held upstairs in Jo’s cramped bedroom. James had never been in a girl’s bedroom before, apart from his sister’s, and he couldn’t help being on tenterhooks the whole time he was there. Everything was pink and soft and fluffy and tidy, and seemed completely ill-suited to the study of Pythagoras and quadratic equations. He'd sit there at her desk, maths textbook open, feeling especially clueless in the presence of a girl, while Jo, by his side, did her best to make him see. But he just couldn't see, despite her valiant efforts. So, each time they ended a lesson and he laid two crumpled pound notes on her bedside cabinet, he felt even worse, for he knew he was flushing his mother's hard-earned cash down the drain. And so it went on, week after week, until it was obvious that no improvement was forthcoming, and the lessons stopped.

The inevitable repercussion came in the Third Year when, in addition to remedial chemistry, he found himself relegated to 3rm1, a remedial maths class. To add insult to injury, lessons were held on the third floor of a dingy school annexe in an abandoned classroom cluttered with broken desks and chairs. By the looks of it, it hadn't seen a cleaning lady since Dunkirk. James got the point loud and clear; remedials were unfit to mix with the rest of The Academy.

Even worse was to come when the outcasts learned that their new maths instructor was to be Mr McCluskie, for his notoriety was second only to that of Duggie Dunbar, the Terror of the Technical Stream. In his forties, Mr McCluskie was equally large and imposing, with floppy black hair and a square, clean-shaven jaw. He could have been a boxer or a rugby player in a former life. His academic gown only served to accentuate his size. But the similarity didn't end there, for Mr McCluskie was just as fearsome as Duggie. There were, however, two differences. Mr McCluskie had a rich sense of humour, albeit warped, and he seldom belted. The fact was that he didn't need to belt, for his tongue was his belt. Many a pupil had been reduced to a quivering wreck by his quick wit, biting sarcasm, cruel mockery and targeted ridicule, all delivered in an educated Morningside accent. And curiously, Mr McCluskie's penchant for addressing his male victims as "Mister" only served to render the sarcasm all that more delicious.

As well, Mr McCluskie had developed a second belting substitute. It was throwing. Mr McCluskie threw things at his troublesome pupils, much in the style of Duggie Dunbar, but more frequently and more imaginatively. In addition to blackboard dusters, he threw chalk. He threw pencils (particularly hazardous when they'd just been sharpened). He threw biros. He threw jotters. He threw crumpled up pieces of paper. He even, once, threw a maths textbook at someone. Fortunately, it missed, which was unusual, for his aim was normally unerring. Perhaps he'd misjudged the unaccustomed weight or the dynamic properties of a four-hundred-page hardback book in flight. The only thing he didn't throw was his prized packet of sandwiches, carefully wrapped in greaseproof paper and an elastic band, which sat on his desk throughout his lessons, awaiting their inevitable fate in the staff room during the midday break. No one in the class escaped his scathing tongue; few escaped his aim. One of the few was James. Taciturn, tractable and well-behaved, he was fearful enough of Mr McCluskie to avoid becoming a target of one of his guided missiles. He simply kept his mouth shut, never put his hand up, copied down what Mr McCluskie chalked on the blackboard and heaved a sigh of relief when each period was over. So successful were these techniques that Mr McCluskie had almost forgotten that James existed.

But as James gazed sideways through the massive grimy windows that had last been cleaned in Edwardian times into the gloom of a Leith morning, another thing puzzled him. Why were there no girls in the class? Were they all so much better at maths than boys? Or had the powers that be, aware of Mr McC's propensity for flinging, lobbing and hurling, not to mention ridicule, decided to keep girls out of harm's way? Whatever the answer, the fact was that the fifteen or so third-year boys were now hostage to at least a year of Mr McCluskie, and possibly two, unless, that was, they were able to improve their maths marks to a level that would see them re-assigned to a normal class.

William Ludwig, known to his pals as Billywig, was one of them. He was a tall, sturdy laddie who'd easily found a place in The Academy First XV. Billywig was happiest covered in mud, head down in a scrum or with folded arms, looking tough, in the annual First XV photograph published in the school magazine. The one thing he was definitely not happy about was maths and particularly being in the remedial maths class. James had thought himself a hopeless case where maths was concerned but he soon realised that Billywig was a strong contender to beat him to the bottom. James wondered how he'd passed the Qualy and concluded that it had either been a clerical error, his prowess at rugby, or shenanigans along the way that had permitted him entry to the scholastic Nirvana that was The Academy. At any rate, Billywig's asinine grasp of maths was to Mr McCluskie like a French railway bridge to a Stuka dive bomber. Day after day, he'd home in on his target, unfailingly calling on Billywig to stand up and reveal to the class his solution to the homework problem.

"Come on Mr Ludwig, get your wig on, take your place at the bench, m'lud, and delight us with the power of your brains!"

Billywig would stand there like a deer caught in a spotlight, aware that no end of rugby practice, no end of scrums and no end of line-outs would help him now. Unable to dance to Mr McCluskie's tune, he'd stutter and stammer his way through his algebra equations. James, forced by circumstance to bear witness, would merely be relieved that it wasn't *his* head on the block, this time at least. Eventually Billywig would be allowed to sit down, leaving the field to his tormentor.

"Next time you come to class Mr Ludwig, remember to bring your brains with you!"

Kenny Hutchinson was quite a different kettle of fish. He was a Cliff Richard lookalike, but unlike Bruce C. Magnus he didn't have to try very hard, for with his dark, slicked-back hair, his smooth cheeks and agreeable features, he really could have passed for Cliff if you half closed your eyes. He was like Cliff, too, in stature, slight and delicately made, and certainly no Billywig, either, where physique or brains were concerned. The strange thing about Kenny, however, was that, if you were to believe his stories, he was the Lothario of Leith if not Edinburgh itself. For Kenny, although he could only have been fifteen-going-on-sixteen at most, claimed to have regular sexual encounters at weekends. Come Monday, while waiting for class to start, he'd lean back in his seat and regale his near neighbours with tales of his exploits and those of his pals in the mean streets of the City.

It seemed that Kenny's favourite locale was Rose Street, particularly of a Friday or Saturday night, and all the drunken chaos that abounded there, for Rose Street was said to have more pubs per mile than any other street in Edinburgh. Kenny and his mates, though very junior teenagers, would hang around the action like Serengeti jackals on the edge of a feeding frenzy, not only taking every opportunity to drink illegally but also darting in to take advantage of whatever, or whomever they could. And this 'taking advantage' often seemed to involve some sort of sexual activity. James, barely fourteen himself, didn't really grasp much of the detail of what Kenny told his classmates and, truth to tell, found his stories far-fetched in the mouth of someone so junior. But they seemed to have a lot to do with drunken women, particularly older women, maybe even prostitutes, up back alleys, and up against walls, and they didn't seem particularly savoury.

It was when Kenny turned up in class with the latest copy of *Reveille* that things took an unusual turn. Availing himself of the delay while the maths teacher made it all the way from the main building to the annexe, Kenny amused himself by displaying to the rest of the boys what was to be found on page 3. It was a photograph of Sophia Loren taken from the waist up. And what a photograph... Of course, she was smiling sexily into the camera, but it wasn't just her smile that captured the boys' imagination. No, no. It was, of course, Sophia's magnificent, braless breasts, the tops of which bulged out of the décolleté of the skimpy white cotton dress, pulling the slender straps taut against her tanned shoulders, and leaving little to the imagination as to their size and shape. It would be fair to say that that morning there was a general erection in class, despite the fact that several of the boys were barely into puberty. Grinning like a champion sportsman displaying his trophy, Kenny was so intent on the effect Sophia's breasts had on his classmates that he failed to look behind him. The Stuka dived and Kenny's *Reveille*, together with Sophia, was in the firm grasp of Mr McCluskie.

For a moment, there were shocked looks all round. Then, when Mr McCluskie strode to the front of the class, still clutching the offending article, the shock turned to surprise, for the expected tirade about their lack of morals never materialised. Instead, Mr McCluskie put down his bag on the table, took the *Reveille* in both hands, gazed at the photograph of Sophia with something akin to admiration, then spoke in his usual caustic tones.

"Mr Hutchinson, stand up."

Kenny obeyed reluctantly.

Mr McCluskie then held up the *Reveille*, displaying Sophia's picture for the whole class to see. Suddenly there were grins all round as they were permitted, yet again, to look on the delights of the Italian goddess. They leaned forward eagerly over their desks. This was undoubtedly the best start to a maths period ever.

"Mr Hutchinson, since you are so keen to show us Miss Loren's, mmm... spherical assets, perhaps you'd be so kind as to remind us, what is the formula for the volume of a sphere?"

Kenny, still pale from the shock loss of his pin-up photo but beginning to surmise that the situation might not be so bad after all, was speechless for, unsurprisingly, he didn't know the answer. After allowing sufficient of a pregnant pause and receiving no response, Mr McCluskie spoke again.

"Anyone?" he said, looking around fourteen upturned heads.

Pawel Przbylski – of course, it had to be him – put up his hand.

"Yes, stand up Mr... Bilski." The maths teacher still hadn't mastered the pronunciation of Pawel's surname. "Pray do provide us with the fruits of your Polish education."

"Please, Sir, it's four over three times pi times the radius cubed," stated Pawel, confidently.

"Quite correct. Well done, Mr Bilski. Sit down."

Still holding up the photo of Sophia, he turned back to Kenny.

"Now, Mr Hutchinson, you will do some special homework. Sit down, get out your maths jotter and start writing."

Kenny did as he was told, self-conscious under the gaze of both class and teacher, and looking up apprehensively when he was ready.

"After class, you will get Mr Bilski here to write down for you the formula for the volume of a sphere. Then, by tomorrow, you will calculate the volume of each of Miss Loren's, er... spheres! You may make three assumptions. One, that her spheres are actually spheres. Two, that they are identical in size. And three, you may make an assumed calculation of their radius. But it must be realistic! You will present the solution to the class tomorrow, together with your working. Do you understand?"

Kenny nodded, still pale and still dumbstruck.

"Any failure on your part to complete this task will result in three of the best from me and a week's detention. Understood?"

Kenny nodded. Mr McCluskie closed the pages of the *Reveille* and placed it carefully on his desk for future perusal, followed closely by the fourteen pairs of eyes, their owners still on the edge of their seats at this unexpected hiatus in what was usually a thoroughly boring morning. Then Kenny put up his hand. Mr McClusky looked at him wordlessly with arched eyebrows.

"Sir, Ah cannae do the homework without the picture!"

Mr McCluskie arched his eyebrows even further.

"Tae calculate the radius Ah mean, Sir!"

Shaking his head in exasperation, the teacher picked up the *Reveille* from his desk, rolled it up, and threw it at Kenny, bouncing it off the top of his head and messing up his pristine Cliff Richard coiffure. In confusion, Kenny bent down from his seat, picked it up, thrust it into his schoolbag and did his best to rearrange his hair sans comb. Then a thought seemed to strike Mr McCluskie, who was already in the throes of selecting a fresh piece of chalk from a green cardboard packet, preparatory to resuming his board work. He looked at Kenny again.

"Mr Hutchinson, am I correct in thinking that I saw you in Rose Street last Friday evening?"

The boys' faces turned from the residue of mild amusement back to shock again. What? Kenny was by far the worst affected. He'd thought the worst was past. Now things had just gone from worst to even worster. Instantly, Mr McCluskie's question implied two things to the remedials, who were hanging onto every word like a Greek chorus. First, that he himself frequented Rose Street on Friday nights. The knowledge zipped through their collective heads like a buzz saw with all the potential ramifications, one of them being that Mr McCluskie had a particular lifestyle, one that must involve booze, and perhaps even other things... And second, Mr McCluskie had a fair idea of what Kenny was up to there. It was the second that was most damaging. Mr McCluskie knew about Kenny, his pack of pals, his underage drinking and maybe even his sexual exploits? This was major. This was earth-shattering. This changed everything!

Speechless again, Kenny just nodded his head.

"I take it, Mr Hutchinson, that your parents are aware of where you hang out of a Friday evening and what you do there?"

Kenny said nothing but his expression said it all.

"It would be a shame, Mr Hutchinson, if they ever found out, wouldn't it?"

Game, set and match. A devastated Kenny lowered his Cliff Richard forehead, together with the little kiss curl, onto the cool wooden surface of the desk and left it there for several moments. All that was left was for the lesson to get underway – at last.

"All right, homework out on your desks!"

Kenny was never the same again. No more Monday morning revelations, no more Sophia in class, no more nonsense. He became a model pupil, almost as invisible as James, and that was saying something.

But one model pupil who certainly wasn't invisible was Pawel Przbylski. Pawel was, to put it mildly, a paradox. The paradox lay in the mystery of why he was in this class at all, for he was, relative to the rest of the no-hopers in the remedial maths class, very smart. Contrary to what Mr McCluskie imagined, Pawel had never had a Polish education. In fact, he'd never been in Poland. Instead, he'd been born in Scotland to a Scottish mother and a Polish father, another refugee from the country that had been carved up between the Fascist and Soviet empires. If anyone could answer one of Mr McCluskie's awkward questions, it was Pawel. If anyone got top marks in tests, it was Pawel. If anyone was the best-behaved pupil in class, it was Pawel.

So why was he here? Why wasn't he in the normal maths stream? After observing Pawel for some time, James had come to a startling conclusion. Pawel was here because he wanted to be here. Pawel preferred to be a rainbow trout among minnows than a minnow among rainbow trout. Pawel knew that, if placed in a class of dimwits, he could only shine. As a result, he'd fabricated poor marks and got himself into the remedial class. Pawel had worked out that what happened between now and the O-Levels at the end of the Fourth Year didn't matter as long as he was presented for the examination by the school. And that would certainly happen. He'd make sure of it in the 'mock' that everyone would have to take. So, in the meantime, he wouldn't be stressed out having to compete with the likes of Eric or Drinda in a crowded classroom among the crème de la crème. Here, among outcasts, there was no competition. Here, he could relax and be top dog. And that was fine by him.

There was another side to the puzzle, though. Mr McCluskie was fully aware of Pawel's obvious mathematical talents. Why didn't he just bump him up to the normal class at the first opportunity? James thought about that too and came to another startling conclusion. Mr McCluskie wanted to keep Pawel in the class because he was Pawel. He was the one bright jewel in a pile of dross. It must have been disheartening for the teacher to have to work with a class of dunces, day in, day out. Having at least one half-decent pupil in the class was sure to make his life more interesting. It was also possible that Mr McCluskie guessed exactly what Pawel was up to and why. If that was true, what was going on amounted to a symbiotic relationship. Both sides were happy. Or at least that's what James concluded. He often wondered if he was right.

But there was someone who wasn't a model and probably never could be. It's said that for every teacher there's at least one pupil in the class that is the bane of that teacher's life, and in Class 3rm1, for Mr McCluskie, that pupil was Gordon Briggs. Or perhaps it would be more accurate to say that Mr McCluskie was the bane of Gordon's life. Whatever the matter, every maths lesson inevitably included fireworks of some sort or other when both were together under the same roof. Whether it was absence, lateness, talking, grinning, not paying attention, forgetting his maths jotter, not doing his homework or not knowing the formula for the volume of a cylinder, Gordon would be in for it from Mr McCluskie as either ridicule or a missile or both were directed his way.

"Mr Briggs," the maths teacher would say, "you will never amount to anything in life. You will pass your days working as a Corporation scaffic, sweeping the gutters and picking up rubbish!"

Gordon's response was, oddly, stoic. He just took it. He never seemed to get upset. He allowed the waves of Mr McCluskie's displeasure to break over him as if he were the Penny Bap at an incoming tide. And the more unaffected he seemed to be, the more belligerent Mr McCluskie became. Somehow, it seemed that for Gordon there was no way out except to toe the line. James couldn't understand it. Gordon clearly wasn't stupid, so why couldn't he get to class on time? Why did he persistently forget his jotter and the formula for the volume of a cylinder? What was wrong with him? The strange thing was, Mr McCluskie's prediction about Gordon seemed to be uncannily in keeping with Gordon's background.

James knew this for the simple reason that he was already acquainted with Gordon, though he assumed Gordon wasn't acquainted with *him*. Gordon had been in a class a year ahead of James at

Bonnybrig. He had come to seven-year-old James's notice because, even then, he was always getting into trouble. As well, James had occasionally seen Gordon in the streets around Leith wielding the very same type of hard-bristled brush and shovel used by Edinburgh Corporation scaffies, for Gordon's father was a ragman. He collected, on his horse-drawn cart, rags and all sorts of junk from around Leith. In return, you could get something for the bairns like an inflated balloon, a goldfish in a jar, or a birlie. And the reason for Gordon's brush and shovel was to clean up after Cuddie the horse whenever the quadruped decided it was time to evacuate his bowels.

James never forgot his first sight of Gordon as he stood in the middle of the little road that connected Brecon Street to Bonnybrig Road, shovelling horse's doovers, as they were known locally, into a battered metal bucket, a grim expression on his young face, as passers-by glanced at him, some sympathetic, others disdainful. On reflection, he found it hard to believe Gordon was somehow rehearsing for the kind of future Mr McCluskie had in mind for him. Nor was he sanitising the highway merely to satisfy the City Fathers of Edinburgh as to the state of their roads. No, there was quite another reason. For horse's doovers were gold. Good money could be made selling them by the bucket load to the well-off gardeners of Trinity for their roses and prize tomatoes. In 1950s Edinburgh it was the ultimate in recycling.

And now, here Gordon was, at The Academy. It was a testament to the system and Gordon himself that the son of a lowly ragman could pass the Qualy at Bonnybrig and get into such a prestigious grammar school. But he was now in the same year as James, although he clearly looked older than anyone else in the class. This could only mean that somewhere along the way he'd repeated a year. Perhaps, thought James, that accounted for his truculence. Or did his background have something to do with it? Had his father somehow kept him off school and made him work instead?

Whatever the reason, as the weeks went by, James looked on while Gordon endured everything that Mr McCluskie threw at him, metaphorical or otherwise. Then suddenly, one day in June 1961, towards the end of the academic year, the throwing stopped, both metaphorical and literal. It gradually dawned on James that in the past week or so neither missiles nor verbal barbs had gone Gordon's way. It wasn't that he'd changed. He was just the same tardy, forgetful, inattentive pupil that he'd been before, but now it didn't seem to matter. The rest of the class weren't so lucky, as Mr McCluskie now switched his whimsical vitriol and his aerial bombardments onto new targets. James was puzzled. Why was the maths teacher leaving Gordon alone? There must be a reason for it. It was two weeks later that he found out what it was.

As luck would have it, he and Gordon were forced to share a urinal in the boys' toilet one day during the midday break. For once, James had stayed at school with a packet of sandwiches for his playpiece because there would be no one home at 68 Chesser Drive today. As they pretended to wash their soapless hands at neighbouring wash hand basins under the trickle of cold water, James happened to look up at Gordon's reflection in the mirror. He was astonished to find that Gordon's loutish features were contorted into what appeared to be a smile. He'd never spoken to Gordon even though they were in the same class. He never went near him. To tell the truth, he was a bit afraid of him, particularly as he was developing a burly physique like his father. Not only that, but James had also never seen him smile. It looked grotesque. Recovering from his shock, James attempted an acknowledging smile. Gordon responded with a greeting.

"How's it gawn, then, Swanston?"

He knew James's name! The second shock!

"Aye, great," James managed to respond. "What about you?"

"Braw," said Gordon. By now they were drying their hands on the week-old damp, grubby textile rolls that passed for towels in The Academy toilets. Then he added, "Were *you* no at Bonnybrig?"

Third shock! How much did Gordon know about him?

"Aye, Ah think you were a class ahead o' me, weren't ye?"

"Aye, ye had Beanie Boyle then ye disappeared. Where did ye go?"

"Oh, we moved out tae Fox Crag."

The ice was broken. It appeared that their common connection to Bonnybrig Primary had done it. Gordon had got a hot pie in a paper bag from the baker in Easter Road. Did James want to join him against a tree in The Links? As they ate and chatted desultorily, James finally plucked up the courage to ask the question that had been bothering him.

"Tell me, Gordon, ye ken McCluskie?"

"Aye."

"Ye ken how 'e's always on at ye, throwin' things at ye an' that?"

"Aye." Gordon was beginning to get James's drift.

"How come 'e's stopped? Ah mean, 'e doesnae do it any more."

"So, *you* noticed as well! Aye, ye're no the only one!"

'But why?"

"Well, it's a funny story. Sure ye want tae hear it?"

James nodded, now intrigued.

It turned out that Mr McCluskie was a keen follower of the gee-gees. Not to put too fine a point on it, his favourite pastime was to bet on horse races. At weekends, he could often be found at Musselburgh racecourse. In the past year, things had only got better for the likes of him as race betting was now legal in Britain and betting shops had been free to open their doors. Legal gambling joints had popped up all over Edinburgh and Leith, meaning that Mr McCluskie no longer had to drive all the way out to Musselburgh to place a legal bet.

"Well," said Gordon, "me an' mah dad were in one o' these new-fangled bettin' places in Easter Road. Mah dad's keen on the horses, ye see. Well, ye ken that, for we had auld Cuddie doon in Brecon Street?"

James remembered. Cuddie had been stabled in a yard near Bonnybrig School.

"Is 'e still wi' ye?" asked James, realising they were getting off the subject, but interested nevertheless.

"Oh, aye. Horses live long if ye treat them well! 'E's still there, pullin' the cart for mah dad!" He stopped and looked at James closely. "Can ye keep a secret?"

James nodded. Gordon was going to share a secret with *him*?

"Are ye sure? Cross yer heart an' hope tae die!"

It seemed childish coming from someone like Gordon, but James did it anyway. Apparently satisfied, Gordon continued.

"Mah dad's got a racehorse!"

James nearly choked on his spam and Pan Yan Pickle sandwich.

"What?" he gasped. "Ye're havin' me on, aren't ye?"

"Naw, gospel. 'E's got a racehorse an' it's stabled out at Musselburgh. It's a two-year-auld called Ragamuffin."

James was dumbstruck. Gordon's father, a ragman, owned a racehorse? Never in a million years! Then he suddenly remembered something Uncle Alistair had once told him. They'd been driving back from Glenogle baths late one Saturday afternoon. It was Saturday because Alistair hadn't been able to make the Monday before. They pulled up at a red traffic light in the Mayflower next to a horse and cart. It was a ragman. He sat on the front of his unladen cart holding the reins, a burly character with a dirty tweed cap and a greasy overcoat. On reflection, James wondered if it had even been Mr Briggs.

"D'ye see that guy?" Alistair had said. Lately, he'd taken to using *guy* a lot, thinking it made him sound American. "Well, I bet he's loaded!"

"How come?"

James couldn't imagine a wealthy ragman. It seemed impossible.

"Easy, he doesn't pay taxes or national insurance. Doesn't keep any books, deals only in cash. And, there's big money in refuse. Mark my words, he might look like a beggar but I bet he's mortgage-free in his own house and has a Rolls Royce tucked away in a garage somewhere."

As they drove away when the lights changed, James had turned and looked back as the old horse, constricted by large leather blinkers, slowly got the cart underway again. He'd still found it hard to believe, but now, it didn't seem so far-fetched. Maybe Alistair had been right after all.

"Really?" was all James could say. Then, "Has 'e won any races?"

"No yet," said Gordon, "'e's too young. But we have high hopes!"

James leaned back and reflected on the strangeness of life. His parents, outwardly fairly well off, were able to afford most of the basic things. But the thought of them being able to own something like a racehorse... well, it was the stuff of dreams. And Mr Briggs, a ragman, the lowest of the low, who, if Gordon was telling the truth, actually did own one...

"So what about McCluskie an' the bettin' shop then?"

"Well, when we went in, the first thing Ah saw was him, standin' in the queue. McCluskie! Did ye ken they had TV in they places, by the way? Well, *he* saw *me* an' *Ah* saw *him*. D'ye ken what Ah did? Ah introduced 'im tae mah dad! Gospel! Mah dad doesnae ken aboot 'im. Ah mean, what 'e does in class. Ah just said this was mah maths teacher at The Academy. Mah dad looks at 'im an' puts oot 'is hand. They shake like auld mates. Then mah dad says, 'Mr McCluskie, would ye like a wee tip?' McCluskie perks up. Dad says 'Hoity Toity in the three o'clock at Goodwood. Put yer shirt on it!'"

Apparently, Hoity-Toity had started at 100-1. What's more, Mr McCluskie, grateful for the inside information, *had* put his shirt on it and had won a small fortune.

"Since then," said Gordon, "Ah'm the teacher's pet! Aye, Ah cannae dae any wrong! An' get this, 'e comes tae *me* now, an' asks if mah dad's got another tip for 'im!"

The bell was ringing for the end of the midday break. They got to their feet and briskly made their way into the playground before the gates were closed on them. As he farewelled Gordon, James was in two minds about what he'd just heard. On the one hand, he was pleased for him if his victimhood under Mr McCluskie had really ceased and for the reason he'd given. On the other hand, he couldn't help wondering if it was just a cock-and-bull story. After all, it *was* Gordon. He decided he was going to keep his eyes open for a horse called Ragamuffin in the racing pages of the *Scottish Daily Express*. And if it really did exist, he might suggest to his mum and dad a wee flutter.

Twenty years later, James happened to pick up a copy of the *Evening News* on one of his rare visits home. A headline caught his eye: *Leith Native Strikes Gold in Canada*. There was a photo. Below it was a name: Gordon Briggs. In the photo was a beaming Gordon, older but still recognisable after all these years with his Leith looks, standing proudly beside some expensive-looking equipment. James skimmed the article. It seemed Gordon was now president of the largest refuse and recycling corporation in Ontario. James was stunned. Gordon Briggs, president of a major company and a millionaire to boot? It didn't sound possible. But there was the evidence right before his eyes. So, Mr McCluskie had been wrong about Gordon, stunningly wrong. He hadn't ended up a scaffie sweeping the streets of Edinburgh. He *had* amounted to something after all. Still, Mr McCluskie had been right about one thing: the nature of Gordon's work. It was just that it wouldn't be Gordon picking up rubbish in the streets. It would be his employees that did it for him. As James digested the story, he couldn't help but speculate on the catalyst for his former classmate's success. Was the credit due to Mr McCluskie for his daily diet of maths, mockery and missiles? Or was it, rather, all down to Gordon's years spent shovelling horse's doovers in the streets of Leith?

9 Yon lone glen o' green breckan

Uncle Willie

It's Uncle Willie!" exclaimed Granny Melrose with more than a hint of excitement in her voice as she peered through the lace curtains of the apartment at Warburton Crescent. James looked over her shoulder to see a black police Jaguar that had just pulled up in front of the building. Two figures could be seen in the darkened interior, a driver whose form, Parkinson's Law-like, seemed to fill all the space available for it, and a small, bulky figure reclining in the back seat. It was a Saturday afternoon in early September 1960. James's first few weeks of the Third Year at The Academy were behind him. In order to escape Saturday mornings at crowded 68 Chesser Drive, and if the Pentland Hills weren't an option, he'd go round to Warburton Crescent to help out his granny and grandad. Once there, he'd get in a load of coal, do food shopping up at Goldenacre, get in a bag of fresh vegetables from the market garden across the road behind the high stone dyke, and do any other chore that needed doing. In return, his granny would give him his dinner, usually mashed potatoes, beef stew or mince and peas, followed by jam roll and custard, not to mention a florin for his pocket money. It had turned into a regular thing over the past few years and it had a useful spin-off: James had established a closer relationship with his grandparents.

And it was through them that Uncle Willie entered his life. He was Chief Constable William Merrilees of the Lothians and Peebles Constabulary, who happened to be a cousin of Alexander Melrose. A legend in his own lifetime, the Chief had risen from abject poverty in

Cochrane's Pend just off The Kirkgate to become one of the top cops in the UK. Forced to end his education at 13, he was put to work in a rope-works in Restalrig where he lost the fingers of his left hand in an accident. But that didn't stop him being a boxer, football player and lifeguard in his spare time. A fitter in the Leith dockyards during World War One, he distinguished himself by saving a large number of people from drowning in Leith harbour, for which he received a string of awards and citations.

Due to his well-publicised exploits, he'd come to the attention of The Lord Provost of Edinburgh who admired not only his heroism but also his innate intelligence, competence, toughness and good character. The Lord Provost recommended him to the Chief Constable who offered him employment as a sworn police officer despite his disability and small stature. An extraordinarily successful career in the City of Edinburgh Police followed. His local knowledge of the Edinburgh and Leith underworld helped him crack cases that had stumped other officers. A flamboyant character, he'd adopt disguises to track and apprehend criminals. Disguised as a railway porter in 1940, he made perhaps his most famous arrest, that of the German spy, Werner Walti, in Waverley Station. Alone and unarmed, he tackled Walti, who was brandishing a fully loaded Mauser pistol, subdued him and arrested him. The high point of his career was the appointment to Chief Constable of the Lothians and Peebles Police in 1950. However, the Chief's success came at a cost. While he was admired by many in Edinburgh and Leith, the Tall Poppy Syndrome was also alive and well. Even in the early days, when he was honoured for his life-saving exploits, jokes were doing the rounds:

Two Leithers are having a pint in a pub.

First Leither: "What aboot that Wee Willie Merrilees, savin' aw' they folk frae drownin' in the harbour! Whit a hero!"

Second Leither: "Aye, that's true. But ye do ken, don't ye, that he was the one that pushed them in, in the first place?"

By the time James came to know Uncle Willie, he was in the final decade of his career. His name was spoken with a mixture of familiarity, awe and reverence in the Melrose family. During the hard times of the 1920s and 1930s Uncle Willie had done his best to help keep the Melrose family afloat. It was said that he and his wife had even offered to adopt one or more of Janet's eight brothers and sisters to take the pressure off her parents, an offer their working-class pride wouldn't allow them to accept. Philanthropy was the other key element in Uncle Willie's life. He supported many local charities, in particular those caring for orphans, disabled children (hence the name *Uncle Willie*) and the aged. Nor did he shrink from extracting donations and favours from the wealthy and famous to benefit Edinburgh's disadvantaged. And it was in this context that James and Uncle Willie were destined to come together.

These two elements of Uncle Willie's life were neatly mirrored in his personality as James came to know him, and know about him, better. On the one hand, he was gentle, with an earthy Scottish sense of humour engendered in the slums of the Kirkgate. On the other hand, he was tough and would, if called on, do the job if it came to a physical confrontation. Even in his old age, Uncle Willie was still a fearsome adversary when it came to a fight. Only a year previously, when he was in his sixty-first year, there had been the widely publicised Wallyford riot of 1959. By some mix-up, Uncle Willie found himself facing over a hundred rioters armed with clubs, chains and flick knives with only two civilians and another police officer on hand. By the time reinforcements arrived, Uncle Willie had already singlehandedly felled three of his far younger attackers.

Up until that day in 1960, Uncle Willie had been to James merely a fabled figure, the subject of family talk. He'd never met him. He knew of his exploits only by repute and had seen him only once. It had been at one of Uncle Willie's famous outings for disadvantaged children. What seemed like a vast battalion of taxis with balloons attached, each one packed with children, had driven out from Edinburgh and had descended on Lord Rosebery's estate near South Queensferry for a mammoth picnic on a Saturday afternoon, all organised by Uncle Willie. Some were orphans; others were in wheelchairs or on crutches; some even in mobile beds attended by nurses. And there in the middle was Uncle Willie. He'd been too busy to approach but now James would see him up close for the first time. When he walked into the Melroses' apartment, James's first impression was of a vigorous, alert man in late middle age wearing police uniform and the flat, diced cap of the Scottish police covered in silver braid. He was slightly shorter than James. He had a generous head of greying hair and a square, craggy face with a pugnacious expression but kind eyes. Although he spoke with a soft, cultured accent, it was unmistakably Scots. He was already smiling and looking around the room as he threw his cap on the settee and hugged Granny Melrose.

"Ah was just passing and thought Ah'd

drop in and see how you were!” he exclaimed.

“Oh, Willie, this is mah grandson, Janet’s laddie,” said Granny Melrose. “He’s…” She paused. “How auld are ye again, son?”

“Thirteen-an’-a-half, Granny.”

James was already standing respectfully. Uncle Willie turned and held out his right hand. In the split second before he did so, James couldn’t help himself glancing down. Yes, there was Uncle Willie’s famous left hand, a mere stump.

“What’s yer name, son?” asked Uncle Willie, as he took James’s juvenile hand firmly in his intact, gnarled paw.

“James Swanston, Sir!”

“Ye’re a fine-lookin’ laddie, a Melrose all right.” He gave James a grin. “Almost as good-lookin’ as me!”

Alexander and his cousin sat down in the two available armchairs and started chatting while Granny Melrose bustled about in the kitchen making tea and sandwiches. James helped, carrying things back and forward, mentally on tiptoe, for he’d never before been in the presence of someone who exuded such power, albeit a member of his own extended family. Nor could he take his eyes off the fabulous black Jaguar, with the police markings and the driver sitting motionless inside. Uncle Willie interrupted his thoughts.

“James, would ye do me a wee favour, son? Would ye take a cup of tea and a sandwich out to mah driver?”

“D’ye no want tae bring ’im in, Willie?” asked Alexander.

“No, no, he’s got to stay by the radio, Ah’m afraid!”

James made fresh tea while his granny put together another couple of sandwiches for the driver. As she held the door open, he stepped into the entry holding the tray, willing himself not to trip on the steps. He walked out into the street and around the Jaguar to the driver’s side, watched by a small crowd of curious local bairns. The driver had already seen him and smartly stepped out. James was confronted by an enormous policeman in his late thirties. He must have been about six feet five and looked even taller in his diced cap. He had a tough, handsome, intelligent face, a prominent nose, a funny left eye and three stripes on the arm of his tunic.

“Uncle Willie asked me tae bring ye a cup o’ tea an’ a sandwich,” announced James, proffering the tray and squinting up at him. He felt weird. He’d never before walked out into the street with a tray, a pot of tea and a plate of sandwiches.

“Well, thank ye kindly, young man,” said the sergeant, taking the tray and balancing it carefully on the bonnet of the Jag while he helped himself. “And who might *you* be?”

"James Swanston, Sir. Alexander Melrose's mah granddad."

"Ah'm Sergeant Seatoun, the Chief's driver an' bodyguard."

A real, live bodyguard? Never had James imagined that he'd be talking to one, especially here in lowly Warburton Crescent, of all places.

"But," said Sergeant Seatoun, in between munching Granny's ham and mustard sandwiches, and gulping down the hot, sweet tea, "you can call me Sandy."

James stood there like an idiot, wondering if that bulge under the Sergeant's tunic could possibly be a revolver.

"What school are ye at?"

"The Academy, Sir, in Leith."

"Oh, a good school. Ah kennt a teacher there, Mr Laidlaw. 'Is wife's only got one arm. D'ye ken 'im?"

"Aye, Ah do, Sir. 'E's mah physics teacher!"

"Well, well, well, it's a sma' world, isn't it? Mrs Laidlaw's from Penicuik, where Ah live." Then he added, "By the way, James, ye neednae call me *Sir*. Sandy will do. Or just Sergeant, if ye like!"

James was beginning to like this man. Sergeant Seatoun drained the teacup, finished his snack and handed the tray back with a smile.

"Thank yer granny for me and maybe we'll see each other again some time!"

He got back into the driver's seat and started fiddling with his radio. Little did either of them realise that they'd be seeing a lot more of each other than they'd ever have imagined. Back inside, James was just in time to tune in to the conversation. Uncle Willie was telling the Melroses about his new venture. He'd successfully persuaded an acquaintance, who happened to be a member of the Scottish nobility and who owned a huge estate near Innerleithen, to let him have a derelict cottage, rent-free. It was on condition that Uncle Willie would restore and renovate it at his expense. The cottage would be used as a country retreat for old folks, orphans, crippled children (as Uncle Willie called them) and any other disadvantaged groups. There was a lot of work to do. It would be done mainly at weekends but he was hoping that it would be completed by the following spring. It even had a name of sorts. It was called The Glen. James pricked up his ears. A cottage in The Borders? *The Glen*. The name was magic. He saw it immediately in his imagination. A small, whitewashed cottage next to a burn below bracken-and-heather-covered slopes. He'd never forgotten his holiday at the caravan near Adelstone. What must it be like, he thought, to have a cottage like that in a glen? Granny Melrose got up.

"Can ye gie me a hand tae redd thir things away, son?"

In the kitchen, he plucked up the courage to ask a question.

"Granny?"

"Aye, son, what is it?"

"Ye ken that cottage o' Uncle Willie's down at Innerleithen?"

"Aye, what aboot it?"

"Ah just wondered if 'e wanted any help wi' it? Ah mean, if 'e says there's a lot o' work tae do, maybe Ah could help?"

Granny looked up, her eyes brightening.

"Well, son, why don't ye ask 'im?"

She took him by his shirt sleeve and pulled him through to the living room.

"Uncle Willie!" she announced, "James has somethin' tae ask ye," and she gave him a nudge forward. But James was tongue-tied.

"Come on, son, out wi' it!" Uncle Willie laughed. "Ah'm no' the Loch Ness Monster!"

"Well, Uncle Willie, Ah just wondered, eh, if ye wanted any help wi' yer cottage, The Glen?"

Uncle Willie considered James's words and looked at him shrewdly. He was wondering what a thirteen-year boy old could possibly do to help *him*. Then he suddenly remembered - how could he forget? - that at thirteen he'd had to endure the clamorous, perilous rope-works at Restalrig where he'd lost his fingers. If *he* could do that at thirteen, why couldn't this wee laddie do something that was far less onerous but far more worthwhile?

"What were ye thinkin' of, son?"

James gulped.

"Anythin', Uncle Willie." He thought for a moment. "Ah can clean up, Ah can help carry stuff, Ah can make tea and cook!"

"Aye, 'e's right, Willie," Granny Melrose put in, "'e *can* cook, simple stuff, that is! 'E's a right dab hand in the kitchen. Janet's learned 'im weel, ye see!"

A light suddenly went on in Uncle Willie's head. Much of the work would be done by tradesmen on Saturdays free of charge. It would be their donation to a worthy cause. Anything for the Chief! Where this wasn't possible, Uncle Willie had negotiated special reduced rates. But the workers would certainly need tea and coffee made, snacks and meals cooked for them in this remote location as part of the arrangement, and at his expense. Without realising it, this wee laddie had highlighted an important point that he'd almost overlooked in his planning. And yes, he could help in a host of other ways as well. By the looks of him he was sturdy and after all, he was one of the family. What could be better? Still sitting, he motioned to James to come over, holding out his good right hand and smiling broadly.

"Son," he said, again shaking James's hand heartily. "Ye've got yerself a bargain. But," he added more seriously, wagging his remaining index finger, "remember ye're doin' this for all the crippled bairns and the old folk, so ye cannae expect any payment." He paused, seeing James nod in agreement. "And ye'd have tae be ready any Saturday Ah need ye, from now on, right through the winter. D'ye think ye can do that?"

"Ah'll do mah best, Uncle Willie."

"Splendid, that's all Ah'm askin'. Right. Away out tae the police car and give yer address tae Sergeant Seatoun. Now, he'll be picking ye up next Saturday at eight o'clock in the morning, so no sleepin' in! OK?"

James was ecstatic. To be picked up at 68 Chesser Drive by Sergeant Seatoun in a police car and driven to The Glen! The nosy parker neighbours would be beside themselves. Grabbing his Granny's notepad and a pen, he hurried outside to carry out Uncle Willie's instructions. When he explained what the Chief had said and given the Sergeant a note of his address, his new friend was delighted.

"Well, well, well, that's just fine an' dandy, son. We could certainly do wi' yer help down at The Glen."

The Sergeant was encouraging but he'd also put James on notice; James had opened his big mouth and now he'd have to deliver. Suddenly he saw things in a different light. What had he done? Make tea, cook some simple meals? Surely he could do that and any other fetching and carrying that was required? He tried to convince himself. Nevertheless, he was uneasy all week and slept badly. What if he made a fool of himself? When he'd told Ian and Janet about his new venture, they were pleased. Uncle Willie was taking their son under his wing. What could be better? And what might it lead to for James, such a prominent person, no matter how distant a relation, taking an interest in him? It had to be good. James was awake most of the following Friday night and up extra early on the Saturday morning. He found Janet already in the kitchen making porridge.

"Ye're gonnae need a good breakfast!" she warned. "It'll be a long day. Now sit yerself doon and git that inside ye!"

With that, she placed a steaming bowl of thick porridge in front of him, together with salt, sugar and milk. Bread was already toasting and a pot of tea was on the way. The Sergeant had warned him not to expect a police patrol car. Yes, it would be a police vehicle equipped with a radio, but it would be unmarked. James was just as enthusiastic. Swanning around in an unmarked police car... At ten to eight, he was already out on the pavement beside the lamppost in his parka against the autumn morning chill, wearing old work clothes and his ex-army black leather boots. As he slung his duffel bag over his shoulder, he tried to hold his excitement in check. Promptly at a minute to eight, a wine-red, 3.8-litre Jaguar Mark 2 appeared at the top of Chesser Drive, snaked its way swiftly and elegantly towards him on the wrong side of the road and stopped right beside him. The window wound down and the cheery face of Sergeant Seaton appeared.

"Good Morning, James!"

"Good morning, Sergeant Seatoun!" He really didn't want to be so familiar so early. And the words *Sergeant Seatoun* sounded far more important in his mouth than just plain *Sandy*, especially since the Sergeant was in full police uniform.

"Well, what are ye waitin' for? Hop in!"

James needed no second telling. Hastening around to the passenger side, he pulled the heavy door open, settled into the plush leather front seat, buckled on the police-issue seat belt and, basking in the certain knowledge that nosy Mrs Pendrich from the next building would be weeing herself with frustration behind her lace curtains, he let himself be whisked away from mundane Chesser Drive into another world.

The Glen

The shrill, two-tone gobble from a nearby thicket was followed by the unmistakable clatter of wings as a pheasant flew up, squawking in alarm. The mist was beginning to dissipate. James emerged from the Jaguar into the cool of a Borders autumn morning. The little glen ran roughly in a northeast to southwest direction. A burn meandered through the cultivated flatlands between grass-covered banks and occasional clumps of alder, directing frothing, peat-brown water down to the River Tweed at Innerleithen. Where the cultivation ended, purple-hued slopes took over, for at this time of the year the heather was coming into bloom and was engulfing the ubiquitous bracken. The land rose steeply on the north side to a high massif of trackless wilderness that had no name on the map but was known locally as Drumbreck. Come winter, there would be snow on its tops. The south side rose to a low ridge clothed in a tract of conifer, mountain ash and birch. They'd approached along a rough, potholed track that peeled off the estate road, crossed the burn by way of a shoogly wooden bridge and led directly to the front door of the cottage which stood by the burn, dwarfed by its surroundings in its own fenced-off grounds. It was as James had imagined it the week before, more or less. However, there were a few significant deviations from his idealised picture.

First, the cottage had no roof to speak of. Most of the area that had once been roof now consisted merely of bare rafters that kept company with the still intact stone-built chimney. The remnants of faded, red roof tiles littered the ground. A sizeable young rowan tree grew out of what appeared to be the kitchen window or at least the hole where the window would have been had there been one. The other windows were missing or smashed. Yes, the outer walls had once been whitewashed but they were now a dirty off-white, the fascia cracked and crumbling in places. The front door was hanging off its hinges. The up side was that the cottage *was* in fact inhabited, that is, by the best part of a flock of blackface ewes accompanied by their strident lambs. James stood and gaped while the Sergeant, who'd already been here several times of course, smiled at his reaction.

"What did ye think, son? That it would be The Peebles Hydro? How d'ye think the Chief got it for nothin'? Aye, they're a canny lot, these big Borders lairds!"

James was nodding his head in agreement. It certainly looked like this particular laird was going to get the better end of the deal. Sergeant Seatoun unbuttoned his tunic, pulled it off and stowed it in the Jag. Then, removing his police regulation tie and opening his collar, he donned a huge pair of wellington boots.

"Are ye ready, son? Up an' at 'em! The builders should be here soon. Our first job is tae clear out the sheep."

And with that, the two budding renovators, now firm friends despite the disparity in their ages, set to work evicting the woolly squatters and shooing them away from the cottage.

The drive down from Edinburgh had taken the best part of an hour. James was to discover that their itinerary would vary from Saturday to Saturday, depending on traffic, weather and personal inclination, as well as whatever had to be done on the way. Sometimes there was police business to be transacted in the likes of Dalkeith, Bonnyrigg or Peebles. Sometimes the Sergeant had to complete some other official or personal errand for the Chief. But a key errand most Saturdays would be to pick up provisions for the builders at the cottage. The Chief's reach throughout the Lothians was long. Over the years he'd developed a network of contacts and associates he could call on. Combined with

Sergeant Seatoun's local knowledge, almost anything could be obtained at the right price. Arrangements had been made to collect, every Saturday, a parcel of whatever was going, butcher meat here, vegetables there, bread, scones and tea bread there, for James to transform into meals for the workmen in the cottage's kitchen.

There were two alternative routes. The western route took them straight down the A 703 past the Pentland Hills to Peebles and then on to Innerleithen. The eastern route was via Dalkeith, straight down the A7 to turn off onto the B709 through Heriot and wild, hilly country on what Sergeant Seatoun called 'the back road', then straight into Innerleithen, neatly bypassing the series of towns on the western route. But on this first day, the western route it was. Autumn was just over the next hill. Poplars were beginning to turn golden. James sat back in the passenger seat of the Jag feeling like royalty being chauffeured to his coronation, silently enjoying the passing landscape while the Sergeant concentrated on the road. First, the soaring easterly flank of Caerketton was behind them, then Turnhouse Hill. Just as Scald Law was coming into view, they were suddenly entering Penicuik and the Sergeant was on his home turf. At this time on a Saturday morning, the small country town seemed deserted. The Jag smoothly came to a stop outside a long, two-storey Georgian building with a black-and-white-painted frontage that took up an entire block. The Sergeant switched off the engine and turned to James who looked at him enquiringly.

"Our first stop, son. We need tae pick up dinner for the lads – and ourselves!"

They stepped out of the Jag. James looked up. Along the front of the building, writ large, was the name Royal Hotel. It seemed that though the town was still sleeping, the Royal Hotel was not, for lights were on and bustle was evident from inside. James followed the Sergeant, who pushed open the heavy wooden door, turned right, and walked with easy familiarity straight through what James realised was the restaurant where breakfast was being served to bleary-eyed guests. Then it was through swing doors into a spacious back room, hot with the sound and aroma of bacon and eggs frying. A beefy chef with a red face waved to them from behind a cooking range as if he'd been expecting them.

"Good mornin', Sergeant Seatoun!"

"Good mornin', Mr Tait!" The Sergeant turned and gestured to James. "This is mah..." He hesitated as if trying to choose the appropriate term. "...apprentice, James Swanston," he added by way of introduction. "'E's the Chief's nephew."

James was to find that he was often referred to as 'the Chief's nephew' or 'Uncle Willie's nephew'. It was a form of shorthand for people who couldn't get their minds around the exact nature of James's familial connection to the Chief. But the fact that the Sergeant also regarded him as his 'apprentice' was news to James. Up until now, the nature of who exactly he was and what exactly he was supposed to be doing at The Glen had been vague, to say the least. But now his new function suddenly had a name. At The Glen, he'd be the Sergeant's apprentice... He glowed inside.

"Oh," said Mr Tait, "Ah thocht for a wee minute 'e was yer son!"

A strange expression crossed the Sergeant's face.

"Well, Mr Tait, tae be honest, Ah wouldnae mind if 'e was!"

It was easy for James to hide his embarrassment in the hot kitchen where everyone had a red face. But if he'd liked the Sergeant before, he liked him even more now.

"Yer order's near ready. The lassie's just finishin' it off!"

Mr Tait nodded to a corner of the kitchen where a girl in a white overall was packing what James took to be sandwiches into several large brown paper bags. It seemed that for the first few Saturdays of the project, James wouldn't be doing any cooking in the cottage. For one thing, there was a tree growing out of the kitchen; for another, there was no roof to speak of; and for a third, a gas stove had yet to be installed. Clearing out the kitchen and starting on the roof were priorities. When that was complete, the stove would come and James could start cooking. So, in the meantime, and until these jobs were done, the fallback position would be sandwiches, tea and soup, supplied by the kitchen of the Royal Hotel.

When the girl was ready, she turned and gestured to two large cardboard boxes. One contained two commercial thermos flasks of soup, two thermos flasks of boiling water and several bags of sandwiches. The other contained several china mugs, cardboard plates, cutlery and condiments, small containers of tea and sugar, a bottle of Camp Coffee, as well as a box of hot pies and another of bridies, each wrapped in newspaper. The Sergeant grabbed the heavier box with the thermos flasks and gestured to James to take the other. They said their goodbyes and walked out together to stow their provisions in the boot of the Jag. For James it was a signature moment. He'd completed his very first task as apprentice on Uncle Willie's project at The Glen. With an increased sense of importance, he hopped in beside the Sergeant and they were off again by way of Peebles and Cardrona.

During the long drives to The Glen and back, James learnt more about Sergeant Seatoun. He'd been the Chief's driver and bodyguard for three years. Before that, he'd been a beat constable and sergeant in various districts of The Lothians. His funny left eye, James learnt, had been the result of an altercation with two violent thugs, one of whom had sliced the Sergeant's eye with a flick knife. Surgeons had saved his sight but he was unable to continue his work as a frontline police officer. He'd been moved to special duties and trained in diplomatic protection, which had led to his present role.

Uncle Alistair was the only driver James had travelled with on a regular basis. The first thing he noticed about the Sergeant was that he drove fast. Very fast. Whenever the road conditions or the traffic permitted, the speedometer was always on, or over, the speed limit. But James never felt in the least nervous. It may have had something to do with the heavy Jaguar and its massive, powerful engine that coped easily with any demands put on it. But it was also to do with the Sergeant's driving. It was clear that he was a professional police driver. Driving fast wasn't the issue. It was all about driving safe.

As James got to know him better, he wanted to satisfy his curiosity about how to drive the Jag on these winding, treacherous country roads. The Sergeant was happy to oblige. He became James's first driving instructor, even though James never got behind the wheel of the Jag, or, at the age of thirteen-going-on-fourteen, any other car. The Sergeant explained the basics. On the curvy, narrow, minor roads of the Borders, he offered his best advice: *Always accelerate into a bend and accelerate out.* He taught James how to read the road ahead, how to use trees, hedges and dykes to anticipate what was coming, to know the signs that there were houses or people up ahead where warning signs were absent. He'd suddenly throw him a question out of the blue: *What's the road going to do after this bend? How do you know there's a T-junction ahead? What hazards do you expect after this village? How do you know there could be sheep on the road?* James was fascinated. This was certainly something he could use when he owned a car himself one day.

In Innerleithen, the Sergeant stopped for ten minutes at the police station to make a courtesy call and so that they could both use the 'facilities'. From there, they backtracked, James guessed, south, on a minor road that was incredibly narrow. An ancient drystane dyke ran on one side and a hedge on the other, with low hills and pasture all around. Then suddenly the Jag slackened off speed. The Sergeant swiftly changed down. Up ahead was a small un-signposted turn-off. The Jag briskly took the corner and suddenly they were on a one-track road with blind corners. They slowed right down. The road meandered through a mix of farmland and woodland, then came a fork in the road. Up to the right, there was a small house on a hill. They went left. Again, the way was un-signposted. An enormous moss-covered arched gateway of ancient stone blocks reaching about fifteen feet up into branches spanned the road ahead. Above the arch, a weatherworn escutcheon of some sort was hewn in the stone. Then they were driving out the other side, through woodland, on a well-maintained gravel road. Through the trees James glimpsed an enormous residence, a pseudo castle with fake crenellations, poised on a hill up to their right. The woodland suddenly opened out, the sun shone, the road dipped sharply and there unmistakeably, straight ahead, was The Glen.

By the time they'd got the ewes and their offspring away from the cottage, through an open gate and into the neighbouring paddock, they were both out of breath.

"Ah'm fair puggled!" exclaimed the Sergeant as he leant on the gate he'd just closed, and cast an eye over the condition of the flock. "Too much sittin' in police cars an' too many meat pies! Tell ye what we need James, a nice wee collie tae do the job for us."

"D'ye mean one like thon?" asked James, pointing in the opposite direction.

The Sergeant turned round and shaded his eyes from the sun with his right hand.

"Well, michty me. Talk o' the devil!"

There, striding in gumboots up the potholed track was a tall figure clad in green check tweeds with a deerstalker cap on his head, a cromach in his right hand and two matched black-and-white Border collies slinking along in his shadow.

"It's Mr Oxnam, the Factor," said the Sergeant matter-of-factly. He waved and advanced to meet the visitor with his apprentice trailing in his wake. James was wondering if he'd heard correctly. They'd been learning algebra at school and he'd struggled with the mere idea of what a factor was and how to find it. Just when he thought he was beginning to understand, here was another factor walking along the road on two legs, with two collie dogs at his side. He sighed. Life was confusing sometimes!

The Factor and the Sergeant greeted each other, James remaining in the background even as he was introduced, yet again, as the Chief's nephew. The two collies had been grounded with a curt growl from Mr Oxnam and they now lay stretched on the grass neatly bracketing their master, tongues lolling and smiling sleekitly at the sheep in the next field, as if to say, *Just you wait, we'll soon be making you jump!* Mr Oxnam's employer, the Laird, had already briefed him on what would be going on over the next few months down at Nether Bankside, as the locale was known on estate maps, and had instructed him to drop by from time to time to keep an eye on things, offer assistance if need be, and report back where appropriate.

This was to be the first of many visits. As befitted his station as estate manager, Mr Oxnam exuded an aura of no-nonsense authority, but when he'd been introduced, James had seen a glint in his eye that hinted at a strong sense of humour. From closer to, James saw a man in his mid-fifties, with a ruddy complexion, bushy eyebrows and a matching bushy grey moustache. He and the Sergeant already seemed to have formed a good working relationship and from their discussion, James was able to glean several titbits of information that he hadn't known before.

The first was that Sergeant Seatoun was the project manager. That wasn't to say that he'd be involved in decisions about the build. No, that was the province of Mr Boswell, the master-builder from Galashiels. But the Sergeant's job was to ensure that everything ran smoothly and that the builders had what they needed outside their own area of expertise to complete the job. The second was that since winter was approaching, there would be a supreme effort in the next couple of weeks to re-roof the cottage before the first snows came. The thinking was that they could continue until early December when winter would shut down operations. They'd look to start up again in late February or early March, weather permitting, and hope to get the whole job completed by April, early May at the latest.

The fact that the Chief had given Sergeant Seatoun this responsibility spoke volumes, for, during the next several months of construction work, not once was James to see Uncle Willie at The Glen. In fact, he never saw him again until the following year. Apparently, Saturdays were busy policing days for the Chief. Occasionally, should circumstances allow, he'd make the trip down from the City on Sundays to check on progress. Other than that, he trusted Sergeant Seatoun, Mr Boswell, his team and his subcontractors, and, of course, James, to complete the job by the following spring.

As if on cue, a new-looking, cream-coloured Bedford TK lorry appeared, grinding down the hill on the Estate road then turning off to cross the burn by the shoogly bridge which must have been stronger than it looked. As it approached slowly over the potholed track, James could make out the words 'Boswell and Sons, Builder' painted on the cab door, and below, the name 'Galashiels'. The flat bed of the lorry was stacked with roofing timbers of various shapes and sizes. It appeared Mr Boswell meant business. The lorry came to a halt, the big six-cylinder diesel engine continued to run with a reassuring throb, then all was silent. The doors opened and three men jumped out, an older man, the driver, wearing a flat cap, who was obviously Mr Boswell, and two young lads in their early twenties.

“Aye, aye!” exclaimed Mr Boswell in greeting, glancing from the Factor to Sergeant Seatoun, surmising who was who. “Ye’ll be the Sergeant, am Ah right?” he suggested in his lilting Border brogue.

“Aye, that Ah am. Seatoun’s the name.” They shook hands. “And this is Mr Oxnam, the Factor.” More handshaking.

“This is mah son, Patrick, and that’s mah worker, Gordon.”

The young men just nodded, unsure how to respond in the presence of a police sergeant.

“And this is the Chief’s nephew, James.”

The three newcomers nodded in James’s direction and he attempted a nod back.

“He’ll be keepin’ yer bellies filled!”

“Well done, laddie! Are we allowed tae make requests?”

Flustered, James could only smile. Anyway, he assumed so.

“Well,” said Mr Oxnam, “ye’ll be wantin’ tae get on.” Turning to the Sergeant, he said, “Let me know if ye need anythin’. Ye ken weel where the estate office is, d’ye no?”

Sergeant Seatoun nodded a yes. Clicking his tongue to release his canine helpers, the Factor set off to move the ewes and the lambs onto the hillside. James stood at the fence, spellbound, as the two black and white streaks rocketed up and down the steep slopes in the sunshine, hastening the ewes on with hardly an instruction from Mr Oxnam. He and the collies seemed to be in telepathic communication.

“Are ye ready tae work, young Swanston?” The Sergeant broke the spell. With a start, James turned and the two made their way to the cottage. The next time James turned round the ewes had disappeared entirely and so had the Factor and his helpers.

In addition to the timber, Mr Boswell had brought a range of tools and a couple of wheelbarrows. While James and Sergeant Seatoun picked and hacked at the rowan growing out of a crack in the concrete floor, the builders made a start on the old rafters, most of which were rotten. With the rowan uprooted, the entire crew spent the rest of the morning at the tricky job of removing the old timber and stacking it at a distance from the cottage. By then, everyone was covered in a century or more of accumulated dirt as well as bird and bat excrement. Mr Boswell and his men then set to installing the new roof beams, all of which had already been cut to size and shape, and numbered for convenience. Meanwhile, with broom, shovel and wheelbarrow, the Sergeant and his apprentice carried on cleaning out the rest of the cottage, which was full, not only of sheep droppings but of broken furniture, abandoned farm implements, piles of bottles and old newspapers, as well as other rubbish left over from years of neglect.

As the debris was gradually removed, James could appreciate the venerable dwelling's finer points. It was single storey but was surprisingly spacious inside as it had been added to over the years. One of the main additions had clearly been the kitchen, which was stuck onto the side like an extra thumb and had a walk-in pantry full of empty pickling jars. Miraculously, there was a supply of running water out of a Verdigris-encrusted brass tap, crystal clear and gravity fed from a lochan named Leuchar up on the ridge. As well as a sprawling living room with an open fireplace, there were three bedrooms, various cupboards and presses and a utility room out the back. The interior walls were universally of plain plaster and had once been white. There was a sizeable shed that could probably take a tractor but seemed to have been used for storage and firewood.

For the morning break at eleven, they dragged an ancient but sturdy rustic bench out of the shed together with some rickety chairs while James made tea and coffee to order and put out sandwiches on plates. They sat at the bench again for the midday break just after one. In the sunshine, James and the Sergeant broke out the pies and bridies and poured Scotch broth into the mugs. There was the remainder of the sandwiches for those still hungry - a choice of cheese and pickle, ham and mustard or corned beef and mayonnaise. They sat around the table, passing the occasional comment and taking in the breath-taking scenery. What was the point of working deep in the Border Country if you didn't take time to appreciate it? Preparations for the installation of the new roof beams and rafters continued into the afternoon, while James and Sergeant Seatoun resumed their clearing out work. By the time four o'clock came round they had a huge pile of rubbish stacked and ready to burn twenty yards or so behind the cottage. Meanwhile, Mr Boswell and his lads had made good progress. Two or three more workdays should see the job completed. Sergeant Seatoun made a point of finishing promptly at five.

"We have tae be out o' here at the back o' five at the latest. The last thing we want is tae be drivin' too long in the dark, especially wi' the nights drawin' in an' winter no' far off!" he warned. The Boswell men agreed and were the first into their Bedford and away home to Galashiels. The Sergeant buttoned his tunic, tied his tie, changed back into his shoes and got into the driving seat while James jumped in beside him. The sun had long disappeared below the mass of Drumbreck and the glen was in shadow as the Jag headed out. It was a fast drive with only a brief stop to drop the two boxes with the empty thermos flasks, cutlery and crockery back to the Royal Hotel in Penicuik. By the time the Jag sped into Chesser Drive, night wasn't far off. Giving the

Sergeant a weary goodbye, and promising to be ready at the same time the following Saturday, James staggered down the garden path, exhausted after what had been the first full day of hard physical work in his life.

"Help mah Boab!" said Ian, who was standing in the kitchen in the middle of making macaroni and cheese for the family's tea, "My, have ye got some colour in yer cheeks! How was it, son? Enjoy yersel'?"

James dropped his duffle bag and dumped himself in a kitchen chair. Even though he was tired, the words tumbled out of his mouth.

"Dad, it was fantastic, ye cannae imagine it! The buildin's a mess but it's in this lovely wee glen! Ye should have seen these two collies..."

His enthusiastic narrative was cut short. Janet had arrived. She ruffled his hair.

"Come on James Swanston, there's a nice hot bath waitin' for ye!" James dragged himself to his feet. "And make sure ye dinnae drop off in the bathtub!"

James assured her that he wouldn't but she made him leave the door unlocked just in case. It was a good thing she did, for no sooner did he feel the velvet embrace of the hot water around his tired bones than his eyelids began to droop, and, but for Janet's knocking, he might soon have been sound asleep.

Better a wee bush than nae bield

"Aye," the Factor was saying, "ye'll be well aware that The Bard himself was in these parts." On seeing the blank looks on the faces of his listeners, he elucidated. "Well, it's no suprisin', is it? Burns Country is barely forty mile tae the west o' us, an' he wantit tae visit The Bush Aboon Traquair."

It was early October. The good weather had held and the renovation team had been able to continue the tradition, begun on that first day a month before, of sitting outside at the wooden bench for their dinner. The build had made progress. The roof was on at last, a brand-new canopy of dark red ochre tiles. They'd made a start on patching and levelling the concrete floor, which, Mr Boswell had adjudged, still had plenty of life in it and just needed a bit of loving care. The kitchen floor was complete – the rowan tree root excised, the hole plugged and smoothed over – and that very morning, as promised, the Boswell Bedford had arrived with a second-hand gas cooker on board, donated by one of the Chief's cronies in Selkirk, along with two large containers of bottled gas. In anticipation, James and the Sergeant had picked up in Dalkeith a large parcel of meat from Sandersons, Purveyors of Fine Meats, By Appointment.

At last, James had been able to set up the kitchen as he wanted it. The pantry was filling with potatoes, carrots, Brussels sprouts, cabbages and turnips, plus a range of condiments, packets and tins. The week before, he and the Sergeant had been directed to pick up several boxes of mismatched crockery and cutlery from a second-hand dealer in Bonnyrigg, yet another donation from a local businessman. From somewhere during the week a small fridge had appeared and was already plugged into the cottage's fickle electrics. At last soup and sandwiches were a thing of the past. James had been able to prepare and cook his first meal for the workers: mashed potatoes, lamb chops, Brussels sprouts and carrots, followed by thick, yellow custard poured over apple charlotte from a local bakery, served on real china plates, with real cutlery. As they'd been leaning back, licking the sticky apple sauce from their lips and stroking their distended bellies, the workmen had taken to complementing James the only way they knew how.

"Aye, laddie, ye'll make a fine wife tae some lassie one day!"

"Keep this up, son, an' ye'll be head chef at The Hydro before long!"

"Man, ye cook better than mah Lizzie!"

James took the chaffing in good part. He'd been saved from further embarrassment by the sudden appearance of the Factor, his two shadows, who, James now knew, were brother and sister and went by the names of Rab and Jean, slinking at his heels. With a greeting to the workers and a growl to his dogs, the Factor took a seat at the bench while James piled the dirty dishes on a tray and carried them back to the kitchen to make coffee. When he returned, the tray heavy with steaming mugs, milk jug, sugar bowl, spoons and a plate of McVitie's digestive biscuits, the Factor was in full flight. It seemed that he was yet another devotee of The Bard.

After James had passed around the mugs and taken his seat, surreptitiously feeding broken bits of digestive to Rab and Jean under the table, he listened in on the conversation, turning over in his mind the puzzling phenomenon of Rabbie and his disciples. They seemed to be everywhere. It wasn't just the Burns Supper Clubs that popped up every 25th of January. Rabbie had a broad vein of devotees throughout

Scottish society, men, almost entirely men, who were ready at the drop of a tam o'shanter to come up with a quote from The Bard to suit any occasion. His grandfather was one of them, Mr Fraser upstairs at Number 68 another, and now Mr Oxnam. It was as if they belonged to some clandestine Burns Underground, dedicated to ensuring that The Bard's memory remained alive and well in the hearts of Scots. For the strange thing was that when it came to formal education in Scotland, at least where James's was concerned, and to anyone who gave the matter a moment's thought, Robert Burns was missing in action.

He'd never rated a mention at either of James's primary schools. As James was to discover, neither Rabbie's name nor his works would appear in any of the curricula he followed in all of his six years at The Academy. It was as if, as far as the Scottish secondary education system was concerned, Rabbie didn't exist. Yet, if you were to hear the ordinary people of Scotland speak, he'd never really expired at all, not even a hundred and seventy years or so after his reported death. It was all a hoax. Reports of his demise were exaggerated. In reality, he was living just around the corner, alive and well, up to his old tricks as usual. And just as usual, Rabbie took on the persona of the rascally nephew, the prodigal son, the lovable rogue. *Almost like Uncle Alistair*, thought James, *but wi' poetry*.

"Aye, that's Rab!" they'd say affectionately, when discussing his exploits, "ye ken what 'e's like wi' the lassies!"

Somehow, it didn't matter that Rab had seduced his way around Scotland, getting lassies 'into trouble' and leaving a trail of bastards in his wake. A wink and a nod and he was forgiven, for the truth was that The Bard wrote fantastic poetry in the Scots tongue and a wealth of love songs besides that lived in the hearts of all True Scots. What could you say about his philandering? It was Rabbie. That's how he was. We might have done the same if we could have got away with it. Maybe we did! Strangely, even James's mother had her own female version of this mostly masculine outlook.

"Aye, Rabbie loved 'is Bonnie Jean!" Janet would say, a gleam in her eye as she sat over her knitting by the coal fire, while Kenneth McKellar gave voice to one of The Bard's evergreens on the wireless, imagining *she* was Bonnie Jean, canoodling with Rab - and more - while comin' through the rye in the gloamin of a Scottish summer's evening or on the banks and braes o' Bonnie Doon.

At a time when Victorian social mores still held sway in Presbyterian Scotland, the single exception seemed to be Rabbie he was allowed to do anything he liked; after all, was he not one of us? And Mr Oxnam's story about how Rabbie and his best pal, Ainslie, came to Innerleithen to father a few more bastards was just another in a long line of similar anecdotes.

"Well," said Mr Oxnam, looking around the blank faces. "Ah can see Ah'm goin' tae have tae fill you lads in. That is, if ye want tae be filled in?"

Nodding heads. Yes, they wanted tae be filled in.

"It was like this," said Mr Oxnam patiently, as if explaining something complicated to a gaggle of toddlers. "It was 1787. Rabbie was, let me think..." He screwed up his face. "...about 28 years old. 'E was just becomin' famous, ye see. 'E'd had 'is first book o' poems published, *The Kilmarnock Edition*. 'E'd started tae make a bit o' money from 'is poetry – no bad for an Ayrshire ploughman! 'E'd gone up tae Edinburgh and been welcomed intae high society. Then 'e decided it was time for a wee holiday in the Borders wi' 'is pal, Ainslie, who was a young lawyer. They went on a tour – on horseback, mind ye, and Rabbie had 'is ain horse, a mare ca'd Jenny Geddes.

"Well, 'e wanted to see The Bush Aboon Traquair – for those of ye who've nae idea what Ah'm talkin' aboot," - which was painfully obvious from further blank expressions - "that was a famous poem by some other poet. Anyway, Burns and Ainslie stopped off in Innerleithen and had a look round the district. Ah dinnae ken, but they might have come along this way on their search for The Bush!" He gestured around him. "Maybe even, this wee glen was the inspiration for a poem. Just imagine, at night in the inn after a guid supper, The Bard lights a candle in 'is room, sits doon at the table, gets oot a sheet o' parchment, a quill an' 'is inkwell, an' starts tae write!"

With that, he suddenly stood up, walked the few yards to where the burn made a small loop, placed himself in the meander and turned to face his audience with a theatrical stance. He grasped his lapels as if he was the President of the Innerleithen and Traquair Burns Club (which, in truth, he was) about to make a speech, and began to declaim verbatim in a booming, sonorous voice, slowly enunciating so that his listeners could savour every word.

Their groves o' sweet myrtle let foreign lands reckon
Where bright beamin' summers exalt the perfume
Far dearer to me yon lone glen o' green breckan...
...Wi' the burn stealin' under the lang yellow broom;
Far dearer tae me are yon humble broom bowers
Where the bluebell and gowan lurk lowly, unseen
For there, lightly tripping amang the wild flowers
A-listening the linnet, aft wanders mah Jean!

Mr Boswell, the lads, the Sergeant, James, they all burst into spontaneous applause and thumped on the table so that the coffee cups jumped. Mr Oxnam, smiling broadly, gave a small bow of acknowledgement, took his place again and resumed his narrative.

"So, Burns and Ainslie, they put up at the inn at Innerleithen for the night. And this is where it gets interestin'." He looked around at the faces. "That's when they meet two braw young Border queynes an' get them both intae trouble."

Pausing, he gazed thoughtfully at James, who was wondering how Rabbie and his friend had got the lassies into trouble. At thirteen-going-on-fourteen, he was beginning to have a clearer idea of how babies were made. Without understanding the intricacies of the mechanics, he'd worked out that babies could result when a man 'slept' with a woman. And that, apparently, was what Rabbie Burns was very good at.

"As we've got a young laddie here, Ah'll leave the rest tae yer imagination!" the Factor continued unhelpfully. He gave his listeners a knowing look and a wink. "Suffice tae say, tradition has it that one o' they lassies was mah great, great, great grandmother. But we dinnae ken which one was which! Was it Burns that got her intae trouble? Or was it Ainslie? Now, nothin' against Ainslie. He was tae become a big lawyer up in the Edinburgh High Street. One o' the High Heid Yins. But just think – there's a fifty-fifty chance Ah could be descended frae The Bard himself!"

With a satisfied expression, the Factor leaned back and picked up his mug, enjoying the reaction to his anecdote. Mr Boswell, his elbows on the table, pursed his lips and gave out, "Well, well, well" under his breath. The two Boswell workers sat silent but nodded their heads, looking mightily impressed. James was too. The Factor's story certainly had a ring of truth about it. What were the chances that Rabbie could have been here, on Jenny Geddes, riding down this road looking for The Bush Aboon Traquair, whatever that was? It put a whole new dimension on things. He looked back at the cottage, shining in the sunlight with its new roof, and wondered how old it was. Could it be two hundred years old? There were plenty of houses that old in Edinburgh and Leith. Why couldn't this cottage have stood at the time of Rabbie? He suddenly had a picture of his mind of Rabbie and Ainslie stopping off at the cottage to water their horses in the burn, and maybe have a wee dram with the householder. Who knew, maybe it was here they got the lassies into trouble? Was it possible? Anything was possible.

But Sergeant Seatoun was more sceptical. These Border loons and young James could believe what they liked. Though he had a lot of time for the Factor, he was beginning to think he might be a teller of tall tales.

And enjoying it. Yes, the fact that Rabbie had visited these parts was a matter of record. But as for being the great, great, great grandfather of the Factor? It could simply be a case of blawin' yer crack. The Sergeant decided it was time to draw a line under the matter.

"That reminds me o' the time," he said with a mock-serious expression, "when Hamish and Sandy were in a pub. Says Sandy, 'Have ye heard, Hamish, that recent research has found half o' the Scottish population is descended frae Rabbie Burns?' 'Aye,' says Hamish, 'an' the other half's descended frae Bonnie Prince Charlie!'"

At that, the whole table cracked up. Mr Boswell nearly choked on his digestive and the Factor had to thump him on the back to help him out. Patrick and Gordon were wiping away tears and James was laughing too. He'd have to make sure he told *that* one at school.

"Well, lads," said the Sergeant, smiling at the very positive response to his wee joke and taking advantage of a lull in the laughter, "time tae get back tae work, Ah think." He looked at his watch and then at James.

"Now, son, ye've done us proud wi' yer dinner the day. There's no too much tae dae this afternoon so if ye want tae go off for a wee dauner after ye've cleared up in the kitchen, that's all right, but make sure ye're back by four at the latest." He looked up at the sky. The sun had suddenly disappeared and dark clouds were sweeping towards them from the direction of Drumbreck. "Better make it short, son, whatever ye do. Looks like the rain's no far off."

The Sergeant well knew by now James's urge to get into the hills whenever he could. He'd got into the habit of letting James off for an hour or two in the afternoon as long as he was no longer needed. In a way, the freedom to wander was recompense for his unpaid contribution to the work at The Glen. To James, it was a very fair trade indeed. The two or three times he'd been out he'd explored the ridge behind the cottage and discovered the hidden lochan called Leuchar, a magic spot, nestling between folds in the range with a small island in the middle. James had lingered there a while, lounging in the heather listening to the curlews, and promised himself he'd come back as often as possible and maybe try and swim over to the island despite the icy water. Then he'd explored further up the estate road. He'd discovered it came to a dead-end where the flat land suddenly stopped and where another lochan, the source of the burn, lapped the edges of the track. But that was as far as he'd gone.

It was then that the Factor, picking up on the Sergeant's message, chimed in.

"Now, James, ye like tae wander the hills, is that right?"

"Aye, Sir, Ah do!" replied James with a grin.

"Now," said the Factor, "Ah'm goin' tae let ye intae a wee secret." He looked around at the others who were listening carefully, winked, and turned back to James. "Did ye ken there's a real braw spot from which ye can see Saint Mary's Loch?"

James had never heard of Saint Mary's Loch but its name sounded important so his interest was immediately aroused. He shook his head.

"Well, this is a place naebody kens aboot. Except for a few estate folk that have been up there." He nodded towards Drumbreck, louring behind James's shoulder. "Now, would ye like tae go there?"

"Aye, Ah would!"

"Right Ah'll tell ye how. But ye need plenty o' time tae get there an' back, and ye need tae be careful. It's sair rough country up there, so ca' canny, all right?"

James nodded. As Mr Boswell and his men finally relinquished their dinner and left for the afternoon shift on the cottage floor, the Factor got up and walked towards the burn, gesturing James to follow, Rab and Jean clinging to his heels like two large black and white leeches. Mr Oxnam stood facing the southwestern corner of Drumbreck and pointed with a straight right arm and a long, lingering index finger. Just visible was a col between two huge masses of upland.

"See that shin? That's where ye have tae go. Now, ye've been along this road tae the wee lochan where the glen tapers oot, haven't ye? Well, that's Kirkscleuch and it's the source o' the Thrashie Burn." He pointed to the peat-coloured water gushing at their feet. "Now, ye'll see a burn that runs intae the lochan comin' doon the hill. It's Kirkscleuch Burn. Follow it up and it'll take ye right up tae a spring on the top. That's mah secret place and that's where ye'll see Saint Mary's Loch on the other side o' the mountain. Now, Ah'm goin' tae tell ye another secret. It has a name. Ye'll no see this name on any map. It's just the name the local folk gie it. It's called the Tulzie Kaime. Now, dinnae ask me what that means, for Ah dinnae ken. It's the auld Scots tongue. It's been called that for as long as folks have lived here aboot. But," he added, looking up at the weather, "Ah doot ye'll be goin' up there the day. Ye'll have tae pick a day when the weather's right and ye've plenty o' time."

"Aye," agreed Sergeant Seatoun, "The Factor's right. Ye'll need the time and ye'll need tae be prepared. Ye've got a rucksack, haven't ye?"

"Aye, of course Ah have!" replied James, struggling to keep up with the stream of information. "It's a Bergen."

"Well, next time, bring yer Bergen, make sure ye have a spare jersey, spare socks, a rain jacket and a toorie."

James didn't have a toorie but he did have a thick, grey balaclava, courtesy of his mother's knitting mania.

"From here, ye'll need," the Sergeant looked to the Factor for confirmation, "maybe two hours there an' back?"

"Mair like three," said the Factor.

"So, maybe next week, son, if the weather plays along?"

James nodded, thanking the Factor for his help. Just imagine, a secret place few people knew about, the Tulzie Kaime! And it was up there on Drumbreck, just waiting for him. He could almost see it in his mind's eye. He would drop into the school library to find out more about Saint Mary's Loch. Then he reluctantly turned away and started clearing away the last of the dinner things. By the time he'd finished in the kitchen, the rain had set in and he had to be satisfied with a scant hour exploring the woods above the cottage. He was back by four-thirty, soaked through, and found the Sergeant waiting. The Boswell crew were already packing up and so would he and James. If they could get away smartly, he was going to stop in Innerleithen to show James something of special interest but wanted to keep it as a surprise.

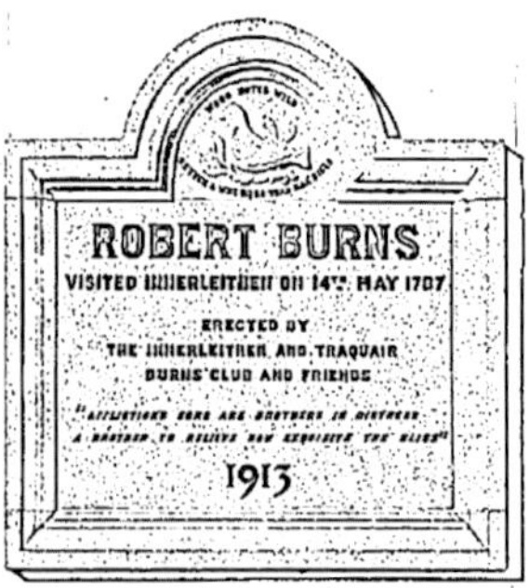

The Bedford left with the Boswell crew and the Sergeant locked the cottage door, now refurbished with a new lock and new hinges. They set off in the rain. The Sergeant told James they'd take the B709 back, for what he wanted to show him would be directly on their route. After Traquair, the Jaguar turned right into Innerleithen High Street and just before their turn off north the Sergeant stopped in front of a strangely shaped corner building of dressed stone in a pseudo-Georgian style. It must have been at least a hundred years old. They got out. The rain had now let off. The Sergeant pointed at the building. There was a large stone plaque let into the wall at about head height. The inscription read:

ROBERT BURNS
VISITED INNERLEITHEN ON 14TH MAY 1787
ERECTED BY
THE INNERLEITHEN AND TRAQUAIR
BURNS CLUB AND FRIENDS
1913

At the top of the plaque was a woodlark sitting on a bush beneath the words *Wood Notes Wild.* Below the bird was the motto: *Better a wee bush than nae bield.* James didn't understand the motto and neither did the Sergeant, who was standing back enjoying James's reaction to his special surprise. But, grabbing a pen from his duffel bag and an old envelope from the Jag, James wrote it down, determined to find out what it meant. Maybe his English teacher, Mr Fluke, would be the most likely to know since he was the only staff member James knew of who dropped Scottish words like 'swither' and 'scunner' into his speech during lessons. So, the Factor had been right; Rabbie *had* been here. At least that part was true. But how much of the rest was? In reality, they'd never know. But it made for a great story, to be puzzled over, recalled and re-told in years to come.

Lucy Ashton

As he neared the ridge, James immediately spotted the spring the Factor had described. A hole had been gouged out of the hillside by the centuries of running water that now dribbled steadily over the bare rock to become the Kirkscleuch burn, a wee trickle of water that got wider as it descended the steep shoulder of Drumbreck and fed Kirkscleuch Lochan, that fed the Thrashie Burn, that flowed into the Tweed. He leant down, cupped his hand under the trickle, let it fill then raised it to his mouth. Pure, crystal clear water, nothing like the stuff you got through the tap in the City, even though it would be hard to fault Edinburgh for the quality of its water these days. He struggled on up the last section of the incline as the ground flattened out. A few more steps and he was on a wide col. It was the Tulzie Kaime. Puggled, his face red from exertion, he stopped to catch his breath, hands on hips, and looked around. On either side was an enormous, steep, heather-and-rock-covered spur of the Drumbreck massif. Though the weather had held, the tops were already shrouded in mist. He'd have to hurry if he wanted a glimpse of the loch. Eagerly, he strode across the floor of the col.

It was the following Saturday and he'd started out as planned. The weather had remained clement for the time of year with scudding clouds and the chance of a shower. He'd served dinner deliberately early – by special request of the Boswells, stovies, sausages, peas and carrots with jam roll and custard to follow. Then, after rushing to clear up the kitchen, he was ready by one o'clock. The Sergeant had insisted on driving him up to Kirkscleuch lochan to save a bit of time and had bid him farewell as he clambered over the wire fence and followed the course of the burn. He watched as the red Jag manoeuvred in the turning space then rapidly disappeared back down the estate track. He had almost three hours to get up there and back. Removing his jersey, he stowed it in his Bergen and set off in shirt sleeves. *When on a climb, always start cold* the clever books had said, and he'd quickly learned the truth of that maxim. The climb to the col took him almost an hour. There was no path; he had to make his own. He zig-zagged across the hillside on the particularly steep bits, keeping within sight of the burn at first, then following it closely as it finally entered the Kirks Cleuch proper, which led him up sodden steps of peat and slippery rock until at last he sighted the spring.

Then he had to cross about a hundred yards of flat ground that was soft but not too muddy; obviously, the spring was helping to drain the col. Approaching the opposite side, he found his outlook opening out. It was misty here as well, but he could clearly see down to the lowlands many hundreds of feet below. Suddenly, there it was, St Mary's Loch away in the distance, glinting in the sunlight with its unmistakable banana shape. In the intervening week, he'd splashed out, paying 4s6d for an Ordinance Survey map of the area. Now, with the little brass compass (7s6d from Millets) he used in the Pentlands, he checked that his identification had been correct. According to his map, the loch should have been almost due south of where he was standing, and so it was. He could even make out the oddly shaped Megget Reservoir, which looked like a horned snail without its shell crawling away westwards.

He stopped abruptly when the ground started to drop away again, noticing that on this slope too, a spring was draining the col. A thought struck him. That wee trickle of water back there would eventually flow via The Tweed into the North Sea, while this spring would eventually find its way to the Irish Sea. He'd learnt about the concept of a watershed in geography classes. Now he was actually standing on top of one that drained both northeast and southwest in the space of a bit over a hundred yards. Suddenly, what had been a mundane school subject took on new meaning. The drop on this side looked to be much greater than on the other. He estimated that he'd probably need three or four hours at least to get down to the Loch itself. Anyway, it was time to rest and earn his reward – the view of St Mary's, the mountain beauty and the solitude. He found a little depression among the rocks shaped almost like an armchair. It was much colder up here and the south-westerly was blowing straight into his face. He put on his sweater and, tucking his rain jacket underneath him, he sat down to enjoy the thermos flask of Camp coffee and the sandwich in his rucksack.

"What are you doing here? Don't you know this is private property?"

James almost jumped out of his skin. The unexpected incursion of a human voice into this silent world was like the screeching of nails across a blackboard. Who else could possibly be here in this isolated spot? Shaken to his core, he leapt to his feet, dropping his sandwich in the process, and spun around. It was hard to credit what he saw. It was a girl. She was older than he was. She looked to be around sixteen. She was tall and thin with thick red hair that flowed over her shoulders in waves. She had a small dog on a lead, some kind of fancy spaniel by the looks of it and not at all the sort of dog you'd have expected to see up here on the mountain. Certainly no Rab or Jean.

She came closer, and James could see that she had a pale, translucent complexion and a freckled face. At the moment, though, her expression was imperious, to say the least. She had on a cream-coloured, long-sleeved shift that had an elaborate lace collar and lace cuffs, and came down below her knees. This was topped by a sleeveless woollen beige tunic with large deer horn buttons down the front and deep pockets that looked as if it would be quite warm. Around her neck was a thin gold chain and on the end of it, just peeping out above her lace collar, was a crucifix. On her feet was a pair of shiny, black, patent boots that were remarkably clean, considering she must have walked a long way to get here.

As James stared in disbelief, his brain was working overtime. His immediate assumption was that she was from The Big House. This deduction was based on, first, the fact that she had a distinct, upper-class, English accent. He'd heard that these lairds were, as the locals opined, 'gey queer folk.' They claimed they were Scottish but spoke with English accents and sent their children to expensive private schools in England or even abroad to Switzerland. Second, her dress was more or less what he'd have expected the daughter of a laird to wear. He'd seen in photos how these anglicised landowners often dressed their offspring, both male and female, in quirky outfits when on their estates. Third, from its noble head, floppy ears and shiny coat, he guessed that the dog had an expensive pedigree. As he hesitated, the girl spoke again.

"Didn't you hear me? I said this is private property! Now get out!"

James was flummoxed. Never having been in this situation before, he didn't know what to say. She was accusing him of trespassing but he was here working at the behest of the Chief who had a free run of the estate courtesy of the Laird. How did you explain that to a hostile, arrogant girl in a few words? He decided that, as his father had tirelessly counselled, attack is often the best means of defence.

"Ah'm not trespassin' if that's what ye think!" he said forcefully. "Ah have permission tae be here!" Seeing doubt creep into her expression, he added in a combative tone, "It's the truth!" and was gratified to note that his outburst seemed to be having the desired effect.

"*Who* gave you permission to be here?" she asked, still imperious but in a softer tone.

"D'ye ken Chief Constable Merrilees?"

"I've never heard of him!"

"Well ye should've! 'E's the police chief for the Lothians and Peebles and this is the Lothians and Peebles, is it not?"

"What about him?"

"'E's mah uncle." James conveniently chose the shorthand version. "'E's rentin' a cottage from the Laird and Ah'm here tae work on renovatin' it." Not exactly right, but near enough.

The girl had stopped a few yards from him now, and, as she considered how to respond, her little spaniel started yapping at him, obviously viewing their closeness as the trigger to defend its mistress.

"Oh, do stop it, Trixie, do!" commanded the girl, and the yapping stopped. "Well," she said, after a pause, "I suppose it's all right but I'll only believe you if you tell me your name and where you're from."

The situation was beginning to calm down.

"Ah'm James Swanston from Edinburgh."

From her expression, she was still weighing him up. He decided to push home his advantage.

"And what's *your* name then?"

"Lucy Ashton," she shot back without a second's hesitation.

Thinking what a posh name it was, but keeping his thoughts to himself, he decided it was time to make a concession of his own.

"Why don't we sit down? Ye can share mah sandwich if ye want." *That is,* he thought, *if Ah can rescue it from the muck!*

He gestured her over and sat back down in his place while she found a spot on a neighbouring rock with the Loch still glinting in the sunlight way below. The sandwich was indeed redeemable, but she declined his offer and merely sat staring at him from her perch, holding on to her dog by the lead. He ventured another question.

"What kind of a name is *Lucy Ashton*, then?"

"I was named after *The Bride of Lammermoor*," she remarked, somewhat petulantly, and continued to stare at him.

"The Bride of Lammermoor? Who's she when she's at home?" he replied, attempting to moderate his dialect to her high English.

She glanced at him with a look of impatience.

"Sir Walter Scott. *The Bride of Lammermoor*!"

James sighed.

"Listen, Lucy Ashton, ye can keep sayin' The Bride of Lammermoor or whatever till ye're blue in the face but, Ah'm sorry tae have tae inform ye that Ah haven't a clue what ye're talkin' about!"

“My goodness,” she replied, “what *do* you learn at school?” And then, switching deftly from sarcasm to incredulity, “You do *go* to school, don’t you?”

“Of course Ah go to school! Ah’m in the Third Year at The Academy in Edinburgh.”

“So you say you attend an academy but you’ve never heard of Sir Walter Scott, one of Scotland’s greatest authors? How is that possible?”

Disbelief was written all over her face. Obviously, James knew the acclaimed Sir Walter. Wasn’t there a fancy-looking monument in Princess Street Gardens that he’d passed countless times? Was it not single-handedly responsible for his claustrophobia, triggered when Janet had fussed him up to the very top when he was a bairn? But he’d never read a single one of his books. He’d once picked one up in Leith Public Library, *Waverley*. He’d been curious about the name – Waverley Station was where Uncle Willie had arrested the German spy. But after struggling to read a couple of paragraphs’ worth of Sir Walter’s turgid prose, he’d realised he’d made a big mistake and decided there and then that the famous literary Scot wasn’t for him.

“Of course Ah’ve *heard* of ’im!” he insisted. “But,” he added lamely, “Ah’ve never actually read anything ’e wrote.” He was embarrassed on two counts. This snooty English girl was questioning the extent of his education. Not only that, she was also claiming acquaintance with Sir Walter’s novels, while he, a Scot, could only admit ignorance.

“Well,” she said as if reading his thoughts, “if you do want to consider yourself educated, you must read Sir Walter Scott. And I strongly suggest you start with *The Bride of Lammermoor*!”

And with that, she got up, delicately dusted bits of heather and twig off her skirt, and made as if to leave.

“Just a minute,” said James. Then he blurted it out without thinking what he was saying. “Will Ah see ye again?”

As soon as he’d said it, he cursed himself inwardly. Why had he said that? She was a total snob. Why would he want to see *her* again? But, inexplicably, he found he was drawn to her. Yes, she seemed obnoxious. But there was something about her he couldn’t explain. Her very contrariness attracted him; not only that, she was obviously educated and might be quite good-looking if she’d only smile.

“Well, I do sometimes come up here on a Saturday afternoon. Maybe I’ll see you again, who knows?” she replied primly.

She coolly turned round and, without saying a word of goodbye, walked off in a northerly direction, first crossing the floor of the col, apparently making for the east face of Drumbreck, her spaniel trotting alongside. James was puzzled. He hadn’t seen any sign of a path there.

She was undoubtedly heading in the direction of The Big House but it was several miles away. It would be a trek, and hazardous, especially as it was turning cold and the mist was now almost down to their level.

He turned away, threw on his rain jacket, pulled on his balaclava, shoved his map, compass and thermos back into the Bergen, swung it on his back and turned round again to go after her. But she was gone. She'd been swallowed up by the mist that was now cascading down the sides of the mountain. He briefly looked for the path she'd taken but could see none. Now the weather was really closing in fast. If he stayed here any longer, he could find himself in a tight spot. He hoped she'd be all right. He looked at his watch. Just after three. He'd need a good hour to get back to the cottage; he'd have to get his skates on. He headed across the col and plunged back down into the muddy delights of the Kirks Cleuch.

The Bride of Lammermoor

James never told anyone about his meeting with Lucy Ashton. There were so many strange aspects to it that he felt anyone he told wouldn't believe him. Who exactly was she? He was picking that she was a daughter of the Laird or one of his relations, but he didn't know. How had she got to the Tulzie Kaime? Where had she gone? Why was she obsessed with Sir Walter Scott? Was she really named after one of his characters? She was, not to put too fine a point on it, an enigma. Anyway, he didn't intend to let anyone into this private corner of his life, at least not yet. Despite his initial shock, then his anger, then his humiliation at being judged uneducated, he knew that something special had occurred. Lucy Ashton was his secret and he was determined to keep it that way.

The first thing he did on Monday morning in the break was to make a beeline for the school library. No, the librarian was sorry, but they didn't keep a copy of *The Bride of Lammermoor*. So, after school, he hurried along Junction Street to Leith Public Library. Again, the answer was no. The librarian there was sorry too. They did have a few works by Walter Scott but they weren't popular any more. Besides, that particular title was a speciality and not the sort of thing you'd find in a public library. He could try one of the University libraries but he wouldn't be able to borrow from there. Or, he might be able to get a cheap copy at one of the second-hand bookshops up the town. Come Tuesday, James's frustration was growing. He just couldn't stop thinking about Lucy. He'd slept badly. He'd dreamt he was up on the Tulzie Kaime in the rain, slogging through the mud, calling into the mist, "Lucy, where are you?"

but he couldn't find her. At breakfast, his mother asked him who Lucy was, as she'd heard him talking in his sleep. Thinking on his feet, he lied that it wasn't 'Lucy' she'd heard. He must have been talking about losing something. Against her better judgement she believed him.

After school, he took the Number 1 bus to the top of the High Street and walked down the right-hand side of George IV Bridge in the direction of Edinburgh University. Not far from the Greyfriars Bobby statue he found a little second-hand bookshop specialising in university texts. The glass-panelled door had a bell attached that rang as he entered. He found himself surrounded by shelf upon shelf of dusty books. A dusty little proprietor who was thin and bald and looked like a superannuated professor suddenly appeared from between the racks, smiling benevolently in anticipation of a sale. Did he have a copy of *The Bride of Lammermoor*? Yes, he did. It was a used university textbook in good condition and he could have it for sixpence. James readily handed over the money. The book, which the dusty proprietor insisted on wrapping nicely in brown paper, was his. He stuffed it in his school bag, which he held onto all the way home as if it contained a gold ingot.

That evening, he was supposed to be swotting for a French test on the subjunctive voice for Miss Ross but instead, he unwrapped his treasured second-hand copy of *The Bride of Lammermoor* and started to read. It was hard going at first. He had to negotiate much the same turgid prose he'd encountered with *Waverley*. The first thing he discovered was that Lucy Ashton hadn't been fibbing up on the Tulzie Kaime, for the heroine of the story *was* called Lucy Ashton. He struggled on, encouraged by the uncanny connection between the living person and the fictitious character. Eventually, helped by the old-fashioned engravings, he found he was getting used to Sir Walter's tortuous style and was growing interested in the plot of the tragic heroine whose love for Edgar Ravenswood was thwarted by her evil, scheming mother. He began to wonder how it would all end but forced himself not to peep at the final pages. Neglecting his school work, every night that week he sat in his parents' bedroom pretending to study but in reality grinding through another, and yet another, page of *The Bride*. He took the book to bed with him and read it under the covers by torchlight. Every time he had the book open in front of him, he was instantly connected to Lucy, the real Lucy. In his mind, *she* was *The Bride*. The heroine's exploits were her exploits. The heroine's love for Edgar was *her* love for... *him*! The realisation hit him like a brick. Lucy was Lucy and *he* was Edgar! No, that was ridiculous. He shook his head to clear his brain of such a moronic idea. But the more he read, the more he found himself identifying with Edgar, no matter how much he tried not to.

At breakfasts, his eyes were noticeably bleary and his mother warned him that he wasn't getting enough sleep. After class, Miss Ross called him over and questioned his poor showing in the French test. Was anything wrong? He really liked Miss Ross so he hated having to lie to her. But he had no choice. And the fact that he was taller than her made it somehow easier. There was a problem at home he said. He hadn't had time to study. But he'd do better next time. Satisfied with his explanation, Miss Ross let him go. This time he'd got off the hook but he was going to have to make a hard decision. His reading of *The Bride* was becoming an obsession, an addiction even. He was going to have to force himself to suspend it for a while. After marking his place with a scrap of paper, he took the book and hid it away at the back of the bottom drawer of the dresser he used in his parents' room. It would stay there until he'd caught up with his studies, until equilibrium had returned to his life.

By late October, the work at The Glen was picking up. The floors were finished and work had commenced on the internal walls, which first had to be re-plastered and pointed and then whitewashed. As well, multiple door frames, window frames and skirting boards had to be replaced. It was a big job. Not only that, a plumber, Mr Hassenden, had turned up from Selkirk with his mate to make a start on upgrading the plumbing which would turn into a major project in itself, for the old Victorian pipes, some even pre-Victorian apparently, had turned out to be rotten.

This meant that James now had seven mouths to feed including his own, sometimes even eight, for the Factor now dropped by regularly and wasn't averse to a spot of James's cooking when it was offered to him. James's workload in the kitchen had increased markedly. The weather having started to turn, meals had moved inside to the bench and chairs that were now set up in the living room.

All week, Lucy Ashton had filled his thoughts and his only wish was to get up to the Tulzie Kaime that Saturday to see if she was there. But it wasn't to be. Not only was there insufficient time, but the autumn storms were starting up and Drumbreck had disappeared in a maelstrom of wind, rain and low cloud. The Saturday after that was the last in October. The Sergeant, aware James was now under more pressure, gallantly stepped in and helped out in the kitchen. His input should have been enough to let James out into the hills for the afternoon, but again, the weather intervened and any thought of going up onto the tops had to be dismissed.

"Just think of the books ye told me about, the ones on walkin' and climbin' in the hills. Surely they tell ye that ye never venture out in filthy weather like this? It's better tae be safe than sorry. Remember, there'll be a next time!"

James had to ruefully agree. And the Sergeant was right. There *was* a next time. The third Saturday after he'd first met Lucy was the first in November. It dawned crisp and clear. Frost had settled overnight and the prospects were for a cold but fine day. As they drove south towards The Glen after picking up provisions in Dalkeith, taking care to safely negotiate the black ice on the roads, both friends were in high spirits.

"It's lookin' good, isn't it, Sergeant? What d'ye think? Can Ah can get up tae the Tulzie Kaime the day?"

"Well, let's say we'll try our best, shall we?"

Of course, the Sergeant knew nothing about Lucy, but he knew that James loved the hills and from his reports, understood well that the Tulzie Kaime had somehow captured his imagination. So again, he did his best to ensure his apprentice could get off early. They were helped by the fact that the workmen had put in a special request the Saturday before. Could they have haggis, neeps and tatties? The Sergeant had registered a special order with Sandersons for a generous haggis to be made ready for pick up but there was one small problem; James had never done haggis before. So, midweek, he'd had a special session with Janet in the kitchen and had learnt all the secrets, courtesy of his mother's memory and Mrs Kirk's *Tried Favourites*. It turned out to be an easy and quick meal to prepare and serve. The lads were pleased by the positive response to their request, especially when they had sherry trifle for afters, courtesy of Mrs Seatoun, containing real sherry and eliciting from Mr Boswell the comment that if she ever got tired of the Sergeant, he'd be happy to take her in. To the accompaniment of laughter, the Sergeant promised to pass on the message.

The good weather having held, James could at last get back up to where he wanted to be. Again, the Sergeant drove him up to the lochan and dropped him off, making him promise that he'd be back by four at the latest. He set off in a hurry, almost racing up the steepness of Drumbreck, entirely ignoring one of the cardinal rules from his books:

When faced with a steep slope never rush up it. You'll just tire fast and soon you'll have to stop. Instead, set off slowly and steadily, regulating your pace and your breathing to your level of fitness.

Inevitably, his first forced stop didn't take long. Red-faced and puggled, he bent over, taking in great gouts of mountain air to replenish his lungs. Then, getting a hold of himself and remembering the sage advice, he set off again, this time slowly and deliberately, pacing himself against the gradient. This new approach had the added advantage that he was now able to look around him as he walked, attending to the call of the curlew and taking in the glories of Drumbreck, now entirely freed from any hint of cloud, rising dark and majestic against an azure sky that seemed to stretch forever.

Slowly ascending the rocks and peat of Kirks Cleuch, he greeted the little spring still flowing steadily towards the North Sea, and breasted the ridge onto the col. The Tulzie Kaime at last! He walked forward over the floor towards the St Mary's Loch lookout. The first thing he saw in the distance was a figure he took to be Lucy from her similar style of dress, sitting on her rock with her back to him, apparently enjoying the view, Trixie curled up at her side.

He was delighted that she was there but instantly decided he'd get his own back. Two could play at this game. He'd creep up on her and give her a scare just as she'd scared him three weeks before. It was childish, he knew, but he didn't care. Quietly approaching the rock, he placed his boots carefully at every step, fearful that Trixie would bark a warning. But strangely, the small bitch never gave a sound, even though she'd obviously spotted him. He'd just got to within five yards of his prey, curbing the sound of his breathing and relishing the mayhem he was about to unleash, when his little scheme was abruptly killed off before it saw the light of day.

"Well, James Swanston, have you made your acquaintance with Sir Walter Scott yet?"

The unmistakeable English accent of Lucy Ashton cut through the mountain silence and gave *him* the very fright he'd been preparing to give *her*. She'd spoken without even looking at him, without turning round. He was stopped in his tracks. How on earth had she known he was there? Still, Trixie didn't bark. How strange. He walked forward. Still, Lucy didn't turn round, her gaze apparently fixed on the view spreading out before her. When he drew level with her, but some yards away, at last she turned her head and looked at him. Yes, it was the same Lucy Ashton, just as before. The same red hair, the same freckles, the same snobby demeanour. But somehow, she looked different. What was it? James thought for a second then realised what it was. Lucy Ashton was smiling.

"Hello, James," she said playfully. "Has the cat got your tongue?"

Yet again she'd bested him. How *did* she do it? No matter what he did or said, she always seemed to be able to demonstrate her superiority. It didn't help of course that he was a naïve gowk with his vulgar accent, and she with the airs of an English lady. From somewhere, he managed to pull himself together.

"Hello, Lucy," he said, trying to sound grown-up. "It's nice to see you again."

"And it's nice to see you, too, James!"

"How did ye know Ah was here?"

"Oh, James, James," she mocked. "I know everything!"

"How can ye know everything?" he scoffed. "That's impossible!"

"Shall we say I know everything that's worth knowing?"

Checked yet again, James dithered. Lucy played a good game.

"You haven't answered my question yet!" she complained, breaking into his silence.

"What question?"

"About Sir Walter Scott!"

"Oh, that question! Well, the answer's yes. Ah'm readin' *The Bride of Lammermoor*."

"Well done, James! And, what do you think? Are you smitten?"

"Well..."

As he wondered what to say, it suddenly occurred to him how bizarre the whole thing must appear to some invisible observer of their encounter. Here he was in the wilds of the Border Country about a thousand feet above sea level in the middle of a mountain massif, apparently about to discuss with an English girl an obscure novel by a long-dead and no longer fashionable Scottish writer. He mentally shook his head. He couldn't have made this up if he'd tried.

"...let's say it's a good story. But Ah'm still only halfway through." When she looked at him disapprovingly, he added, "Ah do have other priorities, ye know. Mah studies at The Academy for one thing!"

Then he decided it was time *he* went on the offensive. He had so many questions.

Where did she live? Why had she been called Lucy? As he'd guessed, she lived in The Big House. Her mother was the Laird's sister. Her father, who came from the wealthy Ashton family, had died when she was a baby but he'd wanted her to be christened Lucy because of his love for Walter Scott's novels and especially *The Bride of Lammermoor*.

Where did she go to school? She'd gone to a private school in Buckinghamshire but didn't any more. She had an English governess who also took charge of her schooling.

Why did she come to this particular place? Her mother had told her that she and her new husband had found this beauty spot when they were young and in love. They kept coming back. The Laird had even commissioned his workmen to build a footpath across the face of

Drumbreck to make access easier. *So that was why she was able to get here and back so quickly.*

Then she asked him about *his* life and the work that was going on down at The Glen. They talked and talked as the sun got lower in the sky and the air started to chill.

"Oh gosh!" James looked at his watch. It was already three-twenty. He scrambled his things together into his Bergen, swung it on his back and looked at Lucy.

"Sorry, but Ah have to go. They'll be waitin' for me!"

She smiled. Their long talk had somehow cemented the beginnings of a tentative friendship. Today she'd been different. She was still snobby but there was a warmth towards him he hadn't sensed before.

"Will Ah see ye again?" he asked.

"If you want to." Then she added, "I'll be here."

"Don't stay too long. It's getting' cold. Bye!"

"Don't worry! Goodbye!"

He hurried across the col floor, cursing to himself that he had to leave her so soon. Just before he dropped down into the Cleuch he turned round and looked one last time. She was still there, sitting on the rock, her back towards him just as she'd been before, but this time in silhouette, as the lowering winter sun shone fully on her motionless form and sank slowly towards the Western Isles.

The weather in November was wet, windy and foul. Excursions up to the Tulzie Kaime were out of the question. Although no snow fell in the lowlands, the tops were white with it. The Sergeant, the tradesmen and James battled on through into the second week of December then, when the first real snows arrived, the build had to be shut down for the year. The snowploughs easily coped with the main highways in The Borders but many of the minor roads were left to themselves. No one could predict what the conditions might be. Drifting snow cut off many a farm and hamlet. Without four-wheel-drive, snow chains and plenty of luck, no journey in the backcountry was feasible.

Christmas came and went, then Hogmanay with the usual round of socialising, family get-togethers and midnight taxis home on black ice. January came in freezing and abominable as it always did, and seemed to go on for ever as it always did. Snow flurries turned the beach at Portobello white. Then, as often happened in this part of Scotland, there was a uncharacteristic warm spell in mid-February. The roads thawed out; early daffodils and optimistic crocuses popped up their heads. James got the message by way of his grandparents. The Sergeant and the Boswell crew would make an attempt to get through to The Glen that Saturday. Was he on board? They didn't have to ask him twice.

The Tulzie Kaime

It was a cheery Sergeant Seatoun who turned up at eight on Saturday morning as usual, but to James's surprise not in the red Jag but a blue police Land Rover. The Sergeant had borrowed it 'just in case' snow conditions turned out to be worse than expected. They heartily shook hands, wishing each other a belated Happy New Year. It had been nearly two months. They chatted all the way there about what they'd done over Christmas and Hogmanay. Snow still blanketed the countryside but the highways were clear. They had to pick up provisions in Dalkeith so they risked the B709 that the Sergeant liked so much. James never forgot that trip. Snow ploughs had been at work along here, but the drifts had been so deep, especially in the bottoms where they had to cross burns, that driving through was like entering one icy canyon after another, with huge white walls of snow twenty feet high on either side of the narrow sliver of road that had been pushed through.

On the estate tracks, an attempt had been made at snow clearing but here among the woodlands, the thaw hadn't yet taken hold, the surface was icy and the Land Rover came into its own. James was wondering if the Bedford would get through, but he hadn't reckoned on the hardy Boswells; these were Border folk, well used to winter's harsh conditions. He and the Sergeant had just driven up to the cottage and were taking stock when the familiar throb of the Bedford's diesel motor could be heard through the clear winter air. Then it appeared, driving slowly down the hill towards them. At once, the Sergeant saw what James didn't until it was pointed out to him. The Boswells had stopped when the going had got rough and had put chains on the back wheels.

Mr Boswell and the lads jumped out and, stamping their feet on the snow, their breath smoking in the icy air, they renewed acquaintance, laughing and joking about what they'd been up to. The snowdrift against the front of the cottage was so deep the front door had disappeared but, as usual, the builders were well prepared with special snow shovels. As soon as the door was freed and opened up, James was first inside with a handful of kindling from the shed to start the fire and waken the place out of its frozen winter slumber. No damage of any kind was evident. The roof was still on, the renovated front and back doors had held firm, the new windows too. Water had been drained from the pipes before they'd left in November to prevent leaks, and the internal plastering and paint jobs hadn't suffered. Then it was just a case of carrying on where they'd left off.

James was busy in the kitchen, the plumbers arrived in a four-wheel drive to continue their work, and the Boswells had more walls to plaster. The cottage was slowly heating up and James made sure to keep piling wood on the fire. That Saturday, the Sergeant strongly advised James not to make an attempt on the Tulzie Kaime, even if there had been time. There was just too much snow around and he didn't want to be responsible for James's safety up there. All he needed to do was turn his ankle and he could freeze to death before anyone found him. James had no problem agreeing. Despite his eagerness to get up there, he'd wait till warmer weather came around. As it happened, he didn't have long to wait. By the beginning of March, the snows had gone, at least for now, and the temperatures were slowly rising. It was their third Saturday back. To James's delight, at last the Sergeant sanctioned an excursion.

All winter, Lucy Ashton hadn't strayed from James's thoughts. There had been end-of-term examinations at The Academy, so swotting had been on the agenda while Walter Scott had definitely been off. But not a day had gone by without Lucy entering his mind along with a picture of the Tulzie Kaime. He imagined what it must look like deep in snow, what the view of St Mary's Loch would be like in winter, and hoped that Lucy wasn't doing anything as foolish as venturing out there in the freezing weather.

It wasn't until after Christmas that his brain had had spare capacity to cope with Sir Walter again. Retrieving the novel from the bottom drawer of the dresser, he'd settled back on the settee after supper one night and tried to get into it again. It was just as hard as the first time round, if not harder. Making headway through the closely spaced lines of dense, early-nineteenth-century English prose was like trying to cut your way through the Amazonian jungle with a butter knife, but it now being the school holidays, he had plenty of time, so he persevered. As he did so, he found that his previous fantasy simply refused to go away: Lucy – his Lucy – was the heroine and he was the hero, Edgar. And the more he read, the more obsessive he became, not just about the literary Lucy but about the real Lucy. When he reached the last few pages, he almost shouted in disbelief to learn that Lucy dies after stabbing her groom on her wedding night and

Edgar is swallowed up by quicksand. He wanted to throw the book into the corner of the living room but didn't because he knew it would upset his mother. But what kind of an ending was that? What a fraud!

He'd dreamt about her again, but this time she was suffocating in the snow. She was freezing. She was dying. They were on the side of a mountain. He was trying to save her, to get her up, to warm her, but every time he tried she slipped away and her face disappeared in the freezing, white mass, her red tresses caught in the snow, then vanishing too. He'd wake with a start, his pyjama jacket soaked in sweat, suddenly relieved it was just a dream. He'd get up in the dark, fumble his way to the bathroom, dry himself with a towel, then put on a fresh T-shirt and try to get back to sleep. But he'd lie awake for hours in the yellow filtered light of the sodium street lamps, listening to the night sounds of Fox Crag; a foghorn from the Forth, a car accelerating up the Drive, a party breaking up loudly nearby. But, of course, his main thought was of her. Where was she? When would he see her again? It wasn't that he had a crush on her. Experience had taught that sixteen-year-old girls weren't remotely interested in fourteen-year-old boys in that way. But he couldn't rid himself of the feeling that something connected them, something defined their relationship. And he didn't know what.

As usual, Sergeant Seatoun dropped him off at the lochan. The day was mild, the southerly breeze encouraging the thaw. Clouds drifted across the sun, still fairly low in the sky just this side of the equinox. But you could be forgiven for thinking spring had already arrived, for early skylarks were hovering and pheasants were calling. He made his way carefully up to the Kirks Cleuch, zig-zagging across the face of Drumbreck, avoiding the deep cracks where snow had drifted to make perfect traps for the unwary. Seeing that the Cleuch was also choked with drift, he detoured on snow-free ground. He breasted the rise further along from his usual route and instantly stopped to take his bearings and look around. There was no sign of Lucy. He walked the hundred yards across the col floor, avoiding dubious patches, and reached his rocky armchair. There down below, steadfast, unchanging, was Saint Mary's Loch, glittering in the sunlight as usual. One day he'd be down there, he promised himself. Maybe he'd walk. Maybe he'd drive. But then, standing at the water's edge, he'd turn and look back at Drumbreck. He'd take out his dad's army binoculars and pick out the Tulzie Kaime tucked between the arms of the massif and he'd tell himself with wonder, *Once, I was up there*!

He hung around, enjoying the view and the solitude, hoping that Lucy might turn up. He drank his coffee from the flask and munched the pie that had been hot when he'd stuffed it into his rucksack. Still no

Lucy. He wandered over to the north side of the col, looking for the path to The Big House that Lucy had described, casting around like a scenting dog, but he found nary a trace of a path. How could that be? He must be looking in the wrong place. Maybe it was covered with snowdrift.

Suddenly he sensed a presence behind him. He was instantly alert. It would be Lucy. She wouldn't catch him unawares this time. He whirled round. There, not five yards from him was a magnificent stag with a huge set of antlers. In attendance were two does, hanging back nervously. James froze. He'd never been this close to a living wild animal before. What should he do? Was it dangerous? They eyed each other for what seemed like an eternity. Then it struck him. The stag was probably just as scared as he was. Slowly, carefully, he reached out his right hand. The stag took a step forward to within inches of the outstretched fingers and sniffed, investigating the unfamiliar scent. Then it suddenly pawed the ground, snorted, wheeled round and trotted off, up and around the back of Drumbreck with the two does mincing behind. James let out his breath with an audible gasp. That was close!

He wandered back over to the rocks and the view of Saint Mary's with a spring in his step, reminding himself that this was his reward in the hills: whatever Nature decided to throw at him at any time on any day. He waited around for a bit, looking at his watch every few minutes. It was still early but something told him Lucy wasn't coming. She'd surely have been here by now. Disappointed, he slowly made his way back down the way he'd come, taking advantage of the time to explore further around Kirkscleuch Lochan where the daffodils were thick along the shore.

The following Saturday was a carbon copy of the previous one except that it was warmer, for April was just over the horizon. One week had made all the difference. All the snow on the bottoms had melted away, raising the level of the lochan and turning the once slowly meandering Thrashie burn into a miniature torrent that overflowed its banks. But large tracts of snow were still visible in drifts along the tops and the Sergeant had stuck with the Land Rover just in case; at this time of the year, sudden snowstorms weren't unknown in the Border Country. James had served up, at the request of the workers, perhaps the most unhealthy meal so far: fried eggs, stovies, black pudding, onions and baked beans, followed by clootie dumpling soaked in syrup. It was a feast for clogged arteries. After a long absence, the Factor had turned up with Rab and Jean and there was much hilarity as he recounted his doings over winter, managing, as usual, to get Rabbie Burns inserted somewhere into the story. Again, there was no problem with James taking time off. The face of Drumbreck was snow-free, the drifts in the dips had melted away and Kirks Cleuch was clear. He greeted the little spring which was now gushing with snowmelt. Standing on the Tulzie Kaime, he looked around him. Still no Lucy. He made his way across to the rocks and the view of the Loch and the tiny dolls' houses around Megget Water. The disappointment began to rise in his throat. Another wasted ascent.

"So, it appears that James Swanston survived the winter!"

The well-known English accent with its hint of mockery broke into his thoughts and he turned to find Lucy Ashton standing not five yards from him with Trixie, as usual, on the end of the lead.

"Hello, Lucy! It's good to see ye again!"

"I thought you'd abandoned me!"

"Well, we couldn't get here sooner for all the snow." Then, in an attempt to impress her, "We've actually been usin' a four-wheel drive to make sure we got through!"

"A what...?"

"A four-wheel drive."

"What's that?"

He almost laughed out loud. The irony! Which was more ignorant, never having heard of some obscure novel of Walter Scott's or not knowing what a four-wheel drive was? But, suppressing the urge to get his own back, he patiently explained.

"Oh, it's a car where the engine can drive all four wheels at once."

"I have no idea what you mean. But never mind, I'm just a girl!"

"Would ye like tae sit down?"

They sat in their usual spot.

"Did ye have a good Christmas?" he asked, trying to make conversation.

"Yes, it was fine. We had family come up from England. All the adults drank the health of the new King, but everyone was worried about maybe war breaking out, so that put a damper on things."

New King? War? He knew that his exclusive focus on Academy homework and swotting for exams meant he was often hermetically sealed from what was going on in the outside world. But war? How had he missed that? Now he was a bit worried. He hoped his dad wouldn't get caught up in it again.

"But of course," she said, incorrectly reading into his expression concern for himself, "you have nothing to worry about James. You're far too young for war!"

"Oh," he announced eagerly, suddenly remembering, "Ah finished the book!"

"*The Bride of Lammermoor*? And? What did you think?"

"Well, Ah have tae say it wasn't easy goin'. But the story was good and Ah got there in the end. It was the end Ah didn't like, though. Why did they have tae die, Lucy and Edgar?"

"Oh, I don't know James. It's just a work of fiction and in fiction, death is the fate of every tragic hero and heroine in love, don't you think? What about Romeo and Juliet?"

James knew the names but they hadn't got that far yet in their English literature class, nor was he equipped to enter into a discussion of tragic heroes and heroines. So he kept his mouth shut. But Lucy's blithe statement was destined to come back to haunt him.

"Lucy, can ye help me with somethin'?" he asked instead.

"Yes, if I can."

"The name o' this place..."

"...the Tulzie Kaime, you mean?"

The Scottish words sounded strangely delicate between English lips.

"Aye. What does it mean? D'ye know?"

She gave him one of her mocking looks.

"James, I am surprised at you! You don't know the meaning of words in your own Scots tongue?"

He sighed. He usually tried to repay sarcasm with sarcasm but somehow this time he couldn't be bothered.

"Aye, ye're quite right. Ah *should* know. But Ah don't. Ah did ask the Factor but he didn't know either. So Ah'm supposin' that you do know what they mean?"

"Of course I do. The Tulzie Kaime's on my own property. How could I not know?"

Well, thought James, that was putting it on a bit thick. The land actually belonged to her uncle. But never mind.

"Lucy, would ye stop beatin' about the bush and put me out o' mah misery!"

It was then that Lucy laughed. She actually laughed! It was the first time she'd done that. Her laughter echoed like silver bells between the spurs of the mountain.

"Oh, James, you are droll! Very well. We have two words, don't we? *Tulzie* means a quarrel or a fight. *Kaime* is something like a mountain ridge or *a* crest. So, this is the mountain ridge where a fight or quarrel took place some time in the past."

"So how did it get that name?" he asked, immediately fascinated.

"Well, James, the legend has it that it all happened somewhere back in the early 18th century, incidentally around about the time of *The Bride of Lammermoor*! This," she said, pointing to the middle of the col floor, "was the boundary between two large estates belonging to two powerful and wealthy families. Of course, that was long before my family owned the land. On this side…" She waved her hand to the south and west, towards Galloway and the Irish Sea. "…were the Fenwick family, and on that side…" She pointed back towards The Glen. "…were the Ruthvens." She pronounced the names *Fenick* and *Riven*. "For your sake, I'll try to be brief.

"Both families had sons and daughters. When Georgina Fenwick was invited to a ball at Ruthven Manor, young Ranald Ruthven asked her to dance. It was, to put it mildly, love at first sight. Their families weren't enemies or anything like that so nothing like Romeo and Juliet. But Georgina was eighteen and said to be beautiful. She'd already been betrothed to some boring, rich old nobleman up in Edinburgh's High Street. Nonetheless, Ranald and Georgina started meeting secretly," she paused, then added with emphasis, "*here*."

James felt a prickle up the back of his neck as the hairs stood straight. *Here?* He looked around as if imagining two young lovers meeting, dressed in the sort of old-fashioned clothes of the period he'd seen in his copy of *The Bride of Lammermoor*.

"Yes, it was a remote spot. But who would find them here? Georgina would come up on a mountain pony attended by a maid, and Ranald rode across the hills on his favourite mare. Well, Georgina's family started to get suspicious and one day her older brother Graham Fenwick and two kinsmen followed her. They caught the lovers together. There was a fight. Ranald happened to be a captain in the First Regiment of Foot and had fought at the Battle of Malplaquet. You can imagine, James, he was no weakling!"

Lucy's eyes sparkled. It seemed she had no time for men who were weaklings. She paused and looked distantly over James's head as if imagining her ideal man.

"So, what happened?" he demanded impatiently.

"With one shot from his pistol, Ranald fatally wounded one of the kinsmen. He tried to draw his sword but the other two were already on to him. He managed to stab Graham with his dirk but the other kinsmen thrust his broadsword through Ranald's heart. He died on the spot." She paused. "Yes, horrible, isn't it?" she said, gauging from his expression the impact of her story. "You know, James, I think about it every time I come here!" She looked around as if reliving the very events she'd recounted.

"And? And?" he asked, on tenterhooks.

"Well, Georgina's parents bundled her off to Edinburgh to marry her old lord. They managed to get Graham Fenwick back to their manor house, but he was dead within a week. And Georgina's maid was threatened that if she ever spoke a word of what had happened – well, you can imagine what the Fenwicks had in mind for her!"

"What about Ranald?"

"Do you know the song about Bonnie George Campbell?"

James shook his head, mesmerised at the way the story was unfolding. Lucy obliged. She opened her mouth and, to James's astonishment, started to sing mournfully, her untrained voice quavering across the silence of the Tulzie Kaime.

High upon Highlands and laigh upon Tay.
Bonnie George Campbell rade oot on a day.
Saddled and bridled and booted rade he
Hame cam his guid horse, but never cam he.

"So 'is horse came home without 'im?" James managed to gulp.

"Yes, she did. Ranald's disappearance was a complete mystery, for none of the Ruthvens had had a clue he was having an affair with Georgina. Of course, they sent out search parties far and wide, but they never found him."

"And what about 'is body?"

"The Fenwicks threw it over a crag somewhere and there it has lain to this day."

James immediately pictured himself on one of his forays across Drumbreck coming upon Ranald's skeleton, with rusting sword in one hand, rusting dirk in the other, and his rusting pistol at his side. Then a thought hit him.

"But wait a minute. If they never found 'is body, how did they know about the fight and what had happened tae 'im?"

"Ah, that's the most interesting part. You see, the maid who was threatened wasn't just some slip of a girl. She was an older woman and she'd been like a mother to Georgina for most of her life. Well, one day, not long afterwards, she disappeared. At first, people thought the Fenwicks had had her murdered, but a few weeks later she turned up in Edinburgh and found Georgina.

"After what had happened Georgina hated her family. And she was now a wealthy noblewoman. She engaged some big lawyer in the Edinburgh High Street. He wrote to the Ruthvens, revealing the truth about Ranald and that they had two witnesses to his murder. The Ruthvens were incensed. They were powerful and had friends in high places. They got their revenge! First, they had the kinsman who'd killed Ranald arrested and tried in the High Court. He was hanged at the Mercat Cross. Then they sued the Fenwicks for damages – after all, they'd lost their eldest son and heir. You could do that sort of thing in the seventeen-hundreds if you were wealthy, of course. With Georgina's and the maid's testimonies, they easily won their case and the Fenwicks had to pay them ten thousand pounds – that was a fortune in those days."

"What happened tae Georgina?"

"Well, she may well have avenged her Ranald, but sadly, life was not all that kind to her. Legend has it that two years later she died in childbirth. Along with her child."

Lucy stopped. Her narrative had clearly exhausted and upset her.

"I have to go now," she said suddenly, a pained expression clouding her face.

"What a story!" James said, shaking his head in awe. "And tae think it all happened here on the Tulzie Kaime."

Then he looked at his watch. With a shock, he saw that he was going to be in trouble. It was after half-past three. He'd never get back to the cottage by four.

"Ah have to go, too," he said.

Pushing his stuff into his rucksack, he stood up, put on his jacket, and looked at Lucy.

"Thank you," he said, "for telling me about Georgina and Ranald!" He paused, and, without thinking, he surprised himself by saying, "This has been one o' the best days o' mah life!"

"What, James? Only *one* of the best days?" Lucy enquired, her eyebrows raised in mock reproach. "Not *the* best?"

"Well, who knows?" he grinned. "Ah'll let ye know, say, in twenty or thirty years' time!" Then, "Really sorry, but Ah'm late. What about next week, same time?"

"I'm not sure, James. Maybe I have to stay at home."

"Well," he said, "we'll see what happens." And then, "Goodbye Lucy – till next time!"

"Goodbye James."

Her gaze was fixed on him as he made his way back across the floor of the Tulzie Kaime. At every step he was wondering if he was treading on the very spot where Ranald's lifeblood had drained away into the peaty soil. He reached the crest, zipped up his jacket and settled the rucksack straps on his shoulders. Just before he dipped down, he turned around. Though the sun was low in the west, he could still make out her features. She was standing waving, with Trixie at her side. As he waved back, a lump came to his throat and his eyes filled with tears. Swearing at himself for a fool, he shot down the hill.

Little did he realise it was his last sight of Lucy Ashton.

My heart is not here

It was the fastest descent of Drumbreck that James had ever made, risking not a few broken bones in the process. Suddenly, about two-thirds of the way down, with the whole glen laid out before him in the late afternoon sunshine, he saw a blue speck in the distance that got larger and larger. It was the Land Rover. It came to a halt by the lochan and the familiar figure of the Sergeant got out. It was already just after four. The Sergeant stared up the hill, shading his eyes with his hand from the weakening rays of the sun. James waved but didn't know if he'd been seen. Increasing his pace, he raced down the hill as fast as he dared. He could see that his friend had at last spotted him and was waving in greeting, even though he was still far away.

"Ah'm really awfy sorry!" James managed to gasp, on flat ground at last, red-faced, and leaning forward, hands on hips, catching his breath. "Ah just lost track o' time!"

"It's aw' right son. Ah was just gettin' a bit worried, that's aw'." Then the Sergeant's eyes wrinkled with mischief. "Have ye got a wee lassie up there or somethin'?"

James would have blushed as he usually did when he was flustered or caught out in a lie but, in any case, his face was already beetroot from his exertions.

"Oh, aye!" he managed to joke between gasps. "Actually, Sergeant, Ah've got a whole harem hidden away on Drumbreck! That's why Ah go tae aw' the bother o' climbin' for a whole hour tae get up there!"

They jumped in the Land Rover and sped off. But James was thanking his lucky stars. That was close. The next four Saturdays were so hectic that a visit to the Tulzie Kaime was out of the question. The Sergeant had fixed on a deadline of mid-April for the work to be finished. With the lighter evenings, longer workdays were possible. More workmen arrived at the cottage. An electrician and his mate from Galashiels had the monumental task of upgrading the cottage's wiring. A carpenter and his apprentice turned up to complete various projects, including a wheelchair ramp and the construction of a prefabricated wooden summerhouse that was sited on piles near the burn. The plumber installed toilets with wheelchair access. There was the track between the estate road and the cottage to resurface. James found himself catering for up to fourteen or fifteen workmen at a time; so many indeed, that he had to serve dinner in two shifts. Thankfully, the Sergeant was there to help out in the kitchen so it never came to a crisis.

The third Saturday of April was to be the big day, for the Chief would be driving down specially in the afternoon for a visit. There would be a formal opening in May with representatives from charities and the first intake of disadvantaged vacationers. But for now, he just wanted to inspect the final product and formally thank everyone for their contribution. That morning, James and Sergeant Seatoun had left Edinburgh an hour earlier than usual in the Jag. The workmen turned up at eight-thirty. There was a host of last-minute jobs to complete. The Glen cottage had never been busier. But by the time two o'clock arrived, dinner had been served and the kitchen detritus cleared away. Able to relax now, James and the Sergeant strolled over to the now completed summerhouse and turned to admire their achievement. They were among the few who'd seen the parlous state the cottage had been in the previous September. They smiled when they reminisced about the rowan growing out of the kitchen window and having to clear out the flock of ewes. The inside was now pristine, with crisply whitewashed walls, new joinery, updated plumbing and wiring, new fixtures everywhere, and the smell of fresh paint. The outside fascia had had a good going over and was now gleaming white in the spring sunshine. The old cottage was unrecognisable.

Suddenly, the Chief's police car was there, driven by his deputy driver. The Chief got out with a broad smile on his face, admiring the finished build, taking in the full extent of the consummation of his vision. Greeting everyone with quips and jokes, he did a quick tour of the inside, praising the progress that had been made since his last Sunday visit a couple of weeks before. Outside again, he asked the team to gather round. In a brief speech, he thanked them on behalf of those less privileged for their largely unpaid donations of work, time and expertise. Meanwhile, his other driver had unloaded the boot of the police car and spread the contents on a table set up outside. The Chief now turned to this and started handing out a gift to each of the men who'd worked on the build; a bottle of Laphroaig malt whisky in a presentation box. Even Sergeant Seatoun got a bottle. Then the Chief turned to James.

"Now a word about the youngest member of the team!"

There was a scattered cheer.

"James, as Ah've heard from the Sergeant, the Factor, Mr Boswell and others at the build, ye've done sterling work over the past six months or so feedin' the crew. Ah think Ah can honestly say, without James's stovies, haggis, black pudden, mashed tatties an' neeps, you men would have starved and this project would never have got off the ground. Am Ah right?" Cheers and shouts. "You and the Sergeant here were the lynchpins that held everything together and without you, Ah'm sure we wouldn't be standin' here now!"

Applause and cheers. James had never blushed so scarlet. He hung his head and wished for the ground to swallow him up.

"Now, son, Ah couldnae get ye a bottle o' whisky..." Laughter. "That would've been against the law, and as ye're all aware, Ah'm meant to be a guardian o' the law!" Guffaws, cheers and some boos. "So, Ah've got a wee special present for ye and Ah hope ye like it."

He handed James a packet wrapped in brown paper.

"Well, open it, son, open it!" came the chorus.

James carefully removed the wrapping. It was an antique book with a green cover and a large medallion on the front. James opened it. It was a collection of Robert Burns poems published in 1861. James was overcome. It must have cost a lot of money and he guessed the Factor had a hand in it somewhere. The Chief put his fingerless left stump on his shoulder and extended his good hand. As James stammered his thanks, they shook.

"Now," said the Chief, "some of ye might know that next tae Harry Lauder, Rabbie Burns is mah favourite Scot!"

The Chief's confession came as no surprise to James who was busy with the sleeves of his jersey. *Aye, as Ah thought, another member of the Burns Underground!*

"So, Ah hope ye don't mind if, in honour o' the occasion, Ah give a wee rendering of one of his songs. Oh, and if ye know it, do join in!"

James knew that as a bairn in the Kirkgate, the Chief had often earned pennies singing for adults around the pubs. He'd heard of the Chief's penchant for breaking, impromptu, into song. So what happened next was not unexpected. The Chief stepped back and, without ado, began to sing *a cappella*, in a true baritone, turning towards the mass of Drumbreck, shadow black against wispy clouds drifting across its tops.

My heart's in the Highlands, my heart is not here,
My heart's in the Highlands, a-chasing the deer,
A-chasing the wild deer and following the roe,
My heart's in the Highlands wherever I go!

Farewell to the Highlands, farewell to the North,
The birth-place of Valour, the country of Worth,
Wherever I wander, wherever I rove,
The hills of the Highlands forever I love.

There he stopped, contenting himself with two verses, and coolly acknowledged the cheers and applause.

"Heh, Chief, if yer hert's in the Highlands, how come ye're still here in the Lowlands?" called out one wag.

The assembly broke up in high spirits. The Chief wanted another confab with a couple of the tradesmen and the others started to pack up, probably for the last time. James and Sergeant Seatoun had set four o'clock for the deadline to leave, in about forty-five minutes' time. James stowed his stuff in the Jag, then pulled the Sergeant aside.

"Sergeant, Ah'm just goin' tae walk up to the estate office tae see the Factor. If Ah'm not back, can ye pick me up there at four?"

The Sergeant nodded and James set off on what was a mere ten-minute walk. All day, despite all the hectic and the kerfuffle, James had had a single thought in his mind: Lucy Ashton. Would he ever see her again? He certainly wanted to. The feeling they were somehow connected rankled like a splinter under a fingernail. What should he do? This was his last day at The Glen. There was no knowing if or when he'd be able to come here again. It was private property and his right to be here would have expired. The Tulzie Kaime would be out of bounds. So he'd made a plan. He'd leave a card at the estate office. He'd ask her to get in touch. Maybe they could work something out. It was a cheap greeting card with the words *Missing You* on the front. Inside, he'd written:

Dear Lucy
Sorry we weren't able to get together again, but my time at The Glen is now over. I would love to hear from you, though. I've written my address and hope you can write.
Until, hopefully, we meet again –
James Swanston

He'd put the card in its envelope, sealed it, and written on the front: *Lucy Ashton, Estate Office, The Glen, please forward*. He was sure they'd be happy to pass it on to her, especially as she was the niece of the Laird. The Factor looked up from his desk and removed his reading glasses as James knocked and entered.

"James, how good tae see ye. Everythin' go all right the day?"

"Fine thanks, Mr Oxnam."

"D'ye want tae take a seat?"

"Well, Ah didn't want tae disturb ye." He remained standing and pulled the envelope out of his jacket pocket. "Ah just wanted tae ask ye tae give this tae Lucy Ashton for me."

He placed the envelope on the desk. The Factor put his glasses back on, took it in both hands and carefully read what was there. Then, he scratched his chin.

"Lucy Ashton, Lucy Ashton," he said. "Now who would *she* be, James? Ah haven't heard of a Lucy Ashton."

"Well, it's a lassie Ah met while Ah was here. She's from the estate."

"From the estate? Ye mean one of the estate worker's families?"

James started to feel jittery. He'd come with a simple request but this was starting to sound like an interrogation.

"Well, no..." He stopped. He'd have to give up something, otherwise his card would never be delivered. He gulped. "Actually, she's the niece o' the Laird."

The Factor leaned back in his chair, his brow furrowed, the envelope still in his hand, and a look on his face James had never seen before.

"James, son, Ah'm sorry tae have tae say this, but tae mah knowledge, the Laird doesn't have a niece, an' Ah've worked on this estate for over thirty year!"

James felt his hands go clammy. He was going to have to choose his words very carefully if he didn't want to appear stupid. He'd have to tell a bit more of the truth.

"Mr Oxnam..." he hesitated. Then, as if reciting something learnt by heart, "Ah met a lassie here on the estate up at the Tulzie Kaime. She told me her name was Lucy Ashton and she was the Laird's niece."

The Factor smiled, shook his head, and spoke with forbearance.

"Ah hate tae spoil yer day son, but that was probably one o' the estate lassies playin' a wee trick on ye!" He paused to gauge James's reaction. "They're aye at it ye ken, especially wi' outsiders that, shall we say, are a bit wet behind the ears! They pretend they're nobility and they're from The Big House. But they aren't."

James realised he was shaking his head dismissively but stopped when he saw the expression on the Factor's face. The last thing he wanted to do was antagonise him. He told himself to calm down. After all, he was fourteen now. And who was to say that Mr Oxnam was actually up to date with things? He forced himself to sound apologetic.

"Ah'm sorry, Mr Oxnam, Ah didn't want tae cause ye any bother. Maybe ye could tell me this. Is there anybody else that could help?"

The Factor's patience was beginning to wear thin. If it had been anyone else, he'd have shown them out of his office by now, but this boy, James Swanston, merited a bit more consideration.

"The only person Ah can think of is old Walter Netherby. 'E's over eighty but what *he* doesn't know about the estate isn't worth knowin'. D'ye want tae try *him*?"

James nodded earnestly. At this point, he'd grasp at any straw. The Factor got out of his chair, handed James his envelope back, showed him to the door and opened it. They stepped out into the road. The estate office was one of a group of stone-built cottages, most of which were the abodes of the estate workers. He pointed down the road.

"See that wee cottage, last on the left, right doon at the end? That's Walter's place. Tell 'im Ah sent ye. Ah hope ye find what ye're after. Good luck!"

With that, the Factor disappeared back into his office. James hurried down the road, aware that four o'clock was fast approaching. He found the cottage, a small building of weathered sandstone blocks and a dilapidated tile roof that looked to be a hundred years or more of age. The front door was of upright wooden boards covered in peeling green paint and next to it a wisteria was struggling into bloom. He knocked. A full-figured Borders wifie of about fifty wearing her street coat opened the door.

"Aye, can Ah help ye?"

"Oh, Ah'm sorry tae bother ye, missus. Mr Oxnam, the Factor, sent me tae see Walter Netherby. Ah'm James Swanston, the nephew o' Chief Constable Merrilees."

"Oh, the Chief! Aye, we've heard aw' aboot the good things goin' on doon at Nether Bankside! Ah'm Mrs Mitchison, Walter's mah faither. Come on in, son!"

She threw the door wide open and James entered. Mrs Mitchison stopped him in the small entrance hall to explain that she came up from Innerleithen every day to cook and clean for her father and that he was almost eighty-five but perfectly clear in his mind.

"Ah dinnae ken exactly what ye want, son, but watch ye dinnae tire 'im oot."

Just then, an old man's voice sounded from a room where the door was ajar.

"Whae's that oot there and what's goin' oan?"

Mrs Mitchison popped her head round the door.

"Oh, Dad, it's just a young laddie come tae hae a crack wi' ye. 'E's Chief Merrilees's nephew. The Factor sent 'im. Is that aw' right?"

"Aye, aye, send 'im in, always happy tae see a young laddie!"

The parlour was tiny, more like the size of a bedroom. Walter Netherby had a wrinkled, weatherbeaten face, wispy white hair and a matching white beard. Wearing a wool cardigan, moleskin trousers and slippers, he was sitting back in an ancient, yellowing, velvet-upholstered armchair in front of a smoky coal fire with a newspaper open on his lap, sipping tea from a cup and munching on a rich tea biscuit.

"Come in! Come in!" he cried, putting down the teacup. "What was yer name, son?" and he cupped his right hand around his ear.

"Er, James Swanston, Mr Netherby. The Factor sent me because he thought ye could help me with somethin'."

"Aye, aye, Ah'll dae mah best. Just remember Ah'm a bit hard o' hearin', so ye'll have tae speak up. Sit doon, sit doon!"

James perched on a chair that must have been an antique when Robert Burns was in the district. He cleared his throat.

"Mr Netherby," he shouted, "Ah'm tryin' tae find a girl called Lucy Ashton. She's from the estate."

"Lucy Ashton, Lucy Ashton, now where have Ah heard that name before?"

"Well, she told me she's the Laird's niece but Mr Oxnam says that's impossible."

Walter sat clutching his teacup, ruminating, apparently scanning his ancient brain for any vestige of a Lucy Ashton.

"What does she look like?" he asked.

"Tall and thin wi' long red hair. An' she has a wee dog, a spaniel."

"Tall, red hair, spaniel. Tall, red hair, spaniel..."

Suddenly, it seemed that a light went on in Walter's head.

"Jeannie! Jeannie!" he shouted.

Mrs Mitchison popped her head round the door.

"Jeannie, hen, go intae the back room and get me that big box o' photies, the grey box on top o' the wardrobe."

While James was wondering how a box of photos would answer his question, Walter took another sip of tea and a bite out of a rich tea. His daughter bustled into the room with a large cardboard box in her hand. She got Walter to put down his teacup, took away his newspaper, and placed the box in his lap. He struggled to remove the lid with misshapen hands. James could see the box was stuffed full with hundreds of black-and-white and sepia photographs.

"When the new laird took over in the nineteen-twenties they threw a lot o' stuff oot onto the rubbish heap," Mrs Mitchison said *sotto voce* by way of explanation. "There were a lot o' auld photies, too. Dad rescued them – didn't ye, Dad?" she added loudly.

"Aye, that's right. Ah saved them. What happened there was a scandal, a damn scandal!" he insisted.

Mrs Mitchison went out to the kitchen. James said nothing but watched patiently while Walter rummaged through the box. Suddenly he seemed to find what he'd been looking for. He pulled a large photograph mounted on card from the middle of the pile, peered at it closely, his spectacles low on his nose, then examined the back.

“Aye, that’s the one!” he muttered. He handed it to James with the back uppermost, at the same time pointing with his arthritic finger at some writing done in pencil.

“There. What does that say, young lad?”

James followed the finger and read the words. *Lucy Ashton, 1910.* He turned it over. The photo was black-and-white and probably professionally done. It was slightly faded but, considering its age, it was still surprisingly sharp. A shiver ran up his spine. A girl with long hair was standing in what was obviously the garden of The Big House since there were fancy leaded windows in the background set into a dressed stone block wall. She looked to be about sixteen. She was tall and thin with flowing dark hair cascading over an off-white shift that had a lace collar and cuffs and that came down to her calves. She was smiling as she held a lead, on the end of which was a dog. It was a spaniel. There was no denying it. The girl was Lucy Ashton, James’s Lucy Ashton.

The room suddenly felt hot and stuffy. He was gasping for air. Sweat was beading on his forehead and he was nauseous. He leant forward in his chair and everything went black. When he came to, he was lying on the floor flat on his back with his legs raised on a cushion, a cold cloth on his forehead and Mrs Mitchison looking down at him anxiously.

“It’s OK, son, ye just fainted,” she reassured him, as Walter gazed around his daughter’s plump form with an equally concerned expression. “Now, you just lie there for a wee minute and Ah’ll get ye some hot, sweet tea. That’s the best thing for a shock!”

James lay there, staring at the ceiling. He tried to unscramble his thoughts. His Lucy? 1910? How was it possible? Mrs Mitchison was back.

“Now, son, d’ye think ye can lie on the settee?”

He managed to crawl onto the settee where his Florence Nightingale propped him up with cushions then went out again, returning with a large mug of tea.

“Michty me, ye dinnae half look pale! Now drink that tea. It’s got plenty o’ sugar an’ mah special ingredient. A good tot o’ brandy!”

James took a sip of the tea, then another one. It really was sweet. He took another sip, then risked a gulp. A warm sensation spread down his throat and across his chest. It was even better than Ian’s toddies. He was beginning to feel better. The room wasn’t spinning as much as before. He wanted to say something but he didn’t know what to say because he didn’t understand the world any more. He lay there, speechless, while Walter sat holding the photo which his daughter had rescued from the carpet, looking at him inquisitively. Still, James remained unable to form a coherent sound. Eventually, it was Walter who broke the silence.

"Listen, son, Ah dinnae ken what the story is wi' you an' Lucy Ashton. But Ah can see ye've had a shock. Ye dinnae have tae speak, but d'ye want me tae tell ye aboot 'er?"

James nodded gratefully, all the while sipping his tea and brandy.

"Well," said Walter, "it was back before The Great War. Ah was thirty and was heid stable hand on the estate. Mah job was tae look efter aw' the horses. Now, here's what Ah remember aboot Lucy Ashton."

Walter went on to tell his story. Lucy Ashton was the daughter of Lord Ashton, who'd married the then laird's sister. He'd died when Lucy was no more than a baby and her mother had come to live with her brother, the Laird, at The Big House.

"Aye, Lucy was a lovely lass, a nice nature, and oh, that red hair tumblin' doon 'er back! Ah can tell ye, she turn't mony a heid! They sent 'er off tae school in England when she was just five. A convent school it was, forbye Lord Ashton had been Catholic and Lucy had tae be brought up in the Catholic faith. She came back here when she was twelve." He raised the photo to his nose again and examined it closely. "That wee dug she got as a puppy fir 'er thirteenth birthday. It was a King Charles Spaniel as Ah recall, a rare dug. What did she ca' it though? Some fancy name, Ah dinnae mind what... And, my, did she no love that dug! She took it everywhere she went."

Befuddled from the faint and the brandy, James listened with a mixture of horror and fascination as Walter's story unfolded. He was in a living nightmare. He wanted it to stop. But he didn't want it to stop.

"Noo," Walter went on, "one o' the heids Lucy turned was a young ghillie oan the estate. He was a fine young loon, twenty-two or twenty-three, in charge o' aw' the shootin', ye ken, the grouse, the pheasant, the deer. Aye, those were the days when there were deer on Drumbreck. What was 'is name again? Let me think." He wrinkled his brow and scratched his beard. Then he gave a start. "Ye ken what, Ah believe 'e had the same name as you! What was yer name again?"

"James," James managed to mumble.

"Naw, naw, yer ither name!"

"Swanston."

"Aye, that's richt, Swanston. Ah cannae mind 'is first name. What was it again? Somethin' queer." He paused, deep in thought, stroking his beard. "Oh aye, Ah have it. It was *Edgar*. That's right, Edgar Swanston, that was him."

Shock upon shock. They washed over James like the waters of the Tweed in spate.

"Aye, she was smitten as weel, for 'e was a guid-lookin' young fellae. Well, they knew the Laird wouldnae approve, so they took tae meetin' in secret aw' ower the estate. Lucy aye had a guid excuse – she had tae take the dug for a walk! Sometimes they even met on Drumbreck tae get away frae pryin' eyes, for Drumbreck was Edgar's stampin' ground, so tae speak. But we aw' kennt what was goin' on – the ordinary folk, Ah mean, the workers, no the Big Folk up at the Hoose, they kennt nothin'."

It would have been no exaggeration to say Edgar's family took it badly when they got wind of the affair. In fact, they were beside themselves. Strict Congregationals, they worshipped at the chapel in Innerleithen. To them, Catholic priests were demons and the Pope was the Devil incarnate. The Laird and his family were High Episcopalian. That particular sect, Edgar's parents could just about stomach; they were at least of the Protestant faith. But Lucy was a Catholic. Their son had been caught in the snare of a Catholic strumpet. Nothing could be worse. After a meeting with their minister and a family conference, a solution was found. Edgar, an equally staunch Congregational, would never have dreamt of going against his parents' wishes. He was hurriedly engaged to the daughter of one of the prominent chapel families and they were married in the time it took to read the banns. But more was to come. It would be impossible for Edgar to remain at the estate. It was far too dangerous. Temptation, in the form of Catholic Lucy, would be constantly before his eyes. Edgar was made to hand in his notice and the newlyweds were shipped off to Edinburgh. A position had been found for Edgar at an estate on the edge of the city, where the factor was a leading light of the local Congregational chapel.

"Aye, it was a sair travail fir the lassie when Edgar suddenly disappeared. For it seemed, or so the estate folk said, she was really in love, aye, a daughter o' one o' the High Heid Yins in love wi' a common man! It was hard tae believe, but true. Aye, she took it hard, Edgar goin' off like that. She wid go oot wi' 'er wee dug, walkin' aw' ower the estate. It was as if she were lookin' fir 'im. Ah saw 'er once at the time, oan one o' 'er walks. Ye could see she was no weel, richt peelie-wallie, an' fair shilpit. It aw' came tae a heid in, let me think, aye, it must hae been at the start o' nineteen-eleven, for that's when mah Jeannie was born. Aye, nineteen-eleven it was. Well, the lassie, Lucy, was oot wi' 'er wee dug as usual. She'd ta'en the path up tae that shin on the edge o' Drumbreck... now what was it called...?"

"...the Tulzie Kaime."

"Aye, that's richt, the Tulzie Kaime," repeated Walter, automatically. Then he stopped abruptly and looked at James in astonishment. "How did ye ken that? Ye're a canny lad an' nae mistake. The Tulzie Kaime, aye. The Laird had the path made special fir 'is sister. Aye, Lucy, she went up tae the Tulzie Kaime wi' 'er wee dug."

There, he paused and looked grave. James knew more or less what was coming. He started to feel sick again.

"Well, the fact is, she never came back," said Walter. "Aye, the lassie never came back! It was March, ye see, winter was still bitin'. Somebody should've stopped 'er frae goin' oot, fir anybody could see snaw was oan the way. Aye, an' so it was. Thir was a muckle storm, a richt blatter oot o' the north, wi' sleet an' snaw. The Laird sent oot search parties weel intae the nicht. Many a man risked 'is life, Ah can tell ye, includin' yours truly. Aye, we went oot in the dark and the snaw wi' oil lamps, but we found nothin' at first." He paused again, pulled a large handkerchief out of his trouser pocket and wiped tears from his rheumy eyes. He blew his nose loudly, then continued. "Aye, it was a dowie day when we did find 'er, me, Jock Binnie an' Angus McLeod, the mornin' efter. There she was, at the Tulzie Kaime, amang the rocks at the lookout, near aboot covered in snaw. We widnae hae fund 'er if it hadnae been fir 'er bonny red hair just keekin' oot o' the drift. We started diggin', wi' oor hauns, ye ken, and tried tae revive 'er, like. But it was nae use. She was stane deid. But she looked sae bonny, jist as if she was asleep. An' there, curled up in 'er airms, deid as weel, was 'er wee dug."

He stopped, wiped away more tears, and looked at James, who was in a state of near-total collapse, softly sobbing to himself.

"Ah'm fair vexed that mah tale's pit ye aboot, son."

James managed a smile. He wiped his tears with his sleeves and asked, "Is that it? Is there any more?"

"Naw, that's it, son. We buried 'er in the family cemetery up at The Big Hoose. Ye can imagine, 'er mither an' the Laird were sair affectit."

It seemed the family never recovered. Lucy's sudden death was bad enough, but then came The Great War. The Laird's only son and heir was killed at Arras by a sniper's bullet. The War had taken almost the entire workforce to serve at the front. Most of them never came back. The land was neglected and the machinery fell into disrepair. The estate was no longer viable. By 1921, The Laird had given up. He sold the estate and moved to the South of France where, it was said, he drank himself into an early grave. Lucy's mother had already passed away several years before, some said of a broken heart.

There was a loud knock on the door. James could hear Mrs Mitchison's voice and then another voice, one he knew so well. There was a brief discussion. The door of the living room opened. Mrs Mitchison was there but she quickly stepped aside to reveal the form of the Sergeant, enormous in Walter Netherby's tiny parlour.

"James!" he cried when he saw his apprentice propped up on the settee. "What's up, son? Ah've been lookin' all over for ye!"

James struggled to speak. Seeing his distress, kind-hearted Mrs Mitchison immediately took over.

"Aye, Sergeant, oor James just had a wee bad turn. He's had a cup o' tea an' brandy, an' Ah think ye're feelin' better now, eh, James?"

Anyway, Mrs Mitchison was hoping he was, for she could see that her father had had enough and was due for his nap. The Sergeant, catching her drift, stepped forward.

"Come on, son, it's half-past four. We'll have tae get on the road."

"Thank you, Mr Netherby," James said, struggling to maintain his composure. "There's just one more thing. Could ye do me a big favour?"

"Aye, son, what is it?"

"Could Ah have the photo?"

"Aye, aye, of course, son, as long as ye look efter it!"

And he handed the photo back to James. Struggling to his feet and offering his thanks, a still dopey James allowed the Sergeant to help him out to the Jag where he dozed off on the wide back seat and slept all the way back to Chesser Drive. After an hour's fast driving, he was just beginning to come to himself when he felt the car stop and the door slam as the Sergeant got out. Janet was surprised to hear a knock at the door. She was expecting James, but he had a door key. She opened the door and there was Sergeant Seatoun filling the door frame. Janet had never met him but had heard so much about him from James that she knew him very well.

"Sergeant!" she said, "come in, come in." Then, when he was standing in the middle of the living room, "Where's James, where's mah son? Is everythin' awright?"

"It's OK, Mrs Swanston, 'e's all right. 'E's just exhausted, Ah think. It's been a long hard day for all of us, an' Ah think 'e's just about had enough." He stopped and looked pointedly at her. "Ye ken, ye've got a fine laddie there. We all think very highly o' 'im, especially the Chief."

Janet smiled awkwardly. For once she was lost for words.

"Ah'll just get 'im in then, an' maybe put 'im tae bed right away?"

Janet did as the Sergeant advised. James slept all day Sunday. Janet called in their GP on Monday. *Mental and physical exhaustion* was Dr Donald's diagnosis. She wasn't to worry. Bed rest was all that was needed, Scotch broth and plenty of fluids. He wrote a sick note which Janet took down to The Academy and handed over to Mrs Tulloch, explaining that her James was 'under the doctor.'

"Ah'm sorry tae hear that Mrs Swanston," was the School Secretary's response. "He's a good boy, James. Ah do hope he gets better!"

Janet walked away feeling uplifted. First Sergeant Seatoun and now Mrs Tulloch. Maybe she hadn't made that many mistakes after all.

Auntie Rose

James had been put in his parents' room; they'd moved out and on to the bed settee for the week. He was supposed to convalesce but his time with Lucy Ashton on the Tulzie Kaime fully occupied him. He'd kept the photograph hidden in his rucksack but propped it on the bedside cabinet when alone, and examined it endlessly. He set his memory of his encounters with Lucy against the details of Walter Netherby's tale and tried to make sense of what had happened. There were only three possibilities.

First, he'd imagined the whole thing. If that was the case, then he could only conclude that he had a serious mental illness. The three episodes had been so real that they'd etched themselves into his brain. He could recall every detail; Lucy's appearance, her looks, her voice, her snobby demeanour, her patronising comments, but also her gentleness at times, her sense of humour and her intelligence. If he'd imagined all that, he needed professional help.

Second, the Factor had suggested he could have been the victim of an elaborate practical joke by one or more of the estate lassies. But there would have been far too many stumbling blocks to staging such a hoax, from finding a King Charles Spaniel that answered to the name Trixie, to knowing exactly when he would be on Drumbreck. As an explanation, it was patently absurd.

That left only the third option. He found it hard to understand how it could be considered an explanation but at the moment, it was all he had. His mother had more than once claimed to be fey. His instinct had always been to scoff. But in spite of himself, he was gradually wondering if *he* was, too. Like her, he was beginning to discern links between events, incidents and circumstances. Sometimes he knew what was going to happen before it happened. That didn't mean he could make things happen, but he could predict them more often than he thought could be explained by mere coincidence. He was convinced of some connection to Lucy. The one thing that stood out was the fact that he and Edgar had the same surname. That couldn't be coincidental, surely?

After he was back on his feet, and several weeks after his collapse, he decided to corner his dad and ask him a question, one that had been niggling him since his session with Walter. The chance came when they were working in the garden together on a balmy late spring evening. Now that the frosts had gone, they could plant potatoes.

"Dad, can Ah ask ye somethin'?"

"Aye, son, what is it?"

"It's about yer family. Did ye ever have a relative called Edgar?"

Ian stopped digging, leant on his spade, and furrowed his brow in thought.

"Edgar, Edgar… That's no really a name Ah'd associate with the Swanstons. It sounds English, doesn't it?"

Ian stared in the direction of Inch Keith, clearly thinking back to his father who'd died too young, and his mother who'd been widowed twice. Suddenly, he raised his eyebrows.

"Ye ken son, Ah'm no sure if ye're just planting this in mah mind, but come tae think o' it, Ah do have a vague memory o' that name. Now, what was it?"

James stayed silent so as not to disturb his concentration.

"Ah've got it. Ah do believe mah dad had a second cousin called Edgar… that would be *his* dad's cousin, Ah suppose. Ah'm no sure exactly. Let's call 'im a distant cousin. Anyway, aye, the name does ring a bell… But why d'ye want tae know?"

"Oh, nothin'. It's just we were learnin' about 1066 at school, an' one o' the kings was called Edgar the Aetheling. Ah just wondered if there was anybody in our family called that…"

"Oh aye, aye… Listen, if ye're really interested, Ah tell ye who'd know. Yer Auntie Rose!"

Rose, Ian's stepsister, was the daughter of Ian's mother and her first husband who'd died of tuberculosis before the First World War. Much older than Ian, at least by ten years, Rose was regarded as pretty much the custodian of the family history. The next day after school, James made a detour and found himself in Gowan Street. He had to get to the bottom of the matter of Edgar and Lucy. The tenement, like the rest of Gowan Street, was on its last legs. The entry stank like a toilet and he had to stand for half a minute to let his eyes get used to the darkness. Unlike Brecon Street, there was no skylight to provide at least a glimmer of light. He cursed. He should have brought a torch. He felt his way up slowly, the soles of his shoes scraping on the cracked, worn sandstone steps, his left hand gripping the invisible banister, hoping there was nothing nasty there. His knock produced no response at first. He knocked again, louder.

The door opened and there stood Auntie Rose. In her sixties but looking older, she was small and round with her grey, straggly hair pinned all over with Kirby Grips, and a sweet face. At first, her elderly eyes couldn't make him out in the gloom of the landing. Then she broke into a huge smile.

"Oh, it's you, James! Come on in, mah bonnie wee laddie!"

"Hello, Auntie Rose, Ah hope Ah'm no disturbin' ye!"

"Naw, naw, mah bonnie wee laddie, no a bit o' it!"

He walked into the cramped flat. It was a room and kitchen like Brecon Street but everything was far smaller and more decrepit.

"Wud ye like a wee salmon sandwich an' a cup o' tea?" asked Auntie Rose as he was finding a seat among the clutter. His heart sank. Auntie Rose's salmon sandwiches were notorious. She'd singlehandedly been responsible for more than one outbreak of salmonella that had kept the emergency department at the Royal Infirmary on its toes. James had been a victim once. He decided once was enough.

"No thanks, Auntie Rose," he replied airily. "Ah'll be getting mah tea at home soon."

"What can Ah dae fir ye, son?" asked Auntie Rose, lowering her arthritic frame into an ancient armchair about six inches from the smouldering coal fire.

"Auntie Rose," James explained, "we're doin' a project at school about families and Ah realised Ah know nothin' about Dad's family."

"Oh, aye, oh aye, son," said Auntie Rose, somewhat relieved, now that the reason for his visit was on the table.

"Ah just had one question." He paused and took a deep breath. He didn't know if Auntie Rose would know the answer and even if she did, he wasn't sure if he wanted to hear it. Anyway, here goes.

"Ah spoke tae Dad an' 'e told me *his* Dad, mah grandfather..." He stopped. "'E was your stepfather, wasn't 'e?"

"Aye, that's right, that would be John Swanston."

"Well, 'e told me John Swanston had a second cousin." He paused again, to make sure Auntie Rose was following. She sat staring at him blankly, then, as if some machinery in her brain had suddenly started up, she looked out through the grimy panes of glass where pigeons were strutting on the window ledge and started to speak as if she were merely repeating what the machine told her to say.

"Aye, John Swanston. 'E did have a second cousin, that would be 'is faither's cousin."

She stopped as if the machine had been paused. James waited, fearful of breaking the thread. The machine started up again.

"'E was a worker on the Earl o' Rosebery's estate at Dalmeny."

James almost fell off his seat. In the cramped, smelly, overheated room, sweat was trickling down his back inside his shirt and he was beginning to feel queasy. It was Walter Netherby's front parlour all over again. The machine seemed to have stopped. Auntie Rose continued to stare out of the window as if waiting for a re-boot, but nothing happened. Finally, James had to say something.

"What was 'is name, this second cousin?"

His words had the desired effect. The re-boot was triggered.

"It was Edgar. Aye, that was 'is name. Ah aye mind that, forbye it's no the sort o' name we wid hae gien oor bairns here in Leith!"

With the fingertips of his right hand, James rubbed the sweat that was beginning to form on his forehead. He felt sick now. But he knew he had to ask.

"Did 'e have any children?"

The machine had clicked over to *pause* again. Then suddenly there it was, back on *play*.

"Aye, 'e did, 'e had a laddie and a lassie. The laddie was ca'd after him, Edgar."

It was all or nothing.

"What was the lassie's name, Auntie Rose?"

The machine was running smoothly now. Auntie Rose spoke without a moment's hesitation.

"It was Lucy," she said.

Saint Mary's Loch

Almost two decades later, James was on leave from an overseas posting. Granny and Grandad Melrose were gone, and now they'd had news that Granny's brother, Uncle George down in Sanquhar, had passed away. Alistair, now the father of two teenagers, would drive three of the sisters down for the funeral; Janet and Effie, along with Flora, who happened to be up visiting from London. Would James come too as the male representative of the Swanston side? Curious about a branch of his family that he'd never known, yes, of course he would.

It was a warm day in July. Though they were off to a funeral, the atmosphere in Alistair's relatively new Ford Cortina was anything but funereal. None of the younger Melroses had known Uncle George very well, James not at all. They couldn't honestly mourn. They were going to honour the memory of their parents, that was all. The weather was stunning, the sisters were squashed together on the back seat, Alistair was driving and they were off for a jaunt to Dumfriesshire. What could be better? They laughed and reminisced the whole way down. The wake was well in progress when they arrived in Sanquhar. After rushing to the toilet, there were the regulation cups of tea and cucumber sandwiches to contend with. While sipping tea and attempting to commiserate with some anonymous relation, James had felt a light touch on his shoulder.

"You'll be cord number eight," said a sombre voice softly. It was one of his elderly uncles or cousins. *Cord number eight?* What on earth did that mean? When he had a chance, he cornered Alistair.

"Oh, cord number eight? That means you'll be holding cord number eight when we lower Uncle George's coffin into the grave. I've got cord number six, by the way!"

The funeral was an object lesson in the strange traditions of the folks of Dumfries and Galloway. For, to James's surprise, Uncle George's burial was a men-only affair. One of the cousins who appeared to be the funeral organiser-in-chief suddenly gave a cryptic signal. It seemed the hearse carrying the coffin had arrived. At that, all the men jumped up, trooped out to cars, formed the cortege, and followed the hearse to the cemetery. The women stayed behind. James was baffled. Men only? How was this possible in Britain in the twentieth century?

The cemetery was a simple affair on a bare hillside overlooking the rolling countryside of southwest Scotland. A cold wind started to come off the Irish Sea as they lowered Uncle George into the ground. James hung on grimly to cord number eight. No one said a word. There was no minister present, no religious service, no elegy. Once Uncle George was down, the men got into their cars and drove home. More cups of tea and then it was a free-for-all. Everyone, women included, piled into cars and it was off to the cemetery again. By then, the hole had been filled in and the ground was flat and covered with fresh earth. Everyone stood around admiring the wreaths and flower sprays that had been positioned over the grave.

There was no reason to stay so the visitors from Edinburgh agreed to leave as soon as possible. They still had most of the afternoon ahead of them. How about a bit of a tour of The Borders before they headed home, suggested Alistair? Oh, yes, said the sisters, great idea. But where? How about Saint Mary's Loch? James's heart leapt. They drove by Elvanfoot and Moffat. The weather had held. The laughter and reminiscing continued. Suddenly an immense sheet of water came into view, sparkling in the sunlight. Alistair stopped the car at a viewpoint near Cappercleuch. They got out and stood looking southeast towards the Loch, savouring the view of the waters and a mellow Borders landscape sinking in the heat haze.

"Alistair?" said James. "D'ye still carry binoculars in yer car?"

Alistair had always carried binoculars in the old days for when he went to golf tournaments. They were de rigeur for the serious fan when it came to spotting the flight and the position of golf balls. He went to the Cortina, came back with an old pair of Zeiss binoculars, and handed them to his nephew. They seemed familiar.

"I borrowed them from your dad and never returned them!" Alistair confessed. "Do not tell him, whatever you do!"

James gave a wry smile. Then, turning away from the group, he looked due north. He put the binoculars to his eyes. The colossal profile of the southwest face of Drumbreck filled the optics. After a few moments' searching, he'd found it. Up there was the Tulzie Kaime, nestling between two arms of the mountain, looking odd from this angle. He strained his eyes, twisting the knurled ring to bring the picture into focus. Yes, there was the lookout. And, was it some trick of the light? Was there a tiny figure, sitting, motionless on a rock? He told himself not to be ridiculous. Alistair was suddenly at his elbow.

"What are you looking at?"

James lowered the binoculars, stretched out his free right arm, and, pointing with his index finger straight at the Tulzie Kaime, he spoke the words formally, as was their due.

"Once," he said, with a catch in his voice, "once, I was up there."

Permissions and copyright

Schule in June: © Robert Bain
From *A Book of Twentieth Century Scots Verse* (1926) Gowans & Gray
UK Intellectual Property Office Licence OWLS000265

Blue Moon: Music by RICHARD RODGERS Lyrics by LORENZ HART
© 1934 (Renewed) METRO-GOLDWYN-MAYER INC.
All Rights (Excluding Print) Controlled and Administered by EMI ROBBINS CATALOG INC.
Exclusive Print Rights Controlled and Administered by ALFRED MUSIC
All Rights Reserved; Used by Permission of ALFRED MUSIC

Illustrations: Adapted as computerised sketches from the original photographs; unless otherwise stated below, sourced from the author's photo archive or from material in the public domain.

By kind permission: Front and back covers © The Scotsman Publications Ltd; p. 2, p. 12 © Crown Copyright, Imperial War Museums; p. 26 © Robert Blomfield Archive; p. 34 © Historic Environment Scotland; p. 39 © Dr Allan Dodds; p. 53, p. 55, p. 68 © The Scotsman Publications Ltd; p. 96 © Flora Hurst; p. 122 © Regentlad; p. 204 © Kenneth G. Williamson.

Creative Commons Licence, copyrighted and licensed for re-use: p. 108 © Kim Traynor (cc-by-sa/2.0); p. 167 © John Erickson (cc-by-sa/3.0); p. 181 © Bristol City Council, Kurt Adams (cc-by-sa/2.0); p. 190 © Mike Smith (cc-by-sa/2.0); p. 238 © Kim Traynor (cc-by-sa/2.0); p. 266 © Kim Traynor (cc-by-sa/2.0); p. 277 © Stephen Roddick (cc-by-sa/2.0); p. 279 © grobertson4 (cc-by-sa/2.0); p. 288 © M J Richardson (cc-by-sa/2.0); p. 311 © Richard Dorrell (cc-by-sa/2.0); p. 315 © Richard Dorrell (cc-by-sa/2.0); p. 320 © Andrew Curtis (cc-by-sa/2.0); p. 365 © John Lindie (cc-by-2.0); p. 379 © Jim Barton (cc-by-sa/2.0); p. 386 © Robert Graham (cc-by-sa/2.0); p. 402 © Walter Baxter (cc-by-sa/2.0); p. 409 © University of Edinburgh Walter Scott Image Collection (cc-by-3.0); p. 415 © Jim Barton (cc-by-sa/2.0); p. 416 © University of Edinburgh Walter Scott Image Collection (cc-by-3.0); p. 424 © Jim Barton (cc-by-sa/2.0); p. 436 © The University of Edinburgh Collection, 1583/58 (cc-by-3.0); p. 439 © Trevor Littlewood (cc-by-sa/2.0); p. 441 © Alan O'Dowd (cc-by-sa/2.0).